# THE ROBERT CHAMBERS COLLECTION:

## Volume I

## The King in Yellow and Other Works

by

Robert Chambers

# Contents

# THE KING IN YELLOW

Along the shore the cloud waves break,
The twin suns sink beneath the lake,
The shadows lengthen
In Carcosa.

Strange is the night where black stars rise,
And strange moons circle through the skies
But stranger still is
Lost Carcosa.

Songs that the Hyades shall sing,
Where flap the tatters of the King,
Must die unheard in
Dim Carcosa.

Song of my soul, my voice is dead;
Die thou, unsung, as tears unshed
Shall dry and die in
Lost Carcosa.

Cassilda's Song in "The King in Yellow," Act i, Scene 2.

# THE REPAIRER OF REPUTATIONS

## I

> "Ne raillons pas les fous; leur folie dure plus longtemps que la nôtre.... Voila toute la différence."

Toward the end of the year 1920 the Government of the United States had practically completed the programme, adopted during the last months of President Winthrop's administration. The country was apparently tranquil. Everybody knows how the Tariff and Labour questions were settled. The war with Germany, incident on that country's seizure of the Samoan Islands, had left no visible scars upon the republic, and the temporary occupation of Norfolk by the invading army had been forgotten in the joy over repeated naval victories, and the subsequent ridiculous plight of General Von Gartenlaube's forces in the State of New Jersey. The Cuban and Hawaiian investments had paid one hundred per cent and the territory of Samoa was well worth its cost as a coaling station. The country was in a superb state of defence. Every coast city had been well supplied with land fortifications; the army under the parental eye of the General Staff, organized according to the Prussian system, had been increased to 300,000 men, with a territorial reserve of a million; and six magnificent squadrons of cruisers and battle-ships patrolled the six stations of the navigable seas, leaving a steam reserve amply fitted to control home waters. The gentlemen from the West had at last been constrained to acknowledge that a college for the training of diplomats was as necessary as law schools are for the training of barristers; consequently we were no longer represented abroad by incompetent patriots. The nation was prosperous; Chicago, for a moment paralyzed after a second great fire, had risen from its ruins, white and imperial, and more beautiful than the white city which had been built for its plaything in 1893. Everywhere good architecture was replacing bad, and even in New York, a sudden craving for decency had swept away a great portion of the existing horrors. Streets had been widened, properly paved and lighted, trees had been planted, squares laid out, elevated structures demolished and underground roads built to replace them. The new government buildings and barracks were fine bits of architecture, and the long system of stone quays which completely surrounded the island had been turned into parks which proved a godsend to the population. The subsidizing of the state theatre and state opera brought its own reward. The United States National Academy of Design was much like European institutions of the same kind. Nobody envied the Secretary of Fine Arts, either his cabinet position or his portfolio. The Secretary of Forestry and Game

Preservation had a much easier time, thanks to the new system of National Mounted Police. We had profited well by the latest treaties with France and England; the exclusion of foreign-born Jews as a measure of self-preservation, the settlement of the new independent negro state of Suanee, the checking of immigration, the new laws concerning naturalization, and the gradual centralization of power in the executive all contributed to national calm and prosperity. When the Government solved the Indian problem and squadrons of Indian cavalry scouts in native costume were substituted for the pitiable organizations tacked on to the tail of skeletonized regiments by a former Secretary of War, the nation drew a long sigh of relief. When, after the colossal Congress of Religions, bigotry and intolerance were laid in their graves and kindness and charity began to draw warring sects together, many thought the millennium had arrived, at least in the new world which after all is a world by itself.

But self-preservation is the first law, and the United States had to look on in helpless sorrow as Germany, Italy, Spain and Belgium writhed in the throes of Anarchy, while Russia, watching from the Caucasus, stooped and bound them one by one.

In the city of New York the summer of 1899 was signalized by the dismantling of the Elevated Railroads. The summer of 1900 will live in the memories of New York people for many a cycle; the Dodge Statue was removed in that year. In the following winter began that agitation for the repeal of the laws prohibiting suicide which bore its final fruit in the month of April, 1920, when the first Government Lethal Chamber was opened on Washington Square.

I had walked down that day from Dr. Archer's house on Madison Avenue, where I had been as a mere formality. Ever since that fall from my horse, four years before, I had been troubled at times with pains in the back of my head and neck, but now for months they had been absent, and the doctor sent me away that day saying there was nothing more to be cured in me. It was hardly worth his fee to be told that; I knew it myself. Still I did not grudge him the money. What I minded was the mistake which he made at first. When they picked me up from the pavement where I lay unconscious, and somebody had mercifully sent a bullet through my horse's head, I was carried to Dr. Archer, and he, pronouncing my brain affected, placed me in his private asylum where I was obliged to endure treatment for insanity. At last he decided that I was well, and I, knowing that my mind had always been as sound as his, if not sounder, "paid my tuition" as he jokingly called it, and left. I told him, smiling, that I would get even with him for his mistake, and he laughed heartily, and asked me to call once in a while. I did so, hoping for a chance to even up accounts, but he gave me none, and I told him I would wait.

The fall from my horse had fortunately left no evil results; on the contrary it had changed my whole character for the better. From a lazy young man about town, I had become active, energetic, temperate, and above all—oh, above all else— ambitious. There was only one thing which troubled me, I laughed at my own uneasiness, and yet it troubled me.

During my convalescence I had bought and read for the first time, *The King in Yellow*. I remember after finishing the first act that it occurred to me that I had better stop. I started up and flung the book into the fireplace; the volume struck the barred grate and fell open on the hearth in the firelight. If I had not caught a glimpse of the opening words in the second act I should never have finished it, but as I stooped to pick it up, my eyes became riveted to the open page, and with a cry of terror, or perhaps it was of joy so poignant that I suffered in every nerve, I snatched the thing out of the coals and crept shaking to my bedroom, where I read it and reread it, and wept and laughed and trembled with a horror which at times assails me yet. This is the thing that troubles me, for I cannot forget Carcosa where black stars hang in the heavens; where the shadows of men's thoughts lengthen in the afternoon, when the twin suns sink into the lake of Hali; and my mind will bear for ever the memory of the Pallid Mask. I pray God will curse the writer, as the writer has cursed the world with this beautiful, stupendous creation, terrible in its simplicity, irresistible in its truth—a world which now trembles before the King in Yellow. When the French Government seized the translated copies which had just arrived in Paris, London, of course, became eager to read it. It is well known how the book spread like an infectious disease, from city to city, from continent to continent, barred out here, confiscated there, denounced by Press and pulpit, censured even by the most advanced of literary anarchists. No definite principles had been violated in those wicked pages, no doctrine promulgated, no convictions outraged. It could not be judged by any known standard, yet, although it was acknowledged that the supreme note of art had been struck in *The King in Yellow*, all felt that human nature could not bear the strain, nor thrive on words in which the essence of purest poison lurked. The very banality and innocence of the first act only allowed the blow to fall afterward with more awful effect.

It was, I remember, the 13th day of April, 1920, that the first Government Lethal Chamber was established on the south side of Washington Square, between Wooster Street and South Fifth Avenue. The block which had formerly consisted of a lot of shabby old buildings, used as cafés and restaurants for foreigners, had been acquired by the Government in the winter of 1898. The French and Italian cafés and restaurants were torn down; the whole block was enclosed by a gilded iron railing, and converted into a lovely garden with lawns, flowers and fountains. In the centre of the garden stood a small, white building, severely classical in architecture, and surrounded by thickets of flowers. Six Ionic columns supported the roof, and the single door was of bronze. A splendid marble group of the "Fates" stood before the door, the work of a young American sculptor, Boris Yvain, who had died in Paris when only twenty-three years old.

The inauguration ceremonies were in progress as I crossed University Place and entered the square. I threaded my way through the silent throng of spectators, but was stopped at Fourth Street by a cordon of police. A regiment of United States lancers were drawn up in a hollow square round the Lethal Chamber. On a raised tribune facing Washington Park stood the Governor of New York, and behind him were grouped the Mayor of New York and Brooklyn, the Inspector-General of Police, the Commandant of the state troops, Colonel Livingston, military aid to the President of the United States, General Blount, commanding at Governor's Island, Major-General Hamilton, commanding the garrison of New York and Brooklyn, Admiral Buffby of the fleet in the North River, Surgeon-General Lanceford, the staff of the National Free Hospital, Senators Wyse and Franklin of New York, and the Commissioner of Public Works. The tribune was surrounded by a squadron of hussars of the National Guard.

The Governor was finishing his reply to the short speech of the Surgeon-General. I heard him say: "The laws prohibiting suicide and providing punishment for any attempt at self-destruction have been repealed. The Government has seen fit to acknowledge the right of man to end an existence which may have become intolerable to him, through physical suffering or mental despair. It is believed that the community will be benefited by the removal of such people from their midst. Since the passage of this law, the number of suicides in the United States has not increased. Now the Government has determined to establish a Lethal Chamber in every city, town and village in the country, it remains to be seen whether or not that class of human creatures from whose desponding ranks new victims of self-destruction fall daily will accept the relief thus provided." He paused, and turned to the white Lethal Chamber. The silence in the street was absolute. "There a painless death awaits him who can no longer bear the sorrows of this life. If death is welcome let him seek it there." Then quickly turning to the military aid of the President's household, he said, "I declare the Lethal Chamber open," and again facing the vast crowd he cried in a clear voice: "Citizens of New York and of the United States of America, through me the Government declares the Lethal Chamber to be open."

The solemn hush was broken by a sharp cry of command, the squadron of hussars filed after the Governor's carriage, the lancers wheeled and formed along Fifth Avenue to wait for the commandant of the garrison, and the mounted police followed them. I left the crowd to gape and stare at the white marble Death Chamber, and, crossing South Fifth Avenue, walked along the western side of that thoroughfare to Bleecker Street. Then I turned to the right and stopped before a dingy shop which bore the sign:

HAWBERK, ARMOURER.

I glanced in at the doorway and saw Hawberk busy in his little shop at the end of the hall. He looked up, and catching sight of me cried in his deep, hearty voice, "Come in, Mr. Castaigne!" Constance, his daughter, rose to meet me as I crossed the threshold, and held out her pretty hand, but I saw the blush of disappointment on her cheeks, and knew that it was another Castaigne she had expected, my cousin Louis. I smiled at her confusion and complimented her on the banner she was embroidering from a coloured plate. Old Hawberk sat riveting the worn greaves of some ancient suit of armour, and the ting! ting! ting! of his little hammer sounded pleasantly in the quaint shop. Presently he dropped his hammer, and fussed about for a moment with a tiny wrench. The soft clash of the mail sent a thrill of pleasure through me. I loved to hear the music of steel brushing against steel, the mellow shock of the mallet on thigh pieces, and the jingle of chain armour. That was the only reason I went to see Hawberk. He had never interested me personally, nor did Constance, except for the fact of her being in love with Louis. This did occupy my attention, and sometimes even kept me awake at night. But I knew in my heart that all would come right, and that I should arrange their future as I expected to arrange that of my kind doctor, John Archer. However, I should never have troubled myself about visiting them just then, had it not been, as I say, that the music of the tinkling hammer had for me this strong fascination. I would sit for hours, listening and listening, and when a stray sunbeam struck the inlaid steel, the sensation it gave me was almost too keen to endure. My eyes would become fixed, dilating with a pleasure that stretched every nerve almost to breaking, until some movement of the old armourer cut off the ray of sunlight, then, still thrilling secretly, I leaned back and listened again to the sound of the polishing rag, swish! swish! rubbing rust from the rivets.

Constance worked with the embroidery over her knees, now and then pausing to examine more closely the pattern in the coloured plate from the Metropolitan Museum.

"Who is this for?" I asked.

Hawberk explained, that in addition to the treasures of armour in the Metropolitan Museum of which he had been appointed armourer, he also had charge of several collections belonging to rich amateurs. This was the missing greave of a famous suit which a client of his had traced to a little shop in Paris on the Quai d'Orsay. He, Hawberk, had negotiated for and secured the greave, and now the suit was complete. He laid down his hammer and read me the history of the suit, traced since 1450 from owner to owner until it was acquired by Thomas Stainbridge. When his superb collection was sold, this client of Hawberk's bought the suit, and since then the search for the missing greave had been pushed until it was, almost by accident, located in Paris.

"Did you continue the search so persistently without any certainty of the greave being still in existence?" I demanded.

"Of course," he replied coolly.

Then for the first time I took a personal interest in Hawberk.

"It was worth something to you," I ventured.

"No," he replied, laughing, "my pleasure in finding it was my reward."

"Have you no ambition to be rich?" I asked, smiling.

"My one ambition is to be the best armourer in the world," he answered gravely.

Constance asked me if I had seen the ceremonies at the Lethal Chamber. She herself had noticed cavalry passing up Broadway that morning, and had wished to see the inauguration, but her father wanted the banner finished, and she had stayed at his request.

"Did you see your cousin, Mr. Castaigne, there?" she asked, with the slightest tremor of her soft eyelashes.

"No," I replied carelessly. "Louis' regiment is manœuvring out in Westchester County." I rose and picked up my hat and cane.

"Are you going upstairs to see the lunatic again?" laughed old Hawberk. If Hawberk knew how I loathe that word "lunatic," he would never use it in my presence. It rouses certain feelings within me which I do not care to explain. However, I answered him quietly: "I think I shall drop in and see Mr. Wilde for a moment or two."

"Poor fellow," said Constance, with a shake of the head, "it must be hard to live alone year after year poor, crippled and almost demented. It is very good of you, Mr. Castaigne, to visit him as often as you do."

"I think he is vicious," observed Hawberk, beginning again with his hammer. I listened to the golden tinkle on the greave plates; when he had finished I replied:

"No, he is not vicious, nor is he in the least demented. His mind is a wonder chamber, from which he can extract treasures that you and I would give years of our life to acquire.'"

Hawberk laughed.

I continued a little impatiently: "He knows history as no one else could know it. Nothing, however trivial, escapes his search, and his memory is so absolute, so precise in details, that were it known in New York that such a man existed, the people could not honour him enough."

"Nonsense," muttered Hawberk, searching on the floor for a fallen rivet.

"Is it nonsense," I asked, managing to suppress what I felt, "is it nonsense when he says that the tassets and cuissards of the enamelled suit of armour commonly known as the 'Prince's Emblazoned' can be found among a mass of rusty theatrical properties, broken stoves and ragpicker's refuse in a garret in Pell Street?"

Hawberk's hammer fell to the ground, but he picked it up and asked, with a great deal of calm, how I knew that the tassets and left cuissard were missing from the "Prince's Emblazoned."

"I did not know until Mr. Wilde mentioned it to me the other day. He said they were in the garret of 998 Pell Street."

"Nonsense," he cried, but I noticed his hand trembling under his leathern apron.

"Is this nonsense too?" I asked pleasantly, "is it nonsense when Mr. Wilde continually speaks of you as the Marquis of Avonshire and of Miss Constance—"

I did not finish, for Constance had started to her feet with terror written on every feature. Hawberk looked at me and slowly smoothed his leathern apron.

"That is impossible," he observed, "Mr. Wilde may know a great many things—"

"About armour, for instance, and the 'Prince's Emblazoned,'" I interposed, smiling.

"Yes," he continued, slowly, "about armour also—may be—but he is wrong in regard to the Marquis of Avonshire, who, as you know, killed his wife's traducer years ago, and went to Australia where he did not long survive his wife."

"Mr. Wilde is wrong," murmured Constance. Her lips were blanched, but her voice was sweet and calm.

"Let us agree, if you please, that in this one circumstance Mr. Wilde is wrong," I said.

## II

I climbed the three dilapidated flights of stairs, which I had so often climbed before, and knocked at a small door at the end of the corridor. Mr. Wilde opened the door and I walked in.

When he had double-locked the door and pushed a heavy chest against it, he came and sat down beside me, peering up into my face with his little light-coloured eyes. Half a dozen new scratches covered his nose and cheeks, and the silver wires which supported his artificial ears had become displaced. I thought I had never seen him so hideously fascinating. He had no ears. The artificial ones, which now stood out at an angle from the fine wire, were his one weakness. They were made of wax and painted a shell pink, but the rest of his face was yellow. He might better have revelled in the luxury of some artificial fingers for his left hand, which was absolutely fingerless, but it seemed to cause him no inconvenience, and he was satisfied with his wax ears. He was very small, scarcely higher than a child of ten, but his arms were magnificently developed, and his thighs as thick as any athlete's. Still, the most remarkable thing about Mr. Wilde was that a man of his marvellous intelligence and knowledge should have such a head. It was flat and pointed, like the heads of many of those unfortunates whom people imprison in asylums for the weak-minded. Many called him insane, but I knew him to be as sane as I was.

I do not deny that he was eccentric; the mania he had for keeping that cat and teasing her until she flew at his face like a demon, was certainly eccentric. I never could understand why he kept the creature, nor what pleasure he found in shutting himself up in his room with this surly, vicious beast. I remember once, glancing up from the manuscript I was studying by the light of some tallow dips, and seeing Mr. Wilde squatting motionless on his high chair, his eyes fairly blazing with excitement, while the cat, which had risen from her place before the stove, came creeping across the floor right at him. Before I could move she flattened her belly to the ground, crouched, trembled, and sprang into his face. Howling and foaming they rolled over and over on the floor, scratching and clawing, until the cat screamed and fled under the cabinet, and Mr. Wilde turned over on his back, his limbs contracting and curling up like the legs of a dying spider. He *was* eccentric.

Mr. Wilde had climbed into his high chair, and, after studying my face, picked up a dog's-eared ledger and opened it.

"Henry B. Matthews," he read, "book-keeper with Whysot Whysot and Company, dealers in church ornaments. Called April 3rd. Reputation damaged on the race-track. Known as a welcher. Reputation to be repaired by August 1st. Retainer Five Dollars." He turned the page and ran his fingerless knuckles down the closely-written columns.

"P. Greene Dusenberry, Minister of the Gospel, Fairbeach, New Jersey. Reputa-tion damaged in the Bowery. To be repaired as soon as possible. Retainer $100."

He coughed and added, "Called, April 6th."

"Then you are not in need of money, Mr. Wilde," I inquired.

"Listen," he coughed again.

"Mrs. C. Hamilton Chester, of Chester Park, New York City. Called April 7th. Reputation damaged at Dieppe, France. To be repaired by October 1st Retainer $500.

"Note.—C. Hamilton Chester, Captain U.S.S. 'Avalanche', ordered home from South Sea Squadron October 1st."

"Well," I said, "the profession of a Repairer of Reputations is lucrative."

His colourless eyes sought mine, "I only wanted to demonstrate that I was cor-rect. You said it was impossible to succeed as a Repairer of Reputations; that even if I did succeed in certain cases it would cost me more than I would gain by it. To-day I have five hundred men in my employ, who are poorly paid, but who pursue the work with an enthusiasm which possibly may be born of fear. These men enter every shade and grade of society; some even are pillars of the most exclusive social tem-ples; others are the prop and pride of the financial world; still others, hold undisputed sway among the 'Fancy and the Talent.' I choose them at my leisure from those who reply to my advertisements. It is easy enough, they are all cowards. I could treble the number in twenty days if I wished. So you see, those who have in their keeping the reputations of their fellow-citizens, I have in my pay."

"They may turn on you," I suggested.

He rubbed his thumb over his cropped ears, and adjusted the wax substitutes. "I think not," he murmured thoughtfully, "I seldom have to apply the whip, and then only once. Besides they like their wages."

"How do you apply the whip?" I demanded.

His face for a moment was awful to look upon. His eyes dwindled to a pair of green sparks.

"I invite them to come and have a little chat with me," he said in a soft voice.

A knock at the door interrupted him, and his face resumed its amiable expression.

"Who is it?" he inquired.

"Mr. Steylette," was the answer.

"Come to-morrow," replied Mr. Wilde.

"Impossible," began the other, but was silenced by a sort of bark from Mr. Wilde.

9

"Come to-morrow," he repeated.

We heard somebody move away from the door and turn the corner by the stairway.

"Who is that?" I asked.

"Arnold Steylette, Owner and Editor in Chief of the great New York daily."

He drummed on the ledger with his fingerless hand adding: "I pay him very badly, but he thinks it a good bargain."

"Arnold Steylette!" I repeated amazed.

"Yes," said Mr. Wilde, with a self-satisfied cough.

The cat, which had entered the room as he spoke, hesitated, looked up at him and snarled. He climbed down from the chair and squatting on the floor, took the creature into his arms and caressed her. The cat ceased snarling and presently began a loud purring which seemed to increase in timbre as he stroked her. "Where are the notes?" I asked. He pointed to the table, and for the hundredth time I picked up the bundle of manuscript entitled—

### "THE IMPERIAL DYNASTY OF AMERICA."

One by one I studied the well-worn pages, worn only by my own handling, and although I knew all by heart, from the beginning, "When from Carcosa, the Hyades, Hastur, and Aldebaran," to "Castaigne, Louis de Calvados, born December 19th, 1877," I read it with an eager, rapt attention, pausing to repeat parts of it aloud, and dwelling especially on "Hildred de Calvados, only son of Hildred Castaigne and Edythe Landes Castaigne, first in succession," etc., etc.

When I finished, Mr. Wilde nodded and coughed.

"Speaking of your legitimate ambition," he said, "how do Constance and Louis get along?"

"She loves him," I replied simply.

The cat on his knee suddenly turned and struck at his eyes, and he flung her off and climbed on to the chair opposite me.

"And Dr. Archer! But that's a matter you can settle any time you wish," he added.

"Yes," I replied, "Dr. Archer can wait, but it is time I saw my cousin Louis."

"It is time," he repeated. Then he took another ledger from the table and ran over the leaves rapidly. "We are now in communication with ten thousand men," he muttered. "We can count on one hundred thousand within the first twenty-eight hours, and in forty-eight hours the state will rise *en masse*. The country follows the state, and the portion that will not, I mean California and the Northwest, might better never have been inhabited. I shall not send them the Yellow Sign."

The blood rushed to my head, but I only answered, "A new broom sweeps clean."

"The ambition of Caesar and of Napoleon pales before that which could not rest until it had seized the minds of men and controlled even their unborn thoughts," said Mr. Wilde.

"You are speaking of the King in Yellow," I groaned, with a shudder.

"He is a king whom emperors have served."

"I am content to serve him," I replied.

Mr. Wilde sat rubbing his ears with his crippled hand. "Perhaps Constance does not love him," he suggested.

I started to reply, but a sudden burst of military music from the street below drowned my voice. The twentieth dragoon regiment, formerly in garrison at Mount St. Vincent, was returning from the manœuvres in Westchester County, to its new barracks on East Washington Square. It was my cousin's regiment. They were a fine lot of fellows, in their pale blue, tight-fitting jackets, jaunty busbys and white riding breeches with the double yellow stripe, into which their limbs seemed moulded. Every other squadron was armed with lances, from the metal points of which fluttered yellow and white pennons. The band passed, playing the regimental march, then came the colonel and staff, the horses crowding and trampling, while their heads bobbed in unison, and the pennons fluttered from their lance points. The troopers, who rode with the beautiful English seat, looked brown as berries from their bloodless campaign among the farms of Westchester, and the music of their sabres against the stirrups, and the jingle of spurs and carbines was delightful to me. I saw Louis riding with his squadron. He was as handsome an officer as I have ever seen. Mr. Wilde, who had mounted a chair by the window, saw him too, but said nothing. Louis turned and looked straight at Hawberk's shop as he passed, and I could see the flush on his brown cheeks. I think Constance must have been at the window. When the last troopers had clattered by, and the last pennons vanished into South Fifth Avenue, Mr. Wilde clambered out of his chair and dragged the chest away from the door.

"Yes," he said, "it is time that you saw your cousin Louis."

He unlocked the door and I picked up my hat and stick and stepped into the corridor. The stairs were dark. Groping about, I set my foot on something soft, which snarled and spit, and I aimed a murderous blow at the cat, but my cane shivered to splinters against the balustrade, and the beast scurried back into Mr. Wilde's room.

Passing Hawberk's door again I saw him still at work on the armour, but I did not stop, and stepping out into Bleecker Street, I followed it to Wooster, skirted the grounds of the Lethal Chamber, and crossing Washington Park went straight to my rooms in the Benedick. Here I lunched comfortably, read the *Herald* and the *Meteor*, and finally went to the steel safe in my bedroom and set the time combination. The three and three-quarter minutes which it is necessary to wait, while the time lock is opening, are to me golden moments. From the instant I set the combination to the moment when I grasp the knobs and swing back the solid steel doors, I live in an ecstasy of expectation. Those moments must be like moments passed in Paradise. I know what I am to find at the end of the time limit. I know what the massive safe holds secure for me, for me alone, and the exquisite pleasure of waiting is hardly enhanced when the safe opens and I lift, from its velvet crown, a diadem of purest gold, blazing with diamonds. I do this every day, and yet the joy of waiting and at last touching again the diadem, only seems to increase as the days pass. It is a diadem fit for a King among kings, an Emperor among emperors. The King in Yellow might scorn it, but it shall be worn by his royal servant.

I held it in my arms until the alarm in the safe rang harshly, and then tenderly, proudly, I replaced it and shut the steel doors. I walked slowly back into my study, which faces Washington Square, and leaned on the window sill. The afternoon sun poured into my windows, and a gentle breeze stirred the branches of the elms and maples in the park, now covered with buds and tender foliage. A flock of pigeons circled about the tower of the Memorial Church; sometimes alighting on the purple tiled roof, sometimes wheeling downward to the lotos fountain in front of the marble arch. The gardeners were busy with the flower beds around the fountain, and the freshly turned earth smelled sweet and spicy. A lawn mower, drawn by a fat white horse, clinked across the green sward, and watering-carts poured showers of spray over the asphalt drives. Around the statue of Peter Stuyvesant, which in 1897 had replaced the monstrosity supposed to represent Garibaldi, children played in the spring sunshine, and nurse girls wheeled elaborate baby carriages with a reckless disregard for the pasty-faced occupants, which could probably be explained by the presence of half a dozen trim dragoon troopers languidly lolling on the benches. Through the trees, the Washington Memorial Arch glistened like silver in the sunshine, and beyond, on the eastern extremity of the square the grey stone barracks of the dragoons, and the white granite artillery stables were alive with colour and motion.

I looked at the Lethal Chamber on the corner of the square opposite. A few curious people still lingered about the gilded iron railing, but inside the grounds the paths were deserted. I watched the fountains ripple and sparkle; the sparrows had already found this new bathing nook, and the basins were covered with the dusty-feathered little things. Two or three white peacocks picked their way across the lawns, and a drab coloured pigeon sat so motionless on the arm of one of the "Fates," that it seemed to be a part of the sculptured stone.

As I was turning carelessly away, a slight commotion in the group of curious loiterers around the gates attracted my attention. A young man had entered, and was advancing with nervous strides along the gravel path which leads to the bronze doors of the Lethal Chamber. He paused a moment before the "Fates," and as he raised his head to those three mysterious faces, the pigeon rose from its sculptured perch, circled about for a moment and wheeled to the east. The young man pressed his hand to his face, and then with an undefinable gesture sprang up the marble steps, the bronze doors closed behind him, and half an hour later the loiterers slouched away, and the frightened pigeon returned to its perch in the arms of Fate.

I put on my hat and went out into the park for a little walk before dinner. As I crossed the central driveway a group of officers passed, and one of them called out, "Hello, Hildred," and came back to shake hands with me. It was my cousin Louis, who stood smiling and tapping his spurred heels with his riding-whip.

"Just back from Westchester," he said; "been doing the bucolic; milk and curds, you know, dairy-maids in sunbonnets, who say 'haeow' and 'I don't think' when you tell them they are pretty. I'm nearly dead for a square meal at Delmonico's. What's the news?"

"There is none," I replied pleasantly. "I saw your regiment coming in this morning."

"Did you? I didn't see you. Where were you?"

"In Mr. Wilde's window."

"Oh, hell!" he began impatiently, "that man is stark mad! I don't understand why you—"

He saw how annoyed I felt by this outburst, and begged my pardon.

"Really, old chap," he said, "I don't mean to run down a man you like, but for the life of me I can't see what the deuce you find in common with Mr. Wilde. He's not well bred, to put it generously; he is hideously deformed; his head is the head of a criminally insane person. You know yourself he's been in an asylum—"

"So have I," I interrupted calmly.

Louis looked startled and confused for a moment, but recovered and slapped me heartily on the shoulder. "You were completely cured," he began; but I stopped him again.

"I suppose you mean that I was simply acknowledged never to have been insane."

"Of course that—that's what I meant," he laughed.

I disliked his laugh because I knew it was forced, but I nodded gaily and asked him where he was going. Louis looked after his brother officers who had now almost reached Broadway.

"We had intended to sample a Brunswick cocktail, but to tell you the truth I was anxious for an excuse to go and see Hawberk instead. Come along, I'll make you my excuse."

We found old Hawberk, neatly attired in a fresh spring suit, standing at the door of his shop and sniffing the air.

"I had just decided to take Constance for a little stroll before dinner," he replied to the impetuous volley of questions from Louis. "We thought of walking on the park terrace along the North River."

At that moment Constance appeared and grew pale and rosy by turns as Louis bent over her small gloved fingers. I tried to excuse myself, alleging an engagement uptown, but Louis and Constance would not listen, and I saw I was expected to remain and engage old Hawberk's attention. After all it would be just as well if I kept my eye on Louis, I thought, and when they hailed a Spring Street horse-car, I got in after them and took my seat beside the armourer.

The beautiful line of parks and granite terraces overlooking the wharves along the North River, which were built in 1910 and finished in the autumn of 1917, had become one of the most popular promenades in the metropolis. They extended from the battery to 190th Street, overlooking the noble river and affording a fine view of the Jersey shore and the Highlands opposite. Cafés and restaurants were scattered here and there among the trees, and twice a week military bands from the garrison played in the kiosques on the parapets.

We sat down in the sunshine on the bench at the foot of the equestrian statue of General Sheridan. Constance tipped her sunshade to shield her eyes, and she and Louis began a murmuring conversation which was impossible to catch. Old Hawberk, leaning on his ivory headed cane, lighted an excellent cigar, the mate to which I politely refused, and smiled at vacancy. The sun hung low above the Staten Island woods, and the bay was dyed with golden hues reflected from the sun-warmed sails of the shipping in the harbour.

Brigs, schooners, yachts, clumsy ferry-boats, their decks swarming with people, railroad transports carrying lines of brown, blue and white freight cars, stately sound steamers, déclassé tramp steamers, coasters, dredgers, scows, and everywhere pervading the entire bay impudent little tugs puffing and whistling officiously;—these were the craft which churned the sunlight waters as far as the eye could reach. In calm contrast to the hurry of sailing vessel and steamer a silent fleet of white warships lay motionless in midstream.

Constance's merry laugh aroused me from my reverie.

"What *are* you staring at?" she inquired.

"Nothing—the fleet," I smiled.

Then Louis told us what the vessels were, pointing out each by its relative position to the old Red Fort on Governor's Island.

"That little cigar shaped thing is a torpedo boat," he explained; "there are four more lying close together. They are the *Tarpon*, the *Falcon*, the *Sea Fox*, and the *Octopus*. The gun-boats just above are the *Princeton*, the *Champlain*, the *Still Water* and the *Erie*. Next to them lie the cruisers *Faragut* and *Los Angeles*, and above them the battle ships *California*, and *Dakota*, and the *Washington* which is the flag ship. Those two squatty looking chunks of metal which are anchored there off Castle William are the double turreted monitors *Terrible* and *Magnificent*; behind them lies the ram, *Osceola*."

Constance looked at him with deep approval in her beautiful eyes. "What loads of things you know for a soldier," she said, and we all joined in the laugh which followed.

Presently Louis rose with a nod to us and offered his arm to Constance, and they strolled away along the river wall. Hawberk watched them for a moment and then turned to me.

"Mr. Wilde was right," he said. "I have found the missing tassets and left cuissard of the 'Prince's Emblazoned,' in a vile old junk garret in Pell Street."

"998?" I inquired, with a smile.

"Yes."

"Mr. Wilde is a very intelligent man," I observed.

"I want to give him the credit of this most important discovery," continued Hawberk. "And I intend it shall be known that he is entitled to the fame of it."

"He won't thank you for that," I answered sharply; "please say nothing about it."

"Do you know what it is worth?" said Hawberk.

"No, fifty dollars, perhaps."

"It is valued at five hundred, but the owner of the 'Prince's Emblazoned' will give two thousand dollars to the person who completes his suit; that reward also belongs to Mr. Wilde."

"He doesn't want it! He refuses it!" I answered angrily. "What do you know about Mr. Wilde? He doesn't need the money. He is rich—or will be—richer than any living man except myself. What will we care for money then—what will we care, he and I, when—when—"

"When what?" demanded Hawberk, astonished.

"You will see," I replied, on my guard again.

He looked at me narrowly, much as Doctor Archer used to, and I knew he thought I was mentally unsound. Perhaps it was fortunate for him that he did not use the word lunatic just then.

"No," I replied to his unspoken thought, "I am not mentally weak; my mind is as healthy as Mr. Wilde's. I do not care to explain just yet what I have on hand, but it is an investment which will pay more than mere gold, silver and precious stones. It will secure the happiness and prosperity of a continent—yes, a hemisphere!"

"Oh," said Hawberk.

"And eventually," I continued more quietly, "it will secure the happiness of the whole world."

"And incidentally your own happiness and prosperity as well as Mr. Wilde's?"

"Exactly," I smiled. But I could have throttled him for taking that tone.

He looked at me in silence for a while and then said very gently, "Why don't you give up your books and studies, Mr. Castaigne, and take a tramp among the mountains somewhere or other? You used to be fond of fishing. Take a cast or two at the trout in the Rangelys."

"I don't care for fishing any more," I answered, without a shade of annoyance in my voice.

"You used to be fond of everything," he continued; "athletics, yachting, shooting, riding—"

"I have never cared to ride since my fall," I said quietly.

"Ah, yes, your fall," he repeated, looking away from me.

I thought this nonsense had gone far enough, so I brought the conversation back to Mr. Wilde; but he was scanning my face again in a manner highly offensive to me.

"Mr. Wilde," he repeated, "do you know what he did this afternoon? He came downstairs and nailed a sign over the hall door next to mine; it read:

## MR. WILDE,
## REPAIRER OF REPUTATIONS.
### Third Bell.

"Do you know what a Repairer of Reputations can be?"

"I do," I replied, suppressing the rage within.

"Oh," he said again.

Louis and Constance came strolling by and stopped to ask if we would join them. Hawberk looked at his watch. At the same moment a puff of smoke shot from the casemates of Castle William, and the boom of the sunset gun rolled across the water and was re-echoed from the Highlands opposite. The flag came running down from the flag-pole, the bugles sounded on the white decks of the warships, and the first electric light sparkled out from the Jersey shore.

As I turned into the city with Hawberk I heard Constance murmur something to Louis which I did not understand; but Louis whispered "My darling," in reply; and again, walking ahead with Hawberk through the square I heard a murmur of "sweetheart," and "my own Constance," and I knew the time had nearly arrived when I should speak of important matters with my cousin Louis.

## III

One morning early in May I stood before the steel safe in my bedroom, trying on the golden jewelled crown. The diamonds flashed fire as I turned to the mirror, and the heavy beaten gold burned like a halo about my head. I remembered Camilla's agonized scream and the awful words echoing through the dim streets of Carcosa. They were the last lines in the first act, and I dared not think of what followed— dared not, even in the spring sunshine, there in my own room, surrounded with familiar objects, reassured by the bustle from the street and the voices of the servants in the hallway outside. For those poisoned words had dropped slowly into my heart, as death-sweat drops upon a bed-sheet and is absorbed. Trembling, I put the diadem from my head and wiped my forehead, but I thought of Hastur and of my own rightful ambition, and I remembered Mr. Wilde as I had last left him, his face all torn and bloody from the claws of that devil's creature, and what he said—ah, what he said. The alarm bell in the safe began to whirr harshly, and I knew my time was up; but I would not heed it, and replacing the flashing circlet upon my head I turned defiantly to the mirror. I stood for a long time absorbed in the changing expression of my own eyes. The mirror reflected a face which was like my own, but whiter, and so thin that I hardly recognized it. And all the time I kept repeating between my clenched teeth, "The day has come! the day has come!" while the alarm in the safe whirred and clamoured, and the diamonds sparkled and flamed above my brow. I heard a door open but did not heed it. It was only when I saw two faces in the mirror:—it was only when another face rose over my shoulder, and two other eyes met mine. I wheeled like a flash and seized a long knife from my dressing-table, and my cousin sprang back very pale, crying: "Hildred! for God's sake!" then as my hand fell, he said: "It is I, Louis, don't you know me?" I stood silent. I could not have spoken for my life. He walked up to me and took the knife from my hand.

"What is all this?" he inquired, in a gentle voice. "Are you ill?"

"No," I replied. But I doubt if he heard me.

"Come, come, old fellow," he cried, "take off that brass crown and toddle into the study. Are you going to a masquerade? What's all this theatrical tinsel anyway?"

I was glad he thought the crown was made of brass and paste, yet I didn't like him any the better for thinking so. I let him take it from my hand, knowing it was best to humour him. He tossed the splendid diadem in the air, and catching it, turned to me smiling.

"It's dear at fifty cents," he said. "What's it for?"

I did not answer, but took the circlet from his hands, and placing it in the safe shut the massive steel door. The alarm ceased its infernal din at once. He watched me curiously, but did not seem to notice the sudden ceasing of the alarm. He did, however, speak of the safe as a biscuit box. Fearing lest he might examine the combination I led the way into my study. Louis threw himself on the sofa and flicked at flies with his eternal riding-whip. He wore his fatigue uniform with the braided jacket and jaunty cap, and I noticed that his riding-boots were all splashed with red mud.

"Where have you been?" I inquired.

"Jumping mud creeks in Jersey," he said. "I haven't had time to change yet; I was rather in a hurry to see you. Haven't you got a glass of something? I'm dead tired; been in the saddle twenty-four hours."

I gave him some brandy from my medicinal store, which he drank with a grimace.

"Damned bad stuff," he observed. "I'll give you an address where they sell brandy that is brandy."

"It's good enough for my needs," I said indifferently. "I use it to rub my chest with." He stared and flicked at another fly.

"See here, old fellow," he began, "I've got something to suggest to you. It's four years now that you've shut yourself up here like an owl, never going anywhere, never taking any healthy exercise, never doing a damn thing but poring over those books up there on the mantelpiece."

He glanced along the row of shelves. "Napoleon, Napoleon, Napoleon!" he read. "For heaven's sake, have you nothing but Napoleons there?"

"I wish they were bound in gold," I said. "But wait, yes, there is another book, *The King in Yellow*." I looked him steadily in the eye.

"Have you never read it?" I asked.

"I? No, thank God! I don't want to be driven crazy."

I saw he regretted his speech as soon as he had uttered it. There is only one word which I loathe more than I do lunatic and that word is crazy. But I controlled myself and asked him why he thought *The King in Yellow* dangerous.

"Oh, I don't know," he said, hastily. "I only remember the excitement it created and the denunciations from pulpit and Press. I believe the author shot himself after bringing forth this monstrosity, didn't he?"

"I understand he is still alive," I answered.

"That's probably true," he muttered; "bullets couldn't kill a fiend like that."

"It is a book of great truths," I said.

"Yes," he replied, "of 'truths' which send men frantic and blast their lives. I don't care if the thing is, as they say, the very supreme essence of art. It's a crime to have written it, and I for one shall never open its pages."

"Is that what you have come to tell me?" I asked.

"No," he said, "I came to tell you that I am going to be married."

I believe for a moment my heart ceased to beat, but I kept my eyes on his face.

"Yes," he continued, smiling happily, "married to the sweetest girl on earth."

"Constance Hawberk," I said mechanically.

"How did you know?" he cried, astonished. "I didn't know it myself until that evening last April, when we strolled down to the embankment before dinner."

"When is it to be?" I asked.

"It was to have been next September, but an hour ago a despatch came ordering our regiment to the Presidio, San Francisco. We leave at noon to-morrow. To-morrow," he repeated. "Just think, Hildred, to-morrow I shall be the happiest fellow that ever drew breath in this jolly world, for Constance will go with me."

I offered him my hand in congratulation, and he seized and shook it like the good-natured fool he was—or pretended to be.

"I am going to get my squadron as a wedding present," he rattled on. "Captain and Mrs. Louis Castaigne, eh, Hildred?"

Then he told me where it was to be and who were to be there, and made me promise to come and be best man. I set my teeth and listened to his boyish chatter without showing what I felt, but—

I was getting to the limit of my endurance, and when he jumped up, and, switching his spurs till they jingled, said he must go, I did not detain him.

"There's one thing I want to ask of you," I said quietly.

"Out with it, it's promised," he laughed.

"I want you to meet me for a quarter of an hour's talk to-night."

"Of course, if you wish," he said, somewhat puzzled. "Where?"

"Anywhere, in the park there."

"What time, Hildred?"

"Midnight."

"What in the name of—" he began, but checked himself and laughingly assented. I watched him go down the stairs and hurry away, his sabre banging at every stride. He turned into Bleecker Street, and I knew he was going to see Constance. I gave him ten minutes to disappear and then followed in his footsteps, taking with me the jewelled crown and the silken robe embroidered with the Yellow Sign. When I turned into Bleecker Street, and entered the doorway which bore the sign—

MR. WILDE,
REPAIRER OF REPUTATIONS.
Third Bell.

I saw old Hawberk moving about in his shop, and imagined I heard Constance's voice in the parlour; but I avoided them both and hurried up the trembling stairways to Mr. Wilde's apartment. I knocked and entered without ceremony. Mr. Wilde lay groaning on the floor, his face covered with blood, his clothes torn to shreds. Drops of blood were scattered about over the carpet, which had also been ripped and frayed in the evidently recent struggle.

"It's that cursed cat," he said, ceasing his groans, and turning his colourless eyes to me; "she attacked me while I was asleep. I believe she will kill me yet."

This was too much, so I went into the kitchen, and, seizing a hatchet from the pantry, started to find the infernal beast and settle her then and there. My search was fruitless, and after a while I gave it up and came back to find Mr. Wilde squatting on his high chair by the table. He had washed his face and changed his clothes. The great furrows which the cat's claws had ploughed up in his face he had filled with collodion, and a rag hid the wound in his throat. I told him I should kill the cat when I came across her, but he only shook his head and turned to the open ledger before him. He read name after name of the people who had come to him in regard to their reputation, and the sums he had amassed were startling.

"I put on the screws now and then," he explained.

"One day or other some of these people will assassinate you," I insisted.

"Do you think so?" he said, rubbing his mutilated ears.

It was useless to argue with him, so I took down the manuscript entitled Imperial Dynasty of America, for the last time I should ever take it down in Mr. Wilde's study. I read it through, thrilling and trembling with pleasure. When I had finished Mr. Wilde took the manuscript and, turning to the dark passage which leads from his study to his bed-chamber, called out in a loud voice, "Vance." Then for the first time, I noticed a man crouching there in the shadow. How I had overlooked him during my search for the cat, I cannot imagine.

"Vance, come in," cried Mr. Wilde.

The figure rose and crept towards us, and I shall never forget the face that he raised to mine, as the light from the window illuminated it.

"Vance, this is Mr. Castaigne," said Mr. Wilde. Before he had finished speaking, the man threw himself on the ground before the table, crying and grasping, "Oh,

God! Oh, my God! Help me! Forgive me! Oh, Mr. Castaigne, keep that man away. You cannot, you cannot mean it! You are different—save me! I am broken down—I was in a madhouse and now—when all was coming right—when I had forgotten the King—the King in Yellow and—but I shall go mad again—I shall go mad—"

His voice died into a choking rattle, for Mr. Wilde had leapt on him and his right hand encircled the man's throat. When Vance fell in a heap on the floor, Mr. Wilde clambered nimbly into his chair again, and rubbing his mangled ears with the stump of his hand, turned to me and asked me for the ledger. I reached it down from the shelf and he opened it. After a moment's searching among the beautifully written pages, he coughed complacently, and pointed to the name Vance.

"Vance," he read aloud, "Osgood Oswald Vance." At the sound of his name, the man on the floor raised his head and turned a convulsed face to Mr. Wilde. His eyes were injected with blood, his lips tumefied. "Called April 28th," continued Mr. Wilde. "Occupation, cashier in the Seaforth National Bank; has served a term of forgery at Sing Sing, from whence he was transferred to the Asylum for the Criminal Insane. Pardoned by the Governor of New York, and discharged from the Asylum, January 19, 1918. Reputation damaged at Sheepshead Bay. Rumours that he lives beyond his income. Reputation to be repaired at once. Retainer $1,500.

"Note.—Has embezzled sums amounting to $30,000 since March 20, 1919, excellent family, and secured present position through uncle's influence. Father, President of Seaforth Bank."

I looked at the man on the floor.

"Get up, Vance," said Mr. Wilde in a gentle voice. Vance rose as if hypnotized. "He will do as we suggest now," observed Mr. Wilde, and opening the manuscript, he read the entire history of the Imperial Dynasty of America. Then in a kind and soothing murmur he ran over the important points with Vance, who stood like one stunned. His eyes were so blank and vacant that I imagined he had become half-witted, and remarked it to Mr. Wilde who replied that it was of no consequence anyway. Very patiently we pointed out to Vance what his share in the affair would be, and he seemed to understand after a while. Mr. Wilde explained the manuscript, using several volumes on Heraldry, to substantiate the result of his researches. He mentioned the establishment of the Dynasty in Carcosa, the lakes which connected Hastur, Aldebaran and the mystery of the Hyades. He spoke of Cassilda and Camilla, and sounded the cloudy depths of Demhe, and the Lake of Hali. "The scolloped tatters of the King in Yellow must hide Yhtill forever," he muttered, but I do not believe Vance heard him. Then by degrees he led Vance along the ramifications of the Imperial family, to Uoht and Thale, from Naotalba and Phantom of Truth, to Aldones, and then tossing aside his manuscript and notes, he began the wonderful story of the Last King. Fascinated and thrilled I watched him. He threw up his head, his long arms were stretched out in a magnificent gesture of pride and power, and his eyes blazed deep in their sockets like two emeralds. Vance listened stupefied. As for me, when at last Mr. Wilde had finished, and pointing to me, cried, "The cousin of the King!" my head swam with excitement.

Controlling myself with a superhuman effort, I explained to Vance why I alone was worthy of the crown and why my cousin must be exiled or die. I made him understand that my cousin must never marry, even after renouncing all his claims, and how that least of all he should marry the daughter of the Marquis of Avonshire and bring England into the question. I showed him a list of thousands of names which Mr. Wilde had drawn up; every man whose name was there had received the Yellow Sign which no living human being dared disregard. The city, the state, the whole land, were ready to rise and tremble before the Pallid Mask.

The time had come, the people should know the son of Hastur, and the whole world bow to the black stars which hang in the sky over Carcosa.

Vance leaned on the table, his head buried in his hands. Mr. Wilde drew a rough sketch on the margin of yesterday's *Herald* with a bit of lead pencil. It was a plan of Hawberk's rooms. Then he wrote out the order and affixed the seal, and shaking like a palsied man I signed my first writ of execution with my name Hildred-Rex.

Mr. Wilde clambered to the floor and unlocking the cabinet, took a long square box from the first shelf. This he brought to the table and opened. A new knife lay in the tissue paper inside and I picked it up and handed it to Vance, along with the order and the plan of Hawberk's apartment. Then Mr. Wilde told Vance he could go; and he went, shambling like an outcast of the slums.

I sat for a while watching the daylight fade behind the square tower of the Judson Memorial Church, and finally, gathering up the manuscript and notes, took my hat and started for the door.

Mr. Wilde watched me in silence. When I had stepped into the hall I looked back. Mr. Wilde's small eyes were still fixed on me. Behind him, the shadows gathered in the fading light. Then I closed the door behind me and went out into the darkening streets.

I had eaten nothing since breakfast, but I was not hungry. A wretched, half-starved creature, who stood looking across the street at the Lethal Chamber, noticed me and came up to tell me a tale of misery. I gave him money, I don't know why, and he went away without thanking me. An hour later another outcast approached and whined his story. I had a blank bit of paper in my pocket, on which was traced the Yellow Sign, and I handed it to him. He looked at it stupidly for a moment, and then with an uncertain glance at me, folded it with what seemed to me exaggerated care and placed it in his bosom.

The electric lights were sparkling among the trees, and the new moon shone in the sky above the Lethal Chamber. It was tiresome waiting in the square; I wandered from the Marble Arch to the artillery stables and back again to the lotos fountain. The flowers and grass exhaled a fragrance which troubled me. The jet of the fountain played in the moonlight, and the musical splash of falling drops reminded me of the tinkle of chained mail in Hawberk's shop. But it was not so fascinating, and the dull sparkle of the moonlight on the water brought no such sensations of exquisite pleasure, as when the sunshine played over the polished steel of a corselet on Hawberk's knee. I watched the bats darting and turning above the water plants in the fountain basin, but their rapid, jerky flight set my nerves on edge, and I went away again to walk aimlessly to and fro among the trees.

The artillery stables were dark, but in the cavalry barracks the officers' windows were brilliantly lighted, and the sallyport was constantly filled with troopers in fatigue, carrying straw and harness and baskets filled with tin dishes.

Twice the mounted sentry at the gates was changed while I wandered up and down the asphalt walk. I looked at my watch. It was nearly time. The lights in the barracks went out one by one, the barred gate was closed, and every minute or two an officer passed in through the side wicket, leaving a rattle of accoutrements and a jingle of spurs on the night air. The square had become very silent. The last homeless loiterer had been driven away by the grey-coated park policeman, the car tracks along Wooster Street were deserted, and the only sound which broke the stillness was the stamping of the sentry's horse and the ring of his sabre against the saddle pommel. In the barracks, the officers' quarters were still lighted, and military servants passed and repassed before the bay windows. Twelve o'clock sounded from the new spire of St. Francis Xavier, and at the last stroke of the sad-toned bell a figure passed through the wicket beside the portcullis, returned the salute of the sentry, and crossing the street entered the square and advanced toward the Benedick apartment house.

"Louis," I called.

The man pivoted on his spurred heels and came straight toward me.

"Is that you, Hildred?"

"Yes, you are on time."

I took his offered hand, and we strolled toward the Lethal Chamber.

He rattled on about his wedding and the graces of Constance, and their future prospects, calling my attention to his captain's shoulder-straps, and the triple gold arabesque on his sleeve and fatigue cap. I believe I listened as much to the music of his spurs and sabre as I did to his boyish babble, and at last we stood under the elms on the Fourth Street corner of the square opposite the Lethal Chamber. Then he laughed and asked me what I wanted with him. I motioned him to a seat on a bench under the electric light, and sat down beside him. He looked at me curiously, with that same searching glance which I hate and fear so in doctors. I felt the insult of his look, but he did not know it, and I carefully concealed my feelings.

"Well, old chap," he inquired, "what can I do for you?"

I drew from my pocket the manuscript and notes of the Imperial Dynasty of America, and looking him in the eye said:

"I will tell you. On your word as a soldier, promise me to read this manuscript from beginning to end, without asking me a question. Promise me to read these notes in the same way, and promise me to listen to what I have to tell later."

"I promise, if you wish it," he said pleasantly. "Give me the paper, Hildred."

He began to read, raising his eyebrows with a puzzled, whimsical air, which made me tremble with suppressed anger. As he advanced his, eyebrows contracted, and his lips seemed to form the word "rubbish."

Then he looked slightly bored, but apparently for my sake read, with an attempt at interest, which presently ceased to be an effort. He started when in the closely written pages he came to his own name, and when he came to mine he lowered the paper, and looked sharply at me for a moment. But he kept his word, and resumed his reading, and I let the half-formed question die on his lips unanswered. When he came to the end and read the signature of Mr. Wilde, he folded the paper carefully and returned it to me. I handed him the notes, and he settled back, pushing his fatigue cap up to his forehead, with a boyish gesture, which I remembered so well in school. I watched his face as he read, and when he finished I took the notes with the manuscript, and placed them in my pocket. Then I unfolded a scroll marked with the Yellow Sign. He saw the sign, but he did not seem to recognize it, and I called his attention to it somewhat sharply.

"Well," he said, "I see it. What is it?"

"It is the Yellow Sign," I said angrily.

"Oh, that's it, is it?" said Louis, in that flattering voice, which Doctor Archer used to employ with me, and would probably have employed again, had I not settled his affair for him.

I kept my rage down and answered as steadily as possible, "Listen, you have engaged your word?"

"I am listening, old chap," he replied soothingly.

I began to speak very calmly.

"Dr. Archer, having by some means become possessed of the secret of the Imperial Succession, attempted to deprive me of my right, alleging that because of a fall from my horse four years ago, I had become mentally deficient. He presumed to place me under restraint in his own house in hopes of either driving me insane or poisoning me. I have not forgotten it. I visited him last night and the interview was final."

Louis turned quite pale, but did not move. I resumed triumphantly, "There are yet three people to be interviewed in the interests of Mr. Wilde and myself. They are my cousin Louis, Mr. Hawberk, and his daughter Constance."

Louis sprang to his feet and I arose also, and flung the paper marked with the Yellow Sign to the ground.

"Oh, I don't need that to tell you what I have to say," I cried, with a laugh of triumph. "You must renounce the crown to me, do you hear, to *me*."

Louis looked at me with a startled air, but recovering himself said kindly, "Of course I renounce the—what is it I must renounce?"

"The crown," I said angrily.

"Of course," he answered, "I renounce it. Come, old chap, I'll walk back to your rooms with you."

"Don't try any of your doctor's tricks on me," I cried, trembling with fury. "Don't act as if you think I am insane."

"What nonsense," he replied. "Come, it's getting late, Hildred."

"No," I shouted, "you must listen. You cannot marry, I forbid it. Do you hear? I forbid it. You shall renounce the crown, and in reward I grant you exile, but if you refuse you shall die."

He tried to calm me, but I was roused at last, and drawing my long knife barred his way.

Then I told him how they would find Dr. Archer in the cellar with his throat open, and I laughed in his face when I thought of Vance and his knife, and the order signed by me.

"Ah, you are the King," I cried, "but I shall be King. Who are you to keep me from Empire over all the habitable earth! I was born the cousin of a king, but I shall be King!"

Louis stood white and rigid before me. Suddenly a man came running up Fourth Street, entered the gate of the Lethal Temple, traversed the path to the bronze doors at full speed, and plunged into the death chamber with the cry of one demented, and I laughed until I wept tears, for I had recognized Vance, and knew that Hawberk and his daughter were no longer in my way.

"Go," I cried to Louis, "you have ceased to be a menace. You will never marry Constance now, and if you marry any one else in your exile, I will visit you as I did my doctor last night. Mr. Wilde takes charge of you to-morrow." Then I turned and darted into South Fifth Avenue, and with a cry of terror Louis dropped his belt and sabre and followed me like the wind. I heard him close behind me at the corner of Bleecker Street, and I dashed into the doorway under Hawberk's sign. He cried, "Halt, or I fire!" but when he saw that I flew up the stairs leaving Hawberk's shop below, he left me, and I heard him hammering and shouting at their door as though it were possible to arouse the dead.

Mr. Wilde's door was open, and I entered crying, "It is done, it is done! Let the nations rise and look upon their King!" but I could not find Mr. Wilde, so I went to the cabinet and took the splendid diadem from its case. Then I drew on the white silk robe, embroidered with the Yellow Sign, and placed the crown upon my head. At last I was King, King by my right in Hastur, King because I knew the mystery of the Hyades, and my mind had sounded the depths of the Lake of Hali. I was King! The first grey pencillings of dawn would raise a tempest which would shake two hemispheres. Then as I stood, my every nerve pitched to the highest tension, faint with the joy and splendour of my thought, without, in the dark passage, a man groaned.

I seized the tallow dip and sprang to the door. The cat passed me like a demon, and the tallow dip went out, but my long knife flew swifter than she, and I heard her screech, and I knew that my knife had found her. For a moment I listened to her tumbling and thumping about in the darkness, and then when her frenzy ceased, I lighted a lamp and raised it over my head. Mr. Wilde lay on the floor with his throat torn open. At first I thought he was dead, but as I looked, a green sparkle came into his sunken eyes, his mutilated hand trembled, and then a spasm stretched his mouth from ear to ear. For a moment my terror and despair gave place to hope, but as I bent over him his eyeballs rolled clean around in his head, and he died. Then while I stood, transfixed with rage and despair, seeing my crown, my empire, every hope and every ambition, my very life, lying prostrate there with the dead master, *they* came, seized me from behind, and bound me until my veins stood out like cords, and my voice failed with the paroxysms of my frenzied screams. But I still raged, bleeding and infuriated among them, and more than one policeman felt my sharp teeth. Then when I could no longer move they came nearer; I saw old Hawberk, and behind him my cousin Louis' ghastly face, and farther away, in the corner, a woman, Constance, weeping softly.

"Ah! I see it now!" I shrieked. "You have seized the throne and the empire. Woe! woe to you who are crowned with the crown of the King in Yellow!"

[EDITOR'S NOTE.—Mr. Castaigne died yesterday in the Asylum for Criminal Insane.]

# THE MASK

Camilla: You, sir, should unmask.
Stranger: Indeed?
Cassilda: Indeed it's time. We all have laid aside disguise but you.
Stranger: I wear no mask.
Camilla: (Terrified, aside to Cassilda.) No mask? No mask!

*The King in Yellow, Act I, Scene 2.*

## I

Although I knew nothing of chemistry, I listened fascinated. He picked up an Easter lily which Geneviève had brought that morning from Notre Dame, and dropped it into the basin. Instantly the liquid lost its crystalline clearness. For a second the lily was enveloped in a milk-white foam, which disappeared, leaving the fluid opalescent. Changing tints of orange and crimson played over the surface, and then what seemed to be a ray of pure sunlight struck through from the bottom where the lily was resting. At the same instant he plunged his hand into the basin and drew out the flower. "There is no danger," he explained, "if you choose the right moment. That golden ray is the signal."

He held the lily toward me, and I took it in my hand. It had turned to stone, to the purest marble.

"You see," he said, "it is without a flaw. What sculptor could reproduce it?"

The marble was white as snow, but in its depths the veins of the lily were tinged with palest azure, and a faint flush lingered deep in its heart.

"Don't ask me the reason of that," he smiled, noticing my wonder. "I have no idea why the veins and heart are tinted, but they always are. Yesterday I tried one of Geneviève's gold-fish,—there it is."

The fish looked as if sculptured in marble. But if you held it to the light the stone was beautifully veined with a faint blue, and from somewhere within came a rosy light like the tint which slumbers in an opal. I looked into the basin. Once more it seemed filled with clearest crystal.

"If I should touch it now?" I demanded.

"I don't know," he replied, "but you had better not try."

"There is one thing I'm curious about," I said, "and that is where the ray of sunlight came from."

"It looked like a sunbeam true enough," he said. "I don't know, it always comes when I immerse any living thing. Perhaps," he continued, smiling, "perhaps it is the vital spark of the creature escaping to the source from whence it came."

I saw he was mocking, and threatened him with a mahl-stick, but he only laughed and changed the subject.

"Stay to lunch. Geneviève will be here directly."

"I saw her going to early mass," I said, "and she looked as fresh and sweet as that lily—before you destroyed it."

"Do you think I destroyed it?" said Boris gravely.

"Destroyed, preserved, how can we tell?"

We sat in the corner of a studio near his unfinished group of the "Fates." He leaned back on the sofa, twirling a sculptor's chisel and squinting at his work.

"By the way," he said, "I have finished pointing up that old academic Ariadne, and I suppose it will have to go to the Salon. It's all I have ready this year, but after the success the 'Madonna' brought me I feel ashamed to send a thing like that."

The "Madonna," an exquisite marble for which Geneviève had sat, had been the sensation of last year's Salon. I looked at the Ariadne. It was a magnificent piece of technical work, but I agreed with Boris that the world would expect something better of him than that. Still, it was impossible now to think of finishing in time for the Salon that splendid terrible group half shrouded in the marble behind me. The "Fates" would have to wait.

We were proud of Boris Yvain. We claimed him and he claimed us on the strength of his having been born in America, although his father was French and his mother was a Russian. Every one in the Beaux Arts called him Boris. And yet there were only two of us whom he addressed in the same familiar way—Jack Scott and myself.

Perhaps my being in love with Geneviève had something to do with his affection for me. Not that it had ever been acknowledged between us. But after all was settled, and she had told me with tears in her eyes that it was Boris whom she loved, I went over to his house and congratulated him. The perfect cordiality of that interview did not deceive either of us, I always believed, although to one at least it was a great comfort. I do not think he and Geneviève ever spoke of the matter together, but Boris knew.

Geneviève was lovely. The Madonna-like purity of her face might have been inspired by the Sanctus in Gounod's Mass. But I was always glad when she changed that mood for what we called her "April Manœuvres." She was often as variable as an April day. In the morning grave, dignified and sweet, at noon laughing, capricious, at evening whatever one least expected. I preferred her so rather than in that Madonna-like tranquillity which stirred the depths of my heart. I was dreaming of Gen-eviève when he spoke again.

"What do you think of my discovery, Alec?"

"I think it wonderful."

"I shall make no use of it, you know, beyond satisfying my own curiosity so far as may be, and the secret will die with me."

"It would be rather a blow to sculpture, would it not? We painters lose more than we ever gain by photography."

Boris nodded, playing with the edge of the chisel.

"This new vicious discovery would corrupt the world of art. No, I shall never confide the secret to any one," he said slowly.

It would be hard to find any one less informed about such phenomena than myself; but of course I had heard of mineral springs so saturated with silica that the leaves and twigs which fell into them were turned to stone after a time. I dimly comprehended the process, how the silica replaced the vegetable matter, atom by atom, and the result was a duplicate of the object in stone. This, I confess, had never interested me greatly, and as for the ancient fossils thus produced, they disgusted me. Boris, it appeared, feeling curiosity instead of repugnance, had investigated the subject, and had accidentally stumbled on a solution which, attacking the immersed object with a ferocity unheard of, in a second did the work of years. This was all I could make out of the strange story he had just been telling me. He spoke again after a long silence.

"I am almost frightened when I think what I have found. Scientists would go mad over the discovery. It was so simple too; it discovered itself. When I think of that formula, and that new element precipitated in metallic scales—"

"What new element?"

"Oh, I haven't thought of naming it, and I don't believe I ever shall. There are enough precious metals now in the world to cut throats over."

I pricked up my ears. "Have you struck gold, Boris?"

"No, better;—but see here, Alec!" he laughed, starting up. "You and I have all we need in this world. Ah! how sinister and covetous you look already!" I laughed too, and told him I was devoured by the desire for gold, and we had better talk of something else; so when Geneviève came in shortly after, we had turned our backs on alchemy.

Geneviève was dressed in silvery grey from head to foot. The light glinted along the soft curves of her fair hair as she turned her cheek to Boris; then she saw me and returned my greeting. She had never before failed to blow me a kiss from the tips of her white fingers, and I promptly complained of the omission. She smiled and held out her hand, which dropped almost before it had touched mine; then she said, looking at Boris—

"You must ask Alec to stay for luncheon." This also was something new. She had always asked me herself until to-day.

"I did," said Boris shortly.

"And you said yes, I hope?" She turned to me with a charming conventional smile. I might have been an acquaintance of the day before yesterday. I made her a low bow. "J'avais bien l'honneur, madame," but refusing to take up our usual bantering tone, she murmured a hospitable commonplace and disappeared. Boris and I looked at one another.

"I had better go home, don't you think?" I asked.

"Hanged if I know," he replied frankly.

While we were discussing the advisability of my departure Geneviève reappeared in the doorway without her bonnet. She was wonderfully beautiful, but her colour was too deep and her lovely eyes were too bright. She came straight up to me and took my arm.

"Luncheon is ready. Was I cross, Alec? I thought I had a headache, but I haven't. Come here, Boris;" and she slipped her other arm through his. "Alec knows that after you there is no one in the world whom I like as well as I like him, so if he sometimes feels snubbed it won't hurt him."

"À la bonheur!" I cried, "who says there are no thunderstorms in April?"

"Are you ready?" chanted Boris. "Aye ready;" and arm-in-arm we raced into the dining-room, scandalizing the servants. After all we were not so much to blame; Geneviève was eighteen, Boris was twenty-three, and I not quite twenty-one.

## II

Some work that I was doing about this time on the decorations for Geneviève's boudoir kept me constantly at the quaint little hotel in the Rue Sainte-Cécile. Boris and I in those days laboured hard but as we pleased, which was fitfully, and we all three, with Jack Scott, idled a great deal together.

One quiet afternoon I had been wandering alone over the house examining curios, prying into odd corners, bringing out sweetmeats and cigars from strange hiding-places, and at last I stopped in the bathing-room. Boris, all over clay, stood there washing his hands.

The room was built of rose-coloured marble excepting the floor, which was tessellated in rose and grey. In the centre was a square pool sunken below the surface of the floor; steps led down into it, sculptured pillars supported a frescoed ceiling. A delicious marble Cupid appeared to have just alighted on his pedestal at the upper end of the room. The whole interior was Boris' work and mine. Boris, in his working-clothes of white canvas, scraped the traces of clay and red modelling wax from his handsome hands, and coquetted over his shoulder with the Cupid.

"I see you," he insisted, "don't try to look the other way and pretend not to see me. You know who made you, little humbug!"

It was always my rôle to interpret Cupid's sentiments in these conversations, and when my turn came I responded in such a manner, that Boris seized my arm and dragged me toward the pool, declaring he would duck me. Next instant he dropped my arm and turned pale. "Good God!" he said, "I forgot the pool is full of the solution!"

I shivered a little, and dryly advised him to remember better where he had stored the precious liquid.

"In Heaven's name, why do you keep a small lake of that gruesome stuff here of all places?" I asked.

"I want to experiment on something large," he replied.

"On me, for instance?"

"Ah! that came too close for jesting; but I do want to watch the action of that solution on a more highly organized living body; there is that big white rabbit," he said, following me into the studio.

Jack Scott, wearing a paint-stained jacket, came wandering in, appropriated all the Oriental sweetmeats he could lay his hands on, looted the cigarette case, and finally he and Boris disappeared together to visit the Luxembourg Gallery, where a new silver bronze by Rodin and a landscape of Monet's were claiming the exclusive attention of artistic France. I went back to the studio, and resumed my work. It was a Renaissance screen, which Boris wanted me to paint for Geneviève's boudoir. But the small boy who was unwillingly dawdling through a series of poses for it, to-day refused all bribes to be good. He never rested an instant in the same position, and inside of five minutes I had as many different outlines of the little beggar.

"Are you posing, or are you executing a song and dance, my friend?" I inquired.

"Whichever monsieur pleases," he replied, with an angelic smile.

Of course I dismissed him for the day, and of course I paid him for the full time, that being the way we spoil our models.

After the young imp had gone, I made a few perfunctory daubs at my work, but was so thoroughly out of humour, that it took me the rest of the afternoon to undo the damage I had done, so at last I scraped my palette, stuck my brushes in a bowl of black soap, and strolled into the smoking-room. I really believe that, excepting Geneviève's apartments, no room in the house was so free from the perfume of tobacco as this one. It was a queer chaos of odds and ends, hung with threadbare tapestry. A sweet-toned old spinet in good repair stood by the window. There were stands of weapons, some old and dull, others bright and modern, festoons of Indian and Turkish armour over the mantel, two or three good pictures, and a pipe-rack. It was here that we used to come for new sensations in smoking. I doubt if any type of pipe ever existed which was not represented in that rack. When we had selected one, we immediately carried it somewhere else and smoked it; for the place was, on the whole, more gloomy and less inviting than any in the house. But this afternoon, the twilight was very soothing, the rugs and skins on the floor looked brown and soft and drowsy; the big couch was piled with cushions—I found my pipe and curled up there for an unaccustomed smoke in the smoking-room. I had chosen one with a long flexible stem, and lighting it fell to dreaming. After a while it went out, but I did not stir. I dreamed on and presently fell asleep.

I awoke to the saddest music I had ever heard. The room was quite dark, I had no idea what time it was. A ray of moonlight silvered one edge of the old spinet, and the polished wood seemed to exhale the sounds as perfume floats above a box of sandalwood. Some one rose in the darkness, and came away weeping quietly, and I was fool enough to cry out "Geneviève!"

She dropped at my voice, and, I had time to curse myself while I made a light and tried to raise her from the floor. She shrank away with a murmur of pain. She was very quiet, and asked for Boris. I carried her to the divan, and went to look for him, but he was not in the house, and the servants were gone to bed. Perplexed and anxious, I hurried back to Geneviève. She lay where I had left her, looking very white.

"I can't find Boris nor any of the servants," I said.

"I know," she answered faintly, "Boris has gone to Ept with Mr. Scott. I did not remember when I sent you for him just now."

"But he can't get back in that case before to-morrow afternoon, and—are you hurt? Did I frighten you into falling? What an awful fool I am, but I was only half awake."

"Boris thought you had gone home before dinner. Do please excuse us for letting you stay here all this time."

"I have had a long nap," I laughed, "so sound that I did not know whether I was still asleep or not when I found myself staring at a figure that was moving toward me, and called out your name. Have you been trying the old spinet? You must have played very softly."

I would tell a thousand more lies worse than that one to see the look of relief that came into her face. She smiled adorably, and said in her natural voice: "Alec, I tripped on that wolf's head, and I think my ankle is sprained. Please call Marie, and then go home."

I did as she bade me, and left her there when the maid came in.

### III

At noon next day when I called, I found Boris walking restlessly about his studio.

"Geneviève is asleep just now," he told me, "the sprain is nothing, but why should she have such a high fever? The doctor can't account for it; or else he will not," he muttered.

"Geneviève has a fever?" I asked.

"I should say so, and has actually been a little light-headed at intervals all night. The idea!—gay little Geneviève, without a care in the world,—and she keeps saying her heart's broken, and she wants to die!"

My own heart stood still.

Boris leaned against the door of his studio, looking down, his hands in his pockets, his kind, keen eyes clouded, a new line of trouble drawn "over the mouth's good mark, that made the smile." The maid had orders to summon him the instant Geneviève opened her eyes. We waited and waited, and Boris, growing restless, wandered about, fussing with modelling wax and red clay. Suddenly he started for the next room. "Come and see my rose-coloured bath full of death!" he cried.

"Is it death?" I asked, to humour his mood.

"You are not prepared to call it life, I suppose," he answered. As he spoke he plucked a solitary gold-fish squirming and twisting out of its globe. "We'll send this one after the other—wherever that is," he said. There was feverish excitement in his voice. A dull weight of fever lay on my limbs and on my brain as I followed him to the fair crystal pool with its pink-tinted sides; and he dropped the creature in. Falling, its scales flashed with a hot orange gleam in its angry twistings and contortions; the moment it struck the liquid it became rigid and sank heavily to the bottom. Then came the milky foam, the splendid hues radiating on the surface and then the shaft of pure serene light broke through from seemingly infinite depths. Boris plunged in his hand and drew out an exquisite marble thing, blue-veined, rose-tinted, and glistening with opalescent drops.

"Child's play," he muttered, and looked wearily, longingly at me,—as if I could answer such questions! But Jack Scott came in and entered into the "game," as he called it, with ardour. Nothing would do but to try the experiment on the white rabbit then and there. I was willing that Boris should find distraction from his cares, but I hated to see the life go out of a warm, living creature and I declined to be present. Picking up a book at random, I sat down in the studio to read. Alas! I had found *The King in Yellow*. After a few moments, which seemed ages, I was putting it away with a nervous shudder, when Boris and Jack came in bringing their marble rabbit. At the same time the bell rang above, and a cry came from the sick-room. Boris was gone like a flash, and the next moment he called, "Jack, run for the doctor; bring him back with you. Alec, come here."

I went and stood at her door. A frightened maid came out in haste and ran away to fetch some remedy. Geneviève, sitting bolt upright, with crimson cheeks and glittering eyes, babbled incessantly and resisted Boris' gentle restraint. He called me to help. At my first touch she sighed and sank back, closing her eyes, and then—then—as we still bent above her, she opened them again, looked straight into Boris' face—poor fever-crazed girl!—and told her secret. At the same instant our three lives turned into new channels; the bond that held us so long together snapped for ever and a new bond was forged in its place, for she had spoken my name, and as the fever tortured her, her heart poured out its load of hidden sorrow. Amazed and dumb I bowed my head, while my face burned like a live coal, and the blood surged in my ears, stupefying me with its clamour. Incapable of movement, incapable of speech, I listened to her feverish words in an agony of shame and sorrow. I could not silence her, I could not look at Boris. Then I felt an arm upon my shoulder, and Boris turned a bloodless face to mine.

"It is not your fault, Alec; don't grieve so if she loves you—" but he could not finish; and as the doctor stepped swiftly into the room, saying—"Ah, the fever!" I seized Jack Scott and hurried him to the street, saying, "Boris would rather be alone." We crossed the street to our own apartments, and that night, seeing I was going to be ill too, he went for the doctor again. The last thing I recollect with any distinctness was hearing Jack say, "For Heaven's sake, doctor, what ails him, to wear a face like that?" and I thought of *The King in Yellow* and the Pallid Mask.

I was very ill, for the strain of two years which I had endured since that fatal May morning when Geneviève murmured, "I love you, but I think I love Boris best," told on me at last. I had never imagined that it could become more than I could endure. Outwardly tranquil, I had deceived myself. Although the inward battle raged night after night, and I, lying alone in my room, cursed myself for rebellious thoughts unloyal to Boris and unworthy of Geneviève, the morning always brought relief, and I returned to Geneviève and to my dear Boris with a heart washed clean by the tempests of the night.

Never in word or deed or thought while with them had I betrayed my sorrow even to myself.

The mask of self-deception was no longer a mask for me, it was a part of me. Night lifted it, laying bare the stifled truth below; but there was no one to see except myself, and when the day broke the mask fell back again of its own accord. These thoughts passed through my troubled mind as I lay sick, but they were hopelessly entangled with visions of white creatures, heavy as stone, crawling about in Boris' basin,—of the wolf's head on the rug, foaming and snapping at Geneviève, who lay smiling beside it. I thought, too, of the King in Yellow wrapped in the fantastic colours of his tattered mantle, and that bitter cry of Cassilda, "Not upon us, oh King, not upon us!" Feverishly I struggled to put it from me, but I saw the lake of Hali, thin and blank, without a ripple or wind to stir it, and I saw the towers of Carcosa behind the moon. Aldebaran, the Hyades, Alar, Hastur, glided through the cloud-rifts which fluttered and flapped as they passed like the scolloped tatters of the King in Yellow. Among all these, one sane thought persisted. It never wavered, no matter what else was going on in my disordered mind, that my chief reason for existing was to meet some requirement of Boris and Geneviève. What this obligation was, its nature, was never clear; sometimes it seemed to be protection, sometimes support, through a great crisis. Whatever it seemed to be for the time, its weight rested only on me, and I was never so ill or so weak that I did not respond with my whole soul.

There were always crowds of faces about me, mostly strange, but a few I recognized, Boris among them. Afterward they told me that this could not have been, but I know that once at least he bent over me. It was only a touch, a faint echo of his voice, then the clouds settled back on my senses, and I lost him, but he *did* stand there and bend over me *once* at least.

At last, one morning I awoke to find the sunlight falling across my bed, and Jack Scott reading beside me. I had not strength enough to speak aloud, neither could I think, much less remember, but I could smile feebly, as Jack's eye met mine, and when he jumped up and asked eagerly if I wanted anything, I could whisper, "Yes— Boris." Jack moved to the head of my bed, and leaned down to arrange my pillow: I did not see his face, but he answered heartily, "You must wait, Alec; you are too weak to see even Boris."

I waited and I grew strong; in a few days I was able to see whom I would, but meanwhile I had thought and remembered. From the moment when all the past grew clear again in my mind, I never doubted what I should do when the time came, and I felt sure that Boris would have resolved upon the same course so far as he was concerned; as for what pertained to me alone, I knew he would see that also as I did. I no longer asked for any one. I never inquired why no message came from them; why during the week I lay there, waiting and growing stronger, I never heard their name spoken. Preoccupied with my own searchings for the right way, and with my feeble but determined fight against despair, I simply acquiesced in Jack's reticence, taking for granted that he was afraid to speak of them, lest I should turn unruly and insist on seeing them. Meanwhile I said over and over to myself, how would it be when life began again for us all? We would take up our relations exactly as they were before Geneviève fell ill. Boris and I would look into each other's eyes, and there would be neither rancour nor cowardice nor mistrust in that glance. I would be with them again for a little while in the dear intimacy of their home, and then, without pretext or explanation, I would disappear from their lives for ever. Boris would know; Geneviève—the only comfort was that she would never know. It seemed, as I thought it over, that I had found the meaning of that sense of obligation which had persisted all through my delirium, and the only possible answer to it. So, when I was quite ready, I beckoned Jack to me one day, and said—

"Jack, I want Boris at once; and take my dearest greeting to Geneviève...."

When at last he made me understand that they were both dead, I fell into a wild rage that tore all my little convalescent strength to atoms. I raved and cursed myself into a relapse, from which I crawled forth some weeks afterward a boy of twenty-one who believed that his youth was gone for ever. I seemed to be past the capability of further suffering, and one day when Jack handed me a letter and the keys to Boris' house, I took them without a tremor and asked him to tell me all. It was cruel of me to ask him, but there was no help for it, and he leaned wearily on his thin hands, to reopen the wound which could never entirely heal. He began very quietly—

"Alec, unless you have a clue that I know nothing about, you will not be able to explain any more than I what has happened. I suspect that you would rather not hear these details, but you must learn them, else I would spare you the relation. God knows I wish I could be spared the telling. I shall use few words.

"That day when I left you in the doctor's care and came back to Boris, I found him working on the 'Fates.' Geneviève, he said, was sleeping under the influence of drugs. She had been quite out of her mind, he said. He kept on working, not talking any more, and I watched him. Before long, I saw that the third figure of the group— the one looking straight ahead, out over the world—bore his face; not as you ever saw it, but as it looked then and to the end. This is one thing for which I should like to find an explanation, but I never shall.

"Well, he worked and I watched him in silence, and we went on that way until nearly midnight. Then we heard the door open and shut sharply, and a swift rush in the next room. Boris sprang through the doorway and I followed; but we were too late. She lay at the bottom of the pool, her hands across her breast. Then Boris shot himself through the heart." Jack stopped speaking, drops of sweat stood under his eyes, and his thin cheeks twitched. "I carried Boris to his room. Then I went back and let that hellish fluid out of the pool, and turning on all the water, washed the marble clean of every drop. When at length I dared descend the steps, I found her lying there as white as snow. At last, when I had decided what was best to do, I went into the laboratory, and first emptied the solution in the basin into the waste-pipe; then I poured the contents of every jar and bottle after it. There was wood in the fireplace, so I built a fire, and breaking the locks of Boris' cabinet I burnt every paper, notebook and letter that I found there. With a mallet from the studio I smashed to pieces all the empty bottles, then loading them into a coal-scuttle, I carried them to the cellar and threw them over the red-hot bed of the furnace. Six times I made the journey, and at last, not a vestige remained of anything which might again aid in seeking for the formula which Boris had found. Then at last I dared call the doctor. He is a good man, and together we struggled to keep it from the public. Without him I never could have succeeded. At last we got the servants paid and sent away into the country, where old Rosier keeps them quiet with stories of Boris' and Geneviève's travels in distant lands, from whence they will not return for years. We buried Boris in the little cemetery of Sèvres. The doctor is a good creature, and knows when to pity a man who can bear no more. He gave his certificate of heart disease and asked no questions of me."

Then, lifting his head from his hands, he said, "Open the letter, Alec; it is for us both."

I tore it open. It was Boris' will dated a year before. He left everything to Geneviève, and in case of her dying childless, I was to take control of the house in the Rue Sainte-Cécile, and Jack Scott the management at Ept. On our deaths the property reverted to his mother's family in Russia, with the exception of the sculptured marbles executed by himself. These he left to me.

The page blurred under our eyes, and Jack got up and walked to the window. Presently he returned and sat down again. I dreaded to hear what he was going to say, but he spoke with the same simplicity and gentleness.

"Geneviève lies before the Madonna in the marble room. The Madonna bends tenderly above her, and Geneviève smiles back into that calm face that never would have been except for her."

His voice broke, but he grasped my hand, saying, "Courage, Alec." Next morning he left for Ept to fulfil his trust.

# IV

The same evening I took the keys and went into the house I had known so well. Everything was in order, but the silence was terrible. Though I went twice to the door of the marble room, I could not force myself to enter. It was beyond my strength. I went into the smoking-room and sat down before the spinet. A small lace handkerchief lay on the keys, and I turned away, choking. It was plain I could not stay, so I locked every door, every window, and the three front and back gates, and went away. Next morning Alcide packed my valise, and leaving him in charge of my apartments I took the Orient express for Constantinople. During the two years that I wandered through the East, at first, in our letters, we never mentioned Geneviève and Boris, but gradually their names crept in. I recollect particularly a passage in one of Jack's letters replying to one of mine—

"What you tell me of seeing Boris bending over you while you lay ill, and feeling his touch on your face, and hearing his voice, of course troubles me. This that you describe must have happened a fortnight after he died. I say to myself that you were dreaming, that it was part of your delirium, but the explanation does not satisfy me, nor would it you."

Toward the end of the second year a letter came from Jack to me in India so unlike anything that I had ever known of him that I decided to return at once to Paris. He wrote: "I am well, and sell all my pictures as artists do who have no need of money. I have not a care of my own, but I am more restless than if I had. I am unable to shake off a strange anxiety about you. It is not apprehension, it is rather a breathless expectancy—of what, God knows! I can only say it is wearing me out. Nights I dream always of you and Boris. I can never recall anything afterward, but I wake in the morning with my heart beating, and all day the excitement increases until I fall asleep at night to recall the same experience. I am quite exhausted by it, and have determined to break up this morbid condition. I must see you. Shall I go to Bombay, or will you come to Paris?"

I telegraphed him to expect me by the next steamer.

When we met I thought he had changed very little; I, he insisted, looked in splendid health. It was good to hear his voice again, and as we sat and chatted about what life still held for us, we felt that it was pleasant to be alive in the bright spring weather.

We stayed in Paris together a week, and then I went for a week to Ept with him, but first of all we went to the cemetery at Sèvres, where Boris lay.

"Shall we place the 'Fates' in the little grove above him?" Jack asked, and I answered—

"I think only the 'Madonna' should watch over Boris' grave." But Jack was none the better for my home-coming. The dreams of which he could not retain even the least definite outline continued, and he said that at times the sense of breathless expectancy was suffocating.

"You see I do you harm and not good," I said. "Try a change without me." So he started alone for a ramble among the Channel Islands, and I went back to Paris. I had not yet entered Boris' house, now mine, since my return, but I knew it must be done. It had been kept in order by Jack; there were servants there, so I gave up my own apartment and went there to live. Instead of the agitation I had feared, I found myself able to paint there tranquilly. I visited all the rooms—all but one. I could not bring myself to enter the marble room where Geneviève lay, and yet I felt the longing growing daily to look upon her face, to kneel beside her.

One April afternoon, I lay dreaming in the smoking-room, just as I had lain two years before, and mechanically I looked among the tawny Eastern rugs for the wolf-skin. At last I distinguished the pointed ears and flat cruel head, and I thought of my dream where I saw Geneviève lying beside it. The helmets still hung against the threadbare tapestry, among them the old Spanish morion which I remembered Geneviève had once put on when we were amusing ourselves with the ancient bits of mail. I turned my eyes to the spinet; every yellow key seemed eloquent of her caressing hand, and I rose, drawn by the strength of my life's passion to the sealed door of the marble room. The heavy doors swung inward under my trembling hands. Sunlight poured through the window, tipping with gold the wings of Cupid, and lingered like a nimbus over the brows of the Madonna. Her tender face bent in compassion over a marble form so exquisitely pure that I knelt and signed myself. Geneviève lay in the shadow under the Madonna, and yet, through her white arms, I saw the pale azure vein, and beneath her softly clasped hands the folds of her dress were tinged with rose, as if from some faint warm light within her breast.

Bending, with a breaking heart, I touched the marble drapery with my lips, then crept back into the silent house.

A maid came and brought me a letter, and I sat down in the little conservatory to read it; but as I was about to break the seal, seeing the girl lingering, I asked her what she wanted.

She stammered something about a white rabbit that had been caught in the house, and asked what should be done with it. I told her to let it loose in the walled garden behind the house, and opened my letter. It was from Jack, but so incoherent that I thought he must have lost his reason. It was nothing but a series of prayers to me not to leave the house until he could get back; he could not tell me why, there were the dreams, he said—he could explain nothing, but he was sure that I must not leave the house in the Rue Sainte-Cécile.

As I finished reading I raised my eyes and saw the same maid-servant standing in the doorway holding a glass dish in which two gold-fish were swimming: "Put them back into the tank and tell me what you mean by interrupting me," I said.

With a half-suppressed whimper she emptied water and fish into an aquarium at the end of the conservatory, and turning to me asked my permission to leave my service. She said people were playing tricks on her, evidently with a design of getting her into trouble; the marble rabbit had been stolen and a live one had been brought into the house; the two beautiful marble fish were gone, and she had just found those common live things flopping on the dining-room floor. I reassured her and sent her away, saying I would look about myself. I went into the studio; there was nothing there but my canvases and some casts, except the marble of the Easter lily. I saw it on a table across the room. Then I strode angrily over to it. But the flower I lifted from the table was fresh and fragile and filled the air with perfume.

Then suddenly I comprehended, and sprang through the hallway to the marble room. The doors flew open, the sunlight streamed into my face, and through it, in a heavenly glory, the Madonna smiled, as Geneviève lifted her flushed face from her marble couch and opened her sleepy eyes.

# IN THE COURT OF THE DRAGON

"Oh, thou who burn'st in heart for those who burn
In Hell, whose fires thyself shall feed in turn;
How long be crying—'Mercy on them.' God!
Why, who art thou to teach and He to learn?"

In the Church of St. Barnabé vespers were over; the clergy left the altar; the little choir-boys flocked across the chancel and settled in the stalls. A Suisse in rich uniform marched down the south aisle, sounding his staff at every fourth step on the stone pavement; behind him came that eloquent preacher and good man, Monseigneur C——.

My chair was near the chancel rail, I now turned toward the west end of the church. The other people between the altar and the pulpit turned too. There was a little scraping and rustling while the congregation seated itself again; the preacher mounted the pulpit stairs, and the organ voluntary ceased.

I had always found the organ-playing at St. Barnabé highly interesting. Learned and scientific it was, too much so for my small knowledge, but expressing a vivid if cold intelligence. Moreover, it possessed the French quality of taste: taste reigned supreme, self-controlled, dignified and reticent.

To-day, however, from the first chord I had felt a change for the worse, a sinister change. During vespers it had been chiefly the chancel organ which supported the beautiful choir, but now and again, quite wantonly as it seemed, from the west gallery where the great organ stands, a heavy hand had struck across the church at the serene peace of those clear voices. It was something more than harsh and dissonant, and it betrayed no lack of skill. As it recurred again and again, it set me thinking of what my architect's books say about the custom in early times to consecrate the choir as soon as it was built, and that the nave, being finished sometimes half a century later, often did not get any blessing at all: I wondered idly if that had been the case at St. Barnabé, and whether something not usually supposed to be at home in a Christian church might have entered undetected and taken possession of the west gallery. I had read of such things happening, too, but not in works on architecture.

Then I remembered that St. Barnabé was not much more than a hundred years old, and smiled at the incongruous association of mediaeval superstitions with that cheerful little piece of eighteenth-century rococo.

But now vespers were over, and there should have followed a few quiet chords, fit to accompany meditation, while we waited for the sermon. Instead of that, the discord at the lower end of the church broke out with the departure of the clergy, as if now nothing could control it.

I belong to those children of an older and simpler generation who do not love to seek for psychological subtleties in art; and I have ever refused to find in music anything more than melody and harmony, but I felt that in the labyrinth of sounds now issuing from that instrument there was something being hunted. Up and down the pedals chased him, while the manuals blared approval. Poor devil! whoever he was, there seemed small hope of escape!

My nervous annoyance changed to anger. Who was doing this? How dare he play like that in the midst of divine service? I glanced at the people near me: not one appeared to be in the least disturbed. The placid brows of the kneeling nuns, still turned towards the altar, lost none of their devout abstraction under the pale shadow of their white head-dress. The fashionable lady beside me was looking expectantly at Monseigneur C——. For all her face betrayed, the organ might have been singing an Ave Maria.

But now, at last, the preacher had made the sign of the cross, and commanded silence. I turned to him gladly. Thus far I had not found the rest I had counted on when I entered St. Barnabé that afternoon.

I was worn out by three nights of physical suffering and mental trouble: the last had been the worst, and it was an exhausted body, and a mind benumbed and yet acutely sensitive, which I had brought to my favourite church for healing. For I had been reading *The King in Yellow*.

"The sun ariseth; they gather themselves together and lay them down in their dens." Monseigneur C—— delivered his text in a calm voice, glancing quietly over the congregation. My eyes turned, I knew not why, toward the lower end of the church. The organist was coming from behind his pipes, and passing along the gallery on his way out, I saw him disappear by a small door that leads to some stairs which descend directly to the street. He was a slender man, and his face was as white as his coat was black. "Good riddance!" I thought, "with your wicked music! I hope your assistant will play the closing voluntary."

With a feeling of relief—with a deep, calm feeling of relief, I turned back to the mild face in the pulpit and settled myself to listen. Here, at last, was the ease of mind I longed for.

"My children," said the preacher, "one truth the human soul finds hardest of all to learn: that it has nothing to fear. It can never be made to see that nothing can really harm it."

"Curious doctrine!" I thought, "for a Catholic priest. Let us see how he will reconcile that with the Fathers."

"Nothing can really harm the soul," he went on, in, his coolest, clearest tones, "because——"

But I never heard the rest; my eye left his face, I knew not for what reason, and sought the lower end of the church. The same man was coming out from behind the organ, and was passing along the gallery *the same way*. But there had not been time for him to return, and if he had returned, I must have seen him. I felt a faint chill, and my heart sank; and yet, his going and coming were no affair of mine. I looked at him: I could not look away from his black figure and his white face. When he was exactly opposite to me, he turned and sent across the church straight into my eyes, a look of hate, intense and deadly: I have never seen any other like it; would to God I might never see it again! Then he disappeared by the same door through which I had watched him depart less than sixty seconds before.

I sat and tried to collect my thoughts. My first sensation was like that of a very young child badly hurt, when it catches its breath before crying out.

To suddenly find myself the object of such hatred was exquisitely painful: and this man was an utter stranger. Why should he hate me so?—me, whom he had never seen before? For the moment all other sensation was merged in this one pang: even fear was subordinate to grief, and for that moment I never doubted; but in the next I began to reason, and a sense of the incongruous came to my aid.

As I have said, St. Barnabé is a modern church. It is small and well lighted; one sees all over it almost at a glance. The organ gallery gets a strong white light from a row of long windows in the clerestory, which have not even coloured glass.

The pulpit being in the middle of the church, it followed that, when I was turned toward it, whatever moved at the west end could not fail to attract my eye. When the organist passed it was no wonder that I saw him: I had simply miscalculated the interval between his first and his second passing. He had come in that last time by the other side-door. As for the look which had so upset me, there had been no such thing, and I was a nervous fool.

I looked about. This was a likely place to harbour supernatural horrors! That clear-cut, reasonable face of Monseigneur C——, his collected manner and easy, graceful gestures, were they not just a little discouraging to the notion of a gruesome mystery? I glanced above his head, and almost laughed. That flyaway lady supporting one corner of the pulpit canopy, which looked like a fringed damask table-cloth in a high wind, at the first attempt of a basilisk to pose up there in the organ loft, she would point her gold trumpet at him, and puff him out of existence! I laughed to myself over this conceit, which, at the time, I thought very amusing, and sat and chaffed myself and everything else, from the old harpy outside the railing, who had made me pay ten centimes for my chair, before she would let me in (she was more like a basilisk, I told myself, than was my organist with the anaemic complexion): from that grim old dame, to, yes, alas! Monseigneur C—— himself. For all devoutness had fled. I had never yet done such a thing in my life, but now I felt a desire to mock.

As for the sermon, I could not hear a word of it for the jingle in my ears of

"The skirts of St. Paul has reached.
Having preached us those six Lent lectures,
More unctuous than ever he preached,"

keeping time to the most fantastic and irreverent thoughts.

It was no use to sit there any longer: I must get out of doors and shake myself free from this hateful mood. I knew the rudeness I was committing, but still I rose and left the church.

A spring sun was shining on the Rue St. Honoré, as I ran down the church steps. On one corner stood a barrow full of yellow jonquils, pale violets from the Riviera, dark Russian violets, and white Roman hyacinths in a golden cloud of mimosa. The street was full of Sunday pleasure-seekers. I swung my cane and laughed with the rest. Some one overtook and passed me. He never turned, but there was the same deadly malignity in his white profile that there had been in his eyes. I watched him as long as I could see him. His lithe back expressed the same menace; every step that carried him away from me seemed to bear him on some errand connected with my destruction.

I was creeping along, my feet almost refusing to move. There began to dawn in me a sense of responsibility for something long forgotten. It began to seem as if I deserved that which he threatened: it reached a long way back—a long, long way back. It had lain dormant all these years: it was there, though, and presently it would rise and confront me. But I would try to escape; and I stumbled as best I could into the Rue de Rivoli, across the Place de la Concorde and on to the Quai. I looked with sick eyes upon the sun, shining through the white foam of the fountain, pouring over the backs of the dusky bronze river-gods, on the far-away Arc, a structure of amethyst mist, on the countless vistas of grey stems and bare branches faintly green. Then I saw him again coming down one of the chestnut alleys of the Cours la Reine.

I left the river-side, plunged blindly across to the Champs Elysées and turned toward the Arc. The setting sun was sending its rays along the green sward of the Rond-point: in the full glow he sat on a bench, children and young mothers all about him. He was nothing but a Sunday lounger, like the others, like myself. I said the words almost aloud, and all the while I gazed on the malignant hatred of his face. But he was not looking at me. I crept past and dragged my leaden feet up the Avenue. I knew that every time I met him brought him nearer to the accomplishment of his purpose and my fate. And still I tried to save myself.

The last rays of sunset were pouring through the great Arc. I passed under it, and met him face to face. I had left him far down the Champs Elysées, and yet he came in with a stream of people who were returning from the Bois de Boulogne. He came so close that he brushed me. His slender frame felt like iron inside its loose black covering. He showed no signs of haste, nor of fatigue, nor of any human feeling. His whole being expressed one thing: the will, and the power to work me evil.

In anguish I watched him where he went down the broad crowded Avenue, that was all flashing with wheels and the trappings of horses and the helmets of the Garde Republicaine.

He was soon lost to sight; then I turned and fled. Into the Bois, and far out beyond it—I know not where I went, but after a long while as it seemed to me, night had fallen, and I found myself sitting at a table before a small café. I had wandered back into the Bois. It was hours now since I had seen him. Physical fatigue and mental suffering had left me no power to think or feel. I was tired, so tired! I longed to hide away in my own den. I resolved to go home. But that was a long way off.

I live in the Court of the Dragon, a narrow passage that leads from the Rue de Rennes to the Rue du Dragon.

It is an "impasse"; traversable only for foot passengers. Over the entrance on the Rue de Rennes is a balcony, supported by an iron dragon. Within the court tall old houses rise on either side, and close the ends that give on the two streets. Huge gates, swung back during the day into the walls of the deep archways, close this court, after midnight, and one must enter then by ringing at certain small doors on the side. The sunken pavement collects unsavoury pools. Steep stairways pitch down to doors that open on the court. The ground floors are occupied by shops of second-hand dealers, and by iron workers. All day long the place rings with the clink of hammers and the clang of metal bars.

Unsavoury as it is below, there is cheerfulness, and comfort, and hard, honest work above.

Five flights up are the ateliers of architects and painters, and the hiding-places of middle-aged students like myself who want to live alone. When I first came here to live I was young, and not alone.

I had to walk a while before any conveyance appeared, but at last, when I had almost reached the Arc de Triomphe again, an empty cab came along and I took it.

From the Arc to the Rue de Rennes is a drive of more than half an hour, especially when one is conveyed by a tired cab horse that has been at the mercy of Sunday fête-makers.

There had been time before I passed under the Dragon's wings to meet my enemy over and over again, but I never saw him once, and now refuge was close at hand.

Before the wide gateway a small mob of children were playing. Our concierge and his wife walked among them, with their black poodle, keeping order; some couples were waltzing on the sidewalk. I returned their greetings and hurried in.

All the inhabitants of the court had trooped out into the street. The place was quite deserted, lighted by a few lanterns hung high up, in which the gas burned dimly.

My apartment was at the top of a house, halfway down the court, reached by a staircase that descended almost into the street, with only a bit of passage-way intervening, I set my foot on the threshold of the open door, the friendly old ruinous stairs rose before me, leading up to rest and shelter. Looking back over my right shoulder, I saw *him*, ten paces off. He must have entered the court with me.

He was coming straight on, neither slowly, nor swiftly, but straight on to me. And now he was looking at me. For the first time since our eyes encountered across the church they met now again, and I knew that the time had come.

Retreating backward, down the court, I faced him. I meant to escape by the entrance on the Rue du Dragon. His eyes told me that I never should escape.

It seemed ages while we were going, I retreating, he advancing, down the court in perfect silence; but at last I felt the shadow of the archway, and the next step brought me within it. I had meant to turn here and spring through into the street. But the shadow was not that of an archway; it was that of a vault. The great doors on the Rue du Dragon were closed. I felt this by the blackness which surrounded me, and at the same instant I read it in his face. How his face gleamed in the darkness, drawing swiftly nearer! The deep vaults, the huge closed doors, their cold iron clamps were all on his side. The thing which he had threatened had arrived: it gathered and bore down on me from the fathomless shadows; the point from which it would strike was his infernal eyes. Hopeless, I set my back against the barred doors and defied him.

There was a scraping of chairs on the stone floor, and a rustling as the congregation rose. I could hear the Suisse's staff in the south aisle, preceding Monseigneur C—— to the sacristy.

The kneeling nuns, roused from their devout abstraction, made their reverence and went away. The fashionable lady, my neighbour, rose also, with graceful reserve. As she departed her glance just flitted over my face in disapproval.

Half dead, or so it seemed to me, yet intensely alive to every trifle, I sat among the leisurely moving crowd, then rose too and went toward the door.

I had slept through the sermon. Had I slept through the sermon? I looked up and saw him passing along the gallery to his place. Only his side I saw; the thin bent arm in its black covering looked like one of those devilish, nameless instruments which lie in the disused torture-chambers of mediaeval castles.

But I had escaped him, though his eyes had said I should not. *Had* I escaped him? That which gave him the power over me came back out of oblivion, where I had hoped to keep it. For I knew him now. Death and the awful abode of lost souls, whither my weakness long ago had sent him—they had changed him for every other eye, but not for mine. I had recognized him almost from the first; I had never doubted what he was come to do; and now I knew while my body sat safe in the cheerful little church, he had been hunting my soul in the Court of the Dragon.

I crept to the door: the organ broke out overhead with a blare. A dazzling light filled the church, blotting the altar from my eyes. The people faded away, the arches, the vaulted roof vanished. I raised my seared eyes to the fathomless glare, and I saw the black stars hanging in the heavens: and the wet winds from the lake of Hali chilled my face.

And now, far away, over leagues of tossing cloud-waves, I saw the moon dripping with spray; and beyond, the towers of Carcosa rose behind the moon.

Death and the awful abode of lost souls, whither my weakness long ago had sent him, had changed him for every other eye but mine. And now I heard *his voice*, rising, swelling, thundering through the flaring light, and as I fell, the radiance increasing, increasing, poured over me in waves of flame. Then I sank into the depths, and I heard the King in Yellow whispering to my soul: "It is a fearful thing to fall into the hands of the living God!"

# THE YELLOW SIGN

"Let the red dawn surmise
What we shall do,
When this blue starlight dies
And all is through."

## I

There are so many things which are impossible to explain! Why should certain chords in music make me think of the brown and golden tints of autumn foliage? Why should the Mass of Sainte Cécile bend my thoughts wandering among caverns whose walls blaze with ragged masses of virgin silver? What was it in the roar and turmoil of Broadway at six o'clock that flashed before my eyes the picture of a still Breton forest where sunlight filtered through spring foliage and Sylvia bent, half curiously, half tenderly, over a small green lizard, murmuring: "To think that this also is a little ward of God!"

When I first saw the watchman his back was toward me. I looked at him indifferently until he went into the church. I paid no more attention to him than I had to any other man who lounged through Washington Square that morning, and when I shut my window and turned back into my studio I had forgotten him. Late in the afternoon, the day being warm, I raised the window again and leaned out to get a sniff of air. A man was standing in the courtyard of the church, and I noticed him again with as little interest as I had that morning. I looked across the square to where the fountain was playing and then, with my mind filled with vague impressions of trees, asphalt drives, and the moving groups of nursemaids and holiday-makers, I started to walk back to my easel. As I turned, my listless glance included the man below in the churchyard. His face was toward me now, and with a perfectly involuntary movement I bent to see it. At the same moment he raised his head and looked at me. Instantly I thought of a coffin-worm. Whatever it was about the man that repelled me I did not know, but the impression of a plump white grave-worm was so intense and nauseating that I must have shown it in my expression, for he turned his puffy face away with a movement which made me think of a disturbed grub in a chestnut.

I went back to my easel and motioned the model to resume her pose. After working a while I was satisfied that I was spoiling what I had done as rapidly as possible, and I took up a palette knife and scraped the colour out again. The flesh tones were sallow and unhealthy, and I did not understand how I could have painted such sickly colour into a study which before that had glowed with healthy tones.

I looked at Tessie. She had not changed, and the clear flush of health dyed her neck and cheeks as I frowned.

"Is it something I've done?" she said.

"No,—I've made a mess of this arm, and for the life of me I can't see how I came to paint such mud as that into the canvas," I replied.

"Don't I pose well?" she insisted.

"Of course, perfectly."

"Then it's not my fault?"

"No. It's my own."

"I am very sorry," she said.

I told her she could rest while I applied rag and turpentine to the plague spot on my canvas, and she went off to smoke a cigarette and look over the illustrations in the *Courrier Français*.

I did not know whether it was something in the turpentine or a defect in the canvas, but the more I scrubbed the more that gangrene seemed to spread. I worked like a beaver to get it out, and yet the disease appeared to creep from limb to limb of the study before me. Alarmed, I strove to arrest it, but now the colour on the breast changed and the whole figure seemed to absorb the infection as a sponge soaks up water. Vigorously I plied palette-knife, turpentine, and scraper, thinking all the time what a *séance* I should hold with Duval who had sold me the canvas; but soon I noticed that it was not the canvas which was defective nor yet the colours of Edward. "It must be the turpentine," I thought angrily, "or else my eyes have become so blurred and confused by the afternoon light that I can't see straight." I called Tessie, the model. She came and leaned over my chair blowing rings of smoke into the air.

"What *have* you been doing to it?" she exclaimed

"Nothing," I growled, "it must be this turpentine!"

"What a horrible colour it is now," she continued. "Do you think my flesh resembles green cheese?"

"No, I don't," I said angrily; "did you ever know me to paint like that before?"

"No, indeed!"

"Well, then!"

"It must be the turpentine, or something," she admitted.

She slipped on a Japanese robe and walked to the window. I scraped and rubbed until I was tired, and finally picked up my brushes and hurled them through the canvas with a forcible expression, the tone alone of which reached Tessie's ears.

Nevertheless she promptly began: "That's it! Swear and act silly and ruin your brushes! You have been three weeks on that study, and now look! What's the good of ripping the canvas? What creatures artists are!"

I felt about as much ashamed as I usually did after such an outbreak, and I turned the ruined canvas to the wall. Tessie helped me clean my brushes, and then danced away to dress. From the screen she regaled me with bits of advice concerning whole or partial loss of temper, until, thinking, perhaps, I had been tormented sufficiently, she came out to implore me to button her waist where she could not reach it on the shoulder.

"Everything went wrong from the time you came back from the window and talked about that horrid-looking man you saw in the churchyard," she announced.

"Yes, he probably bewitched the picture," I said, yawning. I looked at my watch.

"It's after six, I know," said Tessie, adjusting her hat before the mirror.

"Yes," I replied, "I didn't mean to keep you so long." I leaned out of the window but recoiled with disgust, for the young man with the pasty face stood below in the churchyard. Tessie saw my gesture of disapproval and leaned from the window.

"Is that the man you don't like?" she whispered.

I nodded.

"I can't see his face, but he does look fat and soft. Someway or other," she continued, turning to look at me, "he reminds me of a dream,—an awful dream I once had. Or," she mused, looking down at her shapely shoes, "was it a dream after all?"

"How should I know?" I smiled.

Tessie smiled in reply.

"You were in it," she said, "so perhaps you might know something about it."

"Tessie! Tessie!" I protested, "don't you dare flatter by saying that you dream about me!"

"But I did," she insisted; "shall I tell you about it?"

"Go ahead," I replied, lighting a cigarette.

Tessie leaned back on the open window-sill and began very seriously.

"One night last winter I was lying in bed thinking about nothing at all in particular. I had been posing for you and I was tired out, yet it seemed impossible for me to sleep. I heard the bells in the city ring ten, eleven, and midnight. I must have fallen asleep about midnight because I don't remember hearing the bells after that. It seemed to me that I had scarcely closed my eyes when I dreamed that something impelled me to go to the window. I rose, and raising the sash leaned out. Twenty-fifth Street was deserted as far as I could see. I began to be afraid; everything outside seemed so—so black and uncomfortable. Then the sound of wheels in the distance came to my ears, and it seemed to me as though that was what I must wait for. Very slowly the wheels approached, and, finally, I could make out a vehicle moving along the street. It came nearer and nearer, and when it passed beneath my window I saw it was a hearse. Then, as I trembled with fear, the driver turned and looked straight at me. When I awoke I was standing by the open window shivering with cold, but the black-plumed hearse and the driver were gone. I dreamed this dream again in March last, and again awoke beside the open window. Last night the dream came again. You remember how it was raining; when I awoke, standing at the open window, my night-dress was soaked."

"But where did I come into the dream?" I asked.

"You—you were in the coffin; but you were not dead."

"In the coffin?"

"Yes."

"How did you know? Could you see me?"

"No; I only knew you were there."

"Had you been eating Welsh rarebits, or lobster salad?" I began, laughing, but the girl interrupted me with a frightened cry.

"Hello! What's up?" I said, as she shrank into the embrasure by the window.

"The—the man below in the churchyard;—he drove the hearse."

"Nonsense," I said, but Tessie's eyes were wide with terror. I went to the window and looked out. The man was gone. "Come, Tessie," I urged, "don't be foolish. You have posed too long; you are nervous."

"Do you think I could forget that face?" she murmured. "Three times I saw the hearse pass below my window, and every time the driver turned and looked up at me. Oh, his face was so white and—and soft? It looked dead—it looked as if it had been dead a long time."

I induced the girl to sit down and swallow a glass of Marsala. Then I sat down beside her, and tried to give her some advice.

"Look here, Tessie," I said, "you go to the country for a week or two, and you'll have no more dreams about hearses. You pose all day, and when night comes your nerves are upset. You can't keep this up. Then again, instead of going to bed when your day's work is done, you run off to picnics at Sulzer's Park, or go to the Eldorado or Coney Island, and when you come down here next morning you are fagged out. There was no real hearse. There was a soft-shell crab dream."

She smiled faintly.

"What about the man in the churchyard?"

"Oh, he's only an ordinary unhealthy, everyday creature."

"As true as my name is Tessie Reardon, I swear to you, Mr. Scott, that the face of the man below in the churchyard is the face of the man who drove the hearse!"

"What of it?" I said. "It's an honest trade."

"Then you think I *did* see the hearse?"

"Oh," I said diplomatically, "if you really did, it might not be unlikely that the man below drove it. There is nothing in that."

Tessie rose, unrolled her scented handkerchief, and taking a bit of gum from a knot in the hem, placed it in her mouth. Then drawing on her gloves she offered me her hand, with a frank, "Good-night, Mr. Scott," and walked out.


## II


The next morning, Thomas, the bell-boy, brought me the *Herald* and a bit of news. The church next door had been sold. I thanked Heaven for it, not that being a Catholic I had any repugnance for the congregation next door, but because my nerves were shattered by a blatant exhorter, whose every word echoed through the aisle of the church as if it had been my own rooms, and who insisted on his r's with a nasal persistence which revolted my every instinct. Then, too, there was a fiend in human shape, an organist, who reeled off some of the grand old hymns with an interpretation of his own, and I longed for the blood of a creature who could play the doxology with an amendment of minor chords which one hears only in a quartet of very young undergraduates. I believe the minister was a good man, but when he bellowed: "And the Lorrrrd said unto Moses, the Lorrrd is a man of war; the Lorrrd is his name. My wrath shall wax hot and I will kill you with the sworrrrd!" I wondered how many centuries of purgatory it would take to atone for such a sin.

"Who bought the property?" I asked Thomas.

"Nobody that I knows, sir. They do say the gent wot owns this 'ere 'Amilton flats was lookin' at it. 'E might be a bildin' more studios."

I walked to the window. The young man with the unhealthy face stood by the churchyard gate, and at the mere sight of him the same overwhelming repugnance took possession of me.

"By the way, Thomas," I said, "who is that fellow down there?"

Thomas sniffed. "That there worm, sir? 'Es night-watchman of the church, sir. 'E maikes me tired a-sittin' out all night on them steps and lookin' at you insultin' like. I'd a punched 'is 'ed, sir—beg pardon, sir—"

"Go on, Thomas."

"One night a comin' 'ome with 'Arry, the other English boy, I sees 'im a sittin' there on them steps. We 'ad Molly and Jen with us, sir, the two girls on the tray service, an' 'e looks so insultin' at us that I up and sez: 'Wat you looking hat, you fat slug?'—beg pardon, sir, but that's 'ow I sez, sir. Then 'e don't say nothin' and I sez: 'Come out and I'll punch that puddin' 'ed.' Then I hopens the gate an' goes in, but 'e don't say nothin', only looks insultin' like. Then I 'its 'im one, but, ugh! 'is 'ed was that cold and mushy it ud sicken you to touch 'im."

"What did he do then?" I asked curiously.

"'Im? Nawthin'."

50

"And you, Thomas?"

The young fellow flushed with embarrassment and smiled uneasily.

"Mr. Scott, sir, I ain't no coward, an' I can't make it out at all why I run. I was in the 5th Lawncers, sir, bugler at Tel-el-Kebir, an' was shot by the wells."

"You don't mean to say you ran away?"

"Yes, sir; I run."

"Why?"

"That's just what I want to know, sir. I grabbed Molly an' run, an' the rest was as frightened as I."

"But what were they frightened at?"

Thomas refused to answer for a while, but now my curiosity was aroused about the repulsive young man below and I pressed him. Three years' sojourn in America had not only modified Thomas' cockney dialect but had given him the American's fear of ridicule.

"You won't believe me, Mr. Scott, sir?"

"Yes, I will."

"You will lawf at me, sir?"

"Nonsense!"

He hesitated. "Well, sir, it's Gawd's truth that when I 'it 'im 'e grabbed me wrists, sir, and when I twisted 'is soft, mushy fist one of 'is fingers come off in me 'and."

The utter loathing and horror of Thomas' face must have been reflected in my own, for he added:

"It's orful, an' now when I see 'im I just go away. 'E maikes me hill."

When Thomas had gone I went to the window. The man stood beside the church-railing with both hands on the gate, but I hastily retreated to my easel again, sickened and horrified, for I saw that the middle finger of his right hand was missing.

At nine o'clock Tessie appeared and vanished behind the screen with a merry "Good morning, Mr. Scott." When she had reappeared and taken her pose upon the model-stand I started a new canvas, much to her delight. She remained silent as long as I was on the drawing, but as soon as the scrape of the charcoal ceased and I took up my fixative she began to chatter.

"Oh, I had such a lovely time last night. We went to Tony Pastor's."

"Who are 'we'?" I demanded.

"Oh, Maggie, you know, Mr. Whyte's model, and Pinkie McCormick—we call her Pinkie because she's got that beautiful red hair you artists like so much—and Lizzie Burke."

I sent a shower of spray from the fixative over the canvas, and said: "Well, go on."

"We saw Kelly and Baby Barnes the skirt-dancer and—and all the rest. I made a mash."

"Then you have gone back on me, Tessie?"

She laughed and shook her head.

"He's Lizzie Burke's brother, Ed. He's a perfect gen'l'man."

I felt constrained to give her some parental advice concerning mashing, which she took with a bright smile.

"Oh, I can take care of a strange mash," she said, examining her chewing gum, "but Ed is different. Lizzie is my best friend."

Then she related how Ed had come back from the stocking mill in Lowell, Massachusetts, to find her and Lizzie grown up, and what an accomplished young man he was, and how he thought nothing of squandering half-a-dollar for ice-cream and oysters to celebrate his entry as clerk into the woollen department of Macy's. Before she finished I began to paint, and she resumed the pose, smiling and chattering like a sparrow. By noon I had the study fairly well rubbed in and Tessie came to look at it.

"That's better," she said.

I thought so too, and ate my lunch with a satisfied feeling that all was going well. Tessie spread her lunch on a drawing table opposite me and we drank our claret from the same bottle and lighted our cigarettes from the same match. I was very much attached to Tessie. I had watched her shoot up into a slender but exquisitely formed woman from a frail, awkward child. She had posed for me during the last three years, and among all my models she was my favourite. It would have troubled me very much indeed had she become "tough" or "fly," as the phrase goes, but I never noticed any deterioration of her manner, and felt at heart that she was all right. She and I never discussed morals at all, and I had no intention of doing so, partly because I had none myself, and partly because I knew she would do what she liked in spite of me. Still I did hope she would steer clear of complications, because I wished her well, and then also I had a selfish desire to retain the best model I had. I knew that mashing, as she termed it, had no significance with girls like Tessie, and that such things in America did not resemble in the least the same things in Paris. Yet, having lived with my eyes open, I also knew that somebody would take Tessie away some day, in one manner or another, and though I professed to myself that marriage was nonsense, I sincerely hoped that, in this case, there would be a priest at the end of the vista. I am a Catholic. When I listen to high mass, when I sign myself, I feel that everything, including myself, is more cheerful, and when I confess, it does me good. A man who lives as much alone as I do, must confess to somebody. Then, again, Sylvia was Catholic, and it was reason enough for me. But I was speaking of Tessie, which is very different. Tessie also was Catholic and much more devout than I, so, taking it all in all, I had little fear for my pretty model until she should fall in love. But *then* I knew that fate alone would decide her future for her, and I prayed inwardly that fate would keep her away from men like me and throw into her path nothing but Ed Burkes and Jimmy McCormicks, bless her sweet face!

Tessie sat blowing rings of smoke up to the ceiling and tinkling the ice in her tumbler.

"Do you know that I also had a dream last night?" I observed.

"Not about that man," she laughed.

"Exactly. A dream similar to yours, only much worse."

It was foolish and thoughtless of me to say this, but you know how little tact the average painter has. "I must have fallen asleep about ten o'clock," I continued, "and after a while I dreamt that I awoke. So plainly did I hear the midnight bells, the wind in the tree-branches, and the whistle of steamers from the bay, that even now I can scarcely believe I was not awake. I seemed to be lying in a box which had a glass cover. Dimly I saw the street lamps as I passed, for I must tell you, Tessie, the box in which I reclined appeared to lie in a cushioned wagon which jolted me over a stony pavement. After a while I became impatient and tried to move, but the box was too narrow. My hands were crossed on my breast, so I could not raise them to help myself. I listened and then tried to call. My voice was gone. I could hear the trample of the horses attached to the wagon, and even the breathing of the driver. Then another sound broke upon my ears like the raising of a window sash. I managed to turn my head a little, and found I could look, not only through the glass cover of my box, but also through the glass panes in the side of the covered vehicle. I saw houses, empty and silent, with neither light nor life about any of them excepting one. In that house a window was open on the first floor, and a figure all in white stood looking down into the street. It was you."

Tessie had turned her face away from me and leaned on the table with her elbow.

"I could see your face," I resumed, "and it seemed to me to be very sorrowful. Then we passed on and turned into a narrow black lane. Presently the horses stopped. I waited and waited, closing my eyes with fear and impatience, but all was silent as the grave. After what seemed to me hours, I began to feel uncomfortable. A sense that somebody was close to me made me unclose my eyes. Then I saw the white face of the hearse-driver looking at me through the coffin-lid——"

A sob from Tessie interrupted me. She was trembling like a leaf. I saw I had made an ass of myself and attempted to repair the damage.

"Why, Tess," I said, "I only told you this to show you what influence your story might have on another person's dreams. You don't suppose I really lay in a coffin, do you? What are you trembling for? Don't you see that your dream and my unreasonable dislike for that inoffensive watchman of the church simply set my brain working as soon as I fell asleep?"

She laid her head between her arms, and sobbed as if her heart would break. What a precious triple donkey I had made of myself! But I was about to break my record. I went over and put my arm about her.

"Tessie dear, forgive me," I said; "I had no business to frighten you with such nonsense. You are too sensible a girl, too good a Catholic to believe in dreams."

Her hand tightened on mine and her head fell back upon my shoulder, but she still trembled and I petted her and comforted her.

"Come, Tess, open your eyes and smile."

Her eyes opened with a slow languid movement and met mine, but their expression was so queer that I hastened to reassure her again.

"It's all humbug, Tessie; you surely are not afraid that any harm will come to you because of that."

"No," she said, but her scarlet lips quivered.

"Then, what's the matter? Are you afraid?"

"Yes. Not for myself."

"For me, then?" I demanded gaily.

"For you," she murmured in a voice almost inaudible. "I—I care for you."

At first I started to laugh, but when I understood her, a shock passed through me, and I sat like one turned to stone. This was the crowning bit of idiocy I had committed. During the moment which elapsed between her reply and my answer I thought of a thousand responses to that innocent confession. I could pass it by with a laugh, I could misunderstand her and assure her as to my health, I could simply point out that it was impossible she could love me. But my reply was quicker than my thoughts, and I might think and think now when it was too late, for I had kissed her on the mouth.

That evening I took my usual walk in Washington Park, pondering over the occurrences of the day. I was thoroughly committed. There was no back out now, and I stared the future straight in the face. I was not good, not even scrupulous, but I had no idea of deceiving either myself or Tessie. The one passion of my life lay buried in the sunlit forests of Brittany. Was it buried for ever? Hope cried "No!" For three years I had been listening to the voice of Hope, and for three years I had waited for a footstep on my threshold. Had Sylvia forgotten? "No!" cried Hope.

I said that I was no good. That is true, but still I was not exactly a comic opera villain. I had led an easy-going reckless life, taking what invited me of pleasure, deploring and sometimes bitterly regretting consequences. In one thing alone, except my painting, was I serious, and that was something which lay hidden if not lost in the Breton forests.

It was too late for me to regret what had occurred during the day. Whatever it had been, pity, a sudden tenderness for sorrow, or the more brutal instinct of gratified vanity, it was all the same now, and unless I wished to bruise an innocent heart, my path lay marked before me. The fire and strength, the depth of passion of a love which I had never even suspected, with all my imagined experience in the world, left me no alternative but to respond or send her away. Whether because I am so cowardly about giving pain to others, or whether it was that I have little of the gloomy Puritan in me, I do not know, but I shrank from disclaiming responsibility for that thoughtless kiss, and in fact had no time to do so before the gates of her heart opened and the flood poured forth. Others who habitually do their duty and find a sullen satisfaction in making themselves and everybody else unhappy, might have withstood it. I did not. I dared not. After the storm had abated I did tell her that she might better have loved Ed Burke and worn a plain gold ring, but she would not hear of it, and I thought perhaps as long as she had decided to love somebody she could not marry, it had better be me. I, at least, could treat her with an intelligent affection, and whenever she became tired of her infatuation she could go none the worse for it. For I was decided on that point although I knew how hard it would be. I remembered the usual termination of Platonic liaisons, and thought how disgusted I had been whenever I heard of one. I knew I was undertaking a great deal for so unscrupulous a man as I was, and I dreamed the future, but never for one moment did I doubt that she was safe with me. Had it been anybody but Tessie I should not have bothered my head about scruples. For it did not occur to me to sacrifice Tessie as I would have sacrificed a woman of the world. I looked the future squarely in the face and saw the several probable endings to the affair. She would either tire of the whole thing, or become so unhappy that I should have either to marry her or go away. If I married her we would be unhappy. I with a wife unsuited to me, and she with a husband unsuitable for any woman. For my past life could scarcely entitle me to marry. If I went away she might either fall ill, recover, and marry some Eddie Burke, or she might recklessly or deliberately go and do something foolish. On the other hand, if she tired of me, then her whole life would be before her with beautiful vistas of Eddie Burkes and marriage rings and twins and Harlem flats and Heaven knows what. As I strolled along through the trees by the Washington Arch, I decided that she should find a substantial friend in me, anyway, and the future could take care of itself. Then I went into the house and put on my evening dress, for the little faintly-perfumed note on my dresser said, "Have a cab at the stage door at eleven," and the note was signed "Edith Carmichel, Metropolitan Theatre."

I took supper that night, or rather we took supper, Miss Carmichel and I, at Solari's, and the dawn was just beginning to gild the cross on the Memorial Church as I entered Washington Square after leaving Edith at the Brunswick. There was not a soul in the park as I passed along the trees and took the walk which leads from the Garibaldi statue to the Hamilton Apartment House, but as I passed the churchyard I saw a figure sitting on the stone steps. In spite of myself a chill crept over me at the sight of the white puffy face, and I hastened to pass. Then he said something which might have been addressed to me or might merely have been a mutter to himself, but a sudden furious anger flamed up within me that such a creature should address me. For an instant I felt like wheeling about and smashing my stick over his head, but I walked on, and entering the Hamilton went to my apartment. For some time I tossed about the bed trying to get the sound of his voice out of my ears, but could not. It filled my head, that muttering sound, like thick oily smoke from a fat-rendering vat or an odour of noisome decay. And as I lay and tossed about, the voice in my ears seemed more distinct, and I began to understand the words he had muttered. They came to me slowly as if I had forgotten them, and at last I could make some sense out of the sounds. It was this:

"Have you found the Yellow Sign?"

"Have you found the Yellow Sign?"

"Have you found the Yellow Sign?"

I was furious. What did he mean by that? Then with a curse upon him and his I rolled over and went to sleep, but when I awoke later I looked pale and haggard, for I had dreamed the dream of the night before, and it troubled me more than I cared to think.

I dressed and went down into my studio. Tessie sat by the window, but as I came in she rose and put both arms around my neck for an innocent kiss. She looked so sweet and dainty that I kissed her again and then sat down before the easel.

"Hello! Where's the study I began yesterday?" I asked.

Tessie looked conscious, but did not answer. I began to hunt among the piles of canvases, saying, "Hurry up, Tess, and get ready; we must take advantage of the morning light."

When at last I gave up the search among the other canvases and turned to look around the room for the missing study I noticed Tessie standing by the screen with her clothes still on.

"What's the matter," I asked, "don't you feel well?"

"Yes."

"Then hurry."

"Do you want me to pose as—as I have always posed?"

Then I understood. Here was a new complication. I had lost, of course, the best nude model I had ever seen. I looked at Tessie. Her face was scarlet. Alas! Alas! We had eaten of the tree of knowledge, and Eden and native innocence were dreams of the past—I mean for her.

I suppose she noticed the disappointment on my face, for she said: "I will pose if you wish. The study is behind the screen here where I put it."

"No," I said, "we will begin something new;" and I went into my wardrobe and picked out a Moorish costume which fairly blazed with tinsel. It was a genuine costume, and Tessie retired to the screen with it enchanted. When she came forth again I was astonished. Her long black hair was bound above her forehead with a circlet of turquoises, and the ends, curled about her glittering girdle. Her feet were encased in the embroidered pointed slippers and the skirt of her costume, curiously wrought with arabesques in silver, fell to her ankles. The deep metallic blue vest embroidered with silver and the short Mauresque jacket spangled and sewn with turquoises became her wonderfully. She came up to me and held up her face smiling. I slipped my hand into my pocket, and drawing out a gold chain with a cross attached, dropped it over her head.

"It's yours, Tessie."

"Mine?" she faltered.

"Yours. Now go and pose," Then with a radiant smile she ran behind the screen and presently reappeared with a little box on which was written my name.

"I had intended to give it to you when I went home to-night," she said, "but I can't wait now."

I opened the box. On the pink cotton inside lay a clasp of black onyx, on which was inlaid a curious symbol or letter in gold. It was neither Arabic nor Chinese, nor, as I found afterwards, did it belong to any human script.

"It's all I had to give you for a keepsake," she said timidly.

I was annoyed, but I told her how much I should prize it, and promised to wear it always. She fastened it on my coat beneath the lapel.

"How foolish, Tess, to go and buy me such a beautiful thing as this," I said.

"I did not buy it," she laughed.

"Where did you get it?"

Then she told me how she had found it one day while coming from the Aquarium in the Battery, how she had advertised it and watched the papers, but at last gave up all hopes of finding the owner.

"That was last winter," she said, "the very day I had the first horrid dream about the hearse."

I remembered my dream of the previous night but said nothing, and presently my charcoal was flying over a new canvas, and Tessie stood motionless on the model-stand.

## III

The day following was a disastrous one for me. While moving a framed canvas from one easel to another my foot slipped on the polished floor, and I fell heavily on both wrists. They were so badly sprained that it was useless to attempt to hold a brush, and I was obliged to wander about the studio, glaring at unfinished drawings and sketches, until despair seized me and I sat down to smoke and twiddle my thumbs with rage. The rain blew against the windows and rattled on the roof of the church, driving me into a nervous fit with its interminable patter. Tessie sat sewing by the window, and every now and then raised her head and looked at me with such innocent compassion that I began to feel ashamed of my irritation and looked about for something to occupy me. I had read all the papers and all the books in the library, but for the sake of something to do I went to the bookcases and shoved them open with my elbow. I knew every volume by its colour and examined them all, passing slowly around the library and whistling to keep up my spirits. I was turning to go into the dining-room when my eye fell upon a book bound in serpent skin, standing in a corner of the top shelf of the last bookcase. I did not remember it, and from the floor could not decipher the pale lettering on the back, so I went to the smoking-room and called Tessie. She came in from the studio and climbed up to reach the book.

"What is it?" I asked.

"*The King in Yellow.*"

I was dumfounded. Who had placed it there? How came it in my rooms? I had long ago decided that I should never open that book, and nothing on earth could have persuaded me to buy it. Fearful lest curiosity might tempt me to open it, I had never even looked at it in book-stores. If I ever had had any curiosity to read it, the awful tragedy of young Castaigne, whom I knew, prevented me from exploring its wicked pages. I had always refused to listen to any description of it, and indeed, nobody ever ventured to discuss the second part aloud, so I had absolutely no knowledge of what those leaves might reveal. I stared at the poisonous mottled binding as I would at a snake.

"Don't touch it, Tessie," I said; "come down."

Of course my admonition was enough to arouse her curiosity, and before I could prevent it she took the book and, laughing, danced off into the studio with it. I called to her, but she slipped away with a tormenting smile at my helpless hands, and I followed her with some impatience.

"Tessie!" I cried, entering the library, "listen, I am serious. Put that book away. I do not wish you to open it!" The library was empty. I went into both drawing-rooms, then into the bedrooms, laundry, kitchen, and finally returned to the library and began a systematic search. She had hidden herself so well that it was half-an-hour later when I discovered her crouching white and silent by the latticed window in the store-room above. At the first glance I saw she had been punished for her foolishness. *The King in Yellow* lay at her feet, but the book was open at the second part. I looked at Tessie and saw it was too late. She had opened *The King in Yellow*. Then I took her by the hand and led her into the studio. She seemed dazed, and when I told her to lie down on the sofa she obeyed me without a word. After a while she closed her eyes and her breathing became regular and deep, but I could not determine whether or not she slept. For a long while I sat silently beside her, but she neither stirred nor spoke, and at last I rose, and, entering the unused store-room, took the book in my least injured hand. It seemed heavy as lead, but I carried it into the studio again, and sitting down on the rug beside the sofa, opened it and read it through from beginning to end.

When, faint with excess of my emotions, I dropped the volume and leaned wearily back against the sofa, Tessie opened her eyes and looked at me....

We had been speaking for some time in a dull monotonous strain before I realized that we were discussing *The King in Yellow*. Oh the sin of writing such words,— words which are clear as crystal, limpid and musical as bubbling springs, words which sparkle and glow like the poisoned diamonds of the Medicis! Oh the wickedness, the hopeless damnation of a soul who could fascinate and paralyze human creatures with such words,—words understood by the ignorant and wise alike, words which are more precious than jewels, more soothing than music, more awful than death!

We talked on, unmindful of the gathering shadows, and she was begging me to throw away the clasp of black onyx quaintly inlaid with what we now knew to be the Yellow Sign. I never shall know why I refused, though even at this hour, here in my bedroom as I write this confession, I should be glad to know *what* it was that prevented me from tearing the Yellow Sign from my breast and casting it into the fire. I am sure I wished to do so, and yet Tessie pleaded with me in vain. Night fell and the hours dragged on, but still we murmured to each other of the King and the Pallid Mask, and midnight sounded from the misty spires in the fog-wrapped city. We spoke of Hastur and of Cassilda, while outside the fog rolled against the blank window-panes as the cloud waves roll and break on the shores of Hali.

The house was very silent now, and not a sound came up from the misty streets. Tessie lay among the cushions, her face a grey blot in the gloom, but her hands were clasped in mine, and I knew that she knew and read my thoughts as I read hers, for we had understood the mystery of the Hyades and the Phantom of Truth was laid. Then as we answered each other, swiftly, silently, thought on thought, the shadows stirred in the gloom about us, and far in the distant streets we heard a sound. Nearer and nearer it came, the dull crunching of wheels, nearer and yet nearer, and now, outside before the door it ceased, and I dragged myself to the window and saw a black-plumed hearse. The gate below opened and shut, and I crept shaking to my door and bolted it, but I knew no bolts, no locks, could keep that creature out who was coming for the Yellow Sign. And now I heard him moving very softly along the hall. Now he was at the door, and the bolts rotted at his touch. Now he had entered. With eyes starting from my head I peered into the darkness, but when he came into the room I did not see him. It was only when I felt him envelope me in his cold soft grasp that I cried out and struggled with deadly fury, but my hands were useless and he tore the onyx clasp from my coat and struck me full in the face. Then, as I fell, I heard Tessie's soft cry and her spirit fled: and even while falling I longed to follow her, for I knew that the King in Yellow had opened his tattered mantle and there was only God to cry to now.

I could tell more, but I cannot see what help it will be to the world. As for me, I am past human help or hope. As I lie here, writing, careless even whether or not I die before I finish, I can see the doctor gathering up his powders and phials with a vague gesture to the good priest beside me, which I understand.

They will be very curious to know the tragedy—they of the outside world who write books and print millions of newspapers, but I shall write no more, and the father confessor will seal my last words with the seal of sanctity when his holy office is done. They of the outside world may send their creatures into wrecked homes and death-smitten firesides, and their newspapers will batten on blood and tears, but with me their spies must halt before the confessional. They know that Tessie is dead and that I am dying. They know how the people in the house, aroused by an infernal scream, rushed into my room and found one living and two dead, but they do not know what I shall tell them now; they do not know that the doctor said as he pointed to a horrible decomposed heap on the floor—the livid corpse of the watchman from the church: "I have no theory, no explanation. That man must have been dead for months!"

I think I am dying. I wish the priest would—

# THE DEMOISELLE D'YS

"Mais je croy que je
Suis descendu on puiz
Ténébreux onquel disoit
Heraclytus estre Vereté cachée."

"There be three things which are too wonderful for me, yea, four which I know not:

"The way of an eagle in the air; the way of a serpent upon a rock; the way of a ship in the midst of the sea; and the way of a man with a maid."

I

The utter desolation of the scene began to have its effect; I sat down to face the situation and, if possible, recall to mind some landmark which might aid me in extricating myself from my present position. If I could only find the ocean again all would be clear, for I knew one could see the island of Groix from the cliffs.

I laid down my gun, and kneeling behind a rock lighted a pipe. Then I looked at my watch. It was nearly four o'clock. I might have wandered far from Kerselec since daybreak.

Standing the day before on the cliffs below Kerselec with Goulven, looking out over the sombre moors among which I had now lost my way, these downs had appeared to me level as a meadow, stretching to the horizon, and although I knew how deceptive is distance, I could not realize that what from Kerselec seemed to be mere grassy hollows were great valleys covered with gorse and heather, and what looked like scattered boulders were in reality enormous cliffs of granite.

"It's a bad place for a stranger," old Goulven had said: "you'd better take a guide;" and I had replied, "I shall not lose myself." Now I knew that I had lost myself, as I sat there smoking, with the sea-wind blowing in my face. On every side stretched the moorland, covered with flowering gorse and heath and granite boulders. There was not a tree in sight, much less a house. After a while, I picked up the gun, and turning my back on the sun tramped on again.

There was little use in following any of the brawling streams which every now and then crossed my path, for, instead of flowing into the sea, they ran inland to reedy pools in the hollows of the moors. I had followed several, but they all led me to swamps or silent little ponds from which the snipe rose peeping and wheeled away in an ecstasy of fright. I began to feel fatigued, and the gun galled my shoulder in spite of the double pads. The sun sank lower and lower, shining level across yellow gorse and the moorland pools.

As I walked my own gigantic shadow led me on, seeming to lengthen at every step. The gorse scraped against my leggings, crackled beneath my feet, showering the brown earth with blossoms, and the brake bowed and billowed along my path. From tufts of heath rabbits scurried away through the bracken, and among the swamp grass I heard the wild duck's drowsy quack. Once a fox stole across my path, and again, as I stooped to drink at a hurrying rill, a heron flapped heavily from the reeds beside me. I turned to look at the sun. It seemed to touch the edges of the plain. When at last I decided that it was useless to go on, and that I must make up my mind to spend at least one night on the moors, I threw myself down thoroughly fagged out. The evening sunlight slanted warm across my body, but the sea-winds began to rise, and I felt a chill strike through me from my wet shooting-boots. High overhead gulls were wheeling and tossing like bits of white paper; from some distant marsh a solitary curlew called. Little by little the sun sank into the plain, and the zenith flushed with the after-glow. I watched the sky change from palest gold to pink and then to smouldering fire. Clouds of midges danced above me, and high in the calm air a bat dipped and soared. My eyelids began to droop. Then as I shook off the drowsiness a sudden crash among the bracken roused me. I raised my eyes. A great bird hung quivering in the air above my face. For an instant I stared, incapable of motion; then something leaped past me in the ferns and the bird rose, wheeled, and pitched headlong into the brake.

I was on my feet in an instant peering through the gorse. There came the sound of a struggle from a bunch of heather close by, and then all was quiet. I stepped forward, my gun poised, but when I came to the heather the gun fell under my arm again, and I stood motionless in silent astonishment. A dead hare lay on the ground, and on the hare stood a magnificent falcon, one talon buried in the creature's neck, the other planted firmly on its limp flank. But what astonished me, was not the mere sight of a falcon sitting upon its prey. I had seen that more than once. It was that the falcon was fitted with a sort of leash about both talons, and from the leash hung a round bit of metal like a sleigh-bell. The bird turned its fierce yellow eyes on me, and then stooped and struck its curved beak into the quarry. At the same instant hurried steps sounded among the heather, and a girl sprang into the covert in front. Without a glance at me she walked up to the falcon, and passing her gloved hand under its breast, raised it from the quarry. Then she deftly slipped a small hood over the bird's head, and holding it out on her gauntlet, stooped and picked up the hare.

She passed a cord about the animal's legs and fastened the end of the thong to her girdle. Then she started to retrace her steps through the covert. As she passed me I raised my cap and she acknowledged my presence with a scarcely perceptible inclination. I had been so astonished, so lost in admiration of the scene before my eyes, that it had not occurred to me that here was my salvation. But as she moved away I recollected that unless I wanted to sleep on a windy moor that night I had better recover my speech without delay. At my first word she hesitated, and as I stepped before her I thought a look of fear came into her beautiful eyes. But as I humbly explained my unpleasant plight, her face flushed and she looked at me in wonder.

"Surely you did not come from Kerselec!" she repeated.

Her sweet voice had no trace of the Breton accent nor of any accent which I knew, and yet there was something in it I seemed to have heard before, something quaint and indefinable, like the theme of an old song.

I explained that I was an American, unacquainted with Finistère, shooting there for my own amusement.

"An American," she repeated in the same quaint musical tones. "I have never before seen an American."

For a moment she stood silent, then looking at me she said. "If you should walk all night you could not reach Kerselec now, even if you had a guide."

This was pleasant news.

"But," I began, "if I could only find a peasant's hut where I might get something to eat, and shelter."

The falcon on her wrist fluttered and shook its head. The girl smoothed its glossy back and glanced at me.

"Look around," she said gently. "Can you see the end of these moors? Look, north, south, east, west. Can you see anything but moorland and bracken?"

"No," I said.

"The moor is wild and desolate. It is easy to enter, but sometimes they who enter never leave it. There are no peasants' huts here."

"Well," I said, "if you will tell me in which direction Kerselec lies, to-morrow it will take me no longer to go back than it has to come."

She looked at me again with an expression almost like pity.

"Ah," she said, "to come is easy and takes hours; to go is different—and may take centuries."

I stared at her in amazement but decided that I had misunderstood her. Then before I had time to speak she drew a whistle from her belt and sounded it.

"Sit down and rest," she said to me; "you have come a long distance and are tired."

She gathered up her pleated skirts and motioning me to follow picked her dainty way through the gorse to a flat rock among the ferns.

"They will be here directly," she said, and taking a seat at one end of the rock invited me to sit down on the other edge. The after-glow was beginning to fade in the sky and a single star twinkled faintly through the rosy haze. A long wavering triangle of water-fowl drifted southward over our heads, and from the swamps around plover were calling.

"They are very beautiful—these moors," she said quietly.

"Beautiful, but cruel to strangers," I answered.

"Beautiful and cruel," she repeated dreamily, "beautiful and cruel."

"Like a woman," I said stupidly.

"Oh," she cried with a little catch in her breath, and looked at me. Her dark eyes met mine, and I thought she seemed angry or frightened.

"Like a woman," she repeated under her breath, "How cruel to say so!" Then after a pause, as though speaking aloud to herself, "How cruel for him to say that!"

I don't know what sort of an apology I offered for my inane, though harmless speech, but I know that she seemed so troubled about it that I began to think I had said something very dreadful without knowing it, and remembered with horror the pitfalls and snares which the French language sets for foreigners. While I was trying to imagine what I might have said, a sound of voices came across the moor, and the girl rose to her feet.

"No," she said, with a trace of a smile on her pale face, "I will not accept your apologies, monsieur, but I must prove you wrong, and that shall be my revenge. Look. Here come Hastur and Raoul."

Two men loomed up in the twilight. One had a sack across his shoulders and the other carried a hoop before him as a waiter carries a tray. The hoop was fastened with straps to his shoulders, and around the edge of the circlet sat three hooded falcons fitted with tinkling bells. The girl stepped up to the falconer, and with a quick turn of her wrist transferred her falcon to the hoop, where it quickly sidled off and nestled among its mates, who shook their hooded heads and ruffled their feathers till the belled jesses tinkled again. The other man stepped forward and bowing respectfully took up the hare and dropped it into the game-sack.

"These are my piqueurs," said the girl, turning to me with a gentle dignity. "Raoul is a good fauconnier, and I shall some day make him grand veneur. Hastur is incomparable."

The two silent men saluted me respectfully.

"Did I not tell you, monsieur, that I should prove you wrong?" she continued. "This, then, is my revenge, that you do me the courtesy of accepting food and shelter at my own house."

Before I could answer she spoke to the falconers, who started instantly across the heath, and with a gracious gesture to me she followed. I don't know whether I made her understand how profoundly grateful I felt, but she seemed pleased to listen, as we walked over the dewy heather.

"Are you not very tired?" she asked.

I had clean forgotten my fatigue in her presence, and I told her so.

"Don't you think your gallantry is a little old-fashioned?" she said; and when I looked confused and humbled, she added quietly, "Oh, I like it, I like everything old-fashioned, and it is delightful to hear you say such pretty things."

The moorland around us was very still now under its ghostly sheet of mist. The plovers had ceased their calling; the crickets and all the little creatures of the fields were silent as we passed, yet it seemed to me as if I could hear them beginning again far behind us. Well in advance, the two tall falconers strode across the heather, and the faint jingling of the hawks' bells came to our ears in distant murmuring chimes.

Suddenly a splendid hound dashed out of the mist in front, followed by another and another until half-a-dozen or more were bounding and leaping around the girl beside me. She caressed and quieted them with her gloved hand, speaking to them in quaint terms which I remembered to have seen in old French manuscripts.

Then the falcons on the circlet borne by the falconer ahead began to beat their wings and scream, and from somewhere out of sight the notes of a hunting-horn floated across the moor. The hounds sprang away before us and vanished in the twilight, the falcons flapped and squealed upon their perch, and the girl, taking up the song of the horn, began to hum. Clear and mellow her voice sounded in the night air.

"Chasseur, chasseur, chassez encore,
Quittez Rosette et Jeanneton,
Tonton, tonton, tontaine, tonton,
Ou, pour, rabattre, dès l'aurore,
Que les Amours soient de planton,
Tonton, tontaine, tonton."

As I listened to her lovely voice a grey mass which rapidly grew more distinct loomed up in front, and the horn rang out joyously through the tumult of the hounds and falcons. A torch glimmered at a gate, a light streamed through an opening door, and we stepped upon a wooden bridge which trembled under our feet and rose creaking and straining behind us as we passed over the moat and into a small stone court, walled on every side. From an open doorway a man came and, bending in salutation, presented a cup to the girl beside me. She took the cup and touched it with her lips, then lowering it turned to me and said in a low voice, "I bid you welcome."

At that moment one of the falconers came with another cup, but before handing it to me, presented it to the girl, who tasted it. The falconer made a gesture to receive it, but she hesitated a moment, and then, stepping forward, offered me the cup with her own hands. I felt this to be an act of extraordinary graciousness, but hardly knew what was expected of me, and did not raise it to my lips at once. The girl flushed crimson. I saw that I must act quickly.

"Mademoiselle," I faltered, "a stranger whom you have saved from dangers he may never realize empties this cup to the gentlest and loveliest hostess of France."

"In His name," she murmured, crossing herself as I drained the cup. Then stepping into the doorway she turned to me with a pretty gesture and, taking my hand in hers, led me into the house, saying again and again: "You are very welcome, indeed you are welcome to the Château d'Ys."

## II

I awoke next morning with the music of the horn in my ears, and leaping out of the ancient bed, went to a curtained window where the sunlight filtered through little deep-set panes. The horn ceased as I looked into the court below.

A man who might have been brother to the two falconers of the night before stood in the midst of a pack of hounds. A curved horn was strapped over his back, and in his hand he held a long-lashed whip. The dogs whined and yelped, dancing around him in anticipation; there was the stamp of horses, too, in the walled yard.

"Mount!" cried a voice in Breton, and with a clatter of hoofs the two falconers, with falcons upon their wrists, rode into the courtyard among the hounds. Then I heard another voice which sent the blood throbbing through my heart: "Piriou Louis, hunt the hounds well and spare neither spur nor whip. Thou Raoul and thou Gaston, see that the *epervier* does not prove himself *niais*, and if it be best in your judgment, *faites courtoisie à l'oiseau. Jardiner un oiseau*, like the *mué* there on Hastur's wrist, is not difficult, but thou, Raoul, mayest not find it so simple to govern that *hagard*. Twice last week he foamed *au vif* and lost the *beccade* although he is used to the *leurre*. The bird acts like a stupid *branchier. Paître un hagard n'est pas si facile.*"

Was I dreaming? The old language of falconry which I had read in yellow manuscripts—the old forgotten French of the middle ages was sounding in my ears while the hounds bayed and the hawks' bells tinkled accompaniment to the stamping horses. She spoke again in the sweet forgotten language:

"If you would rather attach the *longe* and leave thy *hagard au bloc*, Raoul, I shall say nothing; for it were a pity to spoil so fair a day's sport with an ill-trained *sors. Essimer abaisser,*—it is possibly the best way. *Ça lui donnera des reins.* I was perhaps hasty with the bird. It takes time to pass *à la filière* and the exercises *d'escap.*"

Then the falconer Raoul bowed in his stirrups and replied: "If it be the pleasure of Mademoiselle, I shall keep the hawk."

"It is my wish," she answered. "Falconry I know, but you have yet to give me many a lesson in *Autourserie*, my poor Raoul. Sieur Piriou Louis mount!"

The huntsman sprang into an archway and in an instant returned, mounted upon a strong black horse, followed by a piqueur also mounted.

"Ah!" she cried joyously, "speed Glemarec René! speed! speed all! Sound thy horn, Sieur Piriou!"

The silvery music of the hunting-horn filled the courtyard, the hounds sprang through the gateway and galloping hoof-beats plunged out of the paved court; loud on the drawbridge, suddenly muffled, then lost in the heather and bracken of the moors. Distant and more distant sounded the horn, until it became so faint that the sudden carol of a soaring lark drowned it in my ears. I heard the voice below responding to some call from within the house.

"I do not regret the chase, I will go another time. Courtesy to the stranger, Pelagie, remember!"

And a feeble voice came quavering from within the house, "*Courtoisie!*"

I stripped, and rubbed myself from head to foot in the huge earthen basin of icy water which stood upon the stone floor at the foot of my bed. Then I looked about for my clothes. They were gone, but on a settle near the door lay a heap of garments which I inspected with astonishment. As my clothes had vanished, I was compelled to attire myself in the costume which had evidently been placed there for me to wear while my own clothes dried. Everything was there, cap, shoes, and hunting doublet of silvery grey homespun; but the close-fitting costume and seamless shoes belonged to another century, and I remembered the strange costumes of the three falconers in the courtyard. I was sure that it was not the modern dress of any portion of France or Brittany; but not until I was dressed and stood before a mirror between the windows did I realize that I was clothed much more like a young huntsman of the middle ages than like a Breton of that day. I hesitated and picked up the cap. Should I go down and present myself in that strange guise? There seemed to be no help for it, my own clothes were gone and there was no bell in the ancient chamber to call a servant; so I contented myself with removing a short hawk's feather from the cap, and, opening the door, went downstairs.

By the fireplace in the large room at the foot of the stairs an old Breton woman sat spinning with a distaff. She looked up at me when I appeared, and, smiling frankly, wished me health in the Breton language, to which I laughingly replied in French. At the same moment my hostess appeared and returned my salutation with a grace and dignity that sent a thrill to my heart. Her lovely head with its dark curly hair was crowned with a head-dress which set all doubts as to the epoch of my own costume at rest. Her slender figure was exquisitely set off in the homespun hunting-gown edged with silver, and on her gauntlet-covered wrist she bore one of her petted hawks. With perfect simplicity she took my hand and led me into the garden in the court, and seating herself before a table invited me very sweetly to sit beside her. Then she asked me in her soft quaint accent how I had passed the night, and whether I was very much inconvenienced by wearing the clothes which old Pelagie had put there for me while I slept. I looked at my own clothes and shoes, drying in the sun by the garden-wall, and hated them. What horrors they were compared with the graceful costume which I now wore! I told her this laughing, but she agreed with me very seriously.

"We will throw them away," she said in a quiet voice. In my astonishment I attempted to explain that I not only could not think of accepting clothes from anybody, although for all I knew it might be the custom of hospitality in that part of the country, but that I should cut an impossible figure if I returned to France clothed as I was then.

She laughed and tossed her pretty head, saying something in old French which I did not understand, and then Pelagie trotted out with a tray on which stood two bowls of milk, a loaf of white bread, fruit, a platter of honey-comb, and a flagon of deep red wine. "You see I have not yet broken my fast because I wished you to eat with me. But I am very hungry," she smiled.

"I would rather die than forget one word of what you have said!" I blurted out, while my cheeks burned. "She will think me mad," I added to myself, but she turned to me with sparkling eyes.

"Ah!" she murmured. "Then Monsieur knows all that there is of chivalry—"

She crossed herself and broke bread. I sat and watched her white hands, not daring to raise my eyes to hers.

"Will you not eat?" she asked. "Why do you look so troubled?"

Ah, why? I knew it now. I knew I would give my life to touch with my lips those rosy palms—I understood now that from the moment when I looked into her dark eyes there on the moor last night I had loved her. My great and sudden passion held me speechless.

"Are you ill at ease?" she asked again.

Then, like a man who pronounces his own doom, I answered in a low voice: "Yes, I am ill at ease for love of you." And as she did not stir nor answer, the same power moved my lips in spite of me and I said, "I, who am unworthy of the lightest of your thoughts, I who abuse hospitality and repay your gentle courtesy with bold presumption, I love you."

She leaned her head upon her hands, and answered softly, "I love you. Your words are very dear to me. I love you."

"Then I shall win you."

"Win me," she replied.

But all the time I had been sitting silent, my face turned toward her. She, also silent, her sweet face resting on her upturned palm, sat facing me, and as her eyes looked into mine I knew that neither she nor I had spoken human speech; but I knew that her soul had answered mine, and I drew myself up feeling youth and joyous love coursing through every vein. She, with a bright colour in her lovely face, seemed as one awakened from a dream, and her eyes sought mine with a questioning glance which made me tremble with delight. We broke our fast, speaking of ourselves. I told her my name and she told me hers, the Demoiselle Jeanne d'Ys.

She spoke of her father and mother's death, and how the nineteen of her years had been passed in the little fortified farm alone with her nurse Pelagie, Glemarec René the piqueur, and the four falconers, Raoul, Gaston, Hastur, and the Sieur Piriou Louis, who had served her father. She had never been outside the moorland—never even had seen a human soul before, except the falconers and Pelagie. She did not know how she had heard of Kerselec; perhaps the falconers had spoken of it. She knew the legends of Loup Garou and Jeanne la Flamme from her nurse Pelagie. She embroidered and spun flax. Her hawks and hounds were her only distraction. When she had met me there on the moor she had been so frightened that she almost dropped at the sound of my voice. She had, it was true, seen ships at sea from the cliffs, but as far as the eye could reach the moors over which she galloped were destitute of any sign of human life. There was a legend which old Pelagie told, how any-body once lost in the unexplored moorland might never return, because the moors were enchanted. She did not know whether it was true, she never had thought about it until she met me. She did not know whether the falconers had even been outside, or whether they could go if they would. The books in the house which Pelagie, the nurse, had taught her to read were hundreds of years old.

All this she told me with a sweet seriousness seldom seen in any one but children. My own name she found easy to pronounce, and insisted, because my first name was Philip, I must have French blood in me. She did not seem curious to learn anything about the outside world, and I thought perhaps she considered it had forfeited her interest and respect from the stories of her nurse.

We were still sitting at the table, and she was throwing grapes to the small field birds which came fearlessly to our very feet.

I began to speak in a vague way of going, but she would not hear of it, and before I knew it I had promised to stay a week and hunt with hawk and hound in their company. I also obtained permission to come again from Kerselec and visit her after my return.

"Why," she said innocently, "I do not know what I should do if you never came back;" and I, knowing that I had no right to awaken her with the sudden shock which the avowal of my own love would bring to her, sat silent, hardly daring to breathe.

"You will come very often?" she asked.

"Very often," I said.

"Every day?"

"Every day."

"Oh," she sighed, "I am very happy. Come and see my hawks."

She rose and took my hand again with a childlike innocence of possession, and we walked through the garden and fruit trees to a grassy lawn which was bordered by a brook. Over the lawn were scattered fifteen or twenty stumps of trees—partially im-bedded in the grass—and upon all of these except two sat falcons. They were attached to the stumps by thongs which were in turn fastened with steel rivets to their legs just above the talons. A little stream of pure spring water flowed in a wind-ing course within easy distance of each perch.

The birds set up a clamour when the girl appeared, but she went from one to an-other, caressing some, taking others for an instant upon her wrist, or stooping to adjust their jesses.

"Are they not pretty?" she said. "See, here is a falcon-gentil. We call it 'ignoble,' because it takes the quarry in direct chase. This is a blue falcon. In falconry we call it 'noble' because it rises over the quarry, and wheeling, drops upon it from above. This white bird is a gerfalcon from the north. It is also 'noble!' Here is a merlin, and this tiercelet is a falcon-heroner."

I asked her how she had learned the old language of falconry. She did not remember, but thought her father must have taught it to her when she was very young.

Then she led me away and showed me the young falcons still in the nest. "They are termed *niais* in falconry," she explained. "A *branchier* is the young bird which is just able to leave the nest and hop from branch to branch. A young bird which has not yet moulted is called a *sors*, and a *mué* is a hawk which has moulted in captivity. When we catch a wild falcon which has changed its plumage we term it a *hagard*. Raoul first taught me to dress a falcon. Shall I teach you how it is done?"

She seated herself on the bank of the stream among the falcons and I threw myself at her feet to listen.

Then the Demoiselle d'Ys held up one rosy-tipped finger and began very gravely.

"First one must catch the falcon."

"I am caught," I answered.

She laughed very prettily and told me my *dressage* would perhaps be difficult, as I was noble.

"I am already tamed," I replied; "jessed and belled."

She laughed, delighted. "Oh, my brave falcon; then you will return at my call?"

"I am yours," I answered gravely.

She sat silent for a moment. Then the colour heightened in her cheeks and she held up her finger again, saying, "Listen; I wish to speak of falconry—"

"I listen, Countess Jeanne d'Ys."

But again she fell into the reverie, and her eyes seemed fixed on something beyond the summer clouds.

"Philip," she said at last.

"Jeanne," I whispered.

"That is all,—that is what I wished," she sighed,—"Philip and Jeanne."

She held her hand toward me and I touched it with my lips.

"Win me," she said, but this time it was the body and soul which spoke in unison.

After a while she began again: "Let us speak of falconry."

"Begin," I replied; "we have caught the falcon."

Then Jeanne d'Ys took my hand in both of hers and told me how with infinite patience the young falcon was taught to perch upon the wrist, how little by little it became used to the belled jesses and the *chaperon à cornette*.

"They must first have a good appetite," she said; "then little by little I reduce their nourishment; which in falconry we call *pât*. When, after many nights passed *au bloc* as these birds are now, I prevail upon the *hagard* to stay quietly on the wrist, then the bird is ready to be taught to come for its food. I fix the *pât* to the end of a thong, or *leurre*, and teach the bird to come to me as soon as I begin to whirl the cord in circles about my head. At first I drop the *pât* when the falcon comes, and he eats the food on the ground. After a little he will learn to seize the *leurre* in motion as I whirl it

70

around my head or drag it over the ground. After this it is easy to teach the falcon to strike at game, always remembering to *'faire courtoisie á l'oiseau'*, that is, to allow the bird to taste the quarry."

A squeal from one of the falcons interrupted her, and she arose to adjust the *longe* which had become whipped about the *bloc*, but the bird still flapped its wings and screamed.

"What *is* the matter?" she said. "Philip, can you see?"

I looked around and at first saw nothing to cause the commotion, which was now heightened by the screams and flapping of all the birds. Then my eye fell upon the flat rock beside the stream from which the girl had risen. A grey serpent was moving slowly across the surface of the boulder, and the eyes in its flat triangular head sparkled like jet.

"A couleuvre," she said quietly.

"It is harmless, is it not?" I asked.

She pointed to the black V-shaped figure on the neck.

"It is certain death," she said; "it is a viper."

We watched the reptile moving slowly over the smooth rock to where the sunlight fell in a broad warm patch.

I started forward to examine it, but she clung to my arm crying, "Don't, Philip, I am afraid."

"For me?"

"For you, Philip,—I love you."

Then I took her in my arms and kissed her on the lips, but all I could say was: "Jeanne, Jeanne, Jeanne." And as she lay trembling on my breast, something struck my foot in the grass below, but I did not heed it. Then again something struck my ankle, and a sharp pain shot through me. I looked into the sweet face of Jeanne d'Ys and kissed her, and with all my strength lifted her in my arms and flung her from me. Then bending, I tore the viper from my ankle and set my heel upon its head. I remember feeling weak and numb,—I remember falling to the ground. Through my slowly glazing eyes I saw Jeanne's white face bending close to mine, and when the light in my eyes went out I still felt her arms about my neck, and her soft cheek against my drawn lips.

When I opened my eyes, I looked around in terror. Jeanne was gone. I saw the stream and the flat rock; I saw the crushed viper in the grass beside me, but the hawks and *blocs* had disappeared. I sprang to my feet. The garden, the fruit trees, the drawbridge and the walled court were gone. I stared stupidly at a heap of crumbling ruins, ivy-covered and grey, through which great trees had pushed their way. I crept forward, dragging my numbed foot, and as I moved, a falcon sailed from the tree-tops among the ruins, and soaring, mounting in narrowing circles, faded and vanished in the clouds above.

"Jeanne, Jeanne," I cried, but my voice died on my lips, and I fell on my knees among the weeds. And as God willed it, I, not knowing, had fallen kneeling before a crumbling shrine carved in stone for our Mother of Sorrows. I saw the sad face of the Virgin wrought in the cold stone. I saw the cross and thorns at her feet, and beneath it I read:

> "PRAY FOR THE SOUL OF THE
> DEMOISELLE JEANNE D'Ys,
> WHO DIED
> IN HER YOUTH FOR LOVE OF
> PHILIP, A STRANGER.
> A.D. 1573."

But upon the icy slab lay a woman's glove still warm and fragrant.

# THE PROPHETS' PARADISE

"If but the Vine and Love Abjuring Band
Are in the Prophets' Paradise to stand,
Alack, I doubt the Prophets' Paradise,
Were empty as the hollow of one's hand."

## THE STUDIO

He smiled, saying, "Seek her throughout the world."

I said, "Why tell me of the world? My world is here, between these walls and the sheet of glass above; here among gilded flagons and dull jewelled arms, tarnished frames and canvasses, black chests and high-backed chairs, quaintly carved and stained in blue and gold."

"For whom do you wait?" he said, and I answered, "When she comes I shall know her."

On my hearth a tongue of flame whispered secrets to the whitening ashes. In the street below I heard footsteps, a voice, and a song.

"For whom then do you wait?" he said, and I answered, "I shall know her."

Footsteps, a voice, and a song in the street below, and I knew the song but neither the steps nor the voice.

"Fool!" he cried, "the song is the same, the voice and steps have but changed with years!"

On the hearth a tongue of flame whispered above the whitening ashes: "Wait no more; they have passed, the steps and the voice in the street below."

Then he smiled, saying, "For whom do you wait? Seek her throughout the world!"

I answered, "My world is here, between these walls and the sheet of glass above; here among gilded flagons and dull jewelled arms, tarnished frames and canvasses, black chests and high-backed chairs, quaintly carved and stained in blue and gold."

## THE PHANTOM

The Phantom of the Past would go no further.

"If it is true," she sighed, "that you find in me a friend, let us turn back together. You will forget, here, under the summer sky."

I held her close, pleading, caressing; I seized her, white with anger, but she resisted.

"If it is true," she sighed, "that you find in me a friend, let us turn back together."

The Phantom of the Past would go no further.

## THE SACRIFICE

I went into a field of flowers, whose petals are whiter than snow and whose hearts are pure gold.

Far afield a woman cried, "I have killed him I loved!" and from a jar she poured blood upon the flowers whose petals are whiter than snow and whose hearts are pure gold.

Far afield I followed, and on the jar I read a thousand names, while from within the fresh blood bubbled to the brim.

"I have killed him I loved!" she cried. "The world's athirst; now let it drink!" She passed, and far afield I watched her pouring blood upon the flowers whose petals are whiter than snow and whose hearts are pure gold.

## DESTINY

I came to the bridge which few may pass.

"Pass!" cried the keeper, but I laughed, saying, "There is time;" and he smiled and shut the gates.

To the bridge which few may pass came young and old. All were refused. Idly I stood and counted them, until, wearied of their noise and lamentations, I came again to the bridge which few may pass.

Those in the throng about the gates shrieked out, "He comes too late!" But I laughed, saying, "There is time."

"Pass!" cried the keeper as I entered; then smiled and shut the gates.

## THE THRONG

There, where the throng was thickest in the street, I stood with Pierrot. All eyes were turned on me.

"What are they laughing at?" I asked, but he grinned, dusting the chalk from my black cloak. "I cannot see; it must be something droll, perhaps an honest thief!"

All eyes were turned on me.

"He has robbed you of your purse!" they laughed.

"My purse!" I cried; "Pierrot—help! it is a thief!"

They laughed: "He has robbed you of your purse!"

Then Truth stepped out, holding a mirror. "If he is an honest thief," cried Truth, "Pierrot shall find him with this mirror!" but he only grinned, dusting the chalk from my black cloak.

"You see," he said, "Truth is an honest thief, she brings you back your mirror."

All eyes were turned on me.

"Arrest Truth!" I cried, forgetting it was not a mirror but a purse I lost, standing with Pierrot, there, where the throng was thickest in the street.

## THE JESTER

"Was she fair?" I asked, but he only chuckled, listening to the bells jingling on his cap.

"Stabbed," he tittered. "Think of the long journey, the days of peril, the dreadful nights! Think how he wandered, for her sake, year after year, through hostile lands, yearning for kith and kin, yearning for her!"

"Stabbed," he tittered, listening to the bells jingling on his cap.

"Was she fair?" I asked, but he only snarled, muttering to the bells jingling on his cap.

"She kissed him at the gate," he tittered, "but in the hall his brother's welcome touched his heart."

"Was she fair?" I asked.

"Stabbed," he chuckled. "Think of the long journey, the days of peril, the dreadful nights! Think how he wandered, for her sake, year after year through hostile lands, yearning for kith and kin, yearning for her!"

"She kissed him at the gate, but in the hall his brother's welcome touched his heart."

"Was she fair?" I asked; but he only snarled, listening to the bells jingling in his cap.

## THE GREEN ROOM

The Clown turned his powdered face to the mirror.

"If to be fair is to be beautiful," he said, "who can compare with me in my white mask?"

"Who can compare with him in his white mask?" I asked of Death beside me.

"Who can compare with me?" said Death, "for I am paler still."

"You are very beautiful," sighed the Clown, turning his powdered face from the mirror.

## THE LOVE TEST

"If it is true that you love," said Love, "then wait no longer. Give her these jewels which would dishonour her and so dishonour you in loving one dishonoured. If it is true that you love," said Love, "then wait no longer."

I took the jewels and went to her, but she trod upon them, sobbing: "Teach me to wait—I love you!"

"Then wait, if it is true," said Love.

# THE STREET OF THE FOUR WINDS

"Ferme tes yeux à demi,
Croise tes bras sur ton sein,
Et de ton cœur endormi
Chasse à jamais tout dessein."

"Je chante la nature,
Les étoiles du soir, les larmes du matin,
Les couchers de soleil à l'horizon lointain,
Le ciel qui parle au cœur d'existence future!"

## I

The animal paused on the threshold, interrogative alert, ready for flight if necessary. Severn laid down his palette, and held out a hand of welcome. The cat remained motionless, her yellow eyes fastened upon Severn.

"Puss," he said, in his low, pleasant voice, "come in."

The tip of her thin tail twitched uncertainly.

"Come in," he said again.

Apparently she found his voice reassuring, for she slowly settled upon all fours, her eyes still fastened upon him, her tail tucked under her gaunt flanks.

He rose from his easel smiling. She eyed him quietly, and when he walked toward her she watched him bend above her without a wince; her eyes followed his hand until it touched her head. Then she uttered a ragged mew.

It had long been Severn's custom to converse with animals, probably because he lived so much alone; and now he said, "What's the matter, puss?"

Her timid eyes sought his.

"I understand," he said gently, "you shall have it at once."

Then moving quietly about he busied himself with the duties of a host, rinsed a saucer, filled it with the rest of the milk from the bottle on the window-sill, and kneeling down, crumbled a roll into the hollow of his hand.

The creature rose and crept toward the saucer.

With the handle of a palette-knife he stirred the crumbs and milk together and stepped back as she thrust her nose into the mess. He watched her in silence. From time to time the saucer clinked upon the tiled floor as she reached for a morsel on the rim; and at last the bread was all gone, and her purple tongue travelled over every unlicked spot until the saucer shone like polished marble. Then she sat up, and cool-ly turning her back to him, began her ablutions.

"Keep it up," said Severn, much interested, "you need it."

She flattened one ear, but neither turned nor interrupted her toilet. As the grime was slowly removed Severn observed that nature had intended her for a white cat. Her fur had disappeared in patches, from disease or the chances of war, her tail was bony and her spine sharp. But what charms she had were becoming apparent under vigorous licking, and he waited until she had finished before re-opening the conver-sation. When at last she closed her eyes and folded her forepaws under her breast, he began again very gently: "Puss, tell me your troubles."

At the sound of his voice she broke into a harsh rumbling which he recognized as an attempt to purr. He bent over to rub her cheek and she mewed again, an amiable inquiring little mew, to which he replied, "Certainly, you are greatly improved, and when you recover your plumage you will be a gorgeous bird." Much flattered, she stood up and marched around and around his legs, pushing her head between them and making pleased remarks, to which he responded with grave politeness.

"Now, what sent you here," he said—"here into the Street of the Four Winds, and up five flights to the very door where you would be welcome? What was it that pre-vented your meditated flight when I turned from my canvas to encounter your yellow eyes? Are you a Latin Quarter cat as I am a Latin Quarter man? And why do you wear a rose-coloured flowered garter buckled about your neck?" The cat had climbed into his lap, and now sat purring as he passed his hand over her thin coat.

"Excuse me," he continued in lazy soothing tones, harmonizing with her purring, "if I seem indelicate, but I cannot help musing on this rose-coloured garter, flowered so quaintly and fastened with a silver clasp. For the clasp is silver; I can see the mint mark on the edge, as is prescribed by the law of the French Republic. Now, why is this garter woven of rose silk and delicately embroidered,—why is this silken garter with its silver clasp about your famished throat? Am I indiscreet when I inquire if its owner is your owner? Is she some aged dame living in memory of youthful vanities, fond, doting on you, decorating you with her intimate personal attire? The circum-ference of the garter would suggest this, for your neck is thin, and the garter fits you. But then again I notice—I notice most things—that the garter is capable of being much enlarged. These small silver-rimmed eyelets, of which I count five, are proof of that. And now I observe that the fifth eyelet is worn out, as though the tongue of the clasp were accustomed to lie there. That seems to argue a well-rounded form."

The cat curled her toes in contentment. The street was very still outside.

He murmured on: "Why should your mistress decorate you with an article most necessary to her at all times? Anyway, at most times. How did she come to slip this bit of silk and silver about your neck? Was it the caprice of a moment,—when you, before you had lost your pristine plumpness, marched singing into her bedroom to bid her good-morning? Of course, and she sat up among the pillows, her coiled hair tumbling to her shoulders, as you sprang upon the bed purring: 'Good-day, my lady.' Oh, it is very easy to understand," he yawned, resting his head on the back of the chair. The cat still purred, tightening and relaxing her padded claws over his knee.

"Shall I tell you all about her, cat? She is very beautiful—your mistress," he murmured drowsily, "and her hair is heavy as burnished gold. I could paint her,—not on canvas—for I should need shades and tones and hues and dyes more splendid than the iris of a splendid rainbow. I could only paint her with closed eyes, for in dreams alone can such colours as I need be found. For her eyes, I must have azure from skies untroubled by a cloud—the skies of dreamland. For her lips, roses from the palaces of slumberland, and for her brow, snow-drifts from mountains which tower in fantastic pinnacles to the moons;—oh, much higher than our moon here,—the crystal moons of dreamland. She is—very—beautiful, your mistress."

The words died on his lips and his eyelids drooped.

The cat, too, was asleep, her cheek turned up upon her wasted flank, her paws relaxed and limp.

## II

"It is fortunate," said Severn, sitting up and stretching, "that we have tided over the dinner hour, for I have nothing to offer you for supper but what may be purchased with one silver franc."

The cat on his knee rose, arched her back, yawned, and looked up at him.

"What shall it be? A roast chicken with salad? No? Possibly you prefer beef? Of course,—and I shall try an egg and some white bread. Now for the wines. Milk for you? Good. I shall take a little water, fresh from the wood," with a motion toward the bucket in the sink.

He put on his hat and left the room. The cat followed to the door, and after he had closed it behind him, she settled down, smelling at the cracks, and cocking one ear at every creak from the crazy old building.

The door below opened and shut. The cat looked serious, for a moment doubtful, and her ears flattened in nervous expectation. Presently she rose with a jerk of her tail and started on a noiseless tour of the studio. She sneezed at a pot of turpentine, hastily retreating to the table, which she presently mounted, and having satisfied her curiosity concerning a roll of red modelling wax, returned to the door and sat down with her eyes on the crack over the threshold. Then she lifted her voice in a thin plaint.

When Severn returned he looked grave, but the cat, joyous and demonstrative, marched around him, rubbing her gaunt body against his legs, driving her head enthusiastically into his hand, and purring until her voice mounted to a squeal.

He placed a bit of meat, wrapped in brown paper, upon the table, and with a penknife cut it into shreds. The milk he took from a bottle which had served for medicine, and poured it into the saucer on the hearth.

The cat crouched before it, purring and lapping at the same time.

He cooked his egg and ate it with a slice of bread, watching her busy with the shredded meat, and when he had finished, and had filled and emptied a cup of water from the bucket in the sink, he sat down, taking her into his lap, where she at once curled up and began her toilet. He began to speak again, touching her caressingly at times by way of emphasis.

"Cat, I have found out where your mistress lives. It is not very far away;—it is here, under this same leaky roof, but in the north wing which I had supposed was uninhabited. My janitor tells me this. By chance, he is almost sober this evening. The butcher on the rue de Seine, where I bought your meat, knows you, and old Cabane the baker identified you with needless sarcasm. They tell me hard tales of your mistress which I shall not believe. They say she is idle and vain and pleasure-loving; they say she is hare-brained and reckless. The little sculptor on the ground floor, who was buying rolls from old Cabane, spoke to me to-night for the first time, although we have always bowed to each other. He said she was very good and very beautiful. He has only seen her once, and does not know her name. I thanked him;—I don't know why I thanked him so warmly. Cabane said, 'Into this cursed Street of the Four Winds, the four winds blow all things evil.' The sculptor looked confused, but when he went out with his rolls, he said to me, 'I am sure, Monsieur, that she is as good as she is beautiful.'"

The cat had finished her toilet, and now, springing softly to the floor, went to the door and sniffed. He knelt beside her, and unclasping the garter held it for a moment in his hands. After a while he said: "There is a name engraved upon the silver clasp beneath the buckle. It is a pretty name, Sylvia Elven. Sylvia is a woman's name, Elven is the name of a town. In Paris, in this quarter, above all, in this Street of the Four Winds, names are worn and put away as the fashions change with the seasons. I know the little town of Elven, for there I met Fate face to face and Fate was unkind. But do you know that in Elven Fate had another name, and that name was Sylvia?"

He replaced the garter and stood up looking down at the cat crouched before the closed door.

"The name of Elven has a charm for me. It tells me of meadows and clear rivers. The name of Sylvia troubles me like perfume from dead flowers."

The cat mewed.

"Yes, yes," he said soothingly, "I will take you back. Your Sylvia is not my Sylvia; the world is wide and Elven is not unknown. Yet in the darkness and filth of poorer Paris, in the sad shadows of this ancient house, these names are very pleasant to me."

He lifted her in his arms and strode through the silent corridors to the stairs. Down five flights and into the moonlit court, past the little sculptor's den, and then again in at the gate of the north wing and up the worm-eaten stairs he passed, until he came to a closed door. When he had stood knocking for a long time, something moved behind the door; it opened and he went in. The room was dark. As he crossed the threshold, the cat sprang from his arms into the shadows. He listened but heard nothing. The silence was oppressive and he struck a match. At his elbow stood a table and on the table a candle in a gilded candlestick. This he lighted, then looked around. The chamber was vast, the hangings heavy with embroidery. Over the fireplace towered a carved mantel, grey with the ashes of dead fires. In a recess by the deep-set windows stood a bed, from which the bedclothes, soft and fine as lace, trailed to the polished floor. He lifted the candle above his head. A handker-chief lay at his feet. It was faintly perfumed. He turned toward the windows. In front of them was a *canapé* and over it were flung, pell-mell, a gown of silk, a heap of lace-like garments, white and delicate as spiders' meshes, long, crumpled gloves, and, on the floor beneath, the stockings, the little pointed shoes, and one garter of rosy silk, quaintly flowered and fitted with a silver clasp. Wondering, he stepped forward and drew the heavy curtains from the bed. For a moment the candle flared in his hand; then his eyes met two other eyes, wide open, smiling, and the candle-flame flashed over hair heavy as gold.

She was pale, but not as white as he; her eyes were untroubled as a child's; but he stared, trembling from head to foot, while the candle flickered in his hand.

At last he whispered: "Sylvia, it is I."

Again he said, "It is I."

Then, knowing that she was dead, he kissed her on the mouth. And through the long watches of the night the cat purred on his knee, tightening and relaxing her padded claws, until the sky paled above the Street of the Four Winds.

# THE STREET OF THE FIRST SHELL

"Be of Good Cheer, the Sullen Month will die,
And a young Moon requite us by and by:
Look how the Old one, meagre, bent, and wan
With age and Fast, is fainting from the sky."

The room was already dark. The high roofs opposite cut off what little remained of the December daylight. The girl drew her chair nearer the window, and choosing a large needle, threaded it, knotting the thread over her fingers. Then she smoothed the baby garment across her knees, and bending, bit off the thread and drew the smaller needle from where it rested in the hem. When she had brushed away the stray threads and bits of lace, she laid it again over her knees caressingly. Then she slipped the threaded needle from her corsage and passed it through a button, but as the button spun down the thread, her hand faltered, the thread snapped, and the button rolled across the floor. She raised her head. Her eyes were fixed on a strip of waning light above the chimneys. From somewhere in the city came sounds like the distant beating of drums, and beyond, far beyond, a vague muttering, now growing, swelling, rumbling in the distance like the pounding of surf upon the rocks, now like the surf again, receding, growling, menacing. The cold had become intense, a bitter piercing cold which strained and snapped at joist and beam and turned the slush of yesterday to flint. From the street below every sound broke sharp and metallic—the clatter of sabots, the rattle of shutters or the rare sound of a human voice. The air was heavy, weighted with the black cold as with a pall. To breathe was painful, to move an effort.

In the desolate sky there was something that wearied, in the brooding clouds, something that saddened. It penetrated the freezing city cut by the freezing river, the splendid city with its towers and domes, its quays and bridges and its thousand spires. It entered the squares, it seized the avenues and the palaces, stole across bridges and crept among the narrow streets of the Latin Quarter, grey under the grey of the December sky. Sadness, utter sadness. A fine icy sleet was falling, powdering the pavement with a tiny crystalline dust. It sifted against the window-panes and drifted in heaps along the sill. The light at the window had nearly failed, and the girl bent low over her work. Presently she raised her head, brushing the curls from her eyes.

"Jack?"

"Dearest?"

"Don't forget to clean your palette."

He said, "All right," and picking up the palette, sat down upon the floor in front of the stove. His head and shoulders were in the shadow, but the firelight fell across his knees and glimmered red on the blade of the palette-knife. Full in the firelight beside him stood a colour-box. On the lid was carved,

J. TRENT.

École des Beaux Arts.

1870.

This inscription was ornamented with an American and a French flag.

The sleet blew against the window-panes, covering them with stars and diamonds, then, melting from the warmer air within, ran down and froze again in fern-like traceries.

A dog whined and the patter of small paws sounded on the zinc behind the stove.

"Jack, dear, do you think Hercules is hungry?"

The patter of paws was redoubled behind the stove.

"He's whining," she continued nervously, "and if it isn't because he's hungry it is because—"

Her voice faltered. A loud humming filled the air, the windows vibrated.

"Oh, Jack," she cried, "another—" but her voice was drowned in the scream of a shell tearing through the clouds overhead.

"That is the nearest yet," she murmured.

"Oh, no," he answered cheerfully, "it probably fell way over by Montmartre," and as she did not answer, he said again with exaggerated unconcern, "They wouldn't take the trouble to fire at the Latin Quarter; anyway they haven't a battery that can hurt it."

After a while she spoke up brightly: "Jack, dear, when are you going to take me to see Monsieur West's statues?"

"I will bet," he said, throwing down his palette and walking over to the window beside her, "that Colette has been here to-day."

"Why?" she asked, opening her eyes very wide. Then, "Oh, it's too bad!—really, men are tiresome when they think they know everything! And I warn you that if Monsieur West is vain enough to imagine that Colette—"

From the north another shell came whistling and quavering through the sky, passing above them with long-drawn screech which left the windows singing.

"That," he blurted out, "was too near for comfort."

They were silent for a while, then he spoke again gaily: "Go on, Sylvia, and wither poor West;" but she only sighed, "Oh, dear, I can never seem to get used to the shells."

He sat down on the arm of the chair beside her.

Her scissors fell jingling to the floor; she tossed the unfinished frock after them, and putting both arms about his neck drew him down into her lap.

"Don't go out to-night, Jack."

He kissed her uplifted face; "You know I must; don't make it hard for me."

"But when I hear the shells and—and know you are out in the city—"

"But they all fall in Montmartre—"

"They may all fall in the Beaux Arts; you said yourself that two struck the Quai d'Orsay—"

"Mere accident—"

"Jack, have pity on me! Take me with you!"

"And who will there be to get dinner?"

She rose and flung herself on the bed.

"Oh, I can't get used to it, and I know you must go, but I beg you not to be late to dinner. If you knew what I suffer! I—I—cannot help it, and you must be patient with me, dear."

He said, "It is as safe there as it is in our own house."

She watched him fill for her the alcohol lamp, and when he had lighted it and had taken his hat to go, she jumped up and clung to him in silence. After a moment he said: "Now, Sylvia, remember my courage is sustained by yours. Come, I must go!" She did not move, and he repeated: "I must go." Then she stepped back and he thought she was going to speak and waited, but she only looked at him, and, a little impatiently, he kissed her again, saying: "Don't worry, dearest."

When he had reached the last flight of stairs on his way to the street a woman hobbled out of the house-keeper's lodge waving a letter and calling: "Monsieur Jack! Monsieur Jack! this was left by Monsieur Fallowby!"

He took the letter, and leaning on the threshold of the lodge, read it:

"Dear Jack,

"I believe Braith is dead broke and I'm sure Fallowby is. Braith swears he isn't, and Fallowby swears he is, so you can draw your own conclusions. I've got a scheme for a dinner, and if it works, I will let you fellows in.

"Yours faithfully,
"WEST.

"P.S.—Fallowby has shaken Hartman and his gang, thank the Lord! There is something rotten there,—or it may be he's only a miser.

"P.P.S.—I'm more desperately in love than ever, but I'm sure she does not care a straw for me."

"All right," said Trent, with a smile, to the concierge; "but tell me, how is Papa Cottard?"

The old woman shook her head and pointed to the curtained bed in the lodge.

"Père Cottard!" he cried cheerily, "how goes the wound to-day?"

He walked over to the bed and drew the curtains. An old man was lying among the tumbled sheets.

"Better?" smiled Trent.

"Better," repeated the man wearily; and, after a pause, "Have you any news, Monsieur Jack?"

"I haven't been out to-day. I will bring you any rumour I may hear, though goodness knows I've got enough of rumours," he muttered to himself. Then aloud: "Cheer up; you're looking better."

"And the sortie?"

"Oh, the sortie, that's for this week. General Trochu sent orders last night."

"It will be terrible."

"It will be sickening," thought Trent as he went out into the street and turned the corner toward the rue de Seine; "slaughter, slaughter, phew! I'm glad I'm not going."

The street was almost deserted. A few women muffled in tattered military capes crept along the frozen pavement, and a wretchedly clad gamin hovered over the sewer-hole on the corner of the Boulevard. A rope around his waist held his rags together. From the rope hung a rat, still warm and bleeding.

"There's another in there," he yelled at Trent; "I hit him but he got away."

Trent crossed the street and asked: "How much?"

"Two francs for a quarter of a fat one; that's what they give at the St. Germain Market."

A violent fit of coughing interrupted him, but he wiped his face with the palm of his hand and looked cunningly at Trent.

"Last week you could buy a rat for six francs, but," and here he swore vilely, "the rats have quit the rue de Seine and they kill them now over by the new hospital. I'll let you have this for seven francs; I can sell it for ten in the Isle St. Louis."

"You lie," said Trent, "and let me tell you that if you try to swindle anybody in this quarter the people will make short work of you and your rats."

He stood a moment eyeing the gamin, who pretended to snivel. Then he tossed him a franc, laughing. The child caught it, and thrusting it into his mouth wheeled about to the sewer-hole. For a second he crouched, motionless, alert, his eyes on the bars of the drain, then leaping forward he hurled a stone into the gutter, and Trent left him to finish a fierce grey rat that writhed squealing at the mouth of the sewer.

"Suppose Braith should come to that," he thought; "poor little chap;" and hurrying, he turned in the dirty passage des Beaux Arts and entered the third house to the left.

"Monsieur is at home," quavered the old concierge.

Home? A garret absolutely bare, save for the iron bedstead in the corner and the iron basin and pitcher on the floor.

West appeared at the door, winking with much mystery, and motioned Trent to enter. Braith, who was painting in bed to keep warm, looked up, laughed, and shook hands.

"Any news?"

The perfunctory question was answered as usual by: "Nothing but the cannon."

Trent sat down on the bed.

"Where on earth did you get that?" he demanded, pointing to a half-finished chicken nestling in a wash-basin.

West grinned.

"Are you millionaires, you two? Out with it."

Braith, looking a little ashamed, began, "Oh, it's one of West's exploits," but was cut short by West, who said he would tell the story himself.

"You see, before the siege, I had a letter of introduction to a '*type*' here, a fat bank-er, German-American variety. You know the species, I see. Well, of course I forgot to present the letter, but this morning, judging it to be a favourable opportunity, I called on him.

"The villain lives in comfort;—fires, my boy!—fires in the ante-rooms! The But-tons finally condescends to carry my letter and card up, leaving me standing in the hallway, which I did not like, so I entered the first room I saw and nearly fainted at the sight of a banquet on a table by the fire. Down comes Buttons, very insolent. No, oh, no, his master, 'is not at home, and in fact is too busy to receive letters of introduction just now; the siege, and many business difficulties—'

"I deliver a kick to Buttons, pick up this chicken from the table, toss my card on to the empty plate, and addressing Buttons as a species of Prussian pig, march out with the honours of war."

Trent shook his head.

"I forgot to say that Hartman often dines there, and I draw my own conclusions," continued West. "Now about this chicken, half of it is for Braith and myself, and half for Colette, but of course you will help me eat my part because I'm not hungry."

"Neither am I," began Braith, but Trent, with a smile at the pinched faces before him, shook his head saying, "What nonsense! You know I'm never hungry!"

West hesitated, reddened, and then slicing off Braith's portion, but not eating any himself, said good-night, and hurried away to number 470 rue Serpente, where lived a pretty girl named Colette, orphan after Sedan, and Heaven alone knew where she got the roses in her cheeks, for the siege came hard on the poor.

"That chicken will delight her, but I really believe she's in love with West," said Trent. Then walking over to the bed: "See here, old man, no dodging, you know, how much have you left?"

The other hesitated and flushed.

"Come, old chap," insisted Trent.

Braith drew a purse from beneath his bolster, and handed it to his friend with a simplicity that touched him.

"Seven sons," he counted; "you make me tired! Why on earth don't you come to me? I take it d———d ill, Braith! How many times must I go over the same thing and explain to you that because I have money it is my duty to share it, and your duty and the duty of every American to share it with me? You can't get a cent, the city's blockaded, and the American Minister has his hands full with all the German riff-raff and deuce knows what! Why don't you act sensibly?"

"I—I will, Trent, but it's an obligation that perhaps I can never even in part repay, I'm poor and—"

"Of course you'll pay me! If I were a usurer I would take your talent for security. When you are rich and famous—"

"Don't, Trent—"

"All right, only no more monkey business."

He slipped a dozen gold pieces into the purse, and tucking it again under the mattress smiled at Braith.

"How old are you?" he demanded.

"Sixteen."

Trent laid his hand lightly on his friend's shoulder. "I'm twenty-two, and I have the rights of a grandfather as far as you are concerned. You'll do as I say until you're twenty-one."

"The siege will be over then, I hope," said Braith, trying to laugh, but the prayer in their hearts: "How long, O Lord, how long!" was answered by the swift scream of a shell soaring among the storm-clouds of that December night.

## II

West, standing in the doorway of a house in the rue Serpentine, was speaking angrily. He said he didn't care whether Hartman liked it or not; he was telling him, not arguing with him.

"You call yourself an American!" he sneered; "Berlin and hell are full of that kind of American. You come loafing about Colette with your pockets stuffed with white bread and beef, and a bottle of wine at thirty francs and you can't really afford to give a dollar to the American Ambulance and Public Assistance, which Braith does, and he's half starved!"

Hartman retreated to the curbstone, but West followed him, his face like a thunder-cloud. "Don't you dare to call yourself a countryman of mine," he growled,—"no,—nor an artist either! Artists don't worm themselves into the service of the Public Defence where they do nothing but feed like rats on the people's food! And I'll tell you now," he continued dropping his voice, for Hartman had started as though stung, "you might better keep away from that Alsatian Brasserie and the smug-faced thieves who haunt it. You know what they do with suspects!"

"You lie, you hound!" screamed Hartman, and flung the bottle in his hand straight at West's face. West had him by the throat in a second, and forcing him against the dead wall shook him wickedly.

"Now you listen to me," he muttered, through his clenched teeth. "You are already a suspect and—I swear—I believe you are a paid spy! It isn't my business to detect such vermin, and I don't intend to denounce you, but understand this! Colette don't like you and I can't stand you, and if I catch you in this street again I'll make it somewhat unpleasant. Get out, you sleek Prussian!"

Hartman had managed to drag a knife from his pocket, but West tore it from him and hurled him into the gutter. A gamin who had seen this burst into a peal of laughter, which rattled harshly in the silent street. Then everywhere windows were raised and rows of haggard faces appeared demanding to know why people should laugh in the starving city.

"Is it a victory?" murmured one.

"Look at that," cried West as Hartman picked himself up from the pavement, "look! you miser! look at those faces!" But Hartman gave *him* a look which he never forgot, and walked away without a word. Trent, who suddenly appeared at the corner, glanced curiously at West, who merely nodded toward his door saying, "Come in; Fallowby's upstairs."

"What are you doing with that knife?" demanded Fallowby, as he and Trent entered the studio.

West looked at his wounded hand, which still clutched the knife, but saying, "Cut myself by accident," tossed it into a corner and washed the blood from his fingers.

Fallowby, fat and lazy, watched him without comment, but Trent, half divining how things had turned, walked over to Fallowby smiling.

"I've a bone to pick with you!" he said.

"Where is it? I'm hungry," replied Fallowby with affected eagerness, but Trent, frowning, told him to listen.

"How much did I advance you a week ago?"

"Three hundred and eighty francs," replied the other, with a squirm of contrition.

"Where is it?"

Fallowby began a series of intricate explanations, which were soon cut short by Trent.

"I know; you blew it in;—you always blow it in. I don't care a rap what you did before the siege: I know you are rich and have a right to dispose of your money as you wish to, and I also know that, generally speaking, it is none of my business. But *now* it is my business, as I have to supply the funds until you get some more, which you won't until the siege is ended one way or another. I wish to share what I have, but I won't see it thrown out of the window. Oh, yes, of course I know you will re-imburse me, but that isn't the question; and, anyway, it's the opinion of your friends, old man, that you will not be worse off for a little abstinence from fleshly pleasures. You are positively a freak in this famine-cursed city of skeletons!"

"I *am* rather stout," he admitted.

"Is it true you are out of money?" demanded Trent.

"Yes, I am," sighed the other.

"That roast sucking pig on the rue St. Honoré,—is it there yet?" continued Trent.

"Wh—at?" stammered the feeble one.

"Ah—I thought so! I caught you in ecstasy before that sucking pig at least a doz-en times!"

Then laughing, he presented Fallowby with a roll of twenty franc pieces saying: "If these go for luxuries you must live on your own flesh," and went over to aid West, who sat beside the wash-basin binding up his hand.

West suffered him to tie the knot, and then said: "You remember, yesterday, when I left you and Braith to take the chicken to Colette."

"Chicken! Good heavens!" moaned Fallowby.

"Chicken," repeated West, enjoying Fallowby's grief;—"I—that is, I must explain that things are changed. Colette and I—are to be married—"

"What—what about the chicken?" groaned Fallowby.

"Shut up!" laughed Trent, and slipping his arm through West's, walked to the stairway.

"The poor little thing," said West, "just think, not a splinter of firewood for a week and wouldn't tell me because she thought I needed it for my clay figure. Whew! When I heard it I smashed that smirking clay nymph to pieces, and the rest can freeze and be hanged!" After a moment he added timidly: "Won't you call on your way down and say *bon soir*? It's No. 17."

"Yes," said Trent, and he went out softly closing the door behind.

He stopped on the third landing, lighted a match, scanned the numbers over the row of dingy doors, and knocked at No. 17.

"C'est toi Georges?" The door opened.

"Oh, pardon, Monsieur Jack, I thought it was Monsieur West," then blushing fu-riously, "Oh, I see you have heard! Oh, thank you so much for your wishes, and I'm sure we love each other very much,—and I'm dying to see Sylvia and tell her and—"

"And what?" laughed Trent.

"I am very happy," she sighed.

"He's pure gold," returned Trent, and then gaily: "I want you and George to come and dine with us to-night. It's a little treat,—you see to-morrow is Sylvia's *fête*. She will be nineteen. I have written to Thorne, and the Guernalecs will come with their cousin Odile. Fallowby has engaged not to bring anybody but himself."

The girl accepted shyly, charging him with loads of loving messages to Sylvia, and he said good-night.

He started up the street, walking swiftly, for it was bitter cold, and cutting across the rue de la Lune he entered the rue de Seine. The early winter night had fallen, almost without warning, but the sky was clear and myriads of stars glittered in the heavens. The bombardment had become furious—a steady rolling thunder from the Prussian cannon punctuated by the heavy shocks from Mont Valérien.

The shells streamed across the sky leaving trails like shooting stars, and now, as he turned to look back, rockets blue and red flared above the horizon from the Fort of Issy, and the Fortress of the North flamed like a bonfire.

"Good news!" a man shouted over by the Boulevard St. Germain. As if by magic the streets were filled with people,—shivering, chattering people with shrunken eyes.

"Jacques!" cried one. "The Army of the Loire!"

"Eh! *mon vieux*, it has come then at last! I told thee! I told thee! To-morrow—to-night—who knows?"

"Is it true? Is it a sortie?"

Some one said: "Oh, God—a sortie—and my son?" Another cried: "To the Seine? They say one can see the signals of the Army of the Loire from the Pont Neuf."

There was a child standing near Trent who kept repeating: "Mamma, Mamma, then to-morrow we may eat white bread?" and beside him, an old man swaying, stumbling, his shrivelled hands crushed to his breast, muttering as if insane.

"Could it be true? Who has heard the news? The shoemaker on the rue de Buci had it from a Mobile who had heard a Franctireur repeat it to a captain of the National Guard."

Trent followed the throng surging through the rue de Seine to the river.

Rocket after rocket clove the sky, and now, from Montmartre, the cannon clanged, and the batteries on Montparnasse joined in with a crash. The bridge was packed with people.

Trent asked: "Who has seen the signals of the Army of the Loire?"

"We are waiting for them," was the reply.

He looked toward the north. Suddenly the huge silhouette of the Arc de Triomphe sprang into black relief against the flash of a cannon. The boom of the gun rolled along the quay and the old bridge vibrated.

Again over by the Point du Jour a flash and heavy explosion shook the bridge, and then the whole eastern bastion of the fortifications blazed and crackled, sending a red flame into the sky.

"Has any one seen the signals yet?" he asked again.

"We are waiting," was the reply.

"Yes, waiting," murmured a man behind him, "waiting, sick, starved, freezing, but waiting. Is it a sortie? They go gladly. Is it to starve? They starve. They have no time to think of surrender. Are they heroes,—these Parisians? Answer me, Trent!"

The American Ambulance surgeon turned about and scanned the parapets of the bridge.

"Any news, Doctor," asked Trent mechanically.

"News?" said the doctor; "I don't know any;—I haven't time to know any. What are these people after?"

"They say that the Army of the Loire has signalled Mont Valérien."

"Poor devils." The doctor glanced about him for an instant, and then: "I'm so harried and worried that I don't know what to do. After the last sortie we had the work of fifty ambulances on our poor little corps. To-morrow there's another sortie, and I wish you fellows could come over to headquarters. We may need volunteers. How is madame?" he added abruptly.

"Well," replied Trent, "but she seems to grow more nervous every day. I ought to be with her now."

"Take care of her," said the doctor, then with a sharp look at the people: "I can't stop now—good-night!" and he hurried away muttering, "Poor devils!"

Trent leaned over the parapet and blinked at the black river surging through the arches. Dark objects, carried swiftly on the breast of the current, struck with a grinding tearing noise against the stone piers, spun around for an instant, and hurried away into the darkness. The ice from the Marne.

As he stood staring into the water, a hand was laid on his shoulder. "Hello, Southwark!" he cried, turning around; "this is a queer place for you!"

"Trent, I have something to tell you. Don't stay here,—don't believe in the Army of the Loire:" and the *attaché* of the American Legation slipped his arm through Trent's and drew him toward the Louvre.

"Then it's another lie!" said Trent bitterly.

"Worse—we know at the Legation—I can't speak of it. But that's not what I have to say. Something happened this afternoon. The Alsatian Brasserie was visited and an American named Hartman has been arrested. Do you know him?"

"I know a German who calls himself an American;—his name is Hartman."

"Well, he was arrested about two hours ago. They mean to shoot him."

"What!"

"Of course we at the Legation can't allow them to shoot him off-hand, but the evidence seems conclusive."

"Is he a spy?"

"Well, the papers seized in his rooms are pretty damning proofs, and besides he was caught, they say, swindling the Public Food Committee. He drew rations for fifty, how, I don't know. He claims to be an American artist here, and we have been obliged to take notice of it at the Legation. It's a nasty affair."

"To cheat the people at such a time is worse than robbing the poor-box," cried Trent angrily. "Let them shoot him!"

"He's an American citizen."

"Yes, oh yes," said the other with bitterness. "American citizenship is a precious privilege when every goggle-eyed German—" His anger choked him.

Southwark shook hands with him warmly. "It can't be helped, we must own the carrion. I am afraid you may be called upon to identify him as an American artist," he said with a ghost of a smile on his deep-lined face; and walked away through the Cours la Reine.

Trent swore silently for a moment and then drew out his watch. Seven o'clock. "Sylvia will be anxious," he thought, and hurried back to the river. The crowd still huddled shivering on the bridge, a sombre pitiful congregation, peering out into the night for the signals of the Army of the Loire: and their hearts beat time to the pounding of the guns, their eyes lighted with each flash from the bastions, and hope rose with the drifting rockets.

A black cloud hung over the fortifications. From horizon to horizon the cannon smoke stretched in wavering bands, now capping the spires and domes with cloud, now blowing in streamers and shreds along the streets, now descending from the housetops, enveloping quays, bridges, and river, in a sulphurous mist. And through the smoke pall the lightning of the cannon played, while from time to time a rift above showed a fathomless black vault set with stars.

He turned again into the rue de Seine, that sad abandoned street, with its rows of closed shutters and desolate ranks of unlighted lamps. He was a little nervous and wished once or twice for a revolver, but the slinking forms which passed him in the darkness were too weak with hunger to be dangerous, he thought, and he passed on unmolested to his doorway. But there somebody sprang at his throat. Over and over the icy pavement he rolled with his assailant, tearing at the noose about his neck, and then with a wrench sprang to his feet.

"Get up," he cried to the other.

Slowly and with great deliberation, a small gamin picked himself out of the gutter and surveyed Trent with disgust.

"That's a nice clean trick," said Trent; "a whelp of your age! You'll finish against a dead wall! Give me that cord!"

The urchin handed him the noose without a word.

Trent struck a match and looked at his assailant. It was the rat-killer of the day before.

"H'm! I thought so," he muttered.

"Tiens, c'est toi?" said the gamin tranquilly.

The impudence, the overpowering audacity of the ragamuffin took Trent's breath away.

"Do you know, you young strangler," he gasped, "that they shoot thieves of your age?"

The child turned a passionless face to Trent. "Shoot, then."

That was too much, and he turned on his heel and entered his hotel.

Groping up the unlighted stairway, he at last reached his own landing and felt about in the darkness for the door. From his studio came the sound of voices, West's hearty laugh and Fallowby's chuckle, and at last he found the knob and, pushing back the door, stood a moment confused by the light.

"Hello, Jack!" cried West, "you're a pleasant creature, inviting people to dine and letting them wait. Here's Fallowby weeping with hunger—"

"Shut up," observed the latter, "perhaps he's been out to buy a turkey."

"He's been out garroting, look at his noose!" laughed Guernalec.

"So now we know where you get your cash!" added West; "vive le coup du Père François!"

Trent shook hands with everybody and laughed at Sylvia's pale face.

"I didn't mean to be late; I stopped on the bridge a moment to watch the bombardment. Were you anxious, Sylvia?"

She smiled and murmured, "Oh, no!" but her hand dropped into his and tightened convulsively.

"To the table!" shouted Fallowby, and uttered a joyous whoop.

"Take it easy," observed Thorne, with a remnant of manners; "you are not the host, you know."

Marie Guernalec, who had been chattering with Colette, jumped up and took Thorne's arm and Monsieur Guernalec drew Odile's arm through his.

Trent, bowing gravely, offered his own arm to Colette, West took in Sylvia, and Fallowby hovered anxiously in the rear.

"You march around the table three times singing the Marseillaise," explained Sylvia, "and Monsieur Fallowby pounds on the table and beats time."

Fallowby suggested that they could sing after dinner, but his protest was drowned in the ringing chorus—

"Aux armes! Formez vos bataillons!"

Around the room they marched singing,

"Marchons! Marchons!"

with all their might, while Fallowby with very bad grace, hammered on the table, consoling himself a little with the hope that the exercise would increase his appetite. Hercules, the black and tan, fled under the bed, from which retreat he yapped and whined until dragged out by Guernalec and placed in Odile's lap.

"And now," said Trent gravely, when everybody was seated, "listen!" and he read the menu.

Beef Soup à la Siège de Paris.

———

Fish.
Sardines à la père Lachaise.
(White Wine).

———

Rôti (Red Wine).
Fresh Beef à la sortie.

———

Vegetables.
Canned Beans à la chasse-pot,
Canned Peas Gravelotte,
Potatoes Irlandaises,
Miscellaneous.

———

Cold Corned Beef à la Thieis,
Stewed Prunes à la Garibaldi.

———

Dessert.
Dried prunes—White bread,
Currant Jelly,
Tea—Café,
Liqueurs,
Pipes and Cigarettes.

Fallowby applauded frantically, and Sylvia served the soup.

"Isn't it delicious?" sighed Odile.

Marie Guernalec sipped her soup in rapture.

"Not at all like horse, and I don't care what they say, horse doesn't taste like beef," whispered Colette to West. Fallowby, who had finished, began to caress his chin and eye the tureen.

"Have some more, old chap?" inquired Trent.

"Monsieur Fallowby cannot have any more," announced Sylvia; "I am saving this for the concierge." Fallowby transferred his eyes to the fish.

The sardines, hot from the grille, were a great success. While the others were eating Sylvia ran downstairs with the soup for the old concierge and her husband, and when she hurried back, flushed and breathless, and had slipped into her chair with a happy smile at Trent, that young man arose, and silence fell over the table. For an instant he looked at Sylvia and thought he had never seen her so beautiful.

"You all know," he began, "that to-day is my wife's nineteenth birthday—"

Fallowby, bubbling with enthusiasm, waved his glass in circles about his head to the terror of Odile and Colette, his neighbours, and Thorne, West and Guernalec refilled their glasses three times before the storm of applause which the toast of Sylvia had provoked, subsided.

Three times the glasses were filled and emptied to Sylvia, and again to Trent, who protested.

"This is irregular," he cried, "the next toast is to the twin Republics, France and America?"

"To the Republics! To the Republics!" they cried, and the toast was drunk amid shouts of "Vive la France! Vive l'Amérique! Vive la Nation!"

Then Trent, with a smile at West, offered the toast, "To a Happy Pair!" and everybody understood, and Sylvia leaned over and kissed Colette, while Trent bowed to West.

The beef was eaten in comparative calm, but when it was finished and a portion of it set aside for the old people below, Trent cried: "Drink to Paris! May she rise from her ruins and crush the invader!" and the cheers rang out, drowning for a moment the monotonous thunder of the Prussian guns.

Pipes and cigarettes were lighted, and Trent listened an instant to the animated chatter around him, broken by ripples of laughter from the girls or the mellow chuckle of Fallowby. Then he turned to West.

"There is going to be a sortie to-night," he said. "I saw the American Ambulance surgeon just before I came in and he asked me to speak to you fellows. Any aid we can give him will not come amiss."

Then dropping his voice and speaking in English, "As for me, I shall go out with the ambulance to-morrow morning. There is of course no danger, but it's just as well to keep it from Sylvia."

West nodded. Thorne and Guernalec, who had heard, broke in and offered assistance, and Fallowby volunteered with a groan.

"All right," said Trent rapidly,—"no more now, but meet me at Ambulance headquarters to-morrow morning at eight."

Sylvia and Colette, who were becoming uneasy at the conversation in English, now demanded to know what they were talking about.

"What does a sculptor usually talk about?" cried West, with a laugh.

Odile glanced reproachfully at Thorne, her *fiancé*.

"You are not French, you know, and it is none of your business, this war," said Odile with much dignity.

Thorne looked meek, but West assumed an air of outraged virtue.

"It seems," he said to Fallowby, "that a fellow cannot discuss the beauties of Greek sculpture in his mother tongue, without being openly suspected."

Colette placed her hand over his mouth and turning to Sylvia, murmured, "They are horridly untruthful, these men."

"I believe the word for ambulance is the same in both languages," said Marie Guernalec saucily; "Sylvia, don't trust Monsieur Trent."

"Jack," whispered Sylvia, "promise me—"

A knock at the studio door interrupted her.

"Come in!" cried Fallowby, but Trent sprang up, and opening the door, looked out. Then with a hasty excuse to the rest, he stepped into the hallway and closed the door.

When he returned he was grumbling.

"What is it, Jack?" cried West.

"What is it?" repeated Trent savagely; "I'll tell you what it is. I have received a dispatch from the American Minister to go at once and identify and claim, as a fellow-countryman and a brother artist, a rascally thief and a German spy!"

"Don't go," suggested Fallowby.

"If I don't they'll shoot him at once."

"Let them," growled Thorne.

"Do you fellows know who it is?"

"Hartman!" shouted West, inspired.

Sylvia sprang up deathly white, but Odile slipped her arm around her and supported her to a chair, saying calmly, "Sylvia has fainted,—it's the hot room,—bring some water."

Trent brought it at once.

Sylvia opened her eyes, and after a moment rose, and supported by Marie Guernalec and Trent, passed into the bedroom.

It was the signal for breaking up, and everybody came and shook hands with Trent, saying they hoped Sylvia would sleep it off and that it would be nothing.

When Marie Guernalec took leave of him, she avoided his eyes, but he spoke to her cordially and thanked her for her aid.

"Anything I can do, Jack?" inquired West, lingering, and then hurried downstairs to catch up with the rest.

Trent leaned over the banisters, listening to their footsteps and chatter, and then the lower door banged and the house was silent. He lingered, staring down into the blackness, biting his lips; then with an impatient movement, "I am crazy!" he muttered, and lighting a candle, went into the bedroom. Sylvia was lying on the bed. He bent over her, smoothing the curly hair on her forehead.

"Are you better, dear Sylvia?"

She did not answer, but raised her eyes to his. For an instant he met her gaze, but what he read there sent a chill to his heart and he sat down covering his face with his hands.

At last she spoke in a voice, changed and strained,—a voice which he had never heard, and he dropped his hands and listened, bolt upright in his chair.

"Jack, it has come at last. I have feared it and trembled,—ah! how often have I lain awake at night with this on my heart and prayed that I might die before you should ever know of it! For I love you, Jack, and if you go away I cannot live. I have deceived you;—it happened before I knew you, but since that first day when you found me weeping in the Luxembourg and spoke to me, Jack, I have been faithful to you in every thought and deed. I loved you from the first, and did not dare to tell you this—fearing that you would go away; and since then my love has grown—grown—and oh! I suffered!—but I dared not tell you. And now you know, but you do not know the worst. For him—now—what do I care? He was cruel—oh, so cruel!"

She hid her face in her arms.

"Must I go on? Must I tell you—can you not imagine, oh! Jack—"

He did not stir; his eyes seemed dead.

"I—I was so young, I knew nothing, and he said—said that he loved me—"

Trent rose and struck the candle with his clenched fist, and the room was dark.

The bells of St. Sulpice tolled the hour, and she started up, speaking with feverish haste,—"I must finish! When you told me you loved me—you—you asked me nothing; but then, even then, it was too late, and *that other life* which binds me to him, must stand for ever between you and me! For there *is another* whom he has claimed, and is good to. He must not die,—they cannot shoot him, for that *other's* sake!"

Trent sat motionless, but his thoughts ran on in an interminable whirl.

Sylvia, little Sylvia, who shared with him his student life,—who bore with him the dreary desolation of the siege without complaint,—this slender blue-eyed girl whom he was so quietly fond of, whom he teased or caressed as the whim suited, who sometimes made him the least bit impatient with her passionate devotion to him,—could this be the same Sylvia who lay weeping there in the darkness?

Then he clinched his teeth. "Let him die! Let him die!"—but then,—for Sylvia's sake, and,—for that *other's* sake,—Yes, he would go,—he *must* go,—his duty was plain before him. But Sylvia,—he could not be what he had been to her, and yet a vague terror seized him, now all was said. Trembling, he struck a light.

She lay there, her curly hair tumbled about her face, her small white hands pressed to her breast.

He could not leave her, and he could not stay. He never knew before that he loved her. She had been a mere comrade, this girl wife of his. Ah! he loved her now with all his heart and soul, and he knew it, only when it was too late. Too late? Why? Then he thought of that *other* one, binding her, linking her forever to the creature, who stood in danger of his life. With an oath he sprang to the door, but the door would not open,—or was it that he pressed it back,—locked it,—and flung himself on his knees beside the bed, knowing that he dared not for his life's sake leave what was his all in life.

## III

It was four in the morning when he came out of the Prison of the Condemned with the Secretary of the American Legation. A knot of people had gathered around the American Minister's carriage, which stood in front of the prison, the horses stamping and pawing in the icy street, the coachman huddled on the box, wrapped in furs. Southwark helped the Secretary into the carriage, and shook hands with Trent, thanking him for coming.

"How the scoundrel did stare," he said; "your evidence was worse than a kick, but it saved his skin for the moment at least,—and prevented complications."

The Secretary sighed. "We have done our part. Now let them prove him a spy and we wash our hands of him. Jump in, Captain! Come along, Trent!"

"I have a word to say to Captain Southwark, I won't detain him," said Trent hastily, and dropping his voice, "Southwark, help *me* now. You know the story from the blackguard. You know the—the child is at his rooms. Get it, and take it to my own apartment, and if he is shot, I will provide a home for it."

"I understand," said the Captain gravely.

"Will you do this at once?"

"At once," he replied.

Their hands met in a warm clasp, and then Captain Southwark climbed into the carriage, motioning Trent to follow; but he shook his head saying, "Good-bye!" and the carriage rolled away.

He watched the carriage to the end of the street, then started toward his own quarter, but after a step or two hesitated, stopped, and finally turned away in the opposite direction. Something—perhaps it was the sight of the prisoner he had so recently confronted nauseated him. He felt the need of solitude and quiet to collect his thoughts. The events of the evening had shaken him terribly, but he would walk it off, forget, bury everything, and then go back to Sylvia. He started on swiftly, and for a time the bitter thoughts seemed to fade, but when he paused at last, breathless, under the Arc de Triomphe, the bitterness and the wretchedness of the whole thing—yes, of his whole misspent life came back with a pang. Then the face of the prisoner, stamped with the horrible grimace of fear, grew in the shadows before his eyes.

Sick at heart he wandered up and down under the great Arc, striving to occupy his mind, peering up at the sculptured cornices to read the names of the heroes and battles which he knew were engraved there, but always the ashen face of Hartman followed him, grinning with terror!—or was it terror?—was it not triumph?—At the thought he leaped like a man who feels a knife at his throat, but after a savage tramp around the square, came back again and sat down to battle with his misery.

The air was cold, but his cheeks were burning with angry shame. Shame? Why? Was it because he had married a girl whom chance had made a mother? *Did* he love her? Was this miserable bohemian existence, then, his end and aim in life? He turned his eyes upon the secrets of his heart, and read an evil story,—the story of the past, and he covered his face for shame, while, keeping time to the dull pain throbbing in his head, his heart beat out the story for the future. Shame and disgrace.

Roused at last from a lethargy which had begun to numb the bitterness of his thoughts, he raised his head and looked about. A sudden fog had settled in the streets; the arches of the Arc were choked with it. He would go home. A great horror of being alone seized him. *But he was not alone.* The fog was peopled with phantoms. All around him in the mist they moved, drifting through the arches in lengthening lines, and vanished, while from the fog others rose up, swept past and were engulfed. He was not alone, for even at his side they crowded, touched him, swarmed before him, beside him, behind him, pressed him back, seized, and bore him with them through the mist. Down a dim avenue, through lanes and alleys white with fog, they moved, and if they spoke their voices were dull as the vapour which shrouded them. At last in front, a bank of masonry and earth cut by a massive iron barred gate towered up in the fog. Slowly and more slowly they glided, shoulder to shoulder and thigh to thigh. Then all movement ceased. A sudden breeze stirred the fog. It wavered and eddied. Objects became more distinct. A pallor crept above the horizon, touching the edges of the watery clouds, and drew dull sparks from a thousand bayonets. Bayonets—they were everywhere, cleaving the fog or flowing beneath it in rivers of steel. High on the wall of masonry and earth a great gun loomed, and around it figures moved in silhouettes. Below, a broad torrent of bayonets swept through the iron barred gateway, out into the shadowy plain. It became lighter. Faces grew more distinct among the marching masses and he recognized one.

"You, Philippe!"

The figure turned its head.

Trent cried, "Is there room for me?" but the other only waved his arm in a vague adieu and was gone with the rest. Presently the cavalry began to pass, squadron on squadron, crowding out into the darkness; then many cannon, then an ambulance, then again the endless lines of bayonets. Beside him a cuirassier sat on his steaming horse, and in front, among a group of mounted officers he saw a general, with the astrakan collar of his dolman turned up about his bloodless face.

Some women were weeping near him and one was struggling to force a loaf of black bread into a soldier's haversack. The soldier tried to aid her, but the sack was fastened, and his rifle bothered him, so Trent held it, while the woman unbuttoned the sack and forced in the bread, now all wet with her tears. The rifle was not heavy. Trent found it wonderfully manageable. Was the bayonet sharp? He tried it. Then a sudden longing, a fierce, imperative desire took possession of him.

"*Chouette!*" cried a gamin, clinging to the barred gate, "*encore toi mon vieux?*"

Trent looked up, and the rat-killer laughed in his face. But when the soldier had taken the rifle again, and thanking him, ran hard to catch his battalion, he plunged into the throng about the gateway.

"Are you going?" he cried to a marine who sat in the gutter bandaging his foot.

"Yes."

Then a girl—a mere child—caught him by the hand and led him into the café which faced the gate. The room was crowded with soldiers, some, white and silent, sitting on the floor, others groaning on the leather-covered settees. The air was sour and suffocating.

"Choose!" said the girl with a little gesture of pity; "they can't go!"

In a heap of clothing on the floor he found a capote and képi.

She helped him buckle his knapsack, cartridge-box, and belt, and showed him how to load the chasse-pot rifle, holding it on her knees.

When he thanked her she started to her feet.

"You are a foreigner!"

"American," he said, moving toward the door, but the child barred his way.

"I am a Bretonne. My father is up there with the cannon of the marine. He will shoot you if you are a spy."

They faced each other for a moment. Then sighing, he bent over and kissed the child. "Pray for France, little one," he murmured, and she repeated with a pale smile: "For France and you, beau Monsieur."

He ran across the street and through the gateway. Once outside, he edged into line and shouldered his way along the road. A corporal passed, looked at him, re-passed, and finally called an officer. "You belong to the 60th," growled the corporal looking at the number on his képi.

"We have no use for Franc-tireurs," added the officer, catching sight of his black trousers.

"I wish to volunteer in place of a comrade," said Trent, and the officer shrugged his shoulders and passed on.

Nobody paid much attention to him, one or two merely glancing at his trousers. The road was deep with slush and mud-ploughed and torn by wheels and hoofs. A soldier in front of him wrenched his foot in an icy rut and dragged himself to the edge of the embankment groaning. The plain on either side of them was grey with melting snow. Here and there behind dismantled hedge-rows stood wagons, bearing white flags with red crosses. Sometimes the driver was a priest in rusty hat and gown, sometimes a crippled Mobile. Once they passed a wagon driven by a Sister of Charity. Silent empty houses with great rents in their walls, and every window blank, huddled along the road. Further on, within the zone of danger, nothing of human habitation remained except here and there a pile of frozen bricks or a blackened cellar choked with snow.

For some time Trent had been annoyed by the man behind him, who kept treading on his heels. Convinced at last that it was intentional, he turned to remonstrate and found himself face to face with a fellow-student from the Beaux Arts. Trent stared.

"I thought you were in the hospital!"

The other shook his head, pointing to his bandaged jaw.

"I see, you can't speak. Can I do anything?"

The wounded man rummaged in his haversack and produced a crust of black bread.

"He can't eat it, his jaw is smashed, and he wants you to chew it for him," said the soldier next to him.

Trent took the crust, and grinding it in his teeth morsel by morsel, passed it back to the starving man.

From time to time mounted orderlies sped to the front, covering them with slush. It was a chilly, silent march through sodden meadows wreathed in fog. Along the railroad embankment across the ditch, another column moved parallel to their own. Trent watched it, a sombre mass, now distinct, now vague, now blotted out in a puff of fog. Once for half-an-hour he lost it, but when again it came into view, he noticed a thin line detach itself from the flank, and, bellying in the middle, swing rapidly to the west. At the same moment a prolonged crackling broke out in the fog in front. Other lines began to slough off from the column, swinging east and west, and the crackling became continuous. A battery passed at full gallop, and he drew back with his comrades to give it way. It went into action a little to the right of his battalion, and as the shot from the first rifled piece boomed through the mist, the cannon from the fortifications opened with a mighty roar. An officer galloped by shouting something which Trent did not catch, but he saw the ranks in front suddenly part company with his own, and disappear in the twilight. More officers rode up and stood beside him peering into the fog. Away in front the crackling had become one prolonged crash. It was dreary waiting. Trent chewed some bread for the man behind, who tried to swallow it, and after a while shook his head, motioning Trent to eat the rest himself. A corporal offered him a little brandy and he drank it, but when he turned around to return the flask, the corporal was lying on the ground. Alarmed, he looked at the soldier next to him, who shrugged his shoulders and opened his mouth to speak, but something struck him and he rolled over and over into the ditch below. At that moment the horse of one of the officers gave a bound and backed into the battalion, lashing out with his heels. One man was ridden down; another was kicked in the chest and hurled through the ranks. The officer sank his spurs into the horse and forced him to the front again, where he stood trembling. The cannonade seemed to draw nearer. A staff-officer, riding slowly up and down the battalion suddenly collapsed in his saddle and clung to his horse's mane. One of his boots dangled, crimsoned and dripping, from the stirrup. Then out of the mist in front men came running. The roads, the fields, the ditches were full of them, and many of them fell. For an instant he imagined he saw horsemen riding about like ghosts in the vapours beyond, and a man behind him cursed horribly, declaring he too had seen them, and that they were Uhlans; but the battalion stood inactive, and the mist fell again over the meadows.

The colonel sat heavily upon his horse, his bullet-shaped head buried in the astrakan collar of his dolman, his fat legs sticking straight out in the stirrups.

The buglers clustered about him with bugles poised, and behind him a staff-officer in a pale blue jacket smoked a cigarette and chatted with a captain of hussars. From the road in front came the sound of furious galloping and an orderly reined up beside the colonel, who motioned him to the rear without turning his head. Then on the left a confused murmur arose which ended in a shout. A hussar passed like the wind, followed by another and another, and then squadron after squadron whirled by them into the sheeted mists. At that instant the colonel reared in his saddle, the bugles clanged, and the whole battalion scrambled down the embankment, over the ditch and started across the soggy meadow. Almost at once Trent lost his cap. Something snatched it from his head, he thought it was a tree branch. A good many of his comrades rolled over in the slush and ice, and he imagined that they had slipped. One pitched right across his path and he stopped to help him up, but the man screamed when he touched him and an officer shouted, "Forward! Forward!" so he ran on again. It was a long jog through the mist, and he was often obliged to shift his rifle. When at last they lay panting behind the railroad embankment, he looked about him. He had felt the need of action, of a desperate physical struggle, of killing and crushing. He had been seized with a desire to fling himself among masses and tear right and left. He longed to fire, to use the thin sharp bayonet on his chasse-pot. He had not expected this. He wished to become exhausted, to struggle and cut until incapable of lifting his arm. Then he had intended to go home. He heard a man say that half the battalion had gone down in the charge, and he saw another examining a corpse under the embankment. The body, still warm, was clothed in a strange uniform, but even when he noticed the spiked helmet lying a few inches further away, he did not realize what had happened.

The colonel sat on his horse a few feet to the left, his eyes sparkling under the crimson képi. Trent heard him reply to an officer: "I can hold it, but another charge, and I won't have enough men left to sound a bugle."

"Were the Prussians here?" Trent asked of a soldier who sat wiping the blood trickling from his hair.

"Yes. The hussars cleaned them out. We caught their cross fire."

"We are supporting a battery on the embankment," said another.

Then the battalion crawled over the embankment and moved along the lines of twisted rails. Trent rolled up his trousers and tucked them into his woollen socks: but they halted again, and some of the men sat down on the dismantled railroad track. Trent looked for his wounded comrade from the Beaux Arts. He was standing in his place, very pale. The cannonade had become terrific. For a moment the mist lifted. He caught a glimpse of the first battalion motionless on the railroad track in front, of regiments on either flank, and then, as the fog settled again, the drums beat and the music of the bugles began away on the extreme left. A restless movement passed among the troops, the colonel threw up his arm, the drums rolled, and the battalion moved off through the fog. They were near the front now for the battalion was firing as it advanced. Ambulances galloped along the base of the embankment to the rear, and the hussars passed and repassed like phantoms. They were in the front at last, for all about them was movement and turmoil, while from the fog, close at hand, came cries and groans and crashing volleys. Shells fell everywhere, bursting along the embankment, splashing them with frozen slush. Trent was frightened. He began to dread the unknown, which lay there crackling and flaming in obscurity. The shock of the cannon sickened him. He could even see the fog light up with a dull orange as the thunder shook the earth. It was near, he felt certain, for the colonel shouted "Forward!" and the first battalion was hastening into it. He felt its breath, he trembled, but hurried on. A fearful discharge in front terrified him. Somewhere in the fog men were cheering, and the colonel's horse, streaming with blood plunged about in the smoke.

Another blast and shock, right in his face, almost stunned him, and he faltered. All the men to the right were down. His head swam; the fog and smoke stupefied him. He put out his hand for a support and caught something. It was the wheel of a gun-carriage, and a man sprang from behind it, aiming a blow at his head with a rammer, but stumbled back shrieking with a bayonet through his neck, and Trent knew that he had killed. Mechanically he stooped to pick up his rifle, but the bayonet was still in the man, who lay, beating with red hands against the sod. It sickened him and he leaned on the cannon. Men were fighting all around him now, and the air was foul with smoke and sweat. Somebody seized him from behind and another in front, but others in turn seized them or struck them solid blows. The click! click! click! of bayonets infuriated him, and he grasped the rammer and struck out blindly until it was shivered to pieces.

A man threw his arm around his neck and bore him to the ground, but he throt-tled him and raised himself on his knees. He saw a comrade seize the cannon, and fall across it with his skull crushed in; he saw the colonel tumble clean out of his saddle into the mud; then consciousness fled.

When he came to himself, he was lying on the embankment among the twisted rails. On every side huddled men who cried out and cursed and fled away into the fog, and he staggered to his feet and followed them. Once he stopped to help a com-rade with a bandaged jaw, who could not speak but clung to his arm for a time and then fell dead in the freezing mire; and again he aided another, who groaned: "Trent, c'est moi—Philippe," until a sudden volley in the midst relieved him of his charge.

An icy wind swept down from the heights, cutting the fog into shreds. For an in-stant, with an evil leer the sun peered through the naked woods of Vincennes, sank like a blood-clot in the battery smoke, lower, lower, into the blood-soaked plain.

## IV

When midnight sounded from the belfry of St. Sulpice the gates of Paris were still choked with fragments of what had once been an army.

They entered with the night, a sullen horde, spattered with slime, faint with hunger and exhaustion. There was little disorder at first, and the throng at the gates parted silently as the troops tramped along the freezing streets. Confusion came as the hours passed. Swiftly and more swiftly, crowding squadron after squadron and battery on battery, horses plunging and caissons jolting, the remnants from the front surged through the gates, a chaos of cavalry and artillery struggling for the right of way. Close upon them stumbled the infantry; here a skeleton of a regiment marching with a desperate attempt at order, there a riotous mob of Mobiles crushing their way to the streets, then a turmoil of horsemen, cannon, troops without, officers, officers without men, then again a line of ambulances, the wheels groaning under their heavy loads.

Dumb with misery the crowd looked on.

All through the day the ambulances had been arriving, and all day long the ragged throng whimpered and shivered by the barriers. At noon the crowd was increased ten-fold, filling the squares about the gates, and swarming over the inner fortifications.

At four o'clock in the afternoon the German batteries suddenly wreathed themselves in smoke, and the shells fell fast on Montparnasse. At twenty minutes after four two projectiles struck a house in the rue de Bac, and a moment later the first shell fell in the Latin Quarter.

Braith was painting in bed when West came in very much scared.

"I wish you would come down; our house has been knocked into a cocked hat, and I'm afraid that some of the pillagers may take it into their heads to pay us a visit to-night."

Braith jumped out of bed and bundled himself into a garment which had once been an overcoat.

"Anybody hurt?" he inquired, struggling with a sleeve full of dilapidated lining.

"No. Colette is barricaded in the cellar, and the concierge ran away to the fortifications. There will be a rough gang there if the bombardment keeps up. You might help us—"

"Of course," said Braith; but it was not until they had reached the rue Serpente and had turned in the passage which led to West's cellar, that the latter cried: "Have you seen Jack Trent, to-day?"

"No," replied Braith, looking troubled, "he was not at Ambulance Headquarters."

"He stayed to take care of Sylvia, I suppose."

A bomb came crashing through the roof of a house at the end of the alley and burst in the basement, showering the street with slate and plaster. A second struck a chimney and plunged into the garden, followed by an avalanche of bricks, and another exploded with a deafening report in the next street.

They hurried along the passage to the steps which led to the cellar. Here again Braith stopped.

"Don't you think I had better run up to see if Jack and Sylvia are well entrenched? I can get back before dark."

"No. Go in and find Colette, and I'll go."

"No, no, let me go, there's no danger."

"I know it," replied West calmly; and, dragging Braith into the alley, pointed to the cellar steps. The iron door was barred.

"Colette! Colette!" he called. The door swung inward, and the girl sprang up the stairs to meet them. At that instant, Braith, glancing behind him, gave a startled cry, and pushing the two before him into the cellar, jumped down after them and slammed the iron door. A few seconds later a heavy jar from the outside shook the hinges.

"They are here," muttered West, very pale.

"That door," observed Colette calmly, "will hold for ever."

Braith examined the low iron structure, now trembling with the blows rained on it from without. West glanced anxiously at Colette, who displayed no agitation, and this comforted him.

"I don't believe they will spend much time here," said Braith; "they only rummage in cellars for spirits, I imagine."

"Unless they hear that valuables are buried there."

"But surely nothing is buried here?" exclaimed Braith uneasily.

"Unfortunately there is," growled West. "That miserly landlord of mine—"

A crash from the outside, followed by a yell, cut him short; then blow after blow shook the doors, until there came a sharp snap, a clinking of metal and a triangular bit of iron fell inwards, leaving a hole through which struggled a ray of light.

Instantly West knelt, and shoving his revolver through the aperture fired every cartridge. For a moment the alley resounded with the racket of the revolver, then absolute silence followed.

Presently a single questioning blow fell upon the door, and a moment later another and another, and then a sudden crack zigzagged across the iron plate.

"Here," said West, seizing Colette by the wrist, "you follow me, Braith!" and he ran swiftly toward a circular spot of light at the further end of the cellar. The spot of light came from a barred man-hole above. West motioned Braith to mount on his shoulders.

"Push it over. You *must!*"

With little effort Braith lifted the barred cover, scrambled out on his stomach, and easily raised Colette from West's shoulders.

"Quick, old chap!" cried the latter.

Braith twisted his legs around a fence-chain and leaned down again. The cellar was flooded with a yellow light, and the air reeked with the stench of petroleum torches. The iron door still held, but a whole plate of metal was gone, and now as they looked a figure came creeping through, holding a torch.

"Quick!" whispered Braith. "Jump!" and West hung dangling until Colette grasped him by the collar, and he was dragged out. Then her nerves gave way and she wept hysterically, but West threw his arm around her and led her across the gardens into the next street, where Braith, after replacing the man-hole cover and piling some stone slabs from the wall over it, rejoined them. It was almost dark. They hurried through the street, now only lighted by burning buildings, or the swift glare of the shells. They gave wide berth to the fires, but at a distance saw the flitting forms of pillagers among the *débris*. Sometimes they passed a female fury crazed with drink shrieking anathemas upon the world, or some slouching lout whose blackened face and hands betrayed his share in the work of destruction. At last they reached the Seine and passed the bridge, and then Braith said: "I must go back. I am not sure of Jack and Sylvia." As he spoke, he made way for a crowd which came trampling across the bridge, and along the river wall by the d'Orsay barracks. In the midst of it West caught the measured tread of a platoon. A lantern passed, a file of bayonets, then another lantern which glimmered on a deathly face behind, and Colette gasped, "Hartman!" and he was gone. They peered fearfully across the embankment, holding their breath. There was a shuffle of feet on the quay, and the gate of the barracks slammed. A lantern shone for a moment at the postern, the crowd pressed to the grille, then came the clang of the volley from the stone parade.

One by one the petroleum torches flared up along the embankment, and now the whole square was in motion. Down from the Champs Elysées and across the Place de la Concorde straggled the fragments of the battle, a company here, and a mob there. They poured in from every street followed by women and children, and a great murmur, borne on the icy wind, swept through the Arc de Triomphe and down the dark avenue,—"Perdus! perdus!"

A ragged end of a battalion was pressing past, the spectre of annihilation. West groaned. Then a figure sprang from the shadowy ranks and called West's name, and when he saw it was Trent he cried out. Trent seized him, white with terror.

"Sylvia?"

West stared speechless, but Colette moaned, "Oh, Sylvia! Sylvia!—and they are shelling the Quarter!"

"Trent!" shouted Braith; but he was gone, and they could not overtake him.

The bombardment ceased as Trent crossed the Boulevard St. Germain, but the entrance to the rue de Seine was blocked by a heap of smoking bricks. Everywhere the shells had torn great holes in the pavement. The café was a wreck of splinters and glass, the book-store tottered, ripped from roof to basement, and the little bakery, long since closed, bulged outward above a mass of slate and tin.

He climbed over the steaming bricks and hurried into the rue de Tournon. On the corner a fire blazed, lighting up his own street, and on the bank wall, beneath a shattered gas lamp, a child was writing with a bit of cinder.

## "HERE FELL THE FIRST SHELL."

The letters stared him in the face. The rat-killer finished and stepped back to view his work, but catching sight of Trent's bayonet, screamed and fled, and as Trent staggered across the shattered street, from holes and crannies in the ruins fierce women fled from their work of pillage, cursing him.

At first he could not find his house, for the tears blinded him, but he felt along the wall and reached the door. A lantern burned in the concierge's lodge and the old man lay dead beside it. Faint with fright he leaned a moment on his rifle, then, snatching the lantern, sprang up the stairs. He tried to call, but his tongue hardly moved. On the second floor he saw plaster on the stairway, and on the third the floor was torn and the concierge lay in a pool of blood across the landing. The next floor was his, *theirs*. The door hung from its hinges, the walls gaped. He crept in and sank down by the bed, and there two arms were flung around his neck, and a tear-stained face sought his own.

"Sylvia!"

"O Jack! Jack! Jack!"

From the tumbled pillow beside them a child wailed.

"They brought it; it is mine," she sobbed.

"Ours," he whispered, with his arms around them both.

Then from the stairs below came Braith's anxious voice.

"Trent! Is all well?"

# THE STREET OF OUR LADY OF THE FIELDS

"Et tout les jours passés dans la tristesse
Nous sont comptés comme des jours heureux!"

## I

The street is not fashionable, neither is it shabby. It is a pariah among streets—a street without a Quarter. It is generally understood to lie outside the pale of the aristocratic Avenue de l'Observatoire. The students of the Montparnasse Quarter consider it swell and will have none of it. The Latin Quarter, from the Luxembourg, its northern frontier, sneers at its respectability and regards with disfavour the correctly costumed students who haunt it. Few strangers go into it. At times, however, the Latin Quarter students use it as a thoroughfare between the rue de Rennes and the Bullier, but except for that and the weekly afternoon visits of parents and guardians to the Convent near the rue Vavin, the street of Our Lady of the Fields is as quiet as a Passy boulevard. Perhaps the most respectable portion lies between the rue de la Grande Chaumière and the rue Vavin, at least this was the conclusion arrived at by the Reverend Joel Byram, as he rambled through it with Hastings in charge. To Hastings the street looked pleasant in the bright June weather, and he had begun to hope for its selection when the Reverend Byram shied violently at the cross on the Convent opposite.

"Jesuits," he muttered.

"Well," said Hastings wearily, "I imagine we won't find anything better. You say yourself that vice is triumphant in Paris, and it seems to me that in every street we find Jesuits or something worse."

After a moment he repeated, "Or something worse, which of course I would not notice except for your kindness in warning me."

Dr. Byram sucked in his lips and looked about him. He was impressed by the evident respectability of the surroundings. Then frowning at the Convent he took Hastings' arm and shuffled across the street to an iron gateway which bore the number 201 *bis* painted in white on a blue ground. Below this was a notice printed in English:

1.
For Porter please oppress once.
2.
For Servant please oppress twice.
3.
For Parlour please oppress thrice.

Hastings touched the electric button three times, and they were ushered through the garden and into the parlour by a trim maid. The dining-room door, just beyond, was open, and from the table in plain view a stout woman hastily arose and came toward them. Hastings caught a glimpse of a young man with a big head and several snuffy old gentlemen at breakfast, before the door closed and the stout woman waddled into the room, bringing with her an aroma of coffee and a black poodle.

"It ees a plaisir to you receive!" she cried. "Monsieur is Anglish? No? Americain? Off course. My pension it ees for Americains surtout. Here all spik Angleesh, c'est à dire, ze personnel; ze sairvants do spik, plus ou moins, a little. I am happy to have you comme pensionnaires—"

"Madame," began Dr. Byram, but was cut short again.

"Ah, yess, I know, ah! mon Dieu! you do not spik Frainch but you have come to lairne! My husband does spik Frainch wiss ze pensionnaires. We have at ze moment a family Americaine who learn of my husband Frainch—"

Here the poodle growled at Dr. Byram and was promptly cuffed by his mistress.

"Veux tu!" she cried, with a slap, "veux tu! Oh! le vilain, oh! le vilain!"

"Mais, madame," said Hastings, smiling, "il n'a pas l'air très féroce."

The poodle fled, and his mistress cried, "Ah, ze accent charming! He does spik already Frainch like a Parisien young gentleman!"

Then Dr. Byram managed to get in a word or two and gathered more or less information with regard to prices.

"It ees a pension serieux; my clientèle ees of ze best, indeed a pension de famille where one ees at 'ome."

Then they went upstairs to examine Hastings' future quarters, test the bed-springs and arrange for the weekly towel allowance. Dr. Byram appeared satisfied.

Madame Marotte accompanied them to the door and rang for the maid, but as Hastings stepped out into the gravel walk, his guide and mentor paused a moment and fixed Madame with his watery eyes.

"You understand," he said, "that he is a youth of most careful bringing up, and his character and morals are without a stain. He is young and has never been abroad, never even seen a large city, and his parents have requested me, as an old family friend living in Paris, to see that he is placed under good influences. He is to study art, but on no account would his parents wish him to live in the Latin Quarter if they knew of the immorality which is rife there."

A sound like the click of a latch interrupted him and he raised his eyes, but not in time to see the maid slap the big-headed young man behind the parlour-door.

Madame coughed, cast a deadly glance behind her and then beamed on Dr. Byram.

"It ees well zat he come here. The pension more serious, il n'en existe pas, eet ees not any!" she announced with conviction.

So, as there was nothing more to add, Dr. Byram joined Hastings at the gate.

"I trust," he said, eyeing the Convent, "that you will make no acquaintances among Jesuits!"

Hastings looked at the Convent until a pretty girl passed before the gray façade, and then he looked at her. A young fellow with a paint-box and canvas came swinging along, stopped before the pretty girl, said something during a brief but vigorous handshake at which they both laughed, and he went his way, calling back, "À demain Valentine!" as in the same breath she cried, "À demain!"

"Valentine," thought Hastings, "what a quaint name;" and he started to follow the Reverend Joel Byram, who was shuffling towards the nearest tramway station.

## II

"An' you are pleas wiz Paris, Monsieur' Astang?" demanded Madame Marotte the next morning as Hastings came into the breakfast-room of the pension, rosy from his plunge in the limited bath above.

"I am sure I shall like it," he replied, wondering at his own depression of spirits.

The maid brought him coffee and rolls. He returned the vacant glance of the big-headed young man and acknowledged diffidently the salutes of the snuffy old gentlemen. He did not try to finish his coffee, and sat crumbling a roll, unconscious of the sympathetic glances of Madame Marotte, who had tact enough not to bother him.

Presently a maid entered with a tray on which were balanced two bowls of chocolate, and the snuffy old gentlemen leered at her ankles. The maid deposited the chocolate at a table near the window and smiled at Hastings. Then a thin young lady, followed by her counterpart in all except years, marched into the room and took the table near the window. They were evidently American, but Hastings, if he expected any sign of recognition, was disappointed. To be ignored by compatriots intensified his depression. He fumbled with his knife and looked at his plate.

The thin young lady was talkative enough. She was quite aware of Hastings' presence, ready to be flattered if he looked at her, but on the other hand she felt her superiority, for she had been three weeks in Paris and he, it was easy to see, had not yet unpacked his steamer-trunk.

Her conversation was complacent. She argued with her mother upon the relative merits of the Louvre and the Bon Marché, but her mother's part of the discussion was mostly confined to the observation, "Why, Susie!"

The snuffy old gentlemen had left the room in a body, outwardly polite and inwardly raging. They could not endure the Americans, who filled the room with their chatter.

The big-headed young man looked after them with a knowing cough, murmuring, "Gay old birds!"

"They look like bad old men, Mr. Bladen," said the girl.

To this Mr. Bladen smiled and said, "They've had their day," in a tone which implied that he was now having his.

"And that's why they all have baggy eyes," cried the girl. "I think it's a shame for young gentlemen—"

"Why, Susie!" said the mother, and the conversation lagged.

After a while Mr. Bladen threw down the *Petit Journal*, which he daily studied at the expense of the house, and turning to Hastings, started to make himself agreeable. He began by saying, "I see you are American."

To this brilliant and original opening, Hastings, deadly homesick, replied gratefully, and the conversation was judiciously nourished by observations from Miss Susie Byng distinctly addressed to Mr. Bladen. In the course of events Miss Susie, forgetting to address herself exclusively to Mr. Bladen, and Hastings replying to her general question, the *entente cordiale* was established, and Susie and her mother extended a protectorate over what was clearly neutral territory.

"Mr. Hastings, you must not desert the pension every evening as Mr. Bladen does. Paris is an awful place for young gentlemen, and Mr. Bladen is a horrid cynic."

Mr. Bladen looked gratified.

Hastings answered, "I shall be at the studio all day, and I imagine I shall be glad enough to come back at night."

Mr. Bladen, who, at a salary of fifteen dollars a week, acted as agent for the Pewly Manufacturing Company of Troy, N.Y., smiled a sceptical smile and withdrew to keep an appointment with a customer on the Boulevard Magenta.

Hastings walked into the garden with Mrs. Byng and Susie, and, at their invitation, sat down in the shade before the iron gate.

The chestnut trees still bore their fragrant spikes of pink and white, and the bees hummed among the roses, trellised on the white-walled house.

A faint freshness was in the air. The watering carts moved up and down the street, and a clear stream bubbled over the spotless gutters of the rue de la Grande Chaumière. The sparrows were merry along the curb-stones, taking bath after bath in the water and ruffling their feathers with delight. In a walled garden across the street a pair of blackbirds whistled among the almond trees.

Hastings swallowed the lump in his throat, for the song of the birds and the ripple of water in a Paris gutter brought back to him the sunny meadows of Millbrook.

"That's a blackbird," observed Miss Byng; "see him there on the bush with pink blossoms. He's all black except his bill, and that looks as if it had been dipped in an omelet, as some Frenchman says—"

"Why, Susie!" said Mrs. Byng.

"That garden belongs to a studio inhabited by two Americans," continued the girl serenely, "and I often see them pass. They seem to need a great many models, mostly young and feminine—"

"Why, Susie!"

"Perhaps they prefer painting that kind, but I don't see why they should invite five, with three more young gentlemen, and all get into two cabs and drive away singing. This street," she continued, "is dull. There is nothing to see except the garden and a glimpse of the Boulevard Montparnasse through the rue de la Grande Chaumière. No one ever passes except a policeman. There is a convent on the corner."

"I thought it was a Jesuit College," began Hastings, but was at once overwhelmed with a Baedecker description of the place, ending with, "On one side stand the palatial hotels of Jean Paul Laurens and Guillaume Bouguereau, and opposite, in the little Passage Stanislas, Carolus Duran paints the masterpieces which charm the world."

The blackbird burst into a ripple of golden throaty notes, and from some distant green spot in the city an unknown wild-bird answered with a frenzy of liquid trills until the sparrows paused in their ablutions to look up with restless chirps.

Then a butterfly came and sat on a cluster of heliotrope and waved his crimson-banded wings in the hot sunshine. Hastings knew him for a friend, and before his eyes there came a vision of tall mulleins and scented milkweed alive with painted wings, a vision of a white house and woodbine-covered piazza,—a glimpse of a man reading and a woman leaning over the pansy bed,—and his heart was full. He was startled a moment later by Miss Byng.

"I believe you are homesick!" Hastings blushed. Miss Byng looked at him with a sympathetic sigh and continued: "Whenever I felt homesick at first I used to go with mamma and walk in the Luxembourg Gardens. I don't know why it is, but those old fashioned gardens seemed to bring me nearer home than anything in this artificial city."

"But they are full of marble statues," said Mrs. Byng mildly; "I don't see the resemblance myself."

"Where is the Luxembourg?" inquired Hastings after a silence.

"Come with me to the gate," said Miss Byng. He rose and followed her, and she pointed out the rue Vavin at the foot of the street.

"You pass by the convent to the right," she smiled; and Hastings went.

## III

The Luxembourg was a blaze of flowers. He walked slowly through the long ave-nues of trees, past mossy marbles and old-time columns, and threading the grove by the bronze lion, came upon the tree-crowned terrace above the fountain. Below lay the basin shining in the sunlight. Flowering almonds encircled the terrace, and, in a greater spiral, groves of chestnuts wound in and out and down among the moist thickets by the western palace wing. At one end of the avenue of trees the Observa-tory rose, its white domes piled up like an eastern mosque; at the other end stood the heavy palace, with every window-pane ablaze in the fierce sun of June.

Around the fountain, children and white-capped nurses armed with bamboo poles were pushing toy boats, whose sails hung limp in the sunshine. A dark policeman, wearing red epaulettes and a dress sword, watched them for a while and then went away to remonstrate with a young man who had unchained his dog. The dog was pleasantly occupied in rubbing grass and dirt into his back while his legs waved into the air.

The policeman pointed at the dog. He was speechless with indignation.

"Well, Captain," smiled the young fellow.

"Well, Monsieur Student," growled the policeman.

"What do you come and complain to me for?"

"If you don't chain him I'll take him," shouted the policeman.

"What's that to me, mon capitaine?"

"Wha—t! Isn't that bull-dog yours?"

"If it was, don't you suppose I'd chain him?"

The officer glared for a moment in silence, then deciding that as he was a student he was wicked, grabbed at the dog, who promptly dodged. Around and around the flower-beds they raced, and when the officer came too near for comfort, the bull-dog cut across a flower-bed, which perhaps was not playing fair.

The young man was amused, and the dog also seemed to enjoy the exercise.

The policeman noticed this and decided to strike at the fountain-head of the evil. He stormed up to the student and said, "As the owner of this public nuisance I arrest you!"

"But," objected the other, "I disclaim the dog."

That was a poser. It was useless to attempt to catch the dog until three gardeners lent a hand, but then the dog simply ran away and disappeared in the rue de Medici.

The policeman shambled off to find consolation among the white-capped nurses, and the student, looking at his watch, stood up yawning. Then catching sight of Has-tings, he smiled and bowed. Hastings walked over to the marble, laughing.

"Why, Clifford," he said, "I didn't recognize you."

"It's my moustache," sighed the other. "I sacrificed it to humour a whim of—of—a friend. What do you think of my dog?"

"Then he is yours?" cried Hastings.

"Of course. It's a pleasant change for him, this playing tag with policemen, but he is known now and I'll have to stop it. He's gone home. He always does when the gardeners take a hand. It's a pity; he's fond of rolling on lawns." Then they chatted for a moment of Hastings' prospects, and Clifford politely offered to stand his sponsor at the studio.

"You see, old tabby, I mean Dr. Byram, told me about you before I met you," explained Clifford, "and Elliott and I will be glad to do anything we can." Then looking at his watch again, he muttered, "I have just ten minutes to catch the Versailles train; au revoir," and started to go, but catching sight of a girl advancing by the fountain, took off his hat with a confused smile.

"Why are you not at Versailles?" she said, with an almost imperceptible acknowledgment of Hastings' presence.

"I—I'm going," murmured Clifford.

For a moment they faced each other, and then Clifford, very red, stammered, "With your permission I have the honour of presenting to you my friend, Monsieur Hastings."

Hastings bowed low. She smiled very sweetly, but there was something of malice in the quiet inclination of her small Parisienne head.

"I could have wished," she said, "that Monsieur Clifford might spare me more time when he brings with him so charming an American."

"Must—must I go, Valentine?" began Clifford.

"Certainly," she replied.

Clifford took his leave with very bad grace, wincing, when she added, "And give my dearest love to Cécile!" As he disappeared in the rue d'Assas, the girl turned as if to go, but then suddenly remembering Hastings, looked at him and shook her head.

"Monsieur Clifford is so perfectly hare-brained," she smiled, "it is embarrassing sometimes. You have heard, of course, all about his success at the Salon?"

He looked puzzled and she noticed it.

"You have been to the Salon, of course?"

"Why, no," he answered, "I only arrived in Paris three days ago."

She seemed to pay little heed to his explanation, but continued: "Nobody imagined he had the energy to do anything good, but on varnishing day the Salon was astonished by the entrance of Monsieur Clifford, who strolled about as bland as you please with an orchid in his buttonhole, and a beautiful picture on the line."

She smiled to herself at the reminiscence, and looked at the fountain.

"Monsieur Bouguereau told me that Monsieur Julian was so astonished that he only shook hands with Monsieur Clifford in a dazed manner, and actually forgot to pat him on the back! Fancy," she continued with much merriment, "fancy papa Julian forgetting to pat one on the back."

Hastings, wondering at her acquaintance with the great Bouguereau, looked at her with respect. "May I ask," he said diffidently, "whether you are a pupil of Bouguereau?"

"I?" she said in some surprise. Then she looked at him curiously. Was he permitting himself the liberty of joking on such short acquaintance?

His pleasant serious face questioned hers.

"Tiens," she thought, "what a droll man!"

"You surely study art?" he said.

She leaned back on the crooked stick of her parasol, and looked at him. "Why do you think so?"

"Because you speak as if you did."

"You are making fun of me," she said, "and it is not good taste."

She stopped, confused, as he coloured to the roots of his hair.

"How long have you been in Paris?" she said at length.

"Three days," he replied gravely.

"But—but—surely you are not a nouveau! You speak French too well!"

Then after a pause, "Really are you a nouveau?"

"I am," he said.

She sat down on the marble bench lately occupied by Clifford, and tilting her parasol over her small head looked at him.

"I don't believe it."

He felt the compliment, and for a moment hesitated to declare himself one of the despised. Then mustering up his courage, he told her how new and green he was, and all with a frankness which made her blue eyes open very wide and her lips part in the sweetest of smiles.

"You have never seen a studio?"

"Never."

"Nor a model?"

"No."

"How funny," she said solemnly. Then they both laughed.

"And you," he said, "have seen studios?"

"Hundreds."

"And models?"

"Millions."

"And you know Bouguereau?"

"Yes, and Henner, and Constant and Laurens, and Puvis de Chavannes and Dagnan and Courtois, and—and all the rest of them!"

"And yet you say you are not an artist."

"Pardon," she said gravely, "did I say I was not?"

"Won't you tell me?" he hesitated.

At first she looked at him, shaking her head and smiling, then of a sudden her eyes fell and she began tracing figures with her parasol in the gravel at her feet. Hastings had taken a place on the seat, and now, with his elbows on his knees, sat watching the spray drifting above the fountain jet. A small boy, dressed as a sailor, stood poking his yacht and crying, "I won't go home! I won't go home!" His nurse raised her hands to Heaven.

"Just like a little American boy," thought Hastings, and a pang of homesickness shot through him.

Presently the nurse captured the boat, and the small boy stood at bay.

"Monsieur René, when you decide to come here you may have your boat."

The boy backed away scowling.

"Give me my boat, I say," he cried, "and don't call me René, for my name's Randall and you know it!"

"Hello!" said Hastings,—"Randall?—that's English."

"I am American," announced the boy in perfectly good English, turning to look at Hastings, "and she's such a fool she calls me René because mamma calls me Ranny—"

Here he dodged the exasperated nurse and took up his station behind Hastings, who laughed, and catching him around the waist lifted him into his lap.

"One of my countrymen," he said to the girl beside him. He smiled while he spoke, but there was a queer feeling in his throat.

"Don't you see the stars and stripes on my yacht?" demanded Randall. Sure enough, the American colours hung limply under the nurse's arm.

"Oh," cried the girl, "he is charming," and impulsively stooped to kiss him, but the infant Randall wriggled out of Hastings' arms, and his nurse pounced upon him with an angry glance at the girl.

She reddened and then bit her lips as the nurse, with eyes still fixed on her, dragged the child away and ostentatiously wiped his lips with her handkerchief.

Then she stole a look at Hastings and bit her lip again.

"What an ill-tempered woman!" he said. "In America, most nurses are flattered when people kiss their children."

For an instant she tipped the parasol to hide her face, then closed it with a snap and looked at him defiantly.

"Do you think it strange that she objected?"

"Why not?" he said in surprise.

Again she looked at him with quick searching eyes.

His eyes were clear and bright, and he smiled back, repeating, "Why not?"

"You *are* droll," she murmured, bending her head.

"Why?"

But she made no answer, and sat silent, tracing curves and circles in the dust with her parasol. After a while he said—"I am glad to see that young people have so much liberty here. I understood that the French were not at all like us. You know in America—or at least where I live in Milbrook, girls have every liberty,—go out alone and receive their friends alone, and I was afraid I should miss it here. But I see how it is now, and I am glad I was mistaken."

She raised her eyes to his and kept them there.

He continued pleasantly—"Since I have sat here I have seen a lot of pretty girls walking alone on the terrace there,—and then *you* are alone too. Tell me, for I do not know French customs,—do you have the liberty of going to the theatre without a chaperone?"

For a long time she studied his face, and then with a trembling smile said, "Why do you ask me?"

"Because you must know, of course," he said gaily.

"Yes," she replied indifferently, "I know."

He waited for an answer, but getting none, decided that perhaps she had misunderstood him.

"I hope you don't think I mean to presume on our short acquaintance," he began,—"in fact it is very odd but I don't know your name. When Mr. Clifford presented me he only mentioned mine. Is that the custom in France?"

"It is the custom in the Latin Quarter," she said with a queer light in her eyes. Then suddenly she began talking almost feverishly.

"You must know, Monsieur Hastings, that we are all *un peu sans gêne* here in the Latin Quarter. We are very Bohemian, and etiquette and ceremony are out of place. It was for that Monsieur Clifford presented you to me with small ceremony, and left us together with less,—only for that, and I am his friend, and I have many friends in the Latin Quarter, and we all know each other very well—and I am not studying art, but—but—"

"But what?" he said, bewildered.

"I shall not tell you,—it is a secret," she said with an uncertain smile. On both cheeks a pink spot was burning, and her eyes were very bright.

Then in a moment her face fell. "Do you know Monsieur Clifford very intimately?"

"Not very."

After a while she turned to him, grave and a little pale.

"My name is Valentine—Valentine Tissot. Might—might I ask a service of you on such very short acquaintance?"

"Oh," he cried, "I should be honoured."

"It is only this," she said gently, "it is not much. Promise me not to speak to Monsieur Clifford about me. Promise me that you will speak to no one about me."

"I promise," he said, greatly puzzled.

She laughed nervously. "I wish to remain a mystery. It is a caprice."

"But," he began, "I had wished, I had hoped that you might give Monsieur Clifford permission to bring me, to present me at your house."

"My—my house!" she repeated.

"I mean, where you live, in fact, to present me to your family."

The change in the girl's face shocked him.

"I beg your pardon," he cried, "I have hurt you."

And as quick as a flash she understood him because she was a woman.

"My parents are dead," she said.

Presently he began again, very gently.

"Would it displease you if I beg you to receive me? It is the custom?"

"I cannot," she answered. Then glancing up at him, "I am sorry; I should like to; but believe me. I cannot."

He bowed seriously and looked vaguely uneasy.

"It isn't because I don't wish to. I—I like you; you are very kind to me."

"Kind?" he cried, surprised and puzzled.

"I like you," she said slowly, "and we will see each other sometimes if you will."

"At friends' houses."

"No, not at friends' houses."

"Where?"

"Here," she said with defiant eyes.

"Why," he cried, "in Paris you are much more liberal in your views than we are."

She looked at him curiously.

"Yes, we are very Bohemian."

"I think it is charming," he declared

"You see, we shall be in the best of society," she ventured timidly, with a pretty gesture toward the statues of the dead queens, ranged in stately ranks above the terrace.

He looked at her, delighted, and she brightened at the success of her innocent little pleasantry.

"Indeed," she smiled, "I shall be well chaperoned, because you see we are under the protection of the gods themselves; look, there are Apollo, and Juno, and Venus, on their pedestals," counting them on her small gloved fingers, "and Ceres, Hercules, and—but I can't make out—"

Hastings turned to look up at the winged god under whose shadow they were seated.

"Why, it's Love," he said.

## IV

"There is a nouveau here," drawled Laffat, leaning around his easel and addressing his friend Bowles, "there is a nouveau here who is so tender and green and appetizing that Heaven help him if he should fall into a salad bowl."

"Hayseed?" inquired Bowles, plastering in a background with a broken palette-knife and squinting at the effect with approval.

"Yes, Squeedunk or Oshkosh, and how he ever grew up among the daisies and escaped the cows, Heaven alone knows!"

Bowles rubbed his thumb across the outlines of his study to "throw in a little atmosphere," as he said, glared at the model, pulled at his pipe and finding it out struck a match on his neighbour's back to relight it.

"His name," continued Laffat, hurling a bit of bread at the hat-rack, "his name is Hastings. He *is* a berry. He knows no more about the world,"—and here Mr. Laffat's face spoke volumes for his own knowledge of that planet,—"than a maiden cat on its first moonlight stroll."

Bowles now having succeeded in lighting his pipe, repeated the thumb touch on the other edge of the study and said, "Ah!"

"Yes," continued his friend, "and would you imagine it, he seems to think that everything here goes on as it does in his d——d little backwoods ranch at home; talks about the pretty girls who walk alone in the street; says how sensible it is; and how French parents are misrepresented in America; says that for his part he finds French girls,—and he confessed to only knowing one,—as jolly as American girls. I tried to set him right, tried to give him a pointer as to what sort of ladies walk about alone or with students, and he was either too stupid or too innocent to catch on. Then I gave it to him straight, and he said I was a vile-minded fool and marched off."

"Did you assist him with your shoe?" inquired Bowles, languidly interested.

"Well, no."

"He called you a vile-minded fool."

"He was correct," said Clifford from his easel in front.

"What—what do you mean?" demanded Laffat, turning red.

"*That*," replied Clifford.

"Who spoke to you? Is this your business?" sneered Bowles, but nearly lost his balance as Clifford swung about and eyed him.

"Yes," he said slowly, "it's my business."

No one spoke for some time.

Then Clifford sang out, "I say, Hastings!"

And when Hastings left his easel and came around, he nodded toward the astonished Laffat.

"This man has been disagreeable to you, and I want to tell you that any time you feel inclined to kick him, why, I will hold the other creature."

Hastings, embarrassed, said, "Why no, I don't agree with his ideas, nothing more."

Clifford said "Naturally," and slipping his arm through Hastings', strolled about with him, and introduced him to several of his own friends, at which all the nouveaux opened their eyes with envy, and the studio were given to understand that Hastings, although prepared to do menial work as the latest nouveau, was already within the charmed circle of the old, respected and feared, the truly great.

The rest finished, the model resumed his place, and work went on in a chorus of songs and yells and every ear-splitting noise which the art student utters when studying the beautiful.

Five o'clock struck,—the model yawned, stretched and climbed into his trousers, and the noisy contents of six studios crowded through the hall and down into the street. Ten minutes later, Hastings found himself on top of a Montrouge tram, and shortly afterward was joined by Clifford.

They climbed down at the rue Gay Lussac.

"I always stop here," observed Clifford, "I like the walk through the Luxembourg."

"By the way," said Hastings, "how can I call on you when I don't know where you live?"

"Why, I live opposite you."

"What—the studio in the garden where the almond trees are and the blackbirds—"

"Exactly," said Clifford. "I'm with my friend Elliott."

Hastings thought of the description of the two American artists which he had heard from Miss Susie Byng, and looked blank.

Clifford continued, "Perhaps you had better let me know when you think of coming so,—so that I will be sure to—to be there," he ended rather lamely.

"I shouldn't care to meet any of your model friends there," said Hastings, smiling. "You know—my ideas are rather straitlaced,—I suppose you would say, Puritanical. I shouldn't enjoy it and wouldn't know how to behave."

"Oh, I understand," said Clifford, but added with great cordiality,—"I'm sure we'll be friends although you may not approve of me and my set, but you will like Severn and Selby because—because, well, they are like yourself, old chap."

After a moment he continued, "There is something I want to speak about. You see, when I introduced you, last week, in the Luxembourg, to Valentine—"

"Not a word!" cried Hastings, smiling; "you must not tell me a word of her!"

"Why—"

"No—not a word!" he said gaily. "I insist,—promise me upon your honour you will not speak of her until I give you permission; promise!"

"I promise," said Clifford, amazed.

"She is a charming girl,—we had such a delightful chat after you left, and I thank you for presenting me, but not another word about her until I give you permission."

"Oh," murmured Clifford.

"Remember your promise," he smiled, as he turned into his gateway.

Clifford strolled across the street and, traversing the ivy-covered alley, entered his garden.

He felt for his studio key, muttering, "I wonder—I wonder,—but of course he doesn't!"

He entered the hallway, and fitting the key into the door, stood staring at the two cards tacked over the panels.

FOXHALL CLIFFORD

RICHARD OSBORNE ELLIOTT

"Why the devil doesn't he want me to speak of her?"

He opened the door, and, discouraging the caresses of two brindle bull-dogs, sank down on the sofa.

Elliott sat smoking and sketching with a piece of charcoal by the window.

"Hello," he said without looking around.

Clifford gazed absently at the back of his head, murmuring, "I'm afraid, I'm afraid that man is too innocent. I say, Elliott," he said, at last, "Hastings,—you know the chap that old Tabby Byram came around here to tell us about—the day you had to hide Colette in the armoire—"

"Yes, what's up?"

"Oh, nothing. He's a brick."

"Yes," said Elliott, without enthusiasm.

"Don't you think so?" demanded Clifford.

"Why yes, but he is going to have a tough time when some of his illusions are dispelled."

"More shame to those who dispel 'em!"

"Yes,—wait until he comes to pay his call on us, unexpectedly, of course—"

Clifford looked virtuous and lighted a cigar.

"I was just going to say," he observed, "that I have asked him not to come without letting us know, so I can postpone any orgie you may have intended—"

"Ah!" cried Elliott indignantly, "I suppose you put it to him in that way."

"Not exactly," grinned Clifford. Then more seriously, "I don't want anything to occur here to bother him. He's a brick, and it's a pity we can't be more like him."

"I am," observed Elliott complacently, "only living with you—"

"Listen!" cried the other. "I have managed to put my foot in it in great style. Do you know what I've done? Well—the first time I met him in the street,—or rather, it was in the Luxembourg, I introduced him to Valentine!"

"Did he object?"

"Believe me," said Clifford, solemnly, "this rustic Hastings has no more idea that Valentine is—is—in fact is Valentine, than he has that he himself is a beautiful example of moral decency in a Quarter where morals are as rare as elephants. I heard enough in a conversation between that blackguard Loffat and the little immoral eruption, Bowles, to open my eyes. I tell you Hastings is a trump! He's a healthy, clean-minded young fellow, bred in a small country village, brought up with the idea that saloons are way-stations to hell—and as for women—"

"Well?" demanded Elliott

"Well," said Clifford, "his idea of the dangerous woman is probably a painted Jezabel."

"Probably," replied the other.

"He's a trump!" said Clifford, "and if he swears the world is as good and pure as his own heart, I'll swear he's right."

Elliott rubbed his charcoal on his file to get a point and turned to his sketch saying, "He will never hear any pessimism from Richard Osborne E."

"He's a lesson to me," said Clifford. Then he unfolded a small perfumed note, written on rose-coloured paper, which had been lying on the table before him.

He read it, smiled, whistled a bar or two from "Miss Helyett," and sat down to answer it on his best cream-laid note-paper. When it was written and sealed, he picked up his stick and marched up and down the studio two or three times, whistling.

"Going out?" inquired the other, without turning.

"Yes," he said, but lingered a moment over Elliott's shoulder, watching him pick out the lights in his sketch with a bit of bread.

"To-morrow is Sunday," he observed after a moment's silence.

"Well?" inquired Elliott.

"Have you seen Colette?"

"No, I will to-night. She and Rowden and Jacqueline are coming to Boulant's. I suppose you and Cécile will be there?"

"Well, no," replied Clifford. "Cécile dines at home to-night, and I—I had an idea of going to Mignon's."

Elliott looked at him with disapproval.

"You can make all the arrangements for La Roche without me," he continued, avoiding Elliott's eyes.

"What are you up to now?"

"Nothing," protested Clifford.

"Don't tell me," replied his chum, with scorn; "fellows don't rush off to Mignon's when the set dine at Boulant's. Who is it now?—but no, I won't ask that,—what's the use!" Then he lifted up his voice in complaint and beat upon the table with his pipe. "What's the use of ever trying to keep track of you? What will Cécile say,—oh, yes, what will she say? It's a pity you can't be constant two months, yes, by Jove! and the Quarter is indulgent, but you abuse its good nature and mine too!"

Presently he arose, and jamming his hat on his head, marched to the door.

"Heaven alone knows why any one puts up with your antics, but they all do and so do I. If I were Cécile or any of the other pretty fools after whom you have toddled and will, in all human probabilities, continue to toddle, I say, if I were Cécile I'd spank you! Now I'm going to Boulant's, and as usual I shall make excuses for you and arrange the affair, and I don't care a continental where you are going, but, by the skull of the studio skeleton! if you don't turn up to-morrow with your sketching-kit under one arm and Cécile under the other,—if you don't turn up in good shape, I'm done with you, and the rest can think what they please. Good-night."

Clifford said good-night with as pleasant a smile as he could muster, and then sat down with his eyes on the door. He took out his watch and gave Elliott ten minutes to vanish, then rang the concierge's call, murmuring, "Oh dear, oh dear, why the devil do I do it?"

"Alfred," he said, as that gimlet-eyed person answered the call, "make yourself clean and proper, Alfred, and replace your sabots with a pair of shoes. Then put on your best hat and take this letter to the big white house in the Rue de Dragon. There is no answer, *mon petit* Alfred."

The concierge departed with a snort in which unwillingness for the errand and affection for M. Clifford were blended. Then with great care the young fellow arrayed himself in all the beauties of his and Elliott's wardrobe. He took his time about it, and occasionally interrupted his toilet to play his banjo or make pleasing diversion for the bull-dogs by gambling about on all fours. "I've got two hours before me," he thought, and borrowed a pair of Elliott's silken foot-gear, with which he and the dogs played ball until he decided to put them on. Then he lighted a cigarette and inspected his dress-coat. When he had emptied it of four handkerchiefs, a fan, and a pair of crumpled gloves as long as his arm, he decided it was not suited to add *éclat* to his charms and cast about in his mind for a substitute. Elliott was too thin, and, anyway, his coats were now under lock and key. Rowden probably was as badly off as himself. Hastings! Hastings was the man! But when he threw on a smoking-jacket and sauntered over to Hastings' house, he was informed that he had been gone over an hour.

"Now, where in the name of all that's reasonable could he have gone!" muttered Clifford, looking down the street.

The maid didn't know, so he bestowed upon her a fascinating smile and lounged back to the studio.

Hastings was not far away. The Luxembourg is within five minutes' walk of the rue Notre Dame des Champs, and there he sat under the shadow of a winged god, and there he had sat for an hour, poking holes in the dust and watching the steps which lead from the northern terrace to the fountain. The sun hung, a purple globe, above the misty hills of Meudon. Long streamers of clouds touched with rose swept low on the western sky, and the dome of the distant Invalides burned like an opal through the haze. Behind the Palace the smoke from a high chimney mounted straight into the air, purple until it crossed the sun, where it changed to a bar of smouldering fire. High above the darkening foliage of the chestnuts the twin towers of St. Sulpice rose, an ever-deepening silhouette.

A sleepy blackbird was carolling in some near thicket, and pigeons passed and re-passed with the whisper of soft winds in their wings. The light on the Palace windows had died away, and the dome of the Pantheon swam aglow above the northern terrace, a fiery Valhalla in the sky; while below in grim array, along the terrace ranged, the marble ranks of queens looked out into the west.

From the end of the long walk by the northern façade of the Palace came the noise of omnibuses and the cries of the street. Hastings looked at the Palace clock. Six, and as his own watch agreed with it, he fell to poking holes in the gravel again. A constant stream of people passed between the Odéon and the fountain. Priests in black, with silver-buckled shoes; line soldiers, slouchy and rakish; neat girls without hats bearing milliners' boxes, students with black portfolios and high hats, students with bérets and big canes, nervous, quick-stepping officers, symphonies in turquoise and silver; ponderous jangling cavalrymen all over dust, pastry cooks' boys skipping along with utter disregard for the safety of the basket balanced on the impish head, and then the lean outcast, the shambling Paris tramp, slouching with shoulders bent and little eye furtively scanning the ground for smokers' refuse;—all these moved in a steady stream across the fountain circle and out into the city by the Odeon, whose long arcades were now beginning to flicker with gas-jets. The melancholy bells of St Sulpice struck the hour and the clock-tower of the Palace lighted up. Then hurried steps sounded across the gravel and Hastings raised his head.

"How late you are," he said, but his voice was hoarse and only his flushed face told how long had seemed the waiting.

She said, "I was kept—indeed, I was so much annoyed—and—and I may only stay a moment."

She sat down beside him, casting a furtive glance over her shoulder at the god upon his pedestal.

"What a nuisance, that intruding cupid still there?"

"Wings and arrows too," said Hastings, unheeding her motion to be seated.

"Wings," she murmured, "oh, yes—to fly away with when he's tired of his play. Of course it was a man who conceived the idea of wings, otherwise Cupid would have been insupportable."

"Do you think so?"

"*Ma foi*, it's what men think."

"And women?"

"Oh," she said, with a toss of her small head, "I really forget what we were speaking of."

"We were speaking of love," said Hastings.

"*I* was not," said the girl. Then looking up at the marble god, "I don't care for this one at all. I don't believe he knows how to shoot his arrows—no, indeed, he is a coward;—he creeps up like an assassin in the twilight. I don't approve of cowardice," she announced, and turned her back on the statue.

"I think," said Hastings quietly, "that he does shoot fairly—yes, and even gives one warning."

"Is it your experience, Monsieur Hastings?"

He looked straight into her eyes and said, "He is warning me."

"Heed the warning then," she cried, with a nervous laugh. As she spoke she stripped off her gloves, and then carefully proceeded to draw them on again. When this was accomplished she glanced at the Palace clock, saying, "Oh dear, how late it is!" furled her umbrella, then unfurled it, and finally looked at him.

"No," he said, "I shall not heed his warning."

"Oh dear," she sighed again, "still talking about that tiresome statue!" Then stealing a glance at his face, "I suppose—I suppose you are in love."

"I don't know," he muttered, "I suppose I am."

She raised her head with a quick gesture. "You seem delighted at the idea," she said, but bit her lip and trembled as his eyes met hers. Then sudden fear came over her and she sprang up, staring into the gathering shadows.

"Are you cold?" he said.

But she only answered, "Oh dear, oh dear, it is late—so late! I must go—goodnight."

She gave him her gloved hand a moment and then withdrew it with a start.

"What is it?" he insisted. "Are you frightened?"

She looked at him strangely.

"No—no—not frightened,—you are very good to me—"

"By Jove!" he burst out, "what do you mean by saying I'm good to you? That's at least the third time, and I don't understand!"

The sound of a drum from the guard-house at the palace cut him short. "Listen," she whispered, "they are going to close. It's late, oh, so late!"

The rolling of the drum came nearer and nearer, and then the silhouette of the drummer cut the sky above the eastern terrace. The fading light lingered a moment on his belt and bayonet, then he passed into the shadows, drumming the echoes awake. The roll became fainter along the eastern terrace, then grew and grew and rattled with increasing sharpness when he passed the avenue by the bronze lion and turned down the western terrace walk. Louder and louder the drum sounded, and the echoes struck back the notes from the grey palace wall; and now the drummer loomed up before them—his red trousers a dull spot in the gathering gloom, the brass of his drum and bayonet touched with a pale spark, his epaulettes tossing on his shoulders. He passed leaving the crash of the drum in their ears, and far into the alley of trees they saw his little tin cup shining on his haversack. Then the sentinels began the monotonous cry: "On ferme! on ferme!" and the bugle blew from the barracks in the rue de Tournon.

"On ferme! on ferme!"

"Good-night," she whispered, "I must return alone to-night."

He watched her until she reached the northern terrace, and then sat down on the marble seat until a hand on his shoulder and a glimmer of bayonets warned him away.

She passed on through the grove, and turning into the rue de Medici, traversed it to the Boulevard. At the corner she bought a bunch of violets and walked on along the Boulevard to the rue des Écoles. A cab was drawn up before Boulant's, and a pretty girl aided by Elliott jumped out.

"Valentine!" cried the girl, "come with us!"

"I can't," she said, stopping a moment—"I have a rendezvous at Mignon's."

"Not Victor?" cried the girl, laughing, but she passed with a little shiver, nodding good-night, then turning into the Boulevard St. Germain, she walked a tittle faster to escape a gay party sitting before the Café Cluny who called to her to join them. At the door of the Restaurant Mignon stood a coal-black negro in buttons. He took off his peaked cap as she mounted the carpeted stairs.

"Send Eugene to me," she said at the office, and passing through the hallway to the right of the dining-room stopped before a row of panelled doors. A waiter passed and she repeated her demand for Eugene, who presently appeared, noiselessly skipping, and bowed murmuring, "Madame."

"Who is here?"

"No one in the cabinets, madame; in the half Madame Madelon and Monsieur Gay, Monsieur de Clamart, Monsieur Clisson, Madame Marie and their set." Then he looked around and bowing again murmured, "Monsieur awaits madame since half an hour," and he knocked at one of the panelled doors bearing the number six.

Clifford opened the door and the girl entered.

The garçon bowed her in, and whispering, "Will Monsieur have the goodness to ring?" vanished.

He helped her off with her jacket and took her hat and umbrella. When she was seated at the little table with Clifford opposite she smiled and leaned forward on both elbows looking him in the face.

"What are you doing here?" she demanded.

"Waiting," he replied, in accents of adoration.

For an instant she turned and examined herself in the glass. The wide blue eyes, the curling hair, the straight nose and short curled lip flashed in the mirror an instant only, and then its depths reflected her pretty neck and back. "Thus do I turn my back on vanity," she said, and then leaning forward again, "What are you doing here?"

"Waiting for you," repeated Clifford, slightly troubled.

"And Cécile."

"Now don't, Valentine—"

"Do you know," she said calmly, "I dislike your conduct?"

He was a little disconcerted, and rang for Eugene to cover his confusion.

The soup was bisque, and the wine Pommery, and the courses followed each other with the usual regularity until Eugene brought coffee, and there was nothing left on the table but a small silver lamp.

"Valentine," said Clifford, after having obtained permission to smoke, "is it the Vaudeville or the Eldorado—or both, or the Nouveau Cirque, or—"

"It is here," said Valentine.

"Well," he said, greatly flattered, "I'm afraid I couldn't amuse you—"

"Oh, yes, you are funnier than the Eldorado."

"Now see here, don't guy me, Valentine. You always do, and, and,—you know what they say,—a good laugh kills—"

"What?"

"Er—er—love and all that."

She laughed until her eyes were moist with tears. "Tiens," she cried, "he is dead, then!"

Clifford eyed her with growing alarm.

"Do you know why I came?" she said.

"No," he replied uneasily, "I don't."

"How long have you made love to me?"

"Well," he admitted, somewhat startled,—"I should say,—for about a year."

"It is a year, I think. Are you not tired?"

He did not answer.

"Don't you know that I like you too well to—to ever fall in love with you?" she said. "Don't you know that we are too good comrades,—too old friends for that? And were we not,—do you think that I do not know your history, Monsieur Clifford?"

"Don't be—don't be so sarcastic," he urged; "don't be unkind, Valentine."

"I'm not. I'm kind. I'm very kind,—to you and to Cécile."

"Cécile is tired of me."

"I hope she is," said the girl, "for she deserves a better fate. Tiens, do you know your reputation in the Quarter? Of the inconstant, the most inconstant,—utterly incorrigible and no more serious than a gnat on a summer night. Poor Cécile!"

Clifford looked so uncomfortable that she spoke more kindly.

"I like you. You know that. Everybody does. You are a spoiled child here. Everything is permitted you and every one makes allowance, but every one cannot be a victim to caprice."

"Caprice!" he cried. "By Jove, if the girls of the Latin Quarter are not capricious—"

"Never mind,—never mind about that! You must not sit in judgment—you of all men. Why are you here to-night? Oh," she cried, "I will tell you why! Monsieur receives a little note; he sends a little answer; he dresses in his conquering raiment—"

"I don't," said Clifford, very red.

"You do, and it becomes you," she retorted with a faint smile. Then again, very quietly, "I am in your power, but I know I am in the power of a friend. I have come to acknowledge it to you here,—and it is because of that that I am here to beg of you—a—a favour."

Clifford opened his eyes, but said nothing.

"I am in—great distress of mind. It is Monsieur Hastings."

"Well?" said Clifford, in some astonishment.

"I want to ask you," she continued in a low voice, "I want to ask you to—to—in case you should speak of me before him,—not to say,—not to say,—"

"I shall not speak of you to him," he said quietly.

"Can—can you prevent others?"

"I might if I was present. May I ask why?"

"That is not fair," she murmured; "you know how—how he considers me,—as he considers every woman. You know how different he is from you and the rest. I have never seen a man,—such a man as Monsieur Hastings."

He let his cigarette go out unnoticed.

"I am almost afraid of him—afraid he should know—what we all are in the Quarter. Oh, I do not wish him to know! I do not wish him to—to turn from me—to cease from speaking to me as he does! You—you and the rest cannot know what it has been to me. I could not believe him,—I could not believe he was so good and—and noble. I do not wish him to know—so soon. He will find out—sooner or later, he will find out for himself, and then he will turn away from me. Why!" she cried passionately, "why should he turn from me and not from *you*?"

Clifford, much embarrassed, eyed his cigarette.

The girl rose, very white. "He is your friend—you have a right to warn him."

"He is my friend," he said at length.

They looked at each other in silence.

Then she cried, "By all that I hold to me most sacred, you need not warn him!"

"I shall trust your word," he said pleasantly.

V

The month passed quickly for Hastings, and left few definite impressions after it. It did leave some, however. One was a painful impression of meeting Mr. Bladen on the Boulevard des Capucines in company with a very pronounced young person whose laugh dismayed him, and when at last he escaped from the café where Mr. Bladen had hauled him to join them in a *bock* he felt as if the whole boulevard was looking at him, and judging him by his company. Later, an instinctive conviction regarding the young person with Mr. Bladen sent the hot blood into his cheek, and he returned to the pension in such a miserable state of mind that Miss Byng was alarmed and advised him to conquer his homesickness at once.

Another impression was equally vivid. One Saturday morning, feeling lonely, his wanderings about the city brought him to the Gare St. Lazare. It was early for breakfast, but he entered the Hôtel Terminus and took a table near the window. As he wheeled about to give his order, a man passing rapidly along the aisle collided with his head, and looking up to receive the expected apology, he was met instead by a slap on the shoulder and a hearty, "What the deuce are you doing here, old chap?" It was Rowden, who seized him and told him to come along. So, mildly protesting, he was ushered into a private dining-room where Clifford, rather red, jumped up from the table and welcomed him with a startled air which was softened by the unaffected glee of Rowden and the extreme courtesy of Elliott. The latter presented him to three bewitching girls who welcomed him so charmingly and seconded Rowden in his demand that Hastings should make one of the party, that he consented at once. While Elliott briefly outlined the projected excursion to La Roche, Hastings delightedly ate his omelet, and returned the smiles of encouragement from Cécile and Colette and Jacqueline. Meantime Clifford in a bland whisper was telling Rowden what an ass he was. Poor Rowden looked miserable until Elliott, divining how affairs were turning, frowned on Clifford and found a moment to let Rowden know that they were all going to make the best of it.

"You shut up," he observed to Clifford, "it's fate, and that settles it."

"It's Rowden, and that settles it," murmured Clifford, concealing a grin. For after all he was not Hastings' wet nurse. So it came about that the train which left the Gare St. Lazare at 9.15 a.m. stopped a moment in its career towards Havre and deposited at the red-roofed station of La Roche a merry party, armed with sunshades, trout-rods, and one cane, carried by the non-combatant, Hastings. Then, when they had established their camp in a grove of sycamores which bordered the little river Ept, Clifford, the acknowledged master of all that pertained to sportsmanship, took command.

"You, Rowden," he said, "divide your flies with Elliott and keep an eye on him or else he'll be trying to put on a float and sinker. Prevent him by force from grubbing about for worms."

Elliott protested, but was forced to smile in the general laugh.

"You make me ill," he asserted; "do you think this is my first trout?"

"I shall be delighted to see your first trout," said Clifford, and dodging a fly hook, hurled with intent to hit, proceeded to sort and equip three slender rods destined to bring joy and fish to Cécile, Colette, and Jacqueline. With perfect gravity he ornamented each line with four split shot, a small hook, and a brilliant quill float.

"*I* shall never touch the worms," announced Cécile with a shudder.

Jacqueline and Colette hastened to sustain her, and Hastings pleasantly offered to act in the capacity of general baiter and taker-off of fish. But Cécile, doubtless fascinated by the gaudy flies in Clifford's book, decided to accept lessons from him in the true art, and presently disappeared up the Ept with Clifford in tow.

Elliott looked doubtfully at Colette.

"I prefer gudgeons," said that damsel with decision, "and you and Monsieur Rowden may go away when you please; may they not, Jacqueline?"

"Certainly," responded Jacqueline.

Elliott, undecided, examined his rod and reel.

"You've got your reel on wrong side up," observed Rowden.

Elliott wavered, and stole a glance at Colette.

"I—I—have almost decided to—er—not to flip the flies about just now," he began. "There's the pole that Cécile left—"

"Don't call it a pole," corrected Rowden.

"*Rod*, then," continued Elliott, and started off in the wake of the two girls, but was promptly collared by Rowden.

"No, you don't! Fancy a man fishing with a float and sinker when he has a fly rod in his hand! You come along!"

Where the placid little Ept flows down between its thickets to the Seine, a grassy bank shadows the haunt of the gudgeon, and on this bank sat Colette and Jacqueline and chattered and laughed and watched the swerving of the scarlet quills, while Hastings, his hat over his eyes, his head on a bank of moss, listened to their soft voices and gallantly unhooked the small and indignant gudgeon when a flash of a rod and a half-suppressed scream announced a catch. The sunlight filtered through the leafy thickets awaking to song the forest birds. Magpies in spotless black and white flirted past, alighting near by with a hop and bound and twitch of the tail. Blue and white jays with rosy breasts shrieked through the trees, and a low-sailing hawk wheeled among the fields of ripening wheat, putting to flight flocks of twittering hedge birds.

Across the Seine a gull dropped on the water like a plume. The air was pure and still. Scarcely a leaf moved. Sounds from a distant farm came faintly, the shrill cock-crow and dull baying. Now and then a steam-tug with big raking smoke-pipe, bearing the name "Guêpe 27," ploughed up the river dragging its interminable train of barges, or a sailboat dropped down with the current toward sleepy Rouen.

A faint fresh odour of earth and water hung in the air, and through the sunlight, orange-tipped butterflies danced above the marsh grass, soft velvety butterflies flapped through the mossy woods.

Hastings was thinking of Valentine. It was two o'clock when Elliott strolled back, and frankly admitting that he had eluded Rowden, sat down beside Colette and prepared to doze with satisfaction.

"Where are your trout?" said Colette severely.

"They still live," murmured Elliott, and went fast asleep.

Rowden returned shortly after, and casting a scornful glance at the slumbering one, displayed three crimson-flecked trout.

"And that," smiled Hastings lazily, "that is the holy end to which the faithful plod,—the slaughter of these small fish with a bit of silk and feather."

Rowden disdained to answer him. Colette caught another gudgeon and awoke Elliott, who protested and gazed about for the lunch baskets, as Clifford and Cécile came up demanding instant refreshment. Cécile's skirts were soaked, and her gloves torn, but she was happy, and Clifford, dragging out a two-pound trout, stood still to receive the applause of the company.

"Where the deuce did you get that?" demanded Elliott.

Cécile, wet and enthusiastic, recounted the battle, and then Clifford eulogized her powers with the fly, and, in proof, produced from his creel a defunct chub, which, he observed, just missed being a trout.

They were all very happy at luncheon, and Hastings was voted "charming." He enjoyed it immensely,—only it seemed to him at moments that flirtation went further in France than in Millbrook, Connecticut, and he thought that Cécile might be a little less enthusiastic about Clifford, that perhaps it would be quite as well if Jacqueline sat further away from Rowden, and that possibly Colette could have, for a moment at least, taken her eyes from Elliott's face. Still he enjoyed it—except when his thoughts drifted to Valentine, and then he felt that he was very far away from her. La Roche is at least an hour and a half from Paris. It is also true that he felt a happiness, a quick heart-beat when, at eight o'clock that night the train which bore them from La Roche rolled into the Gare St. Lazare and he was once more in the city of Valentine.

"Good-night," they said, pressing around him. "You must come with us next time!"

He promised, and watched them, two by two, drift into the darkening city, and stood so long that, when again he raised his eyes, the vast Boulevard was twinkling with gas-jets through which the electric lights stared like moons.

## VI

It was with another quick heart-beat that he awoke next morning, for his first thought was of Valentine.

The sun already gilded the towers of Notre Dame, the clatter of workmen's sabots awoke sharp echoes in the street below, and across the way a blackbird in a pink almond tree was going into an ecstasy of trills.

He determined to awake Clifford for a brisk walk in the country, hoping later to beguile that gentleman into the American church for his soul's sake. He found Alfred the gimlet-eyed washing the asphalt walk which led to the studio.

"Monsieur Elliott?" he replied to the perfunctory inquiry, "*je ne sais pas.*"

"And Monsieur Clifford," began Hastings, somewhat astonished.

"Monsieur Clifford," said the concierge with fine irony, "will be pleased to see you, as he retired early; in fact he has just come in."

Hastings hesitated while the concierge pronounced a fine eulogy on people who never stayed out all night and then came battering at the lodge gate during hours which even a gendarme held sacred to sleep. He also discoursed eloquently upon the beauties of temperance, and took an ostentatious draught from the fountain in the court.

"I do not think I will come in," said Hastings.

"Pardon, monsieur," growled the concierge, "perhaps it would be well to see Monsieur Clifford. He possibly needs aid. Me he drives forth with hair-brushes and boots. It is a mercy if he has not set fire to something with his candle."

Hastings hesitated for an instant, but swallowing his dislike of such a mission, walked slowly through the ivy-covered alley and across the inner garden to the studio. He knocked. Perfect silence. Then he knocked again, and this time something struck the door from within with a crash.

"That," said the concierge, "was a boot." He fitted his duplicate key into the lock and ushered Hastings in. Clifford, in disordered evening dress, sat on the rug in the middle of the room. He held in his hand a shoe, and did not appear astonished to see Hastings.

"Good-morning, do you use Pears' soap?" he inquired with a vague wave of his hand and a vaguer smile.

Hastings' heart sank. "For Heaven's sake," he said, "Clifford, go to bed."

"Not while that—that Alfred pokes his shaggy head in here an' I have a shoe left."

Hastings blew out the candle, picked up Clifford's hat and cane, and said, with an emotion he could not conceal, "This is terrible, Clifford,—I—never knew you did this sort of thing."

"Well, I do," said Clifford.

"Where is Elliott?"

"Ole chap," returned Clifford, becoming maudlin, "Providence which feeds—feeds—er—sparrows an' that sort of thing watcheth over the intemperate wander-er—"

"Where is Elliott?"

But Clifford only wagged his head and waved his arm about. "He's out there,—somewhere about." Then suddenly feeling a desire to see his missing chum, lifted up his voice and howled for him.

Hastings, thoroughly shocked, sat down on the lounge without a word. Presently, after shedding several scalding tears, Clifford brightened up and rose with great precaution.

"Ole chap," he observed, "do you want to see er—er miracle? Well, here goes. I'm goin' to begin."

He paused, beaming at vacancy.

"Er miracle," he repeated.

Hastings supposed he was alluding to the miracle of his keeping his balance, and said nothing.

"I'm goin' to bed," he announced, "poor ole Clifford's goin' to bed, an' that's er miracle!"

And he did with a nice calculation of distance and equilibrium which would have rung enthusiastic yells of applause from Elliott had he been there to assist *en connaisseur*. But he was not. He had not yet reached the studio. He was on his way, however, and smiled with magnificent condescension on Hastings, who, half an hour later, found him reclining upon a bench in the Luxembourg. He permitted himself to be aroused, dusted and escorted to the gate. Here, however, he refused all further assistance, and bestowing a patronizing bow upon Hastings, steered a tolerably true course for the rue Vavin.

Hastings watched him out of sight, and then slowly retraced his steps toward the fountain. At first he felt gloomy and depressed, but gradually the clear air of the morning lifted the pressure from his heart, and he sat down on the marble seat under the shadow of the winged god.

The air was fresh and sweet with perfume from the orange flowers. Everywhere pigeons were bathing, dashing the water over their iris-hued breasts, flashing in and out of the spray or nestling almost to the neck along the polished basin. The sparrows, too, were abroad in force, soaking their dust-coloured feathers in the limpid pool and chirping with might and main. Under the sycamores which surrounded the duck-pond opposite the fountain of Marie de Medici, the water-fowl cropped the herbage, or waddled in rows down the bank to embark on some solemn aimless cruise.

Butterflies, somewhat lame from a chilly night's repose under the lilac leaves, crawled over and over the white phlox, or took a rheumatic flight toward some sun-warmed shrub. The bees were already busy among the heliotrope, and one or two grey flies with brick-coloured eyes sat in a spot of sunlight beside the marble seat, or chased each other about, only to return again to the spot of sunshine and rub their fore-legs, exulting.

The sentries paced briskly before the painted boxes, pausing at times to look toward the guard-house for their relief.

They came at last, with a shuffle of feet and click of bayonets, the word was passed, the relief fell out, and away they went, crunch, crunch, across the gravel.

A mellow chime floated from the clock-tower of the palace, the deep bell of St. Sulpice echoed the stroke. Hastings sat dreaming in the shadow of the god, and while he mused somebody came and sat down beside him. At first he did not raise his head. It was only when she spoke that he sprang up.

"You! At this hour?"

"I was restless, I could not sleep." Then in a low, happy voice—"And *you!* at this hour?"

"I—I slept, but the sun awoke me."

"*I* could not sleep," she said, and her eyes seemed, for a moment, touched with an indefinable shadow. Then, smiling, "I am so glad—I seemed to know you were coming. Don't laugh, I believe in dreams."

"Did you really dream of,—of my being here?"

"I think I was awake when I dreamed it," she admitted. Then for a time they were mute, acknowledging by silence the happiness of being together. And after all their silence was eloquent, for faint smiles, and glances born of their thoughts, crossed and recrossed, until lips moved and words were formed, which seemed almost superfluous. What they said was not very profound. Perhaps the most valuable jewel that fell from Hastings' lips bore direct reference to breakfast.

"I have not yet had my chocolate," she confessed, "but what a material man you are."

"Valentine," he said impulsively, "I wish,—I do wish that you would,—just for this once,—give me the whole day,—just for this once."

"Oh dear," she smiled, "not only material, but selfish!"

"Not selfish, hungry," he said, looking at her.

"A cannibal too; oh dear!"

"Will you, Valentine?"

"But my chocolate—"

"Take it with me."

"But *déjeuner*—"

"Together, at St. Cloud."

"But I can't—"

"Together,—all day,—all day long; will you, Valentine?"

She was silent.

"Only for this once."

Again that indefinable shadow fell across her eyes, and when it was gone she sighed. "Yes,—together, only for this once."

"All day?" he said, doubting his happiness.

"All day," she smiled; "and oh, I am so hungry!"

He laughed, enchanted.

"What a material young lady it is."

On the Boulevard St. Michel there is a Crémerie painted white and blue outside, and neat and clean as a whistle inside. The auburn-haired young woman who speaks French like a native, and rejoices in the name of Murphy, smiled at them as they entered, and tossing a fresh napkin over the zinc *tête-à-tête* table, whisked before them two cups of chocolate and a basket full of crisp, fresh croissons.

The primrose-coloured pats of butter, each stamped with a shamrock in relief, seemed saturated with the fragrance of Normandy pastures.

"How delicious!" they said in the same breath, and then laughed at the coincidence.

"With but a single thought," he began.

"How absurd!" she cried with cheeks all rosy. "I'm thinking I'd like a croisson."

"So am I," he replied triumphant, "that proves it."

Then they had a quarrel; she accusing him of behaviour unworthy of a child in arms, and he denying it, and bringing counter charges, until Mademoiselle Murphy laughed in sympathy, and the last croisson was eaten under a flag of truce. Then they rose, and she took his arm with a bright nod to Mile. Murphy, who cried them a merry: "*Bonjour, madame! bonjour, monsieur!*" and watched them hail a passing cab and drive away. "*Dieu! qu'il est beau,*" she sighed, adding after a moment, "Do they be married, I dunno,—*ma foi ils ont bien l'air.*"

The cab swung around the rue de Medici, turned into the rue de Vaugirard, followed it to where it crosses the rue de Rennes, and taking that noisy thoroughfare, drew up before the Gare Montparnasse. They were just in time for a train and scampered up the stairway and out to the cars as the last note from the starting-gong rang through the arched station. The guard slammed the door of their compartment, a whistle sounded, answered by a screech from the locomotive, and the long train glided from the station, faster, faster, and sped out into the morning sunshine. The summer wind blew in their faces from the open window, and sent the soft hair dancing on the girl's forehead.

"We have the compartment to ourselves," said Hastings.

She leaned against the cushioned window-seat, her eyes bright and wide open, her lips parted. The wind lifted her hat, and fluttered the ribbons under her chin. With a quick movement she untied them, and, drawing a long hat-pin from her hat, laid it down on the seat beside her. The train was flying.

The colour surged in her cheeks, and, with each quick-drawn breath, her breath rose and fell under the cluster of lilies at her throat. Trees, houses, ponds, danced past, cut by a mist of telegraph poles.

"Faster! faster!" she cried.

His eyes never left her, but hers, wide open, and blue as the summer sky, seemed fixed on something far ahead,—something which came no nearer, but fled before them as they fled.

Was it the horizon, cut now by the grim fortress on the hill, now by the cross of a country chapel? Was it the summer moon, ghost-like, slipping through the vaguer blue above?

"Faster! faster!" she cried.

Her parted lips burned scarlet.

The car shook and shivered, and the fields streamed by like an emerald torrent. He caught the excitement, and his faced glowed.

"Oh," she cried, and with an unconscious movement caught his hand, drawing him to the window beside her. "Look! lean out with me!"

He only saw her lips move; her voice was drowned in the roar of a trestle, but his hand closed in hers and he clung to the sill. The wind whistled in their ears. "Not so far out, Valentine, take care!" he gasped.

Below, through the ties of the trestle, a broad river flashed into view and out again, as the train thundered along a tunnel, and away once more through the freshest of green fields. The wind roared about them. The girl was leaning far out from the window, and he caught her by the waist, crying, "Not too far!" but she only murmured, "Faster! faster! away out of the city, out of the land, faster, faster! away out of the world!"

"What are you saying all to yourself?" he said, but his voice was broken, and the wind whirled it back into his throat.

She heard him, and, turning from the window looked down at his arm about her. Then she raised her eyes to his. The car shook and the windows rattled. They were dashing through a forest now, and the sun swept the dewy branches with running flashes of fire. He looked into her troubled eyes; he drew her to him and kissed the half-parted lips, and she cried out, a bitter, hopeless cry, "Not that—not that!"

But he held her close and strong, whispering words of honest love and passion, and when she sobbed—"Not that—not that—I have promised! You must—you must know—I am—not—worthy—" In the purity of his own heart her words were, to him, meaningless then, meaningless for ever after. Presently her voice ceased, and her head rested on his breast. He leaned against the window, his ears swept by the furious wind, his heart in a joyous tumult. The forest was passed, and the sun slipped from behind the trees, flooding the earth again with brightness. She raised her eyes and looked out into the world from the window. Then she began to speak, but her voice was faint, and he bent his head close to hers and listened. "I cannot turn from you; I am too weak. You were long ago my master—master of my heart and soul. I have broken my word to one who trusted me, but I have told you all;—what matters the rest?" He smiled at her innocence and she worshipped his. She spoke again: "Take me or cast me away;—what matters it? Now with a word you can kill me, and it might be easier to die than to look upon happiness as great as mine."

He took her in his arms, "Hush, what are you saying? Look,—look out at the sunlight, the meadows and the streams. We shall be very happy in so bright a world."

She turned to the sunlight. From the window, the world below seemed very fair to her.

Trembling with happiness, she sighed: "Is this the world? Then I have never known it."

"Nor have I, God forgive me," he murmured.

Perhaps it was our gentle Lady of the Fields who forgave them both.

# RUE BARRÉE

"For let Philosopher and Doctor preach
Of what they will and what they will not,—each
Is but one link in an eternal chain
That none can slip nor break nor over-reach."

"Crimson nor yellow roses nor
The savour of the mounting sea
Are worth the perfume I adore
That clings to thee.
The languid-headed lilies tire,
The changeless waters weary me;
I ache with passionate desire
Of thine and thee.
There are but these things in the world—
Thy mouth of fire,
Thy breasts, thy hands, thy hair upcurled
And my desire."

## I

One morning at Julian's, a student said to Selby, "That is Foxhall Clifford," pointing with his brushes at a young man who sat before an easel, doing nothing.

Selby, shy and nervous, walked over and began: "My name is Selby,—I have just arrived in Paris, and bring a letter of introduction—" His voice was lost in the crash of a falling easel, the owner of which promptly assaulted his neighbour, and for a time the noise of battle rolled through the studios of MM. Boulanger and Lefebvre, presently subsiding into a scuffle on the stairs outside. Selby, apprehensive as to his own reception in the studio, looked at Clifford, who sat serenely watching the fight.

"It's a little noisy here," said Clifford, "but you will like the fellows when you know them." His unaffected manner delighted Selby. Then with a simplicity that won his heart, he presented him to half a dozen students of as many nationalities. Some were cordial, all were polite. Even the majestic creature who held the position of Massier, unbent enough to say: "My friend, when a man speaks French as well as you do, and is also a friend of Monsieur Clifford, he will have no trouble in this studio. You expect, of course, to fill the stove until the next new man comes?"

"Of course."

"And you don't mind chaff?"

"No," replied Selby, who hated it.

Clifford, much amused, put on his hat, saying, "You must expect lots of it at first."

Selby placed his own hat on his head and followed him to the door.

As they passed the model stand there was a furious cry of "Chapeau! Chapeau!" and a student sprang from his easel menacing Selby, who reddened but looked at Clifford.

"Take off your hat for them," said the latter, laughing.

A little embarrassed, he turned and saluted the studio.

"Et moi?" cried the model.

"You are charming," replied Selby, astonished at his own audacity, but the studio rose as one man, shouting: "He has done well! he's all right!" while the model, laughing, kissed her hand to him and cried: "À demain beau jeune homme!"

All that week Selby worked at the studio unmolested. The French students christened him "l'Enfant Prodigue," which was freely translated, "The Prodigious Infant," "The Kid," "Kid Selby," and "Kidby." But the disease soon ran its course from "Kidby" to "Kidney," and then naturally to "Tidbits," where it was arrested by Clifford's authority and ultimately relapsed to "Kid."

Wednesday came, and with it M. Boulanger. For three hours the students writhed under his biting sarcasms,—among the others Clifford, who was informed that he knew even less about a work of art than he did about the art of work. Selby was more fortunate. The professor examined his drawing in silence, looked at him sharply, and passed on with a non-committal gesture. He presently departed arm in arm with Bouguereau, to the relief of Clifford, who was then at liberty to jam his hat on his head and depart.

The next day he did not appear, and Selby, who had counted on seeing him at the studio, a thing which he learned later it was vanity to count on, wandered back to the Latin Quarter alone.

Paris was still strange and new to him. He was vaguely troubled by its splendour. No tender memories stirred his American bosom at the Place du Châtelet, nor even by Notre Dame. The Palais de Justice with its clock and turrets and stalking sentinels in blue and vermilion, the Place St. Michel with its jumble of omnibuses and ugly water-spitting griffins, the hill of the Boulevard St. Michel, the tooting trams, the policemen dawdling two by two, and the table-lined terraces of the Café Vacehett were nothing to him, as yet, nor did he even know, when he stepped from the stones of the Place St. Michel to the asphalt of the Boulevard, that he had crossed the frontier and entered the student zone,—the famous Latin Quarter.

A cabman hailed him as "bourgeois," and urged the superiority of driving over walking. A gamin, with an appearance of great concern, requested the latest telegraphic news from London, and then, standing on his head, invited Selby to feats of strength. A pretty girl gave him a glance from a pair of violet eyes. He did not see her, but she, catching her own reflection in a window, wondered at the colour burning in her cheeks. Turning to resume her course, she met Foxhall Clifford, and hurried on. Clifford, open-mouthed, followed her with his eyes; then he looked after Selby, who had turned into the Boulevard St. Germain toward the rue de Seine. Then he examined himself in the shop window. The result seemed to be unsatisfactory.

"I'm not a beauty," he mused, "but neither am I a hobgoblin. What does she mean by blushing at Selby? I never before saw her look at a fellow in my life,—neither has any one in the Quarter. Anyway, I can swear she never looks at me, and goodness knows I have done all that respectful adoration can do."

He sighed, and murmuring a prophecy concerning the salvation of his immortal soul swung into that graceful lounge which at all times characterized Clifford. With no apparent exertion, he overtook Selby at the corner, and together they crossed the sunlit Boulevard and sat down under the awning of the Café du Cercle. Clifford bowed to everybody on the terrace, saying, "You shall meet them all later, but now let me present you to two of the sights of Paris, Mr. Richard Elliott and Mr. Stanley Rowden."

The "sights" looked amiable, and took vermouth.

"You cut the studio to-day," said Elliott, suddenly turning on Clifford, who avoided his eyes.

"To commune with nature?" observed Rowden.

"What's her name this time?" asked Elliott, and Rowden answered promptly, "Name, Yvette; nationality, Breton—"

"Wrong," replied Clifford blandly, "it's Rue Barrée."

The subject changed instantly, and Selby listened in surprise to names which were new to him, and eulogies on the latest Prix de Rome winner. He was delighted to hear opinions boldly expressed and points honestly debated, although the vehicle was mostly slang, both English and French. He longed for the time when he too should be plunged into the strife for fame.

The bells of St. Sulpice struck the hour, and the Palace of the Luxembourg answered chime on chime. With a glance at the sun, dipping low in the golden dust behind the Palais Bourbon, they rose, and turning to the east, crossed the Boulevard St. Germain and sauntered toward the École de Médecine. At the corner a girl passed them, walking hurriedly. Clifford smirked, Elliott and Rowden were agitated, but they all bowed, and, without raising her eyes, she returned their salute. But Selby, who had lagged behind, fascinated by some gay shop window, looked up to meet two of the bluest eyes he had ever seen. The eyes were dropped in an instant, and the young fellow hastened to overtake the others.

"By Jove," he said, "do you fellows know I have just seen the prettiest girl—" An exclamation broke from the trio, gloomy, foreboding, like the chorus in a Greek play.

"Rue Barrée!"

"What!" cried Selby, bewildered.

The only answer was a vague gesture from Clifford.

Two hours later, during dinner, Clifford turned to Selby and said, "You want to ask me something; I can tell by the way you fidget about."

"Yes, I do," he said, innocently enough; "it's about that girl. Who is she?"

In Rowden's smile there was pity, in Elliott's bitterness.

"Her name," said Clifford solemnly, "is unknown to any one, at least," he added with much conscientiousness, "as far as I can learn. Every fellow in the Quarter bows to her and she returns the salute gravely, but no man has ever been known to obtain more than that. Her profession, judging from her music-roll, is that of a pianist. Her residence is in a small and humble street which is kept in a perpetual process of repair by the city authorities, and from the black letters painted on the barrier which defends the street from traffic, she has taken the name by which we know her,—Rue Barrée. Mr. Rowden, in his imperfect knowledge of the French tongue, called our attention to it as Roo Barry—"

"I didn't," said Rowden hotly.

"And Roo Barry, or Rue Barrée, is to-day an object of adoration to every rapin in the Quarter—"

"We are not rapins," corrected Elliott.

"*I* am not," returned Clifford, "and I beg to call to your attention, Selby, that these two gentlemen have at various and apparently unfortunate moments, offered to lay down life and limb at the feet of Rue Barrée. The lady possesses a chilling smile which she uses on such occasions and," here he became gloomily impressive, "I have been forced to believe that neither the scholarly grace of my friend Elliott nor the buxom beauty of my friend Rowden have touched that heart of ice."

Elliott and Rowden, boiling with indignation, cried out, "And you!"

"I," said Clifford blandly, "do fear to tread where you rush in."

## II

Twenty-four hours later Selby had completely forgotten Rue Barrée. During the week he worked with might and main at the studio, and Saturday night found him so tired that he went to bed before dinner and had a nightmare about a river of yellow ochre in which he was drowning. Sunday morning, apropos of nothing at all, he thought of Rue Barrée, and ten seconds afterwards he saw her. It was at the flower-market on the marble bridge. She was examining a pot of pansies. The gardener had evidently thrown heart and soul into the transaction, but Rue Barrée shook her head.

It is a question whether Selby would have stopped then and there to inspect a cabbage-rose had not Clifford unwound for him the yarn of the previous Tuesday. It is possible that his curiosity was piqued, for with the exception of a hen-turkey, a boy of nineteen is the most openly curious biped alive. From twenty until death he tries to conceal it. But, to be fair to Selby, it is also true that the market was attractive. Under a cloudless sky the flowers were packed and heaped along the marble bridge to the parapet. The air was soft, the sun spun a shadowy lacework among the palms and glowed in the hearts of a thousand roses. Spring had come,—was in full tide. The watering carts and sprinklers spread freshness over the Boulevard, the sparrows had become vulgarly obtrusive, and the credulous Seine angler anxiously followed his gaudy quill floating among the soapsuds of the lavoirs. The white-spiked chestnuts clad in tender green vibrated with the hum of bees. Shoddy butterflies flaunted their winter rags among the heliotrope. There was a smell of fresh earth in the air, an echo of the woodland brook in the ripple of the Seine, and swallows soared and skimmed among the anchored river craft. Somewhere in a window a caged bird was singing its heart out to the sky.

Selby looked at the cabbage-rose and then at the sky. Something in the song of the caged bird may have moved him, or perhaps it was that dangerous sweetness in the air of May.

At first he was hardly conscious that he had stopped, then he was scarcely conscious why he had stopped, then he thought he would move on, then he thought he wouldn't, then he looked at Rue Barrée.

The gardener said, "Mademoiselle, this is undoubtedly a fine pot of pansies."

Rue Barrée shook her head.

The gardener smiled. She evidently did not want the pansies. She had bought many pots of pansies there, two or three every spring, and never argued. What did she want then? The pansies were evidently a feeler toward a more important transaction. The gardener rubbed his hands and gazed about him.

"These tulips are magnificent," he observed, "and these hyacinths—" He fell into a trance at the mere sight of the scented thickets.

"That," murmured Rue, pointing to a splendid rose-bush with her furled parasol, but in spite of her, her voice trembled a little. Selby noticed it, more shame to him that he was listening, and the gardener noticed it, and, burying his nose in the roses, scented a bargain. Still, to do him justice, he did not add a centime to the honest value of the plant, for after all, Rue was probably poor, and any one could see she was charming.

"Fifty francs, Mademoiselle."

The gardener's tone was grave. Rue felt that argument would be wasted. They both stood silent for a moment. The gardener did not eulogize his prize,—the rose-tree was gorgeous and any one could see it.

"I will take the pansies," said the girl, and drew two francs from a worn purse. Then she looked up. A tear-drop stood in the way refracting the light like a diamond, but as it rolled into a little corner by her nose a vision of Selby replaced it, and when a brush of the handkerchief had cleared the startled blue eyes, Selby himself appeared, very much embarrassed. He instantly looked up into the sky, apparently devoured with a thirst for astronomical research, and as he continued his investigations for fully five minutes, the gardener looked up too, and so did a policeman. Then Selby looked at the tips of his boots, the gardener looked at him and the policeman slouched on. Rue Barrée had been gone some time.

"What," said the gardener, "may I offer Monsieur?"

Selby never knew why, but he suddenly began to buy flowers. The gardener was electrified. Never before had he sold so many flowers, never at such satisfying prices, and never, never with such absolute unanimity of opinion with a customer. But he missed the bargaining, the arguing, the calling of Heaven to witness. The transaction lacked spice.

"These tulips are magnificent!"

"They are!" cried Selby warmly.

"But alas, they are dear."

"I will take them."

"Dieu!" murmured the gardener in a perspiration, "he's madder than most Englishmen."

"This cactus—"

"Is gorgeous!"

"Alas—"

"Send it with the rest."

The gardener braced himself against the river wall.

"That splendid rose-bush," he began faintly.

"That is a beauty. I believe it is fifty francs—"

He stopped, very red. The gardener relished his confusion. Then a sudden cool self-possession took the place of his momentary confusion and he held the gardener with his eye, and bullied him.

"I'll take that bush. Why did not the young lady buy it?"

"Mademoiselle is not wealthy."

"How do you know?"

"*Dame*, I sell her many pansies; pansies are not expensive."

"Those are the pansies she bought?"

"These, Monsieur, the blue and gold."

"Then you intend to send them to her?"

"At mid-day after the market."

"Take this rose-bush with them, and"—here he glared at the gardener—"don't you dare say from whom they came." The gardener's eyes were like saucers, but Selby, calm and victorious, said: "Send the others to the Hôtel du Sénat, 7 rue de Tournon. I will leave directions with the concierge."

Then he buttoned his glove with much dignity and stalked off, but when well around the corner and hidden from the gardener's view, the conviction that he was an idiot came home to him in a furious blush. Ten minutes later he sat in his room in the Hôtel du Sénat repeating with an imbecile smile: "What an ass I am, what an ass!"

An hour later found him in the same chair, in the same position, his hat and gloves still on, his stick in his hand, but he was silent, apparently lost in contemplation of his boot toes, and his smile was less imbecile and even a bit retrospective.


## III


About five o'clock that afternoon, the little sad-eyed woman who fills the position of concierge at the Hôtel du Sénat held up her hands in amazement to see a wagon-load of flower-bearing shrubs draw up before the doorway. She called Joseph, the intemperate garçon, who, while calculating the value of the flowers in *petits verres*, gloomily disclaimed any knowledge as to their destination.

"*Voyons,*" said the little concierge, "*cherchons la femme!*"

"You?" he suggested.

The little woman stood a moment pensive and then sighed. Joseph caressed his nose, a nose which for gaudiness could vie with any floral display.

Then the gardener came in, hat in hand, and a few minutes later Selby stood in the middle of his room, his coat off, his shirt-sleeves rolled up. The chamber originally contained, besides the furniture, about two square feet of walking room, and now this was occupied by a cactus. The bed groaned under crates of pansies, lilies and heliotrope, the lounge was covered with hyacinths and tulips, and the washstand supported a species of young tree warranted to bear flowers at some time or other.

Clifford came in a little later, fell over a box of sweet peas, swore a little, apologized, and then, as the full splendour of the floral *fête* burst upon him, sat down in astonishment upon a geranium. The geranium was a wreck, but Selby said, "Don't mind," and glared at the cactus.

"Are you going to give a ball?" demanded Clifford.

"N—no,—I'm very fond of flowers," said Selby, but the statement lacked enthusiasm.

"I should imagine so." Then, after a silence, "That's a fine cactus."

Selby contemplated the cactus, touched it with the air of a connoisseur, and pricked his thumb.

Clifford poked a pansy with his stick. Then Joseph came in with the bill, announcing the sum total in a loud voice, partly to impress Clifford, partly to intimidate Selby into disgorging a *pourboire* which he would share, if he chose, with the gardener. Clifford tried to pretend that he had not heard, while Selby paid bill and tribute without a murmur. Then he lounged back into the room with an attempt at indifference which failed entirely when he tore his trousers on the cactus.

Clifford made some commonplace remark, lighted a cigarette and looked out of the window to give Selby a chance. Selby tried to take it, but getting as far as—"Yes, spring is here at last," froze solid. He looked at the back of Clifford's head. It expressed volumes. Those little perked-up ears seemed tingling with suppressed glee. He made a desperate effort to master the situation, and jumped up to reach for some Russian cigarettes as an incentive to conversation, but was foiled by the cactus, to whom again he fell a prey. The last straw was added.

"Damn the cactus." This observation was wrung from Selby against his will,—against his own instinct of self-preservation, but the thorns on the cactus were long and sharp, and at their repeated prick his pent-up wrath escaped. It was too late now; it was done, and Clifford had wheeled around.

"See here, Selby, why the deuce did you buy those flowers?"

"I'm fond of them," said Selby.

"What are you going to do with them? You can't sleep here."

"I could, if you'd help me take the pansies off the bed."

"Where can you put them?"

"Couldn't I give them to the concierge?"

As soon as he said it he regretted it. What in Heaven's name would Clifford think of him! He had heard the amount of the bill. Would he believe that he had invested in these luxuries as a timid declaration to his concierge? And would the Latin Quarter comment upon it in their own brutal fashion? He dreaded ridicule and he knew Clifford's reputation.

Then somebody knocked.

Selby looked at Clifford with a hunted expression which touched that young man's heart. It was a confession and at the same time a supplication. Clifford jumped up, threaded his way through the floral labyrinth, and putting an eye to the crack of the door, said, "Who the devil is it?"

This graceful style of reception is indigenous to the Quarter.

"It's Elliott," he said, looking back, "and Rowden too, and their bulldogs." Then he addressed them through the crack.

"Sit down on the stairs; Selby and I are coming out directly."

Discretion is a virtue. The Latin Quarter possesses few, and discretion seldom figures on the list. They sat down and began to whistle.

Presently Rowden called out, "I smell flowers. They feast within!"

"You ought to know Selby better than that," growled Clifford behind the door, while the other hurriedly exchanged his torn trousers for others.

"*We* know Selby," said Elliott with emphasis.

"Yes," said Rowden, "he gives receptions with floral decorations and invites Clifford, while we sit on the stairs."

"Yes, while the youth and beauty of the Quarter revel," suggested Rowden; then, with sudden misgiving; "Is Odette there?"

"See here," demanded Elliott, "is Colette there?"

Then he raised his voice in a plaintive howl, "Are you there, Colette, while I'm kicking my heels on these tiles?"

"Clifford is capable of anything," said Rowden; "his nature is soured since Rue Barrée sat on him."

Elliott raised his voice: "I say, you fellows, we saw some flowers carried into Rue Barrée's house at noon."

"Posies and roses," specified Rowden.

"Probably for her," added Elliott, caressing his bulldog.

Clifford turned with sudden suspicion upon Selby. The latter hummed a tune, selected a pair of gloves and, choosing a dozen cigarettes, placed them in a case. Then walking over to the cactus, he deliberately detached a blossom, drew it through his buttonhole, and picking up hat and stick, smiled upon Clifford, at which the latter was mightily troubled.

# IV

Monday morning at Julian's, students fought for places; students with prior claims drove away others who had been anxiously squatting on coveted tabourets since the door was opened in hopes of appropriating them at roll-call; students squabbled over palettes, brushes, portfolios, or rent the air with demands for Ciceri and bread. The former, a dirty ex-model, who had in palmier days posed as Judas, now dispensed stale bread at one sou and made enough to keep himself in cigarettes. Monsieur Julian walked in, smiled a fatherly smile and walked out. His disappearance was followed by the apparition of the clerk, a foxy creature who flitted through the battling hordes in search of prey.

Three men who had not paid dues were caught and summoned. A fourth was scented, followed, outflanked, his retreat towards the door cut off, and finally captured behind the stove. About that time, the revolution assuming an acute form, howls rose for "Jules!"

Jules came, umpired two fights with a sad resignation in his big brown eyes, shook hands with everybody and melted away in the throng, leaving an atmosphere of peace and good-will. The lions sat down with the lambs, the massiers marked the best places for themselves and friends, and, mounting the model stands, opened the roll-calls.

The word was passed, "They begin with C this week."

They did.

"Clisson!"

Clisson jumped like a flash and marked his name on the floor in chalk before a front seat.

"Caron!"

Caron galloped away to secure his place. Bang! went an easel. "*Nom de Dieu!*" in French,—"Where in h—l are you goin'!" in English. Crash! a paintbox fell with brushes and all on board. "*Dieu de Dieu de*—" spat! A blow, a short rush, a clinch and scuffle, and the voice of the massier, stern and reproachful:

"Cochon!"

Then the roll-call was resumed.

"Clifford!"

The massier paused and looked up, one finger between the leaves of the ledger.

"Clifford!"

Clifford was not there. He was about three miles away in a direct line and every instant increased the distance. Not that he was walking fast,—on the contrary, he was strolling with that leisurely gait peculiar to himself. Elliott was beside him and two bulldogs covered the rear. Elliott was reading the "Gil Blas," from which he seemed to extract amusement, but deeming boisterous mirth unsuitable to Clifford's state of mind, subdued his amusement to a series of discreet smiles. The latter, moodily aware of this, said nothing, but leading the way into the Luxembourg Gardens installed himself upon a bench by the northern terrace and surveyed the landscape with disfavour. Elliott, according to the Luxembourg regulations, tied the two dogs and then, with an interrogative glance toward his friend, resumed the "Gil Blas" and the discreet smiles.

The day was perfect. The sun hung over Notre Dame, setting the city in a glitter. The tender foliage of the chestnuts cast a shadow over the terrace and flecked the paths and walks with tracery so blue that Clifford might here have found encouragement for his violent "impressions" had he but looked; but as usual in this period of his career, his thoughts were anywhere except in his profession. Around about, the sparrows quarrelled and chattered their courtship songs, the big rosy pigeons sailed from tree to tree, the flies whirled in the sunbeams and the flowers exhaled a thousand perfumes which stirred Clifford with languorous wistfulness. Under this influence he spoke.

"Elliott, you are a true friend—"

"You make me ill," replied the latter, folding his paper. "It's just as I thought,—you are tagging after some new petticoat again. And," he continued wrathfully, "if this is what you've kept me away from Julian's for,—if it's to fill me up with the perfections of some little idiot—"

"Not idiot," remonstrated Clifford gently.

"See here," cried Elliott, "have you the nerve to try to tell me that you are in love again?"

"Again?"

"Yes, again and again and again and—by George have you?"

"This," observed Clifford sadly, "is serious."

For a moment Elliott would have laid hands on him, then he laughed from sheer helplessness. "Oh, go on, go on; let's see, there's Clémence and Marie Tellec and Cosette and Fifine, Colette, Marie Verdier—"

"All of whom are charming, most charming, but I never was serious—"

"So help me, Moses," said Elliott, solemnly, "each and every one of those named have separately and in turn torn your heart with anguish and have also made me lose my place at Julian's in this same manner; each and every one, separately and in turn. Do you deny it?"

"What you say may be founded on facts—in a way—but give me the credit of being faithful to one at a time—"

"Until the next came along."

"But this,—this is really very different. Elliott, believe me, I am all broken up."

Then there being nothing else to do, Elliott gnashed his teeth and listened.

"It's—it's Rue Barrée."

"Well," observed Elliott, with scorn, "if you are moping and moaning over *that* girl,—the girl who has given you and myself every reason to wish that the ground would open and engulf us,—well, go on!"

"I'm going on,—I don't care; timidity has fled—"

"Yes, your native timidity."

"I'm desperate, Elliott. Am I in love? Never, never did I feel so d—n miserable. I can't sleep; honestly, I'm incapable of eating properly."

"Same symptoms noticed in the case of Colette."

"Listen, will you?"

"Hold on a moment, I know the rest by heart. Now let me ask you something. Is it your belief that Rue Barrée is a pure girl?"

"Yes," said Clifford, turning red.

"Do you love her,—not as you dangle and tiptoe after every pretty inanity—I mean, do you honestly love her?"

"Yes," said the other doggedly, "I would—"

"Hold on a moment; would you marry her?"

Clifford turned scarlet. "Yes," he muttered.

"Pleasant news for your family," growled Elliott in suppressed fury. "'Dear father, I have just married a charming grisette whom I'm sure you'll welcome with open arms, in company with her mother, a most estimable and cleanly washlady.' Good heavens! This seems to have gone a little further than the rest. Thank your stars, young man, that my head is level enough for us both. Still, in this case, I have no fear. Rue Barrée sat on your aspirations in a manner unmistakably final."

"Rue Barrée," began Clifford, drawing himself up, but he suddenly ceased, for there where the dappled sunlight glowed in spots of gold, along the sun-flecked path, tripped Rue Barrée. Her gown was spotless, and her big straw hat, tipped a little from the white forehead, threw a shadow across her eyes.

Elliott stood up and bowed. Clifford removed his head-covering with an air so plaintive, so appealing, so utterly humble that Rue Barrée smiled.

The smile was delicious and when Clifford, incapable of sustaining himself on his legs from sheer astonishment, toppled slightly, she smiled again in spite of herself. A few moments later she took a chair on the terrace and drawing a book from her music-roll, turned the pages, found the place, and then placing it open downwards in her lap, sighed a little, smiled a little, and looked out over the city. She had entirely forgotten Foxhall Clifford.

After a while she took up her book again, but instead of reading began to adjust a rose in her corsage. The rose was big and red. It glowed like fire there over her heart, and like fire it warmed her heart, now fluttering under the silken petals. Rue Barrée sighed again. She was very happy. The sky was so blue, the air so soft and perfumed, the sunshine so caressing, and her heart sang within her, sang to the rose in her breast. This is what it sang: "Out of the throng of passers-by, out of the world of yesterday, out of the millions passing, one has turned aside to me."

So her heart sang under his rose on her breast. Then two big mouse-coloured pigeons came whistling by and alighted on the terrace, where they bowed and strutted and bobbed and turned until Rue Barrée laughed in delight, and looking up beheld Clifford before her. His hat was in his hand and his face was wreathed in a series of appealing smiles which would have touched the heart of a Bengal tiger.

For an instant Rue Barrée frowned, then she looked curiously at Clifford, then when she saw the resemblance between his bows and the bobbing pigeons, in spite of herself, her lips parted in the most bewitching laugh. Was this Rue Barrée? So changed, so changed that she did not know herself; but oh! that song in her heart which drowned all else, which trembled on her lips, struggling for utterance, which rippled forth in a laugh at nothing,—at a strutting pigeon,—and Mr. Clifford.

"And you think, because I return the salute of the students in the Quarter, that you may be received in particular as a friend? I do not know you, Monsieur, but vanity is man's other name;—be content, Monsieur Vanity, I shall be punctilious—oh, most punctilious in returning your salute."

"But I beg—I implore you to let me render you that homage which has so long—"

"Oh dear; I don't care for homage."

"Let me only be permitted to speak to you now and then,—occasionally—very occasionally."

"And if *you*, why not another?"

"Not at all,—I will be discretion itself."

"Discretion—why?"

Her eyes were very clear, and Clifford winced for a moment, but only for a moment. Then the devil of recklessness seizing him, he sat down and offered himself, soul and body, goods and chattels. And all the time he knew he was a fool and that infatuation is not love, and that each word he uttered bound him in honour from which there was no escape. And all the time Elliott was scowling down on the fountain plaza and savagely checking both bulldogs from their desire to rush to Clifford's rescue,—for even they felt there was something wrong, as Elliott stormed within himself and growled maledictions.

When Clifford finished, he finished in a glow of excitement, but Rue Barrée's response was long in coming and his ardour cooled while the situation slowly assumed its just proportions. Then regret began to creep in, but he put that aside and broke out again in protestations. At the first word Rue Barrée checked him.

"I thank you," she said, speaking very gravely. "No man has ever before offered me marriage." She turned and looked out over the city. After a while she spoke again. "You offer me a great deal. I am alone, I have nothing, I am nothing." She turned again and looked at Paris, brilliant, fair, in the sunshine of a perfect day. He followed her eyes.

"Oh," she murmured, "it is hard,—hard to work always—always alone with never a friend you can have in honour, and the love that is offered means the streets, the boulevard—when passion is dead. I know it,—*we* know it,—we others who have nothing,—have no one, and who give ourselves, unquestioning—when we love,—yes, unquestioning—heart and soul, knowing the end."

She touched the rose at her breast. For a moment she seemed to forget him, then quietly—"I thank you, I am very grateful." She opened the book and, plucking a petal from the rose, dropped it between the leaves. Then looking up she said gently, "I cannot accept."

## V

It took Clifford a month to entirely recover, although at the end of the first week he was pronounced convalescent by Elliott, who was an authority, and his convalescence was aided by the cordiality with which Rue Barrée acknowledged his solemn salutes. Forty times a day he blessed Rue Barrée for her refusal, and thanked his lucky stars, and at the same time, oh, wondrous heart of ours!—he suffered the tortures of the blighted.

Elliott was annoyed, partly by Clifford's reticence, partly by the unexplainable thaw in the frigidity of Rue Barrée. At their frequent encounters, when she, tripping along the rue de Seine, with music-roll and big straw hat would pass Clifford and his familiars steering an easterly course to the Café Vachette, and at the respectful uncovering of the band would colour and smile at Clifford, Elliott's slumbering suspicions awoke. But he never found out anything, and finally gave it up as beyond his comprehension, merely qualifying Clifford as an idiot and reserving his opinion of Rue Barrée. And all this time Selby was jealous. At first he refused to acknowledge it to himself, and cut the studio for a day in the country, but the woods and fields of course aggravated his case, and the brooks babbled of Rue Barrée and the mowers calling to each other across the meadow ended in a quavering "Rue Bar-rée-e!" That day spent in the country made him angry for a week, and he worked sulkily at Julian's, all the time tormented by a desire to know where Clifford was and what he might be doing. This culminated in an erratic stroll on Sunday which ended at the flower-market on the Pont au Change, began again, was gloomily extended to the morgue, and again ended at the marble bridge. It would never do, and Selby felt it, so he went to see Clifford, who was convalescing on mint juleps in his garden.

They sat down together and discussed morals and human happiness, and each found the other most entertaining, only Selby failed to pump Clifford, to the other's unfeigned amusement. But the juleps spread balm on the sting of jealousy, and trickled hope to the blighted, and when Selby said he must go, Clifford went too, and when Selby, not to be outdone, insisted on accompanying Clifford back to his door, Clifford determined to see Selby back half way, and then finding it hard to part, they decided to dine together and "flit." To flit, a verb applied to Clifford's nocturnal prowls, expressed, perhaps, as well as anything, the gaiety proposed. Dinner was ordered at Mignon's, and while Selby interviewed the chef, Clifford kept a fatherly eye on the butler. The dinner was a success, or was of the sort generally termed a success. Toward the dessert Selby heard some one say as at a great distance, "Kid Selby, drunk as a lord."

A group of men passed near them; it seemed to him that he shook hands and laughed a great deal, and that everybody was very witty. There was Clifford opposite swearing undying confidence in his chum Selby, and there seemed to be others there, either seated beside them or continually passing with the swish of skirts on the polished floor. The perfume of roses, the rustle of fans, the touch of rounded arms and the laughter grew vaguer and vaguer. The room seemed enveloped in mist. Then, all in a moment each object stood out painfully distinct, only forms and visages were distorted and voices piercing. He drew himself up, calm, grave, for the moment master of himself, but very drunk. He knew he was drunk, and was as guarded and alert, as keenly suspicious of himself as he would have been of a thief at his elbow. His self-command enabled Clifford to hold his head safely under some running water, and repair to the street considerably the worse for wear, but never suspecting that his companion was drunk. For a time he kept his self-command. His face was only a bit paler, a bit tighter than usual; he was only a trifle slower and more fastidious in his speech. It was midnight when he left Clifford peacefully slumbering in somebody's arm-chair, with a long suede glove dangling in his hand and a plumy boa twisted about his neck to protect his throat from drafts. He walked through the hall and down the stairs, and found himself on the sidewalk in a quarter he did not know. Mechanically he looked up at the name of the street. The name was not familiar. He turned and steered his course toward some lights clustered at the end of the street. They proved farther away than he had anticipated, and after a long quest he came to the conclusion that his eyes had been mysteriously removed from their proper places and had been reset on either side of his head like those of a bird. It grieved him to think of the inconvenience this transformation might occasion him, and he attempted to cock up his head, hen-like, to test the mobility of his neck. Then an immense despair stole over him,—tears gathered in the tear-ducts, his heart melted, and he collided with a tree. This shocked him into comprehension; he stifled the violent tenderness in his breast, picked up his hat and moved on more briskly. His mouth was white and drawn, his teeth tightly clinched. He held his course pretty well and strayed but little, and after an apparently interminable length of time found himself passing a line of cabs. The brilliant lamps, red, yellow, and green annoyed him, and he felt it might be pleasant to demolish them with his cane, but mastering this impulse he passed on. Later an idea struck him that it would save fatigue to take a cab, and he started back with that intention, but the cabs seemed already so far away and the lanterns were so bright and confusing that he gave it up, and pulling himself together looked around.

A shadow, a mass, huge, undefined, rose to his right. He recognized the Arc de Triomphe and gravely shook his cane at it. Its size annoyed him. He felt it was too big. Then he heard something fall clattering to the pavement and thought probably it was his cane but it didn't much matter. When he had mastered himself and regained control of his right leg, which betrayed symptoms of insubordination, he found himself traversing the Place de la Concorde at a pace which threatened to land him at the Madeleine. This would never do. He turned sharply to the right and crossing the bridge passed the Palais Bourbon at a trot and wheeled into the Boulevard St. Germain. He got on well enough although the size of the War Office struck him as a personal insult, and he missed his cane, which it would have been pleasant to drag along the iron railings as he passed. It occurred to him, however, to substitute his hat, but when he found it he forgot what he wanted it for and replaced it upon his head with gravity. Then he was obliged to battle with a violent inclination to sit down and weep. This lasted until he came to the rue de Rennes, but there he became absorbed in contemplating the dragon on the balcony overhanging the Cour du Dragon, and time slipped away until he remembered vaguely that he had no business there, and marched off again. It was slow work. The inclination to sit down and weep had given place to a desire for solitary and deep reflection. Here his right leg forgot its obedience and attacking the left, outflanked it and brought him up against a wooden board which seemed to bar his path. He tried to walk around it, but found the street closed. He tried to push it over, and found he couldn't. Then he noticed a red lantern standing on a pile of paving-stones inside the barrier. This was pleasant. How was he to get home if the boulevard was blocked? But he was not on the boulevard. His treacherous right leg had beguiled him into a detour, for there, behind him lay the boulevard with its endless line of lamps,—and here, what was this narrow dilapidated street piled up with earth and mortar and heaps of stone? He looked up. Written in staring black letters on the barrier was

## RUE BARRÉE.

He sat down. Two policemen whom he knew came by and advised him to get up, but he argued the question from a standpoint of personal taste, and they passed on, laughing. For he was at that moment absorbed in a problem. It was, how to see Rue Barrée. She was somewhere or other in that big house with the iron balconies, and the door was locked, but what of that? The simple idea struck him to shout until she came. This idea was replaced by another equally lucid,—to hammer on the door until she came; but finally rejecting both of these as too uncertain, he decided to climb into the balcony, and opening a window politely inquire for Rue Barrée. There was but one lighted window in the house that he could see. It was on the second floor, and toward this he cast his eyes. Then mounting the wooden barrier and clambering over the piles of stones, he reached the sidewalk and looked up at the façade for a foothold. It seemed impossible. But a sudden fury seized him, a blind, drunken obstinacy, and the blood rushed to his head, leaping, beating in his ears like the dull thunder of an ocean. He set his teeth, and springing at a window-sill, dragged himself up and hung to the iron bars. Then reason fled; there surged in his brain the sound of many voices, his heart leaped up beating a mad tattoo, and gripping at cornice and ledge he worked his way along the façade, clung to pipes and shutters, and dragged himself up, over and into the balcony by the lighted window. His hat fell off and rolled against the pane. For a moment he leaned breathless against the railing—then the window was slowly opened from within.

They stared at each other for some time. Presently the girl took two unsteady steps back into the room. He saw her face,—all crimsoned now,—he saw her sink into a chair by the lamplit table, and without a word he followed her into the room, closing the big door-like panes behind him. Then they looked at each other in silence.

The room was small and white; everything was white about it,—the curtained bed, the little wash-stand in the corner, the bare walls, the china lamp,—and his own face,—had he known it, but the face and neck of Rue were surging in the colour that dyed the blossoming rose-tree there on the hearth beside her. It did not occur to him to speak. She seemed not to expect it. His mind was struggling with the impressions of the room. The whiteness, the extreme purity of everything occupied him—began to trouble him. As his eye became accustomed to the light, other objects grew from the surroundings and took their places in the circle of lamplight. There was a piano and a coal-scuttle and a little iron trunk and a bath-tub. Then there was a row of wooden pegs against the door, with a white chintz curtain covering the clothes underneath. On the bed lay an umbrella and a big straw hat, and on the table, a music-roll unfurled, an ink-stand, and sheets of ruled paper. Behind him stood a wardrobe faced with a mirror, but somehow he did not care to see his own face just then. He was sobering.

The girl sat looking at him without a word. Her face was expressionless, yet the lips at times trembled almost imperceptibly. Her eyes, so wonderfully blue in the daylight, seemed dark and soft as velvet, and the colour on her neck deepened and whitened with every breath. She seemed smaller and more slender than when he had seen her in the street, and there was now something in the curve of her cheek almost infantine. When at last he turned and caught his own reflection in the mirror behind him, a shock passed through him as though he had seen a shameful thing, and his clouded mind and his clouded thoughts grew clearer. For a moment their eyes met then his sought the floor, his lips tightened, and the struggle within him bowed his head and strained every nerve to the breaking. And now it was over, for the voice within had spoken. He listened, dully interested but already knowing the end,—indeed it little mattered;—the end would always be the same for him;—he understood now—always the same for him, and he listened, dully interested, to a voice which grew within him. After a while he stood up, and she rose at once, one small hand resting on the table. Presently he opened the window, picked up his hat, and shut it again. Then he went over to the rose-bush and touched the blossoms with his face. One was standing in a glass of water on the table and mechanically the girl drew it out, pressed it with her lips and laid it on the table beside him. He took it without a word and crossing the room, opened the door. The landing was dark and silent, but the girl lifted the lamp and gliding past him slipped down the polished stairs to the hallway. Then unchaining the bolts, she drew open the iron wicket.

Through this he passed with his rose.

# THE END

# THE MYSTERY
# OF CHOICE

*There is a maid, demure as she is wise,*
*With all of April in her winsome eyes,*
*And to my tales she listens pensively,*
*With slender fingers clasped about her knee,*
*Watching the sparrows on the balcony.*

> *Shy eyes that, lifted up to me,*
> *Free all my heart of vanity;*
> *Clear eyes, that speak all silently,*
> *Sweet as the silence of a nunnery—*
> *Read, for I write my rede for you alone,*
> *Here where the city's mighty monotone*
> *Deepens the silence to a symphony—*
> *Silence of Saints, and Seers, and Sorcery.*

*Arms and the Man! A noble theme, I ween!*
*Alas! I can not sing of these, Eileen—*
*Only of maids and men and meadow-grass,*
*Of sea and fields and woodlands, where I pass;*
*Nothing but these I know, Eileen, alas!*

> *Clear eyes that, lifted up to me,*
> *Free all my soul from vanity;*
> *Gray eyes, that speak all wistfully—*
> *Nothing but these I know, alas!*

R. W. C.

*April, 1896.*

# INTRODUCTION

### I.

*Where two fair paths, deep flowered*
*And leaf-embowered,*
*Creep East and West across a World concealed,*
*Which shall he take who journeys far afield?*

### II.

*Canst thou then say, "I go,"*
*Or "I forego"?*
*What turns thee East or West, as thistles blow?*
*Is fair more fair than fair—and dost thou know?*

### III.

*Turn to the West, unblessed*
*And uncaressed;*
*Turn to the East, and, seated at the Feast*
*Thou shalt find Life, or Death from Life released.*

### IV.

*And thou who lovest best*
*A maid dark-tressed,*
*And passest others by with careless eye,*
*Canst thou tell why thou choosest? Tell, then; why?*

### V.

*So when thy kiss is given*
*Or half-forgiven,*
*Why should she tremble, with her face flame-hot,*
*Or laugh and whisper, "Love, I tremble not"?*

### VI.

*Or when thy hand may catch*
*A half-drawn latch,*
*What draws thee from the door, to turn and pass*
*Through streets unknown, dim, still, and choked with grass?*

### VII.

*What! Canst thou not foresee*
*The Mystery?*
*Heed! For a Voice commands thy every deed!*
*And it hath sounded. And thou needs must heed!*
R. W. C.
*1896.*

# THE PURPLE EMPEROR

Un souvenir heureux est peut-être, sur terre,
Plus vrai que le bonheur.

A. DE MUSSET.

## I.

The Purple Emperor watched me in silence. I cast again, spinning out six feet more of waterproof silk, and, as the line hissed through the air far across the pool, I saw my three flies fall on the water like drifting thistledown. The Purple Emperor sneered.

"You see," he said, "I am right. There is not a trout in Brittany that will rise to a tailed fly."

"They do in America," I replied.

"Zut! for America!" observed the Purple Emperor.

"And trout take a tailed fly in England," I insisted sharply.

"Now do I care what things or people do in England?" demanded the Purple Emperor.

"You don't care for anything except yourself and your wriggling caterpillars," I said, more annoyed than I had yet been.

The Purple Emperor sniffed. His broad, hairless, sunburnt features bore that obstinate expression which always irritated me. Perhaps the manner in which he wore his hat intensified the irritation, for the flapping brim rested on both ears, and the two little velvet ribbons which hung from the silver buckle in front wiggled and fluttered with every trivial breeze. His cunning eyes and sharp-pointed nose were out of all keeping with his fat red face. When he met my eye, he chuckled.

"I know more about insects than any man in Morbihan—or Finistère either, for that matter," he said.

"The Red Admiral knows as much as you do," I retorted.

"He doesn't," replied the Purple Emperor angrily.

"And his collection of butterflies is twice as large as yours," I added, moving down the stream to a spot directly opposite him.

"It is, is it?" sneered the Purple Emperor. "Well, let me tell you, Monsieur Dar-rel, in all his collection he hasn't a specimen, a single specimen, of that magnificent butterfly, Apatura Iris, commonly known as the 'Purple Emperor.'"

"Everybody in Brittany knows that," I said, casting across the sparkling water; "but just because you happen to be the only man who ever captured a 'Purple Emperor' in Morbihan, it doesn't follow that you are an authority on sea-trout flies. Why do you say that a Breton sea-trout won't touch a tailed fly?"

"It's so," he replied.

"Why? There are plenty of May-flies about the stream."

"Let 'em fly!" snarled the Purple Emperor, "you won't see a trout touch 'em."

My arm was aching, but I grasped my split bamboo more firmly, and, half turn-ing, waded out into the stream and began to whip the ripples at the head of the pool. A great green dragon-fly came drifting by on the summer breeze and hung a moment above the pool, glittering like an emerald.

"There's a chance! Where is your butterfly net?" I called across the stream.

"What for? That dragon-fly? I've got dozens—Anax Junius, Drury, characteris-tic, anal angle of posterior wings, in male, round; thorax marked with——"

"That will do," I said fiercely. "Can't I point out an insect in the air without this burst of erudition? Can you tell me, in simple everyday French, what this little fly is—this one, flitting over the eel grass here beside me? See, it has fallen on the wa-ter."

"Huh!" sneered the Purple Emperor, "that's a Linnobia annulus."

"What's that?" I demanded.

Before he could answer there came a heavy splash in the pool, and the fly dis-appeared.

"He! he! he!" tittered the Purple Emperor. "Didn't I tell you the fish knew their business? That was a sea-trout. I hope you don't get him."

He gathered up his butterfly net, collecting box, chloroform bottle, and cyanide jar. Then he rose, swung the box over his shoulder, stuffed the poison bottles into the pockets of his silver-buttoned velvet coat, and lighted his pipe. This latter opera-tion was a demoralizing spectacle, for the Purple Emperor, like all Breton peasants, smoked one of those microscopical Breton pipes which requires ten minutes to find, ten minutes to fill, ten minutes to light, and ten seconds to finish. With true Breton stolidity he went through this solemn rite, blew three puffs of smoke into the air, scratched his pointed nose reflectively, and waddled away, calling back an ironical "Au revoir, and bad luck to all Yankees!"

I watched him out of sight, thinking sadly of the young girl whose life he made a hell upon earth—Lys Trevec, his niece. She never admitted it, but we all knew what the black-and-blue marks meant on her soft, round arm, and it made me sick to see the look of fear come into her eyes when the Purple Emperor waddled into the café of the Groix Inn.

It was commonly said that he half-starved her. This she denied. Marie Joseph and 'Fine Lelocard had seen him strike her the day after the Pardon of the Birds because she had liberated three bullfinches which he had limed the day before. I asked Lys if this were true, and she refused to speak to me for the rest of the week. There was nothing to do about it. If the Purple Emperor had not been avaricious, I should never have seen Lys at all, but he could not resist the thirty francs a week which I offered him; and Lys posed for me all day long, happy as a linnet in a pink thorn hedge. Nevertheless, the Purple Emperor hated me, and constantly threatened to send Lys back to her dreary flax-spinning. He was suspicious, too, and when he had gulped down the single glass of cider which proves fatal to the sobriety of most Bretons, he would pound the long, discoloured oaken table and roar curses on me, on Yves Terrec, and on the Red Admiral. We were the three objects in the world which he most hated: me, because I was a foreigner, and didn't care a rap for him and his butterflies; and the Red Admiral, because he was a rival entomologist.

He had other reasons for hating Terrec.

The Red Admiral, a little wizened wretch, with a badly adjusted glass eye and a passion for brandy, took his name from a butterfly which predominated in his collection. This butterfly, commonly known to amateurs as the "Red Admiral," and to entomologists as Vanessa Atalanta, had been the occasion of scandal among the entomologists of France and Brittany. For the Red Admiral had taken one of these common insects, dyed it a brilliant yellow by the aid of chemicals, and palmed it off on a credulous collector as a South African species, absolutely unique. The fifty francs which he gained by this rascality were, however, absorbed in a suit for damages brought by the outraged amateur a month later; and when he had sat in the Quimperlé jail for a month, he reappeared in the little village of St. Gildas soured, thirsty, and burning for revenge. Of course we named him the Red Admiral, and he accepted the name with suppressed fury.

The Purple Emperor, on the other hand, had gained his imperial title legitimately, for it was an undisputed fact that the only specimen of that beautiful butterfly, Apatura Iris, or the Purple Emperor, as it is called by amateurs—the only specimen that had ever been taken in Finistère or in Morbihan—was captured and brought home alive by Joseph Marie Gloanec, ever afterward to be known as the Purple Emperor.

When the capture of this rare butterfly became known the Red Admiral nearly went crazy. Every day for a week he trotted over to the Groix Inn, where the Purple Emperor lived with his niece, and brought his microscope to bear on the rare newly captured butterfly, in hopes of detecting a fraud. But this specimen was genuine, and he leered through his microscope in vain.

"No chemicals there, Admiral," grinned the Purple Emperor; and the Red Admiral chattered with rage.

To the scientific world of Brittany and France the capture of an Apatura Iris in Morbihan was of great importance. The Museum of Quimper offered to purchase the butterfly, but the Purple Emperor, though a hoarder of gold, was a monomaniac on butterflies, and he jeered at the Curator of the Museum. From all parts of Brittany and France letters of inquiry and congratulation poured in upon him. The French Academy of Sciences awarded him a prize, and the Paris Entomological Society made him an honorary member. Being a Breton peasant, and a more than commonly pig-headed one at that, these honours did not disturb his equanimity; but when the little hamlet of St. Gildas elected him mayor, and, as is the custom in Brittany under such circumstances, he left his thatched house to take up an official life in the little Groix Inn, his head became completely turned. To be mayor in a village of nearly one hundred and fifty people! It was an empire! So he became unbearable, drinking himself viciously drunk every night of his life, maltreating his niece, Lys Trevec, like the barbarous old wretch that he was, and driving the Red Admiral nearly frantic with his eternal harping on the capture of Apatura Iris. Of course he refused to tell where he had caught the butterfly. The Red Admiral stalked his footsteps, but in vain.

"He! he! he!" nagged the Purple Emperor, cuddling his chin over a glass of cider; "I saw you sneaking about the St. Gildas spinny yesterday morning. So you think you can find another Apatura Iris by running after me? It won't do, Admiral, it won't do, d'ye see?"

The Red Admiral turned yellow with mortification and envy, but the next day he actually took to his bed, for the Purple Emperor had brought home not a butterfly but a live chrysalis, which, if successfully hatched, would become a perfect specimen of the invaluable Apatura Iris. This was the last straw. The Red Admiral shut himself up in his little stone cottage, and for weeks now he had been invisible to everybody except 'Fine Lelocard who carried him a loaf of bread and a mullet or langouste every morning.

The withdrawal of the Red Admiral from the society of St. Gildas excited first the derision and finally the suspicion of the Purple Emperor. What deviltry could he be hatching? Was he experimenting with chemicals again, or was he engaged in some deeper plot, the object of which was to discredit the Purple Emperor? Roux, the postman, who carried the mail on foot once a day from Bannalec, a distance of fifteen miles each way, had brought several suspicious letters, bearing English stamps, to the Red Admiral, and the next day the Admiral had been observed at his window grinning up into the sky and rubbing his hands together. A night or two after this apparition the postman left two packages at the Groix Inn for a moment while he ran across the way to drink a glass of cider with me. The Purple Emperor, who was roaming about the café, snooping into everything that did not concern him, came upon the packages and examined the postmarks and addresses. One of the packages was square and heavy, and felt like a book. The other was also square, but very light, and felt like a pasteboard box. They were both addressed to the Red Admiral, and they bore English stamps.

When Roux, the postman, came back, the Purple Emperor tried to pump him, but the poor little postman knew nothing about the contents of the packages, and after he had taken them around the corner to the cottage of the Red Admiral the Purple Emperor ordered a glass of cider, and deliberately fuddled himself until Lys came in and tearfully supported him to his room. Here he became so abusive and brutal that Lys called to me, and I went and settled the trouble without wasting any words. This also the Purple Emperor remembered, and waited his chance to get even with me.

That had happened a week ago, and until to-day he had not deigned to speak to me.

Lys had posed for me all the week, and to-day being Saturday, and I lazy, we had decided to take a little relaxation, she to visit and gossip with her little black-eyed friend Yvette in the neighbouring hamlet of St. Julien, and I to try the appetites of the Breton trout with the contents of my American fly book.

I had thrashed the stream very conscientiously for three hours, but not a trout had risen to my cast, and I was piqued. I had begun to believe that there were no trout in the St. Gildas stream, and would probably have given up had I not seen the sea trout snap the little fly which the Purple Emperor had named so scientifically. That set me thinking. Probably the Purple Emperor was right, for he certainly was an expert in everything that crawled and wriggled in Brittany. So I matched, from my American fly book, the fly that the sea trout had snapped up, and withdrawing the cast of three, knotted a new leader to the silk and slipped a fly on the loop. It was a queer fly. It was one of those unnameable experiments which fascinate anglers in sporting stores and which generally prove utterly useless. Moreover, it was a tailed fly, but of course I easily remedied that with a stroke of my penknife. Then I was all ready, and I stepped out into the hurrying rapids and cast straight as an arrow to the spot where the sea trout had risen. Lightly as a plume the fly settled on the bosom of the pool; then came a startling splash, a gleam of silver, and the line tightened from the vibrating rod-tip to the shrieking reel. Almost instantly I checked the fish, and as he floundered for a moment, making the water boil along his glittering sides, I sprang to the bank again, for I saw that the fish was a heavy one and I should probably be in for a long run down the stream. The five-ounce rod swept in a splendid circle, quivering under the strain. "Oh, for a gaff-hook!" I cried aloud, for I was now firmly convinced that I had a salmon to deal with, and no sea trout at all.

Then as I stood, bringing every ounce to bear on the sulking fish, a lithe, slender girl came hurriedly along the opposite bank calling out to me by name.

"Why, Lys!" I said, glancing up for a second, "I thought you were at St. Julien with Yvette."

"Yvette has gone to Bannalec. I went home and found an awful fight going on at the Groix Inn, and I was so frightened that I came to tell you."

The fish dashed off at that moment, carrying all the line my reel held, and I was compelled to follow him at a jump. Lys, active and graceful as a young deer, in spite of her Pont-Aven sabots, followed along the opposite bank until the fish settled in a deep pool, shook the line savagely once or twice, and then relapsed into the sulks.

"Fight at the Groix Inn?" I called across the water. "What fight?"

"Not exactly fight," quavered Lys, "but the Red Admiral has come out of his house at last, and he and my uncle are drinking together and disputing about butterflies. I never saw my uncle so angry, and the Red Admiral is sneering and grinning. Oh, it is almost wicked to see such a face!"

"But Lys," I said, scarcely able to repress a smile, "your uncle and the Red Admiral are always quarrelling and drinking."

"I know—oh, dear me!—but this is different, Monsieur Darrel. The Red Admiral has grown old and fierce since he shut himself up three weeks ago, and—oh, dear! I never saw such a look in my uncle's eyes before. He seemed insane with fury. His eyes—I can't speak of it—and then Terrec came in."

"Oh," I said more gravely, "that was unfortunate. What did the Red Admiral say to his son?"

Lys sat down on a rock among the ferns, and gave me a mutinous glance from her blue eyes.

Yves Terrec, loafer, poacher, and son of Louis Jean Terrec, otherwise the Red Admiral, had been kicked out by his father, and had also been forbidden the village by the Purple Emperor, in his majestic capacity of mayor. Twice the young ruffian had returned: once to rifle the bedroom of the Purple Emperor—an unsuccessful enterprise—and another time to rob his own father. He succeeded in the latter attempt, but was never caught, although he was frequently seen roving about the forests and moors with his gun. He openly menaced the Purple Emperor; vowed that he would marry Lys in spite of all the gendarmes in Quimperlé; and these same gendarmes he led many a long chase through brier-filled swamps and over miles of yellow gorse.

What he did to the Purple Emperor—what he intended to do—disquieted me but little; but I worried over his threat concerning Lys. During the last three months this had bothered me a great deal; for when Lys came to St. Gildas from the convent the first thing she captured was my heart. For a long time I had refused to believe that any tie of blood linked this dainty blue-eyed creature with the Purple Emperor. Although she dressed in the velvet-laced bodice and blue petticoat of Finistère, and wore the bewitching white coiffe of St. Gildas, it seemed like a pretty masquerade. To me she was as sweet and as gently bred as many a maiden of the noble Faubourg who danced with her cousins at a Louis XV fête champêtre. So when Lys said that Yves Terrec had returned openly to St. Gildas, I felt that I had better be there also.

"What did Terrec say, Lys?" I asked, watching the line vibrating above the placid pool.

The wild rose colour crept into her cheeks. "Oh," she answered, with a little toss of her chin, "you know what he always says."

"That he will carry you away?"

"Yes."

"In spite of the Purple Emperor, the Red Admiral, and the gendarmes?"

"Yes."

"And what do you say, Lys?"

"I? Oh, nothing."

"Then let me say it for you."

Lys looked at her delicate pointed sabots, the sabots from Pont-Aven, made to order. They fitted her little foot. They were her only luxury.

"Will you let me answer for you, Lys?" I asked.

"You, Monsieur Darrel?"

"Yes. Will you let me give him his answer?"

"Mon Dieu, why should you concern yourself, Monsieur Darrel?"

The fish lay very quiet, but the rod in my hand trembled.

"Because I love you, Lys."

The wild rose colour in her cheeks deepened; she gave a gentle gasp, then hid her curly head in her hands.

"I love you, Lys."

"Do you know what you say?" she stammered.

"Yes, I love you."

She raised her sweet face and looked at me across the pool.

"I love you," she said, while the tears stood like stars in her eyes. "Shall I come over the brook to you?"

## II.

That night Yves Terrec left the village of St. Gildas vowing vengeance against his father, who refused him shelter.

I can see him now, standing in the road, his bare legs rising like pillars of bronze from his straw-stuffed sabots, his short velvet jacket torn and soiled by exposure and dissipation, and his eyes, fierce, roving, bloodshot—while the Red Admiral squeaked curses on him, and hobbled away into his little stone cottage.

"I will not forget you!" cried Yves Terrec, and stretched out his hand toward his father with a terrible gesture. Then he whipped his gun to his cheek and took a short step forward, but I caught him by the throat before he could fire, and a second later we were rolling in the dust of the Bannalec road. I had to hit him a heavy blow behind the ear before he would let go, and then, rising and shaking myself, I dashed his muzzle-loading fowling piece to bits against a wall, and threw his knife into the river. The Purple Emperor was looking on with a queer light in his eyes. It was plain that he was sorry Terrec had not choked me to death.

"He would have killed his father," I said, as I passed him, going toward the Groix Inn.

"That's his business," snarled the Purple Emperor. There was a deadly light in his eyes. For a moment I thought he was going to attack me; but he was merely viciously drunk, so I shoved him out of my way and went to bed, tired and disgusted.

The worst of it was I couldn't sleep, for I feared that the Purple Emperor might begin to abuse Lys. I lay restlessly tossing among the sheets until I could stay there no longer. I did not dress entirely; I merely slipped on a pair of chaussons and sabots, a pair of knickerbockers, a jersey, and a cap. Then, loosely tying a handkerchief about my throat, I went down the worm-eaten stairs and out into the moonlit road. There was a candle flaring in the Purple Emperor's window, but I could not see him.

"He's probably dead drunk," I thought, and looked up at the window where, three years before, I had first seen Lys.

"Asleep, thank Heaven!" I muttered, and wandered out along the road. Passing the small cottage of the Red Admiral, I saw that it was dark, but the door was open. I stepped inside the hedge to shut it, thinking, in case Yves Terrec should be roving about, his father would lose whatever he had left.

Then, after fastening the door with a stone, I wandered on through the dazzling Breton moonlight. A nightingale was singing in a willow swamp below, and from the edge of the mere, among the tall swamp grasses, myriads of frogs chanted a bass chorus.

When I returned, the eastern sky was beginning to lighten, and across the meadows on the cliffs, outlined against the paling horizon, I saw a seaweed gatherer going to his work among the curling breakers on the coast. His long rake was balanced on his shoulder, and the sea wind carried his song across the meadows to me:

St. Gildas!

St. Gildas!

Pray for us,

Shelter us,

Us who toil in the sea.

Passing the shrine at the entrance of the village, I took off my cap and knelt in prayer to Our Lady of Faöuet; and if I neglected myself in that prayer, surely I believed Our Lady of Faöuet would be kinder to Lys. It is said that the shrine casts white shadows. I looked, but saw only the moonlight. Then very peacefully I went to bed again, and was only awakened by the clank of sabres and the trample of horses in the road below my window.

"Good gracious!" I thought, "it must be eleven o'clock, for there are the gendarmes from Quimperlé."

I looked at my watch; it was only half-past eight, and as the gendarmes made their rounds every Thursday at eleven, I wondered what had brought them out so early to St. Gildas.

"Of course," I grumbled, rubbing my eyes, "they are after Terrec," and I jumped into my limited bath.

Before I was completely dressed I heard a timid knock, and opening my door, razor in hand, stood astonished and silent. Lys, her blue eyes wide with terror, leaned on the threshold.

"My darling!" I cried, "what on earth is the matter?" But she only clung to me, panting like a wounded sea gull. At last, when I drew her into the room and raised her face to mine, she spoke in a heart-breaking voice:

"Oh, Dick! they are going to arrest you, but I will die before I believe one word of what they say. No, don't ask me," and she began to sob desperately.

When I found that something really serious was the matter, I flung on my coat and cap, and, slipping one arm about her waist, went down the stairs and out into the road. Four gendarmes sat on their horses in front of the café door; beyond them, the entire population of St. Gildas gaped, ten deep.

"Hello, Durand!" I said to the brigadier, "what the devil is this I hear about arresting me?"

"It's true, mon ami," replied Durand with sepulchral sympathy. I looked him over from the tip of his spurred boots to his sulphur-yellow sabre belt, then upward, button by button, to his disconcerted face.

"What for?" I said scornfully. "Don't try any cheap sleuth work on me! Speak up, man, what's the trouble?"

The Purple Emperor, who sat in the doorway staring at me, started to speak, but thought better of it and got up and went into the house. The gendarmes rolled their eyes mysteriously and looked wise.

"Come, Durand," I said impatiently, "what's the charge?"

"Murder," he said in a faint voice.

"What!" I cried incredulously. "Nonsense! Do I look like a murderer? Get off your horse, you stupid, and tell me who's murdered."

Durand got down, looking very silly, and came up to me, offering his hand with a propitiatory grin.

"It was the Purple Emperor who denounced you! See, they found your handkerchief at his door——"

"Whose door, for Heaven's sake?" I cried.

"Why, the Red Admiral's!"

"The Red Admiral's? What has he done?"

"Nothing—he's only been murdered."

I could scarcely believe my senses, although they took me over to the little stone cottage and pointed out the blood-spattered room. But the horror of the thing was that the corpse of the murdered man had disappeared, and there only remained a nauseating lake of blood on the stone floor, in the centre of which lay a human hand. There was no doubt as to whom the hand belonged, for everybody who had ever seen the Red Admiral knew that the shrivelled bit of flesh which lay in the thickening blood was the hand of the Red Admiral. To me it looked like the severed claw of some gigantic bird.

"Well," I said, "there's been murder committed. Why don't you do something?"

"What?" asked Durand.

"I don't know. Send for the Commissaire."

"He's at Quimperlé. I telegraphed."

"Then send for a doctor, and find out how long this blood has been coagulating."

"The chemist from Quimperlé is here; he's a doctor."

"What does he say?"

"He says that he doesn't know."

"And who are you going to arrest?" I inquired, turning away from the spectacle on the floor.

"I don't know," said the brigadier solemnly; "you are denounced by the Purple Emperor, because he found your handkerchief at the door when he went out this morning."

"Just like a pig-headed Breton!" I exclaimed, thoroughly angry. "Did he not mention Yves Terrec?"

"No."

"Of course not," I said. "He overlooked the fact that Terrec tried to shoot his father last night, and that I took away his gun. All that counts for nothing when he finds my handkerchief at the murdered man's door."

"Come into the café," said Durand, much disturbed, "we can talk it over, there. Of course, Monsieur Darrel, I have never had the faintest idea that you were the murderer!"

The four gendarmes and I walked across the road to the Groix Inn and entered the café. It was crowded with Bretons, smoking, drinking, and jabbering in half a dozen dialects, all equally unsatisfactory to a civilized ear; and I pushed through the crowd to where little Max Fortin, the chemist of Quimperlé, stood smoking a vile cigar.

"This is a bad business," he said, shaking hands and offering me the mate to his cigar, which I politely declined.

"Now, Monsieur Fortin," I said, "it appears that the Purple Emperor found my handkerchief near the murdered man's door this morning, and so he concludes"— here I glared at the Purple Emperor—"that I am the assassin. I will now ask him a question," and turning on him suddenly, I shouted, "What were you doing at the Red Admiral's door?"

The Purple Emperor started and turned pale, and I pointed at him triumphantly.

"See what a sudden question will do. Look how embarrassed he is, and yet I do not charge him with murder; and I tell you, gentlemen, that man there knows as well as I do who was the murderer of the Red Admiral!"

"I don't!" bawled the Purple Emperor.

"You do," I said. "It was Yves Terrec."

"I don't believe it," he said obstinately, dropping his voice.

"Of course not, being pig-headed."

"I am not pig-headed," he roared again, "but I am mayor of St. Gildas, and I do not believe that Yves Terrec killed his father."

"You saw him try to kill him last night?"

The mayor grunted.

"And you saw what I did."

He grunted again.

"And," I went on, "you heard Yves Terrec threaten to kill his father. You heard him curse the Red Admiral and swear to kill him. Now the father is murdered and his body is gone."

"And your handkerchief?" sneered the Purple Emperor.

"I dropped it, of course."

"And the seaweed gatherer who saw you last night lurking about the Red Admiral's cottage," grinned the Purple Emperor.

I was startled at the man's malice.

"That will do," I said. "It is perfectly true that I was walking on the Bannalec road last night, and that I stopped to close the Red Admiral's door, which was ajar, although his light was not burning. After that I went up the road to the Dinez Woods, and then walked over by St. Julien, whence I saw the seaweed gatherer on the cliffs. He was near enough for me to hear what he sang. What of that?"

"What did you do then?"

"Then I stopped at the shrine and said a prayer, and then I went to bed and slept until Brigadier Durand's gendarmes awoke me with their clatter."

"Now, Monsieur Darrel," said the Purple Emperor, lifting a fat finger and shooting a wicked glance at me, "Now, Monsieur Darrel, which did you wear last night on your midnight stroll—sabots or shoes?"

I thought a moment. "Shoes—no, sabots. I just slipped on my chaussons and went out in my sabots."

"Which was it, shoes or sabots?" snarled the Purple Emperor.

"Sabots, you fool."

"Are these your sabots?" he asked, lifting up a wooden shoe with my initials cut on the instep.

"Yes," I replied.

"Then how did this blood come on the other one?" he shouted, and held up a sabot, the mate to the first, on which a drop of blood had spattered.

"I haven't the least idea," I said calmly; but my heart was beating very fast and I was furiously angry.

"You blockhead!" I said, controlling my rage, "I'll make you pay for this when they catch Yves Terrec and convict him. Brigadier Durand, do your duty if you think

I am under suspicion. Arrest me, but grant me one favour. Put me in the Red Admiral's cottage, and I'll see whether I can't find some clew that you have overlooked. Of course, I won't disturb anything until the Commissaire arrives. Bah! You all make me very ill."

"He's hardened," observed the Purple Emperor, wagging his head.

"What motive had I to kill the Red Admiral?" I asked them all scornfully. And they all cried:

"None! Yves Terrec is the man!"

Passing out of the door I swung around and shook my finger at the Purple Emperor.

"Oh, I'll make you dance for this, my friend," I said; and I followed Brigadier Durand across the street to the cottage of the murdered man.

### III.

They took me at my word and placed a gendarme with a bared sabre at the gateway by the hedge.

"Give me your parole," said poor Durand, "and I will let you go where you wish." But I refused, and began prowling about the cottage looking for clews. I found lots of things that some people would have considered most important, such as ashes from the Red Admiral's pipe, footprints in a dusty vegetable bin, bottles smelling of Pouldu cider, and dust—oh, lots of dust!—but I was not an expert, only a stupid, everyday amateur; so I defaced the footprints with my thick shooting boots, and I declined to examine the pipe ashes through a microscope, although the Red Admiral's microscope stood on the table close at hand.

At last I found what I had been looking for, some long wisps of straw, curiously depressed and flattened in the middle, and I was certain I had found the evidence that would settle Yves Terrec for the rest of his life. It was plain as the nose on your face. The straws were sabot straws, flattened where the foot had pressed them, and sticking straight out where they projected beyond the sabot. Now nobody in St. Gildas used straw in sabots except a fisherman who lived near St. Julien, and the straw in his sabots was ordinary yellow wheat straw! This straw, or rather these straws, were from the stalks of the red wheat which only grows inland, and which, everybody in St. Gildas knew, Yves Terrec wore in his sabots. I was perfectly satisfied; and when, three hours later, a hoarse shouting from the Bannalec Road brought me to the window, I was not surprised to see Yves Terrec, bloody, dishevelled, hatless, with his strong arms bound behind him, walking with bent head between two mounted gendarmes. The crowd around him swelled every minute, crying: "Parricide! parricide! Death to the murderer!" As he passed my window I saw great clots of mud on his dusty sabots, from the heels of which projected wisps of red wheat straw. Then I walked back into the Red Admiral's study, determined to find what the microscope would show on the wheat straws. I examined each one very carefully, and then, my eyes aching, I rested my chin on my hand and leaned back in the chair. I had not been as fortunate as some detectives, for there was no evidence that the straws had ever been used in a sabot at all. Furthermore, directly across the hallway stood a carved Breton chest, and now I noticed for the first time that, from beneath the closed lid, dozens of similar red wheat straws projected, bent exactly as mine were bent by the weight of the lid.

I yawned in disgust. It was apparent that I was not cut out for a detective, and I bitterly pondered over the difference between clews in real life and clews in a detective story. After a while I rose, walked over to the chest and opened the lid. The interior was wadded with the red wheat straws, and on this wadding lay two curious glass jars, two or three small vials, several empty bottles labelled chloroform, a collecting jar of cyanide of potassium, and a book. In a farther corner of the chest were some letters bearing English stamps, and also the torn coverings of two parcels, all from England, and all directed to the Red Admiral under his proper name of "Sieur Louis Jean Terrec, St. Gildas, par Moëlan, Finistère."

All these traps I carried over to the desk, shut the lid of the chest, and sat down to read the letters. They were written in commercial French, evidently by an Englishman.

Freely translated, the contents of the first letter were as follows:

"LONDON, *June 12, 1894.*

"DEAR MONSIEUR (*sic*): Your kind favour of the 19th inst. received and contents noted. The latest work on the Lepidoptera of England is Blowzer's How to catch British Butterflies, with notes and tables, and an introduction by Sir Thomas Sniffer. The price of this work (in one volume, calf) is £5 or 125 francs of French money. A post-office order will receive our prompt attention. We beg to remain,

"Yours, etc.,
"FRADLEY & TOOMER,
"470 Regent Square, London, S. W."

The next letter was even less interesting. It merely stated that the money had been received and the book would be forwarded. The third engaged my attention, and I shall quote it, the translation being a free one:

"DEAR SIR: Your letter of the 1st of July was duly received, and we at once referred it to Mr. Fradley himself. Mr. Fradley being much interested in your question, sent your letter to Professor Schweineri, of the Berlin Entomological Society, whose note Blowzer refers to on page 630, in his How to catch British Butterflies. We have just received an answer from Professor Schweineri, which we translate into French— (see inclosed slip). Professor Schweineri begs to present to you two jars of cythyl, prepared under his own supervision. We forward the same to you. Trusting that you will find everything satisfactory, we remain,

"Yours sincerely,
"FRADLEY & TOOMER."

The inclosed slip read as follows:

"Messrs. FRADLEY & TOOMER,

"GENTLEMEN: Cythaline, a complex hydrocarbon, was first used by Professor Schnoot, of Antwerp, a year ago. I discovered an analogous formula about the same time and named it cythyl. I have used it with great success everywhere. It is as certain as a magnet. I beg to present you three small jars, and would be pleased to have you forward two of them to your correspondent in St. Gildas with my compliments. Blowzer's quotation of me, on page 630 of his glorious work, How to catch British Butterflies, is correct.

"Yours, etc.,
"HEINRICH SCHWEINERI,
P.H.D., D.D., D.S., M.S."

When I had finished this letter I folded it up and put it into my pocket with the others. Then I opened Blowzer's valuable work, How to catch British Butterflies, and turned to page 630.

Now, although the Red Admiral could only have acquired the book very recently, and although all the other pages were perfectly clean, this particular page was thumbed black, and heavy pencil marks inclosed a paragraph at the bottom of the page. This is the paragraph:

"Professor Schweineri says: 'Of the two old methods used by collectors for the capture of the swift-winged, high-flying Apatura Iris, or Purple Emperor, the first, which was using a long-handled net, proved successful once in a thousand times; and the second, the placing of bait upon the ground, such as decayed meat, dead cats, rats, etc., was not only disagreeable, even for an enthusiastic collector, but also very uncertain. Once in five hundred times would the splendid butterfly leave the tops of his favourite oak trees to circle about the fetid bait offered. I have found cythyl a perfectly sure bait to draw this beautiful butterfly to the ground, where it can be easily captured. An ounce of cythyl placed in a yellow saucer under an oak tree, will draw to it every Apatura Iris within a radius of twenty miles. So, if any collector who possesses a little cythyl, even though it be in a sealed bottle in his pocket—if such a collector does not find a single Apatura Iris fluttering close about him within an hour, let him be satisfied that the Apatura Iris does not inhabit his country.'"

When I had finished reading this note I sat for a long while thinking hard. Then I examined the two jars. They were labelled "*Cythyl.*" One was full, the other *nearly full.* "The rest must be on the corpse of the Red Admiral," I thought, "no matter if it is in a corked bottle——"

I took all the things back to the chest, laid them carefully on the straw, and closed the lid. The gendarme sentinel at the gate saluted me respectfully as I crossed over to the Groix Inn. The Inn was surrounded by an excited crowd, and the hallway was choked with gendarmes and peasants. On every side they greeted me cordially, announcing that the real murderer was caught; but I pushed by them without a word and ran upstairs to find Lys. She opened her door when I knocked and threw both arms about my neck. I took her to my breast and kissed her. After a moment I asked her if she would obey me no matter what I commanded, and she said she would, with a proud humility that touched me.

"Then go at once to Yvette in St. Julien," I said. "Ask her to harness the dog-cart and drive you to the convent in Quimperlé. Wait for me there. Will you do this without questioning me, my darling?"

She raised her face to mine. "Kiss me," she said innocently; the next moment she had vanished.

I walked deliberately into the Purple Emperor's room and peered into the gauze-covered box which had held the chrysalis of Apatura Iris. It was as I expected. The chrysalis was empty and transparent, and a great crack ran down the middle of its back, but, on the netting inside the box, a magnificent butterfly slowly waved its burnished purple wings; for the chrysalis had given up its silent tenant, the butterfly symbol of immortality. Then a great fear fell upon me. I know now that it was the fear of the Black Priest, but neither then nor for years after did I know that the Black Priest had ever lived on earth. As I bent over the box I heard a confused murmur outside the house which ended in a furious shout of "Parricide!" and I heard the gendarmes ride away behind a wagon which rattled sharply on the flinty highway. I went to the window. In the wagon sat Yves Terrec, bound and wild-eyed, two gendarmes at either side of him, and all around the wagon rode mounted gendarmes whose bared sabres scarcely kept the crowd away.

"Parricide!" they howled. "Let him die!"

I stepped back and opened the gauze-covered box. Very gently but firmly I took the splendid butterfly by its closed fore wings and lifted it unharmed between my thumb and forefinger. Then, holding it concealed behind my back, I went down into the café.

Of all the crowd that had filled it, shouting for the death of Yves Terrec, only three persons remained seated in front of the huge empty fireplace. They were the Brigadier Durand, Max Fortin, the chemist of Quimperlé, and the Purple Emperor. The latter looked abashed when I entered, but I paid no attention to him and walked straight to the chemist.

"Monsieur Fortin," I said, "do you know much about hydrocarbons?"

"They are my specialty," he said astonished.

"Have you ever heard of such a thing as cythyl?"

"Schweineri's cythyl? Oh, yes! We use it in perfumery."

"Good!" I said. "Has it an odour?"

"No—and, yes. One is always aware of its presence, but really nobody can affirm it has an odour. It is curious," he continued, looking at me, "it is very curious you should have asked me that, for all day I have been imagining I detected the presence of cythyl."

"Do you imagine so now?" I asked.

"Yes, more than ever."

I sprang to the front door and tossed out the butterfly. The splendid creature beat the air for a moment, flitted uncertainly hither and thither, and then, to my astonishment, sailed majestically back into the café and alighted on the hearthstone. For a moment I was nonplussed, but when my eyes rested on the Purple Emperor I comprehended in a flash.

"Lift that hearthstone!" I cried to the Brigadier Durand; "pry it up with your scabbard!"

The Purple Emperor suddenly fell forward in his chair, his face ghastly white, his jaw loose with terror.

"What is cythyl?" I shouted, seizing him by the arm; but he plunged heavily from his chair, face downward on the floor, and at the same moment a cry from the chemist made me turn. There stood the Brigadier Durand, one hand supporting the hearthstone, one hand raised in horror. There stood Max Fortin, the chemist, rigid with excitement, and below, in the hollow bed where the hearthstone had rested, lay a crushed mass of bleeding human flesh, from the midst of which stared a cheap glass eye. I seized the Purple Emperor and dragged him to his feet.

"Look!" I cried; "look at your old friend, the Red Admiral!" but he only smiled in a vacant way, and rolled his head muttering; "Bait for butterflies! Cythyl! Oh, no, no, no! You can't do it, Admiral, d'ye see. I alone own the Purple Emperor! I alone am the Purple Emperor!"

And the same carriage that bore me to Quimperlé to claim my bride, carried him to Quimper, gagged and bound, a foaming, howling lunatic.

---

This, then, is the story of the Purple Emperor. I might tell you a pleasanter story if I chose; but concerning the fish that I had hold of, whether it was a salmon, a grilse, or a sea trout, I may not say, because I have promised Lys, and she has promised me, that no power on earth shall wring from our lips the mortifying confession that the fish escaped.

# POMPE FUNÈBRE

A wind-swept sky,
The waste of moorland stretching to the west;
The sea, low moaning in a strange unrest—
A seagull's cry.
Washed by the tide,
The rocks lie sullen in the waning light;
The foam breaks in long strips of hungry white,
Dissatisfied.

BATEMAN.

---

POMPE FUNÈBRE.

In the days when the keepers of the house shall tremble.

When I first saw the sexton he was standing motionless behind a stone. Presently he moved on again, pausing at times, and turning right and left with that nervous, jerky motion that always chills me.

His path lay across the blighted moss and withered leaves scattered in moist layers along the bank of the little brown stream, and I, wondering what his errand might be, followed, passing silently over the rotting forest mould. Once or twice he heard me, for I saw him stop short, a blot of black and orange in the sombre woods; but he always started on again, hurrying at times as though the dead might grow impatient.

For the sexton that I followed through the November forest was one of those small creatures that God has sent to bury little things that die alone in the world. Undertaker, sexton, mute, and gravedigger in one, this thing, robed in black and orange, buries all things that die unheeded by the world. And so they call it—this little beetle in black and orange—the "sexton."

How he hurried! I looked up into the gray sky where ashen branches, interlaced, swayed in unfelt winds, and I heard the dry leaves rattle in the tree tops, and the thud of acorns on the mould. A sombre bird peered at me from a heap of brush, then ran pattering over the leaves.

The sexton had reached a bit of broken ground, and was scuffling over sticks and gulleys toward a brown tuft of withered grass above. I dared not help him; besides, I could not bring myself to touch him, he was so horribly absorbed in his errand.

I halted for a moment. The eagerness of this live creature to find his dead and handle it; the odour of death and decay in this little forest world, where I had waited for spring when Lys moved among the flowering gorse, singing like a throstle in the wind—all this troubled me, and I lagged behind.

The sexton scrambled over the dead grass, raising his seared eyes at every wave of wind. The wind brought sadness with it, the scent of lifeless trees, the vague rustle of gorse buds, yellow and dry as paper flowers.

Along the stream, rotting water plants, scorched and frost-blighted, lay massed above the mud. I saw their pallid stems swaying like worms in the listless current.

The sexton had reached a mouldering stump, and now he seemed undecided. I sat down on a fallen tree, moist and bleached, that crumbled under my touch, leaving a stale odour in the air. Overhead a crow rose heavily and flapped out into the moorland; the wind rattled the stark blackthorns; a single drop of rain touched my cheek. I looked into the stream for some sign of life; there was nothing, except a shapeless creature that might have been a blindworm, lying belly upward on the mud bottom. I touched it with a stick. It was stiff and dead.

The wind among the sham paperlike gorse buds filled the woods with a silken rustle. I put out my hand and touched a yellow blossom; it felt like an immortelle on a funeral pillow.

The sexton had moved on again; something, perhaps a musty spider's web, had stuck to one leg, and he dragged it as he laboured on through the wood. Some little field mouse torn by weasel or kestrel, some crushed mole, some tiny dead pile of fur or feather, lay not far off, stricken by God or man or brother creature. And the sexton knew it—how, God knows! But he knew it, and hurried on to his tryst with the dead.

His path now lay along the edge of a tidal inlet from the Groix River. I looked down at the gray water through the leafless branches, and I saw a small snake, head raised, swim from a submerged clot of weeds into the shadow of a rock. There was a curlew, too, somewhere in the black swamp, whose dreary, persistent call cursed the silence.

I wondered when the sexton would fly; for he could fly if he chose; it is only when the dead are near, very near, that he creeps. The soiled mess of cobweb still stuck to him, and his progress was impeded by it. Once I saw a small brown and white spider, striped like a zebra, running swiftly in his tracks, but the sexton turned and raised his two clubbed forelegs in a horrid imploring attitude that still had something of menace under it. The spider backed away and sidled under a stone.

When anything that is dying—sick and close to death—falls upon the face of the earth, something moves in the blue above, floating like a moat; then another, then others. These specks that grow out of the fathomless azure vault are jewelled flies. They come to wait for Death.

The sexton also arranges rendezvous with Death, but never waits; Death must arrive the first.

When the heavy clover is ablaze with painted wings, when bees hum and blunder among the white-thorn, or pass by like swift singing bullets, the sexton snaps open his black and orange wings and hums across the clover with the bees. Death in a scented garden, the tokens of the plague on a fair young breast, the gray flag of fear in the face of one who reels into the arms of Destruction, the sexton scrambling in the lap of spring, folding his sleek wings, unfolding them to ape the buzz of bees, passing over sweet clover tops to the putrid flesh that summons him—these things must be and will be to the end.

The sexton was running now—running fast, trailing the cobweb over twigs and mud. The edge of the wood was near, for I could see the winter wheat, like green scenery in a theatre, stretching for miles across the cliffs, crude as painted grass. And as I crept through the brittle forest fringe, I saw a figure lying face downward in the wheat—a girl's slender form, limp, motionless.

The sexton darted under her breast.

Then I threw myself down beside her, crying, "Lys! Lys!" And as I cried, the icy rain burst out across the moors, and the trees dashed their stark limbs together till the whole spectral forest tossed and danced, and the wind roared among the cliffs.

And through the Dance of Death Lys trembled in my arms, and sobbed and clung to me, murmuring that the Purple Emperor was dead; but the wind tore the words from her white lips, and flung them out across the sea, where the winter lightning lashed the stark heights of Groix.

Then the fear of death was stilled in my soul, and I raised her from the ground, holding her close.

And I saw the sexton, just beyond us, hurry across the ground and seek shelter under a little dead skylark, stiff-winged, muddy, lying alone in the rain.

## POMPE FUNÈBRE

In the storm, above us, a bird hovered singing through the rain. It passed us twice, still singing, and as it passed again we saw the shadow it cast upon the world was whiter than snow.

# THE MESSENGER

Little gray messenger,
Robed like painted Death,
Your robe is dust.
Whom do you seek
Among lilies and closed buds
At dusk?
Among lilies and closed buds
At dusk,
Whom do you seek,
Little gray messenger,
Robed in the awful panoply
Of painted Death?
R. W. C.

---

## THE MESSENGER.

All-wise,
Hast thou seen all there is to see with thy two eyes?
Dost thou know all there is to know, and so,
Omniscient,
Darest thou still to say thy brother lies?
R. W. C.

"The bullet entered here," said Max Fortin, and he placed his middle finger over a smooth hole exactly in the centre of the forehead.

I sat down upon a mound of dry seaweed and unslung my fowling piece.

The little chemist cautiously felt the edges of the shot-hole, first with his middle finger, then with his thumb.

"Let me see the skull again," said I.

Max Fortin picked it up from the sod.

"It's like all the others," he observed. I nodded, without offering to take it from him. After a moment he thoughtfully replaced it upon the grass at my feet.

"It's like all the others," he repeated, wiping his glasses on his handkerchief. "I thought you might care to see one of the skulls, so I brought this over from the gravel pit. The men from Bannalec are digging yet. They ought to stop."

"How many skulls are there altogether?" I inquired.

"They found thirty-eight skulls; there are thirty-nine noted in the list. They lie piled up in the gravel pit on the edge of Le Bihan's wheat field. The men are at work yet. Le Bihan is going to stop them."

"Let's go over," said I; and I picked up my gun and started across the cliffs, Fortin on one side, Môme on the other.

"Who has the list?" I asked, lighting my pipe. "You say there is a list?"

"The list was found rolled up in a brass cylinder," said the little chemist. He added: "You should not smoke here. You know that if a single spark drifted into the wheat——"

"Ah, but I have a cover to my pipe," said I, smiling.

Fortin watched me as I closed the pepper-box arrangement over the glowing bowl of the pipe. Then he continued:

"The list was made out on thick yellow paper; the brass tube has preserved it. It is as fresh to-day as it was in 1760. You shall see it."

"Is that the date?"

"The list is dated 'April, 1760.' The Brigadier Durand has it. It is not written in French."

"Not written in French!" I exclaimed.

"No," replied Fortin solemnly, "it is written in Breton."

"But," I protested, "the Breton language was never written or printed in 1760."

"Except by priests," said the chemist.

"I have heard of but one priest who ever wrote the Breton language," I began.

Fortin stole a glance at my face.

"You mean—the Black Priest?" he asked.

I nodded.

Fortin opened his mouth to speak again, hesitated, and finally shut his teeth obstinately over the wheat stem that he was chewing.

"And the Black Priest?" I suggested encouragingly. But I knew it was useless; for it is easier to move the stars from their courses than to make an obstinate Breton talk. We walked on for a minute or two in silence.

"Where is the Brigadier Durand?" I asked, motioning Môme to come out of the wheat, which he was trampling as though it were heather. As I spoke we came in sight of the farther edge of the wheat field and the dark, wet mass of cliffs beyond.

"Durand is down there—you can see him; he stands just behind the Mayor of St. Gildas."

"I see," said I; and we struck straight down, following a sun-baked cattle path across the heather.

When we reached the edge of the wheat field, Le Bihan, the Mayor of St. Gildas, called to me, and I tucked my gun under my arm and skirted the wheat to where he stood.

"Thirty-eight skulls," he said in his thin, high-pitched voice; "there is but one more, and I am opposed to further search. I suppose Fortin told you?"

I shook hands with him, and returned the salute of the Brigadier Durand.

"I am opposed to further search," repeated Le Bihan, nervously picking at the mass of silver buttons which covered the front of his velvet and broadcloth jacket like a breastplate of scale armour.

Durand pursed up his lips, twisted his tremendous mustache, and hooked his thumbs in his sabre belt.

"As for me," he said, "I am in favour of further search."

"Further search for what—for the thirty-ninth skull?" I asked.

Le Bihan nodded. Durand frowned at the sunlit sea, rocking like a bowl of molten gold from the cliffs to the horizon. I followed his eyes. On the dark glistening cliffs, silhouetted against the glare of the sea, sat a cormorant, black, motionless, its horrible head raised toward heaven.

"Where is that list, Durand?" I asked.

The gendarme rummaged in his despatch pouch and produced a brass cylinder about a foot long. Very gravely he unscrewed the head and dumped out a scroll of thick yellow paper closely covered with writing on both sides. At a nod from Le Bihan he handed me the scroll. But I could make nothing of the coarse writing, now faded to a dull brown.

"Come, come, Le Bihan," I said impatiently, "translate it, won't you? You and Max Fortin make a lot of mystery out of nothing, it seems."

Le Bihan went to the edge of the pit where the three Bannalec men were digging, gave an order or two in Breton, and turned to me.

As I came to the edge of the pit the Bannalec men were removing a square piece of sail-cloth from what appeared to be a pile of cobblestones.

"Look!" said Le Bihan shrilly. I looked. The pile below was a heap of skulls. After a moment I clambered down the gravel sides of the pit and walked over to the men of Bannalec. They saluted me gravely, leaning on their picks and shovels, and wiping their sweating faces with sunburned hands.

"How many?" said I in Breton.

"Thirty-eight," they replied.

I glanced around. Beyond the heap of skulls lay two piles of human bones. Beside these was a mound of broken, rusted bits of iron and steel. Looking closer, I saw that this mound was composed of rusty bayonets, sabre blades, scythe blades, with here and there a tarnished buckle attached to a bit of leather hard as iron.

I picked up a couple of buttons and a belt plate. The buttons bore the royal arms of England; the belt plate was emblazoned with the English arms, and also with the number "27."

"I have heard my grandfather speak of the terrible English regiment, the 27th Foot, which landed and stormed the fort up there," said one of the Bannalec men.

"Oh!" said I; "then these are the bones of English soldiers?"

"Yes," said the men of Bannalec.

Le Bihan was calling to me from the edge of the pit above, and I handed the belt plate and buttons to the men and climbed the side of the excavation.

"Well," said I, trying to prevent Môme from leaping up and licking my face as I emerged from the pit, "I suppose you know what these bones are. What are you going to do with them?"

"There was a man," said Le Bihan angrily, "an Englishman, who passed here in a dog-cart on his way to Quimper about an hour ago, and what do you suppose he wished to do?"

"Buy the relics?" I asked, smiling.

"Exactly—the pig!" piped the mayor of St. Gildas. "Jean Marie Tregunc, who found the bones, was standing there where Max Fortin stands, and do you know what he answered? He spat upon the ground, and said: 'Pig of an Englishman, do you take me for a desecrator of graves?'"

I knew Tregunc, a sober, blue-eyed Breton, who lived from one year's end to the other without being able to afford a single bit of meat for a meal.

"How much did the Englishman offer Tregunc?" I asked.

"Two hundred francs for the skulls alone."

I thought of the relic hunters and the relic buyers on the battlefields of our civil war.

"Seventeen hundred and sixty is long ago," I said.

"Respect for the dead can never die," said Fortin.

"And the English soldiers came here to kill your fathers and burn your homes," I continued.

"They were murderers and thieves, but—they are dead," said Tregunc, coming up from the beach below, his long sea rake balanced on his dripping jersey.

"How much do you earn every year, Jean Marie?" I asked, turning to shake hands with him.

"Two hundred and twenty francs, monsieur."

"Forty-five dollars a year," I said. "Bah! you are worth more, Jean. Will you take care of my garden for me? My wife wished me to ask you. I think it would be worth one hundred francs a month to you and to me. Come on, Le Bihan—come along, Fortin—and you, Durand. I want somebody to translate that list into French for me."

Tregunc stood gazing at me, his blue eyes dilated.

"You may begin at once," I said, smiling, "if the salary suits you?"

"It suits," said Tregunc, fumbling for his pipe in a silly way that annoyed Le Bihan.

"Then go and begin your work," cried the mayor impatiently; and Tregunc started across the moors toward St. Gildas, taking off his velvet-ribboned cap to me and gripping his sea rake very hard.

"You offer him more than my salary," said the mayor, after a moment's contemplation of his silver buttons.

"Pooh!" said I, "what do you do for your salary except play dominoes with Max Fortin at the Groix Inn?"

Le Bihan turned red, but Durand rattled his sabre and winked at Max Fortin, and I slipped my arm through the arm of the sulky magistrate, laughing.

"There's a shady spot under the cliff," I said; "come on, Le Bihan, and read me what is in the scroll."

In a few moments we reached the shadow of the cliff, and I threw myself upon the turf, chin on hand, to listen.

The gendarme, Durand, also sat down, twisting his mustache into needlelike points. Fortin leaned against the cliff, polishing his glasses and examining us with vague, near-sighted eyes; and Le Bihan, the mayor, planted himself in our midst, rolling up the scroll and tucking it under his arm.

"First of all," he began in a shrill voice, "I am going to light my pipe, and while lighting it I shall tell you what I have heard about the attack on the fort yonder. My father told me; his father told him."

He jerked his head in the direction of the ruined fort, a small, square stone structure on the sea cliff, now nothing but crumbling walls. Then he slowly produced a tobacco pouch, a bit of flint and tinder, and a long-stemmed pipe fitted with a microscopical bowl of baked clay. To fill such a pipe requires ten minutes' close attention. To smoke it to a finish takes but four puffs. It is very Breton, this Breton pipe. It is the crystallization of everything Breton.

"Go on," said I, lighting a cigarette.

"The fort," said the mayor, "was built by Louis XIV, and was dismantled twice by the English. Louis XV restored it in 1739. In 1760 it was carried by assault by the English. They came across from the island of Groix—three shiploads—and they stormed the fort and sacked St. Julien yonder, and they started to burn St. Gildas— you can see the marks of their bullets on my house yet; but the men of Bannalec and the men of Lorient fell upon them with pike and scythe and blunderbuss, and those who did not run away lie there below in the gravel pit now—thirty-eight of them."

"And the thirty-ninth skull?" I asked, finishing my cigarette.

The mayor had succeeded in filling his pipe, and now he began to put his tobacco pouch away.

"The thirty-ninth skull," he mumbled, holding the pipestem between his defective teeth—"the thirty-ninth skull is no business of mine. I have told the Bannalec men to cease digging."

"But what is—whose is the missing skull?" I persisted curiously.

The mayor was busy trying to strike a spark to his tinder. Presently he set it aglow, applied it to his pipe, took the prescribed four puffs, knocked the ashes out of the bowl, and gravely replaced the pipe in his pocket.

"The missing skull?" he asked.

"Yes," said I impatiently.

The mayor slowly unrolled the scroll and began to read, translating from the Breton into French. And this is what he read:

> "ON THE CLIFFS OF ST. GILDAS,
> "*April 13, 1760.*

"On this day, by order of the Count of Soisic, general in chief of the Breton forces now lying in Kerselec Forest, the bodies of thirty-eight English soldiers of the

27th, 50th, and 72d regiments of Foot were buried in this spot, together with their arms and equipments."

The mayor paused and glanced at me reflectively.

"Go on, Le Bihan," I said.

"With them," continued the mayor, turning the scroll and reading on the other side, "was buried the body of that vile traitor who betrayed the fort to the English. The manner of his death was as follows: By order of the most noble Count of Soisic, the traitor was first branded upon the forehead with the brand of an arrowhead. The iron burned through the flesh, and was pressed heavily so that the brand should even burn into the bone of the skull. The traitor was then led out and bidden to kneel. He admitted having guided the English from the island of Groix. Although a priest and a Frenchman, he had violated his priestly office to aid him in discovering the pass-word to the fort. This password he extorted during confession from a young Breton girl who was in the habit of rowing across from the island of Groix to visit her hus-band in the fort. When the fort fell, this young girl, crazed by the death of her husband, sought the Count of Soisic and told how the priest had forced her to con-fess to him all she knew about the fort. The priest was arrested at St. Gildas as he was about to cross the river to Lorient. When arrested he cursed the girl, Marie Tre-vec——"

"What!" I exclaimed, "Marie Trevec!"

"Marie Trevec," repeated Le Bihan; "the priest cursed Marie Trevec, and all her family and descendants. He was shot as he knelt, having a mask of leather over his face, because the Bretons who composed the squad of execution refused to fire at a priest unless his face was concealed. The priest was l'Abbé Sorgue, commonly known as the Black Priest on account of his dark face and swarthy eyebrows. He was buried with a stake through his heart."

Le Bihan paused, hesitated, looked at me, and handed the manuscript back to Durand. The gendarme took it and slipped it into the brass cylinder.

"So," said I, "the thirty-ninth skull is the skull of the Black Priest."

"Yes," said Fortin. "I hope they won't find it."

"I have forbidden them to proceed," said the mayor querulously. "You heard me, Max Fortin."

I rose and picked up my gun. Môme came and pushed his head into my hand.

"That's a fine dog," observed Durand, also rising.

"Why don't you wish to find his skull?" I asked Le Bihan. "It would be curious to see whether the arrow brand really burned into the bone."

"There is something in that scroll that I didn't read to you," said the mayor grimly. "Do you wish to know what it is?"

"Of course," I replied in surprise.

"Give me the scroll again, Durand," he said; then he read from the bottom: "I, l'Abbé Sorgue, forced to write the above by my executioners, have written it in my own blood; and with it I leave my curse. My curse on St. Gildas, on Marie Trevec, and on her descendants. I will come back to St. Gildas when my remains are disturbed. Woe to that Englishman whom my branded skull shall touch!"

"What rot!" I said. "Do you believe it was really written in his own blood?"

"I am going to test it," said Fortin, "at the request of Monsieur le Maire. I am not anxious for the job, however."

"See," said Le Bihan, holding out the scroll to me, "it is signed, 'l'Abbé Sorgue.'"

I glanced curiously over the paper.

"It must be the Black Priest," I said. "He was the only man who wrote in the Breton language. This is a wonderfully interesting discovery, for now, at last, the mystery of the Black Priest's disappearance is cleared up. You will, of course, send this scroll to Paris, Le Bihan?"

"No," said the mayor obstinately, "it shall be buried in the pit below where the rest of the Black Priest lies."

I looked at him and recognised that argument would be useless. But still I said, "It will be a loss to history, Monsieur Le Bihan."

"All the worse for history, then," said the enlightened Mayor of St. Gildas.

We had sauntered back to the gravel pit while speaking. The men of Bannalec were carrying the bones of the English soldiers toward the St. Gildas cemetery, on the cliffs to the east, where already a knot of white-coiffed women stood in attitudes of prayer; and I saw the sombre robe of a priest among the crosses of the little graveyard.

"They were thieves and assassins; they are dead now," muttered Max Fortin.

"Respect the dead," repeated the Mayor of St. Gildas, looking after the Bannalec men.

"It was written in that scroll that Marie Trevec, of Groix Island, was cursed by the priest—she and her descendants," I said, touching Le Bihan on the arm. "There was a Marie Trevec who married an Yves Trevec of St. Gildas——"

"It is the same," said Le Bihan, looking at me obliquely.

"Oh!" said I; "then they were ancestors of my wife."

"Do you fear the curse?" asked Le Bihan.

"What?" I laughed.

"There was the case of the Purple Emperor," said Max Fortin timidly.

Startled for a moment, I faced him, then shrugged my shoulders and kicked at a smooth bit of rock which lay near the edge of the pit, almost embedded in gravel.

"Do you suppose the Purple Emperor drank himself crazy because he was descended from Marie Trevec?" I asked contemptuously.

"Of course not," said Max Fortin hastily.

"Of course not," piped the mayor. "I only—— Hello! what's that you're kicking?"

"What?" said I, glancing down, at the same time involuntarily giving another kick. The smooth bit of rock dislodged itself and rolled out of the loosened gravel at my feet.

"The thirty-ninth skull!" I exclaimed. "By jingo, its the noddle of the Black Priest! See! there is the arrowhead branded on the front!"

The mayor stepped back. Max Fortin also retreated. There was a pause, during which I looked at them, and they looked anywhere but at me.

"I don't like it," said the mayor at last, in a husky, high voice. "I don't like it! The scroll says he will come back to St. Gildas when his remains are disturbed. I—I don't like it, Monsieur Darrel——"

"Bosh!" said I; "the poor wicked devil is where he can't get out. For Heaven's sake, Le Bihan, what is this stuff you are talking in the year of grace 1896?"

The mayor gave me a look.

"And he says 'Englishman.' You are an Englishman, Monsieur Darrel," he announced.

"You know better. You know I'm an American."

"It's all the same," said the Mayor of St. Gildas, obstinately.

"No, it isn't!" I answered, much exasperated, and deliberately pushed the skull till it rolled into the bottom of the gravel pit below.

"Cover it up," said I; "bury the scroll with it too, if you insist, but I think you ought to send it to Paris. Don't look so gloomy, Fortin, unless you believe in were-wolves and ghosts. Hey! what the—what the devil's the matter with you, anyway? What are you staring at, Le Bihan?"

"Come, come," muttered the mayor in a low, tremulous voice, "it's time we got out of this. Did you see? Did you see, Fortin?"

"I saw," whispered Max Fortin, pallid with fright.

The two men were almost running across the sunny pasture now, and I hastened after them, demanding to know what was the matter.

"Matter!" chattered the mayor, gasping with exasperation and terror. "The skull is rolling uphill again!" and he burst into a terrified gallop. Max Fortin followed close behind.

I watched them stampeding across the pasture, then turned toward the gravel pit, mystified, incredulous. The skull was lying on the edge of the pit, exactly where it had been before I pushed it over the edge. For a second I stared at it; a singular chilly feeling crept up my spinal column, and I turned and walked away, sweat starting from the root of every hair on my head. Before I had gone twenty paces the absurdity of the whole thing struck me. I halted, hot with shame and annoyance, and retraced my steps.

There lay the skull.

"I rolled a stone down instead of the skull," I muttered to myself. Then with the butt of my gun I pushed the skull over the edge of the pit and watched it roll to the bottom; and as it struck the bottom of the pit, Môme, my dog, suddenly whipped his tail between his legs, whimpered, and made off across the moor.

"Môme!" I shouted, angry and astonished; but the dog only fled the faster, and I ceased calling from sheer surprise.

"What the mischief is the matter with that dog!" I thought. He had never before played me such a trick.

Mechanically I glanced into the pit, but I could not see the skull. I looked down. The skull lay at my feet again, touching them.

"Good heavens!" I stammered, and struck at it blindly with my gunstock. The ghastly thing flew into the air, whirling over and over, and rolled again down the sides of the pit to the bottom. Breathlessly I stared at it, then, confused and scarcely comprehending, I stepped back from the pit, still facing it, one, ten, twenty paces, my eyes almost starting from my head, as though I expected to see the thing roll up from the bottom of the pit under my very gaze. At last I turned my back to the pit and strode out across the gorse-covered moorland toward my home. As I reached the road that winds from St. Gildas to St. Julien I gave one hasty glance at the pit over my shoulder. The sun shone hot on the sod about the excavation. There was something white and bare and round on the turf at the edge of the pit. It might have been a stone; there were plenty of them lying about.

## II.

When I entered my garden I saw Môme sprawling on the stone doorstep. He eyed me sideways and flopped his tail.

"Are you not mortified, you idiot dog?" I said, looking about the upper windows for Lys.

Môme rolled over on his back and raised one deprecating forepaw, as though to ward off calamity.

"Don't act as though I was in the habit of beating you to death," I said, disgusted. I had never in my life raised whip to the brute. "But you are a fool dog," I continued. "No, you needn't come to be babied and wept over; Lys can do that, if she insists, but I am ashamed of you, and you can go to the devil."

Môme slunk off into the house, and I followed, mounting directly to my wife's boudoir. It was empty.

"Where has she gone?" I said, looking hard at Môme, who had followed me. "Oh! I see you don't know. Don't pretend you do. Come off that lounge! Do you think Lys wants tan-coloured hairs all over her lounge?"

I rang the bell for Catherine and 'Fine, but they didn't know where "madame" had gone; so I went into my room, bathed, exchanged my somewhat grimy shooting clothes for a suit of warm, soft knickerbockers, and, after lingering some extra moments over my toilet—for I was particular, now that I had married Lys—I went down to the garden and took a chair out under the fig-trees.

"Where can she be?" I wondered. Môme came sneaking out to be comforted, and I forgave him for Lys's sake, whereupon he frisked.

"You bounding cur," said I, "now what on earth started you off across the moor? If you do it again I'll push you along with a charge of dust shot."

As yet I had scarcely dared think about the ghastly hallucination of which I had been a victim, but now I faced it squarely, flushing a little with mortification at the thought of my hasty retreat from the gravel pit.

"To think," I said aloud, "that those old woman's tales of Max Fortin and Le Bihan should have actually made me see what didn't exist at all! I lost my nerve like a schoolboy in a dark bedroom." For I knew now that I had mistaken a round stone for a skull each time, and had pushed a couple of big pebbles into the pit instead of the skull itself.

"By jingo!" said I, "I'm nervous; my liver must be in a devil of a condition if I see such things when I'm awake! Lys will know what to give me."

I felt mortified and irritated and sulky, and thought disgustedly of Le Bihan and Max Fortin.

But after a while I ceased speculating, dismissed the mayor, the chemist, and the skull from my mind, and smoked pensively, watching the sun low dipping in the western ocean. As the twilight fell for a moment over ocean and moorland, a wistful, restless happiness filled my heart, the happiness that all men know—all men who have loved.

Slowly the purple mist crept out over the sea; the cliffs darkened; the forest was shrouded.

Suddenly the sky above burned with the afterglow, and the world was alight again.

Cloud after cloud caught the rose dye; the cliffs were tinted with it; moor and pasture, heather and forest burned and pulsated with the gentle flush. I saw the gulls turning and tossing above the sand bar, their snowy wings tipped with pink; I saw the sea swallows sheering the surface of the still river, stained to its placid depths with warm reflections of the clouds. The twitter of drowsy hedge birds broke out in the stillness; a salmon rolled its shining side above tide-water.

The interminable monotone of the ocean intensified the silence. I sat motionless, holding my breath as one who listens to the first low rumour of an organ. All at once the pure whistle of a nightingale cut the silence, and the first moonbeam silvered the wastes of mist-hung waters.

I raised my head.

Lys stood before me in the garden.

When we had kissed each other, we linked arms and moved up and down the gravel walks, watching the moonbeams sparkle on the sand bar as the tide ebbed and ebbed. The broad beds of white pinks about us were atremble with hovering white moths; the October roses hung all abloom, perfuming the salt wind.

"Sweetheart," I said, "where is Yvonne? Has she promised to spend Christmas with us?"

"Yes, Dick; she drove me down from Plougat this afternoon. She sent her love to you. I am not jealous. What did you shoot?"

"A hare and four partridges. They are in the gun room. I told Catherine not to touch them until you had seen them."

Now I suppose I knew that Lys could not be particularly enthusiastic over game or guns; but she pretended she was, and always scornfully denied that it was for my sake and not for the pure love of sport. So she dragged me off to inspect the rather meagre game bag, and she paid me pretty compliments and gave a little cry of delight and pity as I lifted the enormous hare out of the sack by his ears.

"He'll eat no more of our lettuce," I said, attempting to justify the assassination.

"Unhappy little bunny—and what a beauty! O Dick, you are a splendid shot, are you not?"

I evaded the question and hauled out a partridge.

"Poor little dead things!" said Lys in a whisper; "it seems a pity—doesn't it, Dick? But then you are so clever——"

"We'll have them broiled," I said guardedly; "tell Catherine."

Catherine came in to take away the game, and presently 'Fine Lelocard, Lys's maid, announced dinner, and Lys tripped away to her boudoir.

I stood an instant contemplating her blissfully, thinking, "My boy, you're the happiest fellow in the world—you're in love with your wife!"

I walked into the dining room, beamed at the plates, walked out again; met Tregunc in the hallway, beamed on him; glanced into the kitchen, beamed at Catherine, and went up stairs, still beaming.

Before I could knock at Lys's door it opened, and Lys came hastily out. When she saw me she gave a little cry of relief, and nestled close to my breast.

"There is something peering in at my window," she said.

"What!" I cried angrily.

"A man, I think, disguised as a priest, and he has a mask on. He must have climbed up by the bay tree."

I was down the stairs and out of doors in no time. The moonlit garden was absolutely deserted. Tregunc came up, and together we searched the hedge and shrubbery around the house and out to the road.

"Jean Marie," said I at length, "loose my bulldog—he knows you—and take your supper on the porch where you can watch. My wife says the fellow is disguised as a priest, and wears a mask."

Tregunc showed his white teeth in a smile. "He will not care to venture in here again, I think, Monsieur Darrel."

I went back and found Lys seated quietly at the table.

"The soup is ready, dear," she said. "Don't worry; it was only some foolish lout from Bannalec. No one in St. Gildas or St. Julien would do such a thing."

I was too much exasperated to reply at first, but Lys treated it as a stupid joke, and after a while I began to look at it in that light.

Lys told me about Yvonne, and reminded me of my promise to have Herbert Stuart down to meet her.

"You wicked diplomat!" I protested. "Herbert is in Paris, and hard at work for the Salon."

"Don't you think he might spare a week to flirt with the prettiest girl in Finistère?" inquired Lys innocently.

"Prettiest girl! Not much!" I said.

"Who is, then?" urged Lys.

I laughed a trifle sheepishly.

"I suppose you mean me, Dick," said Lys, colouring up.

"Now I bore you, don't I?"

"Bore me? Ah, no, Dick."

After coffee and cigarettes were served I spoke about Tregunc, and Lys approved.

"Poor Jean! he will be glad, won't he? What a dear fellow you are!"

"Nonsense," said I; "we need a gardener; you said so yourself, Lys."

But Lys leaned over and kissed me, and then bent down and hugged Môme, who whistled through his nose in sentimental appreciation.

"I am a very happy woman," said Lys.

"Môme was a very bad dog to-day," I observed.

"Poor Môme!" said Lys, smiling.

When dinner was over and Môme lay snoring before the blaze—for the October nights are often chilly in Finistère—Lys curled up in the chimney corner with her embroidery, and gave me a swift glance from under her drooping lashes.

"You look like a schoolgirl, Lys," I said teasingly. "I don't believe you are sixteen yet."

She pushed back her heavy burnished hair thoughtfully. Her wrist was as white as surf foam.

"Have we been married four years? I don't believe it," I said.

She gave me another swift glance and touched the embroidery on her knee, smiling faintly.

"I see," said I, also smiling at the embroidered garment. "Do you think it will fit?"

"Fit?" repeated Lys. Then she laughed.

"And," I persisted, "are you perfectly sure that you—er—we shall need it?"

"Perfectly," said Lys. A delicate colour touched her cheeks and neck. She held up the little garment, all fluffy with misty lace and wrought with quaint embroidery.

"It is very gorgeous," said I; "don't use your eyes too much, dearest. May I smoke a pipe?"

"Of course," she said, selecting a skein of pale blue silk.

For a while I sat and smoked in silence, watching her slender fingers among the tinted silks and thread of gold.

Presently she spoke: "What did you say your crest is, Dick?"

"My crest? Oh, something or other rampant on a something or other——"

"Dick!"

"Dearest?"

"Don't be flippant."

"But I really forget. It's an ordinary crest; everybody in New York has them. No family should be without 'em."

"You are disagreeable, Dick. Send Josephine upstairs for my album."

"Are you going to put that crest on the—the—whatever it is?"

"I am; and my own crest, too."

I thought of the Purple Emperor and wondered a little.

"You didn't know I had one, did you?" she smiled.

"What is it?" I replied evasively.

"You shall see. Ring for Josephine."

I rang, and, when 'Fine appeared, Lys gave her some orders in a low voice, and Josephine trotted away, bobbing her white-coiffed head with a "Bien, madame!"

After a few minutes she returned, bearing a tattered, musty volume, from which the gold and blue had mostly disappeared.

I took the book in my hands and examined the ancient emblazoned covers.

"Lilies!" I exclaimed.

"Fleur-de-lis," said my wife demurely.

"Oh!" said I, astonished, and opened the book.

"You have never before seen this book?" asked Lys, with a touch of malice in her eyes.

"You know I haven't. Hello! what's this? Oho! So there should be a *de* before Trevec? Lys de Trevec? Then why in the world did the Purple Emperor——"

"Dick!" cried Lys.

"All right," said I. "Shall I read about the Sieur de Trevec who rode to Saladin's tent alone to seek for medicine for St. Louis? or shall I read about—what is it? Oh, here it is, all down in black and white—about the Marquis de Trevec who drowned himself before Alva's eyes rather than surrender the banner of the fleur-de-lis to Spain? It's all written here. But, dear, how about that soldier named Trevec who was killed in the old fort on the cliff yonder?"

"He dropped the *de*, and the Trevecs since then have been Republicans," said Lys—"all except me."

"That's quite right," said I; "it is time that we Republicans should agree upon some feudal system. My dear, I drink to the king!" and I raised my wine-glass and looked at Lys.

"To the king," said Lys, flushing. She smoothed out the tiny garment on her knees; she touched the glass with her lips; her eyes were very sweet. I drained the glass to the king.

After a silence I said: "I will tell the king stories. His Majesty shall be amused."

"His Majesty," repeated Lys softly.

"Or hers," I laughed. "Who knows?"

"Who knows?" murmured Lys, with a gentle sigh.

"I know some stories about Jack the Giant-Killer," I announced. "Do you, Lys?"

"I? No, not about a giant-killer, but I know all about the were-wolf, and Jeanne-la-Flamme, and the Man in Purple Tatters, and—O dear me! I know lots more."

"You are very wise," said I. "I shall teach his Majesty English."

"And I Breton," cried Lys jealously.

"I shall bring playthings to the king," said I—"big green lizards from the gorse, little gray mullets to swim in glass globes, baby rabbits from the forest of Kerselec——"

"And I," said Lys, "will bring the first primrose, the first branch of aubepine, the first jonquil, to the king—my king."

"Our king," said I; and there was peace in Finistère.

I lay back, idly turning the leaves of the curious old volume.

"I am looking," said I, "for the crest."

"The crest, dear? It is a priest's head with an arrow-shaped mark on the forehead, on a field——"

I sat up and stared at my wife.

"Dick, whatever is the matter?" she smiled. "The story is there in that book. Do you care to read it? No? Shall I tell it to you? Well, then: It happened in the third crusade. There was a monk whom men called the Black Priest. He turned apostate, and sold himself to the enemies of Christ. A Sieur de Trevec burst into the Saracen camp, at the head of only one hundred lances, and carried the Black Priest away out of the very midst of their army."

"So that is how you come by the crest," I said quietly; but I thought of the branded skull in the gravel pit, and wondered.

"Yes," said Lys. "The Sieur de Trevec cut the Black Priest's head off, but first he branded him with an arrow mark on the forehead. The book says it was a pious action, and the Sieur de Trevec got great merit by it. But I think it was cruel, the branding," she sighed.

"Did you ever hear of any other Black Priest?"

"Yes. There was one in the last century, here in St. Gildas. He cast a white shadow in the sun. He wrote in the Breton language. Chronicles, too, I believe. I never saw them. His name was the same as that of the old chronicler, and of the other priest, Jacques Sorgue. Some said he was a lineal descendant of the traitor. Of course the first Black Priest was bad enough for anything. But if he did have a child, it need not have been the ancestor of the last Jacques Sorgue. They say this one was a holy man. They say he was so good he was not allowed to die, but was caught up to heaven one day," added Lys, with believing eyes.

I smiled.

"But he disappeared," persisted Lys.

"I'm afraid his journey was in another direction," I said jestingly, and thoughtlessly told her the story of the morning. I had utterly forgotten the masked man at her window, but before I finished I remembered him fast enough, and realized what I had done as I saw her face whiten.

"Lys," I urged tenderly, "that was only some clumsy clown's trick. You said so yourself. You are not superstitious, my dear?"

Her eyes were on mine. She slowly drew the little gold cross from her bosom and kissed it. But her lips trembled as they pressed the symbol of faith.

### III.

About nine o'clock the next morning I walked into the Groix Inn and sat down at the long discoloured oaken table, nodding good-day to Marianne Bruyère, who in turn bobbed her white coiffe at me.

"My clever Bannalec maid," said I, "what is good for a stirrup-cup at the Groix Inn?"

"Schist?" she inquired in Breton.

"With a dash of red wine, then," I replied.

She brought the delicious Quimperlé cider, and I poured a little Bordeaux into it. Marianne watched me with laughing black eyes.

"What makes your cheeks so red, Marianne?" I asked. "Has Jean Marie been here?"

"We are to be married, Monsieur Darrel," she laughed.

"Ah! Since when has Jean Marie Tregunc lost his head?"

"His head? Oh, Monsieur Darrel—his heart, you mean!"

"So I do," said I. "Jean Marie is a practical fellow."

"It is all due to your kindness——" began the girl, but I raised my hand and held up the glass.

"It's due to himself. To your happiness, Marianne;" and I took a hearty draught of the schist. "Now," said I, "tell me where I can find Le Bihan and Max Fortin."

"Monsieur Le Bihan and Monsieur Fortin are above in the broad room. I believe they are examining the Red Admiral's effects."

"To send them to Paris? Oh, I know. May I go up, Marianne?"

"And God go with you," smiled the girl.

When I knocked at the door of the broad room above little Max Fortin opened it. Dust covered his spectacles and nose; his hat, with the tiny velvet ribbons fluttering, was all awry.

"Come in, Monsieur Darrel," he said; "the mayor and I are packing up the effects of the Purple Emperor and of the poor Red Admiral."

"The collections?" I asked, entering the room. "You must be very careful in packing those butterfly cases; the slightest jar might break wings and antennæ, you know."

Le Bihan shook hands with me and pointed to the great pile of boxes.

"They're all cork lined," he said, "but Fortin and I are putting felt around each box. The Entomological Society of Paris pays the freight."

The combined collections of the Red Admiral and the Purple Emperor made a magnificent display.

I lifted and inspected case after case set with gorgeous butterflies and moths, each specimen carefully labelled with the name in Latin. There were cases filled with crimson tiger moths all aflame with colour; cases devoted to the common yellow butterflies; symphonies in orange and pale yellow; cases of soft gray and dun-coloured sphinx moths; and cases of garish nettle-bred butterflies of the numerous family of *Vanessa*.

All alone in a great case by itself was pinned the purple emperor, the Apatura Iris, that fatal specimen that had given the Purple Emperor his name and quietus.

I remembered the butterfly, and stood looking at it with bent eyebrows.

Le Bihan glanced up from the floor where he was nailing down the lid of a box full of cases.

"It is settled, then," said he, "that madame, your wife, gives the Purple Emperor's entire collection to the city of Paris?"

I nodded.

"Without accepting anything for it?"

"It is a gift," I said.

"Including the purple emperor there in the case? That butterfly is worth a great deal of money," persisted Le Bihan.

"You don't suppose that we would wish to sell that specimen, do you?" I answered a trifle sharply.

"If I were you I should destroy it," said the mayor in his high-pitched voice.

"That would be nonsense," said I—"like your burying the brass cylinder and scroll yesterday."

"It was not nonsense," said Le Bihan doggedly, "and I should prefer not to discuss the subject of the scroll."

I looked at Max Fortin, who immediately avoided my eyes.

"You are a pair of superstitious old women," said I, digging my hands into my pockets; "you swallow every nursery tale that is invented."

"What of it?" said Le Bihan sulkily; "there's more truth than lies in most of 'em."

"Oh!" I sneered, "does the Mayor of St. Gildas and St. Julien believe in the Loup-garou?"

"No, not in the Loup-garou."

"In what, then—Jeanne-la-Flamme?"

"That," said Le Bihan with conviction, "is history."

"The devil it is!" said I; "and perhaps, monsieur the mayor, your faith in giants is unimpaired?"

"There were giants—everybody knows it," growled Max Fortin.

"And you a chemist!" I observed scornfully.

"Listen, Monsieur Darrel," squeaked Le Bihan; "you know yourself that the Purple Emperor was a scientific man. Now suppose I should tell you that he always refused to include in his collection a Death's Messenger?"

"A what?" I exclaimed.

"You know what I mean—that moth that flies by night; some call it the Death's Head, but in St. Gildas we call it 'Death's Messenger.'"

"Oh!" said I, "you mean that big sphinx moth that is commonly known as the 'death's-head moth.' Why the mischief should the people here call it death's messenger?"

"For hundreds of years it has been known as death's messenger in St. Gildas," said Max Fortin. "Even Froissart speaks of it in his commentaries on Jacques Sorgue's Chronicles. The book is in your library."

"Sorgue? And who was Jacques Sorgue? I never read his book."

"Jacques Sorgue was the son of some unfrocked priest—I forget. It was during the crusades."

"Good Heavens!" I burst out, "I've been hearing of nothing but crusades and priests and death and sorcery ever since I kicked that skull into the gravel pit, and I am tired of it, I tell you frankly. One would think we lived in the dark ages. Do you know what year of our Lord it is, Le Bihan?"

"Eighteen hundred and ninety-six," replied the mayor.

"And yet you two hulking men are afraid of a death's-head moth."

"I don't care to have one fly into the window," said Max Fortin; "it means evil to the house and the people in it."

"God alone knows why he marked one of his creatures with a yellow death's head on the back," observed Le Bihan piously, "but I take it that he meant it as a warning; and I propose to profit by it," he added triumphantly.

"See here, Le Bihan," I said; "by a stretch of imagination one can make out a skull on the thorax of a certain big sphinx moth. What of it?"

"It is a bad thing to touch," said the mayor, wagging his head.

"It squeaks when handled," added Max Fortin.

"Some creatures squeak all the time," I observed, looking hard at Le Bihan.

"Pigs," added the mayor.

"Yes, and asses," I replied. "Listen, Le Bihan: do you mean to tell me that you saw that skull roll uphill yesterday?"

The mayor shut his mouth tightly and picked up his hammer.

"Don't be obstinate," I said; "I asked you a question."

"And I refuse to answer," snapped Le Bihan. "Fortin saw what I saw; let him talk about it."

I looked searchingly at the little chemist.

"I don't say that I saw it actually roll up out of the pit, all by itself," said Fortin with a shiver, "but—but then, how did it come up out of the pit, if it didn't roll up all by itself?"

"It didn't come up at all; that was a yellow cobblestone that you mistook for the skull again," I replied. "You were nervous, Max."

"A—a very curious cobblestone, Monsieur Darrel," said Fortin.

"I also was a victim to the same hallucination," I continued, "and I regret to say that I took the trouble to roll two innocent cobblestones into the gravel pit, imagining each time that it was the skull I was rolling."

"It was," observed Le Bihan with a morose shrug.

"It just shows," said I, ignoring the mayor's remark, "how easy it is to fix up a train of coincidences so that the result seems to savour of the supernatural. Now, last night my wife imagined that she saw a priest in a mask peer in at her window——"

Fortin and Le Bihan scrambled hastily from their knees, dropping hammer and nails.

"W-h-a-t—what's that?" demanded the mayor.

I repeated what I had said. Max Fortin turned livid.

"My God!" muttered Le Bihan, "the Black Priest is in St. Gildas!"

"D-don't you—you know the old prophecy?" stammered Fortin; "Froissart quotes it from Jacques Sorgue:

'When the Black Priest rises from the dead,
St. Gildas folk shall shriek in bed;
When the Black Priest rises from his grave,
May the good God St. Gildas save!'"

"Aristide Le Bihan," I said angrily, "and you, Max Fortin, I've got enough of this nonsense! Some foolish lout from Bannalec has been in St. Gildas playing tricks to frighten old fools like you. If you have nothing better to talk about than nursery legends I'll wait until you come to your senses. Good-morning." And I walked out, more disturbed than I cared to acknowledge to myself.

The day had become misty and overcast. Heavy, wet clouds hung in the east. I heard the surf thundering against the cliffs, and the gray gulls squealed as they tossed and turned high in the sky. The tide was creeping across the river sands, higher, higher, and I saw the seaweed floating on the beach, and the *lançons* springing from the foam, silvery thread-like flashes in the gloom. Curlew were flying up the river in twos and threes; the timid sea swallows skimmed across the moors toward some quiet, lonely pool, safe from the coming tempest. In every hedge field birds were gathering, huddling together, twittering restlessly.

When I reached the cliffs I sat down, resting my chin on my clenched hands. Already a vast curtain of rain, sweeping across the ocean miles away, hid the island of Groix. To the east, behind the white semaphore on the hills, black clouds crowded up over the horizon. After a little the thunder boomed, dull, distant, and slender skeins of lightning unravelled across the crest of the coming storm. Under the cliff at my feet the surf rushed foaming over the shore, and the *lançons* jumped and skipped and quivered until they seemed to be but the reflections of the meshed lightning.

I turned to the east. It was raining over Groix, it was raining at Sainte Barbe, it was raining now at the semaphore. High in the storm whirl a few gulls pitched; a nearer cloud trailed veils of rain in its wake; the sky was spattered with lightning; the thunder boomed.

As I rose to go, a cold raindrop fell upon the back of my hand, and another, and yet another on my face. I gave a last glance at the sea, where the waves were bursting into strange white shapes that seemed to fling out menacing arms toward me. Then something moved on the cliff, something black as the black rock it clutched—a filthy cormorant, craning its hideous head at the sky.

Slowly I plodded homeward across the sombre moorland, where the gorse stems glimmered with a dull metallic green, and the heather, no longer violet and purple, hung drenched and dun-coloured among the dreary rocks. The wet turf creaked under my heavy boots, the black-thorn scraped and grated against knee and elbow. Over all lay a strange light, pallid, ghastly, where the sea spray whirled across the landscape and drove into my face until it grew numb with the cold. In broad bands, rank after rank, billow on billow, the rain burst out across the endless moors, and yet there was no wind to drive it at such a pace.

Lys stood at the door as I turned into the garden, motioning me to hasten; and then for the first time I became conscious that I was soaked to the skin.

"How ever in the world did you come to stay out when such a storm threatened?" she said. "Oh, you are dripping! Go quickly and change; I have laid your warm underwear on the bed, Dick."

I kissed my wife, and went upstairs to change my dripping clothes for something more comfortable.

When I returned to the morning room there was a driftwood fire on the hearth, and Lys sat in the chimney corner embroidering.

"Catherine tells me that the fishing fleet from Lorient is out. Do you think they are in danger, dear?" asked Lys, raising her blue eyes to mine as I entered.

"There is no wind, and there will be no sea," said I, looking out of the window. Far across the moor I could see the black cliffs looming in the mist.

"How it rains!" murmured Lys; "come to the fire, Dick."

I threw myself on the fur rug, my hands in my pockets, my head on Lys's knees.

"Tell me a story," I said. "I feel like a boy of ten."

Lys raised a finger to her scarlet lips. I always waited for her to do that.

"Will you be very still, then?" she said.

"Still as death."

"Death," echoed a voice, very softly.

"Did you speak, Lys?" I asked, turning so that I could see her face.

"No; did you, Dick?"

"Who said 'death'?" I asked, startled.

"Death," echoed a voice, softly.

I sprang up and looked about. Lys rose too, her needles and embroidery falling to the floor. She seemed about to faint, leaning heavily on me, and I led her to the window and opened it a little way to give her air. As I did so the chain lightning split the zenith, the thunder crashed, and a sheet of rain swept into the room, driving with it something that fluttered—something that flapped, and squeaked, and beat upon the rug with soft, moist wings.

We bent over it together, Lys clinging to me, and we saw that it was a death's-head moth drenched with rain.

The dark day passed slowly as we sat beside the fire, hand in hand, her head against my breast, speaking of sorrow and mystery and death. For Lys believed that there were things on earth that none might understand, things that must be nameless forever and ever, until God rolls up the scroll of life and all is ended. We spoke of hope and fear and faith, and the mystery of the saints; we spoke of the beginning and the end, of the shadow of sin, of omens, and of love. The moth still lay on the floor, quivering its sombre wings in the warmth of the fire, the skull and ribs clearly etched upon its neck and body.

"If it is a messenger of death to this house," I said, "why should we fear, Lys?"

"Death should be welcome to those who love God," murmured Lys, and she drew the cross from her breast and kissed it.

"The moth might die if I threw it out into the storm," I said after a silence.

"Let it remain," sighed Lys.

Late that night my wife lay sleeping, and I sat beside her bed and read in the Chronicle of Jacques Sorgue. I shaded the candle, but Lys grew restless, and finally I took the book down into the morning room, where the ashes of the fire rustled and whitened on the hearth.

The death's-head moth lay on the rug before the fire where I had left it. At first I thought it was dead, but, when I looked closer I saw a lambent fire in its amber eyes. The straight white shadow it cast across the floor wavered as the candle flickered.

The pages of the Chronicle of Jacques Sorgue were damp and sticky; the illuminated gold and blue initials left flakes of azure and gilt where my hand brushed them.

"It is not paper at all; it is thin parchment," I said to myself; and I held the discoloured page close to the candle flame and read, translating laboriously:

"I, Jacques Sorgue, saw all these things. And I saw the Black Mass celebrated in the chapel of St. Gildas-on-the-Cliff. And it was said by the Abbé Sorgue, my kinsman: for which deadly sin the apostate priest was seized by the most noble Marquis of Plougastel and by him condemned to be burned with hot irons, until his seared soul quit its body and fly to its master the devil. But when the Black Priest lay in the crypt of Plougastel, his master Satan came at night and set him free, and carried him across land and sea to Mahmoud, which is Soldan or Saladin. And I, Jacques Sorgue, travelling afterward by sea, beheld with my own eyes my kinsman, the Black Priest of St. Gildas, borne along in the air upon a vast black wing, which was the wing of his master Satan. And this was seen also by two men of the crew."

I turned the page. The wings of the moth on the floor began to quiver. I read on and on, my eyes blurring under the shifting candle flame. I read of battles and of saints, and I learned how the great Soldan made his pact with Satan, and then I came to the Sieur de Trevec, and read how he seized the Black Priest in the midst of Saladin's tents and carried him away and cut off his head, first branding him on the forehead. "And before he suffered," said the Chronicle, "he cursed the Sieur de Trevec and his descendants, and he said he would surely return to St. Gildas. 'For the violence you do to me, I will do violence to you. For the evil I suffer at your hands, I will work evil on you and your descendants. Woe to your children, Sieur de Trevec!'" There was a whirr, a beating of strong wings, and my candle flashed up as in a sudden breeze. A humming filled the room; the great moth darted hither and thither, beating, buzzing, on ceiling and wall. I flung down my book and stepped forward. Now it lay fluttering upon the window sill, and for a moment I had it under my hand, but the thing squeaked and I shrank back. Then suddenly it darted across the candle flame; the light flared and went out, and at the same moment a shadow moved in the darkness outside. I raised my eyes to the window. A masked face was peering in at me.

Quick as thought I whipped out my revolver and fired every cartridge, but the face advanced beyond the window, the glass melting away before it like mist, and through the smoke of my revolver I saw something creep swiftly into the room. Then I tried to cry out, but the thing was at my throat, and I fell backward among the ashes of the hearth.

---

When my eyes unclosed I was lying on the hearth, my head among the cold ashes. Slowly I got on my knees, rose painfully, and groped my way to a chair. On the floor lay my revolver, shining in the pale light of early morning. My mind clearing by degrees, I looked, shuddering, at the window. The glass was unbroken. I stooped stiffly, picked up my revolver and opened the cylinder. Every cartridge had been fired. Mechanically I closed the cylinder and placed the revolver in my pocket. The book, the Chronicles of Jacques Sorgue, lay on the table beside me, and as I started to close it I glanced at the page. It was all splashed with rain, and the lettering had run, so that the page was merely a confused blur of gold and red and black. As I stumbled toward the door I cast a fearful glance over my shoulder. The death's-head moth crawled shivering on the rug.

## IV.

The sun was about three hours high. I must have slept, for I was aroused by the sudden gallop of horses under our window. People were shouting and calling in the road. I sprang up and opened the sash. Le Bihan was there, an image of helplessness, and Max Fortin stood beside him, polishing his glasses. Some gendarmes had just arrived from Quimperlé, and I could hear them around the corner of the house, stamping, and rattling their sabres and carbines, as they led their horses into my stable.

Lys sat up, murmuring half-sleepy, half-anxious questions.

"I don't know," I answered. "I am going out to see what it means."

"It is like the day they came to arrest you," Lys said, giving me a troubled look. But I kissed her, and laughed at her until she smiled too. Then I flung on coat and cap and hurried down the stairs.

The first person I saw standing in the road was the Brigadier Durand.

"Hello!" said I, "have you come to arrest me again? What the devil is all this fuss about, anyway?"

"We were telegraphed for an hour ago," said Durand briskly, "and for a sufficient reason, I think. Look there, Monsieur Darrel!"

He pointed to the ground almost under my feet.

"Good heavens!" I cried, "where did that puddle of blood come from?"

"That's what I want to know, Monsieur Darrel. Max Fortin found it at daybreak. See, it's splashed all over the grass, too. A trail of it leads into your garden, across the flower beds to your very window, the one that opens from the morning room. There is another trail leading from this spot across the road to the cliffs, then to the gravel pit, and thence across the moor to the forest of Kerselec. We are going to mount in a minute and search the bosquets. Will you join us? Bon Dieu! but the fellow bled like an ox. Max Fortin says it's human blood, or I should not have believed it."

The little chemist of Quimperlé came up at that moment, rubbing his glasses with a coloured handkerchief.

"Yes, it is human blood," he said, "but one thing puzzles me: the corpuscles are yellow. I never saw any human blood before with yellow corpuscles. But your English Doctor Thompson asserts that he has——"

"Well, it's human blood, anyway—isn't it?" insisted Durand, impatiently.

"Ye-es," admitted Max Fortin.

"Then it's my business to trail it," said the big gendarme, and he called his men and gave the order to mount.

"Did you hear anything last night?" asked Durand of me.

"I heard the rain. I wonder the rain did not wash away these traces."

"They must have come after the rain ceased. See this thick splash, how it lies over and weighs down the wet grass blades. Pah!"

It was a heavy, evil-looking clot, and I stepped back from it, my throat closing in disgust.

"My theory," said the brigadier, "is this: Some of those Biribi fishermen, probably the Icelanders, got an extra glass of cognac into their hides and quarrelled on the road. Some of them were slashed, and staggered to your house. But there is only one trail, and yet—and yet, how could all that blood come from only one person? Well, the wounded man, let us say, staggered first to your house and then back here, and he wandered off, drunk and dying, God knows where. That's my theory."

"A very good one," said I calmly. "And you are going to trail him?"

"Yes."

"When?"

"At once. Will you come?"

"Not now. I'll gallop over by-and-bye. You are going to the edge of the Kerselec forest?"

"Yes; you will hear us calling. Are you coming, Max Fortin? And you, Le Bihan? Good; take the dog-cart."

The big gendarme tramped around the corner to the stable and presently returned mounted on a strong gray horse; his sabre shone on his saddle; his pale yellow and white facings were spotless. The little crowd of white-coiffed women with their children fell back, as Durand touched spurs and clattered away followed by his two troopers. Soon after Le Bihan and Max Fortin also departed in the mayor's dingy dog-cart.

"Are you coming?" piped Le Bihan shrilly.

"In a quarter of an hour," I replied, and went back to the house.

When I opened the door of the morning room the death's-head moth was beating its strong wings against the window. For a second I hesitated, then walked over and opened the sash. The creature fluttered out, whirred over the flower beds a moment, then darted across the moorland toward the sea. I called the servants together and questioned them. Josephine, Catherine, Jean Marie Tregunc, not one of them had heard the slightest disturbance during the night. Then I told Jean Marie to saddle my horse, and while I was speaking Lys came down.

"Dearest," I began, going to her.

"You must tell me everything you know, Dick," she interrupted, looking me earnestly in the face.

"But there is nothing to tell—only a drunken brawl, and some one wounded."

"And you are going to ride—where, Dick?"

"Well, over to the edge of Kerselec forest. Durand and the mayor, and Max Fortin, have gone on, following a—a trail."

"What trail?"

"Some blood."

"Where did they find it?"

"Out in the road there." Lys crossed herself.

"Does it come near our house?"

"Yes."

"How near?"

"It comes up to the morning-room window," said I, giving in.

Her hand on my arm grew heavy. "I dreamed last night——"

"So did I——" but I thought of the empty cartridges in my revolver, and stopped.

"I dreamed that you were in great danger, and I could not move hand or foot to save you; but you had your revolver, and I called out to you to fire——"

"I did fire!" I cried excitedly.

"You—you fired?"

I took her in my arms. "My darling," I said, "something strange has happened—something that I can not understand as yet. But, of course, there is an explanation. Last night I thought I fired at the Black Priest."

"Ah!" gasped Lys.

"Is that what you dreamed?"

"Yes, yes, that was it! I begged you to fire——"

"And I did."

Her heart was beating against my breast. I held her close in silence.

"Dick," she said at length, "perhaps you killed the—the thing."

"If it was human I did not miss," I answered grimly. "And it was human," I went on, pulling myself together, ashamed of having so nearly gone to pieces. "Of course it was human! The whole affair is plain enough. Not a drunken brawl, as Durand thinks; it was a drunken lout's practical joke, for which he has suffered. I suppose I must have filled him pretty full of bullets, and he has crawled away to die in Kerselec forest. It's a terrible affair; I'm sorry I fired so hastily; but that idiot Le Bihan and Max Fortin have been working on my nerves till I am as hysterical as a schoolgirl," I ended angrily.

"You fired—but the window glass was not shattered," said Lys in a low voice.

"Well, the window was open, then. And as for the—the rest—I've got nervous indigestion, and a doctor will settle the Black Priest for me, Lys."

I glanced out of the window at Tregunc waiting with my horse at the gate.

"Dearest, I think I had better go to join Durand and the others."

"I will go too."

"Oh, no!"

"Yes, Dick."

"Don't, Lys."

"I shall suffer every moment you are away."

"The ride is too fatiguing, and we can't tell what unpleasant sight you may come upon. Lys, you don't really think there is anything supernatural in this affair?"

"Dick," she answered gently, "I am a Bretonne." With both arms around my neck, my wife said, "Death is the gift of God. I do not fear it when we are together. But alone—oh, my husband, I should fear a God who could take you away from me!"

We kissed each other soberly, simply, like two children. Then Lys hurried away to change her gown, and I paced up and down the garden waiting for her.

She came, drawing on her slender gauntlets. I swung her into the saddle, gave a hasty order to Jean Marie, and mounted.

Now, to quail under thoughts of terror on a morning like this, with Lys in the saddle beside me, no matter what had happened or might happen, was impossible. Moreover, Môme came sneaking after us. I asked Tregunc to catch him, for I was afraid he might be brained by our horses' hoofs if he followed, but the wily puppy dodged and bolted after Lys, who was trotting along the high-road. "Never mind," I thought; "if he's hit he'll live, for he has no brains to lose."

Lys was waiting for me in the road beside the Shrine of Our Lady of St. Gildas when I joined her. She crossed herself, I doffed my cap, then we shook out our bridles and galloped toward the forest of Kerselec.

We said very little as we rode. I always loved to watch Lys in the saddle. Her exquisite figure and lovely face were the incarnation of youth and grace; her curling hair glistened like threaded gold.

Out of the corner of my eye I saw the spoiled puppy Môme come bounding cheerfully alongside, oblivious of our horses' heels. Our road swung close to the cliffs. A filthy cormorant rose from the black rocks and flapped heavily across our path. Lys's horse reared, but she pulled him down, and pointed at the bird with her riding crop.

"I see," said I; "it seems to be going our way. Curious to see a cormorant in a forest, isn't it?"

"It is a bad sign," said Lys. "You know the Morbihan proverb: 'When the cormorant turns from the sea, Death laughs in the forest, and wise woodsmen build boats.'"

"I wish," said I sincerely, "that there were fewer proverbs in Brittany."

We were in sight of the forest now; across the gorse I could see the sparkle of gendarmes' trappings, and the glitter of Le Bihan's silver-buttoned jacket. The hedge was low and we took it without difficulty, and trotted across the moor to where Le Bihan and Durand stood gesticulating.

They bowed ceremoniously to Lys as we rode up.

"The trail is horrible—it is a river," said the mayor in his squeaky voice. "Monsieur Darrel, I think perhaps madame would scarcely care to come any nearer."

Lys drew bridle and looked at me.

"It is horrible!" said Durand, walking up beside me; "it looks as though a bleeding regiment had passed this way. The trail winds and winds about there in the thickets; we lose it at times, but we always find it again. I can't understand how one man—no, nor twenty—could bleed like that!"

A halloo, answered by another, sounded from the depths of the forest.

"It's my men; they are following the trail," muttered the brigadier. "God alone knows what is at the end!"

"Shall we gallop back, Lys?" I asked.

"No; let us ride along the western edge of the woods and dismount. The sun is so hot now, and I should like to rest for a moment," she said.

"The western forest is clear of anything disagreeable," said Durand.

"Very well," I answered; "call me, Le Bihan, if you find anything."

Lys wheeled her mare, and I followed across the springy heather, Môme trotting cheerfully in the rear.

We entered the sunny woods about a quarter of a kilometre from where we left Durand. I took Lys from her horse, flung both bridles over a limb, and, giving my wife my arm, aided her to a flat mossy rock which overhung a shallow brook gurgling among the beech trees. Lys sat down and drew off her gauntlets. Môme pushed his head into her lap, received an undeserved caress, and came doubtfully toward me. I was weak enough to condone his offence, but I made him lie down at my feet, greatly to his disgust.

I rested my head on Lys's knees, looking up at the sky through the crossed branches of the trees.

"I suppose I have killed him," I said. "It shocks me terribly, Lys."

"You could not have known, dear. He may have been a robber, and—if—not— — Did—have you ever fired your revolver since that day four years ago, when the Red Admiral's son tried to kill you? But I know you have not."

"No," said I, wondering. "It's a fact, I have not. Why?"

"And don't you remember that I asked you to let me load it for you the day when Yves went off, swearing to kill you and his father?"

"Yes, I do remember. Well?"

"Well, I—I took the cartridges first to St. Gildas chapel and dipped them in holy water. You must not laugh, Dick," said Lys gently, laying her cool hands on my lips.

"Laugh, my darling!"

Overhead the October sky was pale amethyst, and the sunlight burned like orange flame through the yellow leaves of beech and oak. Gnats and midges danced and wavered overhead; a spider dropped from a twig halfway to the ground and hung suspended on the end of his gossamer thread.

"Are you sleepy, dear?" asked Lys, bending over me.

"I am—a little; I scarcely slept two hours last night," I answered.

"You may sleep, if you wish," said Lys, and touched my eyes caressingly.

"Is my head heavy on your knees?"

"No, Dick."

I was already in a half doze; still I heard the brook babbling under the beeches and the humming of forest flies overhead. Presently even these were stilled.

The next thing I knew I was sitting bolt upright, my ears ringing with a scream, and I saw Lys cowering beside me, covering her white face with both hands.

As I sprang to my feet she cried again and clung to my knees. I saw my dog rush growling into a thicket, then I heard him whimper, and he came backing out, whining, ears flat, tail down. I stooped and disengaged Lys's hand.

"Don't go, Dick!" she cried. "O God, it's the Black Priest!"

In a moment I had leaped across the brook and pushed my way into the thicket. It was empty. I stared about me; I scanned every tree trunk, every bush. Suddenly I saw him. He was seated on a fallen log, his head resting in his hands, his rusty black robe gathered around him. For a moment my hair stirred under my cap; sweat started on forehead and cheek-bone; then I recovered my reason, and understood that the man was human and was probably wounded to death. Ay, to death; for there, at my feet, lay the wet trail of blood, over leaves and stones, down into the little hollow, across to the figure in black resting silently under the trees.

I saw that he could not escape even if he had the strength, for before him, almost at his very feet, lay a deep, shining swamp.

As I stepped forward my foot broke a twig. At the sound the figure started a little, then its head fell forward again. Its face was masked. Walking up to the man, I bade him tell where he was wounded. Durand and the others broke through the thicket at the same moment and hurried to my side.

"Who are you who hide a masked face in a priest's robe?" said the gendarme loudly.

There was no answer.

"See—see the stiff blood all over his robe!" muttered Le Bihan to Fortin.

"He will not speak," said I.

"He may be too badly wounded," whispered Le Bihan.

"I saw him raise his head," I said; "my wife saw him creep up here."

Durand stepped forward and touched the figure.

"Speak!" he said.

"Speak!" quavered Fortin.

Durand waited a moment, then with a sudden upward movement he stripped off the mask and threw back the man's head. We were looking into the eye sockets of a skull. Durand stood rigid; the mayor shrieked. The skeleton burst out from its rotting robes and collapsed on the ground before us. From between the staring ribs and the grinning teeth spurted a torrent of black blood, showering the shrinking grasses; then the thing shuddered, and fell over into the black ooze of the bog. Little bubbles of iridescent air appeared from the mud; the bones were slowly engulfed, and, as the last fragments sank out of sight, up from the depths and along the bank crept a creature, shiny, shivering, quivering its wings.

It was a death's-head moth.

I wish I had time to tell you how Lys outgrew superstitions—for she never knew the truth about the affair, and she never will know, since she has promised not to read this book. I wish I might tell you about the king and his coronation, and how the coronation robe fitted. I wish that I were able to write how Yvonne and Herbert Stuart rode to a boar hunt in Quimperlé, and how the hounds raced the quarry right through the town, overturning three gendarmes, the notary, and an old woman. But I am becoming garrulous, and Lys is calling me to come and hear the king say that he is sleepy. And his Highness shall not be kept waiting.

## THE KING'S CRADLE SONG.

Seal with a seal of gold
The scroll of a life unrolled;
Swathe him deep in his purple stole;
Ashes of diamonds, crystalled coal,
Drops of gold in each scented fold.
Crimson wings of the Little Death,
Stir his hair with your silken breath;
Flaming wings of sins to be,
Splendid pinions of prophecy,
Smother his eyes with hues and dyes,
While the white moon spins and the winds arise,
And the stars drip through the skies.
Wave, O wings of the Little Death!
Seal his sight and stifle his breath,
Cover his breast with the gemmed shroud pressed;
From north to north, from west to west,
Wave, O wings of the Little Death!
Till the white moon reels in the cracking skies,
And the ghosts of God arise.

# THE WHITE SHADOW

We are no other than a moving row
Of magic shadow-shapes, that come and go
Round with this sun-illumined lantern, held
In midnight by the master of the show.
A moment's halt—a momentary taste
Of being from the well amid the waste—
And lo! the phantom caravan has reached
The nothing it set out from. Oh, make haste!
Ah, Love! could you and I with him conspire
To grasp this sorry scheme of things entire,
Would not we shatter it to bits—and then
Remould it nearer to the heart's desire!
FITZGERALD.

---

## THE WHITE SHADOW.

Listen, then, love, and with your white hand clear
Your forehead from its cloudy hair.

### I.

"Three great hulking cousins," said she, closing her gray eyes disdainfully.

We accepted the rebuke in astonished silence. Presently she opened her eyes, and seemed surprised to see us there yet.

"O," she said, "if you think I am going to stay here until you make up your minds——"

"I've made up mine," said Donald. "We will go to the links. You may come."

"I shall not," she announced. "Walter, what do you propose?"

Walter looked at his cartridge belt and then at the little breech-loader standing in a corner of the arbour.

"Oh, I know," she said, "but I won't! I won't! I won't!"

The uncles and aunts on the piazza turned to look at us; her mother arose from a steamer-chair and came across the lawn.

"Won't what, Sweetheart?" she asked, placing both hands on her daughter's shoulders.

"Mamma, Walter wants me to shoot, and Don wants me to play golf, and I—won't!"

"She doesn't know what she wants," said I.

"Don't I?" she said, flushing with displeasure.

"Her mother might suggest something," hazarded Donald. We looked at our aunt.

"Sweetheart is spoiled," said that lady decisively. "If you children don't go away at once and have a good time, I shall find employment for her."

"Algebra?" I asked maliciously.

"How dare you!" cried Sweetheart, sitting up. "Oh, isn't he mean! isn't he ignoble!—and I've done my algebra; haven't I, mamma?"

"But your French?" I began.

Donald laughed, and so did Walter. As for Sweetheart, she arose in all the dignity of sixteen years, closed her eyes with superb insolence, and, clasping her mother's waist with one round white arm, marched out of the arbour.

"We tease her too much," said Donald.

"She's growing up fast; we ought not to call her 'Sweetheart' when she puts her hair up," added Walter.

"She's going to put it up in October, when she goes back to school," said Donald. "Jack, she will hate you if you keep reminding her of her algebra and French."

"Then I'll stop," said I, suddenly conscious what an awful thing it would be if she hated me.

Donald's two pointers came frisking across the lawn from the kennels, and Donald picked up his gun.

"Here we go again," said I. "Donny's going to the coverts after grouse, Walter's going up on the hill with his dust-shot and arsenic, and I'm going across the fields after butterflies. Why the deuce can't we all go together, just for once?"

"And take Sweetheart? She would like it if we all went together," said Walter; "she is tired of seeing Jack net butterflies."

"Collecting birds and shooting grouse are two different things," began Donald. "You spoil my dogs by shooting your confounded owls and humming birds."

"Oh, your precious dogs!" I cried. "Shut up, Donny, and give Sweetheart a good day's tramp. It's a pity if three cousins can't pool their pleasures for once."

Donald nodded uncertainly.

"Come on," said Walter, "we'll find Sweetheart. Jack, you get your butterfly togs and come back here."

I nodded, and watched my two cousins sauntering across the lawn—big, clean-cut fellows, resembling each other enough to be brothers instead of cousins.

We all resembled each other more or less, Donald, Walter, and I. As for Sweetheart, she looked like none of us.

It was all very well for her mother to call her Sweetheart, and for her aunts to echo it in chorus, but the time was coming when we saw we should have to stop. A girl of sixteen with such a name is ridiculous, and Sweetheart was nearly seventeen; and her hair was "going up" and her gowns were "coming down" in October.

Her own name was pretty enough. I don't know that I ought to tell it, but I will: it was the same as her mother's. We called her Sweetheart sometimes, sometimes "The Aspen Beauty." Donald had given her that name from a butterfly in my collection, the Vanessa Pandora, commonly known as the Aspen beauty, from its never having been captured in America except in our village of Aspen.

Here, in the north of New York State, we four cousins spent our summers in the family house. There was not much to do in Aspen. We used the links, we galloped over the sandy roads, we also trotted our several hobbies, Donald, Walter, and I. Sweetheart had no hobby; to make up for this, however, she owned a magnificent team of bêtes-noires—Algebra and French.

As for me, my butterfly collection languished. I had specimens of nearly every butterfly in New York State, and I rather longed for new states to conquer. Anyway, there were plenty of Aspen beauties—I mean the butterflies—flying about the roads and balm-of-Gilead trees, and perhaps that is why I lingered there long enough to collect hundreds of duplicates for exchange. And perhaps it wasn't.

I thought of these things as I sat in the sun-flecked arbour, watching the yellow elm leaves flutter down from the branches. I thought, too, of Sweetheart, and wondered how she would look with her hair up. And while I sat there smoking, watching the yellow leaves drifting across the lawn, a sharp explosion startled me and I raised my head.

Sweetheart was standing on the lawn, gazing dreamily at the smoking débris of a large firecracker.

"What's that for?" I asked.

"It proclaims my independence," said Sweetheart—"my independence forever. Hereafter my cousins will ask to accompany me on my walks; they need no longer charitably permit me to accompany them. Are you three boys going to ride your hobbies?"

"We are," I said.

"Then good-bye. I am going to walk."

"Can't we come too?" I asked, laughing.

"Oh," she said graciously, "if you put it in that way I could not refuse."

"May we bring our guns?" asked Donald from the piazza.

"May I bring my net?" I added, half amused, half annoyed.

She made a gesture, indifferent, condescending.

"Dear me!" murmured the aunts in chorus from the piazza as we trooped after the Aspen beauty, "Sweetheart is growing very fast."

I smiled vaguely at Sweetheart. I was wondering how she would look in long frocks and coiled hair.

## II.

In the fall of the year the meadows of Aspen glimmer in the sunlight like crumpled sheets of beaten gold; for Aspen is the land of golden-rod, of yellow earth and gilded fern.

There the crisp oaks rustle, every leaf a blot of yellow; there the burnished pines sound, sound, tremble, and resound, like gilt-stringed harps aquiver in the wind.

Sweet fern, sun-dried, bronzed, fills all the hills with incense, vague and delicate as the white down drifting from the frothy milkweed.

And where the meadow brook prattled, limpid, filtered with sunlight, Sweetheart stood knee-deep in fragrant mint, watching the aimless minnows swimming in circles. On a distant hill, dark against the blue, Donald moved with his dogs, and I saw the sun-glint on his gun, and I heard the distant "Hi—on! Hi—on!" long after he disappeared below the brown hill's brow.

Walter, too, had gone, leaving us there by the brook together, Sweetheart and I; and I saw the crows flapping and circling far over the woods, and I heard the soft report of his dust-shot shells among the trees.

"The ruling passion, Sweetheart," I said. "Donny chases the phantom of pleasure with his dogs. The phantom flies from Walter, and he follows with his dust-shot."

"Then," said Sweetheart, "follow your phantom also; there are butterflies everywhere." She raised both arms and turned from the brook. "Everywhere flying I see butterflies—phantoms of pleasure; and, Jack, you do not follow with your net."

"No," said I, "the world to-day is too fair to—slay in. I even doubt that the happiness of empires hinges on the discovery of a new species of anything. Do I bore you?"

"A little," said Sweetheart, touching the powdered gold of the blossoms about her. She laid the tip of her third finger on her lips and then on the golden-rod. "I shall not pick it; the world is too fair to-day," she said. "What are you going to do, Jack?"

"I could doze," I said. "Could you?"

"Yes—if you told me stories."

I contemplated her in silence for a moment. After a while she sat down under an oak and clasped her hands.

"I am growing so old," she sighed, "I no longer take pleasure in childish things—Donald's dogs, Walter's humming birds, your butterflies. Jack?"

"What?"

"Sit down on the grass."

"What for?"

"Because I ask you."

I sat down.

Presently she said: "I am as tall as mamma. Why should I study algebra?"

"Because," I answered evasively.

"Your answer is as rude as though I were twenty, instead of sixteen," said Sweetheart. "If you treat me as a child from this moment, I shall hate you."

"Me—Sweetheart?"

"And that name!—it is good for children and kittens."

I looked at her seriously. "It is good for women, too—when it is time," I said. "I prophesy that one day you will hear it again. As for me, I shall not call you by that name if you dislike it."

"I am a woman—now," she said.

"Oh! at sixteen."

"To-morrow I am to be seventeen."

Presently, looking off at the blue hills, I said: "For a long time I have recognised that that subtle, indefinable attitude—we call it deference—due from men to women is due from us to you. Donny and Walter are slower to accept this. You know what you have been to us as a child; we can't bear to lose you—to meet you in another way—to reckon with you as we reckon with a woman. But it is true: our little Sweetheart has vanished, and—*you* are here!"

The oak leaves began to rustle in the hill winds; the crows cawed from the woods.

"Oui c'est moi," she said at length.

"I shall never call you Sweetheart again," I said, smiling.

"Who knows?" she laughed, and leaned over to pick a blade of wild wheat. She coloured faintly a moment later, and said: "I didn't mean that, Jack."

And so Sweetheart took her first step across that threshold of mystery, the Temple of Idols. And of the gilded idols within the temple, one shall turn to living flesh at the sound of a voice. And lo! where a child had entered, a woman returned with the key to the Temple of Gilded Idols.

"Jack," said Sweetheart, "you are wrong. No day is too fair to kill in. I shall pick my arms full—full of flowers."

Over the yellow fields, red with the stalks of the buckwheat, crowned with a glimmering cloud of the dusty gold of the golden-rod, Sweetheart passed, pensive, sedate, awed by the burden of sixteen years.

I followed.

Over the curling fern and wind-stirred grasses the silken milkweed seeds sailed, sailed, and the great red-brown butterflies drifted above, ruddy as autumn leaves aglow in the sun.

"On the sand-cliff there are marigolds," said Sweetheart.

I looked at the mass of wild flowers in her arms; her white polished skin reflected the blaze of colour, warming like ivory under their glow.

"Marigolds," I repeated; "we will get some."

"The sand slides on the face of the cliff; you must be careful," she said.

"And I may see one of those rare cliff butterflies. I haven't any good examples."

I fancy she was not listening; the crows were clamouring above the beech woods; the hill winds filled our ears with a sound like the sound of the sea on shoals. Her gray eyes, touched with the sky's deep blue and the blue of the misty hills, looked out across the miles of woods and fields, and saw a world; not a world old, scarred, rock-ribbed, and salt with tears, but a new world, youthful, ripe, sunny, hazy with the splendour of wonders hidden behind the horizon—a world jewelled with gems, spanned by rose-mist rainbows—a world of sixteen years.

"We are already at the cliff's edge," I said.

She stepped to the edge and looked over. I drew her back. The sand started among the rocks, running, running with a sound like silver water.

"Then you shall not go either," she said. "I do not care for marigolds."

But I was already on the edge, stooping for a blossom. The next instant I fell.

There was a whistle of sand, a flurry and a rush of wind, a blur of rock, fern, dead grasses—a cry!

For I remember as I fell, falling I called, "Sweetheart!" and again "Sweetheart!" Then my body struck the rocks below.

### III.

Of all the seconds that tick the whole year through, of all the seconds that have slipped onward marking the beat of time since time was loosed, there is one, one brief moment, steeped in magic and heavy with oblivion, that sometimes lingers in the soul of man, annihilating space and time. If, at the feet of God, a year is a second passed unnoted, this magic second, afloat on the tide of time, moves on and on till, caught in the vortex of some life's whirl, it sinks into the soul of a being near to death.

And in that soul the magic second glows and lingers, stretching into minutes, hours, days—aye, days and days, till, if the magic hold, the calm years crowd on one by one; and yet it all is but a second—that magic moment that comes on the tide of time—that came to me and was caught up in my life's whirl as I fell, dropping there between sky and earth.

And so that magic moment grew to minutes, to hours; and when my body, whirling, pitching, struck and lay flung out on the earth, the magic second grew until the crystal days fell from my life, as beads, one by one, fall from the rosaries that saints tell kneeling.

Those days of a life that I have lived, those years that linger still aglow in the sun behind me, dim yet splendid as dust-dimmed jewels, they also have ended, not in vague night, but in the sunburst of another second—such a second as ticks from my watch as I write, quick, sharp, joyous, irrevocable! So, of that magic second, or day, or year, I shall tell—I, as I was, standing beside my body flung there across the earth.

I looked at my body, lying in a heap, then turned to the sand cliff smiling.

"Sweetheart!" I called.

But she was already at my side.

We walked on through fragrant pastures, watching the long shadows stretch from field to field, speaking of what had been and of all that was to be. It was so simple—everything was clear before us. Had there been doubts, fears, sudden alarms, startled heartbeats?

If there had been, now they were ended forever.

"Not forever," said Sweetheart; "who knows how long the magic second may last?"

"But we—what difference can that make?" I asked.

"To us?"

"Yes."

"None," said Sweetheart decisively.

We looked out into the west. The sun turned to a mound of cinders; the hills loomed in opalescent steam.

"But—but—your shadow!" said Sweetheart.

I bent my head, thrilled with happiness.

"And yours," I whispered.

The shadows we cast were whiter than snow.

I still heard the hill winds, soft in my ears as breaking surf; a bird-note came from the dusky woodland; a star broke out overhead.

"What is your pleasure, Sweetheart, now all is said?" I asked.

"The world is all so fair," she sighed; "is it fairer beyond the hills, Jack?"

"It is fair where you pass by, north, south, and from west to west again. In France the poplars are as yellow as our oaks. In Morbihan the gorse gilds all the hills, yellow as golden-rod. Shall we go?"

"But in the spring—let us wait until spring."

"Where?"

"Here."

"Until spring?"

"It is written that Time shall pass as a shadow across the sea. What is that book there under your feet—that iron-bound book, half embedded like a stone in the grass."

"I did not see it!"

"Bring it to me."

I raised the book; it left a bare mark in the sod as a stone that is turned. Then, holding it on my knees, I opened it, and Sweetheart, leaning on my shoulder, read. The tall stars flared like candles, flooding the page with diamond light; the earth, perfumed with blossoms, stirred with the vague vibration of countless sounds, tiny voices swaying breathless in the hidden surge of an endless harmony.

"The white shadow is the shadow of the soul," she read. Even the winds were hushed as her sweet lips moved.

"And what shall make thee to understand what hell is?... When the sun shall be folded up as a garment that is laid away; when the stars fall, and the seas boil, and when souls shall be joined again to their bodies; and when the girl who hath been buried alive shall be asked for what crime; when books shall be laid open, when hell shall burn fiercely, and when paradise shall be brought very near:

"Every soul shall know what it hath wrought!"

I closed my eyes; the splendour of the starlight on the page was more than my eyes could bear.

But she read on; for what can dim her eyes?

"O man, verily, labouring, thou labourest to meet thy LORD.

"And thou shalt meet HIM!

"When the earth shall be stretched like a skin, and shall cast forth that which is therein;

"By the heaven adorned with signs, by the witness and the witnessed;

"By that which appeareth by night; by the daybreak and the ten nights—the ten nights;

"The night of Al Kadr is better than a thousand months.

"Praise be to God, the Lord of all creatures; the Most Merciful, the King of the Day of Judgment. Thee do we worship, and of thee do we beg assistance. Direct us in the right way, in the way of those to whom thou hast been gracious; not of those against whom thou art incensed, nor of those who go astray!"

In the sudden silence that spread across earth and heaven I heard the sound of a voice under the earth, calling, calling, calling.

"It is already spring," said Sweetheart; and she rose, placing her white hands in mine. "Shall we go?"

"But we are already there," I stammered, turning my eyes fearfully; for the tall pines dwindled and clustered and rose again cool and gray in the morning air, all turned to stone, fretted and carved like lacework; and where the pines had faded, the twin towers of a cathedral loomed; and where the hills swept across the horizon, the roofs of a white city glimmered in the morning sun. Bridges and quays and streets and domes and the hum of traffic and rattle of arms; and over all, the veil of haze and the twin gray towers of Notre Dame!

"Sweetheart!" I faltered.

But we were already in my studio.

## IV.

The studio had not changed. The sun flooded it.

Sweetheart sat in the broken armchair and watched me struggle with the packing. Every now and then she made an impulsive movement toward the heap of clothes on the floor, which I checked with a "Thanks! I can fix it all alone, Sweetheart."

Clifford seemed to extract amusement from it all, and said as much to Rowden, who was as usual ruining my zitherine by trying to play it like a banjo.

Elliott, knowing he could be of no use to us, had the decency to sit outside the studio on one of the garden benches. He appeared at intervals at the studio door, saying, "Come along, Clifford; they don't want you messing about. Drop that banjo, Rowden, or Jack will break your head with it—won't you, Jack?"

I said I would, but not with the zitherine.

Clifford flatly refused to move unless Sweetheart would take him out into our garden and show him the solitary goldfish which lurked in the fountain under the almond trees. But Sweetheart, apparently fascinated by the mysteries of packing, turned a deaf ear to Clifford's blandishments and Rowden's discords.

"I imagined," said Clifford, somewhat hurt, "that you would delight in taking upon yourself the duties of a hostess. I should be pleased to believe that I am not an unwelcome guest."

"So should I," echoed Rowden; "I'd be pleased too."

"What a shame for you to bother, Jack!" she said. "Mr. Clifford shall go and make some tea directly. Mr. Rowden, you may take a table out by the fountain—and stay there."

Clifford, motioning Elliott to take the other end of the Japanese table, backed with it through the hallway and out to the gravel walk, expostulating.

"The sugar is there in that tin box by the model stand," she said, when he re-appeared, "and the extra spoons are lying in a long box on Jack's big easel."

When Rowden, reluctantly relinquishing the zitherine, followed Clifford, bearing the cups and alcohol lamp, I raised my head and wiped the dust from my forehead. I believe I swore a little in French. Sweetheart looked startled. She knew more French than I supposed she did.

"What is it, Jack?"

"Mais—rien, ça m'embête—cette espèce de malle——"

"Then why won't you let me help you, Jack? I can at least put in my gowns."

"But I must pack my colour box first, and the gun case, and the box of reels, and the pastel case, and our shooting boots, and the water-colour box, and the cartridge belt, and your golf shoes, and——"

"O dear!" said Sweetheart with a shudder.

I stood up and scowled at the trunk.

"To look at you, Jack," murmured Sweetheart, "one might think you unhappy."

Unhappy! At the thought our eyes met across the table.

"Unhappy!" I whispered.

Then Clifford came stumbling in, wearing a pair of Joseph's sabots, and, imitating that faithful domestic in voice and manner, invited us to tea under the lilacs and almond blossoms.

"In a moment," cried Sweetheart impatiently. "Go and pour the tea."

Clifford looked aghast. "No, no!" he cried; "it's impossible—I won't believe that you two are deliberately getting rid of me so you can be alone to spoon! And your honeymoon already a year old, and——"

Sweetheart frowned, and tapped her foot.

Clifford retired indignant.

Then she raised her eyes to mine, and a delicate colour stained her cheeks and neck.

"Yes," I said, "we have been married nearly a year, Sweetheart."

We looked at our white shadows on the floor.

## V.

Sweetheart sat under the lilac blossoms pouring out tea for Clifford, Elliott, and Rowden. She was gracious to Clifford, gentle to Elliott, and she took Rowden under her wing in the sweetest way possible, to which Clifford stated his objections.

"Mr. Rowden is younger than you are," she said gravely. "Monsieur Clifford, I do not wish you to torment him."

"Rowden's no baby; he's as old as Jack is, and Jack doesn't murder music."

"I am glad to see you acknowledge Jack's superiority in all matters," said Sweetheart with a dangerous smile.

"I don't," cried Clifford laughing; "and I don't see what you find to care about in a man who clips his hair like a gendarme and paints everything purple."

"Everything is purple—if Jack paints it so," said Sweetheart, smiling at her reflected face in the water. She stood at the rim of the little stone fountain with her hands clasped behind her back. Elliott and Clifford were poking about in the water plants to dislodge the solitary goldfish, while Rowden gathered dewy clusters of lilacs as an offering.

"There he goes!" said Elliott.

"Poor fellow, living there all alone!" said Sweetheart. "Jack must leave word with Joseph to get him a little lady fish to pay his court to."

"Better put in another gentleman fish, then, if you're following Nature," said Clifford, with an attempt at cynicism which drew the merriest laugh from Sweetheart.

"Oh, how funny is Monsieur Clifford when he wants to be like Frenchmen!" she murmured.

"Jack," said Elliott, as I came from the studio and picked up a cup of tea grown cold, "Clifford's doing the world-worn disenchanted roué."

"And—and I fear he will next make love to me!" cried Sweetheart.

"You'd better look out, Jack," said Clifford darkly, and pretended to sulk until Sweetheart sent him off to buy the bonbons she would need for the train.

"They're packed," I said, "every trunk of them!"

Sweetheart was enchanted. "All my new gowns, and the shoes from Rix's—O Jack, you didn't forget the shoes—and the bath robes—and——"

"All packed," I said, swallowing the tea with a wry face.

"Oh," she cried reproachfully, "don't drink that! Here, I will have some hot tea in a moment," and she ran over and perched on the arm of the garden bench while I lighted the alcohol lamp and then a cigarette.

Rowden came up with his offering of lilacs, and she decorated each of us with a spray.

It was growing late. The long shadows fell across the gravel walks and flecked the white walls of the sculptor's studio opposite.

"It's the nine-o'clock train, isn't it?" said Elliott.

"We will meet you at the station at eight-thirty," added Rowden.

"You don't mind, do you, our dining alone?" said Sweetheart shyly; "it's our last day—Jack's and mine—in the old studio."

"Not the last, I hope," said Elliott sincerely.

We all sat silent for a moment.

"O Paris, Paris—how I fear it!" murmured Sweetheart to me; and in the same breath, "No, no, we must love it, you and I."

Then Elliott said aloud, "I suppose you have no idea when you will return?"

"No," I replied, thinking of the magic second that had become a year.

And so we dined alone, Sweetheart and I, in the old studio.

At half-past eight o'clock the cab stood at the gate with all our traps piled on top, and Joseph and his wife and the two brats were crying, "Au revoir, madame! au revoir, monsieur! We will keep the studio well dusted. Bon voyage! bon voyage!" and all of a sudden my arm was caught by Sweetheart's little gloved hand, and she drew me back through the long ivy-covered alley to the garden where the studio stood, its doorway closed and silent, the hollow windows black and grim. Truly the light had passed away with the passing of Sweetheart. Her hand slipped from my arm, and she went and knelt down at the threshold and kissed it.

"I first knew happiness when I first crossed it," she said; "it breaks my heart to leave it. Only that magic second! but it seems years that we have lived here."

"It was you who brought happiness to it," I said.

"Good-bye! good-bye, dear, dear, old studio!" she cried. "Oh, if Jack is always the same to me as he has been here—if he will be faithful and true in that new home!"

The new home was to be in a strange land. Sweetheart was a little frightened, but was dying to go there. Sweetheart had never seen the golden gorse ablaze on the moors of Morbihan.

## VI.

I went inside the brass railing and waited my turn to buy the tickets. When it came, I took two first class to Quimperlé, for it was to be an all-night ride, and there was no sleeping car. Clifford had taken charge of the baggage, and I went with him to have it registered, leaving Sweetheart with Elliott and Rowden. All the traps were there—the big trunks, the big valises, my sketching kit, the zitherine in a leather case, two handbags, a bundle of umbrellas and canes, and a huge package of canvases. The toilet case and the rugs and waterproofs we took with us into the compartment.

The compartment was empty. Sweetheart nestled into one corner, and when I had placed our traps in the racks overhead I sat down opposite, while Clifford handed in our sandwiches, a bottle of red wine, and Sweetheart's box of bonbons.

We didn't say much; most had been said before starting. Clifford was more affected than he cared to show—I know by the way he grasped my hand. They are dear fellows, every one. We did not realize that we were actually going—going, perhaps, forever. She laughed, and chatted, and made fun of Clifford, and teased Rowden, aided and abetted by Elliott, until the starting gong clanged and a warning whistle sounded along the gaslit platform.

"Jack," cried Clifford, leaning in the window, "God bless you! God bless you both!"

Elliott touched her hand and wrung mine, and Rowden risked his neck to give us both one last cordial grasp.

"Count on me—on us," cried Clifford, speaking in English, "if you are— troubled!"

By what, my poor Clifford? Can you, with all your gay courage, turn back the hands of the dials? Can you, with all your warm devotion, add one second to the magic second and make it two? The shadows we cast are white.

The train stole out into the night, and I saw them grouped on the platform, silhouettes in the glare of the yellow signals. I drew in my head and shut the window. Sweetheart's face had grown very serious, but now she smiled across from her corner.

"Aren't you coming over by me, Jack?"

## VII.

We must have been moving very swiftly, for the car rocked and trembled, and it was probably that which awoke me. I looked across at Sweetheart. She was lying on her side, one cheek resting on her gloved hand, her travelling cap pushed back, her eyes shut. I smoothed away the curly strands of hair which straggled across her cheeks, and tucked another rug well about her feet. Her feet were small as a child's. I speak as if she were not a child. She was eighteen then.

The next time I awoke we lay in a long gaslit station. Some soldiers were disembarking from the forward carriages, and a gendarme stalked up and down the platform.

I looked sleepily about for the name of the station. It was painted in blue over the buffet—"Petit St. Yves." "Is it possible we are in Brittany?" I thought. Then the voices of the station hands, who were hoisting a small boat upon the forward carriage, settled my doubts. "Allons! tire hardiment, Jean Louis! mets le cannotte deboutte."

"Arrête toi Yves! doucement! doucement! Sacrée garce!"

Somewhere in the darkness a mellow bell tolled. I settled back to slumber, my eyes on Sweetheart.

She slept.

## VIII.

I awoke in a flood of brightest sunshine. From our window I could look into the centre of a most enchanting little town, all built of white limestone and granite. The June sunshine slanted on thatched roof and painted gable, and fairly blazed on the little river slipping by under the stone bridge in the square.

The streets and the square were alive with rosy-faced women in white headdresses. Everywhere the constant motion of blue skirts and spotless coiffes, the twinkle of varnished socks, the clump! clump! of sabots.

Like a black shadow a priest stole across the square. Above him the cross on the church glowed like a live cinder, flashing its reflection along the purple-slated roof from the eaves of which a cloud of ash-gray pigeons drifted into the gutter below. I turned from the window to encounter Sweetheart's eyes. Her lips moved a little, her long lashes heavy with slumber drooped lower, then with a little sigh she sat bolt upright. When I laughed, as I always did, she smiled, a little confused, a little ashamed, murmuring: "Bonjour, mon chéri! Quelle heure est-il?" That was always the way Sweetheart awoke.

"O dear, I am so rumpled!" she said. "Jack, get me the satchel this minute, and don't look at me until I ask you to."

I unlocked the satchel, and then turning to the window again threw it wide open. Oh, how sweet came the morning air from the meadows! Some young fellows below on the bank of the stream were poking long cane fishing-rods under the arches of the bridge.

"Sweetheart," I said over my shoulder, "I believe there are trout in this stream."

"Mr. Elliott says that whenever you see a puddle you always say that," she replied.

"What does he know about it?" I answered, for I am touchy on the subject; "he doesn't know a catfish from a—a dogfish."

"Neither do I, Jack dear, but I'm going to learn. Don't be cross."

She had finished her toilet and came over to the window, leaning out over my shoulder.

"Where are we?" she cried in startled wonder at the little white town and the acres of swaying clover. "Oh, Jack, is—is this the country?"

A man in uniform passing under our window looked up surprised.

"What are you doing here?" he demanded; then, seeing Sweetheart, he took off his gold-laced cap, and added, with a bow: "This carriage goes no farther, monsieur—madame——"

"Merci!" exclaimed Sweetheart, "we wish to go to Quimperlé!"

"And we have tickets for Quimperlé," I insisted.

"But," smiled the official, "this is Quimperlé."

It was true. There was the name written over the end of the station; and, looking ahead, I saw that our car had been detached and was standing in stately seclusion under the freight shed. How long it had been standing so Heaven alone knows; but they evidently had neglected to call us, and there we were inhabiting a detached carriage in the heart of Quimperlé. I managed to get a couple of porters, and presently we found all our traps piled up on the platform, and a lumbering vehicle with a Breton driver waiting to convey us to the hotel.

"Which," said I to the docile Breton, "is the best hotel in Quimperlé?"

"The Hôtel Lion d'Or," he replied.

"How do you know?" I demanded.

"Because," said he mildly, "it is the only hotel in Quimperlé."

Sweetheart observed that this ought to be convincing, even to me, and she tormented me all the way to the square, where I got even by pretending to be horrified at her dishevelled condition incident to a night's railway ride in a stuffy compartment.

"Don't, Jack! people will look at us."

"Let 'em."

"Oh, this is cruel! Oh, I'll pay you for this!"

And they did look at us—or rather at her; for from the time Sweetheart and I had cast our lots together, I noticed that I seemed to escape the observation of passers-by. When I lived alone in Paris I attracted a fair share of observation from the world as it wagged on its Parisian way. It was pleasant to meet a pretty girl's eyes now and then in the throng which flowed through the park and boulevard. I really never flattered myself that it was because of my personal beauty; but in Paris, any young fellow who is dressed in the manner of Albion, hatted and gloved in the same style, is not entirely a cipher. But now it was not the same, by a long shot.

Sweetheart's beauty simply put me in my place as an unnoticed but perhaps correct supplement to her.

She knew she was a beauty, and was delighted when she looked into her mirror. Nothing escaped her. The soft hair threaded with sunshine, which, when loosened, curled to her knees; the clear white forehead and straight brows; the nose delicate and a trifle upturned; the scarlet lips and fine cut chin—she knew the value of each of these. She was pleased with the soft, full curve of her throat, the little ears, and the colour which came and went in her cheeks.

But her eyes were the first thing one noticed. They were the most beautiful gray eyes that ever opened under silken lashes. She approved of my telling her this, which duty I fulfilled daily. Perhaps it may be superfluous to say that we were very much in love. Did I say *were*?

I think that, as I am chanting the graces of Sweetheart, it might not be amiss to say that she is just an inch shorter than I am, and that no Parisienne carried a pretty gown with more perfection than she did. I have seen gowns that looked like the devil on the manikin, but when Sweetheart wore them they were the astonishment and admiration of myself. And I do know when a woman is well dressed, though I am an art critic.

Sweetheart regarded her beauty as an intimate affair between ourselves, a precious gift for our mutual benefit, to be carefully treasured and petted. Her attitude toward the world was unmistakable. The world might look—she was indifferent. With our intimate friends she was above being flattered. Clifford said to me once: "She carries her beauty as a princess would carry the Koh-i-noor—she knows she is worthy of it, and hopes it is worthy of her."

"We ought to be so happy that I am beautiful!" she would say to me. "Just think, supposing I were not!"

I used to try to make her believe that it would have made no difference.

"Oh, not now," she would say gravely. "I know that if I lost it it would be the same to us both, now; but you can't make me believe that, at first, when you used to lean over the terrace of the Luxembourg and wait patiently for hours just to see me walk out of the Odeon."

"I didn't," I would always explain; "I was there by accident."

"Oh, what a funny accident to happen every day for two months!"

"Stop teasing! Of course, after the first week——"

"And what a funny accident that I should pass the same way every day for two months, when before I always went by the Rue de Seine!"

There was once such an accident, and such a girl. I never knew her; she is dead. I wondered sometimes that Sweetheart knew, and believed it was she herself. Yet the other woman's shadow was black.

Sweetheart had a most peculiar and unworldly habit of not embellishing facts. She presently displayed it when we arrived at the Hôtel Lion d'Or.

"Jack," said she nervously, "the cinders have made your face unpleasant. I am ashamed. They may not believe you are my husband."

"As monsieur and madame," I said, "we may have dirty faces and be honest."

"Do you suppose they—they will believe it? These queer people——"

"They'd better!" I said fiercely.

"I—I hadn't thought of that," she said. "You see, in our own little place in Paris everybody knew it, but here——"

I said, "Dearest, what nonsense!" and we marched unceremoniously up to the register, where I wrote our names. Then, with a hasty little squeeze of her gloved hand, she turned to the maid and tripped off to inspect our quarters. While I was pumping the fat-headed old proprietor about the trout fishing in the vicinity, the maid returned with the request that I mount to the room above. I followed her along the tiled passages and found Sweetheart sitting on a trunk.

"It's charming! charming!" she said. "Just look at the roses outside, and the square, and the river! and oh, Jack, the funny little Breton cattle, and the old man with knee-breeches! It's charming! and"—here she caught sight of the enraptured and fascinated maid—"and you are charming, with your red cheeks and white coiffe," she said. "Oh, how pretty!"

"Oh, madame!" murmured the servant in dire confusion.

I said, "Dearest, that will do. Nobody speaks of my peculiar charms, and I wish to be noticed."

The presence of the maid prevented Sweetheart from making amends, so we told her we were satisfied, and we would spare her life if she prepared breakfast in seventeen seconds.

She accepted the gift of existence with a dazed courtsey, and vanished.

It was refreshing to get hold of a sponge and cold water after fourteen hours in a cramped compartment. Hunger drove us to hurry—a thing we rarely did in the morning—and the way we splashed cold water about would have been fatal to any but a tiled floor.

"Dear," I said, "you have not yet seen me in my Tyrolese knickerbockers and beautiful shooting jacket. You have never beheld my legs clothed in Tyrolese stockings, at twenty francs a pair."

"The legs?" she inquired from the depths of a bath robe.

I ignored the question, and parted my hair with care. Then I sat down on the window and whistled.

Of course I was ready first. Sweetheart's hair had got into a tangle and needed to be all combed out.

"Oh, I know you are impatient, because you're whistling the Chant du Départ," she said from the door of her toilet room.

"As usual," I said, "I am ready first."

"If you say that again——" she threatened.

I said it, and dodged a sponge. Presently I was requested to open the trunk and select a gown for her. Dear little Sweetheart! she loved to pretend that she had so many it needed long consultation to decide which.

"The dark blue?" I inquired.

"Don't you think it is too warm?"

"The pale blue, then—or the pink and white?"

"Why not the white, with the cuffs à l'Anglaise, and the canoe hat?"

I hauled it out.

Then, of course, she changed her mind.

"I think the gray is better for the morning; then I can wear the big chip hat."

I fished up the gray. It was light, almost silvery, and had white spots on it.

"Jack, dear," she said, coming out with her hair tucked up in a knot, drawing the bath robe up to her chin with both hands, "I think that the white cloth would be better, and that I can wear the béret."

By this time the trunk was in a pretty mess, which amused her; but at last I ferreted out the white cloth dress, and, refusing to listen to further discussion, sat down on the window seat. Sweetheart enjoyed it.

"Stop telling me to hurry," she said; "I can't, if you keep saying it all the time."

After a while she called me to fasten her corsage, which hooked with about ten hundred hooks along the side and collar. I hated to do it, and my finger ends stung for hours after, but, as Sweetheart very rightly says, "When we are rich enough to have a maid you needn't," I submitted with an air which delighted her. Her tormenting "Thank you, Jack," was the last straw, so I calmly picked her up and carried her out, and almost to the dining room, where I set her down just in time to avoid the proprietor and three domestics issuing from the office.

Sweetheart was half inclined to laugh, half indignant, and wholly scandalized. But she did not dare say anything, for we were at the dining-room door.

There were some people there, but except for a slight inclination we did not notice each other. We had a small table to ourselves by the rose-bowered window.

We were very hungry. Breakfast began with fresh sardines just caught, and ended with little Breton cakes and a demi-tasse. I finished first; I always do, because the wretched habit of bolting my food, contracted while studying under Bouguereau at Julian's, clings to me yet. Oh, I shall have a merry time paying for it when I am forty! I began, as usual, to tease Sweetheart.

"If you continue to eat like this, dear, you will never be able to wear your new frocks. This one seems a trifle too tight now."

Sweetheart, who prided herself as much on her figure as on her lovely face, repelled the insult with disdain and nibbled her Breton biscuit defiantly. When at last she condescended to rise, we strolled out under the trees in front of the hotel, and sat down on the low stone wall surrounding the garden. The noon sun hung in the zenith, flooding the town with a dazzling downpour. Sunbeams glanced and danced on the water; sunbeams filtered through the foliage; sunbeams stole under Sweetheart's big straw hat, searching the depths of the gray eyes. Sunbeams played merry mischief with my ears and neck, which were beginning to sting in the first sunburn of the year. Through the square the white-coiffed women passed and repassed; small urchins with silver-buckled hatbands roamed about the bridge and market-place until collected and trooped off to school by a black-robed Jesuit frère; and in the shade of the trees a dozen sprawling men in Breton costume smoked their microscopical pipes and watched the water.

"They are an industrious race," said I with fine irony, watching a happy inebriate pursuing a serpentine course toward the café opposite.

Sweetheart, who was as patriotic a little girl as ever hummed the Marseillaise, and adopted France as long as she lived in it, was up in arms in an instant.

"I have read," she said with conviction, "that the Bretons are a brave, industrious race. They are French."

"They speak a different language," I said—"not a word of French in it."

"They are French," repeated Sweetheart, with an inflection which decided me to shun the subject until I could unpack my guide-book.

We sat a little while longer under the trees, until we both began nodding and mutually accused each other. Then Sweetheart went up to the room to take a nap, and I, scorning such weakness, lay down in a steamer chair under our window and fell fast asleep in no time.

I was aroused by a big pink rose which hit me squarely on the mouth. Sweetheart was perched in the window seat above, and as I looked up she sent a shower of blossoms down upon me.

"Jack, you lazy creature, it's five o'clock, and I'm dressed and ready for a walk!"

"So am I," I said, jumping up.

"But not like that. You must come up and make yourself nice for dinner."

"Nice? What's the matter with these tweeds? Aren't these new stockings presentable?"

"Look at your hair!" she said evasively. "Come up this minute and brush it."

I went, and was compelled to climb into a white collar and shirt, and trousers of an English cut. But before we had gone far along the great military road that climbed the heights above the little river, I took Sweetheart's hand in mine and imparted to her my views and intentions upon the subject of my costume for the future.

"You see, dearest, we are here in Brittany for three reasons. The first is, that I should paint outdoors. The second is, that we should economize like the deuce. The third is, our shadows——"

"I know," she interrupted faintly. "Never mind, Jack, dear."

We walked silently for a while, hand clasping hand very tightly, for we were both thinking of the third reason.

I broke the silence first, speaking cheerfully, and she looked up with a quick smile while the shadow fell from her brow.

"You see, dear, in this place, where we are going, there are no people but peasants. Your frocks are all right for a place like this; we must both wear our free-and-easy togs—I for painting, and you for scrambling about after your wild flowers or fishing with me. If you get tired of seeing me in corduroys or tweeds, I'll dress for you when you think you can't stand it any longer."

"Oh, Jack, I do like your knickerbockers——"

"And you shall wear your most gorgeous gown for me——"

"Indeed I won't," she laughed, adding impulsively, "indeed I will—every day, if you wish it!"

At the top of the hill stood an ancient Ursuline convent surrounded by a high wall, which also inclosed the broad acres of the wealthy sisterhood. We sat down by the roadside hedge and looked across the valley, where the hurrying river had ceased to hasten and now lingered in placid pools and long, deep reaches. The sun had set behind the forest, and the sky threw a purple light over woods and meadow. The grassy pools below were swept by flocks of whistling martins and swallows. One or two white gulls flapped slowly toward the tide water below, and a young curlew, speeding high overhead, uttered a lonesome cry. The grass—the brilliant green grass of Brittany—had turned a deep metallic blue in the twilight. A pale primrose light grew and died in the sky, and the forest changed from rose to ashes. Then a dull red bar shot across the parting clouds in the west, the forest smouldered an instant, and the pools glowed crimson. Slowly the red bar melted away, the light died out among the branches, the pools turned sombre. Looking up, we saw the new moon flashing in the sky above our heads. Sweetheart sighed in perfect contentment.

"It's beautiful!" I said, with another sigh.

"Ah, yes," she murmured, "beautiful to you, and to me—to me, Jack, who have never before seen this land of Morbihan."

After a while she said, "And the ocean—oh, how I long to see it! Is it near us, Jack?"

"The river runs into it twenty kilometres below. We feel the tide at Quimperlé." I did not add, "Baedeker."

"I wonder," I said presently, "what are the feelings of a little American who sees this country—the real country—for the first time?"

"I suppose you mean me," she said. "I don't know—I don't think I understand it yet, but I know I shall love it, and never want to go back."

"Perhaps we never shall," I said. "The magic second may stretch into years that end at last as all ends."

Then our hands met in that sudden nervous clasp which seemed to help and steady us when we were thinking of the real world, so long, so long forgotten.

## IX.

I was awakened next morning by a spongeful of cold water in the face, which I hate. I started up to wreak vengeance upon Sweetheart, but she fled to the toilet room and locked herself in. From this retreat she taunted me until further sleep was out of the question, and I bowed to the inevitable—indignantly, when I saw my watch pointed to five o'clock.

Sweetheart was perfectly possessed to row; so when I had bolted my coffee and sat watching her placidly sip hers, we decided to go down to the bank of the little stream and hire a boat. The boat was a wretched, shapeless affair, with two enormous oars and the remnants of rowlocks. It was the best boat in town, so we took it. I managed to get away from the bank, and, conscious of Sweetheart's open admiration, pulled boldly down the stream. It was easy work, for the tide was ebbing. The river up to the bridge was tidal, but above the bridge it leaped and flowed, a regular salmon stream. Sweetheart was so impatient to take the oars that I relinquished them and picked up my rod. The boat swung down the stream and under the high stone viaduct, where I insisted on anchoring and whipping the promising-looking water. The water was likely enough, and the sudden splash of a leaping grilse added to its likelihood. I was in hopes a grilse might become entangled with one of the flies, but though a big one shot up out of the water within five feet of Sweetheart, causing her to utter a suppressed scream, neither grilse nor trout rose to the beautiful lures I trailed about, and I only hooked two or three enormous dace, which came up like logs and covered the bottom of the boat with their coarse scales.

Sweetheart had never seen a French trout uncooked, and scarcely shared my disappointment.

"They are splendid fish," she repeated; "you are unreasonable."

There was an ancient Breton squatting on the bank; from his sulky attitude I took him to be a poacher visiting his infernal set lines and snares; but I hailed him pleasantly with a bonjour, which he returned civilly enough.

"Are there trout in this stream?"

"About the bridge," he replied cautiously.

"Have you caught any?"

"I ain't fishing," he said, much alarmed.

"What's that?" I demanded, pointing to as plump a trout as ever I saw, floating on the end of a string under the bank.

"Where?" he asked, looking about him with affected concern.

"There!"

He looked around, everywhere except where I pointed. He examined the horizon, and the tree tops, as though he expected a fish on every twig. I poled the boat up to the bank and pointed out the fish.

"Ma doui!" he exclaimed, "there *is* a fish!"

"Yes, a trout," I said.

"Trout?" He burst into a forced laugh. "Trout! Ha! ha! Why, monsieur, that is a dace—a poor little dace!" He hastily jerked it up with a long homemade gaff which lay—of course quite by accident—at his feet.

"A poor little dace!" he mumbled. "Of course, monsieur would not care to claim such a poor, coarse little fish; but I am only too glad to eat it—ah, yes, only too glad!"

"You see," said Sweetheart impulsively, "that you are wrong. Give him our fish; that will make four dace for the poor fellow."

I placed the three dace across the blade of my oar and held it out to the poacher. He took them as if he were really glad to get them. Then I said, "These are dace, and they don't have red spots."

He stood as if ready to bolt, but I laughed, and settled back on my oars, saying: "You're a poacher; but I don't care a continental, and you can poach all day in this confounded country, where there is about one trout to the kilometre. Don't look scared. What do I care? Only don't tell me I'm unable to distinguish a trout when I can see the tip of his nose."

I then sailed majestically out into the stream.

Sweetheart wanted to know whether that was really a real poacher. She had read about them. Her ideal poacher was a young, stalwart, eagle-eyed giant, with a tangle of hair and a disposition toward assassination. The reality shocked her.

"Anyway," she said, "you frightened the poor old thing. How rough men are!"

We returned to the landing place with difficulty, for the tide was still on the ebb, and we got aground more than once. My hands were in a fine condition when at last I drove that wretched scow into the mud and lifted Sweetheart out to the firm bank. The evil-eyed old man who rented us the boat glanced sardonically at my rod and blistered hands, and I was glad enough to pay him all he asked and break away for the hotel.

We had an hour to lunch in, pack, and be ready for the trap which was to bear us to our destination—the distant village of Faöuet, in Morbihan.

## X.

A long drive on a smooth white road, acres of gorse and broom, beech woods and oak thickets, and the "Heu! heu! Allo! Allons! en route!" of the Breton driver, these are my recollections of the ride to Faöuet. There are others, too—the hedges heavy with bloom, the perfume of the wild honeysuckle, the continual bird chorus from every grove and every bramble patch—and Sweetheart's veil flying into my face.

We have spoken of it since together, but she has few recollections of that journey. She only remembers it as her first steps into our heritage.

And so we entered into our heritage, Sweetheart and I; and our heritage was very fair, for it lay everywhere about us. It was a world which we alone inhabited. Men said, "This land is Gloanec's," "This is Gurnalec's," "This is Kerdec's"; they spoke of "my woods" and "his meadows" and "their pastures." And how we laughed; for when we passed together through their lands, around us, far as the eye could reach, our heritage lay in the sunshine.

## XI.

One day, when Sweetheart had been weeping—for we were thinking of the end to the magic second—I spoke of our heritage which swept far as the eye could reach across the moors of Faöuet.

She said: "The past is ours, Jack; the present is ours; the future———"

We tried to smile, but our hearts were like lead. Yet we know that the future will also be ours. I know it as I write.

## XII.

The letter from St. Gildas, bringing with it a breath of salt air, lay on the table before us. Sweetheart clasped her hands and looked at me.

"I'm in favour of going at once," I said for the third time. Over by the wall were piled my canvases, the result of three months in Faöuet.

The first was a study of Sweetheart under the trees of the ancient orchard in the convent grounds. What trouble I had had with that canvas! I remembered the morning that the old gardener came over and stood behind me as I painted; and when I had replied to his "Good-morning," I recalled the pang his next words gave me:

"I am so sorry, monsieur, but it is forbidden to enter the convent grounds."

My canvas was almost finished, and, as the romancers have it, "my despair was great!" A month's work for nothing—or next to nothing!

Sweetheart rose from her pose on the low bough of the apple tree and came over to my side. "Never mind, Jack; I shall go and ask the Mother Superior about it."

I knew that she would win over the Mother Superior; and when, that evening, she came back radiant, crying, "She is lovely!—she says you may finish the picture, and I think you ought to go and thank her," I put on my cap, and stepping across the street, we rang at the gate.

The old gardener let us in, and in a moment I stood before the latticed windows behind which some one was moving. In a low voice the invisible nun told us that the Superior granted to us the privilege of working in the orchard, but we must be careful of the grass, because it was almost time to cut it.

"I am sure we may have confidence in you," she said.

"We will not trample the grass, my sister, and I thank you for us both."

The lattice trembled, was raised a little, and then fell.

"You are English," said the hidden nun.

"I am American, my sister."

I looked at the lattice a moment, then dropped my eyes. I may have been mistaken, but I think she sighed.

Sweetheart came closer to the lattice and murmured her thanks.

There was a pause.

Then came the voice again, sweet and gentle: "May Our Lady of Saint Gildas protect you"; and we went out by the little iron wicket.

The next picture was another study of Sweetheart in the woods; the next, another study of Sweetheart; and the others were studies of the same young lady.

The light in the room had grown dim, and I walked to the window which overlooked the convent chapel. The chapel windows were open; within, the nuns stood or knelt chanting. Three white-veiled figures were advancing to the altar, and the others, draped in black now knelt behind. I didn't think I had any business to look at them, so I did not. After all, they were cloistered nuns, and it was only on hot nights that they opened the chapel windows. Sweetheart was speaking beside my shoulder.

"Poor things! The ones in white, they are the novices; they will never see parents or friends again. When they enter the gates they never leave—never; they are buried there."

I said: "After all, we are much like them. We have left all; we have nothing now but each other, for the world is dead, and we are bound by vows which keep us within the narrow confines of our heritage."

"But our heritage is everywhere—as far as we can see."

"Ah, yes, but we can only see to the horizon. There is a world beyond."

"I have renounced it," said Sweetheart faintly.

## XIII.

The letter from St. Gildas had been lying on our table for a week before I thought of answering it, and even then it was Sweetheart who wrote:

"DEAR MR. STUART:

"Jack is too lazy to answer your kind note, so, in pure shame for his discourtesy, I hasten to reply to your questions.

"First: Yes; we have been working very hard, and Jack's pictures are charming, though he growls over them all day.

"Second: Yes; we intend to stay in Brittany this winter for lots of reasons—one being economy, and another, Jack's outdoor painting.

"Third: Yes; we are coming to St. Gildas.

"Fourth: To-morrow.

"Fifth: No; we had not heard of Mr. Clifford's affair with the policeman; and oh, I am so sorry he was locked up and fined! Jack laughs. I suspect he, too, was as wicked as you all when he was a student, alone in Paris.

"Sixth: I know you are Jack's oldest and most intimate friend, so I allow you more liberty than I do Messieurs Clifford and Elliott; therefore I will answer your question as to whether the honeymoon is not on the wane. No! no! no! There are three answers to one question. See how generous I can be!"

Sweetheart called me to see whether or not I approved. I did, and added my answer to Stuart's last question as follows: "No, you idiot!" Then I signed the note, and Sweetheart sealed and directed it.

So we left for St. Gildas next morning before sunrise and in the rain. This leaving at such an unearthly hour was not my doing, but Sweetheart was determined, and rose by candlelight in spite of desperate opposition on my part. It was cold, and the rain beat against the windows.

It was many kilometres to St. Gildas, but before we had gone six, the rain had ceased and the eastern sky flushed to a pale rose.

"Thank goodness!" I said, "we shall have the sun."

Then the daily repeated miracle of the coming of dawn was wrought before our eyes. The heavens glowed in rainbow tints; the shredded mist rising along the river was touched with purple and gold, and acres of meadow and pasture dripped precious stones. Shreds of the fading night-mist drifted among the tree tops, now tipped with fire, while in the forest depths faint sparkles came from some lost ray of morning light falling on wet leaves. Then of a sudden up shot the sun, and against it, black and gigantic, a peasant towered, leaning upon his spade.

## XIV.

We were fast nearing the end of our long journey. The sun blazed on us from the zenith, and the wheels creaked with the heat of the white road. The driver leaned back, saying, "We enter Finistère here by this granite post." Presently he added, "The ocean!"

There it lay, a basin of silver and blue. Sweetheart had started to her feet, speechless, one hand holding to my shoulder, the other clasped to her breast. And now, as the road wound through the hills and down to the coast, long stretches of white sand skirted the distant cliffs, and over the cliffs waved miles and miles of yellow gorse. A cluster of white and gray houses lay in the hollow to the left almost at the mouth of the river, and beyond, the waves were beating in the bar—beating the same rhythm which we were to hear so long there together, day and night. There was not a boat to be seen, not a creature, nor was there any sign of life save for the smoke curling from a cottage chimney below. The ocean lay sparkling beneath, and beyond its deeper blue melted into the haze on the horizon.

Suddenly, in the road below, the figure of a man appeared, and at the same moment a pointer pup came gambolling up beside us in an ecstasy of self-abnegation and apology. I sprang out of the lumbering vehicle and lifted Sweetheart to the ground, and in an instant we were shaking hands with a stalwart young fellow in knickerbockers and jersey, who said we were a pretty pair not to have come sooner, and told Sweetheart he pitied her lot—meaning me.

Then we walked arm in arm down a fragrant lane to the river bank, where the dearest old lady toddled out of the granite house to welcome us and show us our rooms. Sweetheart went with her, while I stopped an instant to chat with Stuart.

"That is Madame Ylven," he said. "She is the most stunning peasant woman in Finistère, and you will want for nothing." Then, after a moment, "Good heavens! Jack, what a beauty your wife——" He stopped short, but added, "What a delicious little beauty Sweetheart has grown to be!"

A white-coiffed maid came to the door, and said, "Will monsieur have the goodness to come? Madame wishes him to see the rooms."

The wind blew from the south, and the thunder of the sea was in my ears as I mounted the stairs to our new quarters.

Sweetheart met me at the door, saying, "It seems almost too much happiness to bear, but I feel that we are at home at last—alone together for all time."

Alone together? The ocean at our threshold, the moors and forests at our back, and a good slate roof above us. Before me through the open door I could see the great old-fashioned room, warm in the afternoon sunlight—the room we were to live in so long, the room in which we were to pass the happiest and bitterest moments of our lives.

She hesitated an instant before the threshold. I think we knew that we stood upon the threshold of our destiny. Then I said, half in earnest: "Are you afraid to cross with me into the unknown future? See, the room is filled with sunshine. Are you afraid?"

She sprang across the threshold, and, turning to me, held out both hands.

## XV.

The sun slipped lower and lower into the sea, until a distant tossing wave washed it out against the sky. Light died in the room, and shadows closed around us;

yet it was in the darkness and shadows that we drew nearer to each other, then and after.

## XVI.

Stuart stood under our window and yelled up at me, "Oh, Jack! I say, Jack!"

Sweetheart, who was fussing over the half-unpacked trunk, went to the window and threw open the panes.

"You don't mean to say you have had your coffee?" she said. "Jack isn't up yet."

"Jack is up," I explained, coming to the window in pajamas. "Hello!"

"I only wanted to say that I haven't had my coffee," he explained, "and I'm going to take it with you when you're ready."

Sweetheart picked up her béret, and, passing a hatpin through it, turned to me with a warning, "I shall eat all the breakfast, monsieur!" and vanished down the stairs. A moment later I heard her clear voice below:

Sonnez le chœur,

Chasseur!

Sonnez la mort!

Before I had finished dressing, Sweetheart tripped in with my coffee and toast.

"Of course I've finished," she said, "and you don't deserve this. Mr. Stuart has gone off with his canvases, and says he'll see you at lunch."

I swallowed the coffee and browsed on little squares of toast which she condescendingly buttered for me, and then, lighting a cigarette, I announced my intention of commanding an exploring expedition consisting of Sweetheart and myself. A scratching at the door and a patter of feet announced that I had been overheard.

Sweetheart unlatched the door, and the pointer pup of the evening before charged into the room and covered us with boisterous caresses, which we took to indicate that he not only approved of the expedition, but intended to undertake the general supervision of it himself. I resigned the leadership at once.

"His name," said Sweetheart in the tone of one who presents a distinguished guest, "is 'Luff.'"

I gravely acknowledged the honour by patting his head.

"I'm afraid," I said to Sweetheart, "that there is a bar sinister upon his escutcheon, but possibly it is only the indelible mark of the conquering British foxhound."

Sweetheart said, "Nonsense!" and the expedition moved, Luff leading with a series of ear-splitting orders in the dog language which we perfectly understood.

In ten minutes we stood on the cliffs, the salt wind whipping our faces. Saint-Gildas-des-Prés lay at our feet.

"I know," observed Sweetheart calmly, "all about this place. Captain Ylven told me at breakfast."

"Well," said I, "what's that island on the horizon?"

Then she overwhelmed me with erudition, until I longed for Baedeker and revenge.

"That is the Isle de Groix, and all about us is the Bay of Biscay. This little hamlet on the cliff is St. Julien, and if we follow the coast far enough we come to Lorient."

"Follow the coast? Which way?"

Sweetheart had forgotten, and I triumphed in silence, until she stamped her foot and marched off to assist Luff in investigating a suspicious hole in the cliff.

I went to the edge of the plateau and looked over. The surf thundered against the rocks, tossing long strands of seaweed over the pebbly beach. A man with a wooden rake stood in the water up to his knees. He raked the seaweed from the breakers as a farmer rakes weeds from the lawn. The salt wind began to sting my lips and eyes. My throat felt dry and salty. I turned toward the hamlet of St. Gildas. I had not imagined it so small. Besides our house there were but three others clustered under the river bank. Behind it stretched woods and grain fields broken by patches of yellow gorse. Across the river stood a stone chapel almost lost in the miles of moorland. To the east and west the downs covered with gorse and heather rolled to the horizon. Here and there along the cliffs stood what appeared to be the ruins of ancient forts, and on a rock, just where the river sweeps out into the sea, rose a dirty white signal tower. The tower was low and squatty and wet. It looked like some saline excrescence which had slowly exuded from the brine-soaked rock. On the bar hundreds of white gulls rose and settled as the tide encroached; curlew were running along the foam-splashed shore under the eastern cliffs across the river.

On our side of the river the cliffs were covered with blackthorn and hawthorn, with here and there a stunted oak, probably so placed by Providence as general rendezvous for all the small twittering birds of Finistère. Birds were everywhere. From the clouds came the ceaseless carol of skylarks; from the grain fields and the flowering gorse rose an unbroken chorus, taken up and repeated by flocks of microscopical songsters among the blackthorns on the cliffs.

"This is paradise, this wilderness," I thought.

Then, as I heard Sweetheart's mocking voice from the cliff:

O frère Jacques,
Dormez vous!

"I'm not asleep!" I cried in answer. "What is it?"

"Luff has unearthed a poor little mole, but I won't allow him to hurt it."

"Jack, dear," she said, as I came up, "couldn't we keep it as a pet? See, the poor little thing is blind."

As it was blind we called it "Love," which later was changed to "Cupid," and finally, when we discovered it true gormandizing character, for "Cupid" we substituted "Cupidity," by which name it flourished and fattened.

"What a change," said Sweetheart sadly, "from Blind Love to Blind Greed!"

The mole grew very fat.

## XVII.

When the winds stir the leaves among the poplars, and the long shadows fall athwart the fields; when the winds rise at night, and the branches scrape and crack above the moonlit snow; when in the long hot days the earth is bathed in fragrance, and all the little creatures of the fields are silent; when in the still evenings the flowers perfume the air, and the gravel walks shine white in the moonlight; when the breezes quicken from the distant coast; when the sand shakes beneath the shock of the breakers, and every wave is plumed with white; when the calm eye of the beacon turns to mine, lingers, and turn away, and the surf is yeasty and thick; when I start at the sound of a voice from the cliffs, and my eyes are raised in vain; when the white gulls toss and drift in the storm-clouds, and the water hurries out in the black ebb tide; when I rise and look from the window; when I dress; when I work with pen and colour; when I rest; when I walk; when I sleep—there is one face before my eyes, one name on my lips. For the white shadow is turning gray, and God alone knows the end.

## XVIII.

And God alone knows the end, for the mists are crowding, brooding like angry-browed clouds, and I hear the whistle of unseen winds, and my life-flame wavers and sinks and flares, blown hither and thither, tossing, fading, leaping, but fading, always fading.

In a flash, like a printed picture on a screen, illuminated, keenly etched in the white glare, I see the bed, and the people around me, the black gowns, the pale eyes of the doctor, the sponge and basin, the rolls of lint.

Voices, minute but clean-cut and clear as picked harp-strings, tinkle in my ears; the voice of the doctor, other voices, but always the voice of the doctor—"The splinter of bone on the brain; the splinter pressing on the tissues; the depression."

The doctor! That is the man! That is the man who comes to my side, who follows, follows where I go, who seeks me throughout the world! I saw him as I lay flung on the turf, limp, unconscious, below the cliffs on the Aspen hills; I felt his presence in the studio; I heard him creeping at my heels across the gorse thickets of St. Gildas. And now he has come to cut short the magic second, to turn back time—back, back, into the old worn channels, rock-ribbed and salt with tears.

As a leaf of written paper torn in two, so shall my life be torn in two; and the long tear shall mangle the chapter written in rose and gold.

Then, too, my shadow, already turned from white to gray, shall fall with a deeper stain wherever I pass; and I shall see the yellow gorse glimmer and turn to goldenrod, and the poplars turn to oaks; and the twin towers of Notre Dame, filmy, lace-carved, and gray with centuries, shall dwindle as I look—dwindle and sway and turn to pines, singing pines that murmur to the winds, blowing across the Aspen hills.

---

All that is fair shall pass away; all that I love, all that I fear for—these shall the doctor take away, lifting them from my memory on the point of a steel blade. What has he to give in return? A hell of vapour, distorting sight; a hell of sound, drowning the soul.

---

Gigantic apparitions arise across the world of water, wavering like shadows on the clouds. Steel-clad, clothed in skins, casqued in steel, their winged heads bend and nod and move against the clouds. And even they are changing as clouds change shape. I see steel limbs turn red and naked. I see winged casques trail to the earth, feathered, painted in colours of earth.

Ihó! Inâh! Etó! E-hó!

The bridge of stars spans the vast lake of air; the sun and the moon travel over it.

---

My shadow is turning dark; I can scarcely see the doctor, but now—God have mercy!—*I can touch him.*

All the high spectres are stooping from the clouds, bending above me to watch. I know them and their eyes of shadow—I know them now; Hârpen that was to Chaské what Hárpstinâ shall be to Hapéda; and Hârka shall come after all with the voice of winter winds:

"Aké u, aké u, aké u!"

But the magic second shall never return.

"Mâ cânté maséca!"

Now they leave my bed, the people who crowded there under the shadowy forms of the spectres; now the doctor bends over; I see and feel him. His hands are tangled in the threads of time; he is cutting a thread; he——

## XIX.

When I spoke to him first I spoke in the French language. Before he answered, the scream of a blue jay in the elms outside set my nerves aquiver, and I called for Donald and Walter.

As I lay there I could see the Aspen hills from the window, heaps of crumpled gold bathed in sunshine. Over them sailed the froth from the silken milkweed; over them drifted the big brown-red butterflies, luminous as richest autumn leaves.

Some one closed the door softly. The doctor had gone.

The sunlight poured into the window, etching my shadow on the wall behind. Lying very still there I saw it motionless beside me. *The shadow was black.*

Somebody said in the next room, "Will he die?"

"Die?" I said aloud.

A bird twittered outside my window.

The door opened again, noiselessly.

"Sweetheart?" I whispered.

"Yes, Jack."

After a moment I said, "When do you go back to school?"

"I? I finished school a year ago."

"Come nearer."

"I am here, Jack."

"Time stopped a year ago."

"A year ago to-day."

The same gray eyes, the same face, paler, perhaps.

"We have journeyed far," I sighed, "always together, but in those days our shadows were white as snow. Am I going to die? There are tears in your eyes."

They fell on my cheek; her arms fell too, closer, closer, around my neck.

"Life has begun," she said.

"Life? What was the year that ends to-day? The magic second of life?"

"A year of death, to me!"

Ah, but her soul knows of a life in death! And she shall know it, too, when her shadow turns whiter than snow. For the Temple of Idols has closed its doors at the sound of a voice, and an idol of gilt has turned to flesh and blood.

I-hó!

So shall she know of the life in death when her soul and her body are one.

# PASSEUR

O friends, I've served ye food and bed;
O friends, the mist is rising wet;
Then bide a moment, O my dead,
Where, lonely, I must linger yet!

---

## PASSEUR

Because man goeth to his long home,
And the mourners go about the streets.

When he had finished his pipe he tapped the brier bowl against the chimney until the ashes powdered the charred log smouldering across the andirons. Then he sank back in his chair, absently touching the hot pipe-bowl with the tip of each finger until it grew cool enough to be dropped into his coat pocket.

Twice he raised his eyes to the little American clock ticking upon the mantel. He had half an hour to wait.

The three candles that lighted the room might be trimmed to advantage; this would give him something to do. A pair of scissors lay open upon the bureau, and he rose and picked them up. For a while he stood dreamily shutting and opening the scissors, his eyes roaming about the room. There was an easel in the corner, and a pile of dusty canvases behind it; behind the canvases there was a shadow—that gray, menacing shadow that never moved.

When he had trimmed each candle he wiped the smoky scissors on a paint rag and flung them on the bureau again. The clock pointed to ten; he had been occupied exactly three minutes.

The bureau was littered with neckties, pipes, combs and brushes, matches, reels and fly-books, collars, shirt studs, a new pair of Scotch shooting stockings, and a woman's workbasket.

He picked out all the neckties, folded them once, and hung them over a bit of twine that stretched across the looking-glass; the shirt studs he shovelled into the top drawer along with brushes, combs, and stockings; the reels and fly-books he dusted with his handkerchief and placed methodically along the mantel shelf. Twice he stretched out his hand toward the woman's workbasket, but his hand fell to his side again, and he turned away into the room staring at the dying fire.

Outside the snow-sealed window a shutter broke loose and banged monotonously, until he flung open the panes and fastened it. The soft, wet snow, that had choked the window-panes all day, was frozen hard now, and he had to break the polished crust before he could find the rusty shutter hinge.

He leaned out for a moment, his numbed hands resting on the snow, the roar of a rising snow-squall in his ears; and out across the desolate garden and stark hedgerow he saw the flat black river spreading through the gloom.

A candle sputtered and snapped behind him; a sheet of drawing-paper fluttered across the floor, and he closed the panes and turned back into the room, both hands in his worn pockets.

The little American clock on the mantel ticked and ticked, but the hands lagged, for he had not been occupied five minutes in all. He went up to the mantel and watched the hands of the clock. A minute—longer than a year to him—crept by.

Around the room the furniture stood ranged—a chair or two of yellow pine, a table, the easel, and in one corner the broad curtained bed; and behind each lay shadows, menacing shadows that never moved.

A little pale flame started up from the smoking log on the andirons; the room sang with the sudden hiss of escaping wood gases. After a little the back of the log caught fire; jets of blue flared up here and there with mellow sounds like the lighting of gas-burners in a row, and in a moment a thin sheet of yellow flame wrapped the whole charred log.

Then the shadows moved; not the shadows behind the furniture—they never moved—but other shadows, thin, gray, confusing, that came and spread their slim patterns all around him, and trembled and trembled.

He dared not step or tread upon them, they were too real; they meshed the floor around his feet, they ensnared his knees, they fell across his breast like ropes. Some night, in the silence of the moors, when wind and river were still, he feared these strands of shadow might tighten—creep higher around his throat and tighten. But even then he knew that those other shadows would never move, those gray shapes that knelt crouching in every corner.

When he looked up at the clock again ten minutes had straggled past. Time was disturbed in the room; the strands of shadow seemed entangled among the hands of the clock, dragging them back from their rotation. He wondered if the shadows would strangle Time, some still night when the wind and the flat river were silent.

There grew a sudden chill across the floor; the cracks of the boards let it in. He leaned down and drew his sabots toward him from their place near the andirons, and slipped them over his chaussons; and as he straightened up, his eyes mechanically sought the mantel above, where in the dusk another pair of sabots stood, little, slender, delicate sabots, carved from red beech. A year's dust grayed their surface; a year's rust dulled the silver band across the instep. He said this to himself aloud, knowing that it was within a few minutes of the year.

His own sabots came from Mort-Dieu; they were shaved square and banded with steel. But in days past he had thought that no sabot in Mort-Dieu was delicate enough to touch the instep of the Mort-Dieu passeur. So he sent to the shore lighthouse, and they sent to Lorient, where the women are coquettish and show their hair under the coiffe, and wear dainty sabots; and in this town, where vanity corrupts and there is much lace on coiffe and collarette, a pair of delicate sabots was found, banded with silver and chiselled in red beech. The sabots stood on the mantel above the fire now, dusty and tarnished.

There was a sound from the window, the soft murmur of snow blotting glass panes. The wind, too, muttered under the roof eaves. Presently it would begin to whisper to him from the chimney—he knew it—and he held his hands over his ears and stared at the clock.

In the hamlet of Mort-Dieu the pines sing all day of the sea secrets, but in the night the ghosts of little gray birds fill the branches, singing of the sunshine of past years. He heard the song as he sat, and he crushed his hands over his ears; but the gray birds joined with the wind in the chimney, and he heard all that he dared not hear, and he thought all that he dared not hope or think, and the swift tears scalded his eyes.

In Mort-Dieu the nights are longer than anywhere on earth; he knew it—why should he not know? This had been so for a year; it was different before. There were so many things different before; days and nights vanished like minutes then; the pines told no secrets of the sea, and the gray birds had not yet come to Mort-Dieu. Also, there was Jeanne, passeur at the Carmes.

When he first saw her she was poling the square, flat-bottomed ferry skiff from the Carmes to Mort-Dieu, a red handkerchief bound across her silky black hair, a red skirt fluttering just below her knees. The next time he saw her he had to call to her across the placid river, "Ohé! Ohé, passeur!" She came, poling the flat skiff, her deep blue eyes fixed pensively on him, the scarlet skirt and kerchief idly flapping in the April wind. Then day followed day when the far call "Passeur!" grew clearer and more joyous, and the faint answering cry, "I come!" rippled across the water like music tinged with laughter. Then spring came, and with spring came love—love, carried free across the ferry from the Carmes to Mort-Dieu.

The flame above the charred log whistled, flickered, and went out in a jet of wood vapour, only to play like lightning above the gas and relight again. The clock ticked more loudly, and the song from the pines filled the room. But in his straining eyes a summer landscape was reflected, where white clouds sailed and white foam curled under the square bow of a little skiff. And he pressed his numbed hands tighter to his ears to drown the cry, "Passeur! Passeur!"

And now for a moment the clock ceased ticking. It was time to go—who but he should know it, he who went out into the night swinging his lantern? And he went. He had gone each night from the first—from that first strange winter evening when a strange voice had answered him across the river, the voice of the new passeur. He had never heard *her* voice again.

So he passed down the windy wooden stairs, lantern hanging lighted in his hand, and stepped out into the storm. Through sheets of drifting snow, over heaps of frozen seaweed and icy drift he moved, shifting his lantern right and left, until its glimmer on the water warned him. Then he called out into the night, "Passeur!" The frozen spray spattered his face and crusted the lantern; he heard the distant boom of breakers beyond the bar, and the noise of mighty winds among the seaward cliffs.

"Passeur!"

Across the broad flat river, black as a sea of pitch, a tiny light sparkled a moment. Again he cried, "Passeur!"

"I come!"

He turned ghastly white, for it was her voice—or was he crazy?—and he sprang waist deep into the icy current and cried out again, but his voice ended in a sob.

 Slowly through the snow the flat skiff took shape, creeping nearer and nearer. But she was not at the pole—he saw that; there was only a tall, thin man, shrouded to the eyes in oilskin; and he leaped into the boat and bade the ferryman hasten.

Halfway across he rose in the skiff, and called, "Jeanne!" But the roar of the storm and the thrashing of icy waves drowned his voice. Yet he heard her again, and she called to him by name.

When at last the boat grated upon the invisible shore, he lifted his lantern, trembling, stumbling among the rocks, and calling to her, as though his voice could silence the voice that had spoken a year ago that night. And it could not. He sank shivering upon his knees, and looked out into the darkness, where an ocean rolled across a world. Then his stiff lips moved, and he repeated her name; but the hand of the ferryman fell gently upon his head.

And when he raised his eyes he saw that the ferryman was Death.

# THE KEY TO GRIEF

The moving finger writes, and, having writ,
Moves on; nor all your piety nor wit
Shall lure it back to cancel half a line,
Nor all your tears wash out a word of it.
FITZGERALD.

---

THE KEY TO GRIEF.

The wild hawk to the wind-swept sky
The deer to the wholesome wold,
And the heart of a man to the heart of a maid,
As it was in the days of old.
KIPLING.

## I.

They were doing their work very badly. They got the rope around his neck, and tied his wrists with moose-bush withes, but again he fell, sprawling, turning, twisting over the leaves, tearing up everything around him like a trapped panther.

He got the rope away from them; he clung to it with bleeding fists; he set his white teeth in it, until the jute strands relaxed, unravelled, and snapped, gnawed through by his white teeth.

Twice Tully struck him with a gum hook. The dull blows fell on flesh rigid as stone.

Panting, foul with forest mould and rotten leaves, hands and face smeared with blood, he sat up on the ground, glaring at the circle of men around him.

"Shoot him!" gasped Tully, dashing the sweat from his bronzed brow; and Bates, breathing heavily, sat down on a log and dragged a revolver from his rear pocket. The man on the ground watched him; there was froth in the corners of his mouth.

"Git back!" whispered Bates, but his voice and hand trembled. "Kent," he stammered, "won't ye hang?"

The man on the ground glared.

"Ye've got to die, Kent," he urged; "they all say so. Ask Lefty Sawyer; ask Dyce; ask Carrots.—He's got to swing fur it—ain't he, Tully?—Kent, fur God's sake, swing fur these here gents!"

The man on the ground panted; his bright eyes never moved.

After a moment Tully sprang on him again. There was a flurry of leaves, a crackle, a gasp and a grunt, then the thumping and thrashing of two bodies writhing in the brush. Dyce and Carrots jumped on the prostrate men. Lefty Sawyer caught the rope again, but the jute strands gave way and he stumbled. Tully began to scream, "He's chokin' me!" Dyce staggered out into the open, moaning over a broken wrist.

"Shoot!" shouted Lefty Sawyer, and dragged Tully aside. "Shoot, Jim Bates! Shoot straight, b' God!"

"Git back!" gasped Bates, rising from the fallen log.

The crowd parted right and left; a quick report rang out—another—another. Then from the whirl of smoke a tall form staggered, dealing blows—blows that sounded sharp as the crack of a whip.

"He's off! Shoot straight!" they cried.

There was a gallop of heavy boots in the woods. Bates, faint and dazed, turned his head.

"Shoot!" shrieked Tully.

But Bates was sick; his smoking revolver fell to the ground; his white face and pale eyes contracted. It lasted only a moment; he started after the others, plunging, wallowing through thickets of osier and hemlock underbrush.

Far ahead he heard Kent crashing on like a young moose in November, and he knew he was making for the shore. The others knew too. Already the gray gleam of the sea cut a straight line along the forest edge; already the soft clash of the surf on the rocks broke faintly through the forest silence.

"He's got a canoe there!" bawled Tully. "He'll be into it!"

And he was into it, kneeling in the bow, driving his paddle to the handle. The rising sun gleamed like red lightning on the flashing blade; the canoe shot to the crest of a wave, hung, bows dripping in the wind, dropped into the depths, glided, tipped, rolled, shot up again, staggered, and plunged on.

Tully ran straight out into the cove surf; the water broke against his chest, bare and wet with sweat. Bates sat down on a worn black rock and watched the canoe listlessly.

The canoe dwindled to a speck of gray and silver; and when Carrots, who had run back to the gum camp for a rifle, returned, the speck on the water might have been easier to hit than a loon's head at twilight. So Carrots, being thrifty by nature, fired once, and was satisfied to save the other cartridges. The canoe was still visible, making for the open sea. Somewhere beyond the horizon lay the keys, a string of rocks bare as skulls, black and slimy where the sea cut their base, white on the crests with the excrement of sea birds.

"He's makin' fur the Key to Grief!" whispered Bates to Dyce.

Dyce, moaning, and nursing his broken wrist, turned a sick face out to sea.

The last rock seaward was the Key to Grief, a splintered pinnacle polished by the sea. From the Key to Grief, seaward a day's paddle, if a man dared, lay the long wooded island in the ocean known as Grief on the charts of the bleak coast.

In the history of the coast, two men had made the voyage to the Key to Grief, and from there to the island. One of these was a rum-crazed pelt hunter, who lived to come back; the other was a college youth; they found his battered canoe at sea, and a day later his battered body was flung up in the cove.

So, when Bates whispered to Dyce, and when Dyce called to the others, they knew that the end was not far off for Kent and his canoe; and they turned away into the forest, sullen, but satisfied that Kent would get his dues when the devil got his.

Lefty spoke vaguely of the wages of sin. Carrots, with an eye to thrift, suggested a plan for an equitable division of Kent's property.

When they reached the gum camp they piled Kent's personal effects on a blanket.

Carrots took the inventory: a revolver, two gum hooks, a fur cap, a nickel-plated watch, a pipe, a pack of new cards, a gum sack, forty pounds of spruce gum, and a frying pan.

Carrots shuffled the cards, picked out the joker, and flipped it pensively into the fire. Then he dealt cold decks all around.

When the goods and chattels of their late companion had been divided by chance—for there was no chance to cheat—somebody remembered Tully.

"He's down there on the coast, starin' after the canoe," said Bates huskily.

He rose and walked toward a heap on the ground covered by a blanket. He started to lift the blanket, hesitated, and finally turned away. Under the blanket lay Tully's brother, shot the night before by Kent.

"Guess we'd better wait till Tully comes," said Carrots uneasily. Bates and Kent had been campmates. An hour later Tully walked into camp.

He spoke to no one that day. In the morning Bates found him down on the coast digging, and said: "Hello, Tully! Guess we ain't much hell on lynchin'!"

"Naw," said Tully. "Git a spade."

"Goin' to plant him there?"

"Yep."

"Where he kin hear them waves?"

"Yep."

"Purty spot."

"Yep."

"Which way will he face?"

"Where he kin watch fur that damned canoe!" cried Tully fiercely.

"He—he can't see," ventured Bates uneasily. "He's dead, ain't he?"

"He'll heave up that there sand when the canoe comes back! An' it's a-comin'! An' Bud Kent'll be in it, dead or alive! Git a spade!"

The pale light of superstition flickered in Bates's eyes. He hesitated.

"The—the dead can't see," he began; "kin they?"

Tully turned a distorted face toward him.

"Yer lie!" he roared. "My brother kin see, dead or livin'! An' he'll see the hangin' of Bud Kent! An' he'll git up outer the grave fur to see it, Bill Bates! I'm tellin' ye! I'm tellin' ye! Deep as I'll plant him, he'll heave that there sand and call to me, when the canoe comes in! I'll hear him; I'll be here! An' we'll live to see the hangin' of Bud Kent!"

About sundown they planted Tully's brother, face to the sea.

## II.

On the Key to Grief the green waves rub all day. White at the summit, black at the base, the shafted rocks rear splintered pinnacles, slanting like channel buoys. On the polished pillars sea birds brood—white-winged, bright-eyed sea birds, that nestle and preen and flap and clatter their orange-coloured beaks when the sifted spray drives and drifts across the reef.

As the sun rose, painting crimson streaks criss-cross over the waters, the sea birds sidled together, huddling row on row, steeped in downy drowse.

Where the sun of noon burnished the sea, an opal wave washed, listless, noiseless; a sea bird stretched one listless wing.

And into the silence of the waters a canoe glided, bronzed by the sunlight, jewelled by the salt drops stringing from prow to thwart, seaweed a-trail in the diamond-flashing wake, and in the bow a man dripping with sweat.

Up rose the gulls, sweeping in circles, turning, turning over rock and sea, and their clamour filled the sky, starting little rippling echoes among the rocks.

The canoe grated on a shelf of ebony; the seaweed rocked and washed; the little sea crabs sheered sideways, down, down into limpid depths of greenest shadows. Such was the coming of Bud Kent to the Key to Grief.

He drew the canoe halfway up the shelf of rock and sat down, breathing heavily, one brown arm across the bow. For an hour he sat there. The sweat dried under his eyes. The sea birds came back, filling the air with soft querulous notes.

There was a livid mark around his neck, a red, raw circle. The salt wind stung it; the sun burned it into his flesh like a collar of red-hot steel. He touched it at times; once he washed it with cold salt water.

Far in the north a curtain of mist hung on the sea, dense, motionless as the fog on the Grand Banks. He never moved his eyes from it; he knew what it was. Behind it lay the Island of Grief.

All the year round the Island of Grief is hidden by the banks of mist, ramparts of dead white fog encircling it on every side. Ships give it wide berth. Some speak of warm springs on the island whose waters flow far out to sea, rising in steam eternally.

The pelt hunter had come back with tales of forests and deer and flowers everywhere; but he had been drinking much, and much was forgiven him.

The body of the college youth tossed up in the cove on the mainland was battered out of recognition, but some said, when found, one hand clutched a crimson blossom half wilted, but broad as a sap pan.

So Kent lay motionless beside his canoe, burned with thirst, every nerve vibrating, thinking of all these things. It was not fear that whitened the firm flesh under the tan; it was the fear of fear. He must not think—he must throttle dread; his eyes must never falter, his head never turn from that wall of mist across the sea. With set teeth he crushed back terror; with glittering eyes he looked into the hollow eyes of fright. And so he conquered fear.

He rose. The sea birds whirled up into the sky, pitching, tossing, screaming, till the sharp flapping of their pinions set the snapping echoes flying among the rocks.

Under the canoe's sharp prow the kelp bobbed and dipped and parted; the sunlit waves ran out ahead, glittering, dancing. Splash! splash! bow and stern! And now he knelt again, and the polished paddle swung and dipped, and swept and swung and dipped again.

Far behind, the clamour of the sea birds lingered in his ears, till the mellow dip of the paddle drowned all sound and the sea was a sea of silence.

No wind came to cool the hot sweat on cheek and breast. The sun blazed a path of flame before him, and he followed out into the waste of waters. The still ocean divided under the bows and rippled innocently away on either side, tinkling, foaming, sparkling like the current in a woodland brook. He looked around at the world of flattened water, and the fear of fear rose up and gripped his throat again. Then he lowered his head, like a tortured bull, and shook the fear of fear from his throat, and drove the paddle into the sea as a butcher stabs, to the hilt.

So at last he came to the wall of mist. It was thin at first, thin and cool, but it thickened and grew warmer, and the fear of fear dragged at his head, but he would not look behind.

Into the fog the canoe shot; the gray water ran by, high as the gunwales, oily, silent. Shapes flickered across the bows, pillars of mist that rode the waters, robed in films of tattered shadows. Gigantic forms towered to dizzy heights above him, shaking out shredded shrouds of cloud. The vast draperies of the fog swayed and hung and trembled as he brushed them; the white twilight deepened to a sombre gloom. And now it grew thinner; the fog became a mist, and the mist a haze, and the haze floated away and vanished into the blue of the heavens.

All around lay a sea of pearl and sapphire, lapping, lapping on a silver shoal.

So he came to the Island of Grief.

### III.

On the silver shoal the waves washed and washed, breaking like crushed opals where the sands sang with the humming froth.

Troops of little shore birds, wading on the shoal, tossed their sun-tipped wings and scuttled inland, where, dappled with shadow from the fringing forest, the white beach of the island stretched.

The water all around was shallow, limpid as crystal, and he saw the ribbed sand shining on the bottom, where purple seaweed floated, and delicate sea creatures darted and swarmed and scattered again at the dip of his paddle.

Like velvet rubbed on velvet the canoe brushed across the sand. He staggered to his feet, stumbled out, dragged the canoe high up under the trees, turned it bottom upward, and sank beside it, face downward in the sand. Sleep came to drive away the fear of fear, but hunger, thirst, and fever fought with sleep, and he dreamed—dreamed of a rope that sawed his neck, of the fight in the woods, and the shots. He dreamed, too, of the camp, of his forty pounds of spruce gum, of Tully, and of Bates. He dreamed of the fire and the smoke-scorched kettle, of the foul odour of musty bedding, of the greasy cards, and of his own new pack, hoarded for weeks to please the others. All this he dreamed, lying there face downward in the sand; but he did not dream of the face of the dead.

The shadows of the leaves moved on his blonde head, crisp with clipped curls. A butterfly flitted around him, alighting now on his legs, now on the back of his bronzed hands. All the afternoon the bees hung droning among the wildwood blossoms; the leaves above scarcely rustled; the shore birds brooded along the water's edge; the thin tide, sleeping on the sand, mirrored the sky.

Twilight paled the zenith; a breeze moved in the deeper woods; a star glimmered, went out, glimmered again, faded, and glimmered.

Night came. A moth darted to and fro under the trees; a beetle hummed around a heap of seaweed and fell scrambling in the sand. Somewhere among the trees a sound had become distinct, the song of a little brook, melodious, interminable. He heard it in his dream; it threaded all his dreams like a needle of silver, and like a needle it pricked him—pricked his dry throat and cracked lips. It could not awake him; the cool night swathed him head and foot.

Toward dawn a bird woke up and piped. Other birds stirred, restless, half awakened; a gull spread a cramped wing on the shore, preened its feathers, scratched its tufted neck, and took two drowsy steps toward the sea.

The sea breeze stirred out behind the mist bank; it raised the feathers on the sleeping gulls; it set the leaves whispering. A twig snapped, broke off, and fell. Kent stirred, sighed, trembled, and awoke.

The first thing he heard was the song of the brook, and he stumbled straight into the woods. There it lay, a thin, deep stream in the gray morning light, and he stretched himself beside it and laid his cheek in it. A bird drank in the pool, too—a little fluffy bird, bright-eyed and fearless.

His knees were firmer when at last he rose, heedless of the drops that beaded lips and chin. With his knife he dug and scraped at some white roots that hung half meshed in the bank of the brook, and when he had cleaned them in the pool he ate them.

The sun stained the sky when he went down to the canoe, but the eternal curtain of fog, far out at sea, hid it as yet from sight.

He lifted the canoe, bottom upwards, to his head, and, paddle and pole in either hand, carried it into the forest.

After he had set it down he stood a moment, opening and shutting his knife. Then he looked up into the trees. There were birds there, if he could get at them. He looked at the brook. There were the prints of his fingers in the sand; there, too, was the print of something else—a deer's pointed hoof.

He had nothing but his knife. He opened it again and looked at it.

That day he dug for clams and ate them raw. He waded out into the shallows, too, and jabbed at fish with his setting pole, but hit nothing except a yellow crab.

Fire was what he wanted. He hacked and chipped at flinty-looking pebbles, and scraped tinder from a stick of sun-dried driftwood. His knuckles bled, but no fire came.

That night he heard deer in the woods, and could not sleep for thinking, until the dawn came up behind the wall of mist, and he rose with it to drink his fill at the brook and tear raw clams with his white teeth. Again he fought for fire, craving it as he had never craved water, but his knuckles bled, and the knife scraped on the flint in vain.

His mind, perhaps, had suffered somewhat. The white beach seemed to rise and fall like a white carpet on a gusty hearth. The birds, too, that ran along the sand, seemed big and juicy, like partridges; and he chased them, hurling shells and bits of driftwood at them till he could scarcely keep his feet for the rising, plunging beach— or carpet, whichever it was. That night the deer aroused him at intervals. He heard them splashing and grunting and crackling along the brook. Once he arose and stole after them, knife in hand, till a false step into the brook awoke him to his folly, and he felt his way back to the canoe, trembling.

Morning came, and again he drank at the brook, lying on the sand where count-less heart-shaped hoofs had passed leaving clean imprints; and again he ripped the raw clams from their shells and swallowed them, whimpering.

All day long the white beach rose and fell and heaved and flattened under his bright dry eyes. He chased the shore birds at times, till the unsteady beach tripped him up and he fell full length in the sand. Then he would rise moaning, and creep into the shadow of the wood, and watch the little song-birds in the branches, moan-ing, always moaning.

His hands, sticky with blood, hacked steel and flint together, but so feebly that now even the cold sparks no longer came.

He began to fear the advancing night; he dreaded to hear the big warm deer among the thickets. Fear clutched him suddenly, and he lowered his head and set his teeth and shook fear from his throat again.

Then he started aimlessly into the woods, crowding past bushes, scraping trees, treading on moss and twig and mouldy stump, his bruised hands swinging, always swinging.

The sun set in the mist as he came out of the woods on to another beach—a warm, soft beach, crimsoned by the glow in the evening clouds.

And on the sand at his feet lay a young girl asleep, swathed in the silken garment of her own black hair, round limbed, brown, smooth as the bloom on the tawny beach.

A gull flapped overhead, screaming. Her eyes, deeper than night, unclosed. Then her lips parted in a cry, soft with sleep, "Ihó!"

She rose, rubbing her velvet eyes. "Ihó!" she cried in wonder; "Inâh!"

The gilded sand settled around her little feet. Her cheeks crimsoned.

"E-hó! E-hó!" she whispered, and hid her face in her hair.

### IV.

The bridge of the stars spans the sky seas; the sun and the moon are the travellers who pass over it. This was also known in the lodges of the Isantee, hundreds of years ago. Chaské told it to Hârpam, and when Hârpam knew he told it to Hapéda; and so the knowledge spread to Hârka, and from Winona to Wehârka, up and down, across and ever across, woof and web, until it came to the Island of Grief. And how? God knows!

Wehârka, prattling in the tules, may have told Ne-kâ; and Ne-kâ, high in the November clouds, may have told Kay-óshk, who told it to Shinge-bis, who told it to Skeé-skah, who told it to Sé-só-Kah.

Ihó! Inâh! Behold the wonder of it! And this is the fate of all knowledge that comes to the Island of Grief.

As the red glow died in the sky, and the sand swam in shadows, the girl parted the silken curtains of her hair and looked at him.

"Ehó!" she whispered again in soft delight.

For now it was plain to her that he was the sun! He had crossed the bridge of stars in the blue twilight; he had come!

"E-tó!"

She stepped nearer, shivering, faint with the ecstasy of this holy miracle wrought before her.

He was the Sun! His blood streaked the sky at dawn; his blood stained the clouds at even. In his eyes the blue of the sky still lingered, smothering two blue stars; and his body was as white as the breast of the Moon.

She opened both arms, hands timidly stretched, palm upward. Her face was raised to his, her eyes slowly closed; the deep-fringed lids trembled.

Like a young priestess she stood, motionless save for the sudden quiver of a limb, a quick pulse-flutter in the rounded throat. And so she worshipped, naked and unashamed, even after he, reeling, fell heavily forward on his face; even when the evening breeze stealing over the sands stirred the hair on his head, as winds stir the fur of a dead animal in the dust.

When the morning sun peered over the wall of mist, and she saw it was the sun, and she saw him, flung on the sand at her feet, then she knew that he was a man, only a man, pallid as death and smeared with blood.

And yet—miracle of miracles!—the divine wonder in her eyes deepened, and her body seemed to swoon, and fall a-trembling, and swoon again.

For, although it was but a man who lay at her feet, it had been easier for her to look upon a god.

He dreamed that he breathed fire—fire, that he craved as he had never craved water. Mad with delirium, he knelt before the flames, rubbing his torn hands, washing them in the crimson-scented flames. He had water, too, cool scented water, that sprayed his burning flesh, that washed in his eyes, his hair, his throat. After that came hunger, a fierce rending agony, that scorched and clutched and tore at his entrails; but that, too, died away, and he dreamed that he had eaten and all his flesh was warm. Then he dreamed that he slept; and when he slept he dreamed no more.

One day he awoke and found her stretched beside him, soft palms tightly closed, smiling, asleep.

### V.

Now the days began to run more swiftly than the tide along the tawny beach; and the nights, star-dusted and blue, came and vanished and returned, only to exhale at dawn like perfume from a violet.

They counted hours as they counted the golden bubbles, winking with a million eyes along the foam-flecked shore; and the hours ended, and began, and glimmered, iridescent, and ended as bubbles end in a tiny rainbow haze.

There was still fire in the world; it flashed up at her touch and where she chose. A bow strung with the silk of her own hair, an arrow winged like a sea bird and tipped with shell, a line from the silver tendon of a deer, a hook of polished bone—

these were the mysteries he learned, and learned them laughing, her silken head bent close to his.

The first night that the bow was wrought and the glossy string attuned, she stole into the moonlit forest to the brook; and there they stood, whispering, listening, and whispering, though neither understood the voice they loved.

In the deeper woods, Kaug, the porcupine, scraped and snuffed. They heard Wabóse, the rabbit, pit-a-pat, pit-a-pat, loping across dead leaves in the moonlight. Skeé-skah, the wood-duck, sailed past, noiseless, gorgeous as a floating blossom.

Out on the ocean's placid silver, Shinge-bis, the diver, shook the scented silence with his idle laughter, till Kay-óshk, the gray gull, stirred in his slumber. There came a sudden ripple in the stream, a mellow splash, a soft sound on the sand.

"Ihó! Behold!"

"I see nothing."

The beloved voice was only a wordless melody to her.

"Ihó! Ta-hinca, the red deer! E-hó! The buck will follow!"

"Ta-hinca," he repeated, notching the arrow.

"E-tó! Ta-mdóka!"

So he drew the arrow to the head, and the gray gull feathers brushed his ear, and the darkness hummed with the harmony of the singing string.

Thus died Ta-mdóka, the buck deer of seven prongs.

## VI.

As an apple tossed spinning into the air, so spun the world above the hand that tossed it into space.

And one day in early spring, Sé-só-Kah, the robin, awoke at dawn, and saw a girl at the foot of the blossoming tree holding a babe cradled in the silken sheets of her hair.

At its feeble cry, Kaug, the porcupine, raised his quilled head. Wabóse, the rabbit, sat still with palpitating sides. Kay-óshk, the gray gull, tiptoed along the beach.

Kent knelt with one bronzed arm around them both.

"Ihó! Inâh!" whispered the girl, and held the babe up in the rosy flames of dawn.

But Kent trembled as he looked, and his eyes filled. On the pale green moss their shadows lay—three shadows. But the shadow of the babe was white as froth.

Because it was the firstborn son, they named it Chaské; and the girl sang as she cradled it there in the silken vestments of her hair; all day long in the sunshine she sang:

Wâ-wa, wâ-wa, wâ-we—yeá;

Kah-wéen, nee-zhéka Ke-diaus-âi,

Ke-gâh nau-wâi, ne-mé-go S'weén,

Ne-bâun, ne-bâun, ne-dâun-is âis.

E-we wâ-wa, wâ-we—yeá;

E-we wâ-wa, wâ-we—yeá.

Out in the calm ocean, Shinge-bis, the diver, listened, preening his satin breast in silence. In the forest, Ta-hinca, the red deer, turned her delicate head to the wind.

That night Kent thought of the dead, for the first time since he had come to the Key of Grief.

"Aké-u! aké-u!" chirped Sé-só-Kah, the robin. But the dead never come again.

"Beloved, sit close to us," whispered the girl, watching his troubled eyes. "Ma-cânte maséca."

But he looked at the babe and its white shadow on the moss, and he only sighed: "Ma-cânte maséca, beloved! Death sits watching us across the sea."

Now for the first time he knew more than the fear of fear; he knew fear. And with fear came grief.

He never before knew that grief lay hidden there in the forest. Now he knew it. Still, that happiness, eternally reborn when two small hands reached up around his neck, when feeble fingers clutched his hand—that happiness that Sé-só-Kah understood, chirping to his brooding mate—that Ta-mdóka knew, licking his dappled fawns—that happiness gave him heart to meet grief calmly, in dreams or in the forest depths, and it helped him to look into the hollow eyes of fear.

He often thought of the camp now; of Bates, his blanket mate; of Dyce, whose wrist he had broken with a blow; of Tully, whose brother he had shot. He even seemed to hear the shot, the sudden report among the hemlocks; again he saw the haze of smoke, he caught a glimpse of a tall form falling through the bushes.

He remembered every minute incident of the trial: Bates's hand laid on his shoulder; Tully, red-bearded and wild-eyed, demanding his death; while Dyce spat and spat and smoked and kicked at the blackened log-ends projecting from the fire. He remembered, too, the verdict, and Tully's terrible laugh; and the new jute rope that they stripped off the market-sealed gum packs.

He thought of these things, sometimes wading out on the shoals, shell-tipped fish spear poised: at such times he would miss his fish. He thought of it sometimes when he knelt by the forest stream listening for Ta-hinca's splash among the cresses:

at such moments the feathered shaft whistled far from the mark, and Ta-mdóka stamped and snorted till even the white fisher, stretched on a rotting log, flattened his whiskers and stole away into the forest's blackest depths.

When the child was a year old, hour for hour notched at sunset and sunrise, it prattled with the birds, and called to Ne-Kâ, the wild goose, who called again to the child from the sky: "Northward! northward, beloved!"

When winter came—there is no frost on the Island of Grief—Ne-Kâ, the wild goose, passing high in the clouds, called: "Southward! southward, beloved!" And the child answered in a soft whisper of an unknown tongue, till the mother shivered, and covered it with her silken hair.

"O beloved!" said the girl, "Chaské calls to all things living—to Kaug, the porcupine, to Wabóse, to Kay-óshk, the gray gull—he calls, and they understand."

Kent bent and looked into her eyes.

"Hush, beloved; it is not *that* I fear."

"Then what, beloved?"

"His shadow. It is white as surf foam. And at night—I—I have seen——"

"Oh, what?"

"The air about him aglow like a pale rose."

"Ma cânté maséca. The earth alone lasts. I speak as one dying—I know, O beloved!"

Her voice died away like a summer wind.

"Beloved!" he cried.

But there before him she was changing; the air grew misty, and her hair wavered like shreds of fog, and her slender form swayed, and faded, and swerved, like the mist above a pond.

In her arms the babe was a figure of mist, rosy, vague as a breath on a mirror.

"The earth alone lasts. Inâh! It is the end, O beloved!"

The words came from the mist—a mist as formless as the ether—a mist that drove in and crowded him, that came from the sea, from the clouds, from the earth at his feet. Faint with terror, he staggered forward calling, "Beloved! And thou, Chaské, O beloved! Aké u! Aké u!"

Far out at sea a rosy star glimmered an instant in the mist and went out.

A sea bird screamed, soaring over the waste of fog-smothered waters. Again he saw the rosy star; it came nearer; its reflection glimmered in the water.

"Chaské!" he cried.

He heard a voice, dull in the choking mist.

"O beloved, I am here!" he called again.

There was a sound on the shoal, a flicker in the fog, the flare of a torch, a face white, livid, terrible—the face of the dead.

He fell upon his knees; he closed his eyes and opened them. Tully stood beside him with a coil of rope.

Ihó! Behold the end! The earth alone lasts. The sand, the opal wave on the golden beach, the sea of sapphire, the dusted starlight, the wind, and love, shall die. Death also shall die, and lie on the shores of the skies like the bleached skull there on the Key to Grief, polished, empty, with its teeth embedded in the sand.

# A MATTER OF INTEREST

A MATTER OF INTEREST.

He that knows not, and knows not that he knows not, is a fool. Shun him.

He that knows not, and knows that he knows not, is simple. Teach him.

He that knows, and knows not that he knows, is asleep. Wake him.

He that knows, and knows that he knows, is wise. Follow him.

*Arabian Proverb.*

## I.

Much as I dislike it, I am obliged to include this story in a volume devoted to fiction: I have attempted to tell it as an absolutely true story, but until three months ago, when the indisputable proofs were placed before the British Association by Professor James Holroyd, I was regarded as an impostor. Now that the Smithsonian Institute in Washington, the Philadelphia Zoölogical Society, and the Natural History Museum of New York city, are convinced that the story is truthful and accurate in every particular, I prefer to tell it my own way. Professor Holroyd urges me to do this, although Professor Bruce Stoddard, of Columbia College, is now at work upon a pamphlet, to be published the latter part of next month, describing scientifically the extraordinary discovery which, to the shame of the United States, was first accepted and recognised in England.

Now, having no technical ability concerning the affair in question, and having no knowledge of either comparative anatomy or zoölogy, I am perhaps unfitted to tell this story. But the story is true; the episode occurred under my own eyes—here, within a few hours' sail of the Battery. And as I was one of the first persons to verify what has long been a theory among scientists, and, moreover, as the result of Professor Holroyd's discovery is to be placed on exhibition in Madison Square Garden on the twentieth of next month, I have decided to tell, as simply as I am able, exactly what occurred.

I first wrote out the story on April 1, 1896. The North American Review, the Popular Science Monthly, the Scientific American, Nature, Forest and Stream, and the Fossiliferous Magazine in turn rejected it; some curtly informing me that fiction had no place in their columns. When I attempted to explain that it was not fiction, the editors of these periodicals either maintained a contemptuous silence, or bluntly notified me that my literary services and opinions were not desired. But finally, when several publishers offered to take the story as fiction, I cut short all negotiations and decided to publish it myself. Where I am known at all, it is my misfortune to be known as a writer of fiction. This makes it impossible for me to receive a hearing from a scientific audience. I regret it bitterly, because now, when it is too late, I am prepared to prove certain scientific matters of interest, and to produce the proofs. In this case, however, I am fortunate, for nobody can dispute the existence of a thing when the bodily proof is exhibited as evidence.

This is the story; and if I write it as I write fiction, it is because I do not know how to write it otherwise.

I was walking along the beach below Pine Inlet, on the south shore of Long Island. The railroad and telegraph station is at West Oyster Bay. Everybody who has travelled on the Long Island Railroad knows the station, but few, perhaps, know Pine Inlet. Duck shooters, of course, are familiar with it; but as there are no hotels there, and nothing to see except salt meadow, salt creek, and a strip of dune and sand, the summer-squatting public may probably be unaware of its existence. The local name for the place is Pine Inlet; the maps give its name as Sand Point, I believe, but anybody at West Oyster Bay can direct you to it. Captain McPeek, who keeps the West Oyster Bay House, drives duck shooters there in winter. It lies five miles southeast from West Oyster Bay.

I had walked over that afternoon from Captain McPeek's. There was a reason for my going to Pine Inlet—it embarrasses me to explain it, but the truth is I meditated writing an ode to the ocean. It was out of the question to write it in West Oyster Bay, with the whistle of locomotives in my ears. I knew that Pine Inlet was one of the loneliest places on the Atlantic coast; it is out of sight of everything except leagues of gray ocean. Rarely one might make out fishing smacks drifting across the horizon. Summer squatters never visited it; sportsmen shunned it, except in winter. Therefore, as I was about to do a bit of poetry, I thought that Pine Inlet was the spot for the deed. So I went there.

As I was strolling along the beach, biting my pencil reflectively, tremendously impressed by the solitude and the solemn thunder of the surf, a thought occurred to me: how unpleasant it would be if I suddenly stumbled on a summer boarder. As this joyless impossibility flitted across my mind, I rounded a bleak sand dune.

A summer girl stood directly in my path.

If I jumped, I think the young lady has pardoned me by this time. She ought to, because she also started, and said something in a very faint voice. What she said was "Oh!"

She stared at me as though I had just crawled up out of the sea to bite her. I don't know what my own expression resembled, but I have been given to understand it was idiotic.

Now I perceived, after a few moments, that the young lady was frightened, and I knew I ought to say something civil. So I said, "Are there any mosquitoes here?"

"No," she replied, with a slight quiver in her voice; "I have only seen one, and it was biting somebody else."

I looked foolish; the conversation seemed so futile, and the young lady appeared to be more nervous than before. I had an impulse to say, "Do not run; I have breakfasted," for she seemed to be meditating a plunge into the breakers. What I did say was: "I did not know anybody was here. I do not intend to intrude. I come from Captain McPeek's, and I am writing an ode to the ocean." After I had said this it seemed to ring in my ears like, "I come from Table Mountain, and my name is Truthful James."

I glanced timidly at her.

"She's thinking of the same thing," said I to myself. "What an ass I must appear!"

However, the young lady seemed to be a trifle reassured. I noticed she drew a sigh of relief and looked at my shoes. She looked so long that it made me suspicious, and I also examined my shoes. They seemed to be fairly respectable.

"I—I am sorry," she said, "but would you mind not walking on the beach?"

This was sudden. I had intended to retire and leave the beach to her, but I did not fancy being driven away so abruptly.

"I was about to withdraw, madam," said I, bowing stiffly; "I beg you will pardon any inconvenience——"

"Dear me!" she cried, "you don't understand. I do not—I would not think for a moment of asking you to leave Pine Inlet. I merely ventured to request you to walk on the dunes. I am so afraid that your footprints may obliterate the impressions that my father is studying."

"Oh!" said I, looking about me as though I had been caught in the middle of a flower-bed; "really I did not notice any impressions. Impressions of what—if I may be permitted?"

"I don't know," she said, smiling a little at my awkward pose. "If you step this way in a straight line you can do no damage."

I did as she bade me. I suppose my movements resembled the gait of a wet peacock. Possibly they recalled the delicate manœuvres of the kangaroo. Anyway, she laughed.

This seriously annoyed me. I had been at a disadvantage; I walk well enough when let alone.

"You can scarcely expect," said I, "that a man absorbed in his own ideas could notice impressions on the sand. I trust I have obliterated nothing."

As I said this I looked back at the long line of footprints stretching away in prospective across the sand. They were my own. How large they looked! Was that what she was laughing at?

"I wish to explain," she said gravely, looking at the point of her parasol. "I am very sorry to be obliged to warn you—to ask you to forego the pleasure of strolling on a beach that does not belong to me. Perhaps," she continued, in sudden alarm, "perhaps this beach belongs to you?"

"The beach? Oh, no," I said.

"But—but you were going to write poems about it?"

"Only one—and that does not necessitate owning the beach. I have observed," said I frankly, "that the people who own nothing write many poems about it."

She looked at me seriously.

"I write many poems," I added.

She laughed doubtfully.

"Would you rather I went away?" I asked politely.

"I? Why, no—I mean that you may do as you please—except please do not walk on the *beach*."

"Then I do not alarm you by my presence?" I inquired. My clothes were a bit ancient. I wore them shooting, sometimes. "My family is respectable," I added; and I told her my name.

"Oh! Then you wrote 'Culled Cowslips' and 'Faded Fig-Leaves,' and you imitate Maeterlinck, and you—— Oh, I know lots of people that you know;" she cried with every symptom of relief; "and you know my brother."

"I am the author," said I coldly, "of 'Culled Cowslips,' but 'Faded Fig-Leaves' was an earlier work, which I no longer recognise, and I should be grateful to you if you would be kind enough to deny that I ever imitated Maeterlinck. Possibly," I added, "he imitates me."

"Now, do you know," she said, "I was afraid of you at first? Papa is digging in the salt meadows nearly a mile away."

It was hard to bear.

"Can you not see," said I, "that I am wearing a shooting coat?"

"I do see—now; but it is so—so old," she pleaded.

"It is a shooting coat all the same," I said bitterly.

She was very quiet, and I saw she was sorry.

"Never mind," I said magnanimously, "you probably are not familiar with sporting goods. If I knew your name I should ask permission to present myself."

"Why, I am Daisy Holroyd," she said.

"What! Jack Holroyd's little sister?"

"Little!" she cried.

"I didn't mean that," said I. "You know that your brother and I were great friends in Paris——"

"I know," she said significantly.

"Ahem! Of course," I said, "Jack and I were inseparable——"

"Except when shut in separate cells," said Miss Holroyd coldly.

This unfeeling allusion to the unfortunate termination of a Latin-Quarter celebration hurt me.

"The police," said I, "were too officious."

"So Jack says," replied Miss Holroyd demurely.

We had unconsciously moved on along the sand hills, side by side, as we spoke.

"To think," I repeated, "that I should meet Jack's little——"

"Please," she said, "you are only three years my senior."

She opened the sunshade and tipped it over one shoulder. It was white, and had spots and posies on it.

"Jack sends us every new book you write," she observed. "I do not approve of some things you write."

"Modern school," I mumbled.

"That is no excuse," she said severely; "Anthony Trollope didn't do it."

The foam spume from the breakers was drifting across the dunes, and the little tip-up snipe ran along the beach and teetered and whistled and spread their white-barred wings for a low, straight flight across the shingle, only to tip and skeep and sail on again. The salt sea wind whistled and curled through the crested waves, blowing in perfumed puffs across thickets of sweet bay and cedar. As we passed through the crackling juicy-stemmed marsh weed myriads of fiddler crabs raised their fore-claws in warning and backed away, rustling, through the reeds, aggressive, protesting.

"Like millions of pigmy Ajaxes defying the lightning," I said.

Miss Holroyd laughed.

"Now I never imagined that authors were clever except in print," she said.

She was a most extraordinary girl.

"I suppose," she observed after a moment's silence—"I suppose I am taking you to my father."

"Delighted!" I mumbled. "H'm! I had the honour of meeting Professor Holroyd in Paris."

"Yes; he bailed you and Jack out," said Miss Holroyd serenely.

The silence was too painful to last.

"Captain McPeek is an interesting man," I said. I spoke more loudly than I intended; I may have been nervous.

"Yes," said Daisy Holroyd, "but he has a most singular hotel clerk."

"You mean Mr. Frisby?"

"I do."

"Yes," I admitted, "Mr. Frisby is queer. He was once a bill-poster."

"I know it!" exclaimed Daisy Holroyd, with some heat. "He ruins landscapes whenever he has an opportunity. Do you know that he has a passion for bill-posting? He has; he posts bills for the pure pleasure of it, just as you play golf, or tennis, or billiards."

"But he's a hotel clerk now," I said; "nobody employs him to post bills."

"I know it! He does it all by himself for the pure pleasure of it. Papa has engaged him to come down here for two weeks, and I dread it," said the girl.

What Professor Holroyd might want of Frisby I had not the faintest notion. I suppose Miss Holroyd noticed the bewilderment in my face, for she laughed, and nodded her head twice.

"Not only Mr. Frisby, but Captain McPeek also," she said.

"You don't mean to say that Captain McPeek is going to close his hotel!" I exclaimed.

My trunk was there. It contained guarantees of my respectability.

"Oh, no; his wife will keep it open," replied the girl. "Look! you can see papa now. He's digging."

"Where?" I blurted out.

I remembered Professor Holroyd as a prim, spectacled gentleman, with close-cut, snowy beard and a clerical allure. The man I saw digging wore green goggles, a jersey, a battered sou'wester, and hip-boots of rubber. He was delving in the muck of the salt meadow, his face streaming with perspiration, his boots and jersey splashed with unpleasant-looking mud. He glanced up as we approached, shading his eyes with a sunburnt hand.

"Papa, dear," said Miss Holroyd, "here is Jack's friend, whom you bailed out of Mazas."

The introduction was startling. I turned crimson with mortification. The professor was very decent about it; he called me by name at once.

When he said this he looked at his spade. It was clear that he considered me a nuisance and wished to go on with his digging.

"I suppose," he said, "you are still writing?"

"A little," I replied, trying not to speak sarcastically. My output had rivaled that of "The Duchess"—in quantity, I mean.

"I seldom read—fiction," he said, looking restlessly at the hole in the ground.

Miss Holroyd came to my rescue.

"That was a charming story you wrote last," she said. "Papa should read it— you should, papa; it's all about a fossil."

We both looked narrowly at Miss Holroyd. Her smile was guileless.

"Fossils!" repeated the professor. "Do you care for fossils?"

"Very much," said I.

Now I am not perfectly sure what my object was in lying. I looked at Daisy Holroyd's dark-fringed eyes. They were very grave.

"Fossils," said I, "are my hobby."

I think Miss Holroyd winced a little at this. I did not care. I went on:

"I have seldom had the opportunity to study the subject, but, as a boy, I collected flint arrow-heads——"

"Flint arrow-heads!" said the professor coldly.

"Yes; they were the nearest things to fossils obtainable," I replied, marvelling at my own mendacity.

The professor looked into the hole. I also looked. I could see nothing in it. "He's digging for fossils," thought I to myself.

"Perhaps," said the professor cautiously, "you might wish to aid me in a little research—that is to say, if you have an inclination for fossils." The double-entendre was not lost upon me.

"I have read all your books so eagerly," said I, "that to join you, to be of service to you in any research, however difficult and trying, would be an honour and a privilege that I never dared to hope for."

"That," thought I to myself, "will do its own work."

But the professor was still suspicious. How could he help it, when he remembered Jack's escapades, in which my name was always blended! Doubtless he was satisfied that my influence on Jack was evil. The contrary was the case, too.

"Fossils," he said, worrying the edges of the excavation with his spade, "fossils are not things to be lightly considered."

"No, indeed!" I protested.

"Fossils are the most interesting as well as puzzling things in the world," said he.

"They are!" I cried enthusiastically.

"But I am not looking for fossils," observed the professor mildly.

This was a facer. I looked at Daisy Holroyd. She bit her lip and fixed her eyes on the sea. Her eyes were wonderful eyes.

"Did you think I was digging for fossils in a salt meadow?" queried the professor. "You can have read very little about the subject. I am digging for something quite different."

I was silent. I knew that my face was a trifle flushed. I longed to say, "Well, what the devil are you digging for?" but I only stared into the hole as though hypnotized.

"Captain McPeek and Frisby ought to be here," he said, looking first at Daisy and then across the meadows.

I ached to ask him why he had subpœnaed Captain McPeek and Frisby.

"They are coming," said Daisy, shading her eyes. "Do you see the speck on the meadows?"

"It may be a mud hen," said the professor.

"Miss Holroyd is right," I said. "A wagon and team and two men are coming from the north. There is a dog beside the wagon—it's that miserable yellow dog of Frisby's."

"Good gracious!" cried the professor, "you don't mean to tell me that you see all that at such a distance?"

"Why not?" I said.

"I see nothing," he insisted.

"You will see that I'm right, presently," I laughed.

The professor removed his blue goggles and rubbed them, glancing obliquely at me.

"Haven't you heard what extraordinary eyesight duck shooters have?" said his daughter, looking back at her father. "Jack says that they can tell exactly what kind of a duck is flying before most people could see anything at all in the sky."

"It's true," I said; "it comes to anybody, I fancy, who has had practice."

The professor regarded me with a new interest. There was inspiration in his eyes. He turned toward the ocean. For a long time he stared at the tossing waves on the beach, then he looked far out to where the horizon met the sea.

"Are there any ducks out there?" he asked at last.

"Yes," said I, scanning the sea, "there are."

He produced a pair of binoculars from his coat-tail pocket, adjusted them, and raised them to his eyes.

"H'm! What sort of ducks?"

I looked more carefully, holding both hands over my forehead.

"Surf ducks—scoters and widgeon. There is one bufflehead among them—no, two; the rest are coots," I replied.

"This," cried the professor, "is most astonishing. I have good eyes, but I can't see a blessed thing without these binoculars!"

"It's not extraordinary," said I; "the surf ducks and coots any novice might recognise; the widgeon and buffleheads I should not have been able to name unless they had risen from the water. It is easy to tell any duck when it is flying, even though it looks no bigger than a black pin-point."

But the professor insisted that it was marvellous, and he said that I might render him invaluable service if I would consent to come and camp at Pine Inlet for a few weeks.

I looked at his daughter, but she turned her back—not exactly in disdain either. Her back was beautifully moulded. Her gown fitted also.

"Camp out here?" I repeated, pretending to be unpleasantly surprised.

"I do not think he would care to," said Miss Holroyd without turning.

I had not expected that.

"Above all things," said I, in a clear, pleasant voice, "I like to camp out."

She said nothing.

"It is not exactly camping," said the professor. "Come, you shall see our conservatory. Daisy, come, dear! you must put on a heavier frock; it is getting toward sundown."

At that moment, over a near dune, two horses' heads appeared, followed by two human heads, then a wagon, then a yellow dog.

I turned triumphantly to the professor.

"You are the very man I want," he muttered; "the very man—the very man."

I looked at Daisy Holroyd. She returned my glance with a defiant little smile.

"Waal," said Captain McPeek, driving up, "here we be! Git out, Frisby."

Frisby, fat, nervous, and sentimental, hopped out of the cart.

"Come!" said the professor, impatiently moving across the dunes. I walked with Daisy Holroyd. McPeek and Frisby followed. The yellow dog walked by himself.

## II.

The sun was dipping into the sea as we trudged across the meadows toward a high dome-shaped dune covered with cedars and thickets of sweet bay. I saw no sign of habitation among the sand hills. Far as the eye could reach, nothing broke the gray line of sea and sky save the squat dunes crowned with stunted cedars.

Then, as we rounded the base of the dune, we almost walked into the door of a house. My amazement amused Miss Holroyd, and I noticed also a touch of malice in her pretty eyes. But she said nothing, following her father into the house, with the slightest possible gesture to me. Was it invitation, or was it menace?

The house was merely a light wooden frame, covered with some waterproof stuff that looked like a mixture of rubber and tar. Over this—in fact, over the whole roof—was pitched an awning of heavy sail-cloth. I noticed that the house was anchored to the sand by chains, already rusted red. But this one-storied house was not the only building nestling in the south shelter of the big dune. A hundred feet away stood another structure—long, low, also built of wood. It had rows on rows of round portholes on every side. The ports were fitted with heavy glass, hinged to swing open if necessary. A single big double door occupied the front.

Behind this long, low building was still another, a mere shed. Smoke rose from the sheet-iron chimney. There was somebody moving about inside the open door.

As I stood gaping at this mushroom hamlet the professor appeared at the door and asked me to enter. I stepped in at once.

The house was much larger than I had imagined. A straight hallway ran through the centre from east to west. On either side of this hallway were rooms, the doors swinging wide open. I counted three doors on each side; the three on the south appeared to be bedrooms.

The professor ushered me into a room on the north side, where I found Captain McPeek and Frisby sitting at a table, upon which were drawings and sketches of articulated animals and fishes.

"You see, McPeek," said the professor, "we only wanted one more man, and I think I've got him.—Haven't I?" turning eagerly to me.

"Why, yes," I said, laughing; "this is delightful. Am I invited to stay here?"

"Your bedroom is the third on the south side; everything is ready. McPeek, you can bring his trunk to-morrow, can't you?" demanded the professor.

The red-faced captain nodded, and shifted a quid.

"Then it's all settled," said the professor, and he drew a sigh of satisfaction. "You see," he said, turning to me, "I was at my wit's end to know whom to trust. I never thought of you. Jack's out in China, and I didn't dare trust anybody in my own profession. All you care about is writing verses and stories, isn't it?"

"I like to shoot," I replied mildly.

"Just the thing!" he cried, beaming at us all in turn. "Now I can see no reason why we should not progress rapidly. McPeek, you and Frisby must get those boxes up here before dark. Dinner will be ready before you have finished unloading. Dick, you will wish to go to your room first."

My name isn't Dick, but he spoke so kindly, and beamed upon me in such a fatherly manner, that I let it go. I had occasion to correct him afterward, several times, but he always forgot the next minute. He calls me Dick to this day.

It was dark when Professor Holroyd, his daughter, and I sat down to dinner. The room was the same in which I had noticed the drawings of beast and bird, but the round table had been extended into an oval, and neatly spread with dainty linen and silver.

A fresh-cheeked Swedish girl appeared from a further room, bearing the soup. The professor ladled it out, still beaming.

"Now, this is very delightful!—isn't it, Daisy?" he said.

"Very," said Miss Holroyd, with the faintest tinge of irony.

"Very," I repeated heartily; but I looked at my soup when I said it.

"I suppose," said the professor, nodding mysteriously at his daughter, "that Dick knows nothing of what we're about down here?"

"I suppose," said Miss Holroyd, "that he thinks we are digging for fossils."

I looked at my plate. She might have spared me that.

"Well, well," said her father, smiling to himself, "he shall know everything by morning. You'll be astonished, Dick, my boy."

"His name isn't Dick," corrected Daisy.

The professor said, "Isn't it?" in an absent-minded way, and relapsed into contemplation of my necktie.

I asked Miss Holroyd a few questions about Jack, and was informed that he had given up law and entered the diplomatic service—as what, I did not dare ask, for I know what our diplomatic service is.

"In China," said Daisy.

"Choo Choo is the name of the city," added her father proudly; "it's the terminus of the new trans-Siberian railway."

"It's on the Yellow River," said Daisy.

"He's vice-consul," added the professor triumphantly.

"He'll make a good one," I observed. I knew Jack. I pitied his consul.

So we chatted on about my old playmate, until Freda, the red-cheeked maid, brought coffee, and the professor lighted a cigar, with a little bow to his daughter.

"Of course, you don't smoke," she said to me, with a glimmer of malice in her eyes.

"He mustn't," interposed the professor hastily; "it will make his hand tremble."

"No, it doesn't," said I, laughing; "but my hand will shake if I don't smoke. Are you going to employ me as a draughtsman?"

"You'll know to-morrow," he chuckled, with a mysterious smile at his daughter.—"Daisy, give him my best cigars; put the box here on the table. We can't afford to have his hand tremble."

Miss Holroyd rose, and crossed the hallway to her father's room, returning presently with a box of promising-looking cigars.

"I don't think he knows what is good for him," she said. "He should smoke only one every day."

It was hard to bear. I am not vindictive, but I decided to treasure up a few of Miss Holroyd's gentle taunts. My intimacy with her brother was certainly a disadvantage to me now. Jack had apparently been talking too much, and his sister appeared to be thoroughly acquainted with my past. It was a disadvantage. I remembered her vaguely as a girl with long braids, who used to come on Sundays with her father and take tea with us in our rooms. Then she went to Germany to school, and Jack and I employed our Sunday evenings otherwise. It is true that I regarded her weekly visits as a species of infliction, but I did not think I ever showed it.

"It is strange," said I, "that you did not recognise me at once, Miss Holroyd. Have I changed so greatly in five years?"

"You wore a pointed French beard in Paris," she said—"a very downy one. And you never stayed to tea but twice, and then you only spoke once."

"Oh!" said I blankly. "What did I say?"

"You asked me if I liked plums," said Daisy, bursting into an irresistible ripple of laughter.

I saw that I must have made the same sort of an ass of myself that most boys of eighteen do.

It was too bad. I never thought about the future in those days. Who could have imagined that little Daisy Holroyd would have grown up into this bewildering young lady? It was really too bad. Presently the professor retired to his room, carrying with him an armful of drawings, and bidding us not to sit up late. When he closed his door Miss Holroyd turned to me.

"Papa will work over those drawings until midnight," she said, with a despairing smile.

"It isn't good for him," I said. "What are the drawings?"

"You may know to-morrow," she answered, leaning forward on the table and shading her face with one hand. "Tell me about yourself and Jack in Paris."

I looked at her suspiciously.

"What! There isn't much to tell. We studied. Jack went to the law school, and I attended—er—oh, all sorts of schools."

"Did you? Surely you gave yourself a little recreation occasionally?"

"Occasionally," I nodded.

"I am afraid you and Jack studied too hard."

"That may be," said I, looking meek.

"Especially about fossils."

I couldn't stand that.

"Miss Holroyd," I said, "I do care for fossils. You may think that I am a humbug, but I have a perfect mania for fossils—now."

"Since when?"

"About an hour ago," I said airily. Out of the corner of my eye I saw that she had flushed up. It pleased me.

"You will soon tire of the experiment," she said with a dangerous smile.

"Oh, I may," I replied indifferently.

She drew back. The movement was scarcely perceptible, but I noticed it, and she knew I did.

The atmosphere was vaguely hostile. One feels such mental conditions and changes instantly. I picked up a chessboard, opened it, set up the pieces with elaborate care, and began to move, first the white, then the black. Miss Holroyd watched me coldly at first, but after a dozen moves she became interested and leaned a shade nearer. I moved a black pawn forward.

"Why do you do that?" said Daisy.

"Because," said I, "the white queen threatens the pawn."

"It was an aggressive move," she insisted.

"Purely defensive," I said. "If her white highness will let the pawn alone, the pawn will let the queen alone."

Miss Holroyd rested her chin on her wrist and gazed steadily at the board. She was flushing furiously, but she held her ground.

"If the white queen doesn't block that pawn, the pawn may become dangerous," she said coldly.

I laughed, and closed up the board with a snap.

"True," I said, "it might even take the queen." After a moment's silence I asked, "What would you do in that case, Miss Holroyd?"

"I should resign," she said serenely; then realizing what she had said, she lost her self-possession for a second, and cried: "No, indeed! I should fight to the bitter end! I mean——"

"What?" I asked, lingering over my revenge.

"I mean," she said slowly, "that your black pawn would never have the chance—never! I should take it immediately."

"I believe you would," said I, smiling; "so we'll call the game yours, and—the pawn captured."

"I don't want it," she exclaimed. "A pawn is worthless."

"Except when it's in the king row."

"Chess is most interesting," she observed sedately. She had completely recovered her self-control. Still I saw that she now had a certain respect for my defensive powers. It was very soothing to me.

"You know," said I gravely, "that I am fonder of Jack than of anybody. That's the reason we never write each other, except to borrow things. I am afraid that when I was a young cub in France I was not an attractive personality."

"On the contrary," said Daisy, smiling, "I thought you were very big and very perfect. I had illusions. I wept often when I went home and remembered that you never took the trouble to speak to me but once."

"I was a cub," I said; "not selfish and brutal, but I didn't understand schoolgirls. I never had any sisters, and I didn't know what to say to very young girls. If I had imagined that you felt hurt——"

"Oh, I did—five years ago. Afterward I laughed at the whole thing."

"Laughed?" I repeated, vaguely disappointed.

"Why, of course. I was very easily hurt when I was a child. I think I have outgrown it."

The soft curve of her sensitive mouth contradicted her.

"Will you forgive me now?" I asked.

"Yes. I had forgotten the whole thing until I met you an hour or so ago."

There was something that had a ring not entirely genuine in this speech. I noticed it, but forgot it the next moment.

"Tiger cubs have stripes," said I. "Selfishness blossoms in the cradle, and prophecy is not difficult. I hope I am not more selfish than my brothers."

"I hope not," she said, smiling.

Presently she rose, touched her hair with the tip of one finger, and walked to the door.

"Good-night," she said, courtesying very low.

"Good-night," said I, opening the door for her to pass.

### III.

The sea was a sheet of silver, tinged with pink. The tremendous arch of the sky was all shimmering and glimmering with the promise of the sun. Already the mist above, flecked with clustered clouds, flushed with rose colour and dull gold. I heard the low splash of the waves breaking and curling across the beach. A wandering breeze, fresh and fragrant, blew the curtains of my window. There was the scent of sweet bay in the room, and everywhere the subtile, nameless perfume of the sea.

When at last I stood upon the shore, the air and sea were all aglimmer in a rosy light, deepening to crimson in the zenith. Along the beach I saw a little cove, shelving and all ashine, where shallow waves washed with a mellow sound. Fine as dusted gold the shingle glowed, and the thin film of water rose, receded, crept up again a little higher, and again flowed back, with the low hiss of snowy foam and gilded bubbles breaking.

I stood a little while quiet, my eyes upon the water, the invitation of the ocean in my ears, vague and sweet as the murmur of a shell. Then I looked at my bathing suit and towels.

"In we go!" said I aloud. A second later the prophecy was fulfilled.

I swam far out to sea, and as I swam the waters all around me turned to gold. The sun had risen.

There is a fragrance in the sea at dawn that none can name. Whitethorn abloom in May, sedges asway, and scented rushes rustling in an inland wind recall the sea to me—I can't say why.

Far out at sea I raised myself, swung around, dived, and set out again for shore, striking strong strokes until the flecked foam flew. And when at last I shot through the breakers, I laughed aloud and sprang upon the beach, breathless and happy. Then from the ocean came another cry, clear, joyous, and a white arm rose in the air.

She came drifting in with the waves like a white sea-sprite, laughing at me from her tangled hair, and I plunged into the breakers again to join her.

Side by side we swam along the coast, just outside the breakers, until in the next cove we saw the flutter of her maid's cap strings.

"I will beat you to breakfast!" she cried, as I rested, watching her glide up along the beach.

"Done!" said I—"for a sea-shell!"

"Done!" she called across the water.

I made good speed along the shore, and I was not long in dressing, but when I entered the dining-room she was there, demure, smiling, exquisite in her cool, white frock.

"The sea-shell is yours," said I. "I hope I can find one with a pearl in it."

The professor hurried in before she could reply. He greeted me very cordially, but there was an abstracted air about him, and he called me Dick until I recognised that remonstrance was useless. He was not long over his coffee and rolls.

"McPeek and Frisby will return with the last load, including your trunk, by early afternoon," he said, rising and picking up his bundle of drawings. "I haven't time to explain to you what we are doing, Dick, but Daisy will take you about and instruct you. She will give you the rifle standing in my room—it's a good Winchester. I have sent for an 'Express' for you, big enough to knock over any elephant in India.—

Daisy, take him through the sheds and tell him everything. Luncheon is at noon.— Do you usually take luncheon, Dick?"

"When I am permitted," I smiled.

"Well," said the professor doubtfully, "you mustn't come back here for it. Freda can take you what you want. Is your hand unsteady after eating?"

"Why, papa!" said Daisy. "Do you intend to starve him?"

We all laughed.

The professor tucked his drawings into a capacious pocket, pulled his sea boots up to his hips, seized a spade, and left, nodding to us as though he were thinking of something else.

We went to the door and watched him across the salt meadows until a distant sand dune hid him.

"Come," said Daisy Holroyd, "I am going to take you to the shop."

She put on a broad-brimmed straw hat, a distractingly pretty combination of filmy cool stuffs, and led the way to the long low structure that I had noticed the evening before.

The interior was lighted by the numberless little portholes, and I could see everything plainly. I acknowledge I was nonplussed by what I did see.

In the centre of the shed, which must have been at least a hundred feet long, stood what I thought at first was the skeleton of an enormous whale. After a moment's silent contemplation of the thing I saw that it could not be a whale, for the frames of two gigantic bat-like wings rose from each shoulder. Also I noticed that the animal possessed legs—four of them—with most unpleasant-looking webbed claws fully eight feet long. The bony framework of the head, too, resembled something between a crocodile and a monstrous snapping turtle. The walls of the shanty were hung with drawings and blue prints. A man dressed in white linen was tinkering with the vertebræ of the lizardlike tail.

"Where on earth did such a reptile come from?" I asked at length.

"Oh, it's not real!" said Daisy scornfully; "it's papier-maché."

"I see," said I—"a stage prop."

"A what?" asked Daisy, in hurt astonishment.

"Why, a—a sort of Siegfried dragon—a what's-his-name—er, Pfafner, or Peffer, or——"

"If my father heard you say such things he would dislike you," said Daisy. She looked grieved, and moved toward the door. I apologized—for what, I knew not—

283

and we became reconciled. She ran into her father's room and brought me the rifle, a very good Winchester. She also gave me a cartridge belt, full.

"Now," she smiled, "I shall take you to your observatory, and when we arrive you are to begin your duty at once."

"And that duty?" I ventured, shouldering the rifle.

"That duty is, to watch the ocean. I shall then explain the whole affair—but you mustn't look at me while I speak; you must watch the sea."

"This," said I, "is hardship. I had rather go without the luncheon."

I do not think she was offended at my speech; still she frowned for almost three seconds.

We passed through acres of sweet bay and spear grass, sometimes skirting thickets of twisted cedars, sometimes walking in the full glare of the morning sun, sinking into shifting sand where sun-scorched shells crackled under our feet, and sun-browned seaweed glistened, bronzed and iridescent. Then, as we climbed a little hill, the sea wind freshened in our faces, and lo! the ocean lay below us, far-stretching as the eye could reach, glittering, magnificent.

Daisy sat down flat on the sand. It takes a clever girl to do that and retain the respectful deference due her from men. It takes a graceful girl to accomplish it triumphantly when a man is looking.

"You must sit beside me," she said—as though it would prove irksome to me.

"Now," she continued, "you must watch the water while I am talking."

I nodded.

"Why don't you do it, then?" she asked.

I succeeded in wrenching my head toward the ocean, although I felt sure it would swing gradually round again in spite of me.

"To begin with," said Daisy Holroyd, "there's a thing in that ocean that would astonish you if you saw it. Turn your head!"

"I am," I said meekly.

"Did you hear what I said?"

"Yes—er—a thing in the ocean that's going to astonish me." Visions of mermaids rose before me.

"The thing," said Daisy, "is a Thermosaurus!"

I nodded vaguely, as though anticipating a delightful introduction to a nautical friend.

"You don't seem astonished," she said reproachfully.

"Why should I be?" I asked.

"Please turn your eyes toward the water. Suppose a Thermosaurus should look out of the waves!"

"Well," said I, "in that case the pleasure would be mutual."

She frowned, and bit her upper lip.

"Do you know what a Thermosaurus is?" she asked.

"If I am to guess," said I, "I guess it's a jellyfish."

"It's that big, ugly, horrible creature that I showed you in the shed!" cried Daisy impatiently.

"Eh!" I stammered.

"Not papier-maché either," she continued excitedly; "it's a real one."

This was pleasant news. I glanced instinctively at my rifle and then at the ocean.

"Well," said I at last, "it strikes me that you and I resemble a pair of Andromedas waiting to be swallowed. This rifle won't stop a beast, a live beast, like that Nibelungen dragon of yours."

"Yes, it will," she said; "it's not an ordinary rifle."

Then, for the first time, I noticed, just below the magazine, a cylindrical attachment that was strange to me.

"Now, if you will watch the sea very carefully, and will promise not to look at me," said Daisy, "I will try to explain."

She did not wait for me to promise, but went on eagerly, a sparkle of excitement in her blue eyes:

"You know, of all the fossil remains of the great bat-like and lizard-like creatures that inhabited the earth ages and ages ago, the bones of the gigantic saurians are the most interesting. I think they used to splash about the water and fly over the land during the Carboniferous period; anyway, it doesn't matter. Of course, you have seen pictures of reconstructed creatures such as the Ichthyosaurus, the Plesiosaurus, the Anthracosaurus, and the Thermosaurus?"

I nodded, trying to keep my eyes from hers.

"And you know that the remains of the Thermosaurus were first discovered and reconstructed by papa?"

"Yes," said I. There was no use in saying no.

"I am glad you do. Now, papa has proved that this creature lived entirely in the Gulf Stream, emerging for occasional flights across an ocean or two. Can you imagine how he proved it?"

"No," said I, resolutely pointing my nose at the ocean.

"He proved it by a minute examination of the microscopical shells found among the ribs of the Thermosaurus. These shells contained little creatures that live only in the warm waters of the Gulf Stream. They were the food of the Thermosaurus."

"It was rather slender rations for a thing like that, wasn't it? Did he ever swallow bigger food—er—men?"

"Oh, yes. Tons of fossil bones from prehistoric men are also found in the interior of the Thermosaurus."

"Then," said I, "you, at least, had better go back to Captain McPeek's——"

"Please turn around; don't be so foolish. I didn't say there was a *live* Thermosaurus in the water, did I?"

"Isn't there?"

"Why, no!"

My relief was genuine, but I thought of the rifle and looked suspiciously out to sea.

"What's the Winchester for?" I asked.

"Listen, and I will explain. Papa has found out—how, I do not exactly understand—that there is in the waters of the Gulf Stream the body of a Thermosaurus. The creature must have been alive within a year or so. The impenetrable scale armour that covers its body has, as far as papa knows, prevented its disintegration. We know that it is there still, or was there within a few months. Papa has reports and sworn depositions from steamer captains and seamen from a dozen different vessels, all corroborating each other in essential details. These stories, of course, get into the newspapers—sea-serpent stories—but papa knows that they confirm his theory that the huge body of this reptile is swinging along somewhere on the Gulf Stream."

She opened her sunshade and held it over her. I noticed that she deigned to give me the benefit of about one eighth of it.

"Your duty with that rifle is this: If we are fortunate enough to see the body of the Thermosaurus come floating by, you are to take good aim and fire—fire rapidly every bullet in the magazine; then reload and fire again, and reload and fire as long as you have any cartridges left."

"A self-feeding Maxim is what I should have," I said with gentle sarcasm. "Well, and suppose I make a sieve of this big lizard?"

"Do you see these rings in the sand?" she asked.

Sure enough, somebody had driven heavy piles deep into the sand all around us, and to the tops of these piles were attached steel rings, half buried under the spear grass. We sat almost exactly in the centre of a circle of these rings.

"The reason is this," said Daisy: "every bullet in your cartridges is steel-tipped and armour-piercing. To the base of each bullet is attached a thin wire of pallium. Pallium is that new metal, a thread of which, drawn out into finest wire, will hold a ton of iron suspended. Every bullet is fitted with minute coils of miles of this wire. When the bullet leaves the rifle it spins out this wire as a shot from a life-saver's mortar spins out and carries the life line to a wrecked ship. The end of each coil of wire is attached to that cylinder under the magazine of your rifle. As soon as the shell is automatically ejected this wire flies out also. A bit of scarlet tape is fixed to the end, so that it will be easy to pick up. There is also a snap clasp on the end, and this clasp fits those rings that you see in the sand. Now, when you begin firing, it is my duty to run and pick up the wire ends and attach them to the rings. Then, you see, we have the body of the Thermosaurus full of bullets, every bullet anchored to the shore by tiny wires, each of which could easily hold a ton's strain."

I looked at her in amazement.

"Then," she added calmly, "we have captured the Thermosaurus."

"Your father," said I at length, "must have spent years of labour over this preparation."

"It is the work of a lifetime," she said simply.

My face, I suppose, showed my misgivings.

"It must not fail," she added.

"But—but we are nowhere near the Gulf Stream," I ventured.

Her face brightened, and she frankly held the sunshade over us both.

"Ah, you don't know," she said, "what else papa has discovered. Would you believe that he has found a loop in the Gulf Stream—a genuine loop—that swings in here just outside of the breakers below? It is true! Everybody on Long Island knows that there is a warm current off the coast, but nobody imagined it was merely a sort of backwater from the Gulf Stream that formed a great circular mill-race around the cone of a subterranean volcano, and rejoined the Gulf Stream off Cape Albatross. But it is! That is why papa bought a yacht three years ago and sailed about for two years so mysteriously. Oh, I did want to go with him so much!"

"This," said I, "is most astonishing."

She leaned enthusiastically toward me, her lovely face aglow.

"Isn't it?" she said; "and to think that you and papa and I are the only people in the whole world who know this!"

To be included in such a triology was very delightful.

"Papa is writing the whole thing—I mean about the currents. He also has in preparation sixteen volumes on the Thermosaurus. He said this morning that he was going to ask you to write the story first for some scientific magazine. He is certain that Professor Bruce Stoddard, of Columbia, will write the pamphlets necessary. This will give papa time to attend to the sixteen-volume work, which he expects to finish in three years."

"Let us first," said I, laughing, "catch our Thermosaurus."

"We must not fail," she said wistfully.

"We shall not fail," I said, "for I promise to sit on this sand hill as long as I live—until a Thermosaurus appears—if that is your wish, Miss Holroyd."

Our eyes met for an instant. She did not chide me, either, for not looking at the ocean. Her eyes were bluer, anyway.

"I suppose," she said, bending her head and absently pouring sand between her fingers—"I suppose you think me a blue-stocking, or something odious?"

"Not exactly," I said. There was an emphasis in my voice that made her colour. After a moment she laid the sunshade down, still open.

"May I hold it?" I asked.

She nodded almost imperceptibly.

The ocean had turned a deep marine blue, verging on purple, that heralded a scorching afternoon. The wind died away; the odour of cedar and sweet bay hung heavy in the air.

In the sand at our feet an iridescent flower beetle crawled, its metallic green and blue wings burning like a spark. Great gnats, with filmy, glittering wings, danced aimlessly above the young golden-rod; burnished crickets, inquisitive, timid, ran from under chips of driftwood, waved their antennæ at us, and ran back again. One by one the marbled tiger beetles tumbled at our feet, dazed from the exertion of an aërial flight, then scrambled and ran a little way, or darted into the wire grass, where great brilliant spiders eyed them askance from their gossamer hammocks.

Far out at sea the white gulls floated and drifted on the water, or sailed up into the air to flap lazily for a moment and settle back among the waves. Strings of black surf ducks passed, their strong wings tipping the surface of the water; single wandering coots whirled from the breakers into lonely flight toward the horizon.

We lay and watched the little ring-necks running along the water's edge, now backing away from the incoming tide, now boldly wading after the undertow. The harmony of silence, the deep perfume, the mystery of waiting for that something that all await—what is it? love? death? or only the miracle of another morrow?—troubled me with vague restfulness. As sunlight casts shadows, happiness, too, throws a shadow, and the shadow is sadness.

And so the morning wore away until Freda came with a cool-looking hamper. Then delicious cold fowl and lettuce sandwiches and champagne cup set our tongues wagging as only very young tongues can wag. Daisy went back with Freda after luncheon, leaving me a case of cigars, with a bantering smile. I dozed, half awake, keeping a partly closed eye on the ocean, where a faint gray streak showed plainly amid the azure water all around. That was the Gulf Stream loop.

About four o'clock Frisby appeared with a bamboo shelter tent, for which I was unaffectedly grateful.

After he had erected it over me he stopped to chat a bit, but the conversation bored me, for he could talk of nothing but bill-posting.

"You wouldn't ruin the landscape here, would you?" I asked.

"Ruin it!" repeated Frisby nervously. "It's ruined now; there ain't a place to stick a bill."

"The snipe stick bills—in the sand," I said flippantly.

There was no humour about Frisby. "Do they?" he asked.

I moved with a certain impatience.

"Bills," said Frisby, "give spice an' variety to Nature. They break the monotony of the everlastin' green and what-you-may-call-its."

I glared at him.

"Bills," he continued, "are not easy to stick, lemme tell you, sir. Sign paintin's a soft snap when it comes to bill-stickin'. Now, I guess I've stuck more bills in New York State than ennybody."

"Have you?" I said angrily.

"Yes, siree! I always pick out the purtiest spots—kinder filled chuck full of woods and brooks and things; then I h'ist my paste-pot onto a rock, and I slather that rock with gum, and whoop she goes!"

"Whoop what goes?"

"The bill. I paste her onto the rock, with one swipe of the brush for the edges and a back-handed swipe for the finish—except when a bill is folded in two halves."

"And what do you do then?" I asked, disgusted.

"Swipe twice," said Frisby with enthusiasm.

"And you don't think it injures the landscape?"

"Injures it!" he exclaimed, convinced that I was attempting to joke.

I looked wearily out to sea. He also looked at the water and sighed sentimentally.

"Floatin' buoys with bills onto 'em is a idea of mine," he observed. "That damn ocean is monotonous, ain't it?"

I don't know what I might have done to Frisby—the rifle was so convenient—if his mean yellow dog had not waddled up at this juncture.

"Hi, Davy, sic 'em!" said Frisby, expectorating upon a clamshell and hurling it seaward. The cur watched the flight of the shell apathetically, then squatted in the sand and looked at his master.

"Kinder lost his spirit," said Frisby, "ain't he? I once stuck a bill onto Davy, an' it come off, an' the paste sorter sickened him. He was hell on rats—once!"

After a moment or two Frisby took himself off, whistling cheerfully to Davy, who followed him when he was ready. The rifle burned in my fingers.

It was nearly six o'clock when the professor appeared, spade on shoulder, boots smeared with mud.

"Well," he said, "nothing to report, Dick, my boy?"

"Nothing, professor."

He wiped his shining face with his handkerchief and stared at the water.

"My calculations lead me to believe," he said, "that our prize may be due any day now. This theory I base upon the result of the report from the last sea captain I saw. I can not understand why some of these captains did not take the carcass in tow. They all say that they tried, but that the body sank before they could come within half a mile. The truth is, probably, that they did not stir a foot from their course to examine the thing."

"Have you ever cruised about for it?" I ventured.

"For two years," he said grimly. "It's no use; it's accident when a ship falls in with it. One captain reports it a thousand miles from where the last skipper spoke it, and always in the Gulf Stream. They think it is a different specimen every time, and the papers are teeming with sea-serpent fol-de-rol."

"Are you sure," I asked, "that it will swing in to the coast on this Gulf Stream loop?"

"I think I may say that it is certain to do so. I experimented with a dead right whale. You may have heard of its coming ashore here last summer."

"I think I did," said I with a faint smile. The thing had poisoned the air for miles around.

"But," I continued, "suppose it comes in the night?"

He laughed.

"There I am lucky. Every night this month, and every day, too, the current of the loop runs inland so far that even a porpoise would strand for at least twelve hours. Longer than that I have not experimented with, but I know that the shore trend of the loop runs across a long spur of the submerged volcanic mountain, and that anything heavier than a porpoise would scrape the bottom and be carried so slowly that at least twelve hours must elapse before the carcass could float again into deep water. There are chances of its stranding indefinitely, too, but I don't care to take those chances. That is why I have stationed you here, Dick, my boy."

He glanced again at the water, smiling to himself.

"There is another question I want to ask," I said, "if you don't mind."

"Of course not!" he said warmly.

"What are you digging for?"

"Why, simply for exercise. The doctor told me I was killing myself with my sedentary habits, so I decided to dig. I don't know a better exercise. Do you?"

"I suppose not," I murmured, rather red in the face. I wondered whether he'd mention fossils.

"Did Daisy tell you why we are making our papier-maché Thermosaurus?" he asked.

I shook my head.

"We constructed that from measurements I took from the fossil remains of the Thermosaurus in the Metropolitan Museum. Professor Bruce Stoddard made the drawings. We set it up here, all ready to receive the skin of the carcass that I am expecting."

We had started toward home, walking slowly across the darkening dunes, shoulder to shoulder. The sand was deep, and walking was not easy.

"I wish," said I at last, "that I knew why Miss Holroyd asked me not to walk on the beach. It's much less fatiguing."

"That," said the professor, "is a matter that I intend to discuss with you to-night." He spoke gravely, almost sadly. I felt that something of unparalleled importance was soon to be revealed. So I kept very quiet, watching the ocean out of the corners of my eyes.

## IV.

291

Dinner was ended. Daisy Holroyd lighted her father's pipe for him, and insisted on my smoking as much as I pleased. Then she sat down, and folded her hands like a good little girl, waiting for her father to make the revelation which I felt in my bones must be something out of the ordinary.

The professor smoked for a while, gazing meditatively at his daughter; then, fixing his gray eyes on me, he said:

"Have you ever heard of the kree—that Australian bird, half parrot, half hawk, that destroys so many sheep in New South Wales?"

I nodded.

"The kree kills a sheep by alighting on its back and tearing away the flesh with its hooked beak until a vital part is reached. You know that? Well, it has been discovered that the kree had prehistoric prototypes. These birds were enormous creatures, who preyed upon mammoths and mastodons, and even upon the great saurians. It has been conclusively proved that a few saurians have been killed by the ancestors of the kree, but the favourite food of these birds was undoubtedly the Thermosaurus. It is believed that the birds attacked the eyes of the Thermosaurus, and when, as was its habit, the mammoth creature turned on its back to claw them, they fell upon the thinner scales of its stomach armour and finally killed it. This, of course, is a theory, but we have almost absolute proofs of its correctness. Now, these two birds are known among scientists as the ekaf-bird and the ool-yllik. The names are Australian, in which country most of their remains have been unearthed. They lived during the Carboniferous period. Now it is not generally known, but the fact is, that in 1801 Captain Ransom, of the British exploring vessel Gull, purchased from the natives of Tasmania the skin of an ekaf-bird that could not have been killed more than twenty-four hours previous to its sale. I saw this skin in the British Museum. It was labelled "unknown bird, probably extinct." It took me exactly a week to satisfy myself that it was actually the skin of an ekaf-bird. But that is not all, Dick, my boy," continued the professor excitedly. "In 1854, Admiral Stuart, of our own navy, saw the carcass of a strange gigantic bird floating along the southern coast of Australia. Sharks were after it, and, before a boat could be lowered, these miserable fish got it. But the good old admiral secured a few feathers and sent them to the Smithsonian. I saw them. They were not even labelled, but I knew that they were feathers from the ekaf-bird or its near relative, the ool-yllik."

I had grown so interested that I had leaned far across the table. Daisy, too, bent forward. It was only when the professor paused for a moment that I noticed how close together our heads were—Daisy's and mine. I don't think she realized it. She did not move.

"Now comes the important part of this long discourse," said the professor, smiling at our eagerness. "Ever since the carcass of our derelict Thermosaurus was first noticed, every captain who has seen it has also reported the presence of one or more gigantic birds in the neighbourhood. These birds, at a great distance, appeared to be hovering over the carcass, but on the approach of a vessel they disappeared. Even in midocean they were observed. When I heard about it I was puzzled. A month later I was satisfied that neither the ekaf-bird nor the ool-yllik was extinct. Last Monday I knew that I was right. I found forty-eight distinct impressions of the huge seven-toed claw of the ekaf-bird on the beach here at Pine Inlet. You may imagine my excitement. I succeeded in digging up enough wet sand around one of these impressions to preserve its form. I managed to get it into a soap box, and now it is there in my shop. The tide rose too rapidly for me to save the other footprints."

I shuddered at the possibility of a clumsy misstep on my part obliterating the impression of an ool-yllik.

"That is the reason that my daughter warned you off the beach," he said mildly.

"Hanging would have been too good for the vandal who destroyed such priceless prizes!" I cried out in self-reproach.

Daisy Holroyd turned a flushed face to mine, and impulsively laid her hand on my sleeve.

"How could you know?" she said.

"It's all right now," said her father, emphasizing each word with a gentle tap of his pipe-bowl on the table edge; "don't be hard on yourself, Dick, my boy. You'll do yeoman's service yet."

It was nearly midnight, and still we chatted on about the Thermosaurus, the ekaf-bird, and the ool-yllik, eagerly discussing the probability of the great reptile's carcass being in the vicinity. That alone seemed to explain the presence of these prehistoric birds at Pine Inlet.

"Do they ever attack human beings?" I asked.

The professor looked startled.

"Gracious!" he exclaimed, "I never thought of that. And Daisy running about out of doors! Dear me! it takes a scientist to be an unnatural parent!"

His alarm was half real, half assumed; but all the same, he glanced gravely at us both, shaking his handsome head, absorbed in thought. Daisy herself looked a little doubtful. As for me, my sensations were distinctly queer.

"It is true," said the professor, frowning at the wall, "that human remains have been found associated with the bones of the ekaf-bird—I don't know how intimately. It is a matter to be taken into most serious consideration."

"The problem can be solved," said I, "in several ways. One is, to keep Miss Holroyd in the house——"

"I shall not stay in!" cried Daisy indignantly.

We all laughed, and her father assured her that she should not be abused.

"Even if I did stay in," she said, "one of these birds might alight on Master Dick."

She looked saucily at me as she spoke, but turned crimson when her father observed quietly, "You don't seem to think of me, Daisy."

"Of course I do," she said, getting up and putting both arms around her father's neck; "but Dick—as—as you call him—is so helpless and timid."

My blissful smile froze on my lips.

"Timid!" I repeated.

She came back to the table, making me a mocking reverence.

"Do you think I am to be laughed at with impunity?" she said.

"What are your other plans, Dick, my boy?" asked the professor.—"Daisy, let him alone, you little tease!"

"One is, to haul a lot of cast-iron boilers along the dunes," I said. "If these birds come when the carcass floats in, and if they seem disposed to trouble us, we could crawl into the boilers and be safe."

"Why, that is really brilliant!" cried Daisy.

"Be quiet, my child! Dick, the plan is sound and sensible and perfectly practical. McPeek and Frisby shall go for a dozen loads of boilers to-morrow."

"It will spoil the beauty of the landscape," said Daisy, with a taunting nod to me.

"And Frisby will probably attempt to cover them with bill-posters," I added, laughing.

"That," said Daisy, "I shall prevent, even at the cost of my life." And she stood up, looking very determined.

"Children, children," protested the professor, "go to bed—you bother me."

Then I turned deliberately to Miss Holroyd.

"Good-night, Daisy," I said.

"Good-night, Dick," she said, very gently.

## V.

The week passed quickly for me, leaving but few definite impressions. As I look back to it now I can see the long stretch of beach burning in the fierce sunlight, the endless meadows, with the glimmer of water in the distance, the dunes, the twisted cedars, the leagues of scintillating ocean, rocking, rocking, always rocking. In the starlit nights the curlew came in from the sand-bars by twos and threes; I could hear their faint call as I lay in bed thinking. All day long the little ring-necks whistled from the shore. The plover answered them from distant lonely inland pools. The great white gulls drifted like feathers upon the sea.

One morning, toward the end of the week, I, strolling along the dunes, came upon Frisby. He was bill-posting. I caught him red-handed.

"This," said I, "must stop. Do you understand, Mr. Frisby?"

He stepped back from his work, laying his head on one side, considering first me, then the bill that he had pasted on one of our big boilers.

"Don't like the colour?" he asked. "It goes well on them boilers."

"Colour! No, I don't like the colour either. Can't you understand that there are some people in the world who object to seeing patent-medicine advertisements scattered over a landscape?"

"Hey?" he said perplexed.

"Will you kindly remove that advertisement?" I persisted.

"Too late," said Frisby; "it's sot."

I was too disgusted to speak, but my disgust turned to anger when I perceived that, as far as the eye could reach, our boilers, lying from three to four hundred feet apart, were ablaze with yellow and red posters, extolling the "Eureka Liver Pill Company."

"It don't cost 'em nothin'," said Frisby cheerfully; "I done it fur the fun of it. Purty, ain't it?"

"They are Professor Holroyd's boilers," I said, subduing a desire to beat Frisby with my telescope. "Wait until Miss Holroyd sees this work."

"Don't she like yeller and red?" he demanded anxiously.

"You'll find out," said I.

Frisby gaped at his handiwork and then at his yellow dog. After a moment he mechanically spat on a clamshell and requested Davy to "sic" it.

"Can't you comprehend that you have ruined our pleasure in the landscape?" I asked more mildly.

"I've got some green bills," said Frisby; "I kin stick 'em over the yeller ones——"

"Confound it!" said I, "it isn't the colour!"

"Then," observed Frisby, "you don't like them pills. I've got some bills of the 'Cropper Bicycle,' and a few of 'Bagley, the Gents' Tailor——'"

"Frisby," said I, "use them all—paste the whole collection over your dog and yourself—then walk off the cliff."

He sullenly unfolded a green poster, swabbed the boiler with paste, laid the upper section of the bill upon it, and plastered the whole bill down with a thwack of his brush. As I walked away I heard him muttering.

Next day Daisy was so horrified that I promised to give Frisby an ultimatum. I found him with Freda, gazing sentimentally at his work, and I sent him back to the shop in a hurry, telling Freda at the same time that she could spend her leisure in providing Mr. Frisby with sand, soap, and a scrubbing brush. Then I walked on to my post of observation.

I watched until sunset. Daisy came with her father to hear my report, but there was nothing to tell, and we three walked slowly back to the house.

In the evenings the professor worked on his volumes, the click of his typewriter sounding faintly behind his closed door. Daisy and I played chess sometimes; sometimes we played hearts. I don't remember that we ever finished a game of either—we talked too much.

Our discussions covered every topic of interest: we argued upon politics; we skimmed over literature and music; we settled international differences; we spoke vaguely of human brotherhood. I say we slighted no subject of interest—I am wrong; we never spoke of love.

Now, love is a matter of interest to ten people out of ten. Why it was that it did not appear to interest us is as interesting a question as love itself. We were young, alert, enthusiastic, inquiring. We eagerly absorbed theories concerning any curious phenomena in Nature, as intellectual cocktails to stimulate discussion. And yet we did not discuss love. I do not say that we avoided it. No; the subject was too completely ignored for even that. And yet we found it very difficult to pass an hour separated. The professor noticed this, and laughed at us. We were not even embarrassed.

Sunday passed in pious contemplation of the ocean. Daisy read a little in her prayer-book, and the professor threw a cloth over his typewriter and strolled up and down the sands. He may have been lost in devout abstraction; he may have been looking for footprints. As for me, my mind was very serene, and I was more than happy. Daisy read to me a little for my soul's sake, and the professor came up and said something cheerful. He also examined the magazine of my Winchester.

That night, too, Daisy took her guitar to the sands and sang one or two Armenian hymns. Unlike us, the Armenians do not take their pleasures sadly. One of their pleasures is evidently religion.

The big moon came up over the dunes and stared at the sea until the surface of every wave trembled with radiance. A sudden stillness fell across the world; the wind died out; the foam ran noiselessly across the beach; the cricket's rune was stilled.

I leaned back, dropping one hand upon the sand. It touched another hand, soft and cool.

After a while the other hand moved slightly, and I found that my own had closed above it. Presently one finger stirred a little—only a little—for our fingers were interlocked.

On the shore the foam-froth bubbled and winked and glimmered in the moon-light. A star fell from the zenith, showering the night with incandescent dust.

If our fingers lay interlaced beside us, her eyes were calm and serene as always, wide open, fixed upon the depths of a dark sky. And when her father rose and spoke to us, she did not withdraw her hand.

"Is it late?" she asked dreamily.

"It is midnight, little daughter."

I stood up, still holding her hand, and aided her to rise. And when, at the door, I said good-night, she turned and looked at me for a little while in silence, then passed into her room slowly, with head still turned toward me.

All night long I dreamed of her; and when the east whitened, I sprang up, the thunder of the ocean in my ears, the strong sea wind blowing into the open window.

"She is asleep," I thought, and I leaned from the window and peered out into the east.

The sea called to me, tossing its thousand arms; the soaring gulls, dipping, ris-ing, wheeling above the sand-bar, screamed and clamoured for a playmate. I slipped into my bathing suit, dropped from the window upon the soft sand, and in a mo-ment had plunged head foremost into the surf, swimming beneath the waves toward the open sea.

Under the tossing ocean the voice of the waters was in my ears—a low, sweet voice, intimate, mysterious. Through singing foam and broad, green, glassy depths, by whispering sandy channels atrail with seaweed, and on, on, out into the vague, cool sea, I sped, rising to the top, sinking, gliding. Then at last I flung myself out of water, hands raised, and the clamour of the gulls filled my ears.

As I lay, breathing fast, drifting on the sea, far out beyond the gulls I saw a flash of white, and an arm was lifted, signalling me.

"Daisy!" I called.

A clear hail came across the water, distinct on the sea wind, and at the same in-stant we raised our hands and moved toward each other.

How we laughed as we met in the sea! The white dawn came up out of the depths, the zenith turned to rose and ashes.

And with the dawn came the wind—a great sea wind, fresh, aromatic, that hurled our voices back into our throats and lifted the sheeted spray above our heads. Every wave, crowned with mist, caught us in a cool embrace, cradled us, and slipped away, only to leave us to another wave, higher, stronger, crested with opalescent glory, breathing incense.

We turned together up the coast, swimming lightly side by side, but our words were caught up by the winds and whirled into the sky.

We looked up at the driving clouds; we looked out upon the pallid waste of waters; but it was into each other's eyes we looked, wondering, wistful, questioning the reason of sky and sea. And there in each other's eyes we read the mystery, and we knew that earth and sky and sea were created for us alone.

Drifting on by distant sands and dunes, her white fingers touching mine, we spoke, keying our tones to the wind's vast harmony. And we spoke of love.

Gray and wide as the limitless span of the sky and the sea, the winds gathered from the world's ends to bear us on; but they were not familiar winds; for now, along the coast, the breakers curled and showed a million fangs, and the ocean stirred to its depths, uneasy, ominous, and the menace of its murmur drew us closer as we moved.

Where the dull thunder and the tossing spray warned us from sunken reefs, we heard the harsh challenges of gulls; where the pallid surf twisted in yellow coils of spume above the bar, the singing sands murmured of treachery and secrets of lost souls agasp in the throes of silent undertows.

But there was a little stretch of beach glimmering through the mountains of water, and toward this we turned, side by side. Around us the water grew warmer; the breath of the following waves moistened our cheeks; the water itself grew gray and strange about us.

"We have come too far," I said; but she only answered: "Faster, faster! I am afraid!" The water was almost hot now; its aromatic odour filled our lungs.

"The Gulf loop!" I muttered. "Daisy, shall I help you?"

"No. Swim—close by me! Oh-h! Dick——"

Her startled cry was echoed by another—a shrill scream, unutterably horrible—and a great bird flapped from the beach, splashing and beating its pinions across the water with a thundering noise.

Out across the waves it blundered, rising little by little from the water, and now, to my horror, I saw another monstrous bird swinging in the air above it, squealing as it turned on its vast wings. Before I could speak we touched the beach, and I half lifted her to the shore.

"Quick!" I repeated. "We must not wait."

Her eyes were dark with fear, but she rested a hand on my shoulder, and we crept up among the dune grasses and sank down by the point of sand where the rough shelter stood, surrounded by the iron-ringed piles.

She lay there, breathing fast and deep, dripping with spray. I had no power of speech left, but when I rose wearily to my knees and looked out upon the water my blood ran cold. Above the ocean, on the breast of the roaring wind, three enormous birds sailed, turning and wheeling among each other; and below, drifting with the gray stream of the Gulf loop, a colossal bulk lay half submerged—a gigantic lizard, floating belly upward.

Then Daisy crept kneeling to my side and touched me, trembling from head to foot.

"I know," I muttered. "I must run back for the rifle."

"And—and leave me?"

I took her by the hand, and we dragged ourselves through the wire grass to the open end of a boiler lying in the sand.

She crept in on her hands and knees, and called to me to follow.

"You are safe now," I cried. "I must go back for the rifle."

"The birds may—may attack you."

"If they do I can get into one of the other boilers," I said. "Daisy, you must not venture out until I come back. You won't, will you?"

"No-o," she whispered doubtfully.

"Then—good-by."

"Good-by," she answered, but her voice was very small and still.

"Good-by," I said again. I was kneeling at the mouth of the big iron tunnel; it was dark inside and I could not see her, but, before I was conscious of it, her arms were around my neck and we had kissed each other.

I don't remember how I went away. When I came to my proper senses I was swimming along the coast at full speed, and over my head wheeled one of the birds, screaming at every turn.

The intoxication of that innocent embrace, the close impress of her arms around my neck, gave me a strength and recklessness that neither fear nor fatigue could subdue. The bird above me did not even frighten me; I watched it over my shoulder, swimming strongly, with the tide now aiding me, now stemming my course; but I saw the shore passing quickly and my strength increased, and I shouted when I came in sight of the house, and scrambled up on the sand, dripping and excited. There was nobody in sight, and I gave a last glance up into the air where the bird wheeled, still screeching, and hastened into the house. Freda stared at me in amazement as I seized the rifle and shouted for the professor.

"He has just gone to town, with Captain McPeek in his wagon," stammered Freda.

"What!" I cried. "Does he know where his daughter is?"

"Miss Holroyd is asleep—not?" gasped Freda.

"Where's Frisby?" I cried impatiently.

"Yimmie?" quavered Freda.

"Yes, Jimmie; isn't there anybody here? Good heavens! where's that man in the shop?"

"He also iss gone," said Freda, shedding tears, "to buy papier-maché. Yimmie, he iss gone to post bills."

I waited to hear no more, but swung my rifle over my shoulder, and, hanging the cartridge belt across my chest, hurried out and up the beach. The bird was not in sight.

I had been running for perhaps a minute when, far up on the dunes, I saw a yellow dog rush madly through a clump of sweet bay, and at the same moment a bird soared past, rose, and hung hovering just above the thicket. Suddenly the bird swooped; there was a shriek and a yelp from the cur, but the bird gripped it in one claw and beat its wings upon the sand, striving to rise. Then I saw Frisby—paste, bucket, and brush raised—fall upon the bird, yelling lustily. The fierce creature relaxed its talons, and the dog rushed on, squeaking with terror. The bird turned on Frisby and sent him sprawling on his face, a sticky mass of paste and sand. But this did not end the struggle. The bird, croaking wildly, flew at the prostrate billposter, and the sand whirled into a pillar above its terrible wings. Scarcely knowing what I was about, I raised my rifle and fired twice. A horrid scream echoed each shot, and the bird rose heavily in a shower of sand; but two bullets were embedded in that mass of foul feathers, and I saw the wires and scarlet tape uncoiling on the sand at my feet. In an instant I seized them and passed the ends around a cedar tree, hooking the clasps tight. Then I cast one swift glance upward, where the bird wheeled screeching, anchored like a kite to the pallium wires; and I hurried on across the dunes, the shells cutting my feet, and the bushes tearing my wet swimming suit, until I dripped with blood from shoulder to ankle. Out in the ocean the carcass of the Thermosaurus floated, claws outspread, belly glistening in the gray light, and over him circled two birds. As I reached the shelter I knelt and fired into the mass of scales, and at my first shot a horrible thing occurred: the lizardlike head writhed, the slitted yellow eyes sliding open from the film that covered them. A shudder passed across the undulating body, the great scaled belly heaved, and one leg feebly clawed at the air.

The thing was still alive!

Crushing back the horror that almost paralyzed my hands, I planted shot after shot into the quivering reptile, while it writhed and clawed, striving to turn over and dive; and at each shot the black blood spurted in long, slim jets across the water. And now Daisy was at my side, pale and determined, swiftly clasping each tape-marked wire to the iron rings in the circle around us. Twice I filled the magazine from my belt, and twice I poured streams of steel-tipped bullets into the scaled mass, twisting and shuddering on the sea. Suddenly the birds steered toward us. I felt the wind from their vast wings. I saw the feathers erect, vibrating. I saw the spread claws outstretched, and I struck furiously at them, crying to Daisy to run into the iron shelter. Backing, swinging my clubbed rifle, I retreated, but I tripped across one of the taut pallium wires, and in an instant the hideous birds were on me, and the bone in my forearm snapped like a pipestem at a blow from their wings. Twice I struggled to my knees, blinded with blood, confused, almost fainting; then I fell again, rolling into the mouth of the iron boiler.

When I struggled back to consciousness Daisy knelt silently beside me, while Captain McPeek and Professor Holroyd bound up my shattered arm, talking excitedly. The pain made me faint and dizzy. I tried to speak and could not. At last they got me to my feet and into the wagon, and Daisy came, too, and crouched beside me, wrapped in oilskins to her eyes. Fatigue, lack of food, and excitement had combined with wounds and broken bones to extinguish the last atom of strength in my body; but my mind was clear enough to understand that the trouble was over and the Thermosaurus safe.

I heard McPeek say that one of the birds that I had anchored to a cedar tree had torn loose from the bullets and winged its way heavily out to sea. The professor answered: "Yes, the ekaf-bird; the others were ool-ylliks. I'd have given my right arm to have secured them." Then for a time I heard no more; but the jolting of the wagon over the dunes roused me to keenest pain, and I held out my right hand to Daisy. She clasped it in both of hers, and kissed it again and again.

There is little more to add, I think. Professor Bruce Stoddard has edited this story carefully. His own scientific pamphlet will be published soon, to be followed by Professor Holroyd's sixteen volumes. In a few days the stuffed and mounted Thermosaurus will be placed on free public exhibition in the arena of Madison Square

Garden, the only building in the city large enough to contain the body of this immense winged reptile.

When my arm came out of splints, Daisy and I—— But really that has nothing to do with a detailed scientific description of the Thermosaurus, which, I think, I shall add as an appendix to the book. If you do not find it there it will be because Daisy and I have very little time to write about Thermosaurians.

But what I really want to tell you about is the extraordinary adventures of Captain McPeek and Frisby—how they produced a specimen of Samia Cynthia that dwarfed a hundred of Attacus Atlas, and how the American line steamer St. Louis fouled the thing with her screw.

The more I think of it the more determined I am to tell it to you. It will be difficult to prevent me. And that is not fiction either.

# ENVOI

---

*ENVOI.*

*I.*

*When shadows pass across the grass*
*And April breezes stir the sedge,*
*Along the brimming river's edge*
*I trail my line for silver trout,*
*And smoke, and dream of you, my lass,*
*And wonder why we two fell out,*
*And how the deuce it came about.*

*II.*

*When swallows sheer the meadow-mere*
*And thickets thrill with thrushes' hymns,*
*Along the mill-pond's reedy rims*
*I trail my line for shining dace;*
*But how can finny fishes cheer*
*A fellow, if he find no grace*
*In your sweet eyes and your dear face?*

*III.*

*Let thrushes wing their way and sing*
*Where cresses freshen pebbled nooks;*
*By silent rills and singing brooks*
*I pass my way alone, alas!*
*With your dear name the woodlands ring—*
*Your name is murmured by the grass,*
*By earth, by air, all-where I pass.*

*IV.*

*The painted bream may swim the stream—*

*I'll cast no line to-day, pardi!*
*In vain the river-ripples gleam,*
*In vain the thrushes' minstrelsy.*
*Vain is the wind that whispers, "Lo!*
*Thy fish are waiting—Angler, go!"*
*V.*

*Will you forgive if I forgive?*
*Life is too sad, I think, to live*
*Alone, and dream and smoke and fish;*
*I'll say "Forgive" first—if you wish?*
*VI.*

*For at that word, the Sorcery*
*Of Love shall change the earth and sky*
*To Paradise, with cherubim*
*Instead of birds on every limb.*
*VII.*

*Rivers shall sing our rhapsody;*
*The vaulted forest, tree by tree,*
*High hung with tapestry, shall glow*
*With golden pillars all a-row.*
*VIII.*

*And down the gilded forest aisle*
*Shy throngs of violets shall smile*
*And kiss your feet from tree to tree*
*While blue-bells droop in courtesy.*
*IX.*

*And if the sun incarnadine*
*The clouds—green leaves shall be your screen;*

*And if the clouds with jealousy*
*Should weep—we'll beg of some kind tree*
*A moment's hospitality.*
*X.*

*Good cheer is here, if you incline;*
*Moss-hidden springs shall bubble wine*
*While squirrels chuckle, rank on rank,*

*And strawberries from every bank*
*Shall blush to see how deep we drank.*

### XI.

*Winds of the West shall cool our eyes*
*While every woodland creature tries*
*His voice a little, so that he*
*May know his notes more perfectly*
*When crickets start the symphony.*

### XII.

*Through hazel glade and scented dell*
*Where brooklets ring a tinkling bell,*
*The forest orchestra shall swell,*
*Until the sun-soaked grasses ring*
*With crickets strumming string on string.*

### XIII.

*Then, with your white hand daintily*
*Scarce touching mine, we'll leave our tree*
*And ramble slowly toward the West*
*Where our high castle's flaming crest,*
*Towering behind the setting sun,*
*Flings out its banners, one by one,*
*Signals of fire, that day is done.*

### XIV.

*Deep in that palace we shall find*
*How blind we are, how blind! how blind!*
*And how he'll laugh, who holds the key*
*To the great portal's mystery!*
*And how his joyous laugh will ring*
*When you and I shall bid him fling*
*The gates ajar for you and me!*

### XV.

*Let shadows flee athwart the lea*
*When dark December strips the hedge*
*Along the icy river's edge;*
*Yet, if you will forgive me, lass,*
*The world shall bloom like spring to me,*

*Snow turn to dew upon the grass*
*And fagots blossom where you pass.*
*XVI.*
*Swallows shall sheer the frozen mere,*
*Dead reeds along the mill-pond's rims*
*Shall thrill with summer-thrushes' hymns,*
*While summer breezes blow apace,*
*If you will but forgive me, dear,*
*And let me find a moment's grace,*
*In your sweet eyes and your dear face.*
*R. W. C.*

# THE END.

# IN SEARCH OF THE UNKNOWN

TO
MY FRIEND
E. LE GRAND BEERS

MY DEAR LE GRAND,—You and I were early drawn together by a common love of nature. Your researches into the natural history of the tree-toad, your observations upon the mud-turtles of Providence Township, your experiments with the fresh-water lobster, all stimulated my enthusiasm in a scientific direction, which has crystallized in this helpful little book, dedicated to you.

Pray accept it as an insignificant payment on account for all I owe to you.

THE AUTHOR.

# PREFACE

It appears to the writer that there is urgent need of more "nature books"—books that are scraped clear of fiction and which display only the carefully articulated skeleton of fact. Hence this little volume, presented with some hesitation and more modesty. Various chapters have, at intervals, appeared in the pages of various publications. The continued narrative is now published for the first time; and the writer trusts that it may inspire enthusiasm for natural and scientific research, and inculcate a passion for accurate observation among the young.

THE AUTHOR.

*April 1, 1904.*

---

Shingled tight with greenest leaves,
Sweep the scented meadow-sedge,
Let us snoop along the edge;
Let us pry in hidden nooks,
Laden with our nature books,
Scaring birds with happy cries,
Chloroforming butterflies,
Rooting up each woodland plant,
Pinning beetle, fly, and ant,
So we may identify
What we've ruined, by-and-by.y.

# IN SEARCH OF THE UNKNOWN

## I

Because it all seems so improbable—so horribly impossible to me now, sitting here safe and sane in my own library—I hesitate to record an episode which already appears to me less horrible than grotesque. Yet, unless this story is written now, I know I shall never have the courage to tell the truth about the matter—not from fear of ridicule, but because I myself shall soon cease to credit what I now know to be true. Yet scarcely a month has elapsed since I heard the stealthy purring of what I believed to be the shoaling undertow—scarcely a month ago, with my own eyes, I saw that which, even now, I am beginning to believe never existed. As for the harbor-master—and the blow I am now striking at the old order of things—But of that I shall not speak now, or later; I shall try to tell the story simply and truthfully, and let my friends testify as to my probity and the publishers of this book corroborate them.

On the 29th of February I resigned my position under the government and left Washington to accept an offer from Professor Farrago—whose name he kindly permits me to use—and on the first day of April I entered upon my new and congenial duties as general superintendent of the water-fowl department connected with the Zoological Gardens then in course of erection at Bronx Park, New York.

For a week I followed the routine, examining the new foundations, studying the architect's plans, following the surveyors through the Bronx thickets, suggesting arrangements for water-courses and pools destined to be included in the enclosures for swans, geese, pelicans, herons, and such of the waders and swimmers as we might expect to acclimate in Bronx Park.

It was at that time the policy of the trustees and officers of the Zoological Gardens neither to employ collectors nor to send out expeditions in search of specimens. The society decided to depend upon voluntary contributions, and I was always busy, part of the day, in dictating answers to correspondents who wrote offering their services as hunters of big game, collectors of all sorts of fauna, trappers, snarers, and also to those who offered specimens for sale, usually at exorbitant rates.

To the proprietors of five-legged kittens, mangy lynxes, moth-eaten coyotes, and dancing bears I returned courteous but uncompromising refusals—of course, first submitting all such letters, together with my replies, to Professor Farrago.

One day towards the end of May, however, just as I was leaving Bronx Park to return to town, Professor Lesard, of the reptilian department, called out to me that Professor Farrago wanted to see me a moment; so I put my pipe into my pocket again and retraced my steps to the temporary, wooden building occupied by Professor Farrago, general superintendent of the Zoological Gardens. The professor, who was sitting at his desk before a pile of letters and replies submitted for approval by me, pushed his glasses down and looked over them at me with a whimsical smile that suggested amusement, impatience, annoyance, and perhaps a faint trace of apology.

"Now, here's a letter," he said, with a deliberate gesture towards a sheet of paper impaled on a file—"a letter that I suppose you remember." He disengaged the sheet of paper and handed it to me.

"Oh yes," I replied, with a shrug; "of course the man is mistaken—or—"

"Or what?" demanded Professor Farrago, tranquilly, wiping his glasses.

"—Or a liar," I replied.

After a silence he leaned back in his chair and bade me read the letter to him again, and I did so with a contemptuous tolerance for the writer, who must have been either a very innocent victim or a very stupid swindler. I said as much to Professor Farrago, but, to my surprise, he appeared to waver.

"I suppose," he said, with his near-sighted, embarrassed smile, "that nine hundred and ninety-nine men in a thousand would throw that letter aside and condemn the writer as a liar or a fool?"

"In my opinion," said I, "he's one or the other."

"He isn't—in mine," said the professor, placidly.

"What!" I exclaimed. "Here is a man living all alone on a strip of rock and sand between the wilderness and the sea, who wants you to send somebody to take charge of a bird that doesn't exist!"

"How do you know," asked Professor Farrago, "that the bird in question does not exist?"

"It is generally accepted," I replied, sarcastically, "that the great auk has been extinct for years. Therefore I may be pardoned for doubting that our correspondent possesses a pair of them alive."

"Oh, you young fellows," said the professor, smiling wearily, "you embark on a theory for destinations that don't exist."

He leaned back in his chair, his amused eyes searching space for the imagery that made him smile.

"Like swimming squirrels, you navigate with the help of Heaven and a stiff breeze, but you never land where you hope to—do you?"

Rather red in the face, I said: "Don't you believe the great auk to be extinct?"

"Audubon saw the great auk."

"Who has seen a single specimen since?"

"Nobody—except our correspondent here," he replied, laughing.

I laughed, too, considering the interview at an end, but the professor went on, coolly:

"Whatever it is that our correspondent has—and I am daring to believe that it *is* the great auk itself—I want you to secure it for the society."

When my astonishment subsided my first conscious sentiment was one of pity. Clearly, Professor Farrago was on the verge of dotage—ah, what a loss to the world!

I believe now that Professor Farrago perfectly interpreted my thoughts, but he betrayed neither resentment nor impatience. I drew a chair up beside his desk—there was nothing to do but to obey, and this fool's errand was none of my conceiving.

Together we made out a list of articles necessary for me and itemized the expenses I might incur, and I set a date for my return, allowing no margin for a successful termination to the expedition.

"Never mind that," said the professor. "What I want you to do is to get those birds here safely. Now, how many men will you take?"

"None," I replied, bluntly; "it's a useless expense, unless there is something to bring back. If there is I'll wire you, you may be sure."

"Very well," said Professor Farrago, good-humoredly, "you shall have all the assistance you may require. Can you leave to-night?"

The old gentleman was certainly prompt. I nodded, half-sulkily, aware of his amusement.

"So," I said, picking up my hat, "I am to start north to find a place called Black Harbor, where there is a man named Halyard who possesses, among other household utensils, two extinct great auks—"

We were both laughing by this time. I asked him why on earth he credited the assertion of a man he had never before heard of.

"I suppose," he replied, with the same half-apologetic, half-humorous smile, "it is instinct. I feel, somehow, that this man Halyard *has* got an auk—perhaps two. I can't get away from the idea that we are on the eve of acquiring the rarest of living creatures. It's odd for a scientist to talk as I do; doubtless you're shocked—admit it, now!"

But I was not shocked; on the contrary, I was conscious that the same strange hope that Professor Farrago cherished was beginning, in spite of me, to stir my pulses, too.

"If he has—" I began, then stopped.

The professor and I looked hard at each other in silence.

"Go on," he said, encouragingly.

But I had nothing more to say, for the prospect of beholding with my own eyes a living specimen of the great auk produced a series of conflicting emotions within me which rendered speech profanely superfluous.

As I took my leave Professor Farrago came to the door of the temporary, wooden office and handed me the letter written by the man Halyard. I folded it and put it into my pocket, as Halyard might require it for my own identification.

"How much does he want for the pair?" I asked.

"Ten thousand dollars. Don't demur—if the birds are really—"

"I know," I said, hastily, not daring to hope too much.

"One thing more," said Professor Farrago, gravely; "you know, in that last paragraph of his letter, Halyard speaks of something else in the way of specimens—an undiscovered species of amphibious biped—just read that paragraph again, will you?"

I drew the letter from my pocket and read as he directed:

"When you have seen the two living specimens of the great auk, and have satisfied yourself that I tell the truth, you may be wise enough to listen without prejudice to a statement I shall make concerning the existence of the strangest creature ever fashioned. I will merely say, at this time, that the creature referred to is an amphibious biped and inhabits the ocean near this coast. More I cannot say, for I personally have not seen the animal, but I have a witness who has, and there are many who affirm that they have seen the creature. You will naturally say that my statement amounts to nothing; but when your representative arrives, if he be free from prejudice, I expect his reports to you concerning this sea-biped will confirm the solemn statements of a witness I *know* to be unimpeachable.

"Yours truly,     BURTON HALYARD.

"BLACK HARBOR."

"Well," I said, after a moment's thought, "here goes for the wild-goose chase."

"Wild auk, you mean," said Professor Farrago, shaking hands with me. "You will start to-night, won't you?"

"Yes, but Heaven knows how I'm ever going to land in this man Halyard's door-yard. Good-bye!"

"About that sea-biped—" began Professor Farrago, shyly.

"Oh, don't!" I said; "I can swallow the auks, feathers and claws, but if this fellow Halyard is hinting he's seen an amphibious creature resembling a man—"

"—Or a woman," said the professor, cautiously.

I retired, disgusted, my faith shaken in the mental vigor of Professor Farrago.

---

# II

The three days' voyage by boat and rail was irksome. I bought my kit at Sainte Croix, on the Central Pacific Railroad, and on June 1st I began the last stage of my journey *via* the Sainte Isole broad-gauge, arriving in the wilderness by daylight. A tedious forced march by blazed trail, freshly spotted on the wrong side, of course, brought me to the northern terminus of the rusty, narrow-gauge lumber railway which runs from the heart of the hushed pine wilderness to the sea.

Already a long train of battered flat-cars, piled with sluice-props and roughly hewn sleepers, was moving slowly off into the brooding forest gloom, when I came in sight of the track; but I developed a gratifying and unexpected burst of speed, shouting all the while. The train stopped; I swung myself aboard the last car, where a pleasant young fellow was sitting on the rear brake, chewing spruce and reading a letter.

"Come aboard, sir," he said, looking up with a smile; "I guess you're the man in a hurry."

"I'm looking for a man named Halyard," I said, dropping rifle and knapsack on the fresh-cut, fragrant pile of pine. "Are you Halyard?"

"No, I'm Francis Lee, bossing the mica pit at Port-of-Waves," he replied, "but this letter is from Halyard, asking me to look out for a man in a hurry from Bronx Park, New York."

"I'm that man," said I, filling my pipe and offering him a share of the weed of peace, and we sat side by side smoking very amiably, until a signal from the locomotive sent him forward and I was left alone, lounging at ease, head pillowed on both arms, watching the blue sky flying through the branches overhead.

Long before we came in sight of the ocean I smelled it; the fresh, salt aroma stole into my senses, drowsy with the heated odor of pine and hemlock, and I sat up, peering ahead into the dusky sea of pines.

Fresher and fresher came the wind from the sea, in puffs, in mild, sweet breezes, in steady, freshening currents, blowing the feathery crowns of the pines, setting the balsam's blue tufts rocking.

Lee wandered back over the long line of flats, balancing himself nonchalantly as the cars swung around a sharp curve, where water dripped from a newly propped sluice that suddenly emerged from the depths of the forest to run parallel to the railroad track.

"Built it this spring," he said, surveying his handiwork, which seemed to undulate as the cars swept past. "It runs to the cove—or ought to—" He stopped abruptly with a thoughtful glance at me.

"So you're going over to Halyard's?" he continued, as though answering a question asked by himself.

I nodded.

"You've never been there—of course?"

"No," I said, "and I'm not likely to go again."

I would have told him why I was going if I had not already begun to feel ashamed of my idiotic errand.

"I guess you're going to look at those birds of his," continued Lee, placidly.

"I guess I am," I said, sulkily, glancing askance to see whether he was smiling.

But he only asked me, quite seriously, whether a great auk was really a very rare bird; and I told him that the last one ever seen had been found dead off Labrador in January, 1870. Then I asked him whether these birds of Halyard's were really great auks, and he replied, somewhat indifferently, that he supposed they were—at least, nobody had ever before seen such birds near Port-of-Waves.

"There's something else," he said, running, a pine-sliver through his pipe-stem— "something that interests us all here more than auks, big or little. I suppose I might as well speak of it, as you are bound to hear about it sooner or later."

He hesitated, and I could see that he was embarrassed, searching for the exact words to convey his meaning.

"If," said I, "you have anything in this region more important to science than the great auk, I should be very glad to know about it."

Perhaps there was the faintest tinge of sarcasm in my voice, for he shot a sharp glance at me and then turned slightly. After a moment, however, he put his pipe into his pocket, laid hold of the brake with both hands, vaulted to his perch aloft, and glanced down at me.

"Did you ever hear of the harbor-master?" he asked, maliciously.

"Which harbor-master?" I inquired.

"You'll know before long," he observed, with a satisfied glance into perspective.

This rather extraordinary observation puzzled me. I waited for him to resume, and, as he did not, I asked him what he meant.

"If I knew," he said, "I'd tell you. But, come to think of it, I'd be a fool to go into details with a scientific man. You'll hear about the harbor-master—perhaps you will see the harbor-master. In that event I should be glad to converse with you on the subject."

I could not help laughing at his prim and precise manner, and, after a moment, he also laughed, saying:

"It hurts a man's vanity to know he knows a thing that somebody else knows he doesn't know. I'm damned if I say another word about the harbor-master until you've been to Halyard's!"

"A harbor-master," I persisted, "is an official who superintends the mooring of ships—isn't he?"

But he refused to be tempted into conversation, and we lounged silently on the lumber until a long, thin whistle from the locomotive and a rush of stinging salt-wind brought us to our feet. Through the trees I could see the bluish-black ocean, stretching out beyond black headlands to meet the clouds; a great wind was roaring among the trees as the train slowly came to a stand-still on the edge of the primeval forest.

Lee jumped to the ground and aided me with my rifle and pack, and then the train began to back away along a curved side-track which, Lee said, led to the mica-pit and company stores.

"Now what will you do?" he asked, pleasantly. "I can give you a good dinner and a decent bed to-night if you like—and I'm sure Mrs. Lee would be very glad to have you stop with us as long as you choose."

I thanked him, but said that I was anxious to reach Halyard's before dark, and he very kindly led me along the cliffs and pointed out the path.

"This man Halyard," he said, "is an invalid. He lives at a cove called Black Harbor, and all his truck goes through to him over the company's road. We receive it here, and send a pack-mule through once a month. I've met him; he's a bad-tempered hypochondriac, a cynic at heart, and a man whose word is never doubted. If he says he has a great auk, you may be satisfied he has."

My heart was beating with excitement at the prospect; I looked out across the wooded headlands and tangled stretches of dune and hollow, trying to realize what it might mean to me, to Professor Farrago, to the world, if I should lead back to New York a live auk.

"He's a crank," said Lee; "frankly, I don't like him. If you find it unpleasant there, come back to us."

"Does Halyard live alone?" I asked.

"Yes—except for a professional trained nurse—poor thing!"

"A man?"

"No," said Lee, disgustedly.

Presently he gave me a peculiar glance; hesitated, and finally said: "Ask Halyard to tell you about his nurse and—the harbor-master. Good-bye—I'm due at the quarry. Come and stay with us whenever you care to; you will find a welcome at Port-of-Waves."

We shook hands and parted on the cliff, he turning back into the forest along the railway, I starting northward, pack slung, rifle over my shoulder. Once I met a group of quarrymen, faces burned brick-red, scarred hands swinging as they walked. And, as I passed them with a nod, turning, I saw that they also had turned to look after me, and I caught a word or two of their conversation, whirled back to me on the sea-wind.

They were speaking of the harbor-master.

# III

Towards sunset I came out on a sheer granite cliff where the sea-birds were whirling and clamoring, and the great breakers dashed, rolling in double-thundered reverberations on the sun-dyed, crimson sands below the rock.

Across the half-moon of beach towered another cliff, and, behind this, I saw a column of smoke rising in the still air. It certainly came from Halyard's chimney, although the opposite cliff prevented me from seeing the house itself.

I rested a moment to refill my pipe, then resumed rifle and pack, and cautiously started to skirt the cliffs. I had descended half-way towards the beech, and was examining the cliff opposite, when something on the very top of the rock arrested my attention—a man darkly outlined against the sky. The next moment, however, I knew it could not be a man, for the object suddenly glided over the face of the cliff and slid down the sheer, smooth lace like a lizard. Before I could get a square look at it, the thing crawled into the surf—or, at least, it seemed to—but the whole episode occurred so suddenly, so unexpectedly, that I was not sure I had seen anything at all.

However, I was curious enough to climb the cliff on the land side and make my way towards the spot where I imagined I saw the man. Of course, there was nothing there—not a trace of a human being, I mean. Something *had* been there—a sea-otter, possibly—for the remains of a freshly killed fish lay on the rock, eaten to the backbone and tail.

The next moment, below me, I saw the house, a freshly painted, trim, flimsy structure, modern, and very much out of harmony with the splendid savagery surrounding it. It struck a nasty, cheap note in the noble, gray monotony of headland and sea.

The descent was easy enough. I crossed the crescent beach, hard as pink marble, and found a little trodden path among the rocks, that led to the front porch of the house.

There were two people on the porch—I heard their voices before I saw them—and when I set my foot upon the wooden steps, I saw one of them, a woman, rise from her chair and step hastily towards me.

"Come back!" cried the other, a man with a smooth-shaven, deeply lined face, and a pair of angry, blue eyes; and the woman stepped back quietly, acknowledging my lifted hat with a silent inclination.

The man, who was reclining in an invalid's rolling-chair, clapped both large, pale hands to the wheels and pushed himself out along the porch. He had shawls pinned about him, an untidy, drab-colored hat on his head, and, when he looked down at me, he scowled.

"I know who you are," he said, in his acid voice; "you're one of the Zoological men from Bronx Park. You look like it, anyway."

"It is easy to recognize you from your reputation," I replied, irritated at his discourtesy.

"Really," he replied, with something between a sneer and a laugh, "I'm obliged for your frankness. You're after my great auks, are you not?"

"Nothing else would have tempted me into this place," I replied, sincerely.

"Thank Heaven for that," he said. "Sit down a moment; you've interrupted us." Then, turning to the young woman, who wore the neat gown and tiny cap of a professional nurse, he bade her resume what she had been saying. She did so, with deprecating glance at me, which made the old man sneer again.

"It happened so suddenly," she said, in her low voice, "that I had no chance to get back. The boat was drifting in the cove; I sat in the stern, reading, both oars shipped, and the tiller swinging. Then I heard a scratching under the boat, but thought it might be sea-weed—and, next moment, came those soft thumpings, like the sound of a big fish rubbing its nose against a float."

Halyard clutched the wheels of his chair and stared at the girl in grim displeasure.

"Didn't you know enough to be frightened?" he demanded.

"No—not then," she said, coloring faintly; "but when, after a few moments, I looked up and saw the harbor-master running up and down the beach, I was horribly frightened."

"Really?" said Halyard, sarcastically; "it was about time." Then, turning to me, he rasped out: "And that young lady was obliged to row all the way to Port-of-Waves and call to Lee's quarrymen to take her boat in."

Completely mystified, I looked from Halyard to the girl, not in the least comprehending what all this meant.

"That will do," said Halyard, ungraciously, which curt phrase was apparently the usual dismissal for the nurse.

She rose, and I rose, and she passed me with an inclination, stepping noiselessly into the house.

"I want beef-tea!" bawled Halyard after her; then he gave me an unamiable glance.

"I was a well-bred man," he sneered; "I'm a Harvard graduate, too, but I live as I like, and I do what I like, and I say what I like."

"You certainly are not reticent," I said, disgusted.

"Why should I be?" he rasped; "I pay that young woman for my irritability; it's a bargain between us."

"In your domestic affairs," I said, "there is nothing that interests me. I came to see those auks."

"You probably believe them to be razor-billed auks," he said, contemptuously. "But they're not; they're great auks."

I suggested that he permit me to examine them, and he replied, indifferently, that they were in a pen in his backyard, and that I was free to step around the house when I cared to.

I laid my rifle and pack on the veranda, and hastened off with mixed emotions, among which hope no longer predominated. No man in his senses would keep two such precious prizes in a pen in his backyard, I argued, and I was perfectly prepared to find anything from a puffin to a penguin in that pen.

I shall never forget, as long as I live, my stupor of amazement when I came to the wire-covered enclosure. Not only were there two great auks in the pen, alive, breathing, squatting in bulky majesty on their sea-weed bed, but one of them was gravely contemplating two newly hatched chicks, all bill and feet, which nestled sedately at the edge of a puddle of salt-water, where some small fish were swimming.

For a while excitement blinded, nay, deafened me. I tried to realize that I was gazing upon the last individuals of an all but extinct race—the sole survivors of the gigantic auk, which, for thirty years, has been accounted an extinct creature.

I believe that I did not move muscle nor limb until the sun had gone down and the crowding darkness blurred my straining eyes and blotted the great, silent, bright-eyed birds from sight.

Even then I could not tear myself away from the enclosure; I listened to the strange, drowsy note of the male bird, the fainter responses of the female, the thin plaints of the chicks, huddling under her breast; I heard their flipper-like, embryotic wings beating sleepily as the birds stretched and yawned their beaks and clacked them, preparing for slumber.

"If you please," came a soft voice from the door, "Mr. Halyard awaits your company to dinner."

---

# IV

I dined well—or, rather, I might have enjoyed my dinner if Mr. Halyard had been eliminated; and the feast consisted exclusively of a joint of beef, the pretty nurse, and myself. She was exceedingly attractive—with a disturbing fashion of lowering her head and raising her dark eyes when spoken to.

As for Halyard, he was unspeakable, bundled up in his snuffy shawls, and making uncouth noises over his gruel. But it is only just to say that his table was worth sitting down to and his wine was sound as a bell.

"Yah!" he snapped, "I'm sick of this cursed soup—and I'll trouble you to fill my glass—"

"It is dangerous for you to touch claret," said the pretty nurse.

"I might as well die at dinner as anywhere," he observed.

"Certainly," said I, cheerfully passing the decanter, but he did not appear over-pleased with the attention.

"I can't smoke, either," he snarled, hitching the shawls around until he looked like Richard the Third.

However, he was good enough to shove a box of cigars at me, and I took one and stood up, as the pretty nurse slipped past and vanished into the little parlor beyond.

We sat there for a while without speaking. He picked irritably at the bread-crumbs on the cloth, never glancing in my direction; and I, tired from my long foot-tour, lay back in my chair, silently appreciating one of the best cigars I ever smoked.

"Well," he rasped out at length, "what do you think of my auks—and my veraci-ty?"

I told him that both were unimpeachable.

"Didn't they call me a swindler down there at your museum?" he demanded.

I admitted that I had heard the term applied. Then I made a clean breast of the matter, telling him that it was I who had doubted; that my chief, Professor Farrago, had sent me against my will, and that I was ready and glad to admit that he, Mr. Hal-yard, was a benefactor of the human race.

"Bosh!" he said. "What good does a confounded wobbly, bandy-toed bird do to the human race?"

But he was pleased, nevertheless; and presently he asked me, not unamiably, to punish his claret again.

"I'm done for," he said; "good things to eat and drink are no good to me. Some day I'll get mad enough to have a fit, and then—"

He paused to yawn.

"Then," he continued, "that little nurse of mine will drink up my claret and go back to civilization, where people are polite."

Somehow or other, in spite of the fact that Halyard was an old pig, what he said touched me. There was certainly not much left in life for him—as he regarded life.

"I'm going to leave her this house," he said, arranging his shawls. "She doesn't know it. I'm going to leave her my money, too. She doesn't know that. Good Lord! What kind of a woman can she be to stand my bad temper for a few dollars a month!"

"I think," said I, "that it's partly because she's poor, partly because she's sorry for you."

He looked up with a ghastly smile.

"You think she really is sorry?"

Before I could answer he went on: "I'm no mawkish sentimentalist, and I won't allow anybody to be sorry for me—do you hear?"

"Oh, I'm not sorry for you!" I said, hastily, and, for the first time since I had seen him, he laughed heartily, without a sneer.

We both seemed to feel better after that; I drank his wine and smoked his cigars, and he appeared to take a certain grim pleasure in watching me.

"There's no fool like a young fool," he observed, presently.

As I had no doubt he referred to me, I paid him no attention.

After fidgeting with his shawls, he gave me an oblique scowl and asked me my age.

"Twenty-four," I replied.

"Sort of a tadpole, aren't you?" he said.

As I took no offence, he repeated the remark.

"Oh, come," said I, "there's no use in trying to irritate me. I see through you; a row acts like a cocktail on you—but you'll have to stick to gruel in my company."

"I call that impudence!" he rasped out, wrathfully.

"I don't care what you call it," I replied, undisturbed, "I am not going to be worried by you. Anyway," I ended, "it is my opinion that you could be very good company if you chose."

The proposition appeared to take his breath away—at least, he said nothing more; and I finished my cigar in peace and tossed the stump into a saucer.

"Now," said I, "what price do you set upon your birds, Mr. Halyard?"

"Ten thousand dollars," he snapped, with an evil smile.

"You will receive a certified check when the birds are delivered," I said, quietly.

"You don't mean to say you agree to that outrageous bargain—and I won't take a cent less, either—Good Lord!—haven't you any spirit left?" he cried, half rising from his pile of shawls.

His piteous eagerness for a dispute sent me into laughter impossible to control, and he eyed me, mouth open, animosity rising visibly.

Then he seized the wheels of his invalid chair and trundled away, too mad to speak; and I strolled out into the parlor, still laughing.

The pretty nurse was there, sewing under a hanging lamp.

"If I am not indiscreet—" I began.

"Indiscretion is the better part of valor," said she, dropping her head but raising her eyes.

So I sat down with a frivolous smile peculiar to the appreciated.

"Doubtless," said I, "you are hemming a 'kerchief."

"Doubtless I am not," she said; "this is a night-cap for Mr. Halyard."

A mental vision of Halyard in a night-cap, very mad, nearly set me laughing again.

"Like the King of Yvetot, he wears his crown in bed," I said, flippantly.

"The King of Yvetot might have made that remark," she observed, re-threading her needle.

It is unpleasant to be reproved. How large and red and hot a man's ears feel.

To cool them, I strolled out to the porch; and, after a while, the pretty nurse came out, too, and sat down in a chair not far away. She probably regretted her lost opportunity to be flirted with.

"I have so little company—it is a great relief to see somebody from the world," she said. "If you can be agreeable, I wish you would."

The idea that she had come out to see me was so agreeable that I remained speechless until she said: "Do tell me what people are doing in New York."

So I seated myself on the steps and talked about the portion of the world inhabited by me, while she sat sewing in the dull light that straggled out from the parlor windows.

She had a certain coquetry of her own, using the usual methods with an individuality that was certainly fetching. For instance, when she lost her needle—and, another time, when we both, on hands and knees, hunted for her thimble.

However, directions for these pastimes may be found in contemporary classics.

I was as entertaining as I could be—perhaps not quite as entertaining as a young man usually thinks he is. However, we got on very well together until I asked her tenderly who the harbor-master might be, whom they all discussed so mysteriously.

"I do not care to speak about it," she said, with a primness of which I had not suspected her capable.

Of course I could scarcely pursue the subject after that—and, indeed, I did not intend to—so I began to tell her how I fancied I had seen a man on the cliff that afternoon, and how the creature slid over the sheer rock like a snake.

To my amazement, she asked me to kindly discontinue the account of my adventures, in an icy tone, which left no room for protest.

"It was only a sea-otter," I tried to explain, thinking perhaps she did not care for snake stories.

But the explanation did not appear to interest her, and I was mortified to observe that my impression upon her was anything but pleasant.

"She doesn't seem to like me and my stories," thought I, "but she is too young, perhaps, to appreciate them."

So I forgave her—for she was even prettier than I had thought her at first—and I took my leave, saying that Mr. Halyard would doubtless direct me to my room.

Halyard was in his library, cleaning a revolver, when I entered.

"Your room is next to mine," he said; "pleasant dreams, and kindly refrain from snoring."

"May I venture an absurd hope that you will do the same!" I replied, politely.

That maddened him, so I hastily withdrew.

I had been asleep for at least two hours when a movement by my bedside and a light in my eyes awakened me. I sat bolt upright in bed, blinking at Halyard, who, clad in a dressing-gown and wearing a night-cap, had wheeled himself into my room with one hand, while with the other he solemnly waved a candle over my head.

"I'm so cursed lonely," he said—"come, there's a good fellow—talk to me in your own original, impudent way."

I objected strenuously, but he looked so worn and thin, so lonely and bad-tempered, so lovelessly grotesque, that I got out of bed and passed a spongeful of cold water over my head.

Then I returned to bed and propped the pillows up for a back-rest, ready to quarrel with him if it might bring some little pleasure into his morbid existence.

"No," he said, amiably, "I'm too worried to quarrel, but I'm much obliged for your kindly offer. I want to tell you something."

"What?" I asked, suspiciously.

"I want to ask you if you ever saw a man with gills like a fish?"

"Gills?" I repeated.

"Yes, gills! Did you?"

"No," I replied, angrily, "and neither did you."

"No, I never did," he said, in a curiously placid voice, "but there's a man with gills like a fish who lives in the ocean out there. Oh, you needn't look that way—nobody ever thinks of doubting my word, and I tell you that there's a man—or a thing that looks like a man—as big as you are, too—all slate-colored—with nasty red gills like a fish!—and I've a witness to prove what I say!"

"Who?" I asked, sarcastically.

"The witness? My nurse."

"Oh! She saw a slate-colored man with gills?"

"Yes, she did. So did Francis Lee, superintendent of the Mica Quarry Company at Port-of-Waves. So have a dozen men who work in the quarry. Oh, you needn't laugh, young man. It's an old story here, and anybody can tell you about the harbor-master."

"The harbor-master!" I exclaimed.

"Yes, that slate-colored thing with gills, that looks like a man—and—by Heaven! *is* a man—that's the harbor-master. Ask any quarryman at Port-of-Waves what it is that comes purring around their boats at the wharf and unties painters and changes the mooring of every cat-boat in the cove at night! Ask Francis Lee what it was he saw running and leaping up and down the shoal at sunset last Friday! Ask anybody along the coast what sort of a thing moves about the cliffs like a man and slides over them into the sea like an otter—"

"I saw it do that!" I burst out.

"Oh, did you? Well, *what was it?*"

Something kept me silent, although a dozen explanations flew to my lips.

After a pause, Halyard said: "You saw the harbor-master, that's what you saw!"

I looked at him without a word.

"Don't mistake me," he said, pettishly; "I don't think that the harbor-master is a spirit or a sprite or a hobgoblin, or any sort of damned rot. Neither do I believe it to be an optical illusion."

"What do you think it is?" I asked.

"I think it's a man—I think it's a branch of the human race—that's what I think. Let me tell you something: the deepest spot in the Atlantic Ocean is a trifle over five miles deep—and I suppose you know that this place lies only about a quarter of a mile off this headland. The British exploring vessel, *Gull*, Captain Marotte, discovered and sounded it, I believe. Anyway, it's there, and it's my belief that the profound depths are inhabited by the remnants of the last race of amphibious human beings!"

This was childish; I did not bother to reply.

"Believe it or not, as you will," he said, angrily; "one thing I know, and that is this: the harbor-master has taken to hanging around my cove, and he is attracted by my nurse! I won't have it! I'll blow his fishy gills out of his head if I ever get a shot at him! I don't care whether it's homicide or not—anyway, it's a new kind of murder and it attracts me!"

I gazed at him incredulously, but he was working himself into a passion, and I did not choose to say what I thought.

"Yes, this slate-colored thing with gills goes purring and grinning and spitting about after my nurse—when she walks, when she rows, when she sits on the beach! Gad! It drives me nearly frantic. I won't tolerate it, I tell you!"

"No," said I, "I wouldn't either." And I rolled over in bed convulsed with laughter.

The next moment I heard my door slam. I smothered my mirth and rose to close the window, for the land-wind blew cold from the forest, and a drizzle was sweeping the carpet as far as my bed.

That luminous glare which sometimes lingers after the stars go out, threw a trembling, nebulous radiance over sand and cove. I heard the seething currents under the breakers' softened thunder—louder than I ever heard it. Then, as I closed my window, lingering for a last look at the crawling tide, I saw a man standing, ankle-deep, in the surf, all alone there in the night. But—was it a man? For the figure suddenly began running over the beach on all fours like a beetle, waving its limbs like feelers. Before I could throw open the window again it darted into the surf, and, when I leaned out into the chilling drizzle, I saw nothing save the flat ebb crawling on the coast—I heard nothing save the purring of bubbles on seething sands.

# V

It took me a week to perfect my arrangements for transporting the great auks, by water, to Port-of-Waves, where a lumber schooner was to be sent from Petite Sainte Isole, chartered by me for a voyage to New York.

I had constructed a cage made of osiers, in which my auks were to squat until they arrived at Bronx Park. My telegrams to Professor Farrago were brief. One merely said "Victory!" Another explained that I wanted no assistance; and a third read: "Schooner chartered. Arrive New York July 1st. Send furniture-van to foot of Bluff Street."

My week as a guest of Mr. Halyard proved interesting. I wrangled with that invalid to his heart's content, I worked all day on my osier cage, I hunted the thimble in the moonlight with the pretty nurse. We sometimes found it.

As for the thing they called the harbor-master, I saw it a dozen times, but always either at night or so far away and so close to the sea that of course no trace of it remained when I reached the spot, rifle in hand.

I had quite made up my mind that the so-called harbor-master was a demented darky—wandered from, Heaven knows where—perhaps shipwrecked and gone mad from his sufferings. Still, it was far from pleasant to know that the creature was strongly attracted by the pretty nurse.

She, however, persisted in regarding the harbor-master as a sea-creature; she earnestly affirmed that it had gills, like a fish's gills, that it had a soft, fleshy hole for a mouth, and its eyes were luminous and lidless and fixed.

"Besides," she said, with a shudder, "it's all slate color, like a porpoise, and it looks as wet as a sheet of india-rubber in a dissecting-room."

The day before I was to set sail with my auks in a cat-boat bound for Port-of-Waves, Halyard trundled up to me in his chair and announced his intention of going with me.

"Going where?" I asked.

"To Port-of-Waves and then to New York," he replied, tranquilly.

I was doubtful, and my lack of cordiality hurt his feelings.

"Oh, of course, if you need the sea-voyage—" I began.

"I don't; I need you," he said, savagely; "I need the stimulus of our daily quarrel. I never disagreed so pleasantly with anybody in my life; it agrees with me; I am a hundred per cent. better than I was last week."

I was inclined to resent this, but something in the deep-lined face of the invalid softened me. Besides, I had taken a hearty liking to the old pig.

"I don't want any mawkish sentiment about it," he said, observing me closely; "I won't permit anybody to feel sorry for me—do you understand?"

"I'll trouble you to use a different tone in addressing me," I replied, hotly; "I'll feel sorry for you if I choose to!" And our usual quarrel proceeded, to his deep satisfaction.

By six o'clock next evening I had Halyard's luggage stowed away in the cat-boat, and the pretty nurse's effects corded down, with the newly hatched auk-chicks in a hat-box on top. She and I placed the osier cage aboard, securing it firmly, and then, throwing tablecloths over the auks' heads, we led those simple and dignified birds down the path and across the plank at the little wooden pier. Together we locked up the house, while Halyard stormed at us both and wheeled himself furiously up and down the beach below. At the last moment she forgot her thimble. But we found it, I forget where.

"Come on!" shouted Halyard, waving his shawls furiously; "what the devil are you about up there?"

He received our explanation with a sniff, and we trundled him aboard without further ceremony.

"Don't run me across the plank like a steamer trunk!" he shouted, as I shot him dexterously into the cock-pit. But the wind was dying away, and I had no time to dispute with him then.

The sun was setting above the pine-clad ridge as our sail flapped and partly filled, and I cast off, and began a long tack, east by south, to avoid the spouting rocks on our starboard bow.

The sea-birds rose in clouds as we swung across the shoal, the black surf-ducks scuttered out to sea, the gulls tossed their sun-tipped wings in the ocean, riding the rollers like bits of froth.

Already we were sailing slowly out across that great hole in the ocean, five miles deep, the most profound sounding ever taken in the Atlantic. The presence of great heights or great depths, seen or unseen, always impresses the human mind—perhaps oppresses it. We were very silent; the sunlight stain on cliff and beach deepened to crimson, then faded into sombre purple bloom that lingered long after the rose-tint died out in the zenith.

Our progress was slow; at times, although the sail filled with the rising land breeze, we scarcely seemed to move at all.

"Of course," said the pretty nurse, "we couldn't be aground in the deepest hole in the Atlantic."

"Scarcely," said Halyard, sarcastically, "unless we're grounded on a whale."

"What's that soft thumping?" I asked. "Have we run afoul of a barrel or log?"

It was almost too dark to see, but I leaned over the rail and swept the water with my hand.

Instantly something smooth glided under it, like the back of a great fish, and I jerked my hand back to the tiller. At the same moment the whole surface of the water seemed to begin to purr, with a sound like the breaking of froth in a champagne-glass.

"What's the matter with you?" asked Halyard, sharply.

"A fish came up under my hand," I said; "a porpoise or something—"

With a low cry, the pretty nurse clasped my arm in both her hands.

"Listen!" she whispered. "It's purring around the boat."

"What the devil's purring?" shouted Halyard. "I won't have anything purring around me!"

At that moment, to my amazement, I saw that the boat had stopped entirely, although the sail was full and the small pennant fluttered from the mast-head. Something, too, was tugging at the rudder, twisting and jerking it until the tiller strained and creaked in my hand. All at once it snapped; the tiller swung useless and the boat whirled around, heeling in the stiffening wind, and drove shoreward.

It was then that I, ducking to escape the boom, caught a glimpse of something ahead—something that a sudden wave seemed to toss on deck and leave there, wet and flapping—a man with round, fixed, fishy eyes, and soft, slaty skin.

But the horror of the thing were the two gills that swelled and relaxed spasmodically, emitting a rasping, purring sound—two gasping, blood-red gills, all fluted and scolloped and distended.

Frozen with amazement and repugnance, I stared at the creature; I felt the hair stirring on my head and the icy sweat on my forehead.

"It's the harbor-master!" screamed Halyard.

The harbor-master had gathered himself into a wet lump, squatting motionless in the bows under the mast; his lidless eyes were phosphorescent, like the eyes of living codfish. After a while I felt that either fright or disgust was going to strangle me where I sat, but it was only the arms of the pretty nurse clasped around me in a frenzy of terror.

There was not a fire-arm aboard that we could get at. Halyard's hand crept backward where a steel-shod boat-hook lay, and I also made a clutch at it. The next moment I had it in my hand, and staggered forward, but the boat was already tumbling shoreward among the breakers, and the next I knew the harbor-master ran at me like a colossal rat, just as the boat rolled over and over through the surf, spilling freight and passengers among the sea-weed-covered rocks.

When I came to myself I was thrashing about knee-deep in a rocky pool, blinded by the water and half suffocated, while under my feet, like a stranded porpoise, the harbor-master made the water boil in his efforts to upset me. But his limbs seemed soft and boneless; he had no nails, no teeth, and he bounced and thumped and flapped and splashed like a fish, while I rained blows on him with the boat-hook that sounded like blows on a football. And all the while his gills were blowing out and frothing, and purring, and his lidless eyes looked into mine, until, nauseated and trembling, I dragged myself back to the beach, where already the pretty nurse alternately wrung her hands and her petticoats in ornamental despair.

Beyond the cove, Halyard was bobbing up and down, afloat in his invalid's chair, trying to steer shoreward. He was the maddest man I ever saw.

"Have you killed that rubber-headed thing yet?" he roared.

"I can't kill it," I shouted, breathlessly. "I might as well try to kill a football!"

"Can't you punch a hole in it?" he bawled. "If I can only get at him—"

His words were drowned in a thunderous splashing, a roar of great, broad flippers beating the sea, and I saw the gigantic forms of my two great auks, followed by their chicks, blundering past in a shower of spray, driving headlong out into the ocean.

"Oh, Lord!" I said. "I can't stand that," and, for the first time in my life, I fainted peacefully—and appropriately—at the feet of the pretty nurse.

---

It is within the range of possibility that this story may be doubted. It doesn't matter; nothing can add to the despair of a man who has lost two great auks.

As for Halyard, nothing affects him—except his involuntary sea-bath, and that did him so much good that he writes me from the South that he's going on a walking-tour through Switzerland—if I'll join him. I might have joined him if he had not married the pretty nurse. I wonder whether—But, of course, this is no place for speculation.

In regard to the harbor-master, you may believe it or not, as you choose. But if you hear of any great auks being found, kindly throw a table-cloth over their heads and notify the authorities at the new Zoological Gardens in Bronx Park, New York. The reward is ten thousand dollars.

---

# VI

Before I proceed any further, common decency requires me to reassure my readers concerning my intentions, which, Heaven knows, are far from flippant.

To separate fact from fancy has always been difficult for me, but now that I have had the honor to be chosen secretary of the Zoological Gardens in Bronx Park, I realize keenly that unless I give up writing fiction nobody will believe what I write about science. Therefore it is to a serious and unimaginative public that I shall hereafter address myself; and I do it in the modest confidence that I shall neither be distrusted nor doubted, although unfortunately I still write in that irrational style which suggests covert frivolity, and for which I am undergoing a course of treatment in English literature at Columbia College. Now, having promised to avoid originality and confine myself to facts, I shall tell what I have to tell concerning the dingue, the mammoth, and—something else.

For some weeks it had been rumored that Professor Farrago, president of the Bronx Park Zoological Society, would resign, to accept an enormous salary as manager of Barnum & Bailey's circus. He was now with the circus in London, and had promised to cable his decision before the day was over.

I hoped he would decide to remain with us. I was his secretary and particular favorite, and I viewed, without enthusiasm, the advent of a new president, who might shake us all out of our congenial and carefully excavated ruts. However, it was plain that the trustees of the society expected the resignation of Professor Farrago, for they had been in secret session all day, considering the names of possible candidates to fill Professor Farrago's large, old-fashioned shoes. These preparations worried me, for I could scarcely expect another chief as kind and considerate as Professor Leonidas Farrago.

That afternoon in June I left my office in the Administration Building in Bronx Park and strolled out under the trees for a breath of air. But the heat of the sun soon drove me to seek shelter under a little square arbor, a shady retreat covered with purple wistaria and honeysuckle. As I entered the arbor I noticed that there were three other people seated there—an elderly lady with masculine features and short hair, a younger lady sitting beside her, and, farther away, a rough-looking young man reading a book.

For a moment I had an indistinct impression of having met the elder lady somewhere, and under circumstances not entirely agreeable, but beyond a stony and indifferent glance she paid no attention to me. As for the younger lady, she did not look at me at all. She was very young, with pretty eyes, a mass of silky brown hair, and a skin as fresh as a rose which had just been rained on.

With that delicacy peculiar to lonely scientific bachelors, I modestly sat down beside the rough young man, although there was more room beside the younger lady. "Some lazy loafer reading a penny dreadful," I thought, glancing at him, then at the title of his book. Hearing me beside him, he turned around and blinked over his shabby shoulder, and the movement uncovered the page he had been silently conning. The volume in his hands was Darwin's famous monograph on the monodactyl.

He noticed the astonishment on my face and smiled uneasily, shifting the short clay pipe in his mouth.

"I guess," he observed, "that this here book is too much for me, mister."

"It's rather technical," I replied, smiling.

"Yes," he said, in vague admiration; "it's fierce, ain't it?"

After a silence I asked him if he would tell me why he had chosen Darwin as a literary pastime.

"Well," he said, placidly, "I was tryin' to read about annermals, but I'm up against a word-slinger this time all right. Now here's a gum-twister," and he painfully spelled out m-o-n-o-d-a-c-t-y-l, breathing hard all the while.

"Monodactyl," I said, "means a single-toed creature."

He turned the page with alacrity. "Is that the beast he's talkin' about?" he asked.

The illustration he pointed out was a wood-cut representing Darwin's reconstruction of the dingue from the fossil bones in the British Museum. It was a well-executed wood-cut, showing a dingue in the foreground and, to give scale, a mammoth in the middle distance.

"Yes," I replied, "that is the dingue."

"I've seen one," he observed, calmly.

I smiled and explained that the dingue had been extinct for some thousands of years.

"Oh, I guess not," he replied, with cool optimism. Then he placed a grimy forefinger on the mammoth.

"I've seen them things, too," he remarked.

Again I patiently pointed out his error, and suggested that he referred to the elephant.

"Elephant be blowed!" he replied, scornfully. "I guess I know what I seen. An' I seen that there thing you call a dingue, too."

Not wishing to prolong a futile discussion, I remained silent. After a moment he wheeled around, removing his pipe from his hard mouth.

"Did you ever hear tell of Graham's Glacier?" he demanded.

"Certainly," I replied, astonished; "it's the southernmost glacier in British America."

"Right," he said. "And did you ever hear tell of the Hudson Mountings, mister?"

"Yes," I replied.

"What's behind 'em?" he snapped out.

"Nobody knows," I answered. "They are considered impassable."

"They ain't, though," he said, doggedly; "I've been behind 'em."

"Really!" I replied, tiring of his yarn.

"Ya-as, reely," he repeated, sullenly. Then he began to fumble and search through the pages of his book until he found what he wanted. "Mister," he said, "jest read that out loud, please."

The passage he indicated was the famous chapter beginning:

"Is the mammoth extinct? Is the dingue extinct? Probably. And yet the aborigines of British America maintain the contrary. Probably both the mammoth and the dingue are extinct; but until expeditions have penetrated and explored not only the unknown region in Alaska but also that hidden table-land beyond the Graham Glacier and the Hudson Mountains, it will not be possible to definitely announce the total extinction of either the mammoth or the dingue."

When I had read it, slowly, for his benefit, he brought his hand down smartly on one knee and nodded rapidly.

"Mister," he said, "that gent knows a thing or two, and don't you forget it!" Then he demanded, abruptly, how I knew he hadn't been behind the Graham Glacier.

I explained.

"Shucks!" he said; "there's a road five miles wide inter that there table-land. Mister, I ain't been in New York long; I come inter port a week ago on the *Arctic Belle*, whaler. I was in the Hudson range when that there Graham Glacier bust up—"

"What!" I exclaimed.

"Didn't you know it?" he asked. "Well, mebbe it ain't in the papers, but it busted all right—blowed up by a earthquake an' volcano combine. An', mister, it was oreful. My, how I did run!"

"Do you mean to tell me that some convulsion of the earth has shattered the Graham Glacier?" I asked.

"Convulsions? Ya-as, an' fits, too," he said, sulkily. "The hull blame thing dropped inter a hole. An' say, mister, home an' mother is good enough fur me now."

I stared at him stupidly.

"Once," he said, "I ketched pelts fur them sharps at Hudson Bay, like any yaller husky, but the things I seen arter that convulsion-fit—the *things I seen behind the Hudson Mountings*—don't make me hanker arter no life on the pe-rarie wild, lemme tell yer. I may be a Mother Carey chicken, but this chicken has got enough."

After a long silence I picked up his book again and pointed at the picture of the mammoth.

"What color is it?" I asked.

"Kinder red an' brown," he answered, promptly. "It's woolly, too."

Astounded, I pointed to the dingue.

"One-toed," he said, quickly; "makes a noise like a bell when scutterin' about."

Intensely excited, I laid my hand on his arm. "My society will give you a thousand dollars," I said, "if you pilot me inside the Hudson table-land and show me either a mammoth or a dingue!"

He looked me calmly in the eye.

"Mister," he said, slowly, "have you got a million for to squander on me?"

"No," I said, suspiciously.

"Because," he went on, "it wouldn't be enough. Home an' mother suits me now."

He picked up his book and rose. In vain I asked his name and address; in vain I begged him to dine with me—to become my honored guest.

"Nit," he said, shortly, and shambled off down the path.

But I was not going to lose him like that. I rose and deliberately started to stalk him. It was easy. He shuffled along, pulling on his pipe, and I after him.

It was growing a little dark, although the sun still reddened the tops of the maples. Afraid of losing him in the falling dusk, I once more approached him and laid my hand upon his ragged sleeve.

"Look here," he cried, wheeling about, "I want you to quit follerin' me. Don't I tell you money can't make me go back to them mountings!" And as I attempted to speak, he suddenly tore off his cap and pointed to his head. His hair was white as snow.

"That's what come of monkeyin' inter your cursed mountings," he shouted, fiercely. "There's things in there what no Christian oughter see. Lemme alone er I'll bust yer."

He shambled on, doubled fists swinging by his side. The next moment, setting my teeth obstinately, I followed him and caught him by the park gate. At my hail he whirled around with a snarl, but I grabbed him by the throat and backed him violently against the park wall.

"You invaluable ruffian," I said, "now you listen to me. I live in that big stone building, and I'll give you a thousand dollars to take me behind the Graham Glacier. Think it over and call on me when you are in a pleasanter frame of mind. If you don't come by noon to-morrow I'll go to the Graham Glacier without you."

He was attempting to kick me all the time, but I managed to avoid him, and when I had finished I gave him a shove which almost loosened his spinal column. He went reeling out across the sidewalk, and when he had recovered his breath and his balance he danced with displeasure and displayed a vocabulary that astonished me. However, he kept his distance.

As I turned back into the park, satisfied that he would not follow, the first person I saw was the elderly, stony-faced lady of the wistaria arbor advancing on tiptoe. Behind her came the younger lady with cheeks like a rose that had been rained on.

Instantly it occurred to me that they had followed us, and at the same moment I knew who the stony-faced lady was. Angry, but polite, I lifted my hat and saluted her, and she, probably furious at having been caught tip-toeing after me, cut me dead. The younger lady passed me with face averted, but even in the dusk I could see the tip of one little ear turn scarlet.

Walking on hurriedly, I entered the Administration Building, and found Professor Lesard, of the reptilian department, preparing to leave.

"Don't you do it," I said, sharply; "I've got exciting news."

"I'm only going to the theatre," he replied. "It's a good show—Adam and Eve; there's a snake in it, you know. It's in my line."

"I can't help it," I said; and I told him briefly what had occurred in the arbor.

"But that's not all," I continued, savagely. "Those women followed us, and who do you think one of them turned out to be? Well, it was Professor Smawl, of Barnard College, and I'll bet every pair of boots I own that she starts for the Graham Glacier within a week. Idiot that I was!" I exclaimed, smiting my head with both hands. "I never recognized her until I saw her tip-toeing and craning her neck to listen. Now she knows about the glacier; she heard every word that young ruffian said, and she'll go to the glacier if it's only to forestall me."

Professor Lesard looked anxious. He knew that Miss Smawl, professor of natural history at Barnard College, had long desired an appointment at the Bronx Park gardens. It was even said she had a chance of succeeding Professor Farrago as president, but that, of course, must have been a joke. However, she haunted the gardens, annoying the keepers by persistently poking the animals with her umbrella. On

338

one occasion she sent us word that she desired to enter the tigers' enclosure for the purpose of making experiments in hypnotism. Professor Farrago was absent, but I took it upon myself to send back word that I feared the tigers might injure her. The miserable small boy who took my message informed her that I was afraid she might injure the tigers, and the unpleasant incident almost cost me my position.

"I am quite convinced," said I to Professor Lesard, "that Miss Smawl is perfectly capable of abusing the information she overheard, and of starting herself to explore a region that, by all the laws of decency, justice, and prior claim, belongs to me."

"Well," said Lesard, with a peculiar laugh, "it's not certain whether you can go at all."

"Professor Farrago will authorize me," I said, confidently.

"Professor Farrago has resigned," said Lesard. It was a bolt from a clear sky.

"Good Heavens!" I blurted out. "What will become of the rest of us, then?"

"I don't know," he replied. "The trustees are holding a meeting over in the Administration Building to elect a new president for us. It depends on the new president what becomes of us."

"Lesard," I said, hoarsely, "you don't suppose that they could possibly elect Miss Smawl as our president, do you?"

He looked at me askance and bit his cigar.

"I'd be in a nice position, wouldn't I?" said I, anxiously.

"The lady would probably make you walk the plank for that tiger business," he replied.

"But I didn't do it," I protested, with sickly eagerness. "Besides, I explained to her—"

He said nothing, and I stared at him, appalled by the possibility of reporting to Professor Smawl for instructions next morning.

"See here, Lesard," I said, nervously, "I wish you would step over to the Administration Building and ask the trustees if I may prepare for this expedition. Will you?"

He glanced at me sympathetically. It was quite natural for me to wish to secure my position before the new president was elected—especially as there was a chance of the new president being Miss Smawl.

"You are quite right," he said; "the Graham Glacier would be the safest place for you if our next president is to be the Lady of the Tigers." And he started across the park puffing his cigar.

I sat down on the doorstep to wait for his return, not at all charmed with the prospect. It made me furious, too, to see my ambition nipped with the frost of a possible veto from Miss Smawl.

"If she is elected," thought I, "there is nothing for me but to resign—to avoid the inconvenience of being shown the door. Oh, I wish I had allowed her to hypnotize the tigers!"

Thoughts of crime flitted through my mind. Miss Smawl would not remain president—or anything else very long—if she persisted in her desire for the tigers. And then when she called for help I would pretend not to hear.

Aroused from criminal meditation by the return of Professor Lesard, I jumped up and peered into his perplexed eyes. "They've elected a president," he said, "but they won't tell us who the president is until to-morrow."

"You don't think—" I stammered.

"I don't know. But I know this: the new president sanctions the expedition to the Graham Glacier, and directs you to choose an assistant and begin preparations for four people."

Overjoyed, I seized his hand and said, "Hurray!" in a voice weak with emotion. "The old dragon isn't elected this time," I added, triumphantly.

"By-the-way," he said, "who was the other dragon with her in the park this evening?"

I described her in a more modulated voice.

"Whew!" observed Professor Lesard, "that must be her assistant, Professor Dorothy Van Twiller! She's the prettiest blue-stocking in town!"

With this curious remark my confrère followed me into my room and wrote down the list of articles I dictated to him. The list included a complete camping equipment for myself and three other men.

"Am I one of those other men?" inquired Lesard, with an unhappy smile.

Before I could reply my door was shoved open and a figure appeared at the threshold, cap in hand.

"What do you want?" I asked, sternly; but my heart was beating high with triumph.

The figure shuffled; then came a subdued voice:

"Mister, I guess I'll go back to the Graham Glacier along with you. I'm Billy Spike, an' it kinder scares me to go back to them Hudson Mountains, but somehow, mister, when you choked me and kinder walked me off on my ear, why, mister, I kinder took to you like."

There was absolute silence for a minute; then he said:

"So if you go, I guess I'll go, too, mister."

"For a thousand dollars?"

"Fur nawthin'," he muttered—"or what you like."

"All right, Billy," I said, briskly; "just look over those rifles and ammunition and see that everything's sound."

He slowly lifted his tough young face and gave me a doglike glance. They were hard eyes, but there was gratitude in them.

"You'll get your throat slit," whispered Lesard.

"Not while Billy's with me," I replied, cheerfully.

Late that night, as I was preparing for pleasant dreams, a knock came on my door and a telegraph-messenger handed me a note, which I read, shivering in my bare feet, although the thermometer marked eighty Fahrenheit:

"You will immediately leave for the Hudson Mountains via Wellman Bay, Labrador, there to await further instructions. Equipment for yourself and one assistant will include following articles" [here began a list of camping utensils, scientific paraphernalia, and provisions]. "The steamer *Penguin* sails at five o'clock to-morrow morning. Kindly find yourself on board at that hour. Any excuse for not complying with these orders will be accepted as your resignation.

"SUSAN SMAWL,
"President Bronx Zoological Society."

"Lesard!" I shouted, trembling with fury.

He appeared at his door, chastely draped in pajamas; and he read the insolent letter with terrified alacrity.

"What are you going to do—resign?" he asked, much frightened.

"Do!" I snarled, grinding my teeth; "I'm going—that's what I'm going to do!"

"But—but you can't get ready and catch that steamer, too," he stammered.

He did not know me.

---

# VII

And so it came about that one calm evening towards the end of June, William Spike and I went into camp under the southerly shelter of that vast granite wall called the Hudson Mountains, there to await the promised "further instructions."

It had been a tiresome trip by steamer to Anticosti, from there by schooner to Widgeon Bay, then down the coast and up the Cape Clear River to Port Porpoise. There we bought three pack-mules and started due north on the Great Fur Trail. The second day out we passed Fort Boisé, the last outpost of civilization, and on the sixth day we were travelling eastward under the granite mountain parapets.

On the evening of the sixth day out from Fort Boisé we went into camp for the last time before entering the unknown land.

I could see it already through my field-glasses, and while William was building the fire I climbed up among the rocks above and sat down, glasses levelled, to study the prospect.

There was nothing either extraordinary or forbidding in the landscape which stretched out beyond; to the right the solid palisade of granite cut off the view; to the left the palisade continued, an endless barrier of sheer cliffs crowned with pine and hemlock. But the interesting section of the landscape lay almost directly in front of me—a rent in the mountain-wall through which appeared to run a level, arid plain, miles wide, and as smooth and even as a highroad.

There could be no doubt concerning the significance of that rent in the solid mountain-wall; and, moreover, it was exactly as William Spike had described it. However, I called to him and he came up from the smoky camp-fire, axe on shoulder.

"Yep," he said, squatting beside me; "the Graham Glacier used to meander through that there hole, but somethin' went wrong with the earth's in'ards an' there was a bust-up."

"And you saw it, William?" I said, with a sigh of envy.

"Hey? Seen it? Sure I seen it! I was to Spoutin' Springs, twenty mile west, with a bale o' blue fox an' otter pelt. Fust I knew them geysers begun for to groan egregious like, an' I seen the caribou gallopin' hell-bent south. 'This climate,' sez I, 'is too bracin' for me,' so I struck a back trail an' landed onto a hill. Then them geysers blowed up, one arter the next, an' I heard somethin' kinder cave in between here an' China. I disremember things what happened. Somethin' throwed me down, but I couldn't stay there, for the blamed ground was runnin' like a river—all wavy-like, an' the sky hit me on the back o' me head."

"And then?" I urged, in that new excitement which every repetition of the story revived. I had heard it all twenty times since we left New York, but mere repetition could not apparently satisfy me.

"Then," continued William, "the whole world kinder went off like a fire-cracker, an' I come too, an' ran like—"

"I know," said I, cutting him short, for I had become wearied of the invariable profanity which lent a lurid ending to his narrative.

"After that," I continued, "you went through the rent in the mountains?"

"Sure."

"And you saw a dingue and a creature that resembled a mammoth?"

"Sure," he repeated, sulkily.

"And you saw something else?" I always asked this question; it fascinated me to see the sullen fright flicker in William's eyes, and the mechanical backward glance, as though what he had seen might still be behind him.

He had never answered this third question but once, and that time he fairly snarled in my face as he growled: "I seen what no Christian oughter see."

So when I repeated: "And you saw something else, William?" he gave me a wicked, frightened leer, and shuffled off to feed the mules. Flattery, entreaties, threats left him unmoved; he never told me what the third thing was that he had seen behind the Hudson Mountains.

William had retired to mix up with his mules; I resumed my binoculars and my silent inspection of the great, smooth path left by the Graham Glacier when something or other exploded that vast mass of ice into vapor.

The arid plain wound out from the unknown country like a river, and I thought then, and think now, that when the glacier was blown into vapor the vapor descended in the most terrific rain the world has ever seen, and poured through the newly blasted mountain-gateway, sweeping the earth to bed-rock. To corroborate this theory, miles to the southward I could see the débris winding out across the land towards Wellman Bay, but as the terminal moraine of the vanished glacier formerly ended there I could not be certain that my theory was correct. Owing to the formation of the mountains I could not see more than half a mile into the unknown country. What I could see appeared to be nothing but the continuation of the glacier's path, scored out by the cloud-burst, and swept as smooth as a floor.

Sitting there, my heart beating heavily with excitement, I looked through the evening glow at the endless, pine-crowned mountain-wall with its giant's gateway pierced for me! And I thought of all the explorers and the unknown heroes—trappers, Indians, humble naturalists, perhaps—who had attempted to scale that sheer barricade and had died there or failed, beaten back from those eternal cliffs. Eternal? No! For the Eternal Himself had struck the rock, and it had sprung asunder, thundering obedience.

In the still evening air the smoke from the fire below mounted in a straight, slender pillar, like the smoke from those ancient altars builded before the first blood had been shed on earth.

The evening wind stirred the pines; a tiny spring brook made thin harmony among the rocks; a murmur came from the quiet camp. It was William adjuring his mules. In the deepening twilight I descended the hillock, stepping cautiously among the rocks.

Then, suddenly, as I stood outside the reddening ring of firelight, far in the depths of the unknown country, far behind the mountain-wall, a sound grew on the quiet air. William heard it and turned his face to the mountains. The sound faded to a vibration which was felt, not heard. Then once more I began to divine a vibration in the air, gathering in distant volume until it became a sound, lasting the space of a spoken word, fading to vibration, then silence.

Was it a cry?

I looked at William inquiringly. He had quietly fainted away.

I got him to the little brook and poked his head into the icy water, and after a while he sat up pluckily.

To an indignant question he replied: "Naw, I ain't a-cussin' you. Lemme be or I'll have fits."

"Was it that sound that scared you?" I asked.

"Ya-as," he replied with a dauntless shiver.

"Was it the voice of the mammoth?" I persisted, excitedly. "Speak, William, or I'll drag you about and kick you!"

He replied that it was neither a mammoth nor a dingue, and added a strong request for privacy, which I was obliged to grant, as I could not torture another word out of him.

I slept little that night; the exciting proximity of the unknown land was too much for me. But although I lay awake for hours, I heard nothing except the tinkle of water among the rocks and the plover calling from some hidden marsh. At daybreak I shot a ptarmigan which had walked into camp, and the shot set the echoes yelling among the mountains.

William, sullen and heavy-eyed, dressed the bird, and we broiled it for breakfast.

Neither he nor I alluded to the sound we had heard the night before; he boiled water and cleaned up the mess-kit, and I pottered about among the rocks for another ptarmigan. Wearying of this, presently, I returned to the mules and William, and sat down for a smoke.

"It strikes me," I said, "that our instructions to 'await further orders' are idiotic. How are we to receive 'further orders' here?"

William did not know.

"You don't suppose," said I, in sudden disgust, "that Miss Smawl believes there is a summer hotel and daily mail service in the Hudson Mountains?"

William thought perhaps she did suppose something of the sort.

It irritated me beyond measure to find myself at last on the very border of the unknown country, and yet checked, held back, by the irresponsible orders of a maiden lady named Smawl. However, my salary depended upon the whim of that maiden lady, and although I fussed and fumed and glared at the mountains through my glasses, I realized that I could not stir without the permission of Miss Smawl. At times this grotesque situation became almost unbearable, and I often went away by myself and indulged in fantasies, firing my gun off and pretending I had hit Miss Smawl by mistake. At such moments I would imagine I was free at last to plunge into the strange country, and I would squat on a rock and dream of bagging my first mammoth.

The time passed heavily; the tension increased with each new day. I shot ptarmigan and kept our table supplied with brook-trout. William chopped wood, conversed with his mules, and cooked very badly.

"See here," I said, one morning; "we have been in camp a week to-day, and I can't stand your cooking another minute!"

William, who was washing a saucepan, looked up and begged me sarcastically to accept the *cordon bleu*. But I know only how to cook eggs, and there were no eggs within some hundred miles.

To get the flavor of the breakfast out of my mouth I walked up to my favorite hillock and sat down for a smoke. The next moment, however, I was on my feet, cheering excitedly and shouting for William.

"Here come 'further instructions' at last!" I cried, pointing to the southward, where two dots on the grassy plain were imperceptibly moving in our direction.

"People on mules," said William, without enthusiasm.

"They must be messengers for us!" I cried, in chaste joy. "Three cheers for the northward trail, William, and the mischief take Miss—Well, never mind now," I added.

"On them approachin' mules," observed William, "there is wimmen."

I stared at him for a second, then attempted to strike him. He dodged wearily and repeated his incredible remark: "Ya-as, there is—wimmen—two female ladies onto them there mules."

"Bring me my glasses!" I said, hoarsely; "bring me those glasses, William, because I shall destroy you if you don't!"

Somewhat awed by my calm fury, he hastened back to camp and returned with the binoculars. It was a breathless moment. I adjusted the lenses with a steady hand and raised them.

Now, of all unexpected sights my fate may reserve for me in the future, I trust—nay, I know—that none can ever prove as unwelcome as the sight I perceived through my binoculars. For upon the backs of those distant mules were two women, and the first one was Miss Smawl!

Upon her head she wore a helmet, from which fluttered a green veil. Otherwise she was clothed in tweeds; and at moments she beat upon her mule with a thick umbrella.

Surfeited with the sickening spectacle, I sat down on a rock and tried to cry.

"I told yer so," observed William; but I was too tired to attack him.

When the caravan rode into camp I was myself again, smilingly prepared for the worst, and I advanced, cap in hand, followed furtively by William.

"Welcome," I said, violently injecting joy into my voice. "Welcome, Professor Smawl, to the Hudson Mountains!"

"Kindly take my mule," she said, climbing down to mother earth.

"William," I said, with dignity, "take the lady's mule."

Miss Smawl gave me a stolid glance, then made directly for the camp-fire, where a kettle of game-broth simmered over the coals. The last I saw of her she was smelling of it, and I turned my back and advanced towards the second lady pilgrim, prepared to be civil until snubbed.

Now, it is quite certain that never before had William Spike or I beheld so much feminine loveliness in one human body on the back of a mule. She was clad in the daintiest of shooting-kilts, yet there was nothing mannish about her except the way she rode the mule, and that only accentuated her adorable femininity.

I remembered what Professor Lesard had said about blue stockings—but Miss Dorothy Van Twiller's were gray, turned over at the tops, and disappearing into canvas spats buckled across a pair of slim shooting-boots.

"Welcome," said I, attempting to restrain a too violent cordiality. "Welcome, Professor Van Twiller, to the Hudson Mountains."

"Thank you," she replied, accepting my assistance very sweetly; "it is a pleasure to meet a human being again."

I glanced at Miss Smawl. She was eating game-broth, but she resembled a human being in a general way.

"I should very much like to wash my hands," said Professor Van Twiller, drawing the buckskin gloves from her slim fingers.

I brought towels and soap and conducted her to the brook.

She called to Professor Smawl to join her, and her voice was crystalline; Professor Smawl declined, and her voice was batrachian.

"She is so hungry!" observed Miss Van Twiller. "I am very thankful we are here at last, for we've had a horrid time. You see, we neither of us know how to cook."

I wondered what they would say to William's cooking, but I held my peace and retired, leaving the little brook to mirror the sweetest face that was ever bathed in water.

---

# VIII

That afternoon our expedition, in two sections, moved forward. The first section comprised myself and all the mules; the second section was commanded by Professor Smawl, followed by Professor Van Twiller, armed with a tiny shot-gun. William, loaded down with the ladies' toilet articles, skulked in the rear. I say skulked; there was no other word for it.

"So you're a guide, are you?" observed Professor Smawl when William, cap in hand, had approached her with well-meant advice. "The woods are full of lazy guides. Pick up those Gladstone bags! I'll do the guiding for this expedition."

Made cautious by William's humiliation, I associated with the mules exclusively. Nevertheless, Professor Smawl had her hard eyes on me, and I realized she meant mischief.

The encounter took place just as I, driving the five mules, entered the great mountain gateway, thrilled with anticipation which almost amounted to foreboding. As I was about to set foot across the imaginary frontier which divided the world from the unknown land, Professor Smawl hailed me and I halted until she came up.

"As commander of this expedition," she said, somewhat out of breath, "I desire to be the first living creature who has ever set foot behind the Graham Glacier. Kindly step aside, young sir!"

"Madam," said I, rigid with disappointment, "my guide, William Spike, entered that unknown land a year ago."

"He *says* he did," sneered Professor Smawl.

"As you like," I replied; "but it is scarcely generous to forestall the person whose stupidity gave you the clew to this unexplored region."

"You mean yourself?" she asked, with a stony stare.

"I do," said I, firmly.

Her little, hard eyes grew harder, and she clutched her umbrella until the steel ribs crackled.

"Young man," she said, insolently; "if I could have gotten rid of you I should have done so the day I was appointed president. But Professor Farrago refused to resign unless your position was assured, subject, of course, to your good behavior. Frankly, I don't like you, and I consider your views on science ridiculous, and if an opportunity presents itself I will be most happy to request your resignation. Kindly collect your mules and follow me."

Mortified beyond measure, I collected my mules and followed my president into the strange country behind the Hudson Mountains—I who had aspired to lead, compelled to follow in the rear, driving mules.

The journey was monotonous at first, but we shortly ascended a ridge from which we could see, stretching out below us, the wilderness where, save the feet of William Spike, no human feet had passed.

As for me, tingling with enthusiasm, I forgot my chagrin, I forgot the gross injustice, I forgot my mules. "Excelsior!" I cried, running up and down the ridge in uncontrollable excitement at the sublime spectacle of forest, mountain, and valley all set with little lakes.

"Excelsior!" repeated an excited voice at my side, and Professor Van Twiller sprang to the ridge beside me, her eyes bright as stars.

Exalted, inspired by the mysterious beauty of the view, we clasped hands and ran up and down the grassy ridge.

"That will do," said Professor Smawl, coldly, as we raced about like a pair of distracted kittens. The chilling voice broke the spell; I dropped Professor Van Twiller's hand and sat down on a bowlder, aching with wrath.

Late that afternoon we halted beside a tiny lake, deep in the unknown wilderness, where purple and scarlet bergamot choked the shores and the spruce-partridge strutted fearlessly under our very feet. Here we pitched our two tents. The afternoon sun slanted through the pines; the lake glittered; acres of golden brake perfumed the forest silence, broken only at rare intervals by the distant thunder of a partridge drumming.

Professor Smawl ate heavily and retired to her tent to lie torpid until evening. William drove the unloaded mules into an intervale full of sun-cured, fragrant grasses; I sat down beside Professor Van Twiller.

The wilderness is electric. Once within the influence of its currents, human beings become positively or negatively charged, violently attracting or repelling each other.

"There is something the matter with this air," said Professor Van Twiller. "It makes me feel as though I were desperately enamoured of the entire human race."

She leaned back against a pine, smiling vaguely, and crossing one knee over the other.

Now I am not bold by temperament, and, normally, I fear ladies. Therefore it surprised me to hear myself begin a frivolous *causerie*, replying to her pretty epigrams with epigrams of my own, advancing to the borderland of badinage, fearlessly conducting her and myself over that delicate frontier to meet upon the terrain of undisguised flirtation.

It was clear that she was out for a holiday. The seriousness and restraints of twenty-two years she had left behind her in the civilized world, and now, with a shrug of her young shoulders, she unloosened her burden of reticence, dignity, and responsibility and let the whole load fall with a discreet thud.

"Even hares go mad in March," she said, seriously. "I know you intend to flirt with me—and I don't care. Anyway, there's nothing else to do, is there?"

"Suppose," said I, solemnly, "I should take you behind that big tree and attempt to kiss you!"

The prospect did not appear to appall her, so I looked around with that sneaking yet conciliatory caution peculiar to young men who are novices in the art. Before I had satisfied myself that neither William nor the mules were observing us, Professor Van Twiller rose to her feet and took a short step backward.

"Let's set traps for a dingue," she said, "will you?"

I looked at the big tree, undecided. "Come on," she said; "I'll show you how." And away we went into the woods, she leading, her kilts flashing through the golden half-light.

Now I had not the faintest notion how to trap the dingue, but Professor Van Twiller asserted that it formerly fed on the tender tips of the spruce, quoting Darwin as her authority.

So we gathered a bushel of spruce-tips, piled them on the bank of a little stream, then built a miniature stockade around the bait, a foot high. I roofed this with hemlock, then laboriously whittled out and adjusted a swinging shutter for the entrance, setting it on springy twigs.

"The dingue, you know, was supposed to live in the water," she said, kneeling beside me over our trap.

I took her little hand and thanked her for the information.

"Doubtless," she said, enthusiastically, "a dingue will come out of the lake to-night to feed on our spruce-tips. Then," she added, "we've got him."

"True!" I said, earnestly, and pressed her fingers very gently.

Her face was turned a little away; I don't remember what she said; I don't remember that she said anything. A faint rose-tint stole over her cheek. A few moments later she said: "You must not do that again."

It was quite late when we strolled back to camp. Long before we came in sight of the twin tents we heard a deep voice bawling our names. It was Professor Smawl, and she pounced upon Dorothy and drove her ignominiously into the tent.

"As for you," she said, in hollow tones, "you may explain your conduct at once, or place your resignation at my disposal."

But somehow or other I appeared to be temporarily lost to shame, and I only smiled at my infuriated president, and entered my own tent with a step that was distinctly frolicsome.

"Billy," said I to William Spike, who regarded me morosely from the depths of the tent, "I'm going out to bag a mammoth to-morrow, so kindly clean my elephant-gun and bring an axe to chop out the tusks."

That night Professor Smawl complained bitterly of the cooking, but as neither Dorothy nor I knew how to improve it, she revenged herself on us by eating everything on the table and retiring to bed, taking Dorothy with her.

I could not sleep very well; the mosquitoes were intrusive, and Professor Smawl dreamed she was a pack of wolves and yelped in her sleep.

"Bird, ain't she?" said William, roused from slumber by her weird noises.

Dorothy, much frightened, crawled out of her tent, where her blanket-mate still dreamed dyspeptically, and William and I made her comfortable by the camp-fire.

It takes a pretty girl to look pretty half asleep in a blanket.

"Are you sure you are quite well?" I asked her.

To make sure, I tested her pulse. For an hour it varied more or less, but without alarming either of us. Then she went back to bed and I sat alone by the camp-fire.

Towards midnight I suddenly began to feel that strange, distant vibration that I had once before felt. As before, the vibration grew on the still air, increasing in volume until it became a sound, then died out into silence.

I rose and stole into my tent.

William, white as death, lay in his corner, weeping in his sleep.

I roused him remorselessly, and he sat up scowling, but refused to tell me what he had been dreaming.

"Was it about that third thing you saw—" I began. But he snarled up at me like a startled animal, and I was obliged to go to bed and toss about and speculate.

The next morning it rained. Dorothy and I visited our dingue-trap but found nothing in it. We were inclined, however, to stay out in the rain behind a big tree, but Professor Smawl vetoed that proposition and sent me off to supply the larder with fresh meat.

I returned, mad and wet, with a dozen partridges and a white hare—brown at that season—and William cooked them vilely.

"I can taste the feathers!" said Professor Smawl, indignantly.

"There is no accounting for taste," I said, with a polite gesture of deprecation; "personally, I find feathers unpalatable."

"You may hand in your resignation this evening!" cried Professor Smawl, in hollow tones of passion.

I passed her the pancakes with a cheerful smile, and flippantly pressed the hand next me. Unexpectedly it proved to be William's sticky fist, and Dorothy and I laughed until her tears ran into Professor Smawl's coffee-cup—an accident which kindled her wrath to red heat, and she requested my resignation five times during the evening.

The next day it rained again, more or less. Professor Smawl complained of the cooking, demanded my resignation, and finally marched out to explore, lugging the reluctant William with her. Dorothy and I sat down behind the largest tree we could find.

I don't remember what we were saying when a peculiar sound interrupted us, and we listened earnestly.

It was like a bell in the woods, ding-dong! ding-dong! ding-dong!—a low, mellow, golden harmony, coming nearer, then stopping.

I clasped Dorothy in my arms in my excitement.

"It is the note of the dingue!" I whispered, "and that explains its name, handed down from remote ages along with the names of the behemoth and the coney. It was because of its bell-like cry that it was named! Darling!" I cried, forgetting our short acquaintance, "we have made a discovery that the whole world will ring with!"

Hand in hand we tiptoed through the forest to our trap. There was something in it that took fright at our approach and rushed panic-stricken round and round the interior of the trap, uttering its alarm-note, which sounded like the jangling of a whole string of bells.

I seized the strangely beautiful creature; it neither attempted to bite nor scratch, but crouched in my arms, trembling and eying me.

Delighted with the lovely, tame animal, we bore it tenderly back to the camp and placed it on my blanket. Hand in hand we stood before it, awed by the sight of this beast, so long believed to be extinct.

"It is too good to be true," sighed Dorothy, clasping her white hands under her chin and gazing at the dingue in rapture.

"Yes," said I, solemnly, "you and I, my child, are face to face with the fabled dingue—*Dingus solitarius*! Let us continue to gaze at it, reverently, prayerfully, humbly—"

Dorothy yawned—probably with excitement.

We were still mutely adoring the dingue when Professor Smawl burst into the tent at a hand-gallop, bawling hoarsely for her kodak and note-book.

Dorothy seized her triumphantly by the arm and pointed at the dingue, which appeared to be frightened to death.

"What!" cried Professor Smawl, scornfully; "*that* a dingue? Rubbish!"

"Madam," I said, firmly, "it is a dingue! It's a monodactyl! See! It has but a single toe!"

"Bosh!" she retorted; "it's got four!"

"Four!" I repeated, blankly.

"Yes; one on each foot!"

"Of course," I said; "you didn't suppose a monodactyl meant a beast with one leg and one toe!"

But she laughed hatefully and declared it was a woodchuck.

We squabbled for a while until I saw the significance of her attitude. The unfortunate woman wished to find a dingue first and be accredited with the discovery.

I lifted the dingue in both hands and shook the creature gently, until the chiming ding-dong of its protestations filled our ears like sweet bells jangled out of tune.

Pale with rage at this final proof of the dingue's identity, she seized her camera and note-book.

"I haven't any time to waste over that musical woodchuck!" she shouted, and bounced out of the tent.

"What have you discovered, dear?" cried Dorothy, running after her.

"A mammoth!" bawled Professor Smawl, triumphantly; "and I'm going to photograph him!"

Neither Dorothy nor I believed her. We watched the flight of the infatuated woman in silence.

And now, at last, the tragic shadow falls over my paper as I write. I was never passionately attached to Professor Smawl, yet I would gladly refrain from chronicling the episode that must follow if, as I have hitherto attempted, I succeed in sticking to the unornamented truth.

I have said that neither Dorothy nor I believed her. I don't know why, unless it was that we had not yet made up our minds to believe that the mammoth still existed on earth. So, when Professor Smawl disappeared in the forest, scuttling through the underbrush like a demoralized hen, we viewed her flight with unconcern. There was a large tree in the neighborhood—a pleasant shelter in case of rain. So we sat down behind it, although the sun was shining fiercely.

It was one of those peaceful afternoons in the wilderness when the whole forest dreams, and the shadows are asleep and every little leaflet takes a nap. Under the still tree-tops the dappled sunlight, motionless, soaked the sod; the forest-flies no longer whirled in circles, but sat sunning their wings on slender twig-tips.

The heat was sweet and spicy; the sun drew out the delicate essence of gum and sap, warming volatile juices until they exhaled through the aromatic bark.

The sun went down into the wilderness; the forest stirred in its sleep; a fish splashed in the lake. The spell was broken. Presently the wind began to rise somewhere far away in the unknown land. I heard it coming, nearer, nearer—a brisk wind that grew heavier and blew harder as it neared us—a gale that swept distant branches—a furious gale that set limbs clashing and cracking, nearer and nearer. Crack! and the gale grew to a hurricane, trampling trees like dead twigs! Crack! Crackle! Crash! Crash!

*Was it the wind?*

With the roaring in my ears I sprang up, staring into the forest vista, and at the same instant, out of the crashing forest, sped Professor Smawl, skirts tucked up, thin legs flying like bicycle-spokes. I shouted, but the crashing drowned my voice. Then all at once the solid earth began to shake, and with the rush and roar of a tornado a gigantic living thing burst out of the forest before our eyes—a vast shadowy bulk that rocked and rolled along, mowing down trees in its course.

Two great crescents of ivory curved from its head; its back swept through the tossing tree-tops. Once it bellowed like a gun fired from a high bastion.

The apparition passed with the noise of thunder rolling on towards the ends of the earth. Crack! crash! went the trees, the tempest swept away in a rolling volley of reports, distant, more distant, until, long after the tumult had deadened, then ceased, the stunned forest echoed with the fall of mangled branches slowly dropping.

That evening an agitated young couple sat close together in the deserted camp, calling timidly at intervals for Professor Smawl and William Spike. I say timidly, because it is correct; we did not care to have a mammoth respond to our calls. The lurking echoes across the lake answered our cries; the full moon came up over the forest to look at us. We were not much to look at. Dorothy was moistening my shoulder with unfeigned tears, and I, afraid to light the fire, sat hunched up under the common blanket, wildly examining the darkness around us.

Chilled to the spinal marrow, I watched the gray lights whiten in the east. A single bird awoke in the wilderness. I saw the nearer trees looming in the mist, and the silver fog rolling on the lake.

All night long the darkness had vibrated with the strange monotone which I had heard the first night, camping at the gate of the unknown land. My brain seemed to echo that subtle harmony which rings in the auricular labyrinth after sound has ceased.

There are ghosts of sound which return to haunt long after sound is dead. It was these voiceless spectres of a voice long dead that stirred the transparent silence, intoning toneless tones.

I think I make myself clear.

It was an uncanny night; morning whitened the east; gray daylight stole into the woods, blotting the shadows to paler tints. It was nearly mid-day before the sun became visible through the fine-spun web of mist—a pale spot of gilt in the zenith.

By this pallid light I labored to strike the two empty tents, gather up our equipments and pack them on our five mules. Dorothy aided me bravely, whimpering when I spoke of Professor Smawl and William Spike, but abating nothing of her industry until we had the mules loaded and I was ready to drive them, Heaven knows whither.

"Where shall we go?" quavered Dorothy, sitting on a log with the dingue in her lap.

One thing was certain; this mammoth-ridden land was no place for women, and I told her so.

We placed the dingue in a basket and tied it around the leading mule's neck. Immediately the dingue, alarmed, began dingling like a cow-bell. It acted like a charm on the other mules, and they gravely filed off after their leader, following the bell. Dorothy and I, hand in hand, brought up the rear.

I shall never forget that scene in the forest—the gray arch of the heavens swimming in mist through which the sun peered shiftily, the tall pines wavering through the fog, the preoccupied mules marching single file, the foggy bell-note of the gentle dingue in its swinging basket, and Dorothy, limp kilts dripping with dew, plodding through the white dusk.

We followed the terrible tornado-path which the mammoth had left in its wake, but there were no traces of its human victims—neither one jot of Professor Smawl nor one solitary tittle of William Spike.

And now I would be glad to end this chapter if I could; I would gladly leave myself as I was, there in the misty forest, with an arm encircling the slender body of my little companion, and the mules moving in a monotonous line, and the dingue discreetly jingling—but again that menacing shadow falls across my page, and truth bids me tell all, and I, the slave of accuracy, must remember my vows as the dauntless disciple of truth.

Towards sunset—or that pale parody of sunset which set the forest swimming in a ghastly, colorless haze—the mammoth's trail of ruin brought us suddenly out of the trees to the shore of a great sheet of water.

It was a desolate spot; northward a chaos of sombre peaks rose, piled up like thunder-clouds along the horizon; east and south the darkening wilderness spread like a pall. Westward, crawling out into the mist from our very feet, the gray waste of water moved under the dull sky, and flat waves slapped the squatting rocks, heavy with slime.

And now I understood why the trail of the mammoth continued straight into the lake, for on either hand black, filthy tamarack swamps lay under ghostly sheets of mist. I strove to creep out into the bog, seeking a footing, but the swamp quaked and the smooth surface trembled like jelly in a bowl. A stick thrust into the slime sank into unknown depths.

Vaguely alarmed, I gained the firm land again and looked around, believing there was no road open but the desolate trail we had traversed. But I was in error; already the leading mule was wading out into the water, and the others, one by one, followed.

How wide the lake might be we could not tell, because the band of fog hung across the water like a curtain. Yet out into this flat, shallow void our mules went steadily, slop! slop! slop! in single file. Already they were growing indistinct in the fog, so I bade Dorothy hasten and take off her shoes and stockings.

She was ready before I was, I having to unlace my shooting-boots, and she stepped out into the water, kilts fluttering, moving her white feet cautiously. In a moment I was beside her, and we waded forward, sounding the shallow water with our poles.

When the water had risen to Dorothy's knees I hesitated, alarmed. But when we attempted to retrace our steps we could not find the shore again, for the blank mist shrouded everything, and the water deepened at every step.

I halted and listened for the mules. Far away in the fog I heard a dull splashing, receding as I listened. After a while all sound died away, and a slow horror stole over me—a horror that froze the little net-work of veins in every limb. A step to the right and the water rose to my knees; a step to the left and the cold, thin circle of the flood chilled my breast. Suddenly Dorothy screamed, and the next moment a far cry answered—a far, sweet cry that seemed to come from the sky, like the rushing harmony of the world's swift winds. Then the curtain of fog before us lighted up from behind; shadows moved on the misty screen, outlines of trees and grassy shores, and tiny birds flying. Thrown on the vapory curtain, in silhouette, a man and a woman passed under the lovely trees, arms about each other's necks; near them the shadows of five mules grazed peacefully; a dingue gambolled close by.

"It is a mirage!" I muttered, but my voice made no sound. Slowly the light behind the fog died out; the vapor around us turned to rose, then dissolved, while mile on mile of a limitless sea spread away till, like a quick line pencilled at a stroke, the horizon cut sky and sea in half, and before us lay an ocean from which towered a mountain of snow—or a gigantic berg of milky ice—for it was moving.

"Good Heavens," I shrieked; "it is alive!"

At the sound of my crazed cry the mountain of snow became a pillar, towering to the clouds, and a wave of golden glory drenched the figure to its knees! Figure? Yes—for a colossal arm shot across the sky, then curved back in exquisite grace to a head of awful beauty—a woman's head, with eyes like the blue lake of heaven—ay, a woman's splendid form, upright from the sky to the earth, knee-deep in the sea. The evening clouds drifted across her brow; her shimmering hair lighted the world beneath with sunset. Then, shading her white brow with one hand, she bent, and with the other hand dipped in the sea, she sent a wave rolling at us. Straight out of the horizon it sped—a ripple that grew to a wave, then to a furious breaker which caught us up in a whirl of foam, bearing us onward, faster, faster, swiftly flying through leagues of spray until consciousness ceased and all was blank.

Yet ere my senses fled I heard again that strange cry—that sweet, thrilling harmony rushing out over the foaming waters, filling earth and sky with its soundless vibrations.

And I knew it was the hail of the Spirit of the North warning us back to life again.

———

Looking back, now, over the days that passed before we staggered into the Hudson Bay outpost at Gravel Cove, I am inclined to believe that neither Dorothy nor I were clothed entirely in our proper minds—or, if we were, our minds, no doubt, must have been in the same condition as our clothing. I remember shooting ptarmigan, and that we ate them; flashes of memory recall the steady downpour of rain through the endless twilight of shaggy forests; dim days on the foggy tundra, mudholes from which the wild ducks rose in thousands; then the stunted hemlocks, then the forest again. And I do not even recall the moment when, at last, stumbling into the smooth path left by the Graham Glacier, we crawled through the mountain-wall, out of the unknown land, and once more into a world protected by the Lord Almighty.

A hunting-party of Elbon Indians brought us in to the post, and everybody was most kind—that I remember, just before going into several weeks of unpleasant delirium mercifully mitigated with unconsciousness.

Curiously enough, Professor Van Twiller was not very much battered, physically, for I had carried her for days, pickaback. But the awful experience had produced a shock which resulted in a nervous condition that lasted so long after she returned to New York that the wealthy and eminent specialist who attended her insisted upon taking her to the Riviera and marrying her. I sometimes wonder—but, as I have said, such reflections have no place in these austere pages.

However, anybody, I fancy, is at liberty to speculate upon the fate of the late Professor Smawl and William Spike, and upon the mules and the gentle dingue.

Personally, I am convinced that the suggestive silhouettes I saw on that ghastly curtain of fog were cast by beatified beings in some earthly paradise—a mirage of bliss of which we caught but the colorless shadow-shapes floating 'twixt sea and sky.

At all events, neither Professor Smawl nor her William Spike ever returned; no exploring expedition has found a trace of mule or lady, of William or the dingue. The new expedition to be organized by Barnard College may penetrate still farther. I suppose that, when the time comes, I shall be expected to volunteer. But Professor Van Twiller is married, and William and Professor Smawl ought to be, and altogether, considering the mammoth and that gigantic and splendid apparition that bent from the zenith to the ocean and sent a tidal-wave rolling from the palm of one white hand—I say, taking all these various matters under consideration, I think I shall decide to remain in New York and continue writing for the scientific periodicals. Besides, the mortifying experience at the Paris Exposition has dampened even my perennially youthful enthusiasm. And as for the late expedition to Florida, Heaven knows I am ready to repeat it—nay, I am already forming a plan for the rescue—but though I am prepared to encounter any danger for the sake of my beloved superior, Professor Farrago, I do not feel inclined to commit indiscretions in order to pry into secrets which, as I regard it, concern Professor Smawl and William Spike alone.

But all this is, in a measure, premature. What I now have to relate is the recital of an eye-witness to that most astonishing scandal which occurred during the recent exposition in Paris.

# IX

When the delegates were appointed to the International Scientific Congress at the Paris Exposition of 1900, how little did anybody imagine that the great conference would end in the most gigantic scandal that ever stirred two continents?

Yet, had it not been for the pair of American newspapers published in Paris, this scandal would never have been aired, for the continental press is so well muzzled that when it bites its teeth merely meet in the empty atmosphere with a discreet snap.

But to the Yankee nothing excepting the Monroe Doctrine is sacred, and the unsopped watch-dogs of the press bite right and left, unmuzzled. The biter bites—it is his profession—and that ends the affair; the bitee is bitten, and, in the deplorable argot of the hour, "it is up to him."

So now that the scandal has been well aired and hung out to dry in the teeth of decency and the four winds, and as all the details have been cheerfully and grossly exaggerated, it is, perhaps, the proper moment for the truth to be written by the only person whose knowledge of all the facts in the affair entitles him to speak for himself as well as for those honorable ladies and gentlemen whose names and titles have been so mercilessly criticised.

These, then, are the simple facts:

The International Scientific Congress, now adjourned *sine die*, met at nine o'clock in the morning, May 3, 1900, in the Tasmanian Pavilion of the Paris Exposition. There were present the most famous scientists of Great Britain, France, Germany, Russia, Italy, Switzerland, and the United States.

His Royal Highness the Crown-Prince of Monaco presided.

It is not necessary, now, to repeat the details of that preliminary meeting. It is sufficient to say that committees representing the various known sciences were named and appointed by the Prince of Monaco, who had been unanimously elected permanent chairman of the conference. It is the composition of a single committee that concerns us now, and that committee, representing the science which treats of bird life, was made up as follows:

Chairman—His Royal Highness the Crown-Prince of Monaco. Members—Sir Peter Grebe, Great Britain; Baron de Becasse, France; his Royal Highness King Christian, of Finland; the Countess d'Alzette, of Belgium; and I, from the United States, representing the Smithsonian Institution and the Bronx Park Zoological Society of New York.

This, then, was the composition of that now notorious ornithological committee, a modest, earnest, self-effacing little band of workers, bound together—in the beginning—by those ties of mutual respect and esteem which unite all laborers in the vineyard of science.

From the first meeting of our committee, science, the great leveller, left no artificial barriers of rank or title standing between us. We were enthusiasts in our love for ornithology; we found new inspiration in the democracy of our common interests.

As for me, I chatted with my fellows, feeling no restraint myself and perceiving none. The King of Finland and I discussed his latest monograph on the speckled titmouse, and I was glad to agree with the King in all his theories concerning the nesting habits of that important bird.

Sir Peter Grebe, a large, red gentleman in tweeds, read us some notes he had made on the domestic hen and her reasons for running ahead of a horse and wagon instead of stepping aside to let the disturbing vehicle pass.

The Crown-Prince of Monaco took issue with Sir Peter; so did the Baron de Becasse; and we were entertained by a friendly and marvellously interesting three-cornered dispute, shared in by three of the most profound thinkers of the century.

I shall never forget the brilliancy of that argument, nor the modest, good-humored retorts which gave us all a glimpse into depths of erudition which impressed us profoundly and set the seal on the bonds which held us so closely together.

Alas, that the seal should ever have been broken! Alas, that the glittering apple of discord should have been flung into our midst!—no, not flung, but gently rolled under our noses by the gloved fingers of the lovely Countess d'Alzette.

"Messieurs," said the fair Countess, when all present, excepting she and I, had touched upon or indicated the subjects which they had prepared to present to the congress—"messieurs mes confrères, I have been requested by our distinguished chairman, the Crown-Prince of Monaco, to submit to your judgment the subject which, by favor of the King of the Belgians, I have prepared to present to the International Scientific Congress."

She made a pretty courtesy as she named her own sovereign, and we all rose out of respect to that most austere and moral ruler the King of Belgium.

"But," she said, with a charming smile of depreciation, "I am very, very much afraid that the subject which I have chosen may not meet with your approval, gentlemen."

She stood there in her dainty Parisian gown and bonnet, shaking her pretty head uncertainly, a smile on her lips, her small, gloved fingers interlocked.

"Oh, I know how dreadful it would be if this great congress should be compelled to listen to any hoax like that which Monsieur de Rougemont imposed on the British

Royal Society," she said, gravely; "and because the subject of my paper is as strange as the strangest phenomenon alleged to have been noted by Monsieur de Rougemont, I hesitate—"

She glanced at the silent listeners around her. Sir Peter's red face had hardened; the King of Finland frowned slightly; the Crown-Prince of Monaco and Baron de Becasse wore anxious smiles. But when her violet eyes met mine I gave her a glance of encouragement, and that glance, I am forced to confess, was not dictated by scientific approval, but by something that never entirely dries up in the mustiest and dustiest of savants—the old Adam implanted in us all.

Now, I knew perfectly well what her subject must be; so did every man present. For it was no secret that his Majesty of Belgium had been swindled by some natives in Tasmania, and had paid a very large sum of money for a skin of that gigantic bird, the ux, which has been so often reported to exist among the inaccessible peaks of the Tasmanian Mountains. Needless, perhaps, to say that the skin proved a fraud, being nothing more than a Barnum contrivance made up out of the skins of a dozen ostriches and cassowaries, and most cleverly put together by Chinese workmen; at least, such was the report made on it by Sir Peter Grebe, who had been sent by the British Society to Antwerp to examine the acquisition. Needless, also, perhaps, to say that King Leopold, of Belgium, stoutly maintained that the skin of the ux was genuine from beak to claw.

For six months there had been a most serious difference of opinion among European ornithologists concerning the famous ux in the Antwerp Museum; and this difference had promised to result in an open quarrel between a few Belgian savants on one side and-all Europe and Great Britain on the other.

Scientists have a deep—rooted horror of anything that touches on charlatanism; the taint of trickery not only alarms them, but drives them away from any suspicious subject, and usually ruins, scientifically speaking, the person who has introduced the subject for discussion.

Therefore, it took no little courage for the Countess d'Alzette to touch, with her dainty gloves, a subject which every scientist in Europe, with scarcely an exception, had pronounced fraudulent and unworthy of investigation. And to bring it before the great International Congress required more courage still; for the person who could face, in executive session, the most brilliant intellects in the world, and openly profess faith in a Barnumized bird skin, either had no scientific reputation to lose or was possessed of a bravery far above that of the savants who composed the audience.

Now, when the pretty Countess caught a flash of encouragement in my glance she turned rosy with gratification and surprise. Clearly, she had not expected to find a single ally in the entire congress. Her quick smile of gratitude touched me, and made me ashamed, too, for I had encouraged her out of the pure love of mischief, hoping to hear the whole matter threshed before the congress and so have it settled once for all. It was a thoughtless thing to do on my part. I should have remembered the consequences to the Countess if it were proven that she had been championing a fraud. The ruffled dignity of the congress would never forgive her; her scientific career would practically be at an end, because her theories and observations could no longer command respect or even the attention of those who knew that she herself had once been deceived by a palpable fraud.

I looked at her guiltily, already ashamed of myself for encouraging her to her destruction. How lovely and innocent she appeared, standing there reading her notes in a low, clear voice, fresh as a child's, with now and then a delicious upward sweep of her long, dark lashes.

With a start I came to my senses and bestowed a pinch on myself. This was neither the time nor the place to sentimentalize over a girlish beauty whose small, Parisian head was crammed full of foolish, brave theories concerning an imposition which her aged sovereign had been unable to detect.

I saw the gathering frown on the King of Finland's dark face; I saw Sir Peter Grebe grow redder and redder, and press his thick lips together to control the angry "Bosh!" which need not have been uttered to have been understood. The Baron de Becasse wore a painfully neutral smile, which froze his face into a quaint gargoyle; the Crown-Prince of Monaco looked at his polished fingernails with a startled yet abstracted resignation. Clearly the young Countess had not a sympathizer in the committee.

Something—perhaps it was the latent chivalry which exists imbedded in us all, perhaps it was pity, perhaps a glimmering dawn of belief in the ux skin—set my thoughts working very quickly.

The Countess d'Alzette finished her notes, then glanced around with a deprecating smile, which died out on her lips when she perceived the silent and stony hostility of her fellow-scientists. A quick expression of alarm came into her lovely eyes. Would they vote against giving her a hearing before the congress? It required a unanimous vote to reject a subject. She turned her eyes on me.

I rose, red as fire, my head humming with a chaos of ideas all disordered and vague, yet whirling along in a single, resistless current. I had come to the congress prepared to deliver a monograph on the great auk; but now the subject went overboard as the birds themselves had, and I found myself pleading with the committee to give the Countess a hearing on the ux.

"Why not?" I exclaimed, warmly. "It is established beyond question that the ux does exist in Tasmania. Wallace saw several uxen, through his telescope, walking about upon the inaccessible heights of the Tasmanian Mountains. Darwin acknowledged that the bird exists; Professor Farrago has published a pamphlet containing an accumulation of all data bearing upon the ux. Why should not Madame la Comtesse be heard by the entire congress?"

I looked at Sir Peter Grebe.

"Have *you* seen this alleged bird skin in the Antwerp Museum?" he asked, perspiring with indignation.

"Yes, I have," said I. "It has been patched up, but how are we to know that the skin did not require patching? I have not found that ostrich skin has been used. It is true that the Tasmanians may have shot the bird to pieces and mended the skin with bits of cassowary hide here and there. But the greater part of the skin, and the beak and claws, are, in my estimation, well worth the serious attention of savants. To pronounce them fraudulent is, in my opinion, rash and premature."

I mopped my brow; I was in for it now. I had thrown in my reputation with the reputation of the Countess.

The displeasure and astonishment of my confrères was unmistakable. In the midst of a strained silence I moved that a vote be taken upon the advisability of a hearing before the congress on the subject of the ux. After a pause the young Countess, pale and determined, seconded my motion. The result of the balloting was a foregone conclusion; the Countess had one vote—she herself refraining from voting—and the subject was entered on the committee-book as acceptable and a date set for the hearing before the International Congress.

The effect of this vote on our little committee was most marked. Constraint took the place of cordiality, polite reserve replaced that guileless and open-hearted courtesy with which our proceedings had begun.

With icy politeness, the Crown-Prince of Monaco asked me to state the subject of the paper I proposed to read before the congress, and I replied quietly that, as I was partly responsible for advocating the discussion of the ux, I proposed to associate myself with the Countess d'Alzette in that matter—if Madame la Comtesse would accept the offer of a brother savant.

"Indeed I will," she said, impulsively, her blue eyes soft with gratitude.

"Very well," observed Sir Peter Grebe, swallowing his indignation and waddling off towards the door; "I shall resign my position on this committee—yes, I will, I tell you!"—as the King of Finland laid a fatherly hand on Sir Peter's sleeve—"I'll not be made responsible for this damn—"

He choked, sputtered, then bowed to the horrified Countess, asking pardon, and declaring that he yielded to nobody in respect for the gentler sex. And he retired with the Baron de Becasse.

But out in the hallway I heard him explode. "Confound it! This is no place for petticoats, Baron! And as for that Yankee ornithologist, he's hung himself with the Countess's corset—string—yes, he has! Don't tell me, Baron! The young idiot was all right until the Countess looked at him, I tell you. Gad! how she crumpled him up with those blue eyes of hers! What the devil do women come into such committees for? Eh? It's an outrage, I tell you! Why, the whole world will jeer at us if we sit and listen to her monograph on that fraudulent bird!"

The young Countess, who was writing near the window, could not have heard this outburst; but I heard it, and so did King Christian and the Crown-Prince of Monaco.

"Lord," thought I, "the Countess and I are in the frying-pan this time. I'll do what I can to keep us both out of the fire."

When the King and the Crown-Prince had made their adieux to the Countess, and she had responded, pale and serious, they came over to where I was standing, looking out on the Seine.

"Though we must differ from you," said the King, kindly, "we wish you all success in this dangerous undertaking."

I thanked him.

"You are a young man to risk a reputation already established," remarked the Crown-Prince, then added: "You are braver than I. Ridicule is a barrier to all knowledge, and, though we know that, we seekers after truth always bring up short at that barrier and dismount, not daring to put our hobbies to the fence."

"One can but come a cropper," said I.

"And risk staking our hobbies? No, no, that would make us ridiculous; and ridicule kills in Europe."

"It's somewhat deadly in America, too," I said, smiling.

"The more honor to you," said the Crown-Prince, gravely.

"Oh, I am not the only one," I answered, lightly. "There is my confrère, Professor Hyssop, who studies apparitions and braves a contempt and ridicule which none of us would dare challenge. We Yankees are learning slowly. Some day we will find the lost key to the future while Europe is sneering at those who are trying to pick the lock."

When King Christian, of Finland, and the Crown-Prince of Monaco had taken their hats and sticks and departed, I glanced across the room at the young Countess, who was now working rapidly on a type-writer, apparently quite oblivious of my presence.

I looked out of the window again, and my gaze wandered over the exposition grounds. Gilt and scarlet and azure the palaces rose in every direction, under a wilderness of fluttering flags. Towers, minarets, turrets, golden spires cut the blue sky; in the west the gaunt Eiffel Tower sprawled across the glittering Esplanade; behind it rose the solid golden dome of the Emperor's tomb, gilded once more by the Almighty's sun, to amuse the living rabble while the dead slumbered in his imperial crypt, himself now but a relic for the amusement of the people whom he had despised. O tempora! O mores! O Napoleon!

Down under my window, in the asphalted court, the King of Finland was entering his beautiful victoria. An adjutant, wearing a cocked hat and brilliant uniform, mounted the box beside the green-and-gold coachman; the two postilions straightened up in their saddles; the four horses danced. Then, when the Crown-Prince of Monaco had taken a seat beside the King, the carriage rolled away, and far down the quay I watched it until the flutter of the green-and-white plumes in the adjutant's cocked hat was all I could see of vanishing royalty.

I was still musing there by the window, listening to the click and ringing of the type-writer, when I suddenly became aware that the clicking had ceased, and, turning, I saw the young Countess standing beside me.

"Thank you for your chivalrous impulse to help me," she said, frankly, holding out her bare hand.

I bent over it.

"I had not realized how desperate my case was," she said, with a smile. "I supposed that they would at least give me a hearing. How can I thank you for your brave vote in my favor?"

"By giving me your confidence in this matter," said I, gravely. "If we are to win, we must work together and work hard, madame. We are entering a struggle, not only to prove the genuineness of a bird skin and the existence of a bird which neither of us has ever seen, but also a struggle which will either make us famous forever or render it impossible for either of us ever again to face a scientific audience."

"I know it," she said, quietly "And I understand all the better how gallant a gentleman I have had the fortune to enlist in my cause. Believe me, had I not absolute confidence in my ability to prove the existence of the ux I should not, selfish as I am, have accepted your chivalrous offer to stand or fall with me."

The subtle emotion in her voice touched a responsive chord in me. I looked at her earnestly; she raised her beautiful eyes to mine.

"Will you help me?" she asked.

Would I help her? Faith, I'd pass the balance of my life turning flip-flaps to please her. I did not attempt to undeceive myself; I realized that the lightning had struck me—that I was desperately in love with the young Countess from the tip of her bonnet to the toe of her small, polished shoe. I was curiously cool about it, too, although my heart gave a thump that nigh choked me, and I felt myself going red from temple to chin.

If the Countess d'Alzette noticed it she gave no sign, unless the pink tint under her eyes, deepening, was a subtle signal of understanding to the signal in my eyes.

"Suppose," she said, "that I failed, before the congress, to prove my theory? Suppose my investigations resulted in the exposure of a fraud and my name was held up to ridicule before all Europe? What would become of you, monsieur?"

I was silent.

"You are already celebrated as the discoverer of the mammoth and the great auk," she persisted. "You are young, enthusiastic, renowned, and you have a future before you that anybody in the world might envy."

I said nothing.

"And yet," she said, softly, "you risk all because you will not leave a young woman friendless among her confrères. It is not wise, monsieur; it is gallant and generous and impulsive, but it is not wisdom. Don Quixote rides no more in Europe, my friend."

"He stays at home—seventy million of him—in America," said I.

After a moment she said, "I believe you, monsieur."

"It is true enough," I said, with a laugh. "We are the only people who tilt at windmills these days—we and our cousins, the British, who taught us."

I bowed gayly, and added:

"With your colors to wear, I shall have the honor of breaking a lance against the biggest windmill in the world."

"You mean the Citadel of Science," she said, smiling.

"And its rock-ribbed respectability," I replied.

She looked at me thoughtfully, rolling and unrolling the scroll in her hands. Then she sighed, smiled, and brightened, handing me the scroll.

"Read it carefully," she said; "it is an outline of the policy I suggest that we follow. You will be surprised at some of the statements. Yet every word is the truth. And, monsieur, your reward for the devotion you have offered will be no greater than you deserve, when you find yourself doubly famous for our joint monograph on the ux. Without your vote in the committee I should have been denied a hearing, even though I produced proofs to support my theory. I appreciate that; I do most truly appreciate the courage which prompted you to defend a woman at the risk of your own ruin. Come to me this evening at nine. I hold for you in store a surprise and pleasure which you do not dream of."

"Ah, but I do," I said, slowly, under the spell of her delicate beauty and enthusiasm.

"How can you?" she said, laughing. "You don't know what awaits you at nine this evening?"

"You," I said, fascinated.

The color swept her face; she dropped me a deep courtesy.

"At nine, then," she said. "No. 8 Rue d'Alouette."

I bowed, took my hat, gloves, and stick, and attended her to her carriage below.

Long after the blue-and-black victoria had whirled away down the crowded quay I stood looking after it, mazed in the web of that ancient enchantment whose spell fell over the first man in Eden, and whose sorcery shall not fail till the last man returns his soul.

# X

I lunched at my lodgings on the Quai Malthus, and I had but little appetite, having fed upon such an unexpected variety of emotions during the morning.

Now, although I was already heels over head in love, I do not believe that loss of appetite was the result of that alone. I was slowly beginning to realize what my recent attitude might cost me, not only in an utter collapse of my scientific career, and the consequent material ruin which was likely to follow, but in the loss of all my friends at home. The Zoological Society of Bronx Park and the Smithsonian Institution of Washington had sent me as their trusted delegate, leaving it entirely to me to choose the subject on which I was to speak before the International Congress. What, then, would be their attitude when they learned that I had chosen to uphold the dangerous theory of the existence of the ux.

Would they repudiate me and send another delegate to replace me? Would they merely wash their hands of me and let me go to my own destruction?

"I will know soon enough," thought I, "for this morning's proceedings will have been cabled to New York ere now, and read at the breakfast-tables of every old, moss-grown naturalist in America before I see the Countess d'Alzette this evening." And I drew from my pocket the roll of paper which she had given me, and, lighting a cigar, lay back in my chair to read it.

The manuscript had been beautifully type-written, and I had no trouble in following her brief, clear account of the circumstances under which the notorious ux-skin had been obtained. As for the story itself, it was somewhat fishy, but I manfully swallowed my growing nervousness and comforted myself with the belief of Darwin in the existence of the ux, and the subsequent testimony of Wallace, who simply stated what he had seen through his telescope, and then left it to others to identify the enormous birds he described as he had observed them stalking about on the snowy peaks of the Tasmanian Alps.

My own knowledge of the ux was confined to a single circumstance. When, in 1897, I had gone to Tasmania with Professor Farrago, to make a report on the availability of the so-called "Tasmanian devil," as a substitute for the mongoose in the West Indies, I of course heard a great deal of talk among the natives concerning the birds which they affirmed haunted the summits of the mountains.

Our time in Tasmania was too limited to admit of an exploration then. But although we were perfectly aware that the summits of the Tasmanian Alps are inaccessible, we certainly should have attempted to gain them had not the time set for our departure arrived before we had completed the investigation for which we were sent.

One relic, however, I carried away with me. It was a single greenish bronzed feather, found high up in the mountains by a native, and sold to me for a somewhat large sum of money.

Darwin believed the ux to be covered with greenish plumage; Wallace was too far away to observe the color of the great birds; but all the natives of Tasmania unite in affirming that the plumage of the ux is green.

It was not only the color of this feather that made me an eager purchaser, it was the extraordinary length and size. I knew of no living bird large enough to wear such a feather. As for the color, that might have been tampered with before I bought it, and, indeed, testing it later, I found on the fronds traces of sulphate of copper. But the same thing has been found in the feathers of certain birds whose color is metallic green, and it has been proven that such birds pick up and swallow shining bits of copper pyrites.

Why should not the ux do the same thing?

Still, my only reason for believing in the existence of the bird was this single feather. I had easily proved that it belonged to no known species of bird. I also proved it to be similar to the tail-feathers of the ux-skin in Antwerp. But the feathers on the Antwerp specimen were gray, and the longest of them was but three feet in length, while my huge, bronze-green feather measured eleven feet from tip to tip.

One might account for it supposing the Antwerp skin to be that of a young bird, or of a moulting bird, or perhaps of a different sex from the bird whose feather I had secured.

Still, these ideas were not proven. Nothing concerning the birds had been proven. I had but a single fact to lean on, and that was that the feather I possessed could not have belonged to any known species of bird. Nobody but myself knew of the existence of this feather. And now I meant to cable to Bronx Park for it, and to place this evidence at the disposal of the beautiful Countess d'Alzette.

My cigar had gone out, as I sat musing, and I relighted it and resumed my reading of the type-written notes, lazily, even a trifle sceptically, for all the evidence that she had been able to collect to substantiate her theory of the existence of the ux was not half as important as the evidence I was to produce in the shape of that enormous green feather.

I came to the last paragraph, smoking serenely, and leaning back comfortably, one leg crossed over the other. Then, suddenly, my attention became riveted on the words under my eyes. Could I have read them aright? Could I believe what I read in ever-growing astonishment which culminated in an excitement that stirred the very hair on my head?

369

"The ux exists. There is no longer room for doubt. Ocular proof I can now offer in the shape of *five living eggs* of this gigantic bird. All measures have been taken to hatch these eggs; they are now in the vast incubator. It is my plan to have them hatch, one by one, under the very eyes of the International Congress. It will be the greatest triumph that science has witnessed since the discovery of the New World.

[Signed] "SUSANNE D'ALZETTE."

"Either," I cried out, in uncontrollable excitement—"either that girl is mad or she is the cleverest woman on earth."

After a moment I added:

"In either event I am going to marry her."

# XI

That evening, a few minutes before nine o'clock, I descended from a cab in front of No. 8 Rue d'Alouette, and was ushered into a pretty reception-room by an irreproachable servant, who disappeared directly with my card.

In a few moments the young Countess came in, exquisite in her silvery dinner-gown, eyes bright, white arms extended in a charming, impulsive welcome. The touch of her silky fingers thrilled me; I was dumb under the enchantment of her beauty; and I think she understood my silence, for her blue eyes became troubled and the happy parting of her lips changed to a pensive curve.

Presently I began to tell her about my bronzed-green feather; at my first word she looked up brightly, almost gratefully, I fancied; and in another moment we were deep in eager discussion of the subject which had first drawn us together.

What evidence I possessed to sustain our theory concerning the existence of the ux I hastened to reveal; then, heart beating excitedly, I asked her about the eggs and where they were at present, and whether she believed it possible to bring them to Paris—all these questions in the same breath—which brought a happy light into her eyes and a delicious ripple of laughter to her lips.

"Why, of course it is possible to bring the eggs here," she cried. "Am I sure? Parbleu! The eggs are already here, monsieur!"

"Here!" I exclaimed. "In Paris?"

"In Paris? Mais oui; and in my own house—*this very house*, monsieur. Come, you shall behold them with your own eyes!"

Her eyes were brilliant with excitement; impulsively she stretched out her rosy hand. I took it; and she led me quickly back through the drawing-room, through the dining-room, across the butler's pantry, and into a long, dark hallway. We were almost running now—I keeping tight hold of her soft little hand, she, raising her gown a trifle, hurrying down the hallway, silken petticoats rustling like a silk banner in the wind. A turn to the right brought us to the cellar-stairs; down we hastened, and then across the cemented floor towards a long, glass-fronted shelf, pierced with steam-pipes.

"A match," she whispered, breathlessly.

I struck a wax match and touched it to the gas-burner overhead.

Never, never can I forget what that flood of gas-light revealed. In a row stood five large, glass-mounted incubators; behind the glass doors lay, in dormant majesty, five enormous eggs. The eggs were pale-green—lighter, somewhat, than robins' eggs, but not as pale as herons' eggs. Each egg appeared to be larger than a large hogs-head, and was partly embedded in bales of cotton-wool.

Five little silver thermometers inside the glass doors indicated a temperature of 95° Fahrenheit. I noticed that there was an automatic arrangement connected with the pipes which regulated the temperature.

I was too deeply moved for words. Speech seemed superfluous as we stood there, hand in hand, contemplating those gigantic, pale-green eggs.

There is something in a silent egg which moves one's deeper emotions—something solemn in its embryotic inertia, something awesome in its featureless immobility.

I know of nothing on earth which is so totally lacking in expression as an egg. The great desert Sphinx, brooding through its veil of sand, has not that tremendous and meaningless dignity which wraps the colorless oval effort of a single domestic hen.

I held the hand of the young Countess very tightly. Her fingers closed slightly.

Then and there, in the solemn presence of those emotionless eggs, I placed my arm around her supple waist and kissed her.

She said nothing. Presently she stooped to observe the thermometer. Naturally, it registered 95° Fahrenheit.

"Susanne," I said, softly.

"Oh, we must go up-stairs," she whispered, breathlessly; and, picking up her silken skirts, she fled up the cellar-stairs.

I turned out the gas, with that instinct of economy which early wastefulness has implanted in me, and followed the Countess Suzanne through the suite of rooms and into the small reception-hall where she had first received me.

She was sitting on a low divan, head bent, slowly turning a sapphire ring on her finger, round and round.

I looked at her romantically, and then—

"Please don't," she said.

The correct reply to this is:

"Why not?"—very tenderly spoken.

"Because," she replied, which was also the correct and regular answer.

"Suzanne," I said, slowly and passionately.

She turned the sapphire ring on her finger. Presently she tired of this, so I lifted her passive hand very gently and continued turning the sapphire ring on her finger, slowly, to harmonize with the cadence of our unspoken thoughts.

Towards midnight I went home, walking with great care through a new street in Paris, paved exclusively with rose-colored blocks of air.

# XII

At nine o'clock in the evening, July 31, 1900, the International Congress was to assemble in the great lecture-hall of the Belgian Scientific Pavilion, which adjourned the Tasmanian Pavilion, to hear the Countess Suzanne d'Alzette read her paper on the ux.

That morning the Countess and I, with five furniture vans, had transported the five great incubators to the platform of the lecture-hall, and had engaged an army of plumbers and gas-fitters to make the steam-heating connections necessary to maintain in the incubators a temperature of 100° Fahrenheit.

A heavy green curtain hid the stage from the body of the lecture-hall. Behind this curtain the five enormous eggs reposed, each in its incubator.

The Countess Suzanne was excited and calm by turns, her cheeks were pink, her lips scarlet, her eyes bright as blue planets at midnight.

Without faltering she rehearsed her discourse before me, reading from her type-written manuscript in a clear voice, in which I could scarcely discern a tremor. Then we went through the dumb show of exhibiting the uxen eggs to a frantically applauding audience; she responded to countless supposititious encores, I leading her out repeatedly before the green curtain to face the great, damp, darkened auditorium.

Then, in response to repeated imaginary recalls, she rehearsed the extemporaneous speech, thanking the distinguished audience for their patience in listening to an unknown confrère, and confessing her obligations to me (here I appeared and bowed in self-abasement) for my faith in her and my aid in securing for her a public hearing before the most highly educated audience in the world.

After that we retired behind the curtain to sit on an empty box and eat sandwiches and watch the last lingering plumbers pasting up the steam connections with a pot of molten lead.

The plumbers were Americans, brought to Paris to make repairs on the American buildings during the exposition, and we conversed with them affably as they pottered about, plumber-like, poking under the flooring with lighted candles, rubbing their thumbs up and down musty old pipes, and prying up planks in dark corners.

They informed us that they were union men and that they hoped we were too. And I replied that union was certainly my ultimate purpose, at which the young Countess smiled dreamily at vacancy.

We did not dare leave the incubators. The plumbers lingered on, hour after hour, while we sat and watched the little silver thermometers, and waited.

It was time for the Countess Suzanne to dress, and still the plumbers had not finished; so I sent a messenger for her maid, to bring her trunk to the lecture-hall, and I despatched another messenger to my lodgings for my evening clothes and fresh linen.

There were several dressing-rooms off the stage. Here, about six o'clock, the Countess retired with her maid, to dress, leaving me to watch the plumbers and the thermometers.

When the Countess Suzanne returned, radiant and lovely in an evening gown of black lace, I gave her the roses I had brought for her and hurried off to dress in my turn, leaving her to watch the thermometers.

I was not absent more than half an hour, but when I returned I found the Countess anxiously conversing with the plumbers and pointing despairingly at the thermometers, which now registered only 95°.

"You must keep up the temperature!" I said. "Those eggs are due to hatch within a few hours. What's the trouble with the heat?"

The plumber did not know, but thought the connections were defective.

"But that's why we called you in!" exclaimed the Countess. "Can't you fix things securely?"

"Oh, we'll fix things, lady," replied the plumber, condescendingly, and he ambled away to rub his thumb up and down a pipe.

As we alone were unable to move and handle the enormous eggs, the Countess, whose sweet character was a stranger to vindictiveness or petty resentment, had written to the members of the ornithological committee, revealing the marvellous fortune which had crowned her efforts in the search for evidence to sustain her theory concerning the ux, and inviting these gentlemen to aid her in displaying the great eggs to the assembled congress.

This she had done the night previous. Every one of the gentlemen invited had come post-haste to her "hotel," to view the eggs with their own sceptical and astonished eyes; and the fair young Countess and I tasted our first triumph in her cellar, whither we conducted Sir Peter Grebe, the Crown-Prince of Monaco, Baron de Becasse, and his Majesty King Christian of Finland.

Scepticism and incredulity gave place to excitement and unbounded enthusiasm. The old King embraced the Countess; Baron de Becasse attempted to kiss me; Sir Peter Grebe made a handsome apology for his folly and vowed that he would do open penance for his sins. The poor Crown-Prince, who was of a nervous temperament, sat on the cellar-stairs and wept like a child.

His grief at his own pig-headedness touched us all profoundly.

So it happened that these gentlemen were coming to-night to give their aid to us in moving the priceless eggs, and lend their countenance and enthusiastic support to the young Countess in her maiden effort.

Sir Peter Grebe arrived first, all covered with orders and decorations, and greeted us affectionately, calling the Countess the "sweetest lass in France," and me his un-dutiful Yankee cousin who had landed feet foremost at the expense of the British Empire.

The King of Finland, the Crown-Prince, and Baron de Becasse arrived together, a composite mass of medals, sashes, and academy palms. To see them moving boxes about, straightening chairs, and pulling out rugs reminded me of those golden-embroidered gentlemen who run out into the arena and roll up carpets after the ac-robats have finished their turn in the Nouveau Cirque.

I was aiding the King of Finland to move a heavy keg of nails, when the Countess called out to me in alarm, saying that the thermometers had dropped to 80° Fahren-heit.

I spoke sharply to the plumbers, who were standing in a circle behind the dress-ing-rooms; but they answered sullenly that they could do no more work that day.

Indignant and alarmed, I ordered them to come out to the stage, and, after some hesitation, they filed out, a sulky, silent lot of workmen, with their tools already gath-ered up and tied in their kits. At once I noticed that a new man had appeared among them—a red-faced, stocky man wearing a frock-coat and a shiny silk hat.

"Who is the master-workman here?" I asked.

"I am," said a man in blue overalls.

"Well," said I, "why don't you fix those steam-fittings?"

There was a silence. The man in the silk hat smirked.

"Well?" said I.

"Come, come, that's all right," said the man in the silk hat. "These men know their business without you tellin' them."

"Who are you?" I demanded, sharply.

"Oh, I'm just a walkin' delegate," he replied, with a sneer. "There's a strike in New York and I come over here to tie this here exposition up. See?"

"You mean to say you won't let these men finish their work?" I asked, thunder-struck.

"That's about it, young man," he said, coolly.

Furious, I glanced at my watch, then at the thermometers, which now registered only 75°. Already I could hear the first-comers of the audience arriving in the body of the hall. Already a stage-hand was turning up the footlights and dragging chairs and tables hither and thither.

"What will you take to stay and attend to those steam-pipes?" I demanded, desperately.

"It can't be done nohow," observed the man in the silk hat. "That New York strike is good for a month yet." Then, turning to the workmen, he nodded and, to my horror, the whole gang filed out after him, turning deaf ears to my entreaties and threats.

There was a deathly silence, then Sir Peter exploded into a vivid shower of words. The Countess, pale as a ghost, gave me a heart-breaking look. The Crown-Prince wept.

"Great Heaven!" I cried; "the thermometers have fallen to 70°!"

The King of Finland sat down on a chair and pressed his hands over his eyes. Baron de Becasse ran round and round, uttering subdued and plaintive screams; Sir Peter swore steadily.

"Gentlemen," I cried, desperately, "we must save those eggs! They are on the very eve of hatching! Who will volunteer?"

"To do what?" moaned the Crown-Prince.

"I'll show you," I exclaimed, running to the incubators and beckoning to the Baron to aid me.

In a moment we had rolled out the great egg, made a nest on the stage floor with the bales of cotton-wool, and placed the egg in it. One after another we rolled out the remaining eggs, building for each its nest of cotton; and at last the five enormous eggs lay there in a row behind the green curtain.

"Now," said I, excitedly, to the King, "you must get up on that egg and try to keep it warm."

The King began to protest, but I would take no denial, and presently his Majesty was perched up on the great egg, gazing foolishly about at the others, who were now all climbing up on their allotted eggs.

"Great Heaven!" muttered the King, as Sir Peter settled down comfortably on his egg, "I am willing to give life and fortune for the sake of science, but I can't bear to hatch out eggs like a bird!"

The Crown-Prince was now sitting patiently beside the Baron de Becasse.

"I feel in my bones," he murmured, "that I'm about to hatch something. Can't you hear a tapping on the shell of your egg, Baron?"

"Parbleu!" replied the Baron. "The shell is moving under me."

It certainly was; for, the next moment, the Baron fell into his egg with a crash and a muffled shriek, and floundered out, dripping, yellow as a canary.

"N'importe!" he cried, excitedly. "Allons! Save the eggs! Hurrah! Vive la science!" And he scrambled up on the fourth egg and sat there, arms folded, sublime courage transfiguring him from head to foot.

We all gave him a cheer, which was hushed as the stage-manager ran in, warning us that the audience was already assembled and in place.

"You're not going to raise the curtain while we're sitting, are you?" demanded the King of Finland, anxiously.

"No, no," I said; "sit tight, your Majesty. Courage, gentlemen! Our vindication is at hand!"

The Countess glanced at me with startled eyes; I took her hand, saluted it respectfully, and then quietly led her before the curtain, facing an ocean of upturned faces across the flaring footlights.

She stood a moment to acknowledge the somewhat ragged applause, a calm smile on her lips. All her courage had returned; I saw that at once.

Very quietly she touched her lips to the *eau-sucrée*, laid her manuscript on the table, raised her beautiful head, and began:

"That the ux is a living bird I am here before you to prove—"

A sharp report behind the curtain drowned her voice. She paled; the audience rose amid cries of excitement.

"What was it?" she asked, faintly.

"Sir Peter has hatched out his egg," I whispered. "Hark! There goes another egg!" And I ran behind the curtain.

Such a scene as I beheld was never dreamed of on land or sea. Two enormous young uxen, all over gigantic pin-feathers, were wandering stupidly about. Mounted on one was Sir Peter Grebe, eyes starting from his apoplectic visage; on the other, clinging to the bird's neck, hung the Baron de Becasse.

Before I could move, the two remaining eggs burst, and a pair of huge, scrawny fledglings rose among the débris, bearing off on their backs the King and Crown-Prince.

"Help!" said the King of Finland, faintly. "I'm falling off!"

I sprang to his aid, but tripped on the curtain-spring. The next instant the green curtain shot up, and there, revealed to that vast and distinguished audience, roamed four enormous chicks, bearing on their backs the most respected and exclusive aristocracy of Europe.

The Countess Suzanne turned with a little shriek of horror, then sat down in her chair, laid her lovely head on the table, and very quietly fainted away, unconscious of the frantic cheers which went roaring to the roof.

———————————

This, then, is the *true* history of the famous exposition scandal. And, as I have said, had it not been for the presence in that audience of two American reporters nobody would have known what all the world now knows—nobody would have read of the marvellous feats of bareback riding indulged in by the King of Finland— nobody would have read how Sir Peter Grebe steered his mount safely past the footlights only to come to grief over the prompter's box.

But this *is* scandal. And, as for the charming Countess Suzanne d'Alzette, the public has heard all that it is entitled to hear, and much that it is not entitled to hear.

However, on second thoughts, perhaps the public is entitled to hear a little more. I will therefore say this much—the shock of astonishment which stunned me when the curtain flew up, revealing the King-bestridden uxen, was nothing to the awful blow which smote me when the Count d'Alzette leaped from the orchestra, over the footlights, and bore away with him the fainting form of his wife, the lovely Countess d'Alzette.

I sometimes wonder—but, as I have repeatedly observed, this dull and pedantic narrative of fact is no vehicle for sentimental soliloquy. It is, then, merely sufficient to say that I took the earliest steamer for kinder shores, spurred on to haste by a venomous cable-gram from the Smithsonian, repudiating me, and by another from Bronx Park, ordering me to spend the winter in some inexpensive, poisonous, and unobtrusive spot, and make a collection of isopods. The island of Java appeared to me to be as poisonously unobtrusive and inexpensive a region as I had ever heard of; a steamer sailed from Antwerp for Batavia in twenty-four hours. Therefore, as I say, I took the night-train for Brussels, and the steamer from Antwerp the following evening.

Of my uneventful voyage, of the happy and successful quest, there is little to relate. The Javanese are frolicsome and hospitable. There was a girl there with features that were as delicate as though chiselled out of palest amber; and I remember she wore a most wonderful jewelled, helmet-like head-dress, and jingling bangles on her ankles, and when she danced she made most graceful and poetic gestures with her supple wrists—but that has nothing to do with isopods, absolutely nothing.

Letters from home came occasionally. Professor Farrago had returned to the Bronx and had been re-elected to the high office he had so nobly held when I first became associated with him.

Through his kindness and by his advice I remained for several years in the Far East, until a letter from him arrived recalling me and also announcing his own hurried and sudden departure for Florida. He also mentioned my promotion to the office of subcurator of department; so I started on my homeward voyage very much pleased with the world, and arrived in New York on April 1, 1904, ready for a rest to which I believed myself entitled. And the first thing that they handed me was a letter from Professor Farrago, summoning me South.

---

# XIII

The letter that started me—I was going to say startled me, but only imaginative people are startled—the letter, then, that started me from Bronx Park to the South I print without the permission of my superior, Professor Farrago. I have not obtained his permission, for the somewhat exciting reason that nobody knows where he is. Publicity being now recognized as the annihilator of mysteries, a benevolent purpose alone inspires me to publish a letter so strange, so pathetically remarkable, in view of what has recently occurred.

As I say, I had only just returned from Java with a valuable collection of un-described isopods—an order of edriophthalmous crustaceans with seven free thoracic somites furnished with fourteen legs—and I beg my reader's pardon, but my reader will see the necessity for the author's absolute accuracy in insisting on detail, because the story that follows is a dangerous story for a scientist to tell, in view of the vast amount of nonsense and fiction in circulation masquerading as stories of scientific adventure.

I was, therefore, anticipating a delightful summer's work with pen and micro-scope, when on April 1st I received the following extraordinary letter from Professor Farrago:

"IN CAMP, LITTLE SPRITE LAKE,
"EVERGLADES, FLORIDA, *March 15, 1902.*

"MY DEAR MR. GILLAND,—On receipt of this communication you will immedi-ately secure for me the following articles:

"One complete outfit of woman's clothing.
"One camera.
"One light steel cage, large enough for you to stand in.
"One stenographer (male sex).
"One five-pound steel tank, with siphon and hose attachment.
"One rifle and ammunition.
"Three ounces rosium oxyde.
"One ounce chlorate strontium.

"You will then, within twenty-four hours, set out with the stenographer and the supplies mentioned and join me in camp on Little Sprite Lake. This order is formal and admits of no delay. You will appreciate the necessity of absolute and unquestioning obedience when I tell you that I am practically on the brink of the most astonishing discovery recorded in natural history since Monsieur Zani discovered the purple-spotted zoombok in Nyanza; and that I depend upon you and your zeal and fidelity for success.

"I dare not, lest my letter fall into unscrupulous hands, convey to you more than a hint of what lies before us in these uncharted solitudes of the Everglades.

"You must read between the lines when I say that because one can see through a sheet of glass, the glass is none the less solid and palpable. One can see *through* it—if that is also seeing it; but one can nevertheless hold it and feel it and receive from it sensations of cold or heat according to its temperature.

"Certain jellyfish are absolutely transparent when in the water, and one can only know of their presence by accidental contact, not by sight.

"*Have you ever thought that possibly there might exist larger and more highly organized creatures transparent to eyesight, yet palpable to touch?*

"Little Sprite Lake is the jumping-off place; beyond lie the Everglades, the outskirts of which are haunted by the Seminoles, the interior of which have never been visited by man, as far as we know.

"As you are aware, no general survey of Florida has yet been made; there exist no maps of the Everglades south of Okeechobee; even Little Sprite Lake is but a vague blot on our maps. We know, of course, that south of the eleven thousand square miles of fresh water which is called Lake Okeechobee the Everglades form a vast, delta-like projection of thousands and thousands of square miles. Darkest Africa is no longer a mystery; but the Everglades to-day remain the sombre secret of our continent. And, to-day, this unknown expanse of swamps, barrens, forests, and lagoons is greater than in the days of De Soto, because the entire region has been slowly rising.

"All this, my dear sir, you already know, and I ask your indulgence for recalling the facts to your memory. I do it for this reason—the search for *what I am seeking* may lead us to utter destruction; and therefore my formal orders to you should be modified to this extent:—do you volunteer? If you volunteer, my orders remain; if not, turn this letter over to Mr. Kingsley, who will find for me the companion I require.

"In the event of your coming, you must break your journey at False Cape and ask for an old man named Slunk. He will give you a packet; you will give him a dollar, and drive on to Cape Canaveral, and you will do what is to be done there. From there to Fort Kissimmee, to Okeechobee, traversing the lake to the Rita River, where I have marked the trail to Little Sprite.

"At Little Sprite I shall await you; beyond that point a merciful Providence alone can know what awaits us.

"Yours fraternally,

"FARRAGO.

"P.S.—I think that you had better make your will, and suggest the same idea to the stenographer who is to accompany you.　　　　　F."

And that was the letter I received while seated comfortably on the floor of my work-room, surrounded by innocent isopods, all patiently awaiting scientific investigation.

And this is what I did: Within twenty-four hours I had assembled the supplies required—the cage, the woman's clothing, tank, arms and ammunition, and the chemicals; I had secured accommodations, for that evening, on the Florida, Volusia, and Fort Lauderdale Railway as far as Citron City; and I had been interviewing stenographers all day long, the result of an innocently worded advertisement in the daily newspapers.

It was now very close to the time when I must summon a cab and drive to the ferry; and yet I was still shy one stenographer.

I had seen scores; they simply would not listen to the proposition. "Why does a gentleman in the backwoods of Florida want a stenographer?" they demanded; and as I had not the faintest idea, I could only say so. I think the majority interviewed concluded I had escaped from a State institution.

As the time for departure approached I became desperate, urging and beseeching applicants to accompany me; but neither sympathy for my instant need nor desire for salary moved them.

I waited until the last moment, hoping against hope. Then, with a groan of despair, I seized luggage and raincoat, made for the door and flung it open, only to find myself face to face with an attractive young girl, apparently on the point of pressing the electric button.

"I'm sorry," I said, "but I have a train to catch."

She was noticeably attractive in her storm-coat and pretty hat, and I really was sorry—so sorry that I added:

"I have about twenty-seven seconds to place at your service before I go."

"Twenty will be sufficient," she replied, pleasantly. "I saw your advertisement for a stenographer—"

"We require a man," I interposed, hastily.

"Have you engaged him?"

"N-no."

We looked at each other.

"You wouldn't accept, anyway," I began.

"How do you know?"

"You wouldn't leave town, would you?"

"Yes, if you required it."

"What? Go to Florida?"

"Y-yes—if I must."

"But think of the alligators! Think of the snakes—big, bitey snakes!"

"Gracious!" she exclaimed, eyes growing bigger.

"Indians, too!—unreconciled, sulky Seminoles! Fevers! Mud-puddles! Spiders! And only fifty dollars a week—"

"I—I'll go," she stammered.

"Go?" I repeated, grimly; "then you've exactly two and three-quarter seconds left for preparations."

Instinctively she raised her little gloved hand and patted her hair. "I'm ready," she said, unsteadily.

"One extra second to make your will," I added, stunned by her self-possession.

"I—I have nothing to leave—nobody to leave it to," she said, smiling; "I am ready."

I took that extra second myself for a lightning course in reflection upon effects and consequences.

"It's silly, it's probably murder," I said, "but you're engaged! Now we must run for it!"

And that is how I came to engage the services of Miss Helen Barrison as stenographer.

---

# XIV

At noon on the second day I disembarked from the train at Citron City with all paraphernalia—cage, chemicals, arsenal, and stenographer; an accumulation of very dusty impedimenta—all but the stenographer. By three o'clock our hotel livery-rig was speeding along the beach at False Cape towards the tall lighthouse looming above the dunes.

The abode of a gentleman named Slunk was my goal. I sat brooding in the rickety carriage, still dazed by the rapidity of my flight from New York; the stenographer sat beside me, blue eyes bright with excitement, fair hair blowing in the sea-wind.

Our railway companionship had been of the slightest, also absolutely formal; for I was too absorbed in conjecturing the meaning of this journey to be more than absent-mindedly civil; and she, I fancy, had had time for repentance and perhaps for a little fright, though I could discover traces of neither.

I remember she left the train at some city or other where we were held for an hour; and out of the car-window I saw her returning with a brand-new grip sack.

She must have bought clothes, for she continued to remain cool and fresh in her summer shirt-waists and short outing skirt; and she looked immaculate now, sitting there beside me, the trace of a smile curving her red mouth.

"I'm looking for a personage named Slunk," I observed.

After a moment's silent consideration of the Atlantic Ocean she said, "When do my duties begin, Mr. Gilland?"

"The Lord alone knows," I replied, grimly. "Are you repenting of your bargain?"

"I am quite happy," she said, serenely.

Remorse smote me that I had consented to engage this frail, pink-and-ivory biped for an enterprise which lay outside the suburbs of Manhattan. I glanced guiltily at my victim; she sat there, the incarnation of New York piquancy—a translated denizen of the metropolis—a slender spirit of the back offices of sky-scrapers. Why had I lured her hither?—here where the heavy, lavender-tinted breakers thundered on a lost coast; here where above the dune-jungles vultures soared, and snowy-headed eagles, hulking along the sands, tore dead fish and yelped at us as we passed.

Strange waters, strange skies—a strange, lost land aquiver under an exotic sun; and there she sat with her wise eyes of a child, unconcerned, watching the world in perfect confidence.

"May I pay a little compliment to your pluck?" I asked, amused.

"Certainly," she said, smiling as the maid of Manhattan alone knows how to smile—shyly, inquiringly—with a lingering hint of laughter in the curled lips' corners. Then her sensitive features fell a trifle. "Not pluck," she said, "but necessity; I had no chance to choose, no time to wait. My last dollar, Mr. Gilland, is in my purse!"

With a gay little gesture she drew it from her shirt-front, then, smiling, sat turning it over and over in her lap.

The sun fell on her hands, gilding the smooth skin with the first tint of sunburn. Under the corners of her eyes above the rounded cheeks a pink stain lay like the first ripening flush on a wild strawberry. That, too, was the mark left by the caress of wind and sun. I had had no idea she was so pretty.

"I think we'll enjoy this adventure," I said; "don't you?"

"I try to make the best of things," she said, gazing off into the horizon haze. "Look," she added; "is that a man?"

A spot far away on the beach caught my eye. At first I thought it was a pelican— and small wonder, too, for the dumpy, waddling, goose-necked individual who loomed up resembled a heavy bottomed bird more than a human being.

"Do you suppose that could be Mr. Slunk?" asked the stenographer, as our vehicle drew nearer.

He looked as though his name ought to be Slunk; he was digging coquina clams, and he dug with a pecking motion like a water-turkey mastering a mullet too big for it.

His name was Slunk; he admitted it when I accused him. Our negro driver drew rein, and I descended to the sand and gazed on Mr. Slunk.

He was, as I have said, not impressive, even with the tremendous background of sky and ocean.

"I've come something over a thousand miles to see you," I said, reluctant to admit that I had come as far to see such a specimen of human architecture.

A weather-beaten grin stretched the skin that covered his face, and he shoved a hairy paw into the pockets of his overalls, digging deeply into profound depths. First he brought to light a twist of South Carolina tobacco, which he leisurely inserted in his mouth—not, apparently, for pleasure, but merely to get rid of it.

The second object excavated from the overalls was a small packet addressed to me. This he handed to me; I gravely handed him a silver dollar; he went back to his clam-digging, and I entered the carriage and drove on. All had been carried out according to the letter of my instructions so far, and my spirits brightened.

"If you don't mind I'll read my instructions," I said, in high good-humor.

"Pray do not hesitate," she said, smiling in sympathy.

So I opened the little packet and read:

"Drive to Cape Canaveral along the beach. You will find a gang of men at work on a government breakwater. The superintendent is Mr. Rowan. Show him this letter.

"FARRAGO."

Rather disappointed—for I had been expecting to find in the packet some key to the interesting mystery which had sent Professor Farrago into the Everglades—I thrust the missive into my pocket and resumed a study of the immediate landscape. It had not changed as we progressed: ocean, sand, low dunes crowned with impenetrable tangles of wild bay, sparkleberry, and live-oak, with here and there a weather-twisted palmetto sprawling, and here and there the battered blades of cactus and Spanish-bayonet thrust menacingly forward; and over all the vultures, sailing, sailing—some mere circling motes lost in the blue above, some sheering the earth so close that their swiftly sweeping shadows slanted continually across our road.

"I detest a buzzard," I said, aloud.

"I thought they were crows," she confessed.

"Carrion-crows—yes.

"'The carrion-crows Sing, Caw! caw!'

—only they don't," I added, my song putting me in good-humor once more. And I glanced askance at the pretty stenographer.

"It is a pleasure to be employed by agreeable people," she said, innocently.

"Oh, I can be much more agreeable than that," I said.

"Is Professor Farrago—amusing?" she asked.

"Well—oh, certainly—but not in—in the way I am."

Suddenly it flashed upon me that my superior was a confirmed hater of unmarried women. I had clean forgotten it; and now the full import of what I had done scared me silent.

"Is anything the matter?" asked Miss Barrison.

"No—not yet," I said, ominously.

How on earth could I have overlooked that well-known fact. The hurry and anxiety, the stress of instant preparation and departure, had clean driven it from my absent-minded head.

Jogging on over the sand, I sat silent, cudgelling my brains for a solution of the disastrous predicament I had gotten into. I pictured the astonished rage of my superior—my probable dismissal from employment—perhaps the general overturning and smash-up of the entire expedition.

A distant, dark object on the beach concentrated my distracted thoughts; it must be the breakwater at Cape Canaveral. And it was the breakwater, swarming with negro workmen, who were swinging great blocks of coquina into cemented beds, singing and whistling at their labor.

I forgot my predicament when I saw a thin white man in sun-helmet and khaki directing the work from the beach; and as our horses plodded up, I stepped out and hailed him by name.

"Yes, my name is Rowan," he said, instantly, turning to meet me. His sharp, clear eyes included the vehicle and the stenographer, and he lifted his helmet, then looked squarely at me.

"My name is Gilland," I said, dropping my voice and stepping nearer. "I have just come from Bronx Park, New York."

He bowed, waiting for something more from me; so I presented my credentials.

His formal manner changed at once. "Come over here and let us talk a bit," he said, cordially—then hesitated, glancing at Miss Barrison—"if your wife would excuse us—"

The pretty stenographer colored, and I dryly set Mr. Rowan right—which appeared to disturb him more than his mistake.

"Pardon me, Mr. Gilland, but you do not propose to take this young girl into the Everglades, do you?"

"That's what I had proposed to do," I said, brusquely.

Perfectly aware that I resented his inquiry, he cast a perplexed and troubled glance at her, then slowly led the way to a great block of sun-warmed coquina, where he sat down, motioning me to do the same.

"I see," he said, "that you don't know just where you are going or just what you are expected to do."

"No, I don't," I said.

"Well, I'll tell you, then. You are going into the devil's own country to look for something that I fled five hundred miles to avoid."

"Is that so?" I said, uneasily.

"That is so, Mr. Gilland."

"Oh! And what is this object that I am to look for and from which you fled five hundred miles?"

"I don't know."

"You don't know what you ran away from?"

"No, sir. Perhaps if I had known I should have run a thousand miles."

We eyed one another.

"You think, then, that I'd better send Miss Barrison back to New York?" I asked.

"I certainly do. It may be murder to take her."

"Then I'll do it!" I said, nervously. "Back she goes from the first railroad station."

In a flash the thought came to me that here was a way to avoid the wrath of Professor Farrago—and a good excuse, too. He might forgive my not bringing a man as stenographer in view of my limited time; he never would forgive my presenting him with a woman.

 "She must go back," I repeated; and it rather surprised me to find myself already anticipating loneliness—something that never in all my travels had I experienced before.

"By the first train," I added, firmly, disliking Mr. Rowan without any reason except that he had suddenly deprived me of my stenographer.

"What I have to tell you," he began, lighting a cigarette, the mate to which I declined, "is this: Three years ago, before I entered this contracting business, I was in the government employ as officer in the Coast Survey. Our duties took us into Florida waters; we were months at a time working on shore."

He pulled thoughtfully at his cigarette and blew a light cloud into the air.

"I had leave for a month once; and like an ass I prepared to spend it in a hunting-trip among the Everglades."

He crossed his lean legs and gazed meditatively at his cigarette.

"I believe," he went on, "that we penetrated the Everglades farther than any white man who ever lived to return. There's nothing very dismal about the Everglades—the greater part, I mean. You get high and low hummock, marshes, creeks, lakes, and all that. If you get lost, you're a goner. If you acquire fever, you're as well off as the seraphim—and not a whit better. There are the usual animals there—bears (little black fellows) lynxes, deer, panthers, alligators, and a few stray crocodiles. As for snakes, of course they're there, moccasins a-plenty, some rattlers, but, after all, not as many snakes as one finds in Alabama, or even northern Florida and Georgia.

 "The Seminoles won't help you—won't even talk to you. They're a sullen pack—but not murderous, as far as I know. Beyond their inner limits lie the unknown regions."

He bit the wet end from his cigarette.

"I went there," he said; "I came out as soon as I could."

"Why?"

"Well—for one thing, my companion died of fright."

"Fright? What at?"

"Well, there's something in there."

"What?"

He fixed a penetrating gaze on me. "I don't know, Mr. Gilland."

"Did you see anything to frighten you?" I insisted.

"No, but I felt something." He dropped his cigarette and ground it into the sand viciously. "To cut it short," he said, "I am most unwillingly led to believe that there are—creatures—of some sort in the Everglades—living creatures quite as large as you or I—and that they are perfectly transparent—as transparent as a colorless jelly-fish."

Instantly the veiled import of Professor Farrago's letter was made clear to me. He, too, believed that.

"It embarrasses me like the devil to say such a thing," continued Rowan, digging in the sand with his spurred heels. "It seems so—so like a whopping lie—it seems so childish and ridiculous—so cursed cheap! But I fled; and there you are. I might add," he said, indifferently, "that I have the ordinary portion of courage allotted to normal men."

"But what do you believe these—these animals to be?" I asked, fascinated.

"I don't know." An obstinate look came into his eyes. "I don't know, and I absolutely refuse to speculate for the benefit of anybody. I wouldn't do it for my friend Professor Farrago; and I'm not going to do it for you," he ended, laughing a rather grim laugh that somehow jarred me into realizing the amazing import of his story. For I did not doubt it, strange as it was—fantastic, incredible though it sounded in the ears of a scientist.

What it was that carried conviction I do not know—perhaps the fact that my superior credited it; perhaps the manner of narration. Told in quiet, commonplace phrases, by an exceedingly practical and unimaginative young man who was plainly embarrassed in the telling, the story rang out like a shout in a cañon, startling because of the absolute lack of emphasis employed in the telling.

"Professor Farrago asked me to speak of this to no one except the man who should come to his assistance. He desired the first chance of clearing this—this rather perplexing matter. No doubt he didn't want exploring parties prowling about him," added Rowan, smiling. "But there's no fear of that, I fancy. I never expect to tell that story again to anybody; I shouldn't have told him, only somehow it's worried me for three years, and though I was deadly afraid of ridicule, I finally made up my mind that science ought to have a hack at it.

"When I was in New York last winter I summoned up courage and wrote Professor Farrago. He came to see me at the Holland House that same evening; I told him as much as I ever shall tell anybody. That is all, Mr. Gilland."

For a long time I sat silent, musing over the strange words. After a while I asked him whether Professor Farrago was supplied with provisions; and he said he was; that a great store of staples and tins of concentrated rations had been carried in as far as Little Sprite Lake; that Professor Farrago was now there alone, having insisted upon dismissing all those he had employed.

"There was no practical use for a guide," added Rowan, "because no cracker, no Indian, and no guide knows the region beyond the Seminole country."

I rose, thanking him and offering my hand. He took it and shook it in manly fashion, saying: "I consider Professor Farrago a very brave man; I may say the same of any man who volunteers to accompany him. Good-bye, Mr. Gilland; I most earnestly wish for your success. Professor Farrago left this letter for you."

And that was all. I climbed back into the rickety carriage, carrying my unopened letter; the negro driver cracked his whip and whistled, and the horses trotted inland over a fine shell road which was to lead us across Verbena Junction to Citron City. Half an hour later we crossed the tracks at Verbena and turned into a broad marl road. This aroused me from my deep and speculative reverie, and after a few moments I asked Miss Barrison's indulgence and read the letter from Professor Farrago which Mr. Rowan had given me:

"DEAR MR. GILLAND,—You now know all I dared not write, fearing to bring a swarm of explorers about my ears in case the letter was lost, and found by unscrupulous meddlers. If you still are willing to volunteer, knowing all that I know, join me as soon as possible. If family considerations deter you from taking what perhaps is an insane risk, I shall not expect you to join me. In that event, return to New York immediately and send Kingsley.

"Yours,             F."

"What the deuce is the matter with him!" I exclaimed, irritably. "I'll take any chances Kingsley does!"

Miss Barrison looked up in surprise.

"Miss Barrison," I said, plunging into the subject headfirst, "I'm extremely sorry, but I have news that forces me to believe the journey too dangerous for you to attempt, so I think that it would be much better—" The consternation in her pretty face checked me.

"I'm awfully sorry," I muttered, appalled by her silence.

"But—but you engaged me!"

"I know it—I should not have done it. I only—"

"But you did engage me, didn't you?"

"I believe that I did—er—oh, of course—"

"But a verbal contract is binding between honorable people, isn't it, Mr. Gilland?"

"Yes, but—"

"And ours was a verbal contract; and in consideration you paid me my first week's salary, and I bought shirt-waists and a short skirt and three changes of—and tooth-brushes and—"

"I know, I know," I groaned. "But I'll fix all that."

"You can't if you break your contract."

"Why not?"

"Because," she said, flushing up, "I should not accept."

"You don't understand—"

"Really I do. You are going into a dangerous country and you're afraid I'll be frightened."

"It's something like that."

"Tell me what are the dangers?"

"Alligators, big, bitey snakes—"

"Oh, you've said all that before!"

"Seminoles—"

"And that too. What else is there? Did the young man in the sun-helmet tell you of something worse?"

"Yes—much worse! Something so dreadfully horrible that—"

"What?"

"I am not at liberty to tell you, Miss Barrison," I said, striving to appear shocked.

"It would not make any difference anyway," she observed, calmly. "I'm not afraid of anything in the world."

"Yes, you are!" I said. "Listen to me; I'd be awfully glad to have you go—I—I really had no idea how I'd miss you—miss such pleasant companionship. But it is not possible—" The recollection of Professor Farrago's aversion suddenly returned. "No, no," I said, "it can't be done. I'm most unhappy over this mistake of mine; please don't look as though you were ready to cry!"

"Don't discharge me, Mr. Gilland," she said.

"I'm a brute to do it, but I must; I was a bigger brute to engage you, but I did. Don't—please don't look at me that way, Miss Barrison! As a matter of fact, I'm tender-hearted and I can't endure it."

"If you only knew what I had been through you wouldn't send me away," she said, in a low voice. "It took my last penny to clothe myself and pay for the last lesson at the college of stenography. I—I lived on almost nothing for weeks; every respectable place was filled; I walked and walked and walked, and nobody wanted me—they all required people with experience—and how can I have experience until I begin, Mr. Gilland? I was perfectly desperate when I went to see you, knowing that you had advertised for a man—" The slightest break in her clear voice scared me.

"I'm not going to cry," she said, striving to smile. "If I must go, I will go. I—I didn't mean to say all this—but—but I've been so—so discouraged;—and you were not very cross with me—"

Smitten with remorse, I picked up her hand and fell to patting it violently, trying to think of something to say. The exercise did not appear to stimulate my wits.

"Then—then I'm to go with you?" she asked.

"I will see," I said, weakly, "but I fear there's trouble ahead for this expedition."

"I fear there is," she agreed, in a cheerful voice. "You have a rifle and a cage in your luggage. Are you going to trap Indians and have me report their language?"

"No, I'm not going to trap Indians," I said, sharply. "They may trap us—but that's a detail. What I want to say to you is this: Professor Farrago detests unmarried women, and I forgot it when I engaged you."

"Oh, is that all?" she asked, laughing.

"Not all, but enough to cost me my position."

"How absurd! Why, there are millions of things we might do!—millions!"

"What's one of them?" I inquired.

"Why, we might pretend to be married!" Her frank and absolutely innocent delight in this suggestion was refreshing, but troubling.

"We would have to be demonstrative to make that story go," I said.

"Why? Well-bred people are not demonstrative in public," she retorted, turning a trifle pink.

"No, but in private—"

"I think there is no necessity for carrying a pleasantry into our private life," she said, in a perfectly amiable voice. "Anyway, if Professor Farrago's feelings are to be spared, no sacrifice on the part of a mere girl could be too great," she added, gayly; "I will wear men's clothes if you wish."

"You may have to anyhow in the jungle," I said; "and as it's not an uncommon thing these days, nobody would ever take you for anything except what you are—a very wilful and plucky and persistent and—"

"And what, Mr. Gilland?"

"And attractive," I muttered.

"Thank you, Mr. Gilland."

"You're welcome," I snapped. The near whistle of a locomotive warned us, and I rose in the carriage, looking out across the sand-hills.

"That is probably our train," observed the pretty stenographer.

"*Our* train!"

"Yes; isn't it?"

"Then you insist—"

"Ah, no, Mr. Gilland; I only trust implicitly in my employer."

"We'll wait till we get to Citron City," I said, weakly; "then it will be time enough to discuss the situation, won't it?"

"Yes, indeed," she said, smiling; but she knew, and I already feared, that the situation no longer admitted of discussion. In a few moments more we emerged, without warning, from the scrub-crested sand-hills into the single white street of Citron City, where China-trees hung heavy with bloom, and magnolias, already set with perfumed candelabra, spread soft, checkered shadows over the marl.

The train lay at the station, oceans of heavy, black smoke lazily flowing from the locomotive; negroes were hoisting empty fruit-crates aboard the baggage-car, through the door of which I caught a glimpse of my steel cage and remaining paraphernalia, all securely crated.

"Telegram hyah foh Mistuh Gilland," remarked the operator, lounging at his window as we descended from our dusty vehicle. He had not addressed himself to anybody in particular, but I said that I was Mr. Gilland, and he produced the envelope. "Toted in from Okeechobee?" he inquired, listlessly.

"Probably; it's signed 'Farrago,' isn't it?"

"It's foh yoh, suh, I reckon," said the operator, handing it out with a yawn. Then he removed his hat and fanned his head, which was perfectly bald.

I opened the yellow envelope. "Get me a good dog with points," was the laconic message; and it irritated me to receive such idiotic instructions at such a time and in such a place. A good dog? Where the mischief could I find a dog in a town consisting of ten houses and a water-tank? I said as much to the bald-headed operator, who smiled wearily and replaced his hat: "Dawg? They's moh houn'-dawgs in Citron City than they's wood-ticks to keep them busy. I reckon a dollah 'll do a heap foh you, suh."

"Could you get me a dog for a dollar?" I asked;—"one with points?"

"Points? I sholy can, suh;—plenty of points. What kind of dawg do yoh requiah, suh?—live dawg? daid dawg? houn'-dawg? raid-dawg? hawg-dawg? coon-dawg?—"

The locomotive emitted a long, lazy, softly modulated and thoroughly Southern toot. I handed the operator a silver dollar, and he presently emerged from his office and slouched off up the street, while I walked with Miss Barrison to the station platform, where I resumed the discussion of her future movements.

"You are very young to take such a risk," I said, gravely. "Had I not better buy your ticket back to New York? The north-bound train meets this one. I suppose we are waiting for it now—" I stopped, conscious of her impatience.

Her face flushed brightly: "Yes; I think it best. I have embarrassed you too long already—"

"Don't say that!" I muttered. "I—I—shall be deadly bored without you."

"I am not an entertainer, only a stenographer," she said, curtly. "Please get me my ticket, Mr. Gilland."

She gazed at me from the car-platform; the locomotive tooted two drawling toots.

"It is for your sake," I said, avoiding her gaze as the far-off whistle of the north-bound express came floating out of the blue distance.

She did not answer; I fished out my watch, regarding it in silence, listening to the hum of the approaching train, which ought presently to bear her away into the North, where nothing could menace her except the brilliant pitfalls of a Christian civilization. But I stood there, temporizing, unable to utter a word as her train shot by us with a rush, slower, slower, and finally stopped, with a long-drawn sigh from the air-brakes.

At that instant the telegraph-operator appeared, carrying a dog by the scruff of the neck—a sad-eyed, ewe-necked dog, from the four corners of which dangled enormous, cushion-like paws. He yelped when he beheld me. Miss Barrison leaned down from the car-platform and took the animal into her arms, uttering a suppressed exclamation of pity as she lifted him.

"You have your hands full," she said to me; "I'll take him into the car for you."

She mounted the steps; I followed with the valises, striving to get a good view of my acquisition over her shoulder.

"That isn't the kind of dog I wanted!" I repeated again and again, inspecting the animal as it sprawled on the floor of the car at the edge of Miss Barrison's skirt. "That dog is all voice and feet and emotion! What makes it stick up its paws like that? I don't want that dog and I'm not going to identify myself with it! Where's the operator—"

I turned towards the car-window; the operator's bald head was visible on a line with the sill, and I made motions at him. He bowed with courtly grace, as though I were thanking him.

"I'm not!" I cried, shaking my head. "I wanted a dog with points—not the kind of points that stick up all over this dog. Take him away!"

The operator's head appeared to be gliding out of my range of vision; then the windows of the north-bound train slid past, faster and faster. A melancholy grace-note from the dog, a jolt, and I turned around, appalled.

"This train is going," I stammered, "and you are on it!"

Miss Barrison sprang up and started towards the door, and I sped after her.

"I can jump," she said, breathlessly, edging out to the platform; "please let me! There is time yet—if you only wouldn't hold me—so tight—"

A few moments later we walked slowly back together through the car and took seats facing one another.

Between us sat the hound-dog, a prey to melancholy unutterable.

# XV

It was on Sunday when I awoke to the realization that I had quitted civilization and was afloat on an unfamiliar body of water in an open boat containing—

One light steel cage,One rifle and ammunition,One stenographer,Three ounces rosium oxide,One hound-dog,Two valises.

A playful wave slopped over the bow and I lost count; but the pretty stenographer made the inventory, while I resumed the oars, and the dog punctured the primeval silence with staccato yelps.

A few minutes later everything and everybody was accounted for; the sky was blue and the palms waved, and several species of dicky-birds tuned up as I pulled with powerful strokes out into the sunny waters of Little Sprite Lake, now within a few miles of my journey's end.

From ponds hidden in the marshes herons rose in lazily laborious flight, flapping low across the water; high in the cypress yellow-eyed ospreys bent crested heads to watch our progress; sun-baked alligators, lying heavily in the shoreward sedge, slid open, glassy eyes as we passed.

"Even the 'gators make eyes at you," I said, resting on my oars.

We were on terms of badinage.

"Who was it who shed crocodile tears at the prospect of shipping me North?" she inquired.

"Speaking of tears," I observed, "somebody is likely to shed a number when Professor Farrago is picked up."

"Pooh!" she said, and snapped her pretty, sun-tanned fingers; and I resumed the oars in time to avoid shipwreck on a large mud-bar.

She reclined in the stern, serenely occupied with the view, now and then caressing the discouraged dog, now and then patting her hair where the wind had loosened a bright strand.

"If Professor Farrago didn't expect a woman stenographer," she said, abruptly, "why did he instruct you to bring a complete outfit of woman's clothing?"

"I don't know," I said, tartly.

"But you bought them. Are they for a young woman or an old woman?"

"I don't know; I sent a messenger to a department store. I don't know what he bought."

"Didn't you look them over?"

"No. Why? I should have been no wiser. I fancy they're all right, because the bill was eighteen hundred dollars—"

The pretty stenographer sat up abruptly.

"Is that much?" I asked, uneasily. "I've always heard women's clothing was expensive. Wasn't it enough? I told the boy to order the best;—Professor Farrago always requires the very best scientific instruments, and—I listed the clothes as scientific accessories—that being the object of this expedition—*What* are you laughing at?"

When it pleased her to recover her gravity she announced her desire to inspect and repack the clothing; but I refused.

"They're for Professor Farrago," I said. "I don't know what he wants of them. I don't suppose he intends to wear 'em and caper about the jungle, but they're his. I got them because he told me to. I bought a cage, too, to fit myself, but I don't suppose he means to put me in it. Perhaps," I added, "he may invite you into it."

"Let me refold the gowns," she pleaded, persuasively. "What does a clumsy man know about packing such clothing as that? If you don't, they'll be ruined. It's a shame to drag those boxes about through mud and water!"

So we made a landing, and lifted out and unlocked the boxes. All I could see inside were mounds of lace and ribbons, and with a vague idea that Miss Barrison needed no assistance I returned to the boat and sat down to smoke until she was ready.

When she summoned me her face was flushed and her eyes bright.

"Those are certainly the most beautiful things!" she said, softly. "Why, it is like a bride's trousseau—absolutely complete—all except the bridal gown—"

"Isn't there a dress there?" I exclaimed, in alarm.

"No—not a day-dress."

"Night-dresses!" I shrieked. "He doesn't want women's night-dresses! He's a bachelor! Good Heavens! I've done it this time!"

"But—but who is to wear them?" she asked.

"How do I know? I don't know anything; I can only presume that he doesn't intend to open a department store in the Everglades. And if any lady is to wear garments in his vicinity, I assume that those garments are to be anything except diaphanous!... Please take your seat in the boat, Miss Barrison. I want to row and think."

I had had my fill of exercise and thought when, about four o'clock in the afternoon, Miss Barrison directed my attention to a point of palms jutting out into the water about a mile to the southward.

"That's Farrago!" I exclaimed, catching sight of a United States flag floating majestically from a bamboo-pole. "Give me the megaphone, if you please."

She handed me the instrument; I hailed the shore; and presently a man appeared under the palms at the water's edge.

"Hello!" I roared, trying to inject cheerfulness into the hollow bellow. "How are you, professor?"

The answer came distinctly across the water:

"*Who* is that with you?"

My lips were buried in the megaphone; I strove to speak; I only produced a ghastly, chuckling sound.

"Of course you expect to tell the truth," observed the pretty stenographer, quietly.

I removed my lips from the megaphone and looked around at her. She returned my gaze with a disturbing smile.

"I want to mitigate the blow," I said, hoarsely. "Tell me how."

"I'm sure I don't know," she said, sweetly.

"Well, *I* do!" I fairly barked, and seizing the megaphone again, I set it to my lips and roared, "My fiancée!"

"Good gracious!" exclaimed Miss Barrison, in consternation, "I thought you were going to tell the truth!"

"Don't do that or you'll upset us," I snapped—"I'm telling the truth; I've engaged myself to you; I did it mentally before I bellowed."

"But—"

"You know as well as I do what engagements mean," I said, picking up the oars and digging them deep in the blue water.

She assented uncertainly.

A few minutes more of vigorous rowing brought us to a muddy landing under a cluster of tall palmettos, where a gasoline launch lay. Professor Farrago came down to the shore as I landed, and I walked ahead to meet him. He was the maddest man I ever saw. But I was his match, for I was desperate.

"What the devil—" he began, under his breath.

"Nonsense!" I said, deliberately. "An engaged woman is practically married already, because marriages are made in heaven."

"Good Lord!" he gasped, "are you mad, Gilland? I sent for a stenographer—"

"Miss Barrison is a stenographer," I said, calmly; and before he could recover I had presented him, and left them face to face, washing my hands of the whole affair.

Unloading the boat and carrying the luggage up under the palms, I heard her saying:

"No, I am not in the least afraid of snakes, and I am quite ready to begin my duties."

And he: "Mr. Gilland is a young man who—er—lacks practical experience."

And she: "Mr. Gilland has been most thoughtful for my comfort. The journey has been perfectly heavenly."

And he, clumsily: "Ahem!—the—er—celestial aspect of your journey has—er—doubtless been colored by—er—the prospect of your—er—approaching nuptials—"

She, hastily: "Oh, I do not think so, professor."

"Idiot!" I muttered, dragging the dog to the shore, where his yelps brought the professor hurrying.

"Is *that* the dog?" he inquired, adjusting his spectacles.

"That's the dog," I said. "He's full of points, you see?"

"Oh," mused the professor; "I thought he was full of—" He hesitated, inspecting the animal, who, nose to the ground, stood investigating a smell of some sort.

"See," I said, with enthusiasm, "he's found a scent; he's trailing it already! Now he's rolling on it!"

"He's rolling on one of our concentrated food lozenges," said the professor, dryly. "Tie him up, Mr. Gilland, and ask Mrs. Gilland to come up to camp. Your room is ready."

"Rooms," I corrected; "she isn't Mrs. Gilland yet," I added, with a forced smile.

"But you're practically married," observed the professor, "as you pointed out to me. And if she's practically Mrs. Gilland, why not say so?"

"Don't, all the same," I snarled.

"But marriages are made in—"

I cast a desperate eye upon him.

From that moment, whenever we were alone together, he made a target of me. I never had supposed him humorously vindictive; he was, and his apparently innocent mistakes almost turned my hair gray.

But to Miss Barrison he was kind and courteous, and for a time over-serious. Observing him, I could never detect the slightest symptom of dislike for her sex—a failing which common rumor had always credited him with to the verge of absolute rudeness.

On the contrary, it was perfectly plain to anybody that he liked her. There was in his manner towards her a mixture of business formality and the deferential attitude of a gentleman.

We were seated, just before sunset, outside of the hut built of palmetto logs, when Professor Farrago, addressing us both, began the explanation of our future duties.

Miss Barrison, it appeared, was to note everything said by himself, making several shorthand copies by evening. In other words, she was to report every scrap of conversation she heard while in the Everglades. And she nodded intelligently as he finished, and drew pad and pencil from the pocket of her walking-skirt, jotting down his instructions as a beginning. I could see that he was pleased.

"The reason I do this," he said, "is because I do not wish to hide anything that transpires while we are on this expedition. Only the most scrupulously minute record can satisfy me; no details are too small to merit record; I demand and I court from my fellow-scientists and from the public the fullest investigation."

He smiled slightly, turning towards me.

"You know, Mr. Gilland, how dangerous to the reputation of a scientific man is any line of investigation into the unusual. If a man once is even suspected of charlatanism, of sensationalism, of turning his attention to any phenomena not strictly within the proper pale of scientific investigation, that man is doomed to ridicule; his profession disowns him; he becomes a man without honor, without authority. Is it not so?"

"Yes," I said.

"Therefore," he resumed, thoughtfully, "as I do most firmly believe in the course I am now pursuing, whether I succeed or fail I desire a true and minute record made, hiding nothing of what may be said or done. A stenographer alone can give this to the world, while I can only supplement it with a description of events—if I live to transcribe them."

Sunk in profound reverie he sat there silent under the great, smooth palm-tree—a venerable figure in his yellow dressing-gown and carpet slippers. Seated side by side, we waited, a trifle awed. I could hear the soft breathing of the pretty stenographer beside me.

"First of all," said Professor Farrago, looking up, "I must be able to trust those who are here to aid me."

"I—I will be faithful," said the girl, in a low voice.

"I do not doubt you, my child," he said; "nor you, Gilland. And so I am going to tell you this much now—more, I hope, later."

And he sat up straight, lifting an impressive forefinger.

"Mr. Rowan, lately an officer of our Coast Survey, wrote me a letter from the Holland House in New York—a letter so strange that, on reading it, I immediately repaired to his hotel, where for hours we talked together.

"The result of that conference is this expedition.

"I have now been here two months, and I am satisfied of certain facts. First, there do exist in this unexplored wilderness certain forms of life which are solid and palpable, but transparent and practically invisible. Second, these living creatures belong to the animal kingdom, are warm-blooded vertebrates, possess powers of locomotion, but whether that of flight I am not certain. Third, they appear to possess such senses as we enjoy—smell, touch, sight, hearing, and no doubt the sense of taste. Fourth, their skin is smooth to the touch, and the temperature of the epidermis appears to approximate that of a normal human being. Fifth and last, whether bipeds or quadrupeds I do not know, though all evidence appears to confirm my theory that they walk erect. One pair of their limbs appear to terminate in a sort of foot—like a delicately shaped human foot, except that there appear to be no toes. The other pair of limbs terminate in something that, from the single instance I experienced, seemed to resemble soft but firm antennæ or, perhaps, digitated palpi—"

"Feelers!" I blurted out.

"I don't know, but I think so. Once, when I was standing in the forest, perfectly aware that creatures I could not see had stealthily surrounded me, the tension was brought to a crisis when over my face, from cheek to chin, stole a soft something, brushing the skin as delicately as a child's fingers might brush it."

"Good Lord!" I breathed.

A care-worn smile crept into his eyes. "A test for nerves, you think, Mr. Gilland? I agree with you. Nobody fears what anybody can see."

There came the slightest movement beside me.

"Are you trembling?" I asked, turning.

"I was writing," she replied, steadily. "Did my elbow touch you?"

"By-the-way," said Professor Farrago, "I fear I forgot to congratulate you upon your choice of a stenographer, Mr. Gilland."

A rosy light stole over her pale face.

"Am I to record that too?" she asked, raising her blue eyes.

"Certainly," he replied, gravely.

"But, professor," I began, a prey to increasing excitement, "do you propose to attempt the capture of one of these animals?"

"That is what the cage is for," he said. "I supposed you had guessed that."

"I had," murmured the pretty stenographer.

"I do not doubt it," said Professor Farrago, gravely.

"What are the chemicals for—and the tank and hose attachment?"

"Think, Mr. Gilland."

"I can't; I'm almost stunned by what you tell me."

He laughed. "The rosium oxide and salts of strontium are to be dumped into the tank together. They'll effervesce, of course."

"Of course," I muttered.

"And I can throw a rose-colored spray over any object by the hose attachment, can't I?"

"Yes."

"Well, I tried it on a transparent jelly-fish and it became perfectly visible and of a beautiful rose-color: and I tried it on rock-crystal, and on glass, and on pure gelatine, and all became suffused with a delicate pink glow, which lasted for hours or minutes according to the substance.... Now you understand, don't you?"

"Yes; you want to see what sort of creature you have to deal with."

"Exactly; so when I've trapped it I am going to spray it." He turned half humorously towards the stenographer: "I fancy you understood long before Mr. Gilland did."

"I don't think so," she said, with a sidelong lifting of the heavy lashes; and I caught the color of her eyes for a second.

"You see how Miss Barrison spares your feelings," observed Professor Farrago, dryly. "She owes you little gratitude for bringing her here, yet she proves a generous victim."

"Oh, I am very grateful for this rarest of chances!" she said, shyly. "To be among the first in the world to discover such wonders ought to make me very grateful to the man who gave me the opportunity."

"Do you mean Mr. Gilland?" asked the professor, laughing.

I had never before seen Professor Farrago laugh such a care-free laugh; I had never suspected him of harboring even an embryo of the social graces. Dry as dust, sapless as steel, precise as the magnetic needle, he had hitherto been to me the mummified embodiment of science militant. Now, in the guise of a perfectly human and genial old gentleman, I scarcely recognized my superior of the Bronx Park society. And as a woman-hater he was a miserable failure.

"Heavens," I thought to myself, "am I becoming jealous of my revered professor's social success with a stray stenographer?" I felt mean, and I probably looked it, and I was glad that telepathy did not permit Miss Barrison to record my secret and unworthy ruminations.

The professor was saying: "These transparent creatures break off berries and fruits and branches; I have seen a flower, too, plucked from its stem by invisible digits and borne swiftly through the forest—only the flower visible, apparently speeding through the air and out of sight among the thickets.

"I have found the footprints that I described to you, usually on the edge of a stream or in the soft loam along some forest lake or lost lagoon.

"Again and again I have been conscious in the forest that unseen eyes were fixed on me, that unseen shapes were following me. Never but that one time did these invisible creatures close in around me and venture to touch me.

"They may be weak; their structure may be frail, and they may be incapable of violence or harm, but the depth of the footprints indicates a weight of at least one hundred and thirty pounds, and it certainly requires some muscular strength to break off a branch of wild guavas."

He bent his noble head, thoughtfully regarding the design on his slippers.

"What was the rifle for?" I asked.

"Defence, not aggression," he said, simply.

"And the camera?"

"A camera record is necessary in these days of bad artists."

I hesitated, glancing at Miss Barrison. She was still writing, her pretty head bent over the pad in her lap.

"And the clothing?" I asked, carelessly.

"Did you get it?" he demanded.

"Of course—" I glanced at Miss Barrison. "There's no use writing down everything, is there?"

"Everything must be recorded," said Professor Farrago, inflexibly. "What clothing did you buy?"

"I forgot the gown," I said, getting red about the ears.

"Forgot the gown!" he repeated.

"Yes—one kind of gown—the day kind. I—I got the other kind."

He was annoyed; so was I. After a moment he got up, and crossing to the log cabin, opened one of the boxes of apparel.

"Is it what you wanted?" I inquired.

"Y-es, I presume so," he replied, visibly perplexed.

"It's the best to be had," said I.

"That's quite right," he said, musingly. "We use only the best of everything at Bronx Park. It is traditional with us, you know."

Curiosity pushed me. "Well, what on earth is it for?" I broke out.

He looked at me gravely over the tops of his spectacles—a striking and inspiring figure in his yellow flannel dressing-gown and slippers.

"I shall tell you some day—perhaps," he said, mildly. "Good-night, Miss Barrison; good-night, Mr. Gilland. You will find extra blankets on your bunk—"

"What!" I cried.

"Bunks," he said, and shut the door.

# XVI

"There is something weird about this whole proceeding," I observed to the pretty stenographer next morning.

"These pies will be weird if you don't stop talking to me," she said, opening the doors of Professor Farrago's portable camping-oven and peeping in at the fragrant pastry.

The professor had gone off somewhere into the woods early that morning. As he was not in the habit of talking to himself, the services of Miss Barrison were not required. Before he started, however, he came to her with a request for a dozen pies, the construction of which he asked if she understood. She had been to cooking-school in more prosperous days, and she mentioned it; so at his earnest solicitation she undertook to bake for him twelve apple-pies; and she was now attempting it, assisted by advice from me.

"Are they burned?" I asked, sniffing the air.

"No, they are not burned, Mr. Gilland, but my finger is," she retorted, stepping back to examine the damage.

I offered sympathy and witch-hazel, but she would have none of my offerings, and presently returned to her pies.

"We can't eat all that pastry," I protested.

"Professor Farrago said they were not for us to eat," she said, dusting each pie with powdered sugar.

"Well, what are they for? The dog? Or are they simply objets d'art to adorn the shanty—"

"You annoy me," she said.

"The pies annoy me; won't you tell me what they're for?"

"I have a pretty fair idea what they're for," she observed, tossing her head. "Haven't you?"

"No. What?"

"These pies are for bait."

"To bait hooks with?" I exclaimed.

"Hooks! No, you silly man. They're for baiting the cage. He means to trap these transparent creatures in a cage baited with pie."

She laughed scornfully; inserted the burned tip of her finger in her mouth and stood looking at me defiantly like a flushed and bright-eyed school-girl.

"You think you're teasing me," she said; "but you do not realize what a singularly slow-minded young man you are."

I stopped laughing. "How did you come to the conclusion that pies were to be used for such a purpose?" I asked.

"I deduce," she observed, with an airy wave of her disengaged hand.

"Your deductions are weird—like everything else in this vicinity. Pies to catch invisible monsters? Pooh!"

"You're not particularly complimentary, are you?" she said.

"Not particularly; but I could be, with you for my inspiration. I could even be enthusiastic—"

"About my pies?"

"No—about your eyes."

"You are very frivolous—for a scientist," she said, scornfully; "please subdue your enthusiasm and bring me some wood. This fire is almost out."

When I had brought the wood, she presented me with a pail of hot water and pointed at the dishes on the breakfast-table.

"Never!" I cried, revolted.

"Then I suppose I must do them—"

She looked pensively at her scorched finger-tip, and, pursing up her red lips, blew a gentle breath to cool it.

"I'll do the dishes," I said.

Splashing and slushing the cups and saucers about in the hot water, I reflected upon the events of the last few days. The dog, stupefied by unwonted abundance of food, lay in the sunshine, sleeping the sleep of repletion; the pretty stenographer, all rosy from her culinary exertions, was removing the pies and setting them in neat rows to cool.

"There," she said, with a sigh; "now I will dry the dishes for you.... You didn't mention the fact, when you engaged me, that I was also expected to do general housework."

"I didn't engage you," I said, maliciously; "you engaged me, you know."

She regarded me disdainfully, nose uptilted.

"How thoroughly disagreeable you can be!" she said. "Dry your own dishes. I'm going for a stroll."

"May I join—"

"You may *not*! I shall go so far that you cannot possibly discover me."

I watched her forestward progress; she sauntered for about thirty yards along the lake and presently sat down in plain sight under a huge live-oak.

A few moments later I had completed my task as general bottle-washer, and I cast about for something to occupy me.

First I approached and politely caressed the satiated dog. He woke up, regarded me with dully meditative eyes, yawned, and went to sleep again. Never a flop of tail to indicate gratitude for blandishments, never the faintest symptom of canine appreciation.

Chilled by my reception, I moused about for a while, poking into boxes and bundles; then raised my head and inspected the landscape. Through the vista of trees the pink shirt-waist of the pretty stenographer glimmered like a rose blooming in the wilderness.

From whatever point I viewed the prospect that pink spot seemed to intrude; I turned my back and examined the jungle, but there it was repeated in a hundred pink blossoms among the massed thickets; I looked up into the tree-tops, where pink mosses spotted the palms; I looked out over the lake, and I saw it in my mind's eye pinker than ever. It was certainly a case of pink-eye.

"I'll go for a stroll, too; it's a free country," I muttered.

After I had strolled in a complete circle I found myself within three feet of a pink shirt-waist.

"I beg your pardon," I said; "I had no inten—"

"I thought you were never coming," she said, amiably.

"How is your finger?" I asked.

She held it up. I took it gingerly; it was smooth and faintly rosy at the tip.

"Does it hurt?" I inquired.

"Dreadfully. Your hands feel so cool—"

After a silence she said, "Thank you, that has cooled the burning."

"I am determined," said I, "to expel the fire from your finger if it takes hours and hours." And I seated myself with that intention.

For a while she talked, making innocent observations concerning the tropical foliage surrounding us. Then silence crept in between us, accentuated by the brooding stillness of the forest.

"I am afraid your hands are growing tired," she said, considerately.

I denied it.

Through the vista of palms we could see the lake, blue as a violet, sparkling with silvery sunshine. In the intense quiet the splash of leaping mullet sounded distinctly.

Once a tall crane stalked into view among the sedges; once an unseen alligator shook the silence with his deep, hollow roaring. Then the stillness of the wilderness grew more intense.

We had been sitting there for a long while without exchanging a word, dreamily watching the ripple of the azure water, when all at once there came a scurrying patter of feet through the forest, and, looking up, I beheld the hound-dog, tail between his legs, bearing down on us at lightning speed. I rose instantly.

"What is the matter with the dog?" cried the pretty stenographer. "Is he going mad, Mr. Gilland?"

"Something has scared him," I exclaimed, as the dog, eyes like lighted candles, rushed frantically between my legs and buried his head in Miss Barrison's lap.

"Poor doggy!" she said, smoothing the collapsed pup; "poor, p-oor little beast! Did anything scare him? Tell aunty all about it."

When a dog flees *without yelping* he's a badly frightened creature. I instinctively started back towards the camp whence the beast had fled, and before I had taken a dozen steps Miss Barrison was beside me, carrying the dog in her arms.

"I've an idea," she said, under her breath.

"What?" I asked, keeping my eyes on the camp.

"It's this: I'll wager that we find those pies gone!"

"Pies gone?" I repeated, perplexed; "what makes you think—"

"They *are* gone!" she exclaimed. "Look!"

I gaped stupidly at the rough pine table where the pies had stood in three neat rows of four each. And then, in a moment, the purport of this robbery flashed upon my senses.

"The transparent creatures!" I gasped.

"Hush!" she whispered, clinging to the trembling dog in her arms.

I listened. I could hear nothing, see nothing, yet slowly I became convinced of the presence of something unseen—something in the forest close by, watching us out of invisible eyes.

A chill, settling along my spine, crept upward to my scalp, until every separate hair wiggled to the roots. Miss Barrison was pale, but perfectly calm and self-possessed.

"Let us go in-doors," I said, as steadily as I could.

"Very well," she replied.

I held the door open; she entered with the dog; I followed, closing and barring the door, and then took my station at the window, rifle in hand.

There was not a sound in the forest. Miss Barrison laid the dog on the floor and quietly picked up her pad and pencil. Presently she was deep in a report of the phenomena, her pencil flying, leaf after leaf from the pad fluttering to the floor.

Nor did I at the window change my position of scared alertness, until I was aware of her hand gently touching my elbow to attract my attention, and her soft voice at my ear—

"You don't suppose by any chance that the dog ate those pies?"

I collected my tumultuous thoughts and turned to stare at the dog.

"Twelve pies, twelve inches each in diameter," she reflected, musingly. "One dog, twenty inches in diameter. How many times will the pies go into the dog? Let me see." She made a few figures on her pad, thought awhile, produced a tape-measure from her pocket, and, kneeling down, measured the dog.

"No," she said, looking up at me, "he couldn't contain them."

Inspired by her coolness and perfect composure, I set the rifle in the corner and opened the door. Sunlight fell in bars through the quiet woods; nothing stirred on land or water save the great, yellow-striped butterflies that fluttered and soared and floated above the flowering thickets bordering the jungle.

The heat became intense; Miss Barrison went to her room to change her gown for a lighter one; I sat down under a live-oak, eyes and ears strained for any sign of our invisible neighbors.

When she emerged in the lightest and filmiest of summer gowns, she brought the camera with her; and for a while we took pictures of each other, until we had used up all but one film.

Desiring to possess a picture of Miss Barrison and myself seated together, I tied a string to the shutter-lever and attached the other end of the string to the dog, who had resumed his interrupted slumbers. At my whistle he jumped up nervously, snapping the lever, and the picture was taken.

With such innocent and harmless pastime we whiled away the afternoon. She made twelve more apple-pies. I mounted guard over them. And we were just beginning to feel a trifle uneasy about Professor Farrago, when he appeared, tramping sturdily through the forest, green umbrella and butterfly-net under one arm, shot-gun and cyanide-jar under the other, and his breast all criss-crossed with straps, from which dangled field-glasses, collecting-boxes, and botanizing-tins—an inspiring figure indeed—the embodied symbol of science indomitable, triumphant!

We hailed him with three guilty cheers; the dog woke up with a perfunctory bark—the first sound I had heard from him since he yelped his disapproval of me on the lagoon.

Miss Barrison produced three bowls full of boiling water and dropped three pellets of concentrated soup-meat into them, while I prepared coffee. And in a few moments our simple dinner was ready—the red ants had been dusted from the biscuits, the spiders chased off the baked beans, the scorpions shaken from the napkins, and we sat down at the rough, improvised table under the palms.

The professor gave us a brief but modest account of his short tour of exploration. He had brought back a new species of orchid, several undescribed beetles, and a pocketful of coontie seed. He appeared, however, to be tired and singularly depressed, and presently we learned why.

It seemed that he had gone straight to that section of the forest where he had hitherto always found signs of the transparent and invisible creatures which he had determined to capture, and he had not found a single trace of them.

"It alarms me," he said, gravely. "If they have deserted this region, it might take a lifetime to locate them again in this wilderness."

Then, very quietly, sinking her voice instinctively, as though the unseen might be at our very elbows listening, Miss Barrison recounted the curious adventure which had befallen the dog and the first batch of apple-pies.

With visible and increasing excitement the professor listened until the very end. Then he struck the table with clinched fist—a resounding blow which set the concentrated soup dancing in the bowls and scattered the biscuits and the industrious red ants in every direction.

"Eureka!" he whispered. "Miss Barrison, your deduction was not only perfectly reasonable, but brilliant. You are right; the pies are for that very purpose. I conceived the idea when I first came here. Again and again the pies that my guide made out of dried apples disappeared in a most astonishing and mysterious manner when left to cool. At length I determined to watch them every second; and did so, with the result that late one afternoon I was amazed to see a pie slowly rise from the table and move swiftly away through the air about four feet above the ground, finally disappearing into a tangle of jasmine and grape-vine.

"The apparently automatic flight of that pie solved the problem; these transparent creatures cannot resist that delicacy. Therefore I decided to bait the cage for them this very night—Look! What's the matter with that dog?"

The dog suddenly bounded into the air, alighted on all fours, ears, eyes, and muzzle concentrated on a point directly behind us.

"Good gracious! The pies!" faltered Miss Barrison, half rising from her seat; but the dog rushed madly into her skirts, scrambling for protection, and she fell back almost into my arms.

Clasping her tightly, I looked over my shoulder; the last pie was snatched from the table before my eyes and I saw it borne swiftly away by something unseen, straight into the deepening shadows of the forest.

The professor was singularly calm, even slightly ironical, as he turned to me, saying:

"Perhaps if you relinquish Miss Barrison she may be able to free herself from that dog."

I did so immediately, and she deposited the cowering dog in my arms. Her face had suddenly become pink.

I passed the dog on to Professor Farrago, dumping it viciously into his lap—a proceeding which struck me as resembling a pastime of extreme youth known as "button, button, who's got the button?"

The professor examined the animal gravely, feeling its pulse, counting its respirations, and finally inserting a tentative finger in an attempt to examine its tongue. The dog bit him.

"Ouch! It's a clear case of fright," he said, gravely. "I wanted a dog to aid me in trailing these remarkable creatures, but I think this dog of yours is useless, Gilland."

"It's given us warning of the creatures' presence twice already," I argued.

"Poor little thing," said Miss Barrison, softly; "I don't know why, but I love that dog.... He has eyes like yours, Mr. Gilland—"

Exasperated, I rose from the table. "He's got eyes like holes burned in a blanket!" I said. "And if ever a flicker of intelligence lighted them I have failed to observe it."

The professor regarded me dreamily. "We ought to have more pies," he observed. "Perhaps if you carried the oven into the shanty—"

"Certainly," said Miss Barrison; "we can lock the door while I make twelve more pies."

I carried the portable camping-oven into the cabin, connected the patent asbestos chimney-pipes, and lighted the fire. And in a few minutes Miss Barrison, sleeves rolled up and pink apron pinned under her chin, was busily engaged in rolling pie-crust, while Professor Farrago measured out spices and set the dried apples to soak.

The swift Southern twilight had already veiled the forest as I stepped out of the cabin to smoke a cigar and promenade a bit and cogitate. A last trace of color lingering in the west faded out as I looked; the gray glimmer deepened into darkness, through which the white lake vapors floated in thin, wavering strata across the water.

For a while the frog's symphony dominated all other sounds, then lagoon and forest and cypress branch awoke; and through the steadily sustained tumult of woodland voices I could hear the dry bark of the fox-squirrel, the whistle of the raccoon, ducks softly quacking or whimpering as they prepared for sleep among the reeds, the soft booming of bitterns, the clattering gossip of the heronry, the Southern whippoorwill's incessant call.

At regular intervals the howling note of a lone heron echoed the strident screech of a crimson-crested crane; the horned owl's savage hunting-cry haunted the night, now near, now floating from infinite distances.

And after a while I became aware of a nearer sound, low-pitched but ceaseless—the hum of thousands of lesser living creatures blending to a steady monotone.

Then the theatrical moon came up through filmy draperies of waving Spanish moss thin as cobwebs; and far in the wilderness a cougar fell a-crying and coughing like a little child with a bad cold.

I went in after that. Miss Barrison was sitting before the oven, knees gathered in her clasped hands, languidly studying the fire. She looked up as I appeared, opened the oven-doors, sniffed the aroma, and resumed her attitude of contented indifference.

"Where is the professor?" I asked.

"He has retired. He's been talking in his sleep at moments."

"Better take it down; that's what you're here for," I observed, closing and holding the outside door. "Ugh! there's a chill in the air. The dew is pelting down from the pines like a steady fall of rain."

"You will get fever if you roam about at night," she said. "Mercy! your coat is soaking. Sit here by the fire."

So I pulled up a bench and sat down beside her like the traditional spider.

"Miss Muffitt," I said, "don't let me frighten you away—"

"I was going anyhow—"

"Please don't."

"Why?" she demanded, reseating herself.

"Because I like to sit beside you," I said, truthfully.

"Your avowal is startling and not to be substantiated by facts," she remarked, resting her chin on one hand and gazing into the fire.

"You mean because I went for a stroll by moonlight? I did that because you always seem to make fun of me as soon as the professor joins us."

"Make fun of you? You surely don't expect me to make eyes at you!"

There was a silence; I toasted my shins, thoughtfully.

"How is your burned finger?" I asked.

She lifted it for my inspection, and I began a protracted examination.

"What would you prescribe?" she inquired, with an absent-minded glance at the professor's closed door.

"I don't know; perhaps a slight but firm pressure of the finger-tips—"

"You tried that this afternoon."

"But the dog interrupted us—"

"Interrupted *you*. Besides—"

"What?"

"I don't think you ought to," she said.

Sitting there before the oven, side by side, hand innocently clasped in hand, we heard the drumming of the dew on the roof, the night-wind stirring the palms, the muffled snoring of the professor, the faint whisper and crackle of the fire.

A single candle burned brightly, piling our shadows together on the wall behind us; moonlight silvered the window-panes, over which crawled multitudes of soft-winged moths, attracted by the candle within.

"See their tiny eyes glow!" she whispered. "How their wings quiver! And all for a candle-flame! Alas! alas! fire is the undoing of us all."

She leaned forward, resting as though buried in reverie. After a while she extended one foot a trifle and, with the point of her shoe, carefully unlatched the oven-door. As it swung outward a delicious fragrance filled the room.

"They're done," she said, withdrawing her hand from mine. "Help me to lift them out."

Together we arranged the delicious pastry in rows on the bench to cool. I opened the door for a few minutes, then closed and bolted it again.

"Do you suppose those transparent creatures will smell the odor and come around the cabin?" she suggested, wiping her fingers on her handkerchief.

I walked to the window uneasily. Outside the pane the moths crawled, some brilliant in scarlet and tan-color set with black, some snow-white with black tracings on their wings, and bodies peacock-blue edged with orange. The scientist in me was aroused; I called her to the window, and she came and leaned against the sill, nose pressed to the glass.

"I don't suppose you know that the antennæ of that silvery-winged moth are distinctly pectinate," I said.

"Of course I do," she said. "I took my degree as D.E. at Barnard College."

"What!" I exclaimed in astonishment. "You've been through Barnard? You are a Doctor of Entomology?"

"It was my undoing," she said. "The department was abolished the year I graduated. There was no similar vacancy, even in the Smithsonian."

She shrugged her shoulders, eyes fixed on the moths. "I had to make my own living. I chose stenography as the quickest road to self-sustenance."

She looked up, a flush on her cheeks.

"I suppose you took me for an inferior?" she said. "But do you suppose I'd flirt with you if I was?"

She pressed her face to the pane again, murmuring that exquisite poem of Andrew Lang:

"Spooning is innocuous and needn't have a sequel, But recollect, if spoon you must, spoon only with your equal."

Standing there, watching the moths, we became rather silent—I don't know why.

The fire in the range had gone out; the candle-flame, flaring above a saucer of melted wax, sank lower and lower.

Suddenly, as though disturbed by something inside, the moths all left the window-pane, darting off in the darkness.

"That's curious," I said.

"What's curious?" she asked, opening her eyes languidly. "Good gracious! Was that a bat that beat on the window?"

"I saw nothing," I said, disturbed. "Listen!"

A soft sound against the glass, as though invisible fingers were feeling the pane—a gentle rubbing—then a tap-tap, all but inaudible.

"Is it a bird? Can you see?" she whispered.

The candle-flame behind us flashed and expired. Moonlight flooded the pane. The sounds continued, but there was nothing there.

We understood now what it was that so gently rubbed and patted the glass outside. With one accord we noiselessly gathered up the pies and carried them into my room.

Then she walked to the door of her room, turned, held out her hand, and whispering, "Good-night! A demain, monsieur!" slipped into her room and softly closed the door.

And all night long I lay in troubled slumber beside the pies, a rifle resting on the blankets beside me, a revolver under my pillow. And I dreamed of moths with brilliant eyes and vast silvery wings harnessed to a balloon in which Miss Barrison and I sat, arms around each other, eating slice after slice of apple-pie.

---

# XVII

Dawn came—the dawn of a day that I am destined never to forget. Long, rosy streamers of light broke through the forest, shaking, quivering, like unstable beams from celestial search-lights. Mist floated upward from marsh and lake; and through it the spectral palms loomed, drooping fronds embroidered with dew.

For a while the ringing outburst of bird music dominated all; but it soon ceased with dropping notes from the crimson cardinals repeated in lengthening minor intervals; and then the spell of silence returned, broken only by the faint splash of mullet, mocking the sun with sinuous, silver flashes.

"Good-morning," said a low voice from the door as I stood encouraging the camp-fire with splinter wood and dead palmetto fans.

Fresh and sweet from her toilet as a dew-drenched rose, Miss Barrison stood there sniffing the morning air daintily, thoroughly.

"Too much perfume," she said—"too much like ylang-ylang in a department-store. Central Park smells sweeter on an April morning."

"Are you criticising the wild jasmine?" I asked.

"I'm criticising an exotic smell. Am I not permitted to comment on the tropics?"

Fishing out a cedar log from the lumber-stack, I fell to chopping it vigorously. The axe-strokes made a cheerful racket through the woods.

"Did you hear anything last night after you retired?" I asked.

"Something was at my window—something that thumped softly and seemed to be feeling all over the glass. To tell you the truth, I was silly enough to remain dressed all night."

"You don't look it," I said.

"Oh, when daylight came I had a chance," she added, laughing.

"All the same," said I, leaning on the axe and watching her, "you are about the coolest and pluckiest woman I ever knew."

"We were all in the same fix," she said, modestly.

"No, we were not. Now I'll tell you the truth—my hair stood up the greater part of the night. You are looking upon a poltroon, Miss Barrison."

"Then there was something at your window, too?"

"Something? A dozen! They were monkeying with the sashes and panes all night long, and I imagined that I could hear them breathing—as though from effort of intense eagerness. Ouch! I came as near losing my nerve as I care to. I came within an ace of hurling those cursed pies through the window at them. I'd bolt to-day if I wasn't afraid to play the coward."

"Most people are brave for that reason," she said.

The dog, who had slept under my bunk, and who had contributed to my entertainment by sighing and moaning all night, now appeared ready for business— business in his case being the operation of feeding. I presented him with a concentrated tablet, which he cautiously investigated and then rolled on.

"Nice testimonial for the people who concocted it," I said, in disgust. "I wish I had an egg."

"There are some concentrated egg tablets in the shanty," said Miss Barrison; but the idea was not attractive.

"I refuse to fry a pill for breakfast," I said, sullenly, and set the coffee-pot on the coals.

In spite of the dewy beauty of the morning, breakfast was not a cheerful function. Professor Farrago appeared, clad in sun-helmet and khaki. I had seldom seen him depressed; but he was now, and his very efforts to disguise it only emphasized his visible anxiety.

His preparations for the day, too, had an ominous aspect to me. He gave his orders and we obeyed, instinctively suppressing questions. First, he and I transported all personal luggage of the company to the big electric launch—Miss Barrison's effects, his, and my own. His private papers, the stenographic reports, and all memoranda were tied up together and carried aboard.

Then, to my surprise, two weeks' concentrated rations for two and mineral water sufficient for the same period were stowed away aboard the launch. Several times he asked me whether I knew how to run the boat, and I assured him that I did.

In a short time nothing was left ashore except the bare furnishings of the cabin, the female wearing-apparel, the steel cage and chemicals which I had brought, and the twelve apple-pies—the latter under lock and key in my room.

As the preparations came to an end, the professor's gentle melancholy seemed to deepen. Once I ventured to ask him if he was indisposed, and he replied that he had never felt in better physical condition.

Presently he bade me fetch the pies; and I brought them, and, at a sign from him, placed them inside the steel cage, closing and locking the door.

"I believe," he said, glancing from Miss Barrison to me, and from me to the dog—"I believe that we are ready to start."

He went to the cabin and locked the door on the outside, pocketing the key.

Then he backed up to the steel cage, stooped and lifted his end as I lifted mine, and together we started off through the forest, bearing the cage between us as porters carry a heavy piece of luggage.

Miss Barrison came next, carrying the trousseau, the tank, hose, and chemicals; and the dog followed her—probably not from affection for us, but because he was afraid to be left alone.

We walked in silence, the professor and I keeping an instinctive lookout for snakes; but we encountered nothing of that sort. On every side, touching our shoulders, crowded the closely woven and impenetrable tangle of the jungle; and we threaded it along a narrow path which he, no doubt, had cut, for the machete marks were still fresh, and the blazes on hickory, live-oak, and palm were all wet with dripping sap, and swarming with eager, brilliant butterflies.

At times across our course flowed shallow, rapid streams of water, clear as crystal, and most alluring to the thirsty.

"There's fever in every drop," said the professor, as I mentioned my thirst; "take the bottled water if you mean to stay a little longer."

"Stay where?" I asked.

"On earth," he replied, tersely; and we marched on.

The beauty of the tropics is marred somewhat for me; under all the fresh splendor of color death lurks in brilliant tints. Where painted fruit hangs temptingly, where great, silky blossoms exhale alluring scent, where the elaps coils inlaid with scarlet, black, and saffron, where in the shadow of a palmetto frond a succession of velvety black diamonds mark the rattler's swollen length, there death is; and his invisible consort, horror, creeps where the snake whose mouth is lined with white creeps— where the tarantula squats, hairy, motionless; where a bit of living enamel fringed with orange undulates along a mossy log.

Thinking of these things, and watchful lest, unawares, terror unfold from some blossoming and leafy covert, I scarcely noticed the beauty of the glade we had entered—a long oval, cross-barred with sunshine which fell on hedges of scrub-palmetto, chin high, interlaced with golden blossoms of the jasmine. And all around, like pillars supporting a high green canopy above a throne, towered the silvery stems of palms fretted with pale, rose-tinted lichens and hung with draperies of grape-vine.

"This is the place," said Professor Farrago.

His quiet, passionless voice sounded strange to me; his words seemed strange, too, each one heavily weighted with hidden meaning.

We set the cage on the ground; he unlocked and opened the steel-barred door, and, kneeling, carefully arranged the pies along the centre of the cage.

"I have a curious presentiment," he said, "that I shall not come out of this experiment unscathed."

"Don't, for Heaven's sake, say that!" I broke out, my nerves on edge again.

"Why not?" he asked, surprised. "I am not afraid."

"Not afraid to die?" I demanded, exasperated.

"Who spoke of dying?" he inquired, mildly. "What I said was that I do not expect to come out of this affair unscathed."

I did not comprehend his meaning, but I understood the reproof conveyed.

He closed and locked the cage door again and came towards us, balancing the key across the palm of his hand.

Miss Barrison had seated herself on the leaves; I stood back as the professor sat down beside her; then, at a gesture from him, took the place he indicated on his left.

"Before we begin," he said, calmly, "there are several things you ought to know and which I have not yet told you. The first concerns the feminine wearing apparel which Mr. Gilland brought me."

He turned to Miss Barrison and asked her whether she had brought a complete outfit, and she opened the bundle on her knees and handed it to him.

"I cannot," he said, "delicately explain in so many words what use I expect to make of this apparel. Nor do I yet know whether I shall have any use at all for it. That can only be a theoretical speculation until, within a few more hours, my theory is proven or disproven—and," he said, suddenly turning on me, "my theory concerning these invisible creatures is the most extraordinary and audacious theory ever entertained by man since Columbus presumed that there must lie somewhere a hidden continent which nobody had ever seen."

He passed his hand over his protruding forehead, lost for a moment in deepest reflection. Then, "Have you ever heard of the Sphyx?" he asked.

"It seems to me that Ponce de Leon wrote of something—" I began, hesitating.

"Yes, the famous lines in the third volume which have set so many wise men guessing. You recall them:

"'*And there, alas! within sound of the Fountain of Youth whose waters tint the skin till the whole body glows softly like the petal of a rose—there, alas! in the new world already blooming,* THE ETERNAL ENIGMA *I beheld, in the flesh living; yet it faded even as I looked, although I swear it lived and breathed. This is the Sphyx.*'"

A silence; then I said, "Those lines are meaningless to me."

"Not to me," said Miss Barrison, softly.

The professor looked at her. "Ah, child! Ever subtler, ever surer—the Eternal Enigma is no enigma to you."

"What is the Sphyx?" I asked.

"Have you read De Soto? Or Goya?"

"Yes, both. I remember now that De Soto records the Syachas legend of the Sphyx—something about a goddess—"

"Not a goddess," said Miss Barrison, her lips touched with a smile.

"Sometimes," said the professor, gently. "And Goya said:

"*It has come to my ears while in the lands of the Syachas that the Sphyx surely lives, as bolder and more curious men than I may, God willing, prove to the world hereafter.*"

"But what is the Sphyx?" I insisted.

"For centuries wise men and savants have asked each other that question. I have answered it for myself; I am now to prove it, I trust."

His face darkened, and again and again he stroked his heavy brow.

"If anything occurs," he said, taking my hand in his left and Miss Barrison's hand in his right, "promise me to obey my wishes. Will you?"

"Yes," we said, together.

"If I lose my life, or—or disappear, promise me on your honor to get to the electric launch as soon as possible and make all speed northward, placing my private papers, the reports of Miss Barrison, and your own reports in the hands of the authorities in Bronx Park. Don't attempt to aid me; don't delay to search for me. Do you promise?"

"Yes," we breathed together.

He looked at us solemnly. "If you fail me, you betray me," he said.

We swore obedience.

"Then let us begin," he said, and he rose and went to the steel cage. Unlocking the door, he flung it wide and stepped inside, leaving the cage door open.

"The moment a single pie is disturbed," he said to me, "I shall close the steel door from the inside, and you and Miss Barrison will then dump the rosium oxide and the strontium into the tank, clap on the lid, turn the nozzle of the hose on the cage, and spray it thoroughly. Whatever is invisible in the cage will become visible and of a faint rose color. And when the trapped creature becomes visible, hold yourselves ready to aid me as long as I am able to give you orders. After that either all will go well or all will go otherwise, and you must run for the launch." He seated himself in the cage near the open door.

I placed the steel tank near the cage, uncoiled the hose attachment, unscrewed the top, and dumped in the salts of strontium. Miss Barrison unwrapped the bottle of rosium oxide and loosened the cork. We examined this pearl-and-pink powder and shook it up so that it might run out quickly. Then Miss Barrison sat down, and presently became absorbed in a stenographic report of the proceedings up to date.

When Miss Barrison finished her report she handed me the bundle of papers. I stowed them away in my wallet, and we sat down together beside the tank.

Inside the cage Professor Farrago was seated, his spectacled eyes fixed on the row of pies. For a while, although realizing perfectly that our quarry was transparent and invisible, we unconsciously strained our eyes in quest of something stirring in the forest.

"I should think," said I, in a low voice, "that the odor of the pies might draw at least one out of the odd dozen that came rubbing up against my window last night."

"Hush! Listen!" she breathed. But we heard nothing save the snoring of the overfed dog at our feet.

"He'll give us ample notice by butting into Miss Barrison's skirts," I observed. "No need of our watching, professor."

The professor nodded. Presently he removed his spectacles and lay back against the bars, closing his eyes.

At first the forest silence seemed cheerful there in the flecked sunlight. The spotted wood-gnats gyrated merrily, chased by dragon-flies; the shy wood-birds hopped from branch to twig, peering at us in friendly inquiry; a lithe, gray squirrel, plumy tail undulating, rambled serenely around the cage, sniffing at the pastry within.

Suddenly, without apparent reason, the squirrel sprang to a tree-trunk, hung a moment on the bark, quivering all over, then dashed away into the jungle.

"Why did he act like that?" whispered Miss Barrison. And, after a moment: "How still it is! Where have the birds gone?"

In the ominous silence the dog began to whimper in his sleep and his hind legs kicked convulsively.

"He's dreaming—" I began.

The words were almost driven down my throat by the dog, who, without a yelp of warning, hurled himself at Miss Barrison and alighted on my chest, fore paws around my neck.

I cast him scornfully from me, but he scrambled back, digging like a mole to get under us.

"The transparent creatures!" whispered Miss Barrison. "Look! See that pie move!"

I sprang to my feet just as the professor, jamming on his spectacles, leaned forward and slammed the cage door.

"I've got one!" he shouted, frantically. "There's one in the cage! Turn on that hose!"

"Wait a second," said Miss Barrison, calmly, uncorking the bottle and pouring a pearly stream of rosium oxide into the tank. "Quick! It's fizzing! Screw on the top!"

In a second I had screwed the top fast, seized the hose, and directed a hissing cloud of vapor through the cage bars.

For a moment nothing was heard save the whistling rush of the perfumed spray escaping; a delicious odor of roses filled the air. Then, slowly, there in the sunshine, a misty something grew in the cage—a glistening, pearl-tinted phantom, imperceptibly taking shape in space—vague at first as a shred of lake vapor, then lengthening, rounding into flowing form, clearer, clearer.

"The Sphyx!" gasped the professor. "In the name of Heaven, play that hose!"

As he spoke the treacherous hose burst. A showery pillar of rose-colored vapor enveloped everything. Through the thickening fog for one brief instant a human form appeared like magic—a woman's form, flawless, exquisite as a statue, pure as marble. Then the swimming vapor buried it, cage, pies, and all.

We ran frantically around, the cage in the obscurity, appealing for instructions and feeling for the bars. Once the professor's muffled voice was heard demanding the wearing apparel, and I groped about and found it and stuffed it through the bars of the cage.

"Do you need help?" I shouted. There was no response. Staring around through the thickening vapor of rosium rolling in clouds from the overturned tank, I heard Miss Barrison's voice calling:

"I can't move! A transparent lady is holding me!"

Blindly I rushed about, arms outstretched, and the next moment struck the door of the cage so hard that the impact almost knocked me senseless. Clutching it to steady myself, it suddenly flew open. A rush of partly visible creatures passed me like a burst of pink flames, and in the midst, borne swiftly away on the crest of the outrush, the professor passed like a bolt shot from a catapult; and his last cry came wafted back to me from the forest as I swayed there, drunk with the stupefying perfume: "Don't worry! I'm all right!"

I staggered out into the clearer air towards a figure seen dimly through swirling vapor.

"Are you hurt?" I stammered, clasping Miss Barrison in my arms.

"No—oh no," she said, wringing her hands. "But the professor! I saw him! I could not scream; I could not move! *They* had him!"

"I saw him too," I groaned. "There was not one trace of terror on his face. He was actually smiling."

Overcome at the sublime courage of the man, we wept in each other's arms.

————————————

True to our promise to Professor Farrago, we made the best of our way northward; and it was not a difficult journey by any means, the voyage in the launch across Okeechobee being perfectly simple and the trail to the nearest railroad station but a few easy miles from the landing-place.

Shocking as had been our experience, dreadful as was the calamity which had not only robbed me of a life-long friend, but had also bereaved the entire scientific world, I could not seem to feel that desperate and hopeless grief which the natural decease of a close friend might warrant. No; there remained a vague expectancy which so dominated my sorrow that at moments I became hopeful—nay, sanguine, that I should one day again behold my beloved superior in the flesh. There was something so happy in his last smile, something so artlessly pleased, that I was certain no fear of impending dissolution worried him as he disappeared into the uncharted depth of the unknown Everglades.

I think Miss Barrison agreed with me, too. She appeared to be more or less dazed, which was, of course, quite natural; and during our return voyage across Okeechobee and through the lagoons and forests beyond she was very silent.

When we reached the railroad at Portulacca, a thrifty lemon-growing ranch on the Volusia and Chinkapin Railway, the first thing I did was to present my dog to the station-agent—but I was obliged to give him five dollars before he consented to accept the dog.

However, Miss Barrison interviewed the station-master's wife, a kindly, pitiful soul, who promised to be a good mistress to the creature. We both felt better after that was off our minds; we felt better still when the north-bound train rolled leisurely into the white glare of Portulacca, and presently rolled out again, quite as leisurely, bound, thank Heaven, for that abused aggregation of sinful boroughs called New York.

Except for one young man whom I encountered in the smoker, we had the train to ourselves, a circumstance which, curiously enough, appeared to increase Miss Barrison's depression, and my own as a natural sequence. The circumstances of the taking off of Professor Farrago appeared to engross her thoughts so completely that it made me uneasy during our trip out from Little Sprite—in fact it was growing plainer to me every hour that in her brief acquaintance with that distinguished scientist she had become personally attached to him to an extent that began to worry me. Her personal indignation at the caged Sphyx flared out at unexpected intervals, and there could be no doubt that her unhappiness and resentment were becoming morbid.

I spent an hour or two in the smoking compartment, tenanted only by a single passenger and myself. He was an agreeable young man, although, in the natural acquaintanceship that we struck up, I regretted to learn that he was a writer of popular fiction, returning from Fort Worth, where he had been for the sole purpose of composing a poem on Florida.

I have always, in common with other mentally balanced savants, despised writers of fiction. All scientists harbor a natural antipathy to romance in any form, and that antipathy becomes a deep horror if fiction dares to deal flippantly with the exact sciences, or if some degraded intellect assumes the warrantless liberty of using natural history as the vehicle for silly tales.

Never but once had I been tempted to romance in any form; never but once had sentiment interfered with a passionless transfer of scientific notes to the sanctuary of the unvarnished note-book or the cloister of the juiceless monograph. Nor have I the slightest approach to that superficial and doubtful quality known as literary skill. Once, however, as I sat alone in the middle of the floor, classifying my isopods, I was not only astonished but totally unprepared to find myself repeating aloud a verse that I myself had unconsciously fashioned:

"An isopod  Is a work of God."

Never before in all my life had I made a rhyme; and it worried me for weeks, ringing in my brain day and night, confusing me, interfering with my thoughts.

I said as much to the young man, who only laughed good-naturedly and replied that it was the Creator's purpose to limit certain intellects, nobody knows why, and that it was apparent that mine had not escaped.

"There's one thing, however," he said, "that might be of some interest to you and come within the circumscribed scope of your intelligence."

"And what is that?" I asked, tartly.

"A scientific experience of mine," he said, with a careless laugh. "It's so much stranger than fiction that even Professor Bruce Stoddard, of Columbia, hesitated to credit it."

I looked at the young fellow suspiciously. His bland smile disarmed me, but I did not invite him to relate his experience, although he apparently needed only that encouragement to begin.

"Now, if I could tell it exactly as it occurred," he observed, "and a stenographer could take it down, word for word, exactly as I relate it—"

"It would give me great pleasure to do so," said a quiet voice at the door. We rose at once, removing the cigars from our lips; but Miss Barrison bade us continue smoking, and at a gesture from her we resumed our seats after she had installed herself by the window.

"Really," she said, looking coldly at me, "I couldn't endure the solitude any longer. Isn't there anything to do on this tiresome train?"

"If you had your pad and pencil," I began, maliciously, "you might take down a matter of interest—"

She looked frankly at the young man, who laughed in that pleasant, good-tempered manner of his, and offered to tell us of his alleged scientific experience if we thought it might amuse us sufficiently to vary the dull monotony of the journey north.

"Is it fiction?" I asked, point-blank.

"It is absolute truth," he replied.

I rose and went off to find pad and pencil. When I returned Miss Barrison was laughing at a story which the young man had just finished.

"But," he ended, gravely, "I have practically decided to renounce fiction as a means of livelihood and confine myself to simple, uninteresting statistics and facts."

"I am very glad to hear you say that," I exclaimed, warmly. He bowed, looked at Miss Barrison, and asked her when he might begin his story.

"Whenever you are ready," replied Miss Barrison, smiling in a manner which I had not observed since the disappearance of Professor Farrago. I'll admit that the young fellow was superficially attractive.

"Well, then," he began, modestly, "having no technical ability concerning the affair in question, and having no knowledge of either comparative anatomy or zoology, I am perhaps unfitted to tell this story. But the story is true; the episode occurred under my own eyes—within a few hours' sail of the Battery. And as I was one of the first persons to verify what has long been a theory among scientists, and, moreover, as the result of Professor Holroyd's discovery is to be placed on exhibition in Madison Square Garden on the 20th of next month, I have decided to tell you, as simply as I am able, exactly what occurred.

"I first told the story on April 1, 1903, to the editors of the *North American Review*, *The Popular Science Monthly*, the *Scientific American*, *Nature*, *Outing*, and the *Fossiliferous Magazine*. All these gentlemen rejected it; some curtly informing me that fiction had no place in their columns. When I attempted to explain that it was not fiction, the editors of these periodicals either maintained a contemptuous silence, or bluntly notified me that my literary services and opinions were not desired. But finally, when several publishers offered to take the story as fiction, I cut short all negotiations and decided to publish it myself. Where I am known at all, it is my misfortune to be known as a writer of fiction. This makes it impossible for me to receive a hearing from a scientific audience. I regret it bitterly, because now, when it is too late, I am prepared to prove certain scientific matters of interest, and to produce the proofs. In this case, however, I am fortunate, for nobody can dispute the existence of a thing when the bodily proof is exhibited as evidence.

"This is the story; and if I tell it as I write fiction, it is because I do not know how to tell it otherwise.

"I was walking along the beach below Pine Inlet, on the south shore of Long Island. The railroad and telegraph station is at West Oyster Bay. Everybody who has travelled on the Long Island Railroad knows the station, but few, perhaps, know Pine Inlet. Duck-shooters, of course, are familiar with it; but as there are no hotels there, and nothing to see except salt meadow, salt creek, and a strip of dune and sand, the summer-squatting public may probably be unaware of its existence. The local name for the place is Pine Inlet; the maps give its name as Sand Point, I believe, but anybody at West Oyster Bay can direct you to it. Captain McPeek, who keeps the West Oyster Bay House, drives duck-shooters there in winter. It lies five miles southeast from West Oyster Bay.

"I had walked over that afternoon from Captain McPeek's. There was a reason for my going to Pine Inlet—it embarrasses me to explain it, but the truth is I meditated writing an ode to the ocean. It was out of the question to write it in West Oyster Bay, with the whistle of locomotives in my ears. I knew that Pine Inlet was one of the loneliest places on the Atlantic coast; it is out of sight of everything except leagues of gray ocean. Rarely one might make out fishing-smacks drifting across the horizon. Summer squatters never visited it; sportsmen shunned it, except in winter. Therefore, as I was about to do a bit of poetry, I thought that Pine Inlet was the spot for the deed. So I went there.

"As I was strolling along the beach, biting my pencil reflectively, tremendously impressed by the solitude and the solemn thunder of the surf, a thought occurred to me—how unpleasant it would be if I suddenly stumbled on a summer boarder. As this joyless impossibility flitted across my mind, I rounded a bleak sand-dune.

"A girl stood directly in my path.

"She stared at me as though I had just crawled up out of the sea to bite her. I don't know what my own expression resembled, but I have been given to understand it was idiotic.

"Now I perceived, after a few moments, that the young lady was frightened, and I knew I ought to say something civil. So I said, 'Are there many mosquitoes here?'

"'No,' she replied, with a slight quiver in her voice; 'I have only seen one, and it was biting somebody else.'

"The conversation seemed so futile, and the young lady appeared to be more nervous than before. I had an impulse to say, 'Do not run; I have breakfasted,' for she seemed to be meditating a flight into the breakers. What I did say was: 'I did not know anybody was here. I do not intend to intrude. I come from Captain McPeek's, and I am writing an ode to the ocean.' After I had said this it seemed to ring in my ears like, 'I come from Table Mountain, and my name is Truthful James.'

"I glanced timidly at her.

"'She's thinking of the same thing,' said I to myself.

"However, the young lady seemed to be a trifle reassured. I noticed she drew a sigh of relief and looked at my shoes. She looked so long that it made me suspicious, and I also examined my shoes. They seemed to be in a fair state of repair.

"'I—I am sorry,' she said, 'but would you mind not walking on the beach?'

"This was sudden. I had intended to retire and leave the beach to her, but I did not fancy being driven away so abruptly.

"'Dear me!' she cried; 'you don't understand. I do not—I would not think for a moment of asking you to leave Pine Inlet. I merely ventured to request you to walk on the dunes. I am so afraid that your footprints may obliterate the impressions that my father is studying.'

"'Oh!' said I, looking about me as though I had been caught in the middle of a flower-bed; 'really I did not notice any impressions. Impressions of what?'

"'I don't know,' she said, smiling a little at my awkward pose. 'If you step this way in a straight line you can do no damage.'

"I did as she bade me. I suppose my movements resembled the gait of a wet peacock. Possibly they recalled the delicate manœuvres of the kangaroo. Anyway, she laughed.

"This seriously annoyed me. I had been at a disadvantage; I walk well enough when let alone.

"'You can scarcely expect,' said I, 'that a man absorbed in his own ideas could notice impressions on the sand. I trust I have obliterated nothing.'

"As I said this I looked back at the long line of footprints stretching away in prospective across the sand. They were my own. How large they looked! Was that what she was laughing at?

"'I wish to explain,' she said, gravely, looking at the point of her parasol. 'I am very sorry to be obliged to warn you—to ask you to forego the pleasure of strolling on a beach that does not belong to me. Perhaps,' she continued, in sudden alarm, 'perhaps this beach belongs to you?'

"'The beach? Oh no,' I said.

"'But—but you were going to write poems about it?'

"'Only one—and that does not necessitate owning the beach. I have observed,' said I, frankly, 'that the people who own nothing write many poems about it.'

"She looked at me seriously.

"'I write many poems,' I added.

"She laughed doubtfully.

"'Would you rather I went away?' I asked, politely. 'My family is respectable,' I added; and I told her my name.

"'Oh! Then you wrote *Culled Cowslips* and *Faded Fig-Leaves* and you imitate Maeterlinck, and you—Oh, I know lots of people that you know;' she cried, with every symptom of relief; 'and you know my brother.'

"'I am the author,' said I, coldly, 'of *Culled Cowslips*, but *Faded Fig-Leaves* was an earlier work, which I no longer recognize, and I should be grateful to you if you would be kind enough to deny that I ever imitated Maeterlinck. Possibly,' I added, 'he imitates me.'

"She was very quiet, and I saw she was sorry.

"'Never mind,' I said, magnanimously, 'you probably are not familiar with modern literature. If I knew your name I should ask permission to present myself.'

"'Why, I am Daisy Holroyd,' she said.

"'What! Jack Holroyd's little sister?'

"'Little?' she cried.

"'I didn't mean that,' said I. 'You know that your brother and I were great friends in Paris—'

"'I know,' she said, significantly.

"'Ahem! Of course,' I said, 'Jack and I were inseparable—'

"'Except when shut in separate cells,' said Miss Holroyd, coldly.

"This unfeeling allusion to the unfortunate termination of a Latin-Quarter celebration hurt me.

"'The police,' said I, 'were too officious.'

"'So Jack says,' replied Miss Holroyd, demurely.

"We had unconsciously moved on along the sand-hills, side by side, as we spoke.

"'To think,' I repeated, 'that I should meet Jack's little—'

"'Please,' she said, 'you are only three years my senior.'

"She opened the sunshade and tipped it over one shoulder. It was white, and had spots and posies on it.

"'Jack sends us every new book you write,' she observed. 'I do not approve of some things you write.'

"'Modern school,' I mumbled.

"'That is no excuse,' she said, severely; 'Anthony Trollope didn't do it.'

"The foam spume from the breakers was drifting across the dunes, and the little tip-up snipe ran along the beach and teetered and whistled and spread their white-barred wings for a low, straight flight across the shingle, only to tip and run and sail on again. The salt sea-wind whistled and curled through the crested waves, blowing in perfumed puffs across thickets of sweet bay and cedar. As we passed through the crackling juicy-stemmed marsh-weed myriads of fiddler crabs raised their fore-claws in warning and backed away, rustling, through the reeds, aggressive, protesting.

"'Like millions of pygmy Ajaxes defying the lightning,' I said.

"Miss Holroyd laughed.

"'Now I never imagined that authors were clever except in print,' she said.

"She was a most extraordinary girl.

"'I suppose,' she observed, after a moment's silence—'I suppose I am taking you to my father.'

"'Delighted!' I mumbled. 'H'm! I had the honor of meeting Professor Holroyd in Paris.'

"'Yes; he bailed you and Jack out,' said Miss Holroyd, serenely.

"The silence was too painful to last.

"'Captain McPeek is an interesting man,' I said. I spoke more loudly than I intended. I may have been nervous.

"'Yes,' said Daisy Holroyd, 'but he has a most singular hotel clerk.'

"'You mean Mr. Frisby?'

"'I do.'

"'Yes,' I admitted, 'Mr. Frisby is queer. He was once a bill-poster.'

"'I know it!' exclaimed Daisy Holroyd, with some heat. 'He ruins landscapes whenever he has an opportunity. Do you know that he has a passion for bill-posting? He has; he posts bills for the pure pleasure of it, just as you play golf, or tennis, or squash.'

"'But he's a hotel clerk now,' I said; 'nobody employs him to post bills.'

"'I know it! He does it all by himself for the pure pleasure of it. Papa has engaged him to come down here for two weeks, and I dread it,' said the girl.

"What Professor Holroyd might want of Frisby I had not the faintest notion. I suppose Miss Holroyd noticed the bewilderment in my face, for she laughed and nodded her head twice.

"'Not only Mr. Frisby, but Captain McPeek also,' she said.

"'You don't mean to say that Captain McPeek is going to close his hotel!' I exclaimed.

"My trunk was there. It contained guarantees of my respectability.

"'Oh no; his wife will keep it open,' replied the girl. 'Look! you can see papa now. He's digging.'

"'Where?' I blurted out.

"I remembered Professor Holroyd as a prim, spectacled gentleman, with close-cut, snowy beard and a clerical allure. The man I saw digging wore green goggles, a jersey, a battered sou'wester, and hip-boots of rubber. He was delving in the muck of the salt meadow, his face streaming with perspiration, his boots and jersey splashed with unpleasant-looking mud. He glanced up as we approached, shading his eyes with a sunburned hand.

"'Papa, dear,' said Miss Holroyd, 'here is Jack's friend, whom you bailed out of Mazas.'

"The introduction was startling. I turned crimson with mortification. The professor was very decent about it; he called me by name at once. Then he looked at his spade. It was clear he considered me a nuisance and wished to go on with his digging.

"'I suppose,' he said, 'you are still writing?'

"'A little,' I replied, trying not to speak sarcastically. My output had rivalled that of 'The Duchess'—in quantity, I mean.

"'I seldom read—fiction,' he said, looking restlessly at the hole in the ground.

"Miss Holroyd came to my rescue.

"'That was a charming story you wrote last,' she said. 'Papa should read it—you should, papa; it's all about a fossil.'

"We both looked narrowly at Miss Holroyd. Her smile was guileless.

"'Fossils!' repeated the professor. 'Do you care for fossils?'

"'Very much,' said I.

"Now I am not perfectly sure what my object was in lying. I looked at Daisy Holroyd's dark-fringed eyes. They were very grave.

"'Fossils,' said I, 'are my hobby.'

"I think Miss Holroyd winced a little at this. I did not care. I went on:

"'I have seldom had the opportunity to study the subject, but, as a boy, I collected flint arrow-heads—"

"'Flint arrow-heads!' said the professor coldly.

"'Yes; they were the nearest things to fossils obtainable,' I replied, marvelling at my own mendacity.

"The professor looked into the hole. I also looked. I could see nothing in it. 'He's digging for fossils,' thought I to myself.

"'Perhaps,' said the professor, cautiously, 'you might wish to aid me in a little research—that is to say, if you have an inclination for fossils.' The double-entendre was not lost upon me.

"'I have read all your books so eagerly,' said I, 'that to join you, to be of service to you in any research, however difficult and trying, would be an honor and a privilege that I never dared to hope for.'

"'That,' thought I to myself, 'will do its own work.'

"But the professor was still suspicious. How could he help it, when he remembered Jack's escapades, in which my name was always blended! Doubtless he was satisfied that my influence on Jack was evil. The contrary was the case, too.

"'Fossils,' he said, worrying the edge of the excavation with his spade—'fossils are not things to be lightly considered.'

"'No, indeed!' I protested.

"'Fossils are the most interesting as well as puzzling things in the world,' said he.

"'They are!' I cried, enthusiastically.

"'But I am not looking for fossils,' observed the professor, mildly.

"This was a facer. I looked at Daisy Holroyd. She bit her lip and fixed her eyes on the sea. Her eyes were wonderful eyes.

"'Did you think I was digging for fossils in a salt meadow?' queried the professor. 'You can have read very little about the subject. I am digging for something quite different.'

"I was silent. I knew that my face was flushed. I longed to say, 'Well, what the devil are you digging for?' but I only stared into the hole as though hypnotized.

"'Captain McPeek and Frisby ought to be here,' he said, looking first at Daisy and then across the meadows.

"I ached to ask him why he had subpœnaed Captain McPeek and Frisby.

"'They are coming,' said Daisy, shading her eyes. 'Do you see the speck on the meadows?'

"'It may be a mud-hen,' said the professor.

"'Miss Holroyd is right,' I said. 'A wagon and team and two men are coming from the north. There's a dog beside the wagon—it's that miserable yellow dog of Frisby's.'

"'Good gracious!' cried the professor, 'you don't mean to tell me that you see all that at such a distance?'

"'Why not?' I said.

"'I see nothing,' he insisted.

"'You will see that I'm right, presently,' I laughed.

"The professor removed his blue goggles and rubbed them, glancing obliquely at me.

"'Haven't you heard what extraordinary eyesight duck-shooters have?' said his daughter, looking back at her father. 'Jack says that he can tell exactly what kind of a duck is flying before most people could see anything at all in the sky.'

"'It's true,' I said; 'it comes to anybody, I fancy, who has had practice.'

"The professor regarded me with a new interest. There was inspiration in his eyes. He turned towards the ocean. For a long time he stared at the tossing waves on the beach, then he looked far out to where the horizon met the sea.

"'Are there any ducks out there?' he asked, at last.

"'Yes,' said I, scanning the sea, 'there are.'

"He produced a pair of binoculars from his coat-tail pocket, adjusted them, and raised them to his eyes.

"'H'm! What sort of ducks?'

"I looked more carefully, holding both hands over my forehead.

"'Surf-ducks and widgeon. There is one bufflehead among them—no, two; the rest are coots,' I replied.

"'This,' cried the professor, 'is most astonishing. I have good eyes, but I can't see a blessed thing without these binoculars!'

"'It's not extraordinary,' said I; 'the surf-ducks and coots any novice might recognize; the widgeon and buffleheads I should not have been able to name unless they had risen from the water. It is easy to tell any duck when it is flying, even though it looks no bigger than a black pin-point.'

"But the professor insisted that it was marvellous, and he said that I might render him invaluable service if I would consent to come and camp at Pine Inlet for a few weeks.

"I looked at his daughter, but she turned her back. Her back was beautifully moulded. Her gown fitted also.

"'Camp out here?' I repeated, pretending to be unpleasantly surprised.

"'I do not think he would care to,' said Miss Holroyd, without turning.

"I had not expected that.

"'Above all things,' said I, in a clear, pleasant voice, 'I like to camp out.'

"She said nothing.

"'It is not exactly camping,' said the professor. 'Come, you shall see our conservatory. Daisy, come, dear! You must put on a heavier frock; it is getting towards sundown.'

"At that moment, over a near dune, two horses' heads appeared, followed by two human heads, then a wagon, then a yellow dog.

"I turned triumphantly to the professor.

"'You are the very man I want,' he muttered—'the very man—the very man.'

"I looked at Daisy Holroyd. She returned my glance with a defiant little smile.

"'Waal,' said Captain McPeek, driving up, 'here we be! Git out, Frisby.'

"Frisby, fat, nervous, and sentimental, hopped out of the cart.

"'Come,' said the professor, impatiently moving across the dunes. I walked with Daisy Holroyd. McPeek and Frisby followed. The yellow dog walked by himself.

---

# XVIII

"The sun was dipping into the sea as we trudged across the meadows towards a high, dome-shaped dune covered with cedars and thickets of sweet bay. I saw no sign of habitation among the sand-hills. Far as the eye could reach, nothing broke the gray line of sea and sky save the squat dunes crowned with stunted cedars.

"Then, as we rounded the base of the dune, we almost walked into the door of a house. My amazement amused Miss Holroyd, and I noticed also a touch of malice in her pretty eyes. But she said nothing, following her father into the house, with the slightest possible gesture to me. Was it invitation or was it menace?

"The house was merely a light wooden frame, covered with some waterproof stuff that looked like a mixture of rubber and tar. Over this—in fact, over the whole roof—was pitched an awning of heavy sail-cloth. I noticed that the house was anchored to the sand by chains, already rusted red. But this one-storied house was not the only building nestling in the south shelter of the big dune. A hundred feet away stood another structure—long, low, also built of wood. It had rows on rows of round port-holes on every side. The ports were fitted with heavy glass, hinged to swing open if necessary. A single, big double door occupied the front.

"Behind this long, low building was still another, a mere shed. Smoke rose from the sheet-iron chimney. There was somebody moving about inside the open door.

"As I stood gaping at this mushroom hamlet the professor appeared at the door and asked me to enter. I stepped in at once.

"The house was much larger than I had imagined. A straight hallway ran through the centre from east to west. On either side of this hallway were rooms, the doors swinging wide open. I counted three doors on each side; the three on the south appeared to be bedrooms.

"The professor ushered me into a room on the north side, where I found Captain McPeek and Frisby sitting at a table, upon which were drawings and sketches of articulated animals and fishes.

"'You see, McPeek,' said the professor, 'we only wanted one more man, and I think I've got him—Haven't I?' turning eagerly to me.

"'Why, yes,' I said, laughing; 'this is delightful. Am I invited to stay here?'

"'Your bedroom is the third on the south side; everything is ready. McPeek, you can bring his trunk to-morrow, can't you?' demanded the professor.

"The red-faced captain nodded, and shifted a quid.

"'Then it's all settled,' said the professor, and he drew a sigh of satisfaction. 'You see,' he said, turning to me, 'I was at my wit's end to know whom to trust. I never thought of you. Jack's out in China, and I didn't dare trust anybody in my own profession. All you care about is writing verses and stories, isn't it?'

"'I like to shoot,' I replied, mildly.

"'Just the thing!' he cried, beaming at us all in turn. 'Now I can see no reason why we should not progress rapidly. McPeek, you and Frisby must get those boxes up here before dark. Dinner will be ready before you have finished unloading. Dick, you will wish to go to your room first.'

"My name isn't Dick, but he spoke so kindly, and beamed upon me in such a fatherly manner, that I let it go. I had occasion to correct him afterwards, several times, but he always forgot the next minute. He calls me Dick to this day.

"It was dark when Professor Holroyd, his daughter, and I sat down to dinner. The room was the same in which I had noticed the drawings of beast and bird, but the round table had been extended into an oval, and neatly spread with dainty linen and silver.

"A fresh-cheeked Swedish girl appeared from a farther room, bearing the soup. The professor ladled it out, still beaming.

"'Now, this is very delightful—isn't it, Daisy?' he said.

"'Very,' said Miss Holroyd, with a tinge of irony.

"'Very,' I repeated, heartily.

"'I suppose,' said the professor, nodding mysteriously at his daughter, 'that Dick knows nothing of what we're about down here?'

"'I suppose,' said Miss Holroyd, 'that he thinks we are digging for fossils.'

"I looked at my plate. She might have spared me that.

"'Well, well,' said her father, smiling to himself, 'he shall know everything by morning. You'll be astonished, Dick, my boy.'

"'His name isn't Dick,' corrected Daisy.

"The professor said, 'Isn't it?' in an absent-minded way, and relapsed into contemplation of my necktie.

"I asked Miss Holroyd a few questions about Jack, and was informed that he had given up law and entered the consular service—as what, I did not dare ask, for I know what our consular service is.

"'In China,' said Daisy.

"'Choo Choo is the name of the city,' added her father, proudly; 'it's the terminus of the new trans-Siberian railway.'

"'It's on the Pong Ping,' said Daisy.

"'He's vice-consul,' added the professor, triumphantly.

"'He'll make a good one,' I observed. I knew Jack. I pitied his consul.

"So we chatted on about my old playmate, until Freda, the red-cheeked maid, brought coffee, and the professor lighted a cigar, with a little bow to his daughter.

"'Of course, you don't smoke,' she said to me, with a glimmer of malice in her eyes.

"'He mustn't,' interposed the professor, hastily; 'it will make his hand tremble.'

"'No, it won't,' said I, laughing; 'but my hand will shake if I don't smoke. Are you going to employ me as a draughtsman?'

"'You'll know to-morrow,' he chuckled, with a mysterious smile at his daughter. 'Daisy, give him my best cigars—put the box here on the table. We can't afford to have his hand tremble.'

"Miss Holroyd rose and crossed the hallway to her father's room, returning presently with a box of promising-looking cigars.

"'I don't think he knows what is good for him,' she said. 'He should smoke only one every day.'

"It was hard to bear. I am not vindictive, but I decided to treasure up a few of Miss Holroyd's gentle taunts. My intimacy with her brother was certainly a disadvantage to me now. Jack had apparently been talking too much, and his sister appeared to be thoroughly acquainted with my past. It was a disadvantage. I remembered her vaguely as a girl with long braids, who used to come on Sundays with her father and take tea with us in our rooms. Then she went to Germany to school, and Jack and I employed our Sunday evenings otherwise. It is true that I regarded her weekly visits as a species of infliction, but I did not think I ever showed it.

"'It is strange,' said I, 'that you did not recognize me at once, Miss Holroyd. Have I changed so greatly in five years?'

"'You wore a pointed French beard in Paris,' she said—'a very downy one. And you never stayed to tea but twice, and then you only spoke once.'

"'Oh!' said I, blankly. 'What did I say?'

"'You asked me if I liked plums,' said Daisy, bursting into an irresistible ripple of laughter.

"I saw that I must have made the same sort of an ass of myself that most boys of eighteen do.

"It was too bad. I never thought about the future in those days. Who could have imagined that little Daisy Holroyd would have grown up into this bewildering young lady? It was really too bad. Presently the professor retired to his room, carrying with him an armful of drawings, and bidding us not to sit up late. When he closed his door Miss Holroyd turned to me.

"'Papa will work over those drawings until midnight,' she said, with a despairing smile.

"'It isn't good for him,' I said. 'What are the drawings?'

"'You may know to-morrow,' she answered, leaning forward on the table and shading her face with one hand. 'Tell me about yourself and Jack in Paris.'

"I looked at her suspiciously.

"'What! There isn't much to tell. We studied. Jack went to the law school, and I attended—er—oh, all sorts of schools.'

"'Did you? Surely you gave yourself a little recreation occasionally?'

"'Occasionally,' I nodded.

"'I am afraid you and Jack studied too hard.'

"'That may be,' said I, looking meek.

"'Especially about fossils.'

"I couldn't stand that.

"'Miss Holroyd,' I said, 'I do care for fossils. You may think that I am a humbug, but I have a perfect mania for fossils—now.'

"'Since when?'

"'About an hour ago,' I said, airily. Out of the corner of my eye I saw that she had flushed up. It pleased me.

"'You will soon tire of the experiment,' she said, with a dangerous smile.

"'Oh, I may,' I replied, indifferently.

"She drew back. The movement was scarcely perceptible, but I noticed it, and she knew I did.

"The atmosphere was vaguely hostile. One feels such mental conditions and changes instantly. I picked up a chess-board, opened it, set up the pieces with elaborate care, and began to move, first the white, then the black. Miss Holroyd watched me coldly at first, but after a dozen moves she became interested and leaned a shade nearer. I moved a black pawn forward.

"'Why do you do that?' said Daisy.

"'Because,' said I, 'the white queen threatens the pawn.'

"'It was an aggressive move,' she insisted.

"'Purely defensive,' I said. 'If her white highness will let the pawn alone, the pawn will let the queen alone.'

"Miss Holroyd rested her chin on her wrist and gazed steadily at the board. She was flushing furiously, but she held her ground.

"'If the white queen doesn't block that pawn, the pawn may become dangerous,' she said, coldly.

"I laughed, and closed up the board with a snap.

"'True,' I said, 'it might even take the queen.' After a moment's silence I asked, 'What would you do in that case, Miss Holroyd?'

"'I should resign,' she said, serenely; then, realizing what she had said, she lost her self-possession for a second, and cried: 'No, indeed! I should fight to the bitter end! I mean—'

"'What?' I asked, lingering over my revenge.

"'I mean,' she said, slowly, 'that your black pawn would never have the chance— never! I should take it immediately.'

"'I believe you would,' said I, smiling; 'so we'll call the game yours, and—the pawn captured.'

"'I don't want it,' she exclaimed. 'A pawn is worthless.'

"'Except when it's in the king row.'

"'Chess is most interesting,' she observed, sedately. She had completely recovered her self-possession. Still I saw that she now had a certain respect for my defensive powers. It was very soothing to me.

"'You know,' said I, gravely, 'that I am fonder of Jack than of anybody. That's the reason we never write each other, except to borrow things. I am afraid that when I was a young cub in France I was not an attractive personality.'

"'On the contrary,' said Daisy, smiling, 'I thought you were very big and very perfect. I had illusions. I wept often when I went home and remembered that you never took the trouble to speak to me but once.'

"'I was a cub,' I said—'not selfish and brutal, but I didn't understand school-girls. I never had any sisters, and I didn't know what to say to very young girls. If I had imagined that you felt hurt—'

"'Oh, I did—five years ago. Afterwards I laughed at the whole thing.'

"'Laughed?' I repeated, vaguely disappointed.

"'Why, of course. I was very easily hurt when I was a child. I think I have out-grown it.'

"The soft curve of her sensitive mouth contradicted her.

"'Will you forgive me now?' I asked.

"'Yes. I had forgotten the whole thing until I met you an hour or so ago.'

"There was something that had a ring not entirely genuine in this speech. I noticed it, but forgot it the next moment.

"Presently she rose, touched her hair with the tip of one finger, and walked to the door.

"'Good-night,' she said.

"'Good-night,' said I, opening the door for her to pass.

---

# XIX

"The sea was a sheet of silver tinged with pink. The tremendous arch of the sky was all shimmering and glimmering with the promise of the sun. Already the mist above, flecked with clustered clouds, flushed with rose color and dull gold. I heard the low splash of the waves breaking and curling across the beach. A wandering breeze, fresh and fragrant, blew the curtains of my window. There was the scent of sweet bay in the room, and everywhere the subtle, nameless perfume of the sea.

"When at last I stood upon the shore, the air and sea were all a-glimmer in a rosy light, deepening to crimson in the zenith. Along the beach I saw a little cove, shelving and all a-shine, where shallow waves washed with a mellow sound. Fine as dusted gold the shingle glowed, and the thin film of water rose, receded, crept up again a little higher, and again flowed back, with the low hiss of snowy foam and gilded bubbles breaking.

"I stood a little while quiet, my eyes upon the water, the invitation of the ocean in my ears, vague and sweet as the murmur of a shell. Then I looked at my bathing-suit and towels.

"'In we go!' said I, aloud. A second later the prophecy was fulfilled.

"I swam far out to sea, and as I swam the waters all around me turned to gold. The sun had risen.

"There is a fragrance in the sea at dawn that none can name. Whitethorn a-bloom in May, sedges a-sway, and scented rushes rustling in an inland wind recall the sea to me—I can't say why.

"Far out at sea I raised myself, swung around, dived, and set out again for shore, striking strong strokes until the necked foam flew. And when at last I shot through the breakers, I laughed aloud and sprang upon the beach, breathless and happy. Then from the ocean came another cry, clear, joyous, and a white arm rose in the air.

"She came drifting in with the waves like a white sea-sprite, laughing at me, and I plunged into the breakers again to join her.

"Side by side we swam along the coast, just outside the breakers, until in the next cove we saw the flutter of her maid's cap-strings.

"'I will beat you to breakfast!' she cried, as I rested, watching her glide up along the beach.

"'Done!' said I—'for a sea-shell!'

"'Done!' she called, across the water.

"I made good speed along the shore, and I was not long in dressing, but when I entered the dining-room she was there, demure, smiling, exquisite in her cool, white frock.

"'The sea-shell is yours,' said I. 'I hope I can find one with a pearl in it.'

"The professor hurried in before she could reply. He greeted me very cordially, but there was an abstracted air about him, and he called me Dick until I recognized that remonstrance was useless. He was not long over his coffee and rolls.

"'McPeek and Frisby will return with the last load, including your trunk, by early afternoon,' he said, rising and picking up his bundle of drawings. 'I haven't time to explain to you what we are doing, Dick, but Daisy will take you about and instruct you. She will give you the rifle standing in my room—it's a good Winchester. I have sent for an 'Express' for you, big enough to knock over any elephant in India. Daisy, take him through the sheds and tell him everything. Luncheon is at noon. Do you usually take luncheon, Dick?'

"'When I am permitted,' I smiled.

"'Well,' said the professor, doubtfully, 'you mustn't come back here for it. Freda can take you what you want. Is your hand unsteady after eating?'

"'Why, papa!' said Daisy. 'Do you intend to starve him?'

"We all laughed.

"The professor tucked his drawings into a capacious pocket, pulled his sea-boots up to his hips, seized a spade, and left, nodding to us as though he were thinking of something else.

"We went to the door and watched him across the salt meadows until the distant sand-dune hid him.

"'Come,' said Daisy Holroyd, 'I am going to take you to the shop.'

"She put on a broad-brimmed straw hat, a distractingly pretty combination of filmy cool stuffs, and led the way to the long, low structure that I had noticed the evening before.

"The interior was lighted by the numberless little port-holes, and I could see everything plainly. I acknowledge I was nonplussed by what I did see.

"In the centre of the shed, which must have been at least a hundred feet long, stood what I thought at first was the skeleton of an enormous whale. After a moment's silent contemplation of the thing I saw that it could not be a whale, for the frames of two gigantic, batlike wings rose from each shoulder. Also I noticed that the animal possessed legs—four of them—with most unpleasant-looking webbed claws fully eight feet long. The bony framework of the head, too, resembled something between a crocodile and a monstrous snapping-turtle. The walls of the shanty were hung with drawings and blue prints. A man dressed in white linen was tinkering with the vertebrae of the lizard-like tail.

"'Where on earth did such a reptile come from?' I asked at length.

"'Oh, it's not real!' said Daisy, scornfully; 'it's papier-maché.'

"'I see,' said I; 'a stage prop.'

"'A what?' asked Daisy, in hurt astonishment.

"'Why, a—a sort of Siegfried dragon—a what's-his-name—er, Pfafner, or Peffer, or—'

"'If my father heard you say such things he would dislike you,' said Daisy. She looked grieved, and moved towards the door. I apologized—for what, I knew not—and we became reconciled. She ran into her father's room and brought me the rifle, a very good Winchester. She also gave me a cartridge-belt, full.

"'Now,' she smiled, 'I shall take you to your observatory, and when we arrive you are to begin your duty at once.'

"'And that duty?' I ventured, shouldering the rifle.

"'That duty is to watch the ocean. I shall then explain the whole affair—but you mustn't look at me while I speak; you must watch the sea.'

"'This,' said I, 'is hardship. I had rather go without the luncheon.'

"I do not think she was offended at my speech; still she frowned for almost three seconds.

"We passed through acres of sweet bay and spear grass, sometimes skirting thickets of twisted cedars, sometimes walking in the full glare of the morning sun, sinking into shifting sand where sun-scorched shells crackled under our feet, and sun-browned sea-weed glistened, bronzed and iridescent. Then, as we climbed a little hill, the sea-wind freshened in our faces, and lo! the ocean lay below us, far-stretching as the eye could reach, glittering, magnificent.

"Daisy sat down flat on the sand. It takes a clever girl to do that and retain the respectful deference due her from men. It takes a graceful girl to accomplish it triumphantly when a man is looking.

"'You must sit beside me,' she said—as though it would prove irksome to me.

"'Now,' she continued, 'you must watch the water while I am talking.'

"I nodded.

"'Why don't you do it, then?' she asked.

"I succeeded in wrenching my head towards the ocean, although I felt sure it would swing gradually round again in spite of me.

"'To begin with,' said Daisy Holroyd, 'there's a thing in that ocean that would astonish you if you saw it. Turn your head!'

"'I am,' I said, meekly.

"'Did you hear what I said?'

"'Yes—er—a thing in the ocean that's going to astonish me.' Visions of mermaids rose before me.

"'The thing,' said Daisy, 'is a thermosaurus!'

"I nodded vaguely, as though anticipating a delightful introduction to a nautical friend.

"'You don't seem astonished,' she said, reproachfully.

"'Why should I be?' I asked.

"'Please turn your eyes towards the water. Suppose a thermosaurus should look out of the waves!'

"'Well,' said I, 'in that case the pleasure would be mutual.'

"She frowned and bit her upper lip.

"'Do you know what a thermosaurus is?' she asked.

"'If I am to guess,' said I, 'I guess it's a jelly-fish.'

"'It's that big, ugly, horrible creature that I showed you in the shed!' cried Daisy, impatiently.

"'Eh!' I stammered.

"'Not papier-maché, either,' she continued, excitedly; 'it's a real one.'

"This was pleasant news. I glanced instinctively at my rifle and then at the ocean.

"'Well,' said I at last, 'it strikes me that you and I resemble a pair of Andromedas waiting to be swallowed. This rifle won't stop a beast, a live beast, like that Nibelung-en dragon of yours.'

"'Yes, it will,' she said; 'it's not an ordinary rifle.'

"Then, for the first time, I noticed, just below the magazine, a cylindrical attach-ment that was strange to me.

"'Now, if you will watch the sea very carefully, and will promise not to look at me,' said Daisy, 'I will try to explain.'

"She did not wait for me to promise, but went on eagerly, a sparkle of excitement in her blue eyes:

"'You know, of all the fossil remains of the great batlike and lizard-like creatures that inhabited the earth ages and ages ago, the bones of the gigantic saurians are the most interesting. I think they used to splash about the water and fly over the land during the carboniferous period; anyway, it doesn't matter. Of course you have seen pictures of reconstructed creatures such as the ichthyosaurus, the plesiosaurus, the anthracosaurus, and the thermosaurus?'

"I nodded, trying to keep my eyes from hers.

"'And you know that the remains of the thermosaurus were first discovered and reconstructed by papa?'

"'Yes,' said I. There was no use in saying no.

"'I am glad you do. Now, papa has proved that this creature lived entirely in the Gulf Stream, emerging for occasional flights across an ocean or two. Can you imagine how he proved it?'

"'No,' said I, resolutely pointing my nose at the ocean.

"'He proved it by a minute examination of the microscopical shells found among the ribs of the thermosaurus. These shells contained little creatures that live only in the warm waters of the Gulf Stream. They were the food of the thermosaurus.'

"'It was rather slender rations for a thing like that, wasn't it? Did he ever swallow bigger food—er—men?'

"'Oh yes. Tons of fossil bones from prehistoric men are also found in the interior of the thermosaurus.'

"'Then,' said I, 'you, at least, had better go back to Captain McPeek's—'

"'Please turn around; don't be so foolish. I didn't say there was a live thermosaurus in the water, did I?'

"'Isn't there?'

"'Why, no!'

"My relief was genuine, but I thought of the rifle and looked suspiciously out to sea.

"'What's the Winchester for?' I asked.

"'Listen, and I will explain. Papa has found out—how, I do not exactly understand—that there is in the waters of the Gulf Stream the body of a thermosaurus. The creature must have been alive within a year or so. The impenetrable scale-armor that covers its body has, as far as papa knows, prevented its disintegration. We know that it is there still, or was there within a few months. Papa has reports and sworn depositions from steamer captains and seamen from a dozen different vessels, all corroborating one another in essential details. These stories, of course, get into the newspapers—sea-serpent stories—but papa knows that they confirm his theory that the huge body of this reptile is swinging along somewhere in the Gulf Stream.'

"She opened her sunshade and held it over her. I noticed that she deigned to give me the benefit of about one-eighth of it.

"'Your duty with that rifle is this: if we are fortunate enough to see the body of the thermosaurus come floating by, you are to take good aim and fire—fire rapidly every bullet in the magazine; then reload and fire again, and reload and fire as long as you have any cartridges left.'

"'A self-feeding Maxim is what I should have,' I said, with gentle sarcasm. 'Well, and suppose I make a sieve of this big lizard?'

"'Do you see these rings in the sand?' she asked.

"Sure enough, somebody had driven heavy piles deep into the sand all around us, and to the tops of these piles were attached steel rings, half buried under the spear-grass. We sat almost exactly in the centre of a circle of these rings.

"'The reason is this,' said Daisy; 'every bullet in your cartridges is steel-tipped and armor-piercing. To the base of each bullet is attached a thin wire of pallium. Pallium is that new metal, a thread of which, drawn out into finest wire, will hold a ton of iron suspended. Every bullet is fitted with minute coils of miles of this wire. When the bullet leaves the rifle it spins out this wire as a shot from a life-saver's mortar spins out and carries the life-line to a wrecked ship. The end of each coil of wire is attached to that cylinder under the magazine of your rifle. As soon as the shell is automatically ejected this wire flies out also. A bit of scarlet tape is fixed to the end, so that it will be easy to pick up. There is also a snap-clasp on the end, and this clasp fits those rings that you see in the sand. Now, when you begin firing, it is my duty to run and pick up the wire ends and attach them to the rings. Then, you see, we have the body of the thermosaurus full of bullets, every bullet anchored to the shore by tiny wires, each of which could easily hold a ton's strain.'

"I looked at her in amazement.

"'Then,' she added, calmly, 'we have captured the thermosaurus.'

"'Your father,' said I, at length, 'must have spent years of labor over this preparation.'

"'It is the work of a lifetime,' she said, simply.

"My face, I suppose, showed my misgivings.

"'It must not fail,' she added.

"'But—but we are nowhere near the Gulf Stream,' I ventured.

"Her face brightened, and she frankly held the sunshade over us both.

"'Ah, you don't know,' she said, 'what else papa has discovered. Would you believe that he has found a loop in the Gulf Stream—a genuine loop—that swings in here just outside of the breakers below? It is true! Everybody on Long Island knows that there is a warm current off the coast, but nobody imagined it was merely a sort of backwater from the Gulf Stream that formed a great circular mill-race around the cone of a subterranean volcano, and rejoined the Gulf Stream off Cape Albatross. But it is! That is why papa bought a yacht three years ago and sailed about for two years so mysteriously. Oh, I did want to go with him so much!'

"'This,' said I, 'is most astonishing.'

"She leaned enthusiastically towards me, her lovely face aglow.

"'Isn't it?' she said; 'and to think that you and papa and I are the only people in the whole world who know this!'

"To be included in such a triology was very delightful.

"'Papa is writing the whole thing—I mean about the currents. He also has in preparation sixteen volumes on the thermosaurus. He said this morning that he was going to ask you to write the story first for some scientific magazine. He is certain that Professor Bruce Stoddard, of Columbia, will write the pamphlets necessary. This will give papa time to attend to the sixteen-volume work, which he expects to finish in three years.'

"'Let us first,' said I, laughing, 'catch our thermosaurus.'

"'We must not fail,' she said, wistfully.

"'We shall not fail,' I said, 'for I promise to sit on this sand-hill as long as I live—until a thermosaurus appears—if that is your wish, Miss Holroyd.'

"Our eyes met for an instant. She did not chide me, either, for not looking at the ocean. Her eyes were bluer, anyway.

"'I suppose,' she said, bending her head and absently pouring sand between her fingers—'I suppose you think me a blue-stocking, or something odious?'

"'Not exactly,' I said. There was an emphasis in my voice that made her color. After a moment she laid the sunshade down, still open.

"'May I hold it?' I asked.

"She nodded almost imperceptibly.

"The ocean had turned a deep marine blue, verging on purple, that heralded a scorching afternoon. The wind died away; the odor of cedar and sweet-bay hung heavy in the air.

"In the sand at our feet an iridescent flower-beetle crawled, its metallic green-and-blue wings burning like a spark. Great gnats, with filmy, glittering wings, danced aimlessly above the young golden-rod; burnished crickets, inquisitive, timid, ran from under chips of driftwood, waved their antennæ at us, and ran back again. One by one the marbled tiger-beetles tumbled at our feet, dazed from the exertion of an aërial flight, then scrambled and ran a little way, or darted into the wire grass, where great, brilliant spiders eyed them askance from their gossamer hammocks.

"Far out at sea the white gulls floated and drifted on the water, or sailed up into the air to flap lazily for a moment and settle back among the waves. Strings of black surf-ducks passed, their strong wings tipping the surface of the water; single wandering coots whirled from the breakers into lonely flight towards the horizon.

"We lay and watched the little ring-necks running along the water's edge, now backing away from the incoming tide, now boldly wading after the undertow. The harmony of silence, the deep perfume, the mystery of waiting for that something that all await—what is it? love? death? or only the miracle of another morrow?—troubled me with vague restlessness. As sunlight casts shadows, happiness, too, throws a shadow, an the shadow is sadness.

"And so the morning wore away until Freda came with a cool-looking hamper. Then delicious cold fowl and lettuce sandwiches and champagne cup set our tongues wagging as only very young tongues can wag. Daisy went back with Freda after luncheon, leaving me a case of cigars, with a bantering smile. I dozed, half awake, keeping a partly closed eye on the ocean, where a faint gray streak showed plainly amid the azure water all around. That was the Gulf Stream loop.

"About four o'clock Frisby appeared with a bamboo shelter-tent, for which I was unaffectedly grateful.

"After he had erected it over me he stopped to chat a bit, but the conversation bored me, for he could talk of nothing but bill-posting.

"'You wouldn't ruin the landscape here, would you?' I asked.

"'Ruin it!' repeated Frisby, nervously. 'It's ruined now; there ain't a place to stick a bill.'

"'The snipe stick bills—in the sand,' I said, flippantly.

"There was no humor about Frisby. 'Do they?' he asked.

"I moved with a certain impatience.

"'Bills,' said Frisby, 'give spice an' variety to nature. They break the monotony of the everlastin' green and what-you-may-call-its.'

"I glared at him.

"'Bills,' he continued, 'are not easy to stick, lemme tell you, sir. Sign-paintin's a soft snap when it comes to bill-stickin'. Now, I guess I've stuck more bills onto New York State than ennybody.'

"'Have you?' I said, angrily.

"'Yes, siree! I always pick out the purtiest spots—kinder filled chuck full of woods and brooks and things; then I h'ist my paste-pot onto a rock, and I slather that rock with gum, and whoop she goes!'

"'Whoop what goes?'

"'The bill. I paste her onto the rock, with one swipe of the brush for the edges and a back-handed swipe for the finish—except when a bill is folded in two halves.'

"'And what do you do then?' I asked, disgusted.

"'Swipe twice,' said Frisby, with enthusiasm.

"'And you don't think it injures the landscape?'

"'Injures it!' he exclaimed, convinced that I was attempting to joke.

"I looked wearily out to sea. He also looked at the water and sighed sentimentally.

"'Floatin' buoys with bills onto 'em is a idea of mine,' he observed. 'That damn ocean is monotonous, ain't it?'

"I don't know what I might have done to Frisby—the rifle was so convenient—if his mean yellow dog had not waddled up at this juncture.

"'Hi, Davy, sic 'em!' said Frisby, expectorating upon a clam-shell and hurling it seaward. The cur watched the flight of the shell apathetically, then squatted in the sand and looked at his master.

"'Kinder lost his spirit,' said Frisby, 'ain't he? I once stuck a bill onto Davy, an' it come off, an' the paste sorter sickened him. He was hell on rats—once!'

"After a moment or two Frisby took himself off, whistling cheerfully to Davy, who followed him when he was ready. The rifle burned in my fingers.

"It was nearly six o'clock when the professor appeared, spade on shoulder, boots smeared with mud.

"'Well,' he said, 'nothing to report, Dick, my boy?'

"'Nothing, professor.'

"He wiped his shining face with his handkerchief and stared at the water.

"'My calculations lead me to believe,' he said, 'that our prize may be due any day now. This theory I base upon the result of the report from the last sea-captain I saw. I cannot understand why some of these captains did not take the carcass in tow. They all say that they tried, but that the body sank before they could come within half a mile. The truth is, probably, that they did not stir a foot from their course to examine the thing.'

"'Have you ever cruised about for it?' I ventured.

"'For two years,' he said, grimly. 'It's no use; it's accident when a ship falls in with it. One captain reports it a thousand miles from where the last skipper spoke it, and always in the Gulf Stream. They think it is a different specimen every time, and the papers are teeming with sea-serpent fol-de-rol.'

"'Are you sure,' I asked, 'that it will swing into the coast on this Gulf Stream loop?'

"'I think I may say that it is certain to do so. I experimented with a dead right-whale. You may have heard of its coming ashore here last summer.'

"'I think I did,' said I, with a faint smile. The thing had poisoned the air for miles around.

"'But,' I continued, 'suppose it comes in the night?'

"He laughed.

"'There I am lucky. Every night this month, and every day, too, the current of the loop runs inland so far that even a porpoise would strand for at least twelve hours. Longer than that I have not experimented with, but I know that the shore trend of the loop runs across a long spur of the submerged volcanic mountain, and that any-thing heavier than a porpoise would scrape the bottom and be carried so slowly that at least twelve hours must elapse before the carcass could float again into deep water. There are chances of its stranding indefinitely, too, but I don't care to take those chances. That is why I have stationed you here, Dick.'

"He glanced again at the water, smiling to himself.

"'There is another question I want to ask,' I said, 'if you don't mind.'

"'Of course not!' he said, warmly.

"'What are you digging for?'

"'Why, simply for exercise. The doctor told me I was killing myself with my sed-entary habits, so I decided to dig. I don't know a better exercise. Do you?'

"'I suppose not,' I murmured, rather red in the face. I wondered whether he'd mention fossils.

"'Did Daisy tell you why we are making our papier-maché thermosaurus?' he asked.

"I shook my head.

"'We constructed that from measurements I took from the fossil remains of the thermosaurus in the Metropolitan Museum. Professor Bruce Stoddard made the drawings. We set it up here, all ready to receive the skin of the carcass that I am expecting.'

"We had started towards home, walking slowly across the darkening dunes, shoulder to shoulder. The sand was deep, and walking was not easy.

"'I wish,' said I at last, 'that I knew why Miss Holroyd asked me not to walk on the beach. It's much less fatiguing.'

"'That,' said the professor, 'is a matter that I intend to discuss with you to-night.' He spoke gravely, almost sadly. I felt that something of unparalleled importance was soon to be revealed. So I kept very quiet, watching the ocean out of the corners of my eyes.

---

# XX

"Dinner was ended. Daisy Holroyd lighted her father's pipe for him, and insisted on my smoking as much as I pleased. Then she sat down, and folded her hands like a good little girl, waiting for her father to make the revelation which I felt in my bones must be something out of the ordinary.

"The professor smoked for a while, gazing meditatively at his daughter; then, fixing his gray eyes on me, he said:

"'Have you ever heard of the kree—that Australian bird, half parrot, half hawk, that destroys so many sheep in New South Wales?'

"I nodded.

"'The kree kills a sheep by alighting on its back and tearing away the flesh with its hooked beak until a vital part is reached. You know that? Well, it has been discovered that the kree had prehistoric prototypes. These birds were enormous creatures, who preyed upon mammoths and mastodons, and even upon the great saurians. It has been conclusively proved that a few saurians have been killed by the ancestors of the kree, but the favorite food of these birds was undoubtedly the thermosaurus. It is believed that the birds attacked the eyes of the thermosaurus, and when, as was its habit, the mammoth creature turned on its back to claw them, they fell upon the thinner scales of its stomach armor and finally killed it. This, of course, is a theory, but we have almost absolute proofs of its correctness. Now, these two birds are known among scientists as the ekaf-bird and the ool-yllik. The names are Australian, in which country most of their remains have been unearthed. They lived during the Carboniferous period. Now, it is not generally known, but the fact is, that in 1801 Captain Ransom, of the British exploring vessel *Gull*, purchased from the natives of Tasmania the skin of an ekaf-bird that could not have been killed more than twenty-four hours previous to its sale. I saw this skin in the British Museum. It was labelled, "Unknown bird, probably extinct." It took me exactly a week to satisfy myself that it was actually the skin of an ekaf-bird. But that is not all, Dick,' continued the professor, excitedly. 'In 1854 Admiral Stuart, of our own navy, saw the carcass of a strange, gigantic bird floating along the southern coast of Australia. Sharks were after it, and before a boat could be lowered these miserable fish got it. But the good old admiral secured a few feathers and sent them to the Smithsonian. I saw them. They were not even labelled, but I knew that they were feathers from the ekaf-bird or its near relative, the ool-yllik.'

"I had grown so interested that I had leaned far across the table. Daisy, too, bent forward. It was only when the professor paused for a moment that I noticed how close together our heads were—Daisy's and mine. I don't think she realized it. She did not move.

"'Now comes the important part of this long discourse,' said the professor, smiling at our eagerness. "'Ever since the carcass of our derelict thermosaurus was first noticed, every captain who has seen it has also reported the presence of one or more gigantic birds in the neighborhood. These birds, at a great distance, appeared to be hovering over the carcass, but on the approach of a vessel they disappeared. Even in mid-ocean they were observed. When I heard about it I was puzzled. A month later I was satisfied that neither the ekaf-bird nor the ool-yllik was extinct. Last Monday I knew that I was right. I found forty-eight distinct impressions of the huge, seven-toed claw of the ekaf-bird on the beach here at Pine Inlet. You may imagine my excitement. I succeeded in digging up enough wet sand around one of these impressions to preserve its form. I managed to get it into a soap-box, and now it is there in my shop. The tide rose too rapidly for me to save the other footprints.'

"I shuddered at the possibility of a clumsy misstep on my part obliterating the impression of an ool-yllik.

"'That is the reason that my daughter warned you off the beach,' he said, mildly.

"'Hanging would have been too good for the vandal who destroyed such priceless prizes,' I cried out, in self-reproach.

"Daisy Holroyd turned a flushed face to mine and impulsively laid her hand on my sleeve.

"'How could you know?' she said.

"'It's all right now,' said her father, emphasizing each word with a gentle tap of his pipe-bowl on the table-edge; 'don't be hard on yourself, Dick. You'll do yeoman's service yet.'

"It was nearly midnight, and still we chatted on about the thermosaurus, the ekaf-bird, and the ool-yllik, eagerly discussing the probability of the great reptile's carcass being in the vicinity. That alone seemed to explain the presence of these prehistoric birds at Pine Inlet.

"'Do they ever attack human beings?' I asked.

"The professor looked startled.

"'Gracious!' he exclaimed, 'I never thought of that. And Daisy running about out-of-doors! Dear me! It takes a scientist to be an unnatural parent!'

"His alarm was half real, half assumed; but, all the same, he glanced gravely at us both, shaking his handsome head, absorbed in thought. Daisy herself looked a little doubtful. As for me, my sensations were distinctly queer.

"'It is true,' said the professor, frowning at the wall, 'that human remains have been found associated with the bones of the ekaf-bird—I don't know how intimately. It is a matter to be taken into most serious consideration.'

"'The problem can be solved,' said I, 'in several ways. One is, to keep Miss Holroyd in the house—'

"'I shall not stay in,' cried Daisy, indignantly.

"We all laughed, and her father assured her that she should not be abused.

"'Even if I did stay in,' she said, 'one of these birds might alight on Master Dick.'

"She looked saucily at me as she spoke, but turned crimson when her father observed, quietly, 'You don't seem to think of me, Daisy!'

"'Of course I do,' she said, getting up and putting both arms around her father's neck; 'but Dick—as—as you call him—is so helpless and timid.'

"My blissful smile froze on my lips.

"'Timid!' I repeated.

"She came back to the table, making me a mocking reverence.

"'Do you think I am to be laughed at with impunity?' she said.

"'What are your other plans, Dick?' asked the professor. 'Daisy, let him alone, you little tease!'

"'One is, to haul a lot of cast-iron boilers along the dunes,' I said. 'If these birds come when the carcass floats in, and if they seem disposed to trouble us, we could crawl into the boilers and be safe.'

"'Why, that is really brilliant!' cried Daisy.

"'Be quiet, my child. Dick, the plan is sound and sensible and perfectly practical. McPeek and Frisby shall go for a dozen loads of boilers to-morrow.'

"'It will spoil the beauty of the landscape,' said Daisy, with a taunting nod to me.

"'And Frisby will probably attempt to cover them with bill-posters,' I added, laughing.

"'That,' said Daisy, 'I shall prevent, even at the cost of his life.' And she stood up, looking very determined.

"'Children, children,' protested the professor, 'go to bed—you bother me.'

"Then I turned deliberately to Miss Holroyd.

"'Good-night, Daisy,' I said.

"'Good-night, Dick,' she said, very gently.

---

# XXI

"The week passed quickly for me, leaving but few definite impressions. As I look back to it now I can see the long stretch of beach burning in the fierce sunlight, the endless meadows, with the glimmer of water in the distance, the dunes, the twisted cedars, the leagues of scintillating ocean, rocking, rocking, always rocking. In the starlit nights the curlew came in from the sand-bars by twos and threes; I could hear their querulous call as I lay in bed thinking. All day long the little ring-necks whistled from the shore. The plover answered them from distant, lonely inland pools. The great white gulls drifted like feathers upon the sea.

"One morning towards the end of the week, I, strolling along the dunes, came upon Frisby. He was bill-posting. I caught him red-handed.

"'This,' said I, 'must stop. Do you understand, Mr. Frisby?'

"He stepped back from his work, laying his head on one side, considering first me, then the bill that he had pasted on one of our big boilers.

"'Don't you like the color?' he asked. 'It goes well on them black boilers.'

"'Color! No, I don't like the color, either. Can't you understand that there are some people in the world who object to seeing patent-medicine advertisements scattered over a landscape?'

"'Hey?' he said, perplexed.

"'Will you kindly remove that advertisement?' I persisted.

"'Too late,' said Frisby; 'it's sot.'

"I was too disgusted to speak, but my disgust turned to anger when I perceived that, as far as the eye could reach, our boilers, lying from three to four hundred feet apart, were ablaze with yellow-and-red posters extolling the 'Eureka Liver Pill Company.'

"'It don't cost 'em nothin',' said Frisby, cheerfully; 'I done it fur the fun of it. Purty, ain't it?'

"'They are Professor Holroyd's boilers,' I said, subduing a desire to beat Frisby with my telescope. 'Wait until Miss Holroyd sees this work.'

"'Don't she like yeller and red?' he demanded, anxiously.

"'You'll find out,' said I.

"Frisby gaped at his handiwork and then at his yellow dog. After a moment he mechanically spat on a clam-shell and requested Davy to 'sic' it.

"'Can't you comprehend that you have ruined our pleasure in the landscape?' I asked, more mildly.

"'I've got some green bills,' said Frisby; 'I kin stick 'em over the yeller ones—'

"'Confound it,' said I, 'it isn't the color!'

"'Then,' observed Frisby, 'you don't like them pills. I've got some bills of the "Cropper Automobile" and a few of "Bagley, the Gents' Tailor"—'

"'Frisby,' said I, 'use them all—paste the whole collection over your dog and your-self—then walk off the cliff.'

"He sullenly unfolded a green poster, swabbed the boiler with paste, laid the up-per section of the bill upon it, and plastered the whole bill down with a thwack of his brush. As I walked away I heard him muttering.

"Next day Daisy was so horrified that I promised to give Frisby an ultimatum. I found him with Freda, gazing sentimentally at his work, and I sent him back to the shop in a hurry, telling Freda at the same time that she could spend her leisure in providing Mr. Frisby with sand, soap, and a scrubbing-brush. Then I walked on to my post of observation.

"I watched until sunset. Daisy came with her father to hear my report, but there was nothing to tell, and we three walked slowly back to the house.

"In the evenings the professor worked on his volumes, the click of his type-writer sounding faintly behind his closed door. Daisy and I played chess sometimes; some-times we played hearts. I don't remember that we ever finished a game of either—we talked too much.

"Our discussions covered every topic of interest: we argued upon politics; we skimmed over literature and music; we settled international differences; we spoke vaguely of human brotherhood. I say we slighted no subject of interest—I am wrong; we never spoke of love.

"Now, love is a matter of interest to ten people out of ten. Why it was that it did not appear to interest us is as interesting a question as love itself. We were young, alert, enthusiastic, inquiring. We eagerly absorbed theories concerning any curious phenomena in nature, as intellectual cocktails to stimulate discussion. And yet we did not discuss love. I do not say that we avoided it. No; the subject was too completely ignored for even that. And yet we found it very difficult to pass an hour separated. The professor noticed this, and laughed at us. We were not even embarrassed.

"Sunday passed in pious contemplation of the ocean. Daisy read a little in her prayer-book, and the professor threw a cloth over his type-writer and strolled up and down the sands. He may have been lost in devout abstraction; he may have been looking for footprints. As for me, my mind was very serene, and I was more than happy. Daisy read to me a little for my soul's sake, and the professor came up and said something cheerful. He also examined the magazine of my Winchester.

"That night, too, Daisy took her guitar to the sands and sang one or two Basque hymns. Unlike us, the Basques do not take their pleasures sadly. One of their pleasures is evidently religion.

"The big moon came up over the dunes and stared at the sea until the surface of every wave trembled with radiance. A sudden stillness fell across the world; the wind died out; the foam ran noiselessly across the beach; the cricket's rune was stilled.

"I leaned back, dropping one hand upon the sand. It touched another hand, soft and cool.

"After a while the other hand moved slightly, and I found that my own had closed above it. Presently one finger stirred a little—only a little—for our fingers were inter-locked.

"On the shore the foam-froth bubbled and winked and glimmered in the moon-light. A star fell from the zenith, showering the night with incandescent dust.

"If our fingers lay interlaced beside us, her eyes were calm and serene as always, wide open, fixed upon the depths of a dark sky. And when her father rose and spoke to us, she did not withdraw her hand.

"'Is it late?' she asked, dreamily.

"'It is midnight, little daughter.'

"I stood up, still holding her hand, and aided her to rise. And when, at the door, I said good-night, she turned and looked at me for a little while in silence, then passed into her room slowly, with head still turned towards me.

"All night long I dreamed of her; and when the east whitened, I sprang up, the thunder of the ocean in my ears, the strong sea-wind blowing into the open window.

"'She's asleep,' I thought, and I leaned from the window and peered out into the east.

"The sea called to me, tossing its thousand arms; the soaring gulls, dipping, rising, wheeling above the sandbar, screamed and clamored for a playmate. I slipped into my bathing-suit, dropped from the window upon the soft sand, and in a moment had plunged head foremost into the surf, swimming beneath the waves towards the open sea.

"Under the tossing ocean the voice of the waters was in my ears—a low, sweet voice, intimate, mysterious. Through singing foam and broad, green, glassy depths, by whispering sandy channels atrail with sea-weed, and on, on, out into the vague, cool sea, I sped, rising to the top, sinking, gliding. Then at last I flung myself out of water, hands raised, and the clamor of the gulls filled my ears.

"As I lay, breathing fast, drifting on the sea, far out beyond the gulls I saw a flash of white, and an arm was lifted, signalling me.

"'Daisy!' I called.

"A clear hail came across the water, distinct on the sea-wind, and at the same instant we raised our hands and moved towards each other.

"How we laughed as we met in the sea! The white dawn came up out of the depths, the zenith turned to rose and ashes.

"And with the dawn came the wind—a great sea-wind, fresh, aromatic, that hurled our voices back into our throats and lifted the sheeted spray above our heads. Every wave, crowned with mist, caught us in a cool embrace, cradled us, and slipped away, only to leave us to another wave, higher, stronger, crested with opalescent glory, breathing incense.

"We turned together up the coast, swimming lightly side by side, but our words were caught up by the winds and whirled into the sky.

"We looked up at the driving clouds; we looked out upon the pallid waste of waters, but it was into each other's eyes we looked, wondering, wistful, questioning the reason of sky and sea And there in each other's eyes we read the mystery, and we knew that earth and sky and sea were created for us alone.

"Drifting on by distant sands and dunes, her white fingers touching mine, we spoke, keying our tones to the wind's vast harmony. And we spoke of love.

"Gray and wide as the limitless span of the sky and the sea, the winds gathered from the world's ends to bear us on; but they were not familiar winds; for now, along the coast, the breakers curled and showed a million fangs, and the ocean stirred to its depths, uneasy, ominous, and the menace of its murmur drew us closer as we moved.

"Where the dull thunder and the tossing spray warned us from sunken reefs, we heard the harsh challenges of gulls; where the pallid surf twisted in yellow coils of spume above the bar, the singing sands murmured of treachery and secrets of lost souls agasp in the throes of silent undertows.

"But there was a little stretch of beach glimmering through the mountains of water, and towards this we turned, side by side. Around us the water grew warmer; the breath of the following waves moistened our cheeks; the water itself grew gray and strange about us.

"'We have come too far,' I said; but she only answered:

"'Faster, faster! I am afraid!' The water was almost hot now; its aromatic odor filled our lungs.

"'The Gulf loop!' I muttered. 'Daisy, shall I help you?'

"'No. Swim—close by me! Oh-h! Dick—'

"Her startled cry was echoed by another—a shrill scream, unutterably horrible—and a great bird flapped from the beach, splashing and beating its pinions across the water with a thundering noise.

"Out across the waves it blundered, rising little by little from the water, and now, to my horror, I saw another monstrous bird swinging in the air above it, squealing as it turned on its vast wings. Before I could speak we touched the beach, and I half lifted her to the shore.

"'Quick!' I repeated. 'We must not wait.'

"Her eyes were dark with fear, but she rested a hand on my shoulder, and we crept up among the dune-grasses and sank down by the point of sand where the rough shelter stood, surrounded by the iron-ringed piles.

"She lay there, breathing fast and deep, dripping with spray. I had no power of speech left, but when I rose wearily to my knees and looked out upon the water my blood ran cold. Above the ocean, on the breast of the roaring wind, three enormous birds sailed, turning and wheeling among one another; and below, drifting with the gray stream of the Gulf loop, a colossal bulk lay half submerged—a gigantic lizard, floating belly upward.

"Then Daisy crept kneeling to my side and touched me, trembling from head to foot.

"'I know,' I muttered. 'I must run back for the rifle.'

"'And—and leave me?'

"I took her by the hand, and we dragged ourselves through the wire-grass to the open end of a boiler lying in the sand.

"She crept in on her hands and knees, and called to me to follow.

"'You are safe now,' I cried. 'I must go back for the rifle.'

"'The birds may—may attack you.'

"'If they do I can get into one of the other boilers,' I said. 'Daisy, you must not venture out until I come back. You won't, will you?'

"'No-o,' she whispered, doubtfully.

"'Then—good-bye.'

"'Good-bye,' she answered, but her voice was very small and still.

"'Good-bye,' I said again. I was kneeling at the mouth of the big iron tunnel; it was dark inside and I could not see her, but, before I was conscious of it, her arms were around my neck and we had kissed each other.

"I don't remember how I went away. When I came to my proper senses I was swimming along the coast at full speed, and over my head wheeled one of the birds, screaming at every turn.

"The intoxication of that innocent embrace, the close impress of her arms around my neck, gave me a strength and recklessness that neither fear nor fatigue could subdue. The bird above me did not even frighten me. I watched it over my shoulder, swimming strongly, with the tide now aiding me, now stemming my course; but I saw the shore passing quickly, and my strength increased, and I shouted when I came in sight of the house, and scrambled up on the sand, dripping and excited. There was nobody in sight, and I gave a last glance up into the air where the bird wheeled, still screeching, and hastened into the house. Freda stared at me in amazement as I seized the rifle and shouted for the professor.

"'He has just gone to town, with Captain McPeek in his wagon,' stammered Freda.

"'What!' I cried. 'Does he know where his daughter is?'

"'Miss Holroyd is asleep—not?' gasped Freda.

"'Where's Frisby?' I cried, impatiently.

"'Yimmie?' quavered Freda.

"'Yes, Jimmie; isn't there anybody here? Good Heavens! where's that man in the shop?'

"'He also iss gone,' said Freda, shedding tears, 'to buy papier-maché. Yimmie, he iss gone to post bills.'

"I waited to hear no more, but swung my rifle over my shoulder, and, hanging the cartridge-belt across my chest, hurried out and up the beach. The bird was not in sight.

"I had been running for perhaps a minute when, far up on the dunes, I saw a yellow dog rush madly through a clump of sweet-bay, and at the same moment a bird soared past, rose, and hung hovering just above the thicket. Suddenly the bird swooped; there was a shriek and a yelp from the cur, but the bird gripped it in one claw and beat its wings upon the sand, striving to rise. Then I saw Frisby—paste, bucket, and brush raised—fall upon the bird, yelling lustily. The fierce creature relaxed its talons, and the dog rushed on, squeaking with terror. The bird turned on Frisby and sent him sprawling on his face, a sticky mass of paste and sand. But this did not end the struggle. The bird, croaking horridly, flew at the prostrate bill-poster,

461

and the sand whirled into a pillar above its terrible wings. Scarcely knowing what I was about, I raised my rifle and fired twice. A scream echoed each shot, and the bird rose heavily in a shower of sand; but two bullets were embedded in that mass of foul feathers, and I saw the wires and scarlet tape uncoiling on the sand at my feet. In an instant I seized them and passed the ends around a cedar-tree, hooking the clasps tight. Then I cast one swift glance upward, where the bird wheeled, screeching, anchored like a kite to the pallium wires; and I hurried on across the dunes, the shells cutting my feet and the bushes tearing my wet swimming-suit, until I dripped with blood from shoulder to ankle. Out in the ocean the carcass of the thermosaurus floated, claws outspread, belly glistening in the gray light, and over him circled two birds. As I reached the shelter I knelt and fired into the mass of scales, and at my first shot a horrible thing occurred—the lizard-like head writhed, the slitted yellow eyes sliding open from the film that covered them. A shudder passed across the undulating body, the great scaled belly heaved, and one leg feebly clawed at the air.

"The thing was still alive!

"Crushing back the horror that almost paralyzed my hands, I planted shot after shot into the quivering reptile, while it writhed and clawed, striving to turn over and dive; and at each shot the black blood spurted in long, slim jets across the water. And now Daisy was at my side, pale and determined, swiftly clasping each tape-marked wire to the iron rings in the circle around us. Twice I filled the magazine from my belt, and twice I poured streams of steel-tipped bullets into the scaled mass, twisting and shuddering on the sea. Suddenly the birds steered towards us. I felt the wind from their vast wings. I saw the feathers erect, vibrating. I saw the spread claws outstretched, and I struck furiously at them, crying to Daisy to run into the iron shelter. Backing, swinging my clubbed rifle, I retreated, but I tripped across one of the taut pallium wires, and in an instant the hideous birds were on me, and the bone in my forearm snapped like a pipe-stem at a blow from their wings. Twice I struggled to my knees, blinded with blood, confused, almost fainting; then I fell again, rolling into the mouth of the iron boiler.

---

"When I struggled back to consciousness Daisy knelt silently beside me, while Captain McPeek and Professor Holroyd bound up my shattered arm, talking excitedly. The pain made me faint and dizzy. I tried to speak and could not. At last they got me to my feet and into the wagon, and Daisy came, too, and crouched beside me, wrapped in oilskins to her eyes. Fatigue, lack of food, and excitement had combined with wounds and broken bones to extinguish the last atom of strength in my body; but my mind was clear enough to understand that the trouble was over and the thermosaurus safe.

"I heard McPeek say that one of the birds that I had anchored to a cedar-tree had torn loose from the bullets and had winged its way heavily out to sea. The professor answered: 'Yes, the ekaf-bird; the others were ool-ylliks. I'd have given my right arm to have secured them.' Then for a time I heard no more; but the jolting of the wagon over the dunes roused me to keenest pain, and I held out my right hand to Daisy. She clasped it in both of hers, and kissed it again and again.

———————

"There is little more to add, I think. Professor Bruce Stoddard's scientific pamphlet will be published soon, to be followed by Professor Holroyd's sixteen volumes. In a few days the stuffed and mounted thermosaurus will be placed on free public exhibition in the arena of Madison Square Garden, the only building in the city large enough to contain the body of this immense winged reptile."

———————

The young man hesitated, looking long and earnestly at Miss Barrison.

"Did you marry her?" she asked, softly.

"You wouldn't believe it," said the young man, earnestly—"you wouldn't believe it, after all that happened, if I should tell you that she married Professor Bruce Stoddard, of Columbia—would you?"

"Yes, I would," said Miss Barrison. "You never can tell what a girl will do."

"That story of yours," I said, "is to me the most wonderful and valuable contribution to nature study that it has ever been my fortune to listen to. You are fitted to write; it is your sacred mission to produce. Are you going to?"

"I am writing," said the young man, quietly, "a nature book. Sir Peter Grebe's magnificent monograph on the speckled titmouse inspired me. But nature study is not what I have chosen as my life's mission."

He looked dreamily across at Miss Barrison. "No, not natural phenomena," he repeated, "but unnatural phenomena. What Professor Hyssop has done for Columbia, I shall attempt to do for Harvard. In fact, I have already accepted the chair of Psychical Phenomena at Cambridge."

I gazed upon him with intense respect.

"A personal experience revealed to me my life's work," he, went on, thoughtfully stroking his blond mustache. "If Miss Barrison would care to hear it—"

"Please tell it," she said, sweetly.

"I shall have to relate it clothed in that artificial garb known as literary style," he explained, deprecatingly.

"It doesn't matter," I said, "I never noticed any style at all in your story of the thermosaurus."

He smiled gratefully, and passed his hand over his face; a far-away expression came into his eyes, and he slowly began, hesitating, as though talking to himself:

---

# XXII

"It was high noon in the city of Antwerp. From slender steeples floated the mellow music of the Flemish bells, and in the spire of the great cathedral across the square the cracked chimes clashed discords until my ears ached.

"When the fiend in the cathedral had jerked the last tuneless clang from the chimes, I removed my fingers from my ears and sat down at one of the iron tables in the court. A waiter, with his face shaved blue, brought me a bottle of Rhine wine, a tumbler of cracked ice, and a siphon.

"'Does monsieur desire anything else?' he inquired.

"'Yes—the head of the cathedral bell-ringer; bring it with vinegar and potatoes,' I said, bitterly. Then I began to ponder on my great-aunt and the Crimson Diamond.

"The white walls of the Hôtel St. Antoine rose in a rectangle around the sunny court, casting long shadows across the basin of the fountain. The strip of blue overhead was cloudless. Sparrows twittered under the eaves the yellow awnings fluttered, the flowers swayed in the summer breeze, and the jet of the fountain splashed among the water-plants. On the sunny side of the piazza the tables were vacant; on the shady side I was lazily aware that the tables behind me were occupied, but I was indifferent as to their occupants, partly because I shunned all tourists, partly because I was thinking of my great-aunt.

"Most old ladies are eccentric, but there is a limit, and my great-aunt had overstepped it. I had believed her to be wealthy—she died bankrupt. Still, I knew there was one thing she did possess, and that was the famous Crimson Diamond. Now, of course, you know who my great-aunt was.

"Excepting the Koh-i-noor and the Regent, this enormous and unique stone was, as everybody knows, the most valuable gem in existence. Any ordinary person would have placed that diamond in a safe-deposit. My great-aunt did nothing of the kind. She kept it in a small velvet bag, which she carried about her neck. She never took it off, but wore it dangling openly on her heavy silk gown.

"In this same bag she also carried dried catnip-leaves, of which she was inordinately fond. Nobody but myself, her only living relative, knew that the Crimson Diamond lay among the sprigs of catnip in the little velvet bag.

"'Harold,' she would say, 'do you think I'm a fool? If I place the Crimson Diamond in any safe-deposit vault in New York, somebody will steal it, sooner or later.' Then she would nibble a sprig of catnip and peer cunningly at me. I loathed the odor of catnip and she knew it. I also loathed cats. This also she knew, and of course sur-rounded herself with a dozen. Poor old lady! One day she was found dead in her bed in her apartments at the Waldorf. The doctor said she died from natural causes. The only other occupant of her sleeping-room was a cat. The cat fled when we broke open the door, and I heard that she was received and cherished by some eccentric people in a neighboring apartment.

"Now, although my great-aunt's death was due to purely natural causes, there was one very startling and disagreeable feature of the case. The velvet bag containing the Crimson Diamond had disappeared. Every inch of the apartment was searched, the floors torn up, the walls dismantled, but the Crimson Diamond had vanished. Chief of Police Conlon detailed four of his best men on the case, and, as I had nothing better to do, I enrolled myself as a volunteer. I also offered $25,000 reward for the recovery of the gem. All New York was agog.

"The case seemed hopeless enough, although there were five of us after the thief. McFarlane was in London, and had been for a month, but Scotland Yard could give him no help, and the last I heard of him he was roaming through Surrey after a man with a white spot in his hair. Harrison had gone to Paris. He kept writing me that clews were plenty and the scent hot, but as Dennet, in Berlin, and Clancy, in Vienna, wrote me the same thing, I began to doubt these gentlemen's ability.

"'You say,' I answered Harrison, 'that the fellow is a Frenchman, and that he is now concealed in Paris; but Dennet writes me by the same mail that the thief is un-doubtedly a German, and was seen yesterday in Berlin. To-day I received a letter from Clancy, assuring me that Vienna holds the culprit, and that he is an Austrian from Trieste. Now, for Heaven's sake,' I ended, 'let me alone and stop writing me letters until you have something to write about.'

"The night-clerk at the Waldorf had furnished us with our first clew. On the night of my aunt's death he had seen a tall, grave-faced man hurriedly leave the hotel. As the man passed the desk he removed his hat and mopped his forehead, and the night-clerk noticed that in the middle of his head there was a patch of hair as white as snow.

"We worked this clew for all it was worth, and, a month later, I received a cable despatch from Paris, saying that a man answering to the description of the Waldorf suspect had offered an enormous crimson diamond for sale to a jeweller in the Palais Royal. Unfortunately the fellow took fright and disappeared before the jeweller could send for the police, and since that time McFarlane in London, Harrison in Paris, Dennet in Berlin, and Clancy in Vienna had been chasing men with white patches on their hair until no gray-headed patriarch in Europe was free from suspicion. I myself had sleuthed it through England, France, Holland, and Belgium, and now I found myself in Antwerp at the Hôtel St. Antoine, without a clew that promised anything except another outrage on some respectable white-haired citizen. The case seemed hopeless enough, unless the thief tried again to sell the gem. Here was our only hope, for, unless he cut the stone into smaller ones, he had no more chance of selling it than he would have had if he had stolen the Venus of Milo and peddled her about the Rue de Seine. Even were he to cut up the stone, no respectable gem collector or jeweller would buy a crimson diamond without first notifying me; for although a few red stones are known to collectors, the color of the Crimson Diamond was absolutely unique, and there was little probability of an honest mistake.

"Thinking of all these things, I sat sipping my Rhine wine in the shadow of the yellow awnings. A large white cat came sauntering by and stopped in front of me to perform her toilet, until I wished she would go away. After a while she sat up, licked her whiskers, yawned once or twice, and was about to stroll on, when, catching sight of me, she stopped short and looked me squarely in the face. I returned the attention with a scowl, because I wished to discourage any advances towards social intercourse which she might contemplate; but after a while her steady gaze disconcerted me, and I turned to my Rhine wine. A few minutes later I looked up again. The cat was still eying me.

"'Now what the devil is the matter with the animal,' I muttered; 'does she recognize in me a relative?'

"'Perhaps,' observed a man at the next table.

"'What do you mean by that?' I demanded.

"'What I say,' replied the man at the next table.

"I looked him full in the face. He was old and bald and appeared weak-minded. His age protected his impudence. I turned my back on him. Then my eyes fell on the cat again. She was still gazing earnestly at me.

"Disgusted that she should take such pointed public notice of me, I wondered whether other people saw it; I wondered whether there was anything peculiar in my own personal appearance. How hard the creature stared! It was most embarrassing.

"'What has got into that cat?' I thought. 'It's sheer impudence. It's an intrusion, and I won't stand it!' The cat did not move. I tried to stare her out of countenance. It was useless. There was aggressive inquiry in her yellow eyes. A sensation of uneasiness began to steal over me—a sensation of embarrassment not unmixed with awe. All cats looked alike to me, and yet there was something about this one that bothered me—something that I could not explain to myself, but which began to occupy me.

"She looked familiar—this Antwerp cat. An odd sense of having seen her before, of having been well acquainted with her in former years, slowly settled in my mind, and, although I could never remember the time when I had not detested cats, I was almost convinced that my relations with this Antwerp tabby had once been intimate if not cordial. I looked more closely at the animal. Then an idea struck me—an idea which persisted and took definite shape in spite of me. I strove to escape from it, to evade it, to stifle and smother it; an inward struggle ensued which brought the perspiration in beads upon my cheeks—a struggle short, sharp, decisive. It was useless—useless to try to put it from me—this idea so wretchedly bizarre, so grotesque and fantastic, so utterly inane—it was useless to deny that the cat bore a distinct resemblance to my great-aunt!

"I gazed at her in horror. What enormous eyes the creature had!

"'Blood is thicker than water,' said the man at the next table.

"'What does he mean by that?' I muttered, angrily, swallowing a tumbler of Rhine wine and seltzer. But I did not turn. What was the use?

"'Chattering old imbecile,' I added to myself, and struck a match, for my cigar was out; but, as I raised the match to relight it, I encountered the cat's eyes again. I could not enjoy my cigar with the animal staring at me, but I was justly indignant, and I did not intend to be routed. 'The idea! Forced to leave for a cat!' I sneered. 'We will see who will be the one to go!' I tried to give her a jet of seltzer from the siphon, but the bottle was too nearly empty to carry far. Then I attempted to lure her nearer, calling her in French, German, and English, but she did not stir. I did not know the Flemish for 'cat.'

"'She's got a name, and won't come,' I thought. 'Now, what under the sun can I call her?'

"'Aunty,' suggested the man at the next table.

"I sat perfectly still. Could that man have answered my thoughts?—for I had not spoken aloud. Of course not—it was a coincidence—but a very disgusting one.

"'Aunty,' I repeated, mechanically, 'aunty, aunty—good gracious, how horribly human that cat looks!' Then, somehow or other, Shakespeare's words crept into my head and I found myself repeating: 'The soul of my grandam might haply inhabit a bird; the soul of—nonsense!' I growled—'it isn't printed correctly! One might possibly say, speaking in poetical metaphor, that the soul of a bird might haply inhabit one's grandam—' I stopped short, flushing painfully. 'What awful rot!' I murmured, and lighted another cigar. The cat was still staring; the cigar went out. I grew more and more nervous. 'What rot!' I repeated. 'Pythagoras must have been an ass, but I do believe there are plenty of asses alive to-day who swallow that sort of thing.'

"'Who knows?' sighed the man at the next table, and I sprang to my feet and wheeled about. But I only caught a glimpse of a pair of frayed coat-tails and a bald head vanishing into the dining-room. I sat down again, thoroughly indignant. A moment later the cat got up and went away.

---

# XXIII

"Daylight was fading in the city of Antwerp. Down into the sea sank the sun, tinting the vast horizon with flakes of crimson, and touching with rich deep undertones the tossing waters of the Scheldt. Its glow fell like a rosy mantle over red-tiled roofs and meadows; and through the haze the spires of twenty churches pierced the air like sharp, gilded flames. To the west and south the green plains, over which the Spanish armies tramped so long ago, stretched away until they met the sky; the enchantment of the after-glow had turned old Antwerp into fairy-land; and sea and sky and plain were beautiful and vague as the night-mists floating in the moats below.

"Along the sea-wall from the Rubens Gate all Antwerp strolled, and chattered, and flirted, and sipped their Flemish wines from slender Flemish glasses, or gossiped over krugs of foaming beer.

"From the Scheldt came the cries of sailors, the creaking of cordage, and the puff! puff! of the ferry-boats. On the bastions of the fortress opposite, a bugler was standing. Twice the mellow notes of the bugle came faintly over the water, then a great gun thundered from the ramparts, and the Belgian flag fluttered along the lanyards to the ground.

"I leaned listlessly on the sea-wall and looked down at the Scheldt below. A battery of artillery was embarking for the fortress. The tublike transport lay hissing and whistling in the slip, and the stamping of horses, the rumbling of gun and caisson, and the sharp cries of the officers came plainly to the ear.

"When the last caisson was aboard and stowed, and the last trooper had sprung jingling to the deck, the transport puffed out into the Scheldt, and I turned away through the throng of promenaders; and found a little table on the terrace, just outside of the pretty café. And as I sat down I became aware of a girl at the next table—a girl all in white—the most ravishingly and distractingly pretty girl that I had ever seen. In the agitation of the moment I forgot my name, my fortune, my aunt, and the Crimson Diamond—all these I forgot in a purely human impulse to see clearly; and to that end I removed my monocle from my left eye. Some moments later I came to myself and feebly replaced it. It was too late; the mischief was done. I was not aware at first of the exact state of my feelings—for I had never been in love more than three or four times in all my life—but I did know that at her request I would have been proud to stand on my head, or turn a flip-flap into the Scheldt.

"I did not stare at her, but I managed to see her most of the time when her eyes were in another direction. I found myself drinking something which a waiter brought, presumably upon an order which I did not remember having given. Later I noticed that it was a loathsome drink which the Belgians call 'American grog,' but I swallowed it and lighted a cigarette. As the fragrant cloud rose in the air, a voice, which I recognized with a chill, broke, into my dream of enchantment. Could *he* have been there all the while—there sitting beside that vision in white? His hat was off, and the ocean-breezes whispered about his bald head. His frayed coat-tails were folded carefully over his knees, and between the thumb and forefinger of his left hand he balanced a bad cigar. He looked at me in a mildly cheerful way, and said, 'I know now.'

"'Know what?' I asked, thinking it better to humor him, for I was convinced that he was mad.

"'I know why cats bite.'

"This was startling. I hadn't an idea what to say.

"'I know why,' he repeated; 'can you guess why?' There was a covert tone of triumph in his voice and he smiled encouragement. 'Come, try and guess,' he urged.

"I told him that I was unequal to problems.

"'Listen, young man,' he continued, folding his coat-tails closely about his legs—'try to reason it out: why should cats bite? Don't you know? I do.'

"He looked at me anxiously.

"'You take no interest in this problem?' he demanded.

"'Oh yes.'

"'Then why do you not ask me why?' he said, looking vaguely disappointed.

"'Well,' I said, in desperation, 'why do cats bite?—hang it all!' I thought, 'it's like a burned-cork show, and I'm Mr. Bones and he's Tambo!'

"Then he smiled gently. 'Young man,' he said, 'cats bite because they feed on catnip. I have reasoned it out.'

"I stared at him in blank astonishment. Was this benevolent-looking old party poking fun at me? Was he paying me up for the morning's snub? Was he a malignant and revengeful old party, or was he merely feeble-minded? Who might he be? What was he doing here in Antwerp—what was he doing now?—for the bald one had turned familiarly to the beautiful girl in white.

"'Wilhelmina,' he said, 'do you feel chilly?' The girl shook her head.

"'Not in the least, papa.'

"'Her father!' I thought—'her father!' Thank God she did not say 'popper'!

"'I have been to the Zoo to-day,' announced the bald one, turning towards me.

"'Ah, indeed,' I observed; 'er—I trust you enjoyed it.'

"'I have been contemplating the apes,' he continued, dreamily. 'Yes, contemplating the apes.'

"I tried to look interested.

"'Yes, the apes,' he murmured, fixing his mild eyes on me. Then he leaned towards me confidentially and whispered, 'Can you tell me what a monkey thinks?'

"'I cannot,' I replied, sharply.

"'Ah,' he sighed, sinking back in his chair, and patting the slender hand of the girl beside him—'ah, who can tell what a monkey thinks?' His gentle face lulled my suspicions, and I replied, very gravely:

"'Who can tell whether they think at all?'

"'True, true! Who can tell whether they think at all; and if they do think, ah! who can tell what they think?'

"'But,' I began, 'if you can't tell whether they think at all, what's the use of trying to conjecture what they *would* think if they *did* think?'

"He raised his hand in deprecation. 'Ah, it is exactly that which is of such absorbing interest—exactly that! It is the abstruseness of the proposition which stimulates research—which stirs profoundly the brain of the thinking world. The question is of vital and instant importance. Possibly you have already formed an opinion.'

"I admitted that I had thought but little on the subject.

"'I doubt,' he continued, swathing his knees in his coat-tails—'I doubt whether you have given much attention to the subject lately discussed by the Boston Dodo Society of Pythagorean Research.'

"'I am not sure,' I said, politely, 'that I recall that particular discussion. May I ask what was the question brought up?'

"'The Felis domestica question.'

"'Ah, that must indeed be interesting! And—er—what may be the Felis do—do—
'

"'Domestica—not dodo. Felis domestica, the common or garden cat.'

"'Indeed,' I murmured.

"'You are not listening,' he said.

"I only half heard him. I could not turn my eyes from his daughter's face.

"'Cat!' shouted the bald one, and I almost leaped from my chair. 'Are you deaf?' he inquired, sympathetically.

"'No—oh no!' I replied, coloring with confusion; 'you were—pardon me—you were—er—speaking of the dodo. Extraordinary bird that—'

"'I was not discussing the dodo,' he sighed. 'I was speaking of cats.'

"'Of course,' I said.

"'The question is,' he continued, twisting his frayed coat-tails into a sort of rope—'the question is, how are we to ameliorate the present condition and social status of our domestic cats?'

"'Feed 'em,' I suggested.

"He raised both hands. They were eloquent with patient expostulation. 'I mean their spiritual condition,' he said.

"I nodded, but my eyes reverted to that exquisite face. She sat silent, her eyes fixed on the waning flecks of color in the western sky.

"'Yes,' repeated the bald one, 'the spiritual welfare of our domestic cats.'

"'Toms and tabbies?' I murmured.

"'Exactly,' he said, tying a large knot in his coat-tails.

"'You will ruin your coat,' I observed.

"'Papa!' exclaimed the girl, turning in dismay, as that gentleman gave a guilty start, 'stop it at once!'

"He smiled apologetically and made a feeble attempt to conceal his coat-tails.

"'My dear,' he said, with gentle deprecation, 'I am so absent-minded—I always do it in the heat of argument.'

"The girl rose, and, bending over her untidy parent, deftly untied the knot in his flapping coat. When he was disentangled, she sat down and said, with a ghost of a smile, 'He is so very absent-minded.'

"'Your father is evidently a great student,' I ventured, pleasantly. How I pitied her, tied to this old lunatic!

"'Yes, he is a great student,' she said, quietly.

"'I am,' he murmured; 'that's what makes me so absent-minded. I often go to bed and forget to sleep.' Then, looking at me, he asked me my name, adding, with a bow, that his name was P. Royal Wyeth, Professor of Pythagorean Research and Abstruse Paradox.

"'My first name is Penny—named after Professor Penny, of Harvard,' he said; 'but I seldom use my first name in connection with my second, as the combination suggests a household remedy of penetrating odor.'

"'My name is Kensett,' I said, 'Harold Kensett, of New York.'

"'Student?'

"'Er—a little.'

"'Student of diamonds?'

"I smiled. 'Oh, I see you know who my great-aunt was,' I said.

"'I know her,' he said.

"'Ah—perhaps you are unaware that my great-aunt is not now living.'

"'I know her,' he repeated, obstinately.

"I bowed. What a crank he was!

"'What do you study? You don't fiddle away all your time, do you?' he asked.

"Now that was just what I did, but I was not pleased to have Miss Wyeth know it. Although my time was chiefly spent in killing time, I had once, in a fit of energy, succeeded in writing some verses 'To a Tomtit,' so I evaded a humiliating confession by saying that I had done a little work in ornithology.

"'Good!' cried the professor, beaming all over. 'I knew you were a fellow-scientist. Possibly you are a brother-member of the Boston Dodo Society of Pythagorean Research. Are you a dodo?'

"I shook my head. 'No, I am not a dodo.'

"'Only a jay?'

"'A—what?' I said, angrily.

"'A jay. We call the members of the Junior Ornithological Jay Society of New York, jays, just as we refer to ourselves as dodos. Are you not even a jay?'

"'I am not,' I said, watching him suspiciously.

"'I must convert you, I see,' said the professor, smiling.

"'I'm afraid I do not approve of Pythagorean research,' I began, but the beautiful Miss Wyeth turned to me very seriously, and, looking me frankly in the eyes, said:

"'I trust you will be open to conviction.'

"'Good Lord!' I thought. 'Can she be another lunatic?' I looked at her steadily. What a little beauty she was! She also, then, belonged to the Pythagoreans—a sect I despised. Everybody knows all about the Pythagorean craze, its rise in Boston, its rapid spread, and its subsequent consolidation with mental and Christian science, theosophy, hypnotism, the Salvation Army, the Shakers, the Dunkards, and the mind-cure cult, upon a business basis. I had hitherto regarded all Pythagoreans with the same scornful indifference which I accorded to the faith-curists; being a member of no particular church, I was scarcely prepared to take any of them seriously. Least of all did I approve of the 'business basis,' and I looked very much askance indeed at the 'Scientific and Religious Trust Company,' duly incorporated and generally known as the Pythagorean Trust, which, consolidating with mind-curists, faith-curists, and other flourishing salvation syndicates, actually claimed a place among ordinary trusts, and at the same time pretended to a control over man's future life. No, I could never listen—I was ashamed of even entertaining the notion, and I shook my head.

"'No, Miss Wyeth, I am afraid I do not care to listen to any reasoning on this subject.'

"'Don't you believe in Pythagoras?' demanded the professor, subduing his excitement with difficulty, and adding another knot to his coat-tails.

"'No,' I said, 'I do not.'

"'How do you know you don't?' inquired the professor.

"'Because,' I said, firmly, 'it is nonsense to say that the soul of a human being can inhabit a hen!'

"'Put it in a more simplified form!' insisted the professor. 'Do you believe that the soul of a hen can inhabit a human being?'

"'No, I don't!'

"'Did you ever hear of a hen-pecked man?' cried the professor, his voice ending in a shout.

"I nodded, intensely annoyed.

"'Will you listen to reason, then?' he continued, eagerly.

"'No,' I began, but I caught Miss Wyeth's blue eyes fixed on mine with an expression so sad, so sweetly appealing, that I faltered.

"'Yes, I will listen,' I said, faintly.

"'Will you become my pupil?' insisted the professor.

"I was shocked to find myself wavering, but my eyes were looking into hers, and I could not disobey what I read there. The longer I looked the greater inclination I felt to waver. I saw that I was going to give in, and, strangest of all, my conscience did not trouble me. I felt it coming—a sort of mild exhilaration took possession of me. For the first time in my life I became reckless—I even gloried in my recklessness.

"'Yes, yes,' I cried, leaning eagerly across the table, 'I shall be glad—delighted! Will you take me as your pupil?' My single eye-glass fell from its position unheeded. 'Take me! Oh, will you take me?' I cried. Instead of answering, the professor blinked rapidly at me for a moment. I imagined his eyes had grown bigger, and were assuming a greenish tinge. The corners of his mouth began to quiver, emitting queer, caressing little noises, and he rapidly added knot after knot to his twitching coat-tails. Suddenly he bent forward across the table until his nose almost touched mine. The pupils of his eyes expanded, the iris assuming a beautiful, changing, golden-green tinge, and his coat-tails switched violently. Then he began to mew.

"I strove to rouse myself from my paralysis—I tried to shrink back, for I felt the end of his cold nose touch mine. I could not move. The cry of terror died in my straining throat, my hands tightened convulsively; I was incapable of speech or motion. At the same time my brain became wonderfully clear. I began to remember everything that had ever happened to me—everything that I had ever done or said. I even remembered things that I had neither done nor said; I recalled distinctly much that had never happened. How fresh and strong my memory! The past was like a mirror, crystal clear, and there, in glorious tints and hues, the scenes of my childhood grew and glowed and faded, and gave place to newer and more splendid scenes. For a moment the episode of the cat at the Hôtel St. Antoine flashed across my mind. When it vanished a chilly stupor slowly clouded my brain; the scenes, the memories, the brilliant colors, faded, leaving me enveloped in a gray vapor, through which the two great eyes of the professor twinkled with a murky light. A peculiar longing stirred me—a strange yearning for something, I knew not what—but, oh! how I longed and yearned for it! Slowly this indefinite, incomprehensible longing became a living pain. Ah, how I suffered, and how the vapors seemed to crowd around me! Then, as at a great distance, I heard her voice, sweet, imperative:

"'Mew!' she said.

"For a moment I seemed to see the interior of my own skull, lighted as by a flash of fire; the rolling eyeballs, veined in scarlet, the glistening muscles quivering along the jaw, the humid masses of the convoluted brain; then awful darkness—a darkness almost tangible—an utter blackness, through which now seemed to creep a thin, silver thread, like a river crawling across a world—like a thought gliding to the brain—like a song, a thin, sharp song which some distant voice was singing—which I was singing.

"And I knew that I was mewing!

"I threw myself back in my chair and mewed with all my heart. Oh, that heavy load which was lifted from my breast! How good, how satisfying it was to mew! And how I did miaul and yowl!

"I gave myself up to it, heart and soul; my whole being thrilled with the passionate outpourings of a spirit freed. My voice trembled in the upper bars of a feline love-song, quavered, descended, swelling again into an intimation that I brooked no rival, and ended with a magnificent crescendo.

"I finished, somewhat abashed, and glanced askance at the professor and his daughter, but the one sat nonchalantly disentangling his coat-tails, and the other was apparently absorbed in the distant landscape. Evidently they did not consider me ridiculous. Flushing painfully, I turned in my chair to see how my grewsome solo had affected the people on the terrace. Nobody even looked at me. This, however, gave me little comfort, for, as I began to realize what I had done, my mortification and rage knew no bounds. I was ready to die of shame. What on earth had induced me to mew? I looked wildly about for escape—I would leap up—rush home to bury my burning face in my pillows, and, later, in the friendly cabin of a homeward-bound steamer. I would fly—fly at once! Woe to the man who blocked my way! I started to my feet, but at that moment I caught Miss Wyeth's eyes fixed on mine.

"'Don't go,' she said.

"What in Heaven's name lay in those blue eyes? I slowly sank back into my chair.

"Then the professor spoke: 'Wilhelmina, I have just received a despatch.'

"'Where from, papa?'

"'From India. I'm going at once.'

"She nodded her head, without turning her eyes from the sea. 'Is it important, papa?'

"'I should say so. The cashier of the local trust has compromised an astral body, and has squandered on her all our funds, including a lot of first mortgages on Nirvana. I suppose he's been dabbling in futures and is short in his accounts. I sha'n't be gone long.'

"'Then, good-night, papa,' she said, kissing him; 'try to be back by eleven.' I sat stupidly staring at them.

"'Oh, it's only to Bombay—I sha'n't go to Thibet to-night—good-night, my dear,' said the professor.

"Then a singular thing occurred. The professor had at last succeeded in disentangling his coat-tails, and now, jamming his hat over his ears, and waving his arms with a batlike motion, he climbed upon the seat of his chair and ejaculated the word 'Presto!' Then I found my voice.

"'Stop him!' I cried, in terror.

"'Presto! Presto!' shouted the professor, balancing himself on the edge of his chair and waving his arms majestically, as if preparing for a sudden flight across the Scheldt; and, firmly convinced that he not only meditated it, but was perfectly capable of attempting it, I covered my eyes with my hands.

"'Are you ill, Mr. Kensett?' asked the girl, quietly.

"I raised my head indignantly. 'Not at all, Miss Wyeth, only I'll bid you good-evening, for this is the nineteenth century, and I'm a Christian.'

"'So am I,' she said. 'So is my father.'

"'The devil he is,' I thought.

"Her next words made me jump.

"'Please do not be profane, Mr. Kensett.'

"How did she know I was profane? I had not spoken a word! Could it be possible she was able to read my thoughts? This was too much, and I rose.

"'I have the honor to bid you good-evening,' I began, and reluctantly turned to include the professor, expecting to see that gentleman balancing himself on his chair. The professor's chair was empty.

"'Oh,' said the girl, smiling, 'my father has gone.'

"'Gone! Where?'

"'To—to India, I believe.'

"I sank helplessly into my own chair.

"'I do not think he will stay very long—he promised to return by eleven,' she said, timidly.

"I tried to realize the purport of it all. 'Gone to India? Gone! How? On a broom-stick? Good Heavens,' I murmured, 'am I insane?'

"'Perfectly,' she said, 'and I am tired; you may take me back to the hotel.'

"I scarcely heard her; I was feebly attempting to gather up my numbed wits. Slowly I began to comprehend the situation, to review the startling and humiliating events of the day. At noon, in the court of the Hôtel St. Antoine, I had been annoyed by a man and a cat. I had retired to my own room and had slept until dinner. In the evening I met two tourists on the sea-wall promenade. I had been beguiled into conversation—yes, into intimacy with these two tourists! I had had the intention of embracing the faith of Pythagoras! Then I had mewed like a cat with all the strength of my lungs. Now the male tourist vanishes—and leaves me in charge of the female tourist, alone and at night in a strange city! And now the female tourist proposes that I take her home!

"With a remnant of self-possession I groped for my eye-glass, seized it, screwed it firmly into my eye, and looked long and earnestly at the girl. As I looked, my eyes softened, my monacle dropped, and I forgot everything in the beauty and purity of the face before me. My heart began to beat against my stiff, white waistcoat. Had I dared—yes, dared to think of this wondrous little beauty as a female tourist? Her pale, sweet face, turned towards the sea, seemed to cast a spell upon the night. How loud my heart was beating! The yellow moon floated, half dipping in the sea, flooding land and water with enchanted lights. Wind and wave seemed to feel the spell of her eyes, for the breeze died away, the heaving Scheldt tossed noiselessly, and the dark Dutch luggers swung idly on the tide with every sail adroop.

"A sudden hush fell over land and water, the voices on the promenade were stilled; little by little the shadowy throng, the terrace, the sea itself vanished, and I only saw her face, shadowed against the moon.

"It seemed as if I had drifted miles above the earth, through all space and eternity, and there was naught between me and high heaven but that white face. Ah, how I loved her! I knew it—I never doubted it. Could years of passionate adoration touch her heart—her little heart, now beating so calmly with no thought of love to startle it from its quiet and send it fluttering against the gentle breast? In her lap her clasped hands tightened—her eyelids drooped as though some pleasant thought was passing. I saw the color dye her temples, I saw the blue eyes turn, half frightened, to my own, I saw—and I knew she had read my thoughts. Then we both rose, side by side, and she was weeping softly, yet for my life I dared not speak. She turned away, touching her eyes with a bit of lace, and I sprang to her side and offered her my arm.

"'You cannot go back alone,' I said.

"She did not take my arm.

"'Do you hate me, Miss Wyeth?'

"'I am very tired,' she said; 'I must go home.'

"'You cannot go alone.'

"'I do not care to accept your escort.'

"'Then—you send me away?'

"'No,' she said, in a hard voice. 'You can come if you like.' So I humbly attended her to the Hôtel St. Antoine.

---

# XXIV

"As we reached the Place Verte and turned into the court of the hotel, the sound of the midnight bells swept over the city, and a horse-car jingled slowly by on its last trip to the railroad station.

"We passed the fountain, bubbling and splashing in the moonlit court, and, crossing the square, entered the southern wing of the hotel. At the foot of the stairway she leaned for an instant against the banisters.

"'I am afraid we have walked too fast,' I said.

"She turned to me coldly. 'No—conventionalities must be observed. You were quite right in escaping as soon as possible.'

"'But,' I protested, 'I assure you—'

"She gave a little movement of impatience. 'Don't,' she said, 'you tire me—conventionalities tire me. Be satisfied—nobody has seen you.'

"'You are cruel,' I said, in a low voice—'what do you think I care for conventionalities?'

"'You care everything—you care what people think, and you try to do what they say is good form. You never did such an original thing in your life as you have just done.'

"'You read my thoughts,' I exclaimed, bitterly. 'It is not fair—'

"'Fair or not, I know what you consider me—ill-bred, common, pleased with any sort of attention. Oh! why should I waste one word—one thought on you?'

"'Miss Wyeth—' I began, but she interrupted me.

"'Would you dare tell me what you think of me?—Would you dare tell me what you think of my father?'

"I was silent. She turned and mounted two steps of the stairway, then faced me again.

"'Do you think it was for my own pleasure that I permitted myself to be left alone with you? Do you imagine that I am flattered by your attention?—do you venture to think I ever could be? How dared you think what you did think there on the sea-wall?'

"'I cannot help my thoughts!' I replied.

"'You turned on me like a tiger when you awoke from your trance. Do you really suppose that you mewed? Are you not aware that my father hypnotized you?'

"'No—I did not know it,' I said. The hot blood tingled in my finger-tips, and I looked angrily at her.

"'Why do you imagine that I waste my time on you?' she said. 'Your vanity has answered that question—now let your intelligence answer it. I am a Pythagorean; I have been chosen to bring in a convert, and you were the convert selected for me by the Mahatmas of the Consolidated Trust Company. I have followed you from New York to Antwerp, as I was bidden, but now my courage fails, and I shrink from fulfilling my mission, knowing you to be the type of man you are. If I could give it up—if I could only go away—never, never again to see you! Ah, I fear they will not permit it!—until my mission is accomplished. Why was I chosen—I, with a woman's heart and a woman's pride. I—I hate you!'

"'I love you,' I said, slowly.

"She paled and looked away.

"'Answer me,' I said.

"Her wide, blue eyes turned back again, and I held them with mine. At last she slowly drew a long-stemmed rose from the bunch at her belt, turned, and mounted the shadowy staircase. For a moment I thought I saw her pause on the landing above, but the moonlight was uncertain. After waiting for a long time in vain, I moved away, and in going raised my hand to my face, but I stopped short, and my heart stopped too, for a moment. In my hand I held a long-stemmed rose.

"With my brain in a whirl I crept across the court and mounted the stairs to my room. Hour after hour I walked the floor, slowly at first, then more rapidly, but it brought no calm to the fierce tumult of my thoughts, and at last I dropped into a chair before the empty fireplace, burying my head in my hands.

"Uncertain, shocked, and deadly weary, I tried to think—I strove to bring order out of the chaos in my brain, but I only sat staring at the long-stemmed rose. Slowly I began to take a vague pleasure in its heavy perfume, and once I crushed a leaf between my palms, and, bending over, drank in the fragrance.

"Twice my lamp flickered and went out, and twice, treading softly, I crossed the room to relight it. Twice I threw open the door, thinking that I heard some sound without. How close the air was!—how heavy and hot! And what was that strange, subtle odor which had insensibly filled the room? It grew stronger and more penetrating, and I began to dislike it, and to escape it I buried my nose in the half-opened rose. Horror! The odor came from the rose—and the rose itself was no longer a rose—not even a flower now—it was only a bunch of catnip; and I dashed it to the floor and ground it under my heel.

"'Mountebank!' I cried, in a rage. My anger grew cold—and I shivered, drawn per-force to the curtained window. Something was there, outside. I could not hear it, for it made no sound, but I knew it was there, watching me. What was it? The damp hair stirred on my head. I touched the heavy curtains. Whatever was outside them sprang up, tore at the window, and then rushed away.

"Feeling very shaky, I crept to the window, opened it, and leaned out. The night was calm. I heard the fountain splashing in the moonlight and the sea-winds sough-ing through the palms. Then I closed the window and turned back into the room; and as I stood there a sudden breeze, which could not have come from without, blew sharply in my face, extinguishing the candle and sending the long curtains belly-ing out into the room. The lamp on the table flashed and smoked and sputtered; the room was littered with flying papers and catnip leaves. Then the strange wind died away, and somewhere in the night a cat snarled.

"I turned desperately to my trunk and flung it open. Into it I threw everything I owned, pell-mell, closed the lid, locked it, and, seizing my mackintosh and travelling-bag, ran down the stairs, crossed the court, and entered the night-office of the hotel. There I called up the sleepy clerk, settled my reckoning, and sent a porter for a cab.

"'Now,' I said, 'what time does the next train leave?'

"'The next train for where?'

"'Anywhere!'

"The clerk locked the safe, and, carefully keeping the desk between himself and me, motioned the office-boy to look at the time-tables.

"'Next train, 2.10. Brussels—Paris,' read the boy.

"At that moment the cab rattled up by the curbstone, and I sprang in while the porter tossed my traps on top. Away we bumped over the stony pavement, past street after street lighted dimly by tall gas-lamps, and alley after alley brilliant with the glare of villanous all-night café-concerts, and then, turning, we rumbled past the Cir-cus and the Eldorado, and at last stopped with a jolt before the Brussels station.

"I had not a moment to lose. 'Paris!' I cried—'first-class!' and, pocketing the book of coupons, hurried across the platform to where the Brussels train lay. A guard came running up, flung open the door of a first-class carriage, slammed and locked it after I had jumped in, and the long train glided from the arched station out into the starlit morning.

"I was all alone in the compartment. The wretched lamp in the roof flickered dim-ly, scarcely lighting the stuffy box. I could not see to read my time-table, so I wrapped my legs in the travelling-rug and lay back, staring out into the misty morn-ing. Trees, walls, telegraph-poles flashed past, and the cinders drove in showers against the rattling windows. I slept at times, fitfully, and once, springing up, peered sharply at the opposite seat, possessed with the idea that somebody was there.

"When the train reached Brussels I was sound asleep, and the guard awoke me with difficulty.

"'Breakfast, sir?' he asked.

"'Anything,' I sighed, and stepped out to the platform, rubbing my legs and shivering. The other passengers were already breakfasting in the station café, and I joined them and managed to swallow a cup of coffee and a roll.

"The morning broke gray and cloudy, and I bundled myself into my mackintosh for a tramp along the platform. Up and down I stamped, puffing a cigar, and digging my hands deep in my pockets, while the other passengers huddled into the warmer compartments of the train or stood watching the luggage being lifted into the forward mail-carriage. The wait was very long; the hands of the great clock pointed to six, and still the train lay motionless along the platform. I approached a guard and asked him whether anything was wrong.

"'Accident on the line,' he replied; 'monsieur had better go to his compartment and try to sleep, for we may be delayed until noon.'

"I followed the guard's advice, and, crawling into my corner, wrapped myself in the rug and lay back watching the rain-drops spattering along the window-sill. At noon the train had not moved, and I lunched in the compartment. At four o'clock in the afternoon the station-master came hurrying along the platform, crying, 'Montez! montez! messieurs, s'il vous plaît'—and the train steamed out of the station and whirled away through the flat, treeless Belgian plains. At times I dozed, but the shaking of the car always awoke me, and I would sit blinking out at the endless stretch of plain, until a sudden flurry of rain blotted the landscape from my eyes. At last a long, shrill whistle from the engine, a jolt, a series of bumps, and an apparition of red trousers and bayonets warned me that we had arrived at the French frontier. I turned out with the others, and opened my valise for inspection, but the customs officials merely chalked it, without examination, and I hurried back to my compartment amid the shouting of guards and the clanging of station bells. Again I found that I was alone in the compartment, so I smoked a cigarette, thanked Heaven, and fell into a dreamless sleep.

"How long I slept I do not know, but when I awoke the train was roaring through a tunnel. When again it flashed out into the open country I peered through the grimy, rain-stained window and saw that the storm had ceased and stars were twinkling in the sky. I stretched my legs, yawned, pushed my travelling-cap back from my forehead, and, stumbling to my feet, walked up and down the compartment until my cramped muscles were relieved. Then I sat down again, and, lighting a cigar, puffed great rings and clouds of fragrant smoke across the aisle.

"The train was flying; the cars lurched and shook, and the windows rattled accompaniment to the creaking panels. The smoke from my cigar dimmed the lamp in the ceiling and hid the opposite seat from view. How it curled and writhed in the corners, now eddying upward, now floating across the aisle like a veil! I lounged back in my cushioned seat, watching it with interest. What queer shapes it took! How thick it was becoming!—how strangely luminous! Now it had filled the whole compartment, puff after puff crowding upward, waving, wavering, clouding the windows, and blotting the lamp from sight. It was most interesting. I had never before smoked such a cigar. What an extraordinary brand! I examined the end, flicking the ashes away. The cigar was out. Fumbling for a match to relight it, my eyes fell on the drifting smoke-curtain which swayed across the corner opposite. It seemed almost tangible. How like a real curtain it hung, gray, impenetrable! A man might hide behind it. Then an idea came into my head, and it persisted until my uneasiness amounted to a vague terror. I tried to fight it off—I strove to resist—but the conviction slowly settled upon me that something was behind that smoke-veil—something which had entered the compartment while I slept.

"'It can't be,' I muttered, my eyes fixed on the misty drapery; 'the train has not stopped.'

"The car creaked and trembled. I sprang to my feet and swept my arm through the veil of smoke. Then my hair rose on my head. For my hand touched another hand, and my eyes had met two other eyes.

"I heard a voice in the gloom, low and sweet, calling me by name; I saw the eyes again, tender and blue; soft fingers touched my own.

"'Are you afraid?' she said.

"My heart began to beat again, and my face warmed with returning blood.

"'It is only I,' she said, gently.

"I seemed to hear my own voice speaking as if at a great distance, 'You here—alone?'

"'How cruel of you!' she faltered; 'I am not alone.' At the same instant my eyes fell upon the professor, calmly seated by the farther window. His hands were thrust into the folds of a corded and tasselled dressing-gown, from beneath which peeped two enormous feet encased in carpet slippers. Upon his head towered a yellow night-cap. He did not pay the slightest attention to either me or his daughter, and, except for the lighted cigar which he kept shifting between his lips, he might have been taken for a wax dummy.

"Then I began to speak, feebly, hesitating like a child.

"'How did you come into this compartment? You—you do not possess wings, I suppose? You could not have been here all the time. Will you explain—explain to me? See, I ask you very humbly, for I do not understand. This is the nineteenth century, and these things don't fit in. I'm wearing a Dunlap hat—I've got a copy of the New York *Herald* in my bag—President Roosevelt is alive, and everything is so very unromantic in the world! Is this real magic? Perhaps I'm filled with hallucinations.

Perhaps I'm asleep and dreaming. Perhaps you are not really here—nor I—nor anybody, nor anything!'

"The train plunged into a tunnel, and when again it dashed out from the other end the cold wind blew furiously in my face from the farther window. It was wide open; the professor was gone.

"'Papa has changed to another compartment,' she said, quietly. 'I think perhaps you were beginning to bore him.'

"Her eyes met mine and she smiled.

"'Are you very much bewildered?'

"I looked at her in silence. She sat very quietly, her hands clasped above her knee, her curly hair glittering to her girdle. A long robe, almost silvery in the twilight, clung to her young figure; her bare feet were thrust deep into a pair of shimmering Eastern slippers.

"'When you fled,' she sighed, 'I was asleep and there was no time to lose. I barely had a moment to go to Bombay, to find papa, and return in time to join you. This is an East-Indian costume.'

"Still I was silent.

"'Are you shocked?' she asked, simply.

"'No,' I replied, in a dull voice, 'I'm past that.'

"'You are very rude,' she said, with the tears starting to her eyes.

"'I do not mean to be. I only wish to go away—away somewhere and find out what my name is.'

"'Your name is Harold Kensett.'

"'Are you sure?' I asked, eagerly.

"'Yes—what troubles you?'

"'Is everything plain to you? Are you a sort of prophet and second-sight medium? Is nothing hidden from you?' I asked.

"'Nothing,' she faltered. My head ached and I clasped it in my hand.

"A sudden change came over her. 'I am human—believe me!' she said, with piteous eagerness. 'Indeed, I do not seem strange to those who understand. You wonder, because you left me at midnight in Antwerp and you wake to find me here. If, because I find myself reincarnated, endowed with senses and capabilities which few at present possess—if I am so made, why should it seem strange? It is all so natural to me. If I appear to you—'

"'Appear?'

"'Yes—'

"'Wilhelmina!' I cried; 'can you vanish?'

"'Yes,' she murmured; 'does it seem to you unmaidenly?'

"'Great Heaven!' I groaned.

"'Don't!' she cried, with tears in her voice—'oh, please don't! Help me to bear it! If you only knew how awful it is to be different from other girls—how mortifying it is to me to be able to vanish—oh, how I hate and detest it all!'

"'Don't cry,' I said, looking at her pityingly.

"'Oh, dear me!' she sobbed. 'You shudder at the sight of me because I can vanish.'

"'I don't!' I cried.

"'Yes, you do! You abhor me—you shrink away! Oh, why did I ever see you?— why did you ever come into my life?—what have I done in ages past, that now, re-born, I suffer cruelly—cruelly?'

"'What do you mean?' I whispered. My voice trembled with happiness.

"'I?—nothing; but you think me a fabled monster.'

"'Wilhelmina—my sweet Wilhelmina,' I said, 'I don't think you a fabled monster. I love you; see—see—I am at your feet; listen to me, my darling—'

"She turned her blue eyes to mine. I saw tears sparkling on the curved lashes.

"'Wilhelmina, I love you,' I said again.

"Slowly she raised her hands to my head and held it a moment, looking at me strangely. Then her face grew nearer to my own, her glittering hair fell over my shoulders, her lips rested on mine.

"In that long, sweet kiss the beating of her heart answered mine, and I learned a thousand truths, wonderful, mysterious, splendid; but when our lips fell apart, the memory of what I learned departed also.

"'It was so very simple and beautiful,' she sighed, 'and I—I never saw it. But the Mahatmas knew—ah, they knew that my mission could only be accomplished through love.'

"'And it is,' I whispered, 'for you shall teach me—me, your husband.'

"'And—and you will not be impatient? You will try to believe?'

"'I will believe what you tell me, my sweetheart.'

"'Even about—cats?'

"Before I could reply the farther window opened and a yellow night-cap, followed by the professor, entered from somewhere without. Wilhelmina sank back on her sofa, but the professor needed not to be told, and we both knew he was already busi-ly reading our thoughts.

"For a moment there was dead silence—long enough for the professor to grasp the full significance of what had passed. Then he uttered a single exclamation, 'Oh!'

"After a while, however, he looked at me for the first time that evening, saying, 'Congratulate you, Mr. Kensett, I'm sure,' tied several knots in the cord of his dress-ing-gown, lighted a cigar, and paid no further attention to either of us. Some moments later he opened the window again and disappeared. I looked across the aisle at Wilhelmina.

"'You may come over beside me,' she said, shyly.

---

# XXV

"It was nearly ten o'clock and our train was rapidly approaching Paris. We passed village after village wrapped in mist, station after station hung with twinkling red and blue and yellow lanterns, then sped on again with the echo of the switch-bells ringing in our ears.

"When at length the train slowed up and stopped, I opened the window and looked out upon a long, wet platform, shining under the electric lights.

"A guard came running by, throwing open the doors of each compartment, and crying, 'Paris next! Tickets, if you please.'

"I handed him my book of coupons, from which he tore several and handed it back. Then he lifted his lantern and peered into the compartment, saying, 'Is monsieur alone?'

"I turned to Wilhelmina.

"'He wants your ticket—give it to me.'

"'What's that?' demanded the guard.

"I looked anxiously at Wilhelmina.

"'If your father has the tickets—' I began, but was interrupted by the guard, who snapped:

"'Monsieur will give himself the trouble to remember that I do not understand English.'

"'Keep quiet!' I said, sharply, in French. 'I am not speaking to you.'

"The guard stared stupidly at me, then, at my luggage, and finally, entering the car, knelt down and peered under the seats. Presently he got up, very red in the face, and went out slamming the door. He had not paid the slightest attention to Wilhelmina, but I distinctly heard him say, 'Only Englishmen and idiots talk to themselves!'

"'Wilhelmina,' I faltered, 'do you mean to say that that guard could not see you?'

"She began to look so serious again that I merely added, 'Never mind, I don't care whether you are invisible or not, dearest.'

"'I am not invisible to you,' she said; 'why should you care?'

"A great noise of bells and whistles drowned our voices, and, amid the whirring of switch-bells, the hissing of steam, and the cries of 'Paris! All out!' our train glided into the station.

"It was the professor who opened the door of our carriage. There he stood, calmly adjusting his yellow night-cap and drawing his dressing-gown closer with the corded tassels.

"'Where have you been?' I asked.

"'On the engine.'

"'*In* the engine, I suppose you mean,' I said.

"'No, I don't; I mean *on* the engine—on the pilot. It was very refreshing. Where are we going now?'

"'Do you know Paris?' asked Wilhelmina, turning to me.

"'Yes. I think your father had better take you to the Hôtel Normandie on the Rue de l'Échelle—'

"'But you must stay there, too!'

"'Of course—if you wish—'

"She laughed nervously.

"'Don't you see that my father and I could not take rooms—now? You must engage three rooms for yourself.'

"'Why?' I asked, stupidly.

"'Oh, dear—why, because we are invisible.'

"I tried to repress a shudder. The professor gave Wilhelmina his arm, and, as I studied his ensemble, I thanked Heaven that he was invisible.

"At the gate of the station I hailed a four-seated cab, and we rattled away through the stony streets, brilliant with gas-jets, and in a few moments rolled smoothly across the Avenue de l'Opéra, turned into the Rue de l'Échelle, and stopped. A bright little page, all over buttons, came out, took my luggage, and preceded us into the hallway.

"I, with Wilhelmina on my arm and the professor shuffling along beside me, walked over to the desk.

"'Room?' said the clerk. 'We have a very desirable room on the second, fronting the Rue St. Honoré—'

"'But we—that is, I want three rooms—three separate rooms!' I said.

"The clerk scratched his chin. 'Monsieur is expecting friends?'

"'Say yes,' whispered Wilhelmina, with a suspicion of laughter in her voice.

"'Yes,' I repeated, feebly.

"'Gentlemen, of course?' said the clerk, looking at me narrowly.

"'One lady.'

"'Married, of course?'

"'What's that to you?' I said, sharply. 'What do you mean by speaking to us—'

"'Us!'

"'I mean to me,' I said, badly rattled; 'give me the rooms and let me get to bed, will you?'

"'Monsieur will remember,' said the clerk, coldly, 'that this is an old and respectable hotel.'

"'I know it,' I said, smothering my rage.

"The clerk eyed me suspiciously.

"'Front!' he called, with irritating deliberation. 'Show this gentleman to apartment ten.'

"'How many rooms are there!' I demanded.

"'Three sleeping-rooms and a parlor.'

"'I will take it,' I said, with composure.

"'On probation,' muttered the clerk, insolently.

"Swallowing the insult, I followed the bell-boy up the stairs, keeping between him and Wilhelmina, for I dreaded to see him walk through her as if she were thin air. A trim maid rose to meet us and conducted us through a hallway into a large apartment. She threw open all the bedroom-doors and said, 'Will monsieur have the goodness to choose?'

"'Which will you take,' I began, turning to Wilhelmina.

"'I? Monsieur!' cried the startled maid.

"That completely upset me. 'Here,' I muttered, slipping some silver into her hand; 'now, for the love of Heaven, run away!'

"When she had vanished with a doubtful 'Merci, monsieur!' I handed the professor the keys and asked him to settle the thing with Wilhelmina.

"Wilhelmina took the corner room, the professor rambled into the next one, and I said good-night and crept wearily into my own chamber. I sat down and tried to think. A great feeling of fatigue weighted my spirits.

"'I can think better with my clothes off,' I said, and slipped the coat from my shoulders. How tired I was! 'I can think better in bed,' I muttered, flinging my cravat on the dresser and tossing my shirt-studs after it. I was certainly very tired. 'Now,' I yawned, grasping the pillow and drawing it under my head—'now I can think a bit.' But before my head fell on the pillow sleep closed my eyes.

"I began to dream at once. It seemed as though my eyes were wide open and the professor was standing beside my bed.

"'Young man,' he said, 'you've won my daughter and you must pay the piper!'

"'What piper?' I said.

"'The Pied Piper of Hamelin, I don't think,' replied the professor, vulgarly, and before I could realize what he was doing he had drawn a reed pipe from his dressing-gown and was playing a strangely annoying air. Then an awful thing occurred. Cats began to troop into the room, cats by the hundred—toms and tabbies, gray, yellow, Maltese, Persian, Manx—all purring and all marching round and round, rubbing against the furniture, the professor, and even against me. I struggled with the nightmare.

"'Take them away!' I tried to gasp.

"'Nonsense!' he said; 'here is an old friend.'

"I saw the white tabby cat of the Hôtel St. Antoine.

"'An old friend,' he repeated, and played a dismal melody on his reed.

"I saw Wilhelmina enter the room, lift the white tabby in her arms, and bring her to my side.

"'Shake hands with him,' she commanded.

"To my horror the tabby deliberately extended a paw and tapped me on the knuckles.

"'Oh!' I cried, in agony; 'this is a horrible dream! Why, oh, why can't I wake!'

"'Yes,' she said, dropping the cat, 'it is partly a dream, but some of it is real. Remember what I say, my darling; you are to go to-morrow morning and meet the twelve-o'clock train from Antwerp at the Gare du Nord. Papa and I are coming to Paris on that train. Don't you know that we are not really here now, you silly boy? Good-night, then. I shall be very glad to see you.'

"I saw her glide from the room, followed by the professor, playing a gay quickstep, to which the cats danced two and two.

"'Good-night, sir,' said each cat as it passed my bed; and I dreamed no more.

"When I awoke, the room, the bed had vanished; I was in the street, walking rapidly; the sun shone down on the broad, white pavements of Paris, and the streams of busy life flowed past me on either side. How swiftly I was walking! Where the devil was I going? Surely I had business somewhere that needed immediate attention. I tried to remember when I had awakened, but I could not. I wondered where I had dressed myself; I had apparently taken great pains with my toilet, for I was immaculate, monocle and all, even down to a long-stemmed rose nestling in my button-hole. I knew Paris and recognized the streets through which I was hurrying. Where could I be going? What was my hurry? I glanced at my watch and found I had not a moment to lose. Then, as the bells of the city rang out mid-day, I hastened into the railroad station on the Rue Lafayette and walked out to the platform. And as I looked down the glittering track, around the distant curve shot a locomotive followed by a long line of cars. Nearer and nearer it came, while the station-gongs sounded and the switch-bells began ringing all along the track.

"'Antwerp express!' cried the sous-chef de gare, and as the train slipped along the tiled platform I sprang upon the steps of a first-class carriage and threw open the door.

"'How do you do, Mr. Kensett?' said Wilhelmina Wyeth, springing lightly to the platform. 'Really it is very nice of you to come to the train.' At the same moment a bald, mild-eyed gentleman emerged from the depths of the same compartment, carrying a large, covered basket.

"'How are you, Kensett?' he said. 'Glad to see you again. Rather warm in that compartment—no, I will not trust this basket to an expressman; give Wilhelmina your arm and I'll follow. We go to the Normandie, I believe?'

"All the morning I had Wilhelmina to myself, and at dinner I sat beside her, with the professor opposite. The latter was cheerful enough, but he nearly ruined my appetite, for he smelled strongly of catnip. After dinner he became restless and fidgeted about in his chair until coffee was brought, and we went up to the parlor of our apartment. Here his restlessness increased to such an extent that I ventured to ask him if he was in good health.

"'It's that basket—the covered basket which I have in the next room,' he said.

"'What's the trouble with the basket?' I asked.

"'The basket's all right—but the contents worry me.'

"'May I inquire what the contents are?' I ventured.

"The professor rose.

"'Yes,' he said, 'you may inquire of my daughter.' He left the room, but reappeared shortly, carrying a saucer of milk.

"I watched him enter the next room, which was mine.

"'What on earth is he taking that into my room for?' I asked Wilhelmina. 'I don't keep cats.'

"'But you will,' she said.

"'I? Never!'

"'You will if I ask you to.'

"'But—but you won't ask me.'

"'But I do.'

"'Wilhelmina!'

"'Harold!'

"'I detest cats.'

"'You must not.'

"'I can't help it.'

"'You will when I ask it. Have I not given myself to you? Will you not make a little sacrifice for me?'

"'I don't understand—'

"'Would you refuse my first request?'

"'No,' I said, miserably, 'I will keep dozens of cats—'

"'I do not ask that; I only wish you to keep one.'

"'Was that what your father had in that basket?' I asked, suspiciously.

"'Yes, the basket came from Antwerp.'

"'What! The white Antwerp cat!' I cried.

"'Yes.'

"'And you ask me to keep that cat? Oh, Wilhelmina!'

"'Listen!' she said. 'I have a long story to tell you; come nearer, close to me. You say you love me?'

"I bent and kissed her.

"'Then I shall put you to the proof,' she murmured.

"'Prove me!'

"'Listen. That cat is the same cat that ran out of the apartment in the Waldorf when your great-aunt ceased to exist—in human shape. My father and myself, having received word from the Mahatmas of the Trust Company, sheltered and cherished the cat. We were ordered by the Mahatmas to convert you. The task was appalling—but there is no such thing as refusing a command, and we laid our plans. That man with a white spot in his hair was my father—'

"'What! Your father is bald.'

"'He wore a wig then. The white spot came from dropping chemicals on the wig while experimenting with a substance which you could not comprehend.'

"'Then—then that clew was useless; but who could have taken the Crimson Diamond? And who was the man with the white spot on his head who tried to sell the stone in Paris?'

"'That was my father.'

"'He—he—st—took the Crimson Diamond!' I cried, aghast.

"'Yes and no. That was only a paste stone that he had in Paris. It was to draw you over here. He had the real Crimson Diamond also.'

"'Your father?'

"'Yes. He has it in the next room now. Can you not see how it disappeared, Harold? Why, the cat swallowed it!'

"'Do you mean to say that the white tabby swallowed the Crimson Diamond?'

"'By mistake. She tried to get it out of the velvet bag, and, as the bag was also full of catnip, she could not resist a mouthful, and unfortunately just then you broke in the door and so startled the cat that she swallowed the Crimson Diamond.'

"There was a painful pause. At last I said:

"'Wilhelmina, as you are able to vanish, I suppose you also are able to converse with cats.'

"'I am,' she replied, trying to keep back the tears of mortification.

"'And that cat told you this?'

"'She did.'

"'And my Crimson Diamond is inside that cat?'

"'It is.'

"'Then,' said I, firmly, 'I am going to chloroform the cat.'

"'Harold!' she cried, in terror, 'that cat is your great-aunt!'

"I don't know to this day how I stood the shock of that announcement, or how I managed to listen while Wilhelmina tried to explain the transmigration theory, but it was all Chinese to me. I only knew that I was a blood relation of a cat, and the thought nearly drove me mad.

"'Try, my darling, try to love her,' whispered Wilhelmina; 'she must be very precious to you—'

"'Yes, with my diamond inside her,' I replied, faintly.

"'You must not neglect her,' said Wilhelmina.

493

"'Oh no, I'll always have my eye on her—I mean I will surround her with luxury—er, milk and bones and catnip and books—er—does she read?'

"'Not the books that human beings read. Now, go and speak to your aunt, Harold.'

"'Eh! How the deuce—'

"'Go; for my sake try to be cordial.'

"She rose and led me unresistingly to the door of my room.

"'Good Heavens!' I groaned; 'this is awful.'

"'Courage, my darling!' she whispered. 'Be brave for love of me.'

"I drew her to me and kissed her. Beads of cold perspiration started in the roots of my hair, but I clenched my teeth and entered the room alone. The room was dark and I stood silent, not knowing where to turn, fearful lest I step on my aunt! Then, through the dreary silence, I called, 'Aunty!'

"A faint noise broke upon my ear, and my heart grew sick, but I strode into the darkness, calling, hoarsely:

"'Aunt Tabby! It is your nephew!'

"Again the faint sound. Something was stirring there among the shadows—a shape moving softly along the wall, a shade which glided by me, paused, wavered, and darted under the bed. Then I threw myself on the floor, profoundly moved, begging, imploring my aunt to come to me.

"'Aunty! Aunty!' I murmured. 'Your nephew is waiting to take you to his heart!'

"At last I saw my great-aunt's eyes shining in the dark."

The young man's voice grew hushed and solemn, and he lifted his hand in silence:

"Close the door. That meeting is not for the eyes of the world! Close the door upon that sacred scene where great-aunt and nephew are united at last."

—————————

A long pause followed; deep emotion was visible in Miss Barrison's sensitive face. She said:

"Then—you are married?"

"No," replied Mr. Kensett, in a mortified voice.

"Why not?" I asked, amazed.

"Because," he said, "although my fiancée was prepared to accept a cat as her great-aunt, she could not endure the complications that followed."

"What complications?" inquired Miss Barrison.

The young man sighed profoundly, shaking his head.

"My great-aunt had kittens," he said, softly.

---

The tremendous scientific importance of these experiences excited me beyond measure. The simplicity of the narrative, the elaborate attention to corroborative detail, all bore irresistible testimony to the truth of these accounts of phenomena vitally important to the entire world of science.

We all dined together that night—a little earnest company of knowledge-seekers in the vast wilderness of the unexplored; and we lingered long in the dining-car, propounding questions, advancing theories, speculating upon possibilities of most intense interest. Never before had I known a man whose relatives were cats and kittens, but he did not appear to share my enthusiasm in the matter.

"You see," he said, looking at Miss Barrison, "it may be interesting from a purely scientific point of view, but it has already proved a bar to my marrying."

"Were the kittens black?" I inquired.

"No," he said, "my aunt drew the color-line, I am proud to say."

"I don't see," said Miss Barrison, "why the fact that your great-aunt is a cat should prevent you from marrying."

"It wouldn't prevent *me*!" said the young man, quickly.

"Nor me," mused Miss Barrison—"if I were really in love."

Meanwhile I had been very busy thinking about Professor Farrago, and, coming to an interesting theory, advanced it.

"If," I began, "he marries one of those transparent ladies, what about the children?"

"Some would be, no doubt, transparent," said Kensett.

"They might be only translucent," suggested Miss Barrison.

"Or partially opaque," I ventured. "But it's a risky marriage—not to be able to see what one's wife is about—"

"That is a silly reflection on women," said Miss Barrison, quietly. "Besides, a girl need not be transparent to conceal what she's doing."

This observation seemed to end our postprandial and tripartite conference; Miss Barrison retired to her stateroom presently; after a last cigar, smoked almost in silence, the young man and I bade each other a civil good-night and retired to our re-respective berths.

I think it was at Richmond, Virginia, that I was awakened by the negro porter shaking me very gently and repeating, in a pleasant, monotonous voice: "Teleg'am foh you, suh! Teleg'am foh Mistuh Gilland, suh. 'Done call you 'lev'm times sense breakfass, suh! Las' call foh luncheon, suh. Teleg'am foh—"

"Heavens!" I muttered, sitting up in my bunk, "is it as late as that! Where are we?" I slid up the window-shade and sat blinking at a flood of sunshine.

"Telegram?" I said, yawning and rubbing my eyes. "Let me have it. All right, I'll be out presently. Shut that curtain! I don't want the entire car to criticise my pink pajamas!"

"Ain' nobody in de cyar, 'scusin yo'se'f, suh," grinned the porter, retiring.

I heard him, but did not comprehend, sitting there sleepily unfolding the scrawled telegram. Suddenly my eyes flew wide open; I scanned the despatch with stunned incredulity:

"ATLANTA, GEORGIA.

"We couldn't help it. Love at first sight. Married this morning in Atlanta. Wildly happy. Forgive. Wire blessing.

"(Signed) HAROLD KENSETT,
"HELEN BARRISON KENSETT."

"Porter!" I shouted. "Porter! Help!"

There was no response.

"Oh, Lord!" I groaned, and rolled over, burying my head in the blankets; for I understood at last that Science, the most jealous, most exacting of mistresses, could never brook a rival.


**THE END**

www.ingramcontent.com/pod-product-compliance
Lightning Source LLC
Chambersburg PA
CBHW080944020726
47505CB00009B/2136